James H. Graff, Dutton Cook

Leo

A Novel

James H. Graff, Dutton Cook

Leo
A Novel

ISBN/EAN: 9783337349295

Printed in Europe, USA, Canada, Australia, Japan

Cover: Foto ©Andreas Hilbeck / pixelio.de

More available books at **www.hansebooks.com**

L E O

A NOVEL.

BY

DUTTON COOK,

AUTHOR OF "A PRODIGAL SON," "PAUL FOSTER'S DAUGHTER," ETC., ETC.

NEW EDITION.

LONDON:

CHAPMAN AND HALL, 193, PICCADILLY.

CONTENTS.

L E O.

CHAPTER I.

A DRONE IN THE HIVE.

OUR Babylon has been seldom afflicted with the violent improvements which have often ravaged continental cities. We sometimes tender to the genius of alteration a corner building here and there, or permit a rookery to be pierced, or oust poverty from a back slum—but we never sacrifice a whole hecatomb of houses; we never sweep away at once an entire street, to establish a new boulevard or open up a magnificent vista. Our changes are in the nature of nibblings rather than great bites. Yet is our London gradually wearing a new face. By careful cosmeticising and adroit dressing it grows more and more comely of aspect. Light is permitted to penetrate where once it was barely known, save by hearsay and accidental reflection; gas-pipes thread the thoroughfares, and water is generally laid on, and a subterranean city toils for the sake of order, and decency, and cleanliness, in the world above ground; and of course these things are matters of congratulation. Still, it is with regret we learn now and then of the loss of some relic of an older age—even though it may have been an abuse, it was yet a landmark in our own history, in our town's, in our globe's. The new white teeth we buy of our dentist are very excellent, admirable, ornamental—even useful—but that preceding extraction of stumps was decidedly a painful business.

I

Has Improvement gone round with double-tie brush and set a mark of destruction in whitewash upon a pleasant row of houses known as Sun-dial Buildings, in the Temple? Have these been partitioned into lots, and numbered and lined until they resemble the diagrams of dishes in the cookery books which profess to give instruction how to carve? Has the iconoclastic labourer, pickaxe in hand, mounted on the walls, and with aid of pulley and rope, been busy sending baskets of bricks—mockeries of game-hampers, presents from the country—to his fellows below, toiling behind a high hoarding, as though ashamed, as well they might be, of their occupation? The reader must for himself answer these queries. But if Sun-dial Buildings yet exist, as of yore, red-tiled, ramshackle, worm-eaten, smoke-grimed, defiant of architectural and sanitary reformers —gifted with all the inevitable picturesqueness of age and dirt—I pray you go view the premises. And should incentive be wanting to this mission, problematical and unsatisfactory as I concede it may be under the progressive economy of metropolitan improvements, why then, let me give you motive for inquiry. It is in Sun-dial Buildings that the first scene of our novel is laid.

Unto which of the learned and illustrious Inns did the Buildings pertain? Were they of the Middle or the Inner Temple? Did their inhabitants fight beneath the armorial ensign of the Pegasus or of the Holy Lamb? Nay, why should I pause to set down such particulars? To these questions, also, it were better to obtain answer on the spot.

On a certain black door on the first-floor landing of one of the houses in Sun-dial Buildings two names were inscribed in thick white paint. It was quite necessary that they should be marked with some distinctness, for the staircase was very dark, and visitors had to grope their way, poring over the names they were in quest of, as travellers at night strain their eyes to read finger-posts. By making out each letter separately—perhaps by feeling them after the manner of blind people reading their embossed books—the words finally deciphered were " Mr. A. PAGE : " and underneath, " Mr. R. HOOPER."

The black door gave entrance, however, to very light and pleasant rooms. These had formerly been tenanted by old

Mr. Tangleton, the veteran special pleader, who was said to have lived in Sun-dial Buildings for nearly half a century, and during that period to have consumed more port wine (fruity and full-bodied), played more rubbers at whist (long, guinea points), and produced pleas of more cunning and curiousness, and of a higher degree of intricacy and incomprehensibility, than any three other men in the Inn put together—which was saying a good deal, undoubtedly. For some years preceding his demise, the old gentleman had never stirred outside his black door, seldom from his great greasy armchair by the fire-place, hindered partly by increasing age and infirmity, and partly by a love of ease and a stanchly conservative hatred of alteration; and at the time of his death he had grown to a size so enormous—having been always a man of gigantesque mould—that, it was rumoured throughout the Buildings, his coffin had to be lowered from his front windows by means of strong ropes, the undertaker's men having positively declined the responsibility of conveying a burden so extraordinary down the rather tortuous staircase in the usual way. The chambers were then found to be in a state of terrible dilapidation. The white-washer had never once set foot in the place during the period of Mr. Tangleton's tenancy. In the corners of the rooms swung cobwebs, so thick, and interwoven, and strong, that they would probably have made very trustworthy hammocks for middle-weight rats. The Turkey carpet was in holes, and every trace of pattern had been trodden out, or was else secreted beneath a closely-sown surface of dust. The walls, not hidden by the shelves upon shelves of law-books, were black with dirt and age, the paint peeling from them, and curling off in large sheets here and there, as though, like snakes, they were shedding their skins. The ceilings were so cracked that they looked as though they were tesselated with a brown, monotone material unskilfully put together; they were clouded angrily with dust and smoke, while in places the plaster had fallen, and an interlacing of laths was exposed to view—just as the warp and woof of cloth are visible when the nap is thoroughly rubbed away. But the old special pleader dead and buried—(he left no will, and the great bulk of his enormous wealth devolved upon his laundress, a one-eyed woman of eighty, who, it seemed, had been also his wife for some years,)—Mr. Arnold Page entered upon possession of the chambers, and wrote A. PAGE upon the exact spot on the black door which had formerly borne the memorable name of TANGLETON.

Certainly the rooms hardly looked the same as when they were under the rule of Tangleton. The painter, the decorator, the upholsterer, had rendered valuable aid. Silken curtains profusely gimped, and corded, and tasselled, now draped windows which had once stood nude, and dirty, and cracked. Outside were Venetian blinds to ward off the fierceness of the sun, and diminish the glare of light from the river. Gold-mouldings edged the rooms; velvet pile carpets caressed the feet of the visitor, and deadened the creaking of boots and the noise of footfalls: antique, carved, oaken book-cases replaced the common shelves of the late special pleader; and light literature now reigned in places which had known before nothing but reading of the heaviest and most legal description. Bronze and gilt chandeliers depended from the ceilings; pier glasses towered up from the marble mantelpieces above the polished steel stoves; paintings in admirable frames adorned the walls; while scattered about the room, were statuettes in Parian, real and good bronzes, cut-glass candelabra, and various delicate specimens of Dresden and old Chelsea china. Substantial furniture—all oak — chairs of various patterns; and elaborately easy, padded couches. Yes, and a grand piano, and a flower-stand in the window crowded with plants, and positively a canary bird hopping about from perch to perch, proud of his golden plumage, which eclipsed even the brilliant lacquer of his cage.

It was hardly to be wondered at, therefore, that the gentleman who had brought about all this splendour should be the object of some curiosity and canvassing amongst his fellow diners and students in Hall. Of course, information about him was speedily forthcoming, as it is forthcoming concerning any and everybody, if you are careful to ask for it often, and loudly, and persistently enough.

" Page?—oh, yes!—Arnold Page—Pages of Woodland-shire—good family—tidy estate, I believe. Yes!—he's a swell—lots of money—wish I had. Oh, no! he isn't going to practise at the bar—only called for the fun of the thing.

Why, he keeps a man-servant, who wears a cockade in his hat; an awful chap, because Page holds a commission in the Woodlandshire Yeomanry, I suppose; or because his father was a Waterloo man. Oh, no! he aint proud; not a bit; very good sort of fellow, I believe, and clever too, when he likes to give his mind to a thing. You see, he started with odds in his favour—two to one, I should say. Born with a silver spoon in his mouth, that's the fact— wish I had been. No, he don't care for the Temple port; he's got a better tap over at his chambers; such a swell place—fitted up like a drawing-room, bless you," &c., &c.

Some such statement, containing the above particulars, was not unfrequently asked for and given. As to why a gentleman so prosperous as Mr. Page had chosen to eat his terms and abide in old Tangleton's chambers in the Temple, it was less easy to arrive at a satisfactory explanation. Fortune having made already other and better provision for him, he could not be said to aspire to any of those political preferments which involve a seven years' standing as an indispensable qualification. Mr. Arnold Page, of Oakmere Court, Woodlandshire, was secure in the possession of very considerable wealth and first-rate social position. His father—a soldier who had seen active service under the great Duke, and who had been dead many years—had sat for the county, and the rumour went that young Mr. Page would offer himself as a candidate on the occasion, if not of the next vacancy certainly of the next but one, without a doubt being entertained that his so doing would result in success. It was only, people said, his disinclination to place himself in opposition to the present member, a very old gentleman, and a connexion of the Page family, that had prevented his long ago contesting the election and taking his seat in Parliament as one of the members for the county of Woodlandshire. In that case, he would, of course, as his father and grandfather had done before him, have found his way to the benches occupied by the influential party in the House who are presumed to represent the landed and agricultural interests of the country; for political conviction runs through a family and is as hereditary as gout or insanity. In his Eton and Oxford days, of course, a young fellow takes up with revolutionary

sentiments, or entertains odd notions about Venetian
constitutions, Doges, and Councils of Ten ; but he passes
through these as through the measles and the chicken-pox,
to arrive finally at those confirmed mental disorders which
have ranged his progenitors before him sturdy combatants
under a prescribed Parliamentary standard and converts to
the political creed of a party.   At present, however, it might
be premature to discuss what course Mr. Page would pursue
in the event of his return as a member for Woodlandshire.
There was little evidence as yet of his having assigned to
himself any special career other than that of an independent
gentleman residing *en garçon* in very admirable apartments
in the Temple.

You could obtain from Mr. Page's windows, between the
massive old walls and buttresses of the Hall on the one side,
and a graceful group of limes on the other, very pleasant
glimpses of the river Thames—now silver-bright in the
sun, now rather jaundiced by the heavy-laden London
clouds brooding over it.   You could watch the hare and
tortoise progresses of the smart little steamboats and the
round-shouldered barges ; you could note youthful amateurs
plying their oars in the wherries in a manner singularly
unlike the steady, ready, adroit performance of the water-
man in the burletta, and also the dapper boating gentleman poised so dexterously in his skeleton outrigger, looking almost as though he were riding on a walking-stick
with a two-pronged fork on either side by way of row-
locks ; and you could trace out, too, the low-lying Lambeth
shore, very patched and uneven, brown and Dutch-like,
bristling with chimneys and canopied with smoke.   You
were within ear-shot of the spirt, and pelt, and clatter of
the fountain, and of the chatter of the birds, and the
prattle of the children, and the rustle of the leaves in the
memorable and historic gardens of the Temple.

The London season quite in decadence : autumn weather
setting in ; mist quenching heat ; the last drawing-room
held, and the Court already from town ; the closing performances of the opera announced, grouse-shooting at hand,
Parliament up, more, dissolved : candidates busy courting
their constituents, unparliamentary society thinking of paper-
ing its blinds, and having made up its book and its party

for Goodwood, of taking its jaded, fevered cheeks to be fanned and renovated by cordial sea-breezes and beach exposure and exercise ; Jane busy with her bandbox, sewing it up in canvas after the manner of her sex *en voyage;* John engaged with the straps and buckles of his knapsack ; much over-hauling of *Murray,* discussions upon passports, *visas,* and railway and steamboat time-tables ; great productions of alpenstocks ; small men once more slapping their chests and talking of doing the Matterhorn, and Captain Martingale starting yet again to break the bank at Baden Baden—this time for certain.

Dusk : the birds and children asleep, the gardens deserted and quiet, Mr. Arnold Page sits at his open window, and the fragrance of cigars floats out into the evening air. A half emptied bottle of claret stands upon a small table at his side. Mr. Page looks at his watch.

Another quarter of an hour, Jack," he says, " and I must be off. I promised to meet the Carrs at the opera. It's their last Tuesday. I ought by rights to have gone down to Westbourne Terrace and dined with them ; but I must now join them at the theatre. I shan't be long after the overture. Help yourself, Jack."

Jack was a rather small, spare gentleman, curled up in a large arm chair. A tumbled sort of gentleman—careless in his dress, not particular as to the brushing of his coat, or his boots, or his hair. He looked as if he had rolled himself accidentally or been hurled by somebody else into the chair, rather than as though he sat down in it deliberately in an ordinary way. He was huddled together in a creased mass ; though sometimes he would stretch a leg over the arm of the chair, sometimes, indeed, over the back, and leave it hanging there, whilom exposing a wide expanse of sock between the end of his trousers and the commencement of his unskilfully-laced boots.

Lazily, listlessly, and as though the slight effort necessary were a matter of considerable inconvenience and trouble, Jack filled his glass, puffed at his cigar, and then buried his hands deep in his pockets, sinking his chin upon his chest. Arnold Page looked at him quietly. There was a pause.

" Well, Jack, you don't seem to say much," said Mr. Page, at length, in a tone of reproach.

"Forgive me. You see I get rather knocked over when important news comes too suddenly upon me. And I never could make up my mind in a hurry about anything."

Jack sipped his claret; this speech was evidently rather an effort for him, and he needed refreshment after it. He surrounded himself with smoke, jerked his hair from his eyes, and resumed.

"Of course, you know, I should like to say all that's right and do what's proper and that. But—matrimony—isn't it rather serious and responsible, and that sort of thing, you know, old fellow?—I think I've heard so."

"So have I," Mr. Page remarks, rather drily; "but you see, Jack, a man must marry at some time or other."

"Do you think so?"

"Isn't marriage inevitable?"

"Hum. I've heard that death is. They can't mean the same thing, I should think."

"What a Pagan you are!" and Mr. Page rises from his seat and begins to pace up and down the room. "Of course I'm quite aware that the announcement of an event of this nature is accepted by one's friends as a hint to cultivate whatever talent for epigram they may happen to possess. I'm prepared for all manner of smart things being levelled at me. They'll not be sharp enough to cut very deeply. So I scorn even to hold up a buckler of any kind before me. We'll talk of the feeling of the business by-and-by. Mere sentiment, and heart, and that, are, of course, quite secondary considerations, according to the modern plan of looking at things. Isn't it a good reason for getting married, that one's bored with single life, as it seems to be a good reason for getting a divorce that one's bored with matrimony?"

"Please don't talk like a man in a play, old fellow," says Jack, imploringly; "I can't keep up with you: I can't, indeed. You see, you've got no end the pull of me. You've rehearsed your part. If I do happen to pump up a smart impromptu on the occasion—and I aint a good hand at that sort of thing at any time, I admit, freely—why, you've a lot of smashing speeches, all ready cut and dried, to come down upon a fellow with. Don't stalk about, swinging your arms, like a restless light comedian. Do sit down. I'm not going to say anything horrid on the subject.

I merely want to understand it. If you put sentiment out of the question, I confess I don't see my way."

"I marry," Mr. Page says, sitting down laughing, "for a nurse for my old age. I'm getting on, Jack. I detected three grey hairs in this front curl this morning. At a ball the other night, a child of seventeen—a pretty little bit of a thing, that looked like a rosebud in tarlatan—declined to waltz with me, and whispered to her sister that I was too old. It was rather hard to say that of a man under thirty. But one can trace one's age in the faces of one's contemporaries. *You* don't look anything like so young as you used to, Jack. For Fanny Clipperton—whose first season I remember well—she was quite the town rage—well, she's now the mother of seven children, and looks forty."

"Rubbish! a man's no older than he looks. You'll pass for a youngster for a good many more years, in spite of what chits of seventeen may choose to say, with their idiotic nursery notions. Why should you grow old, who've never had a care, or a trouble, or a gloomy thought? When *your* face wrinkles, it will only be from your having had to smile too often and bear an overload of happiness."

"Well, then, I'll marry because it's the right thing to do. And I'll go and live with my wife at Oakmere Court, and look after my tenants. I'll cram Burns's *Justice of the Peace*, sit on the magistrate's bench, and come down hot and strong upon poachers. I don't see why I shouldn't play the part of country gentleman very well; and I'll take my seat, perhaps even office, when the time arrives for the innings of our side of the House. Besides, marriage gives one importance, strengthens one's hand—I shall gain in political influence."

"Hum! and the lady is——"

"Is the daughter of old Carr, who owns Croxall Chase— a very fine estate; it adjoins mine in Woodlandshire."

"An old family?"

"Well, no—a railway contractor; the grandfather founded iron and the family and made all the money, or nearly all. But what of that? Family doesn't matter in these days; and I've no great right to stickle about the matter. It's true that when I'm bullied I go back to the bishop of Queen Elizabeth. But *entre nous*, I've grave doubts about it. Certainly there are a good many missing links. I can only be sure of the serjeant-at-law of Queen Anne, and that isn't much, though he did bring Oakmere into the family; and I've a horrid suspicion that *his* father was a tradesman in an adjoining county. We ask no questions as to ancestry now. It's only the insurance offices who are curious on that subject, and then only to find out whether or not one's progenitors died of consumption or insanity : not out of any respect for a pedigree."

"I thought you'd let Oakmere to that prig Lomax, of the Wafer Stamp Office. I beg your pardon, I forgot he was your brother-in-law."

"He's my brother-in-law, and a prig too, and he's tenant of Oakmere—what does that matter? Of course, when I marry, he turns out. My living there as a bachelor would be too absurd."　.

"Hum. Do you know, Arnold, I think we'd better pass to the sentimental side of the question. Somehow, I don't see *you* in all these motives, and they only make me giddy."

"You're right, Jack. I was only submitting to convention. The modern view of marriage is that it's a transaction, or a partnership, from which both members of the firm are to derive commercial advantages. Men are for ever taking up this sort of tone now; but then men are always making themselves out to be both wiser and worse than they really are—it's the reaction from cant—it's the converse of hypocrisy—sham venality—the compliment that virtue pays to vice. For we live in a very polite, easy-going age. We bow and smile when we used to call names and cudgel. We rather like to hold a candle to the old gentleman now and then—two candles, if he prefers it. You see he's a very old institution, and it's safest to be well with him. One can't tell what may happen."

"I'm sure you've studied all this beforehand."

"No matter, if I have; I marry old Carr's daughter."

"Well, why?"

"Because I love her."

"Earnest?"

"Infidel! Yes. Why not?"

"Is it a great passion this time? Are we as tremendously *épris*—may I say spoony—as in the old days with Miss— what was her name?—Miss Angela——?"

"Be quiet. No; I've got over the attitudinising part of love. That old *grand sérieux* style of thing doesn't do often ; one goes in at first for a fancy sort of article. Very pretty, and attractive, and showy ; but no wear in it, bless you—not a bit—I've got a stout, steady, broadcloth now, Sir, that will last my life and look well to the last. That first love is like a first tooth : very pearly and charming ; and a great fuss is made over it, of course ; but it's not very serviceable, and it drops out one fine morning, replaced by a better, stronger, more durable affair."

"Well, here's *her* health. Is she pretty?"

"Judge for yourself. Here's a sketch of her : it's rather slight, but I did it myself, and I'm to have more sittings." (He produced a water-colour drawing from a portfolio.) "Don't look upon it as finished."

"A brunette ! I think I like a brunette best. You talk to a blonde, but a brunette talks to you. It saves no end of trouble. By George ! this is very capitally done. You've a great talent for this sort of free-handed sketchy work. How stunning that strong light is upon the waves of her hair. How well you've given the reflection from that white gush of lace round her neck. You'd have made a hit in Art, Arnold. It's awfully jolly."

"For Heaven's sake, sink the artist, look upon it as a man."

"She's pretty. Very pretty. Are her eyes really such a charming soft brown as that? Are her eyebrows so beautifully marked? Her nose so delicate in form? No ; you've flattered her, of course."

"I have done her but half justice," said Arnold Page, stoutly.

"I beg your pardon. I was thinking you were already a husband. One ought not to expect candour from a lover. Anyhow, it's a very first-rate drawing, Arnold."

"Thank you. Now amuse yourself with that claret, while I put myself into a dress-coat and choker." And Mr. Page left the room.

"A very pretty little darling," mused his friend, still contemplating the portrait; "though, of course, she doesn't really come up to this. People, somehow, never do come up to their pictures. There's always something hid—some

dodge about the business. Has he taken a three-quarter
view of her because her eyes aint straight, or to conceal a
slight defect on the off-side of her nose? Anyhow though,
I think she must be nice-looking. Certainly she's very jolly
colour; but that may be all his doing. She seems the sort
of woman a fellow might be deuced happy with. He's a
lucky dog, that Arnold. He'll be fortunate in his marriage
as in everything else. But it will be an awful business for
us others when he marries. We shan't see anything of him :
a house in Belgravia—Mrs. P. in satin—and flunkeys in
plush—grand dinners ; you come away, and feel as though
you'd just escaped from custody ; the wife turns up her dear
little nose, and thinks it's only right to wean her husband
from the dreadful set he knew before their marriage ; and
A. P. is as much hid from us as though he'd gone up into
the clouds. Sometimes I think I'll marry myself. Only I
never seem to have any money ; and the bride's aunts and
uncles—what beasts the bride's aunts and uncles always
are !—invariably regard that as an objection. Why will
people make such a bore, and a nuisance, and an ignominy
of marriage? But it's an awful world. Life's nothing but
one great trouble."

He refilled his glass, and curled himself in his chair again
more slothfully than ever.

"Look here, Jack Lackington," said Arnold, full dressed,
returning.

"Yes, I see, you look stunning."

"I don't mean that. I want you to listen to what I'm going
to say. One talks a lot of fearful nonsense about all sorts of
things. It's as well to be serious for a little now and then.
Don't make any mistake about what I've been telling you.
I marry for no nonsensical motive about estates, and Parliament, and politics, and that ; it's not for her fortune, but
distinctly for herself, that I love old Carr's daughter."

"One loves every fortune, but one doesn't love every
girl," murmured Jack Lackington, interrupting. But Arnold
did not heed him.

"If she had not a rap in the whole world, I should love
her, and I should marry her all the same. She's a dear,
good, tender little soul, whom, as a child, I played with and
loved. I have known her quite from her baby days, and

I'll make her a good husband, and do all man can to make her happy—and that although I couldn't make a long speech to her about my love, and could no more write verses to her—believing in them myself—than I could fly. It's a sober sort of love I offer her; a little dull perhaps; but it's not the less honest. There, old boy, I've done, and I'm off. I shall miss the overture for certain, and barely be in time for the grand duet, going as hard as I can pelt. Sit here as long as you like. You've got the cigar-box before you; if you want more claret, you know where to find it, and by all means help yourself. I shall be back after the opera, but it will be late, for *William Tell's* a prodigious length. I shan't go to the club; I hate the club at midnight. I shall have a smoke here before I turn in. If you get sick of waiting and make off, mind you close the door after you. Good-bye."

"Good-bye," said Mr. Lackington, without moving; and he added, as his friend left the room, "He was getting decidedly prosy, talking of his love and his marriage—decidedly prosy—no mistake at all about it."

For some time Mr. Lackington continued to sit, or to lounge rather, smoking cigars and sipping claret. A second bottle had been opened prior to the departure of Page. Apparently, Mr. Lackington was possessed with the importance of finishing this bottle.

"It's no use leaving any," he said, as he held it up to the light to see how much it contained; "and it's very tidy drink. Arnold has a neat taste in wines. So have I, for that matter; but, as I don't know a confiding wine-merchant, I can't say that it's of much use to me."

It was getting a little cold now as the night came over. Mr. Lackington moved uneasily in his chair, shivering rather.

"I wish Arnold were here. He'd shut the window for me."

Presently there was a knock at the door.

"I wonder who that is! I suppose I ought to go and see. Never mind. If it's important, they'll go on knocking; if it isn't they'll go away, and I shan't have to move. I think I should prefer that."

But the knocking continued. Slowly Mr. Lackington uncoiled himself and went to the door.

"Is Mr. Page in?" asked a strong, rather harsh voice.

A tall, gaunt-looking man, with ragged black whiskers, rusty clothes, his hat set carelessly on the back of his head —perhaps because he could not get his broad protuberant forehead into it—stood in the doorway.

"Oh, it's you, Wood, is it? Won't you come in?"

"Isn't Arnold in?"

"No, he's gone out—into society somewhere—the opera, I think he said. Come in."

"No—I won't come in," said the tall man addressed as Wood; but he entered as he said so, and Jack Lackington closed the door behind him.

"Where's Robin?" asked Wood.

"He's out somewhere. I think it's one of his practising evenings. He's vĕry musical, you know."

"Yes, I know. But it was Arnold I wanted to see: how is he?"

"Oh, he's all right. No, by the way, I'm forgetting. I can only give you bad news of him."

"Bad news!—why, what's the matter?"

"Don't look so serious. He's the victim of a bad attack from which he'll probably not recover: at least, he'll feel the effects of it all his life."

"Don't worry me with these infernal enigmas, which you think good jokes," said Wood, sternly. "What do you mean?"

"I mean that Arnold's going to be married."

"Is he, indeed? I'm sure I'm very glad to hear it."

"Glad, are you? Yes, of course that's the right, and conventional, and usual thing to say; it's what is expected of one. But that apart, I know I'm not glad—I know I'm deuced sorry."

"Why should you be sorry? Is there anything to be regretted in the marriage? I'm sure Arnold would do nothing that was unworthy of him, and that there must be every chance of his being happy, as he well deserves to be, in his marriage."

"Yes, that's all very well; but I like to look a little deeper into the matter than that. Do you know what it means, Arnold's getting married? Please to look at it from another point of view than the genial, pleasant, complimentary one that you are so fond of. Arnold's getting married means our losing him ; it means his giving up this crib, and all the jollity of his life here ; it means cutting us —altogether—dead. You don't suppose that Mrs. Arnold Page, whoever she may be—I've never seen her, for that matter, but I've not a doubt about the line of conduct she'll adopt—you don't suppose that Mrs. Arnold Page will care to see the grim mug of Mr. Hugh Wood reflected on the brilliant surface of her mahogany, or will be particularly anxious for the strong-smelling pipe of Mr. Phil Gossett perfuming her house, or the sprawling figure of your humble servant tumbling her furniture. Don't you know what an intense stunner Arnold Page is, and don't you feel that his getting married is enough to plunge all us poor beggars into the deepest crape and the densest mourning ? By George ! Sir, there'll never be another ray of sunshine in this place when Arnold's out of it—the birds will leave off singing, the fountain will give over playing, the river will sparkle no more—it will all be as dreary as a prison ; our lives without Arnold Page will be like a picture by an old master —with all its golden glazing peeled off."

"You're a very selfish fellow, Lackington, it seems to me," said Hugh Wood, gravely.

"Well, isn't selfishness natural — isn't it good to be natural ? "

"I think it's good to rejoice in a friend's happiness, and not to turn away moodily, wrapping oneself up in twopenny regrets that one's personal comforts and likings may be a little interfered with. Can't you think more of Arnold Page and less of Jack Lackington ? "

"I can't, honestly. To me, the latter — a trumpery dog, no doubt—seems very much the first to be considered."

"I don't understand you, Lackington—I tell you frankly, —and I don't think I ever shall, any more than I shall ever understand your art, as it appears in those pictures on the wall yonder. It seems to me a very poor thing, at a time when Arnold's happiness is in the scale, to be weighing against it the loss of the patron it may entail upon you, or the claret and cigars it will deprive you of."

Jack Lackington flung the end of his cigar out of the

window, with a brisker action than was usual with him, as he said,—

"Perhaps you don't, as you say, understand me—and, of course, that's a very good reason for abusing me. I don't set up for much. I know I'm a lazy, idle, good-for-nothing sort of fellow, and that I'm fonder of lying on my back smoking, than I am of work; and that I'm hard up, and in debt, and seedy, and down-at-heel altogether; and that such art as I produce is incomprehensible to you—(that mayn't be altogether such a bad compliment to the art as you perhaps imagine). I can admit all this; and more; that Arnold's been a good friend to me, and bought pictures of me, perhaps because he understood and liked them, perhaps because he didn't do either, but wanted to put money in my pocket, and bread in my mouth, and clothes on my back, and keep me straight generally and out of prison. I know all about all this—no one better. But it seems to me that if Arnold chooses to call me his friend, and make me welcome here, and give me all the claret and cigars in the place, it doesn't become Mr. Hugh Wood to step in and cry 'halt,' and put the cork in the bottle and shut up the cigar-box; that's my notion of the case, as it's my notion also, that if Arnold had need of the pictures, or any work that I could do for him, he should have had them without price being once thought of between us. Only as it is, money isn't much to him and it's a good deal to me. So he gives it to me, and I take it; and it doesn't occur to either of us that we've been the least soiled by the transaction."

Hugh gazed at the artist, amazed, evidently, at so unaccustomed a manifestation of earnestness.

"I said more than I ought," he remarked, quietly; "put it down please to my not understanding you."

"I will," and Mr. Lackington's languid manner returned. "I'm not a fighting-man, Hugh. I make you a present of that information. I sometimes hold up my fists bravely enough; but I always put them down again, if I find the other side really means business. I dare say what you said was right enough. Sit down and smoke."

"No; it's tempting Providence. We don't like each other; we understand that: we should only quarrel. I'll be off. I merely wanted to tell Arnold that I was going to spend part of the vacation in Woodlandshire, and to ask if I could do anything for him."

" I'll tell him if he comes back before I leave."

Hugh Wood moved to the door; but he returned to say, in a softer, kinder tone than he had hitherto employed,

" By-the-way, Lackington, if you're really hard up, can I lend you some money?"

" Well," the artist replied, after a pause; " five shillings *would* be an accommodation."

With a puzzled air, as though half afraid that he was being laughed at, Wood drew a handful of silver from his pocket, and held it to Lackington.

"Well; thank you," he said, simply; " as you're so pressing, I'll make it seven and sixpence—an extra half-crown is always useful."

He picked out the money with a deliberation that seemed fairly to bewilder Hugh Wood.

"What's the name of the lady Arnold is going to marry?" he asked, by way of saying something.

"She's of a Woodlandshire family living near Arnold's place. Carr, I think, he said the name was," and Mr. Lackington filled his glass again.

This occupation perhaps prevented his remarking that Hugh Wood left the room with a pale face and a strange look in his eyes.

"The great question now is," said the artist, once more alone, "whether it is or not worth while to open another bottle. Oh! if drawing the cork wasn't such a trouble!"

CHAPTER II.

AN OPERA BY ROSSINI.

F you can fancy a cherub who habitually stuck a disc of glass in his right eye, who had cultivated a streak of floss silk upon his upper lip; who had left off wings and taken to tiny shirtcollars, and a gauzy strip of white neckerchief; who had also, by an extraordinary process of development, put forth under his head a little light trunk, with limbs and extremities complete ; making his height in all about five feet three inches, and his weight seven stones and two pounds : if, I say, you can fancy all this, why you then have a very respectable notion of the personal appearance of Lord Adolphus Fairfield (Lord Dolly he was commonly called : he was just the man to have his name abbreviated ; people felt it was too long for him and did not fit him, and that it was necessary to dock it and run a tuck in it, as it were), the grandson of the late, and the younger brother of the present, Marquis of Southernwood : Lord Marigold, who filled the office of Chancellor of the Duchy of Brompton during the brief administration of the Earl of Birmingham, and to whom, as the reader is, of course, well aware, the country is indebted for that admirable provision known as the Marigold clause, contained in the Franchise Bill, and of so vital an importance to the interests of the half-a-crown householders, having predeceased his father, the late Marquis of Southernwood, some years : falling a victim, indeed, to an acute cerebral disorder at Naples in the spring of 18— (*vide* Burke).   The body, embalmed and brought home, was interred with much splendour in the mausoleum attached to Gashleigh Abbey, the family seat, in the county of Woodlandshire.   By his marriage with the Honourable Blanche Guinever, daughter of John Logwood, second Baron Lambeth, his lordship had issue one son, George Arthur Lancelot Gaston, who succeeded in due course to the titles of his father and grandfather, and is, indeed, at this period of our history, the present (being the sixth) Marquis of Southernwood. It is to the brother of this distinguished nobleman that we have now the honour of introducing the reader.

Lord Dolly Fairfield's little hands were covered with the smartest and smallest of blush-tinted gloves ; they were made expressly for him (I could name the shop at which he obtained them, but I should require to be paid heavily for an announcement so much in the nature of an advertisement) ; his little feet were cased in the trimmest and brightest of lacquered boots ; his flaxen locks were arranged in the daintiest curls ; if I dared I would say that he was the prettiest little nobleman that ever was seen. At the mess-table of the 600th Light Dragoons (of which crack regiment he was a distinguished officer), he was known as "Cupid" and "Tiny." He was too good-natured to resent these liberties. He was always laughing his pleasant noisy school-boy laugh—about an octave of notes—all musical and agreeable ; and he seemed quite as well pleased (unlike some eminent jesters), to laugh at himself as at anyone else. And the courage of the little gentleman was beyond dispute. He was a mere child when the 600th went into action in the south-east of Europe on the occasion of a great charge being made by the British cavalry. His superior officers were left dead upon the field, but the boy cornet rallied the remnant of his troop, and was able to bring them in tolerable order from under fire. He was wounded in three places, but he never lost heart nor presence of mind, nor, it was said, his glass from his right eye.

There was no question about the pluck of little Lord Dolly after that eventful day.

Smiling and nodding many recognitions, Lord Dolly made his way with some difficulty and stumbling over hats, and feet, and crinolines, to his stall at the opera. His graceful bows of apology and conciliation on the occasion of any little contretemps of this nature were delightful to witness. He tripped along with volatile ease and eventually tossed himself lightly, as though he had been an omelette, into his arm-chair. He looked about him for a few moments, then thrust two of his fingers into the large hand of a

2—2

tall, abstracted gentleman, occupying the next seat, as he whispered,—

"Hullo! Chalker, old man, how are you?"

His friend, I may say, at once, for I deprecate needless mystery, was the Honourable Dudley Chalker, eldest son of Lord Sandstone. Chalker was a melancholy-looking man, with weak eyes and a strong moustache; his nose projected and his chin receded a little too much for intellectual expression; the parting of his hair was so beautifully and accurately in the centre of his head, that it looked as though a result so marvellous must have been obtained by machinery; he passed for handsome in certain circles, and entertained a strong opinion upon that subject himself. He tried to smile upon his lively little friend; the result of his efforts was not a success; indeed, it might almost have been called a painful exhibition.

Lord Dolly, it must be confessed, did not pay much heed to the music. He was busy with a colossal opera-glass, examining the occupants of the boxes—"spotting his friends" he termed the process.

The theatre was a London opera-house, with a European reputation for the excellence of its performances. The bills at the door announced in bright green letters the opera of the evening to be Rossini's *Guglielmo Tell*.

The conclusion of the first act permitted Lord Dolly to talk with greater freedom and noise.

"Rum lot of people here to-night, aint there, Chalker? Evidently a party from Hounsditch up there with the diamonds on the first tier. Eminent butcher, I should say, in the stage box. Who's got into Plumer's stall? He aint such a bad sort of fellow, Plumer, you know, is he? But that man must be his tailor, I should think. *Do* look at his shirt-front, my dear Chalker, *do*, as a personal favour. I knew that Plumer owed him money, but I didn't think that he was going to pay him in this sort of way. Seems to me they let anybody in just now at the butt end of the season. The house is pretty full though, isn't it? only they won't bear looking into much; not with a glass. Where *did* they pick up that dear old lady in the Veres' box? My eye! what a turban! Everybody's going away—that's the fact. I suppose you'll be off soon, Chalker, won't you?

Going to the family dungeon in Wales this time? I pity you! I know what that is. Southernwood wanted to come that dodge over me, only I wouldn't stand it. I had enough of Gashleigh Abbey in the winter. They go in so awfully for High Church, and that sort of thing now, you know : it's the marchioness's doing. If Southernwood ever asks you to dine with him on a Friday, take my advice, and don't you go. Nothing but salt fish, Sir : second course, prayer-books served up with hymn sauce, I call it. It's pious, perhaps, but it isn't filling, not at the price. He aint such a bad sort of fellow, though, you know, Southernwood : stumped up like a man when I got into that hole about little Solomon's bill. You weren't here on Saturday. We had a new woman in the *Puritani;* not bad looking, by any means—but such ankles! They say she's a good singer, though, and we're to have her next year. I thought myself she was rather a squaller ; but the people seemed to like her. Yes ; I was to have gone away with Flukemore in his yacht, with Storkfort, Clipstone, and a lot more fellows. I don't know why we go, I'm sure. We all hate yachting, I do believe : I know we're always awful ill. We were to do the Mediterranean, or Spitzbergen or somewhere : I forget the name of the place ; but old Flukey he gets muddle-headed somehow ; never thought about Parliament being dissolved—up, you know : goes walking about Piccadilly as bold as brass. Of course Barney Levy was on to him in a moment. Poor Flukey! he was quite knocked over with astonishment. He's done nothing but cry out, ' By Jove!'—you know his way—every five minutes, ever since. We shall get him out to-morrow, though, if no more detainers have come in. He aint such a bad sort of fellow, Flukemore, you know. That looks deuced like little Polly Trevor there in the pit-tier. Don't you see?—in a blue wreath ; black-muzzled party with her ; dirty hands and diamond rings—that sort of thing ; something in the Manchester warehouse line, I should say."

Lord Dolly, it will be seen, had a pleasant flow of conversation. In this respect, he had decidedly the advantage of his friend, the Honourable Dudley Chalker, whose powers of speech were limited, or who made but slight calls upon his vocabulary. Mr. Chalker confined himself almost entirely to two words, or rather utterance. He jerked out "Aw!" when he desired to convey acquiescence or approval, while to express dissent or reprobation, he produced a sound something like "Baw!" It was astonishing what long conversations he was able to maintain by means of these two simple sounds, especially when the person he conversed with possessed the volubility of little Lord Dolly.

"You look a little seedy, Chalker, old boy, I think. I'm afraid you overdo it with soda-water, you know. It's very nice, but a fellow can't live on it; and having it brought to you in bed is, I think, an excess. Is it true that the governor found out about the deferred annuity? It was deucedly well managed: did the Ostrich Insurance Office no end of credit, only Sandstone's such an infernally wide-awake old bird. You see he has done all that sort of thing himself. Hullo! the Carrs haven't gone away yet. You know them, don't you, Chalker? Nice sort of people; simple and that, you know: no ·humbug, or pretence, or anything of that kind. That little girl will be worth a doose of a lot of money, I believe. 'Pon my soul, she's very pretty; don't you think so, Chalker? Oh, you like those great lumpy blonde women with ringlets, like Flukemore's mother-in-law. She really is a charming little girl, though. I sometimes feel quite spoony about her. I know Southernwood was very anxious for me to take up the case. But, you see, Arnold Page is in it; at least, so everybody says. You know him. He aint such a bad sort of fellow, you know, Arnold:—rather eccentric, and that. Cut his rooms in the Albany to go and live down in the City somewhere—the Temple, I believe. Queer fellow! Going in to be Lord Chancellor, or something of that sort, I suppose: got a wig and gown already. He has—'pon my soul! showed them me; kept in a box in his library. Very eccentric—but a good sort—knows a queer lot of people; artists, you know, and singers, and that. He does all that sort of thing himself, you know—very well, too—deuced clever! I often wonder he don't send things to *Punch.* Why, he's up there in the Carrs' box. Yes; I'm afraid that's a decided case. He's a good-looking fellow, Arnold, don't you think so, Chalker? I'll go up and talk to the Carrs after the next act. By George! how those Chol-

mondeley girls have gone off—do look! Why, they're quite
pale and scraggy; and they've only been out two seasons—
shocking! only just left off sugar-plums, and going in for
liver pills already. By George! it's serious."

The box occupied by the Carrs was on the tier above the
grand tier. It was engaged for every Tuesday of the sub-
scription, and was well situated on the curve of the theatre.
Mr. and Mrs. Carr wore a homely aspect; there was between
them the likeness so often to be remarked between a husband and wife, who have passed together many years of
married life. The assimilation of habits of thought and
action had produced at last a resemblance of expression
and even feature. They were elderly people, solid, rather
stolid-looking. Mr. Carr crowned a creased red face with a
flaxen whig of an old-fashioned pyramidic form, that well
covered his forehead, and interfered a little with his tufted
grey eyebrows: these repeated the angular line of his wig,
rising to a point some inches above his nose—of the flabby
Roman order—and imparting a resigned and melancholy expression to his face. He sat in a compact mass—very still
—giving drowsy attention to the music, and as though
motion would break some important spell, and the downfall
of his wig, or the crumpling up of his collar or cravat, or
shirt-front would result. His hands, in loosely-fitting white
gloves, with a superfluous inch, like a harmless talon, projecting at the end of each finger, he kept constantly before
him, folded one above the other in a neat and compact
parcel. He had the appearance of being very harmless
and respectable and a little over-fed. The same characteristics distinguished his wife. She was gorgeously attired in
maroon velvet. She wore a blonde head-dress a trifle
excessive in regard to flowers, and on her shoulders a superb
orange-tawny India shawl. In her youth, many years back,
she had been noted for the beauty of her raven tresses.
For some inscrutable reason, unless it was as a matter of compliment to the taste of her husband, she now substituted for
these a front of light flaxen, retained in its place by a fillet
of black velvet and a diamond. She was kind-hearted and
good-natured, although inclined to fits of silence and dulness
that looked almost like aberration of mind. For this, however, explanation might be offered. She could never be said

to have fairly recovered the loss of her only and darling son, Jordan Carr, who had been unfortunately drowned, while bathing at Oxford, some ten years prior to the date at which our history has commenced.   To this poor young man and his melancholy fate the good old lady's thoughts were continually recurring.   Hence, perhaps, her frequent attacks of speechlessness and dejection.

The only surviving child of the Carrs was the child of their old age, a daughter, Leonora Agnes Carr, born many years after their son Jordan.   Most tenderly did they cherish this their only treasure.   For the old gentleman he quite idolised his little Leo.

She was a beauty; if it be permissible to put size altogether on one side as having nothing to do with the question : for she was very little.   Contemplate her as she occupies the best chair in the opera-box; her parents persistently in the background as though thrown into shadow by the radiance of her loveliness.   A dainty little brunette, with a complexion not hard and tough as that of some dark beauties I wot of, whose only chance of producing colour on their dusky cheeks is by a thick application of it artificially on the outside; but fine and satiny, and delicate in texture, permitted now and then a beautiful rosy underflush to glow through it; luminous, melting brown eyes, made still more soft in colour by the shadow of her superb fringe of silken eyelashes; her features small and delicate, the mouth being quite perfection in form and colour; the shape of her head admirable ; the profuse dense brown hair growing in a charming curved line with a peak in the centre, rather low on her forehead, as the hair of the brunette beauty should always grow; her eyebrows well marked, her figure, though very slight in frame, very limber and graceful in movement. When she turned or bent quickly you did not hear the creaking of cordage, pulleys and busks—awful sound, which accompanies the change of position of certain graceful creatures, whose waists and shoulders have been brought by ingenuity into quite the three-cornered tart style of female figure, and are of course, as a consequence, greatly admired by the world in general.   Upon her head Leonora wore no ornament save that natural one of her soft hair, dexterously twisted and plaited and twined in shining cables at the back.

Round her neck was a cord of gold suspending a locket set with diamonds. Her slender wrists were decked with bracelets of coral and dead gold. Through her lace dress was to be seen the rich gleams of maize-coloured satin ; while her ample skirts were caught and confined by bunches of corn-flowers. Her toilet altogether was excellent in taste and effect and did great credit to all concerned in it. (I may as well say at once that to secure accuracy in regard to all matters of millinery that may from time to time be under mention in the course of this narrative, and to obviate all chance of impeachment upon a subject of importance so vital, the proof sheets have been submitted to the careful supervision of an eminent court dressmaker in Bond Street, whose decisions as coming from an adept would of course be recognised as final anywhere. In the same way I have not ventured to introduce any topic of a legal character without having first obtained the assurance of an eminent sheriff's officer, that the law as stated by me was beyond all question.)

Leonora Carr leant upon the damask cushions of the box, listening to the honied music of Rossini. Perhaps after a pretty woman's smile, the next charming thing is a pretty woman's frown. Just as the best singers can execute musical difficulties without disfiguring the arrangement of their features, so a pretty woman can frown and still look very winning and beautiful indeed. There was the slight plait of a frown upon the brow of Leonora. The immediate effect upon the spectator of the air of melancholy so produced was an earnest desire to kiss the red lips of the little lady very tenderly, and ask her what was the matter. To my certain knowledge there were six gentlemen in the stalls, their ages varying from twenty-two to seventy, and ten in the pit (one of them being connected with a newspaper), who were moved by a burning anxiety to go through such a proceeding. But another moment and they might turn away their opera-glasses : there was no longer need for their intervention, Leonora's frown had vanished. A gentleman had entered the Carrs' box. The sunny beauty of Leonora's smile ! Look to the stage, gentlemen of the stalls and pit. That smile of happiness is not for you !

" Dear Arnold, how late you are ! "

So the gentleman who entered the box was greeted. He pressed the hands of both Mr. and Mrs. Carr, and then the tiny fingers of Leonora; as though he had kept the best for the last, after the manner of judicious school-boys with respect to their choicest sweetmeat.

The old people made room for him; they retreated still farther to the background of the box; Arnold Page took the vacant chair in the front close to pretty Miss Leonora.

"I thought you were to come and dine with us?" said the lady, rather reproachfully. "I expected you; why didn't you come, Sir?"

"Forgive me, Leo dear, I was prevented. Someone called, I couldn't well get away, and Westbourne's such a long way off."

"That horrid Temple," she murmured, and she pouted. I have made mention of both her frown and her smile. Well, her pout, in point of attraction, was somewhere midway between the two; possessing certain of the charms of both.

"Town gets very empty," said Arnold, looking through his opera-glass round the house. "I see our friend Dolly's still here, though. I suppose the yachting expedition he was telling us of has gone off. Do you like this opera, Leo?"

"Yes, very much," she answered, with rather an air of indifference though, it must be owned.

"How well Tamberlik's singing to-night," said Arnold. "I don't think I ever heard him in better voice. I'm glad I got in time for the 'Dove sono;' I heard Duprez in this part some years back in Paris, but I don't think I liked him so much: true, he was gone by then. He had more passion, but I don't think he was so musical as Tamberlik. What an exquisite air this 'Chère Mathilde' is! I do believe it's one of the finest love-songs ever composed. It's almost as sublime as the 'Il mio tesoro' of Mozart."

Leonora was pouting again. Indeed the pout grew to a frown at last, as she said,

"Don't talk like a newspaper critic."

Arnold laughed good-naturedly.

"Don't laugh at me either, Sir."

"Wnat shall I do, then?" Her little hand came near him on the cushion. It was concealed from the audience by a superb bouquet: Arnold gave the little hand ever so gentle a little squeeze. The frown dwindled into a pout which subsided into a glorious smile. Leonora looked perfectly satisfied and happy again.

"There's only one more Tuesday," she said, "and perhaps then we shall not be in town—only think—this may be our last opera night; so I want you to be very good, and nice, and kind to me. I shan't be sorry to go away, I'm getting rather tired of London. I don't know where we shall go to; some quiet sea-side place, I suppose, where I shall read all the novels I'm supposed to have read this season—at least all of them I can get from the circulating library—and I shall sit on the beach all the morning, and wear a hat. Ah, such a hat, so pretty: with such a dear little scarlet feather! if you're very good, I'll show it to you the next time you come to Westbourne Terrace. And we're to go down to Woodlandshire. It's dull there, but very pretty; and I shall make great friends this time with dear Mrs. Lomax. You know why, Sir; and I've promised before I go to drive down to Kew to see little Edith and Rosy at Miss Bigg's school. Your nieces, Sir."

"*Your* nieces, too," Arnold interrupted, laughing, "or shall we say *our* nieces?"

"Be quiet, Sir," and Leonora laughed too, with very brilliant eyes. "You must be very good, or else I shall change my mind about that. I'll drive down to-morrow if it's fine. Have you any message, Uncle Arnold?"

"No, Aunt Leo; I know you will take care of the sugar-plum department. I've, therefore, only kisses to send to the little ducks. I'll give them to you, twelve for Edith, and twenty for little Rosy; you shall have them by-and-by. Take care to remind me to give them to you, in case I should forget."

"I'll ask mamma if that's a proper observation. I'm sure people didn't talk like that when she was a girl. Do you think that Madame —— is pretty? I think she is, decidedly. Her voice is beautiful; only Mathilde is not a very good part, is it? One thing's quite clear, she doesn't know what to do with her train. Who's that next to Lord Dolly in the stalls?"

"His friend Chalker, Dudley Chalker. He's related distantly to Lomax."

"Oh, I know! he danced with me at the Veres'. Isn't he rather a silly? I think he is; he did nothing all through the quadrille but pull his moustache."

"Ask Arabella Vere what her opinion is on that subject."

"I don't believe Arabella cares the least tiddy bit about him. You men are always fancying that girls are in love with you."

"Well! I suppose they are sometimes."

"Very seldom, indeed; I should think it's a most unusual occurrence." And Leonora gave a very bright kindly glance—perhaps to prevent Arnold's putting too serious a construction upon her words; and added a silvery little laugh, still further for his comforting; and presently I think the little hand was having another little squeeze behind the bouquet.

Arnold turned to the background figures in the box; he had been neglecting them rather.

"Do you like this music, Mrs. Carr?" he inquired.

"Charming, charming," the old gentleman answered, rousing himself, thinking probably that the question was addressed to him And he began to make believe great interest in what was going on; and to nod his head to the music in a way that rather endangered his pyramidic wig, and to beat time with an extended finger.

"It's pretty; very pretty," said Mrs. Carr, vacantly. "I'm fond of music. I don't know anything about it, but I'm fond of it. I never could play myself, but I always liked to hear others play. Leonora plays sweetly on the piano; she was taught by Signor Fuoco, at Miss Bigg's school, and afterwards had lessons of the celebrated Da Capo. My son Jordan—you've heard me speak of him I dare say, Arnold, though I don't think you ever knew him: he'd have been just your age if he'd lived, your age to a day, Arnold—my son Jordan had great musical ability; he played on the cornopean and the German flute: and played beautifully—entirely by ear;

he was self-taught. Jordan would have liked this opera;
he could play part of the overture on the piano with one
hand; it sounded beautifully with the soft pedal down.
Carr, dear, move your chair, you're on my dress. Leo,
darling, you look pale. Would you like my salts?"

The old lady had a way of speaking rapidly a few
sentences without pause between them, and then relaps-
ing into complete quietude just as a clock which only
strikes after long intervals of silence. And it was very
rarely that she spoke without mention of her late son
Jordan. To Arnold it may be said she always evinced
an almost maternal affection, probably for the reason
that he constantly reminded her of her lost darling, who
would have been the same age to a day had he lived,
as she was often stating. She sometimes even would
maintain that there was a strong likeness between
the two—though this was believed to be a matter of
sheer delusion on the part of the old lady. Certainly
whenever she appealed to her husband for confirmation of her idea, he would always reply kindly but
simply,

"No, Agnes dear; I don't see the likeness. I have
told you so before."

But she none the less persisted in her opinion.

" I hope Lord Dolly will come up and see us, don't you,
Ar?" said Leo. " I shouldn't like to leave London without
saying good-bye to him."

" Oh, he's sure to come up, I should think; he always
does, you know. I'll go and fetch him if he doesn't come
soon."

" I like little Lord Dolly, don't you, Ar?"

"It's impossible to help liking him. He's such a good
little fellow. He's a great friend of mine."

" He's a darling to waltz with. You're such a monster.
You are a great deal too big for waltzing. Do you know
that, Ar?"

"You can't think what an intense comfort it is to me."

" Where *are* you turning your opera-glass. Oh, I know:
you're looking for your friends in the gallery! How can
you, Arnold?"

" I'm not a bit ashamed of them, Leo."

"But you don't call them *gentlemen*, do you, Ar?" and the little lady began to pout again.

"I call them my friends, Leo. Isn't that a sufficient answer?"

Leo glanced at him quickly, probably to ascertain if he were really in earnest, perhaps to question too a certain rather sharp ring in his voice.

"I think you must be a Radical, Sir. I shall talk to papa upon that subject, and ascertain his opinions. I don't like Radicals. They want to make out that all people are equal, and that ladies ought to be taken down to dinner by coal-heavers, and dance with dustmen, and do unpleasant things of that kind. Isn't that what you want, Arnold?"

"Not quite, dearest. I've no very intimate friend in the coal-heaving interest, and I don't think I should introduce him to you if I had. And I'm not at all a Radical, Leo. Don't be at all alarmed. My political sentiments are quite safe and sound."

"Oh, of course women don't understand anything about politics," and Leo tossed out her little chin with a droll air of impatience. "But I know who you're looking for in the gallery, Mr. Red Republican. There's *that* Mr. Hugh Wood, for one person."

"You've nothing to say against him, I should think. You met him at the Comptons', and his father's a Woodlandshire rector."

"I don't like his father and I don't like him. He's very ugly, and he never knows what to say. Then there's Mr. Lackington " (she laid in each case an ironical stress upon the *mister*)—"you see I know all their names—a pre-Raphaelite painter—isn't that what he calls himself? I'm sure I tried hard to understand his pictures because you seemed to think so much of them, though they were hung up so high at the Academy, and I thought them very foolish and affected, and not at all nice and pretty, as I like pictures to be. And I saw you shaking hands with Mr. Lackington,—such a shabby, badly-dressed, *gauche* young man. Then there's Mr. Gossett, a medical man, isn't he, Ar? I've never seen him; but he must be an awful creature from all accounts. And Mr. Hooper, a farmer's son, one of papa's tenants, a poor little humpbacked——"

" Leo ! " Arnold interrupted, in a tone of reproach.

" I beg your pardon, Ar, but you know I can't like him. He frightened my pony once down in the park at home, and I was very nearly thrown."

" But he stopped the pony for you afterwards."

" Yes, he did ; and I was very much obliged to him ; but still, you know, I don't think I could ever like him ; that is, not much—and, then, a farmer's son, you know, Ar ! What makes you like them, Ar ? I should like to like what you like, if I only could."

" I'm afraid their great offence in your eyes, Leo, is that they are not often met with in society, and that they go to the gallery of the opera-house because they are fond of music, and find it cheaper up there than down below in the stalls, next to brilliant Mr. Chalker. If you prefer Chalker to Hugh Wood, and Lackington, and Robin Hooper, why I don't, that's all, Leo."

" Don't be cross with me, Sir. I don't prefer Mr. Chalker —I don't like Mr. Chalker. But I do like Lord Dolly."

" Hush ! here he is."

" How d'ye do, Mrs. Carr ? How d'ye do, Miss Carr ? How d'ye do, Mr. Carr ? How are you, Arnold ? " And his little lordship was pressing their hands with his slender fingers, laughing his merry boy's laugh, bowing and bending, pouring out his usual stream of pleasant small talk with a fashionable seasoning of " chaff," his gibus under his arm, his colossal opera-glass in his left hand, and, of course, his glass in his eye.

" Like this opera, Miss Carr ? Oh, yes ; first-rate, you know—classical music—good as Beethoven—that sort of thing ; but just a little heavy—ever so little, don't you think so ? Yes ; capital singer, Tamberlik. No end of a good singer—getting a little fat though, don't you think ? Good fun when the man what's-his-name shoots the apple off his son's head. First-rate—know how it's done ? No ; he don't fire off at all—arrow comes out of the apple, through the post at the back. Good trick, eh ? Pretty-looking woman danced the Tyrolienne to-night, wasn't she ? Soon leave town now, I suppose, Mrs. Carr ? You'll be glad to get into the country again, I dare say. Oh, yes—long season— knocked up—awful bore—that sort of thing. Lose the best

part of the season in London? Yes; so we do, very
foolish, and absurd, and that. Weather's changing now—
getting quite autumn—dear me, yes. What are our chances
as to grouse this year, Mr. Carr? Yes; I was going yachting with Flukemore—postponed the thing for the present.
Don't think I shall be down in Woodlandshire until the
winter. Much obliged. Yes; I'll certainly ride over to the
Chase, if I should come down. Where are you going,
Arnold? Tyrol—Alps—that sort of thing. Very true—
sick of it myself. Switzerland does get chuck-full of snobs,
somehow. Sort of continental Margate—that sort of thing.
Are you going to contest Woodlandshire? not this time, I
suppose. You'd have Southernwood's support, I think.
Yes, Miss Carr, it was Dudley Chalker; he's been admiring
you awful—made quite a conquest of him, I assure you.
No, Littledale went away without proposing. Poor Fanny
Forde quite ill in consequence—old Forde raging like a
mad bull—made sure of his daughter being a countess.
No; it's quite true, 'pon my word. Bra! Br-r-ra! Fine
fellow, Tamberlik. He don't sing the 'Suivez moi' badly,
does he, Miss Carr? I wish I could chuck up my voice and
catch it again like that. Are you going? You'll be sure to
give my kind regards to Mr. and Mrs. Lomax, when you see
them. Hope I shall have the pleasure of seeing you again.
Not next Tuesday? Dear me, the theatre *will* look empty
without you." And so on.

"Don't leave us at the door of the theatre," Leonora
whispered coaxingly to Arnold. "Come round to Westbourne Terrace, do, there's a dear. I've so many things to
say to you."

"Come out after the opera, Arnold, old man, and have a
cigar, will you? or come on to the club, or to the Albany.
I've got some decent hock now—Southernwood sent it to
me; or we'll go a little round, if you like, for a change.
We'll get old Chalker to come too. He aint such a bad
sort of a fellow, Chalker, you know—is he?"

But Arnold found the lady's proposition the more tempting.

"I think going round by Westbourne must be quite the
nearest way to the Temple," he said, laughing.

"Well, but the carriage can take you there afterwards.
Papa will speak to Andrews about it."

"No, darling, we won't make Andrews' life a burden to him. It's a fine night, I believe: and I can easily get a cab from Oxford Street."

"You ought to keep a cab, Arnold. I'm sure you'd find it very convenient."

"I tried it once; but I found it very troublesome. Somehow the cab was always at one end of the town when I was at the other. It seemed to me at last that I was only keeping it to enable my tiger to enjoy carriage exercise. I thought that reason was barely a sufficient one, so I put down the cab."

"When Jordan was at Oxford he used to drive a tandem," Mrs. Carr said. "Jordan drove beautifully, though he was sometimes upset. He was fond of very spirited horses. I was frightened to death to see him drive. But his father and myself always agreed that he should be humoured in everything that was reasonable. He'd have been just your age if he'd lived, Arnold; your age to a day. No; I never drive myself—not now—I used to drive a pony phaeton round our park, but I'm not equal to it now. Leo, dear, you'd better have that window up or you'll catch cold, coming out of the hot theatre. Poor Jordan once caught a dreadful cold from merely sitting with his back to an open window. Do you remember, Carr?"

"Yes, Agnes, I remember," said the old gentleman, quietly.

"I nursed him for weeks. Dear me, how ill he was." And Mrs. Carr relapsed again into silence.

"That's a regular case, you know, Chalker, old man, between that fellow Arnold and that little girl—a regular case; and a very nice little girl she is too, let me tell you, Chalker—not at all a bad sort of girl in point of fact. A man might do a deuced sight worse. I call her a—a howling poppet!"

This designation of little Miss Carr, from its possessing a sort of Ojibbeway smack, or from some other remarkable characteristics, evidently struck the Hon. Dudley Chalker as being intense and forcible. It had all the effect upon him that a blow in the chest might be expected to produce upon an ordinary man. He lost his breath to begin with:

3

he opened his weak eyes very widely indeed, pulled wildly at his moustache, and ejaculated "Aw!" three distinct times, with effusion; as a supplementary demonstration of surprise, he next took to blinking violently for some minutes.

Lord Dolly was apparently all the better for the relief to his feelings occasioned by his open expression of opinion relative to Leonora Carr. He returned to the consideration of everyday interests.

"This is the neatest thing you've had in cheroots, Chalker, for no end of time. It does you great credit."

The little nobleman blew as big a cloud as a giant might have blown.

"To-morrow we must see about getting old Flukey out of that lock-up. •It makes a fellow awful nervous though, trusting himself in those places; one never knows what may happen. Suppose, you know, Chalker, they were to nobble on to me!"

Chalker murmured—"Baw!"

The utterance seemed to be as eloquent as the occasion demanded.

"I want to speak to you, Ar, before you go," said Leonora, joining him in the hall as he prepared to leave the house in Westbourne Terrace.

"What is it, Leo?" he asked, kindly.

She took his hand, pressing it gently between her two soft little palms.

"Have I done wrong to-night, Ar; tell me?"

"No, dearest; how can you do wrong?"

"But I have; I've said things I ought not to have said. I have spoken of your friends badly—and it was foolish and wicked of me—and you, Ar, so good and kind to me always. I had no right to say what I did. Forgive me, Ar; I won't do it again, at least, I'll try not to. Forgive me."

"Silly little Leo," said Arnold, smoothing her silky tresses, "there is nothing to forgive."

"Yes, but there is."

"Why will you think so seriously of such nonsense?"

"It isn't nonsense. But I see you forgive me; thank you, Ar. And you won't think the worse of me for what I said? You won't love me the less?"

"Surely not, Leo."

The soft brown eyes looked strangely bright even through a veil of tears, but this on the whole perhaps decked rather than dimmed their lustre. A pause of a minute.

"You may kiss me, Ar, if you like," she said, gently, with a little winning smile running along the line of her lips. She held up her face : so that he shouldn't have to stoop too low, perhaps.

What a commingling of innocence and half-conscious coquetry and tenderness and merriment, the tears still dewing her eyelashes !

Mr. Arnold Page availed himself of the privilege permitted him. Probably under like circumstances most people would have done as he did.

"Darling little Leo !" he said, as he looked about for a cab to take him to the Temple.

Soon after he added—

" I wonder if that fellow Lackington has left my place yet ? I feel inclined for a cigar and a chat before turning in."

He found Mr. Lackington in the chambers in Sun-dial Buildings, but asleep on a sofa with an empty bottle at his side. He was in the dark ; he had been too lazy to light a candle.

" It will be a shame to disturb him ; but it will be better for him to have the window shut," said Arnold Page, and he closed the window, leaving the painter to his repose.

"Dear little Leo !" he said again. She was a pleasant subject to return to, unquestionably.

We need not follow further the steps of Lord Dolly and his friend, nor is it immediately material to the objects of our history whether or not Flukemore obtained his liberty. Sufficient to say, for the present, that on the morning after his visit to the opera, the Honourable Dudley Chalker required a large dose of his favourite soda-water before he could be put upon his feet, and even then he was for a long time speechless, and not a very exhilarating spectacle. Some hours later, however, he was sufficiently recovered to show himself at his club (the Junior Adonis, St. James's Street), and give a friendly " Aw," to certain of his acquaintances there, including Lord Dolly—as pink and fresh, flaxen and trim, as a school-girl. No wonder they called him "Cupid;" he looked the part; only you are required to imagine the son of Cytherea as a modern, very fashionable divinity, attired in broadcloth, and "about town:" smoking cheroots when not sucking his ivory-topped cane; and a splendid seat upon a colossal, rakish looking, bay blood mare, prancing in the Row—now thinning like the trees in the park, for the glory of the season had departed.

CHAPTER III.

THE MISSES BIGGS' SEMINARY FOR YOUNG LADIES.

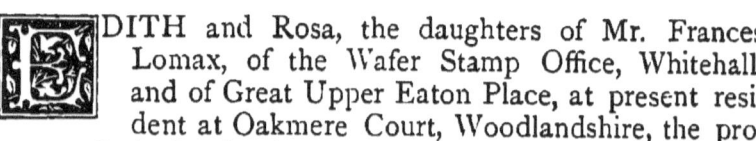DITH and Rosa, the daughters of Mr. Frances Lomax, of the Wafer Stamp Office, Whitehall, and of Great Upper Eaton Place, at present resident at Oakmere Court, Woodlandshire, the property of his brother-in-law, Mr. Arnold Page—Edith and Rosa, little girls of the respective ages of eleven and nine years, were pupils at the Misses Biggs' seminary for young ladies, Chapone House, Kew Green. This establishment was of no mean fame. It had been in existence many years. It was expensive—it was exclusive. It recognised in no way the "mutual system." A coal-merchant could not place his daughter under the charge of the Misses Bigg—still less could he hope to pay for his child's education with so many tons of fuel per quarter. The Misses Bigg steadily declined to receive into their academy the children of persons engaged in trade. They had even entertained doubts at one time in regard to the offspring of professional men. It was with a sigh that Miss Adelaide Bigg had accepted the charge of the two daughters of that eminent advocate Lisper, Q.C., of the Northern Circuit. She admitted, with tears in her eyes, that she perceived distinctly in that proceeding "the thin end of the wedge." But Miss Adelaide Bigg entertained strong opinions. She

had been heard to declare that the secrets of scholastic success were exclusiveness—exclusiveness—exclusiveness. Her cry at one time had been the peerage, the whole peerage, and nothing but the peerage. She was one of those alarming creatures known as "superior women." She adhered to her opinions with a tenacity that had something terrible in it. But she was compelled to yield to what it pleased her to designate "the frightful inroads of democracy." She confessed that she had suffered deeply for the cause of the aristocratic families. It was believed that the books of the establishment could have shown a sad list of debts due to the Misses Bigg in respect of some of their most distinguished pupils. She was found one morning quite dead in her chair. She had been reading the *Court Circular.* In the list of presentations at a drawing-room of the Sovereign, she had discovered the names of no less than six of her former pupils. It is not known how much loss in money those pupils represented.

The surviving sister, Miss Dorothea Bigg, was a less superior woman than the late Miss Adelaide. She had not the firmness of mind nor the dignity of manner, nor, it was said, the intellectual culture of her departed sister. It is possible, indeed, that the seminary was existing rather on the strength of its reputation in the past than because of the extent of its merits in the present. Yet Miss Dorothea did all in her power to cherish the fair fame of the institution. The children of commerce were still kept without the gates. The terms had not been reduced—the number of the pupils were still limited—the name of "the Misses Bigg" was still preserved on the door-plate, still headed the half-yearly bills and the prospectuses. The nobility and gentry were informed now, as of old, that at the Misses Biggs' seminary, Chapone House, Kew Green, a limited number of young ladies were received. TERMS—One hundred and fifty guineas per annum, including board and instruction in every essential of a sound English education. RELIGIOUS AND MORAL CULTURE under the immediate and personal superintendence of Miss Dorothea Bigg. (This had reference, probably, to an examination of the pupils every Sunday afternoon in the catechism and collect of the day). There were said to be reasons why Miss Bigg did not venture to interfere in any other educational matters. Certainly, her French was Britannic in point of accent, while, grammatically considered, it could only be called shaky. The FRENCH, GERMAN, and ITALIAN languages constantly spoken, and French made the medium of instruction (whatever that might mean). The PIANO, HARP, GUITAR, DRAWING, PAINTING IN OIL AND WATER COLOURS, GERMAN, FRENCH, ITALIAN AND LATIN by first-rate professors, each twelve guineas. DANCING, three guineas a quarter. SEAT AT CHURCH, two guineas. USE OF INSTRUMENTS, two or three guineas, according to age. The USE OF THE GLOBES and CALISTHENICS, four guineas. LAUNDRESS, eight guineas. Charge for remaining during vacations, twelve guineas. A half year's notice required before the removal of a pupil. Each lady providing her own plate and linen. While, after these announcements, the prospectus went on to state that "the Misses Bigg, deeply impressed with the intense responsibility devolving upon those to whom may be entrusted the absolute charge of children at a distance from their homes, desire that it may be understood that young people from abroad or the colonies consigned to their protection, it will be their especial care to make the objects of an untiring, affectionate, and maternal solicitude; not simply in so far as their educational progress may be concerned, but also in regard to the even more important considerations affecting their religious and moral welfare and training, their personal comfort and happiness, and their health, for the preservation and promotion of which last Chapone House presents peculiar advantages. It is most favourably situated, on a gravelly soil, overlooking the Royal Gardens of Kew, the air being at the same time both mild and bracing, and particularly recommended by the Faculty. References rigorously insisted on, and permitted to the Right Reverend Blackman Savage, Lord Bishop of Otaheite; the Venerable G. Todd, Archdeacon of Bunglowputty, East Indies; the Hon. J. Crow, Secretary of the Legation, Dixie's Land; and to the numerous parents of pupils who have received the blessings of education at the Misses Biggs' Seminary, Chapone House, Kew Green."

This excellently planned prospectus had all the effect of what is called, I believe, "a strong bill" at the theatres. It attracted attention—it drew. The limited number of pupils was generally complete, even though it had been necessary for particular reasons to look a little lower than the aristocratic families, and to receive the children of the professional classes.

But among the Misses Biggs' pupils you could not always distinguish those who sprung from an aristocratic and those from a less precious stock. When Miss Leonora Agnes Carr was one of the limited number of young ladies, you would have been inclined, I think, to attribute to her an origin quite as *recherché* as that of the Hon. Maud Eve Elaine, only daughter of Hubert Lord Stonehenge. There had been no question about the reception of little Leonora into the school. Miss Dorothea was pleased, she said, to see Miss Carr an inmate of Chapone House; and she was able to rely for certain, as she well knew, on the periodical receipt of old Mr. Carr's cheques in payment for the education of his child.

But the Misses Bigg had other claims to the estimation of the world. They were the daughters of the eminent poet Bigg, the author of that superb epic, so favourably noticed by all the Low Church reviews of the period, *The Course of Life*, in twenty cantos. (Alas! Dorothea would pronounce the word *canters*, now that Adelaide was no longer alive to correct her.) Bigg, in his youth the gentleman of *ton*, the friend of Fox and Sheridan, the companion of George the Debonair, a grand man and a handsome, as is evident from his portrait still hanging in the Misses Biggs' best drawing-room, at Chapone House—a massive personage with brilliant eyes and a fascinating smile, a bottle nose, and his hair well combed over his forehead : Bigg, the beauty, the girth and symmetry of whose leg had been even the envy of his sovereign, and, indeed, the subject of a bet on the part of that urbane monarch (was not Sheridan invited to decide the wager? and did he not give his opinion in favour of the superior size of calf being on the side of his royal master?—a partial judgment, as it was always believed, and for which Bigg never forgave him)—Bigg, who in his maturity had repented of the unwisdom of his youth, and his money gone and the gout come in his hands and feet, had invoked the Muse—how successfully, there was his sublime work—that was the proper phrase to employ concerning it—to bear witness. It went rapidly through sixteen editions. "Can you 'ave anythink more sublime than that?" asked Binks, the publisher. *The Course of Life*, a soul poem, in twenty cantos. It was considered at certain prayer and tea parties a great thing that Bigg should have had a call so beneficial as was implied in the production of *The Course of Life*, while unquestionably it was a great thing for Bigg that he could make so advantageous a call upon the public as was comprehended in the sixteen editions of his great work. Did he not also receive a pension from the Earl of Birmingham's government?—not a large sum, of course, but still sufficient to supply the bard with as much of his favourite snuff and beloved rum-punch as he could possibly require for the rest of his life—his needs in these respects not being trifling; while, *au reste*, he lived upon the exertions of his daughters, the Misses Bigg, of Chapone House. Altogether, Bigg had probably enjoyed his life as much as most of us, and rather more than some. A youth of pleasure and an old age of comfort, and all at the expense of other people.

There are some Ministers who keep office under all forms of government. Bigg had hobnobbed in tokay with giddiness and gaiety; by-and-by he was enjoying tea and muffins with primness and prudery. Of course it's easy to be inconsistent and to change your convictions; the difficulty is to bring to a good market your altered opinions. Bigg was successful in this respect. He posed himself as a convert. Now, in the case of a convert, of course it is an advantage for him to have enjoyed previously as bad a character as possible. If we are to wash the black man white, let us have him as jetty as may be at starting, and there will be so much more credit in the concern; let us have a whole-bred negro rather than an octoroon. The well-known early naughtiness of Bigg were so many testimonials in his favour. An influential evangelical congregation straightway took up Bigg, and he took up them and their sentiments hot and strong. He became a valuable member of their body. His success was tremendous. He lectured in the chapels of the party. He could point to himself as at once the frightful example and the moral result of his own teaching. Money was turned away from the doors, and he crowned his triumph by the production of *The Course of Life* in twenty cantos. This is not the place to review that remarkable book. Its enormous sale has been already the subject of observation. Passages of it were set to music and sung in the chapels of the faithful. It was the gift-book of families of the persuasion; and it was, of course, bound in calf, whole extra, with gilt edges, and, with the autograph of Miss Dorothea on the fly-leaf, one of the prizes bestowed upon successful students at Chapone House, Kew Green. I am afraid that some of these did not rate highly either the poetry or the piety of Bigg's book.

" Portrait of my father, at the age of thirty-seven, by Cadmium, R.A., well-known as the rival of Lawrence, exhibited at Somerset House in 18—," Miss Dorothea would say, for the edification of visitors, pointing a gristly, knuckly, black-mittened hand in the direction of the picture over the mantelpiece. " Black shade of the poet Bigg at the age of sixty-two, considered a wonderful likeness. My father, when a boy, with Epping Forest in the background ; he was born in Essex, at the village of Chingford, in the year 17— Water-colour study of my father when a child, by the celebrated artist, P. Madder. My father, even quite as an infant, was remarkable for the beauty of his countenance ; those works of art in the corner are two other portraits of the poet Bigg, by the eminent and fashionable amatoor, Prince Ernest Blisterhazy. My father with his hat on ; my father with his hat off. Medallion portrait of my father, by Moulder, the sculptor ; the shape of my father's head was generally considered to be very remarkable. The protooberances on the forehead are certainly singular ; they are not in the least exaggerated. The bust on the staircase, which you passed as you came up, was by Chiswell, R.A., a very admirable work, slightly idealised, very highly estimated by persons of distinction ; it was on seeing that bust that his majesty, the late King George the Fourth, struck by the likeness, gave an order for his own bust in his coronation robes to be executed by Chiswell. It was the same bust that his Majesty afterwards most graciously presented to the Emperor of China, and it is now one of the most cherished ornaments of the imperial palace at Pekin. Favourite chair of the poet Bigg ; the desk at which the poem of *The Course of Life* was written ; the poet's table ; the poet's pen-wiper ; the poet's pen ; a copy of the first edition of *The Course of Life,* bound in morocco—valuable from its possessing on the title-page impromptu lines upon his work, addressed to my father and in her own handwriting by the poetess, Lady Grinderstone, the authoress of *Strains of the Soul, or the Evangelical Hymnal.* From this window you can perceive the poet's favourite seat in the little arbour at the bottom of the garden ; it is completely covered with nasturtiums in the summer time. The poet would often sit there for hours meditating upon his great poem, and generally upon philosophical and sacred topics. He would sometimes take his tea in that arbour " (more often, however, his hot rum-and-water, and clay pipe ; only Miss Dorothea made no mention of those constant friends and companions of the poet, probably because they appeared to convey too material a notion of the poet's manner of life) ; "he would rather remain hours in that spot than enter the house, and be liable to the interruption of an important train of thought. Specimen of my father's handwriting at the age of eighty-three, considered very remarkable for its distinctness, being written at so advanced an age ;" and so on. It will be seen that there was little danger of the fame of the late Bigg dying out in the seminary ; certainly, whatever else he was, he was a poet in his own household.

"The picture over the 'shiffoneer' is by the celebrated Cromer ; he was formerly professor of drawing and painting at this institution. It represents a fancy sketch of my late sister Adelaide " (at this moment Miss Dorothea was popularly supposed to remove a stray tear from the corner of her eye with the aid of a long bony finger, that looked rather like a stick of yellow sealing-wax). "It is considered a good likeness by many, though it always appeared to me that it did not do justice to the intellectual expression of my late sister, which was very remarkable. Upon her head she wears a turban of primrose-coloured satin. She is depicted in the character of St. Cecilia. It was a fancy of the artist's which my late sister did not approve, and which I am not prepared to defend. She is playing upon an organ of the form supposed to be in use at that early period." (The musical instrument thus described, it is needless to say, was of the pattern with which happily art has made us fully acquainted, and which appears to have resulted from an accidental combination, admirable for a still-life study,—of a patent mangle and a row of gas-pipes).

The drawing-room of Chapone House was rather grim and gaunt, hard and white. It was crowded with straight lines; it looked as though it had been starched and ironed. The visitor was always possessed with a doubt and a difficulty as to where he should sit; the forbidding aspect of the formal files of chairs lining the room at once compelled him to abandon all thought of finding relief in those quarters. He would no more have dreamt of removing one from its place against the wall than he would have contemplated pulling out one of Miss Bigg's front teeth. The furniture was all shrouded in white holland, just as though it was so much furniture that had departed this life, and had got its grave-clothes on already whenever the undertaker might come to announce that he was prepared to complete the business by decent interment. A chandelier in a white bag, like an inverted and collapsed balloon, hung from the centre of the ceiling. The steel grates, glittering with polish, looked as though they knew nothing about fire, and wood, and coals, and such vulgarities; while they concealed their emptiness, like diners-out before dinner, behind superb shirt-fronts, thick with frilled decorations. For the poker, smooth, shining, slender—if it had been a gold stick in waiting it could not have enjoyed more of a sinecure.

Miss Dorothea Bigg was a very tall woman: she looked even taller than she really was, from her strenuous forbearance to diminish her appearance of height by amplitude of skirt. She resorted to no artificial means to project the folds of her dress, and, as a consequence, these hung limply in long lines: so that, in point of fact, the drapery screening her ankles was but little wider than where it covered her shoulders. Her figure was rectangular in pattern, her face very long and thin; the stiffly plaited cap exactly followed the outline of her head, and its sad-coloured ribbons were tied under her chin with a tightness that was most probably painful. Her eyebrows were strongly marked, her eyes a dull black, her mouth large, showing when she spoke not merely many of her discoloured teeth, but a good margin of the gums in which these were set. The little black dab of a front that she wore upon her forehead might almost have been a petrifaction, it was so harsh and rigid. She had a general complaint that the weather was "very chilly" (certainly the climate in the Chapone House drawing-room was rather severe) ; and was for ever huddling a shabby cachmere shawl about her sharply-pointed shoulders, while she rubbed her hands one over the other briskly, until the grating of her mittens, as they came in contact with each other, became quite audible. She was not very erect, being almost too tall and slight for that; so that she advanced with rather a bending, sloping air, like the progress of a fire-escape or a cameleopard.

The limited number of young ladies could perceive from the windows that a handsome barouche had stopped at the gate of Chapone House. The Mangnall's Questions class were undergoing examination by Miss Mullins, who, being Irish by birth and accent, was engaged to teach English at the Misses Biggs' seminary.

"I think it's Leo Carr," whispered the young lady nearest the window to her neighbour, and soon the information went round the class. Soon two pink-cheeked, blue-eyed, yellow-haired, thoroughly English-looking little girls began to blush with pleasure, and their little hearts to thump quite anxiously.

"It's for *us*," murmured the daughters of Francis Lomax, Esq., of the Wafer Stamp Office.

"Silence!" cried Miss Mullins. "I'll have no looking out of the whindow during studhies. Miss Mhortimer, I'll throuble you to name some of the eminent men who flourished in the reign of Heliogabalus. Oh, so you didn't hear the question ! Thin, perhaps, Miss Hengist will inform you."

"Origen of Alexandria, one of the fathers of the Church, who repulsed the attacks of Celsus, the Epicurean philosopher," Miss Hengist, with breathless eagerness, jerked out in reply.

"Quite right, Miss Hengist," remarked Miss Mullins.

"Miss Mhortimer will be so good as to write the lesson out six times. Miss Lomax—" little Edith started like a pony making a first acquaintance with whipcord—"what kings in ancient history afford the most striking proof of the vicissitudes to which human life is subject?"

Poor Edith's cheeks became yet more crimson, and her breathing very quick indeed. Like Miss Mortimer, she had permitted her attention to wander from Mangnall to the barouche at the gates. The hawk-eyes of Miss Mullins were detecting the deficiencies of the little lamb; a severe sentence was about to be pronounced, when the door of the school-room was flung wide open, and Miss Dorothea Bigg entered.

Leonora Carr was alone in the gaunt drawing-room. Mrs. Carr had accompanied her daughter to the school, but the old lady had declined the trouble of descending from the carriage to enter Chapone House, and attempt conversation with Miss Bigg.

"Don't ask me to get out, Leo dear," said Mrs. Carr, "for I can't do it. I don't like Miss Bigg. I never did like schoolmistresses, they're so formal, and so hungry-looking. Miss Bigg is a very estimable person, I dare say, and her school was very highly recommended to me, or I should not have entrusted you to her care; but it always seems to me that she wants to pick holes in everything I say, and it makes me quite nervous: and it's so long since I went to school that I begin to think I'm talking bad grammar. Bring Edith and Rosy out and we'll take them for a drive—children like a drive—and we can go on to the pastry-cook's on Richmond Hill. Children are fond of the pastry-cooks. Take my card-case; you can leave my card and your papa's."

And Mrs. Carr leant back in the well-padded barouche, while Leonora tripped lightly up the vividly white steps of Chapone House. The old lady struggled at first with the drowsiness with which the gentle rocking of the well-built and balanced carriage always affected her. By-and-by she was nodding and dozing comfortably. (She took her three glasses of sherry at lunch regularly, in pursuance of the advice of her favourite physician, the famous Sir Cupper Leech.) Leonora had entered the drawing-room and confronted her former instructress, Miss Dorothea Bigg : who, on the sound of carriage wheels, had—according to her custom—made for that apartment, so that, on the entrance of visitors, she might be—to use a theatrical term—"discovered" seated on the hard sofa, at right angles with the icy-looking fireplace, studying the penultimate canto of the poet Bigg's *Course of Life*. As "Miss Carr" was announced, she rose to greet her visitor, having first carefully marked the place at which her reading had been interrupted, by means of an elaborately embroidered card bookmarker ; the words "Read, mark, and digest," appearing on it in coloured beads almost like an illumination legend, with long streamers of sea-green ribbon at either end.

Leonora, in spite of her slight form and not tall stature, was possessed of a good share of courage and strength of will. She was prepared for something of a conflict with her old schoolmistress, whom, I may as well say at once, she cordially hated ; in fact, as a rule, it is only those ultra and impossibly well-conducted children of the story-books (who, by-the-way, generally die young, I notice—and what a comfort that is !) who love their teachers. She had made up her mind as to the part she would play in the interview. She would be very cold, and stiff, and dignified. She had dressed for the part evidently, under the idea of impressing the schoolmistress : a superb brocaded silk, rustling noisily as she moved and struck the furniture with her ample skirts ; her tiny hands in the most delicately tinted gloves, holding her card-case, and a handkerchief that was, in fact, a mere filmy square of lace.

"She'll try to kiss me, I know her," the little lady said to herself ; "but I'll take care that she doesn't. I don't know that I'll even shake hands with her—I hate her."

"My dear Leonora," said Miss Dorothea, rising from the sofa with a great cordiality, and showing her teeth freely, which proceeding, indeed, constituted her notion of a smile, "how kee-ind this is. How glad I am to see you, my dear che-ild. Welcome again to our 'umble dwelling, Chapone House."

She extended her arms ; she was evidently about to fall upon her late pupil and embrace her affectionately. (They bore about the relation to each other in size and form, that

a lighthouse would bear to a diving-bell.) But the aspect
of little Leo rather quenched this needless ardour. The
expression of her face was very prim and demure indeed ;
her lips were drawn together into a compact little line ; the
brown eyes beamed very steadily and solemnly. She made
a profound curtsey ; the edges of her dress quite crackled
upon the carpet as she descended among her flounces.
She put forward two fingers of her left hand, as she said,
feebly, languidly, half closing her eyes, as though she were
short-sighted and could so see better—

"Miss Bigg, I believe ? I hope I see you well."

The schoolmistress felt the effect of this demeanour.

"I hope your ma is well, Leonora. I hope your excellent pa enjoys his health," she said, with rather a dashed
manner.

Leonora listlessly produced two cards and pushed them
gently across the table.

"Kind regards and inquiries," she murmured affectedly.
"I have come to see Edith and Rosa Lomax, by request of
their mamma. Will you let them come to me ? "

"They are now in class," Miss Bigg adopting the formula
usual on like occasions, and with a pretended hesitation.
"As a rule we don't like the studies of our young ladies to
be interrupted."

"That is of no consequence," Leo said grandly. "Of
course I must see them. I have come here with that object
only."

"Little minx," muttered Miss Dorothea, as she left the
drawing-room in quest of the young ladies inquired for. "I
should like to give her a good shaking, I should."

Leo's face changed as her enemy departed. She wore
quite an expression of triumph.

"Oh, if she only knew how frightened I really am of
her," she exclaimed, and by way of relief to her feelings
she made a disrespectful *moue* at Cadmium's portrait of the
author of *The Course of Life* over the mantelpiece, and another at Cromer's sketch above the " shiffoneer " of Miss
Adelaide Bigg in the character of St. Cecilia. Leonora had
known Adelaide in the flesh (she had not had much to
speak of), and had not loved her greatly.

" How I hate this room ! it gives me quite a creepy,

crawly sensation," soliloquised Leonora. "How well I remember that great, ugly, upright piano in the corner, with its frayed, faded yellow silk. And all those dreadful pictures. Bigg was a hideous-looking man, although he was a poet— at least, they say here that he was. Ah! and that precious china card-basket, riveted in three places; and those old-fashioned bronze and brass and glass lustres, and that looking-glass, which makes one look quite green. What yards and yards of brown holland; wax flowers in the middle of the table; stuffed birds between the windows; Bigg's poems, first edition, in morocco, and his chair, and desk, and pen-wiper, the old fright; and Miss Adelaide's album, with original lines never published, by Hannah More, or Mrs. Hemans, or Mrs. Barbauld, or someone, I'm sure I forget. I never could make out what they meant, I know *that*. And old Dorothea's Church Service in dirty red velvet with brass edges. How I hate the whole place! Ah! here she comes again." And Leonora hurriedly resumed a studied position of much grace, but considerable affectation.

Edith and Rosa Lomax entered the room. There had just been time to perform a hurried toilette as to their countenances: these had been rubbed with a moist towel by an expeditious servant, who had also, being a clever and handy woman, found time to apply a brush vigorously to their yellow hair; the process being almost as brief and rapid as when a brisk baker rasps a burnt French roll. After Leonora had kissed the fresh, cool cheeks of her young friends she detected a distinct flavour of soap lingering upon her lips.

"How do you do, dear?" she inquired, still preserving her fine-lady manner, for Miss Dorothea was still present.

"I'm before Edith in French," says little Rosy with a triumphant sparkle in her blue eyes.

"Are you, dear? I'm sure you ought to be very grateful to those who take so much pains to instruct you."

Leonora's languid eyes rest for a moment on the schoolmistress, who, not entirely free from suspicion, bows a grim acknowledgment of the compliment conveyed by the remark.

"I hope your pupils give you satisfaction, Miss Bigg," and Leonora bows her head with wonderful courtesy.

"I have no grave cause of complaint against them," Miss Bigg replies, slowly sighing.

Soon a reluctant permission is obtained for the little girls having a drive in Mrs. Carr's barouche.

"It's unusual," the schoolmistress remarks, "very unusual; yes, and inconvenient; and against the rules. It is only the relatives of the young ladies who are permitted to remove them from my care for ever so short a time."

She watched the effect of these observations upon Leonora. They had no success in the way of quelling that young lady. She adhered to her demand; the children by their anxious glances and gleaming eyes endorsing her views of the case as earnestly as they dared.

"I suppose I must consent," Miss Bigg said. "I suppose I must make an exception in *your* case, Leonora, my former esteemed pupil. Though it's to be much regretted that they should be deprived of the benefit of Miss Mullins' admirable instructions in English; she is now occupied with her class."

"Somehow," little Rosy said to her sister, as they put on their bonnets, "I don't think I like Leo so much as I used to do; do you, Edith? She's rather fine and grand, and stuck up; don't you think so?"

"What nice gloves she has on, and what a darling parasol," Edith remarks. (She is already acquiring a taste in dress.)

"I suppose they'll drive to Richmond. I hope they'll take us to the pastry-cook's," and Rosy claps her little red hands, moved to that demonstration by visions of tarts.

"For shame, Rosy, thinking of such things. How *can* you be so greedy?"

"Oh, yes, Miss: but you'll eat quite as many things as I shall, if you get the chance. If Mrs. Carr asks me if I'll have some ginger-beer I shall say, yes. I like to see it fizz up. It's so nice, only it always brings the tears into my eyes. Don't you love ginger-beer, Edith? I do."

Meanwhile Miss Carr has visited the school-room, interrupting, by permission of Miss Bigg, hesitatingly accorded, Miss Mullins' Mangnall's Questions class. She has resumed her acquaintance with certain of her old fellow pupils and playmates; she is very kind and smiling

4

and gracious; a little too condescending, they agreed afterwards; but she is rather full of her grand manner in the
neighbourhood of Miss Bigg. The young ladies crowd
round her, admiring her greatly. Miss Mortimer thinks
"her bonnet lovely, and in charming taste." Miss Hengist
holds that her brocaded silk is sweetly pretty, and most
fashionably made. It is true that *that* Miss Bobbin ventures
to sneer at the visitor after her withdrawal, denouncing her
even as a "judy," and a "guy" (whatever those terms may
signify; they were regarded by her associates as bitterly
and needlessly hostile). But then Miss Bobbin had never
been admitted to the friendship of Leonora. Miss Bobbin
was notoriously a rude girl: rude in her speech, and
opinions, and actions. She had been known to call Miss
Mullins names èven to her face, while she had on one occasion actually slapped the French teacher. There had even
been a talk at one time of expelling her the school: so the
girls whispered to each other. No one could be surprised
at anything Miss Bobbin might say. No one could care
either. What could you expect? Was not her father the
large millowner, the member for that dreadful place Shuttle-
combe, in the north of England—a fiery Radical and de-
mocrat; a dangerous man, as many country gentlemen had
freely stated. Lord Stonehenge had at one time meditated
removing his daughter from contact with the man Bobbin's
daughter. But somehow that nobleman's intentions were
constantly a very long way ahead of his conduct.

"Take care of your fingers, dears, as he shuts the door.
Mind their frocks, Andrews. Richmond, and, Andrews,
stop at the pastry-cook's." So Mrs. Carr gives instructions.
"Well, my dears, you look very well. Your mamma will
be glad to hear that. I shall see her next week. I suppose you're already looking forward to the Michaelmas holidays. Talk to them, Leo—amuse them—there's a dear."

Leo's manner had undergone a complete change. Even
critical Rosy was satisfied upon that subject now.

"You darlings," she cried presently, quite boisterously,
"how glad I am to see you! Come and kiss me again both
of you. I was obliged to be grand and stately before that
horrid old thing, Bigg. Isn't she an old dragon, Rosy?"

"She is," Rosy says at once, with frank acquiescence.

" Now we can have some fun ! "

And there is great prattling and laughing, and something between a squeak and a crow from Rosy ; very noisy indeed, waking up echoes amongst the stately elms of Kew Gardens —amazing Mrs. Carr.

" Oh, Leo ! You do tickle me so dreadfully ! "

" Ah ! this is all very well," Leo remarks with mock sedateness. " You'll have to behave very differently, by-and-by. You'll have both of you to treat me with great cere-mony and respect. A whisper to both of you. Perhaps I'm going to become Aunt Leo. Think of that ! "

" You're not ; what stuff ! " Rosy exclaims, incredulous.

" Suppose that I and Uncle Arnold—— "

" Are you going to marry Uncle Ar, Leo ? " Edith asks— she is a little girl of quick perception.

" Perhaps, Edie."

" Marry Uncle Ar ; oh, what fun ! " and Rosy claps her hands again, partly, perhaps, because the carriage stopped just then at the foot of Richmond Hill, at a well-known shop.

What a feast they had at that pastry-cook's ! What a number of maids-of-honour they consumed (how cannibally it sounds !) ; and Rosy had ginger-beer, and tears in her eyes, and the froth and bubbles of the draught all over her lips, and nose, and cheeks. She enjoyed herself immensely, and did not feel in the least ill after her exertions. She was blessed with the digestive powers of a young ostrich.

" And now tell me, dears, something about the school. When did my pet little Baby Gill go away? I did not see her in the class-room, and I forgot to make inquiry about her."

Four blue eyes opened very widely at this question.

" She hasn't gone away at all."

" Where is she then ? "

" She's very bad. Haven't you heard, Leo ? "

" Naughty? no, she was never naughty."

" No, she's ill. We haven't seen her for days. No one has seen her. She's up at quite the top of the house. No one has seen her. We don't know what's the matter with her."

" How cruel of me to be laughing and talking here, and

4—2

never thinking of the poor little soul before. I'll see her when I go back though," Leo says, self-reproachfully.

"I don't think Miss Bigg will let you see her."

"Hum! I'm of a different opinion, Miss Edie."

"Miss Bigg," said Leonora, "before I return to town, I am most anxious to renew my acquaintance with my little friend, Barbara Gill. I am sorry to learn that she is unwell —confined to her room, indeed."

"I regret, Miss Carr, to inform you that it is quite impossible to comply with your request."

"Miss Bigg, I should wish you to understand," said Leo, firmly, "that I don't leave the house until I have seen Barbara Gill."

Miss Bigg turned quite pale. It was hard to say whether with anger or from alarm. Her hand shook so that she removed it from the table.

"Miss Carr, it is impossible," she muttered.

"Miss Bigg, I don't think so," and Leo turned the light of her brilliant eyes full on the white face of the schoolmistress.

CHAPTER IV

APARTMENTS FURNISHED.

INE o'clock and past. A thickening mist: lost in it, London looks like a huge fresco, over which some barbarous hand has spread a first coat of whitewash; or a giant corpse, strange and blurred, and awful in its outlines, swathed in grave-clothes of gauze. All colour has gone, with all distinctness and delicacy of drawing. Nothing now save confused masses of shadow, more or less opaque; and here and there suggestions of shape, that speedily dwindle into vagueness: the lamps in the roadways seem to be mere sparks glimmering behind thick horn or ground glass, they emit so dim and feeble a light. The mist everywhere; now setting in a dense inanimate cloud; now shifting capriciously in wreathed streaky vapour. Not the saffron-hued fog of evenings later in the year: not the fine old tawny November, with plenty of body in it and crust about it. The light India muslin mist floating round the traveller, rather than the yellow India shawl fog that wraps so suffocatingly tight, with a consistency so dense and oppressive.

A woman hurrying, running, arrives breathless at the toll-gate on the Surrey side of Hungerford Suspension Bridge. With trembling eagerness she thrusts a piece of money into the gate-keeper's hand, and then pushes at the turnstile.

"Stop a minute."

"For God's sake let me through," she cries passionately. The man is not greatly moved; he examines the coin she has given him, bites it, and examines it anew.

"I can't take this."

"Is it bad?" and she takes out her purse with quick nervous fingers.

"Not as I knows on; but I can't take it. It's furrin money."

She gives him an English shilling.

" Here, stop ! Your change ! "

But she has hurried through, and is now some yards on her way, running as fast as she can. She heeds not even if she hears him. Soon she is lost in the mist.

" Rum uns, women are," the gate-keeper remarks. " I never could make out whether they like saving or spending money most. Sometimes they'll stand higgle-haggle for hours all about twopence halfpenny, the next moment they'll fling all they've got in the world out o' window. Rum uns I call them."

He nodded and winked, and shook his head, entirely, would seem, for his own gratification ; for he was quite alone, and even his blackbird in a wicker cage in a corner of the room was fast asleep ; and spun the shilling in the air, and commenced to conjure with it—swallowing it and bringing it by turns out of his eyes and his ears and his nose, a neat performance ; it was a pity there were no spectators to enjoy it and applaud.

" Hi, hillo ! Oh ! oho ! "

How thick it is on the Surrey side of the river. A cab-man has mistaken his way, and believes himself at Waterloo Bridge when he is only at Hungerford. He is now backing on the pavement, coming with a thump on the kerb-stone, or trying to turn round a lamp-post in a peculiarly purpose-less manner.

" Cabby's lost his 'ead ; or the fog's been and got in it and fuddled him." So the gate-keeper comments.

The woman runs on, very quickly and lightly ; yet, evidently, she is distressed. She is painfully breathless. She holds one hand to her side and presses it tightly there : she suffers from what the faculty would call " lancinating pains in the side ; " what the people describe briefly as " the stitch." She stops for a moment to lean against the chain of the bridge and recover herself. She is quite hot with running, and she dabs her forehead with her handker-chief, and loosens the strings of her bonnet and the wrap-pings round her throat.

" This is better than the darkest night," she murmurs, glancing round approvingly. " How my heart beats. I feel quite sick with running. I must rest for a minute, only for a minute. Surely there will be no danger in that." And she appears to discuss with herself the propriety of pausing.

A fragile-looking woman, with a pallid face and large, limpid, intent eyes—one can see so much, the mist notwithstanding—her dress of a neutral tint that readily blends with the prevailing obscurity. Flying along as she had been, she looked like a creature of air, an incarnation of the mist : her face discernible long before the lines of her figure and the shape of her flowing skirts were to be traced with any degree of distinctness.

"Directly, directly ; I will start again directly."

She is occupied with self-communing.

The mist becomes very dense. The bridge seems as though it were hung in the clouds : the water below, the land at either end, are alike screened from sight. The few passengers grow bewildered. Some shout as they advance, to warn those coming in an opposite direction. A footstep is heard close to where the woman is resting : another second, and a hand as though groping its way along, touches her shoulder.

"What's this ? " asks someone puzzled.

How the woman starts, as though she had been stabbed with sharp steel or seared with hot iron.

"Let me go ! don't touch me ! "

And she is off running again at her utmost speed.

"Well I never," says the voice, gruffly, and as though indignant at such unnecessary vehemence ; " who wants to touch you ? Women should never come out in fogs, they always get frightened. People should never lose their presence of mind. God bless me ! How thick the mist is over the river. I wish I was well home. But I dare say it will be better on the Middlesex side."

It *was* better on the Middlesex side ; the woman found it so. It would vary a good deal—now coming densely over, now lifting off, as it were, and growing thinner and lighter ; remaining so for a few minutes, then darkening again, like a coquette at a masquerade toying with her mask, now showing, now hiding her face.

On flew our fugitive, fog or no fog. She was soon in the Strand. She stood for a moment as though in doubt whether to proceed eastward or westward. Then she turned to the east, running again. The mist was decidedly clearer now, and many people looked back wonderingly after she had passed them. Some even, with that broad, wilful jocoseness common in the London streets, seeing her advance rapidly, set up a cry to startle her, or stretched out a hand, as though to detain her. This frightened her terribly. She sprung aside or dashed across the road, and then, as though convinced that there was greater safety in the quieter thoroughfares, she turned abruptly out of the Strand and soon found herself in a tangle of streets in the neighbourhood of Clare Market. She went on, however, at random apparently, and at last emerged in Lincoln's Inn Fields. The mist seemed here, as it always does seem in open places, to be denser again, as bad even as it had been on the bridge. Again she stopped.

"Where am I? where shall I go? what place is this? Oh, if I had but *one* friend in London!"

The words were uttered breathlessly; yet in tones very soft and plaintive.

"Have you lost your way?"

She started back, a policeman stood at her elbow.

"Holborn," she gasped out; "where is it? is it near?"

She was trembling with fright.

"Cross the square, go through that farther corner, and you're in it."

Again she was hurrying on. But she soon quitted Holborn for the same reason, as it seemed, that she had turned from the Strand. The noise and stir, the number of passengers and vehicles alarmed her. She was in Gray's Inn Lane; but she left it abruptly by a street on the right hand. A little way on, and she was leaning against the dense walls of the House of Correction, Cold Bath Fields. She was on higher ground now, the fog was comparatively slight and transparent. But she could run no more. She tottered as she walked—she was so fatigued and exhausted —almost fainting. A few more paces, and she stopped to read the name of a street inscribed on a corner house, well lit up by a lamp close at hand, and the glare of a public-house on the opposite side of the way, the proprietor of which was evidently bent upon brilliance, at no matter what expenditure in gas.

"Coppice Row," she made out with some little difficulty. "I wonder where that is? in what part of London? I must have come some miles." Her voice was broken, and she was now pressing both hands to her side. "I can go no farther. Oh, that I could sit down and rest."

The corner house was a newsvender's—the shop window crowded with publications of various kinds; newspapers suspended by strings covering even the door-posts, so that they looked something like the masts of a ship in full sail. All sorts of particoloured placards spotted the outside of the house and drew attention to the merits of *this* wonderfully cheap newspaper, or *that* intensely interesting miscellany. And the proprietor of the shop dealt also in tobacco, snuff, cigars, and pipes. Mechanically the woman's eyes wandered over the shop window; suddenly they rested upon a piece of paper wafered against the glass; it announced in feeble characters and faint ink that furnished apartments were to be let, and that inquiry was to be made within.

"Why not here as well as anywhere else?" she asked herself. "It cannot be dear here;" and she passed in at the door of the shop.

A fat man, in a Scotch bonnet, behind the counter, was ladling snuff out of an earthen jar by means of an instrument in form something between a spoon and a shoe-horn twisted the wrong way. The customer was a child waiting in the shop, pressing its nose against the edge of the counter, and clutching tightly a few warm halfpence in its tiny, not clean, red hands.

"A quarter of a hounce of blackguard for father—there you 'ave it," said the man, wrapping up the snuff in a scrap of paper adorned with a rude representation of a Scotchman performing a national dance over a vapid conundrum. "Anything helse? What's for mother?"

"No. 103 of the Felon's Aunt, and this week's number of the Chronicle of Crime," the child cried out in a shrill treble; the sentence pointed rather by breathlessness and anxiety, than any strict system of punctuation.

"Very good;" and the man, from a confused huddle of periodical publications, looked out those required.

The transaction completed, and the hot halfpence thrust into the till, the child looked up with wide-open inquiring eyes—it had probably never been taught that it was rude to stare—an early lesson in well-regulated nurseries—at the pale woman who now entered the shop.

"You let apartments, I believe?" she asked in a low voice.

"Private door, please," answered the man in the Scotch bonnet. "This is the shop entrance; don't ask here, but at the private door."

He spoke pompously, but not unkindly. A fat bland man, with a weak streak of hair upon his upper lip; a meaningless face, dull grey eyes, and a husky voice.

The woman seemed a little alarmed at this rebuff. She left the shop, however, and slowly approached a private door at the side. She raised her hand to the knocker, apparently unaware that another person was standing close to her on the step.

"I *have* knocked," a voice said calmly. She was so startled that she gave quite a scream of alarm.

"Pray forgive me. I'm afraid I have frightened you."

The words were spoken in tones so kind and sympathetic as to dispel at once all fear or suspicion. Still her heart was beating with painful violence.

She then perceived, close in the angle of the doorway, a small figure, a boy crouching, as she was at first inclined to believe. Upon a closer examination, however, she discovered that a man was leaning against the door-post in a position almost as upright as he could assume, for indeed he was deformed; a very short man, his head sunk deep between his shoulders; one foot twisted and clubbed. He must have been less than five feet in height altogether.

"Pray pardon me," he went on in rather a troubled voice. "I ought to have been more careful. You have been out in the fog, perhaps, and that has made you timid, and inclined to start at trifles. I know what it is to do that. I am dreadfully nervous myself at times; at least, I *was*, I should say. I am better and stronger now. (How long they are at the door!) But now you are quite safe, you know, and the fog is clearing off. You will soon be quite well again, when you have rested."

The deformed's manner was so gentle, and his tone of voice so tender, that the woman seemed quite moved. She turned in order to see him better. She found that he had small delicate features, not regular, yet prepossessing; long fair hair that fell on his shoulders, but then they were very high and rounded ; a pale complexion and earnest-looking eyes. Some feeling of sympathy seemed to be established at once between the man and the woman. But she was at a loss, apparently, how to address him. She spoke at last with effort, and as though at a loss for words.

"Help me," she said to him simply—faintly.

Her hands clasped together as she made this appeal.

"Indeed I will, if I can. Show me how to help you."

"I am most wretched—most miserable !" and she covered her face sobbing.

"Don't cry, don't cry !" The deformed took her hand. He started. "How hot your hand is. It quite burns. You are ill. You are suffering from fever."

Her face was deathly pale.

"Hush !" she said in a low voice. "Help me. They let lodgings here ; I must take them. I grow quite giddy. I must go in and lie down."

"I'll knock again ;" and he plied the knocker boldly. "Why do they keep us so long ? You should not be standing here."

The door was opened almost immediately by the news-vender in the Scotch bonnet.

"Now what is it ?" he asked, peevishly, "what *is* it ? I have nothink to do with this department. I have nothink to do with the 'ouse or the lodgings, nothink whatever. They are entirely under Mrs. S.'s control, and I never interfere, never. My sphere" (he said *spere*) "is the shop, and, if you please, I'll stick to it."

The words came from him flaccidly. Perhaps the fact of his tongue being too large for his mouth, aggravated his slip-shod manner of speech. But he seemed proud of his elocution, nevertheless, and gazed, while he spoke, above the heads of those whom he addressed. Suddenly he recognised the deformed.

"Ah ! Mr. Hooper " (of course he omitted the H.), "how de do. I beg your pardin, I'm sure. I didn't see it was you. Mr. Gossett *is* in. You see it aint my place to attend to the door, only Mrs. S. haven't come in yet ; and as for that girl Nancy, one might as well keep no servant at all, as I'm always a telling Mrs. S. : 'alf-an-hour fetching the supper beer, or filling a scuttle of coal or what not. Oh! here comes Mr. Gossett."

The newsvender withdrew; of the woman standing at the side of Mr. Hooper he took no notice.

"Robin, old man, how are you?" cried a deep, strong, hearty voice. "Why, I thought you were lost in the mist. Come in. I'm in splendid voice. I've touched G below the line." And he commenced to sing—

> L'or est une chimère,
> Sachons-nous en servir
> Le vrai bien sur la terre
> N'est-il pas le plaisir?
> Rum-ti-iddity, Rum-ti-iddity, &c. &c.

"That's getting near Levasseur, I think? But what is the matter?"

A short broad gentleman, with a rather bald head, a long moustache, and a pipe in his mouth, appeared at the door. He had been talking as he descended the staircase, and was unaware of what had been happening on the step.

"Why, what's the matter, Robin? You're as white as a sheet."

"Look here, Phil. Help me, for Heaven's sake! Here's a woman fainting, I think; help her in; carry her; we can never leave her like this. Help her, Phil, for God's sake!"

Thus appealed to, Mr. Gossett, as the newsvender had called him, without a word threw away his pipe, took up the woman, and carried her up stairs into the room over the shop. It was a comfortable looking room, in spite of the rather shabby, over-worn furniture. Mr. Gossett, who had carried her as though she had weighed but a few ounces, gently laid the poor woman on the sofa.

"Thank you," she murmured, drowsily, raising herself. "I shall be better soon." But she closed her eyes and fell back.

"How did this happen, Rob? How pale she is."

"She came to the door just as I was knocking. I know no more. She seemed very faint and exhausted then, and was panting for breath, and trembling. I am afraid I frightened her rather," he added sadly. "I'm so little, and in the darkness of the doorway she overlooked me, and afterwards gave quite a scream and shook all over. There's no danger, Phil, is there? Tell me, you don't think there is any danger? Say so, Phil."

"I don't know what to think, to tell you the truth."

"Oh, Phil, but you *should* know. You're a doctor—you're a medical student. Is there any danger?"

Mr. Gossett looked rather bewildered. He tugged at his black moustache.

"I'm *only* a student, Rob, remember. Don't expect too much." There was a half comical glance in his eyes as he said this. Then he turned again with all seriousness to the sufferer.

"If she should be dead," cried Robin, in a tone of agony.

"Don't be frightened, Rob; she's not dead; her pulse still beats—though—though,"—and the face of the medical student grew grave—"indeed it's hardly perceptible. Get some cold water, Rob; quick as you can, old boy. You'll find some in my bed-room, close by;" and he unfastened the top of her dress. Loosening her collar, he smoothed the hair from her face, fanning her with his handkerchief.

"How white she is," said Robin Hooper. "She's like marble; and how beautiful, isn't she? Oh, Phil! don't let her die."

"Hush! She is better, I think; the cold water has roused her."

Slowly the woman opened her eyes; her lips parted; the colour had quite gone from them; gradually she seemed to become conscious of her situation. Her eyes rested upon Robin Hooper, the deformed man. She made an effort to speak.

"Save me," she moaned, very feebly, and stretched forth a small, thin, white hand. He pressed it reverently — tenderly.

"There's a knock at the door," said the student. "It must be Mrs. Simmons. Run, Rob, and beg her to come here."

He spoke with seriousness, if not alarm. Robin hurried from the room. He moved rapidly, though his foot com-

pelled him to limp very much. He was heard talking
eagerly on the staircase.

"You must, Mrs. Simmons, indeed you must; do, there's
a dear soul."

A tall, stout woman, rather red-faced, entered the room.
She spoke loudly, and her manner was a little abrupt.

"Oh, Mr. Hooper," she said, "when once you get an idea
into your head there's certainly no getting it out again.
What am I to do? Haven't I troubles enough? I am sure
one would think so. What with this house over my head,
and a pack of noisy lodgers, like that Mr. Gossett there, and
only me to do for them all, and a slut of a girl to look after
—that isn't worth her salt, let alone her tea and sugar—and
a good-for-nothing husband that's all plague and no profit,
and a lot of children quarrelling and bothering after me from
morning till night,—haven't I enough to do, but what you
must bring home a sick woman here—a woman, by all that's
respectable — and turn the place into a hospital and me
into a nurse? Anything else? What next? Well, where's
the patient?"

She had advanced by this time to the sofa, upon which
the woman was lying in a deplorable state. Her tone and
manner changed at once, and she went down on her knees,
taking the woman's hand and chafing it.

"Poor soul, how ill she looks; very ill indeed, poor
woman. Poor girl, rather. Why, she's a mere child. How
slight, how pretty, too But we must rouse her from this
faint, Mr. Gossett, or ——"

Robin could not repress a cry of alarm.

"Bless the man, what's the good of making that noise?"
Mrs. Simmons said, sternly. "What use do you expect that
will be? You'd better by half run and fetch a doctor. It's
always safest to have one in. There's no knowing what
may happen."

"I'll go round to St. Lazarus—it's only a step from here,"
said Mr. Gossett, starting up.

"As quick as you like; the poor child's very white, very
weak."

"I'll go, I'll go," cried Robin. "Pray let me go. I
can run very fast, very fast indeed, I can; as fast as anybody."

"I think not," said Gossett, kindly. "I think you had better let me go. Trust me, Rob, I'll go full speed."

Robin glanced sadly at his mis-shapen foot, and sighed.

"Perhaps you *can* go quicker than I can. Only make haste, there's a good old Phil!"

Mr. Gossett was off without another word.

"Oh, Mrs. Simmons, do you think she's really **very** bad?"

"Look at that face. Did you ever see anything more like a corpse?"

Robin turned away as he said in a broken voice—

"Half an hour ago she was nothing to me. I am a poor over-sensitive deformed fool, very likely; but, if she were to die, I should never be happy again."

He spoke with some passion, trembling, and his eyes shining very brightly, as he tossed his long fair hair from his forehead.

"You've a kind heart, Mr. Robin," said Mrs. Simmons, gently; "a very kind heart;" and she shook his hand.

"Do all you can for her."

"Indeed I will. If for no other reason, why then for your sake, Mr. Robin. But the poor thing looks very bad."

Some time passed before the doctor arrived. All the ordinary efforts to rouse the sufferer were without effect.

"Now, then, what's all this about?" asked Dr. Hawkshaw, from St. Lazarus Hospital, entering with Mr. Gossett. "What have you brought me from the hospital for? It was a mere chance I was there—an interesting case in the accident ward." He seized the woman's wrist, a little roughly, so Robin thought; but probably the doctor knew what he was about.

"Did she look like this when you first met her?" he inquired of Robin Hooper, as he placed his hand upon her heart.

"Yes, very much like that," answered Robin. "Indeed I remember thinking at the time that she looked like——"

"Like what?" asked the doctor, sharply.

"Like a woman who had seen a ghost."

"Pooh! Stuff! What's a ghost?—a symptom of disease, not a disease itself. It proceeds from the stomach. Ghosts always proceed from the stomach; they signify bile, disordered brain, inactive liver ; the system in a devil of a state, and so on. Never lose your head, Mr. Gossett. It's an important thing to recollect in our profession. But the fact is, men have a great tendency towards losing their heads: especially young men. Throw that window open. The young girl's in a weak state of health ; her nerves have been acted upon violently ; she's been over-exerting herself — frightening herself. More cold water, Mrs. Simmons ; don't be afraid of it. There, she's better already. She breathes. A little sal volatile as soon as she can swallow, and we'll soon put her on her legs again," &c. &c.

It was some short time after this that Mrs. Simmons descended to the very small parlour at the back of the news-shop, now closed for the night.

"What *is* the matter, Mrs. S ? " asked the fat man, in his husky peevish voice. "What *as* been going on up stairs ? "

"Don't bother," said his wife, sharply. "Have you eaten all the supper, or have you left me anything ? I've had nothing since my tea at five o'clock, and I'm quite famished. Why don't you answer, Simmons ? "

"Lor', Eliza, don't snap at one like that. There's a sassage on the 'ob. I left it a purpose for you. I've 'ad my supper 'ours ago. I really couldn't wait. That shop do fatigue a feller so. Dear me, I'm afraid that sassage is quite cold. You see I didn't think to keep the fire in, because I was just agoing to bed when you come down."

"You're a selfish pig, Simmons," said his wife, so calmly, and with so complete an air of conviction, that the reproach seemed to be almost deprived of offence. "Give me a pickle, and pour me out a glass of beer. I shall be better presently."

Mr. Simmons did not hurry himself, but eventually attended to his wife's requirements. Suddenly she put down her knife and fork, and looked sternly at her lord.

"There's a smell of spirts here. Simmons, you've been drinking."

He turned very red in the face. He removed his Scotch bonnet, to rub his shining bald head with a large many-coloured handkerchief. Perhaps the bonnet was worn so constantly to conceal his loss of hair.

"Now, Eliza, there's no call to rail at me," he said, deprecatingly; "supposing it being a misty, depressing evening, and me knocked up with working 'ard all day in the shop, and having a symptom of a coff upon me, which you know, Eliza, I'm delicate on my chess, and 'ow my ashmer troubles me at times; and supposing I sit down to a bit of supper quite alone, and you, Eliza, absent—and which you know I never like to have my supper by myself—and supposing I do mix myself just a small glass of 'ollands, or what not, before I go to bed, surely, Eliza——"

"There, there, that will do," said Mrs. Simmons, abruptly. But the stream of her husband's oratory was not to be stayed so easily.

"And which, of course, Eliza," he went on, "if I'd thought you would have objected, or would have liked me to have kept supper waiting for you, or the kettle biling, or the fire in, or the sassages 'ot, or have mixed a glass of 'ollands for you, with pleasure I'd have done it; or——"

"There, Simmons, do stop and let me eat my supper; when once you get the talks on there's no bearing you. It's the Hollands gets into your head, and makes more a fool of you than ever."

Mr. Simmons, with a rather fatuous expression of face, twirled the ends of his feeble moustache. He gazed with a half-frightened, half-admiring air at his wife, as she made steady progress with her supper.

"But what *'as* been going on up stairs?" he soon recommenced; "are any of the children ill?"

"No, thank Heaven! or I don't know what we should do."

"What *is* the matter, then? Have Mr. Gossett got a party?"

"No, he hasn't. But there's a poor girl up stairs been very faint and ill. I'm sure at one time I didn't think she'd live from one minute to another."

"In *my* house!" and Mr. Simmons started up. "I won't have it. Suppose she were to die?—only think!"

"You be quiet; sit down!" she said angrily. "What made it your house? what have you got to do with the lodgers? If I choose, I'll have a score of people come and be sick and ill and die here; and I'll have a coroner's

5

inquest in every room in the house—attics included.
Lor' bless me ! haven't I enough to do without your chatter-
ing and worrying?   I've to play in a new part of I don't
know how many lengths, at the Paroquet, on Monday, and
I haven't looked at a line of it yet.   I've all the children's
socks to mend : I've the lodgers to attend to ; and this poor
girl half dead in Phil Gossett's room.   Little enough sleep
shall I get to-night, I know that."

She had turned away for a minute; when she looked at her
husband again he had dozed off quietly in his chair—very
fat and placid, and not wise-looking.   Whereas his own
talk had a certain enlivening effect upon him, the observations of others were often attended with a directly contrary
result.

"The fool·I was to marry Simmons !" she exclaimed,
quietly.   " I thought him a handsome man and a love of a
figure, I remember, years ago, when he was playing
Harlequin at Bath.   Clever he never was ; but who would
ever have expected then he would have grown so fat,
and so ugly, and so selfish.   Ugh !   But here's the doctor
again.   Let's hear how the patient goes on."

CHAPTER V.

HARLEQUIN AND COLUMBINE.

OVELY woman *will* stoop to folly; to do so is part of her graceful, tender, pliant nature—she can't help it. Ever since the world began—and so on, I suppose, until it ends—Eve and her daughters have been and will be prone to commit numberless silly, charming, absurd, fond, admirable actions. Like those fashionable West-End mercers, who seem to be unable to carry on their business without periodically snapping the bonds of rational trade ; inoculating their shops with a Bedlamite virus, and breaking out into a delirious " SALE WITHOUT RESERVE ! " " AN ALARMING SACRIFICE ! " or a " SELLING OFF UNDER COST PRICE, WITH NO REASONABLE OFFER REFUSED ! "—who, with the poetical untidiness of mad Ophelia sticking sordid straws and hedge-flowers amid her beautiful tresses, glory every now and then in soiling their superb plate-glass with shabby bills and placards, littering their floors and counters with valuable merchandise, hanging silk dresses from second-story windows, and crinolines from chimney-pots—just so, lovely woman is afflicted with a re-current passionate desire to break the even pathway of her life by landmarks of events—to star her career with crises— to sell off occasionally, so to speak, at an alarming sacrifice, and without any sort of reserve, and to let herself go to any-one that will bid, refusing no kind of offer, reasonable or unreasonable—perhaps the more unreasonable the better.

If, to enforce some such teaching as this, an example were required, it might be found in the story of Miss Montresor, of the T. R., Bath, who, some years ago now, ran away with handsome Jemmy Simmons, the harlequin. It was in days when a flavour of the old Ellistonian glory still lingered about the T. R., Bath. The city of King Bladud and Beau Nash—like a faded coquette who yet promises herself one or two more seasons of low dresses, galops, and ball-room champagne, before she is resigned to a poke bonnet and the *rôle* of a sister of charity—was still playing *écarté* while drifting to evangelicalism. A remnant of the old guard remained, keeping up, as it were, a running fight with time; their numbers were frightfully diminished, but they closed their ranks; they kept shoulder to shoulder, they presented a bold front—many bold fronts, I may say. A limited phalanx of bewigged old ladies, radiant with diamonds, burning with rouge, furiously fragrant with musk and bergamot, in glossy satins and beautiful blonde—their threadbare necks richly jewelled, and their rather palsied hands glittering with rings and bracelets—often filled certain boxes of the theatre, and bestowed a persistent patronage upon the manager—for one reason, that the theatre offered a good, open, public mode of defying the opposition, of running counter to, and manifesting contempt for, the opinions of prudery and Puritanism. And to match the old ladies, there were plenty of old gentlemen—nicely padded and buckled, curled, dyed, toupéed, well-repaired, and made up altogether—headed by the old Marquis of Southernwood, who had engaged a box for the whole season, and lolled in it night after night, leering at the actresses and ogling the ladies of the audience—a juvenile, flaxen-headed gentleman of seventy-eight, with bloodshot eyes and artificial teeth, debonnaire manners, and most free conversation. Under these auspices a certain air of fashion still remained to the T. R., Bath, and the manager put money in his purse, and secured all available metropolitan and provincial talent, and included many attractive-looking young ladies in his troupe; and amongst others, Arabella Montresor—her real name was Eliza Perkins, and she was said to be the daughter of old Tom Perkins, well known as the proprietor of Perkins's Dairy, Kentish Town. (I know that once, during a squabble in the ladies'-room of the theatre, Miss Montresor fairly burst into tears when that giddy Miss Vivian— Polly Vivian she was often known as—screamed out with markedly offensive shrillness, 'Milk below, oh!' and appeared to insinuate that Miss Montresor, at an early period of her life, had even carried out the cans.) And in addition to Miss Montresor and Miss Vivian, there was also the fascinating singing chambermaid, Louisa Delafosse.

The career of Lord Southernwood is, I am thankful to

say, so well known that I am spared the necessity of setting
it forth here with any particularity. In nursery books and
infant stories, as we are all aware, a wicked ogre every now
and then makes his appearance, to the agony of childhood.
So in turning over that grown-up, drawing-room collection of
fairy tales, the *Peerage*, we come here and there upon Bogey
noblemen—(at least, we used to : the Bogey nobleman is
becoming extinct almost, or is seldom to be lighted on now
out of fashionable works of fiction). George Henry Ernest
Gaston, fifth Marquis of Southernwood, had become a little
too notorious. He was a Bogey nobleman if there ever was
one. He was rusticated for a time. He retreated from
London to Bath ; the air of which city has been often found
beneficial to invalid reputations—balmy to battered characters. The marquis was not unkindly received. The
Dowager Lady Rougeminster, a giddy flirt of sixty-six, said
he was a naughty old thing, and that she was quite shocked
at him, and wondered how he dared to come near her; and
then hid her face with her fan (trimmed with marabouts
and a mirror in the centre), and made room for him by her
side on the sofa. After this, of course, other thoughtless
young creatures, ranging in age from sixty to eighty,
could not but follow suit. They owned that he was too
bad—a great deal too bad—and the things he said sometimes were really dreadful, my dear, quite dreadful ; but still
they listened, and laughed, and told the free old cavalier to
go along with him, while they took care not to lose sight of
him, and to pamper, and flatter, and pay court to him. So
he occupied an important position in Bath society.

What great things people are always missing by a very
little ! Arabella Montresor missed being Marchioness of
Southernwood by just five minutes. The very night she
eloped with handsome Jemmy Simmons, the harlequin—but
five minutes before she started—there had been thrown to
her from the Southernwood box, a bouquet circling a billet
from the Marquis of Southernwood, proffering her his hand
in marriage. She smiled her thanks for the bouquet. She
never knew of the billet until some time afterwards. How
the old gentleman, heated with his wine and trembling with
age and excitement, roared applause and thumped his kidt
gloved old hands upon the box-cushions till a cloud of dust

arose, and his flaxen curls nearly fell into the orchestra ! She flung the flowers aside and herself into the arms of her harlequin.

Poor Arabella Montresor—or Eliza Perkins, if you prefer it—stooped to folly with a vengeance. She gave herself away without reserve—an awful sacrifice : and she didn't love the harlequin a bit. It was pure madness, and impulse, and accident. She was pretty, good—intelligent, if not very accomplished or refined. He was low, dull, selfish, heartless. He had only his good looks, his charming figure, his agile feet, to recommend him. Why then did she marry him ? Because she hated Louisa Delafosse, who—poor Louisa !—adored the harlequin.

Louisa was a favourite at the T. R., Bath. The remnant of the old guard honoured her with their especial approval. The old gallants applauded her until their chalk-stoned fingers ached again. She fairly divided the favour of the house with Arabella. And she could sing nicely, too, perfectly in tune; whereas Arabella's ear was defective, and when she attempted to be musical, the audience held their heads. Now, on the occasion of that very eminent tragedian Calverley visiting Bath—secured at an enormous sum for six nights only—Arabella was cast for Gertrude, and the part of Ophelia was given to Louisa Delafosse—Calverley, of course, appearing in his favourite character of Hamlet. The Queen is not a very grateful *rôle*, and Arabella did not get a hand. But Louisa—what a hit she made—how charmingly she sang ! She fairly took away the honours of the evening even from Calverley. He was in a tremendous rage, of course. He said he had never been so insulted in his life. *She* said that he pinched her shamefully, on purpose, till she nearly screamed in the "go to a nunnery" scene, and that she could and did show the marks of his ill-usage to the whole company for days afterwards. Arabella cried herself to sleep, dreaming of vengeance.

Perhaps she could have overlooked, and in time forgiven, this her rival's triumph. But her troubles were not to end here. The success of Miss Delafosse as Ophelia induced the management to entrust the charming lady with other important parts. Hitherto her position in the theatre had not been a high one. She had only smiled and sung in burlettas, or prattled and danced in farces. She had even been one of the fairies—how derogatory! but then her figure was very admirable—in the opening scenes of the pantomime. Now she was told to study Cordelia, to play to Calverley's Lear :— Desdemona to Calverley's Othello. Arabella was to be content with Goneril—with Emilia. So the night before one of these disgraces was to be inflicted upon her, after playing Mrs. Beverley to a crowded house, and after the episode of the Southernwood bouquet, Miss Montresor ran away with Jemmy Simmons. She would make her rival, she said, pay a high price for her success—that price was the harlequin. The news was brought to Miss Delafosse during her performance of Cordelia, and she went straightway into hysterics on the stage. Her screams quite terrified the audience. The Marquis of Southernwood was extremely angry. He looked quite livid, by contrast with the velvet cushions of his box. He hated to hear even, much more see anything of illness. "Don't let that woman come on the stage again!" he screamed with an oath. His will was law.

Jemmy Simmons was of the style of beauty which women and hair-dressers have agreed to estimate very highly. The reader will not require that he should be more particularly described. For Arabella, she was avenged : and, of course, miserable for the rest of her life. She soon probed to the bottom of her husband's motive for marrying her. She was simply in his eyes the woman who drew the largest salary in the theatre. They quarrelled desperately. He would have beaten her if he had dared. He contented himself with squandering her money. He could do nothing on the stage but dance. He had no other talent of any kind whatever. He was a good harlequin, that was all : but he was a favourite with the public, and always commanded a good engagement at Christmas. At last his habits began to tell upon him; he failed in his leaps; he fell down in his dances; the stage manager apologised to the house :—Mr. Simmons had sprained his ankle at the rehearsal that morning; indulgence was requested, and, of course, given with applause. What a wretchedly deboshed sot he was, in spite of his splendid figure and his beautifully spangled dress! But at last his figure went. He grew fat, his breath became

so short he could no longer play through the part. Handsome Jemmy Simmons's harlequin days were over for
ever.

Arabella Montresor had by her marriage lost the chance
of advancement in her profession. Even if she had declined
to become Marchioness of Southernwood, she might have
secured, through his lordship's interest, a liberal engagement
on metropolitan boards. But her marriage, and then her
family! Young Simmonses began to flock round her, and
she looked very matronly; she grew stout; her complexion
might almost be called rubicund now. She wearied of wandering about from town to town in the provinces. An engagement had been offered her at the Paroquet Theatre,
Hoxton, and she had accepted it. The terms were not very
liberal: but a, permanency was secured. The Simmons'
family wandered no more. They settled in the house at the
corner of Coppice Row.

Mr. Simmons—he could fairly be called Jemmy no longer
—the father of a large family, and the husband of Mrs.
Montresor (so she was called in the bills of the Paroquet),
Mr. Simmons was no longer handsome. A fat man, with a
meaningless face, hiding his bald head in a Glengarry cap—
with dull, sodden-looking eyes and husky voice; his beauty
had gone with his spangles. He had been always fond of
smoking pipes and reading the papers: there was a sort of
ironical justice in fixing the man behind the counter of a
shop that dealt in tobacco and news. He yielded to his
wife now more than he had done in his old, gay, good-looking times. She insisted upon his doing work of some kind,
or she knew that he would be at mischief, which, in his case,
meant the public-house. So he presided over the news-shop;
upon the express stipulation, however, that he was not to be
called upon to interfere in any of the arrangements of the
other parts of the house. Mrs. Simmons was an industrious,
hard-working woman. She let as many rooms as she could
spare to lodgers; she superintended the whole house; and
with her lodgers, and her children, and her appearances as
the heroine of Paroquet melodramas, indeed she had enough
to do.

Mr. Philip Gossett (he answered also to the name of
"Phil"), student at St. Lazarus's Hospital, was one of Mr.

Simmons's lodgers. He had come up from the country to
pursue his medical studies in the metropolis. He had at
first taken expensive apartments at the West End of the
town. Gradually, however, the straightened condition of
his funds had compelled him to remove to less costly
regions ; and he had drifted away accordingly, like a ship
ineffectually anchored, until he had run ashore at Coppice
Row. Mrs. Simmons welcomed him to her first floor.
Other people might possibly have objected to a medical
student lodger. At least, I have understood that lodging-
house keepers often do object, on the ground that, as a
class, medical students are addicted to noise. But Mrs.
Simmons made no demur. She was accustomed to noise ;
she had been in noise all her life ; she was noisy herself
(particularly in last acts at the Paroquet) ; her husband was
often noisy (especially when he came home late at night—
unwell) ; her children were always noisy. Mr. Gossett was
at liberty to make as much noise as he pleased, provided he
paid for his rooms.

Mr. Gossett availed himself to the full of his privileges in
Mrs. Simmons's house. But, perhaps, he was not noisy
precisely in the way contemplated. Ostensibly, he studied
medicine ; in reality, it would seem, he practised music.
Through all his wanderings from house to house, from the
West End to Coppice Row—and he had tarried in a good
many apartments on his way—moving when the noise he
made was objected to, or his purse became too light—he
had carried with him his dearly-beloved piccolo piano, and,
of course, his grand, deep bass voice. He was for ever
thumping on his piccolo ; he was for ever bawling out bass
melodies, or busied in producing notes of a depth and
volume sufficiently alarming to his audience. He studied
fierce dramatic music ; he affected long, passionate scenas,
of a wild and demoniac character. He was acquainted
more especially, it may be noted, with the music of the parts
of Caspar in Der Frieschütz and Bertram in Robert le Diable.
He frightened the infant Simmonses dreadfully at first with
his vehement delivery of incantation music. Even Mr.
Simmons admitted that, in all his life, he had never heard so
powerful a voice—" He never 'ad, never, though he'd known
'Icks of Birmingham, who was thought a sight of for lungs,

as likewise Borleigh and Barker; but he didn't think they come up to Mr. Gossett, blessed if he did—not for row. While Mrs. Simmons was of opinion that Mr. Gossett had decided operatic talent. Mr. Gossett was pleased with this homage; he decided to remain in Coppice Row, and sung thenceforth louder than ever. He permitted his moustache to grow as long as it would, and brushed back his hair from his face; it was said at one time that he "shaved up," as the technical term is; that is, that he made himself artificially bald, shaving his hair to a peak on his forehead, turning up the points of his moustache, and cultivating a tuft upon his chin, to carry out thoroughly the prescribed theatrical notion of a demon bass singer. Such was the friend of crippled Robin Hooper — Philip Gossett, of St. Lazarus's Hospital, medical student—in whose rooms a poor, fainting, friendless woman had been nursed by Mrs. Simmons and attended by Dr. Hawkshaw.

She had now been removed, however—very weak and suffering—to another part of the house, but the friends were still occupied with the strange occurrence. If for a few minutes they wandered from it to other topics, they were always sure to return to it again. There was in it for them, actors in the scene, a kind of fascination.

Robin lay curled on the sofa, exhausted and fatigued, yet wakeful and restless from nervous excitement; his back dreadfully twisted, and his head deeply sunk in his shoulders, his thin fingers plaiting themselves together, and his eyes hectically bright. His sensibilities were ever acutely, almost painfully alive—his organisation febrile, his fancy morbidly vivid. If pain were inflicted on another in his presence, he seemed to suffer by the reflection of it—he writhed and winced with the sufferer. He was haunted by that pale face and look of pain.

Phil Gossett had been interested—alarmed even; but the impression was wearing off, for now some hours had passed. He was able to hum at intervals, and as in his heavy promenades about the room he neared the corner in which his piccolo was placed, he could seldom resist playing (with the soft pedal down) a few notes of one of his favourite airs, or gently testing his depth of voice by the piano. He did this, however, without too much noise; for Robin had more than once implored him to desist, lest any annoyance should be occasioned to Dr. Hawkshaw's patient up stairs.

"How I wish," said Robin, "that I had studied medicine!"

"You made a good beginning, Rob, though it seems quite a long time now since you were entered at St. Lazarus."

"Ah! but I couldn't go on. It killed me, that place. To see all those poor suffering people in the wards turning their sad eyes to me as I entered. I never grew reconciled to it. It was just as dreadful to me every day. I could shut my eyes and yet see their faces, as I can see hers now. Will the colour never come back? Will her eyes always shine so—like stars, in her hollow face? I wonder how she is now, Phil—shall I go and ask Mrs. Simmons?"

"Better not. She's a good soul; she'll do all she can, I'll answer for her. How kind she was to me when I had that bad throat, you remember. Besides, it's all right now, you know; Hawkshaw said so."

"But do *you* think so, Phil? *Really?* Don't cheat me with telling me so, if you don't think so really. I'm quite well and strong now, and calm. You know I could bear to hear it."

"Let me feel your pulse. Feverish, old boy, feverish. You're not too strong, Rob."

"But I could bear to hear the truth."

"You thought you could bear the dissecting-room—do you remember? Yet you swooned dead away."

"Don't speak of it;" and Robin covered his face with his hands. Then he started up. "But I could bear this, Phil. After all, what is it? A woman picked half-dead out of the streets—whom I have never seen before—whom, likely enough, I shall never see again—what does it matter to me whether she lives or dies? I say, Phil, why should I care?——Yet no"—and he shuddered—"for God's sake, don't let me talk like that! Yes, it *does* matter—*dead*—it would be cruel suffering to me. Tell me you don't think she'll die, Phil—do tell me so!"

"This is what you call calmness, is it? Why, you're all of a tremble, you silly old Rob you. No; I tell you, I don't think she'll die. Her state was a little critical for a time. Hawkshaw owned as much; but it's all right now.

Hawkshaw wouldn't have left her if he hadn't been sure of that."

"Thank you, Phil."

"And now you'd better get some rest, Rob; though I fear Arnold will be anxious about you."

"He knew I was coming here; and, indeed, he must forgive me, for I cannot go now; not that I'm sleepy, but I want to hear how she goes on."

"I little thought when I heard your knock, Rob, of all that was going to happen. I looked forward to lots of music. You've a jolly tenor. I'm certain we could manage that '*Ah l'honnête homme*' duet splendidly. Shall we try softly, just for five minutes?"

"No," said the cripple, firmly; "I wouldn't do it for worlds."   .

Mr. Gossett saw that his friend was in earnest, and, with a sigh, closed the piano.

CHAPTER VI.

DR. HAWKSHAW'S PATIENT.

RS. SIMMONS entered a small room on an upper floor in the house in Coppice Row, treading very softly indeed. You would hardly have imagined that a lady of her size could have passed along so lightly. For the figure of Arabella Montresor was much less delicate than it had been; she had increased in weight since the time when she was playing, at Bath, Mrs. Beverley in *The Gamester* to the delight of the late lamented fifth Marquis of Southernwood.

Mrs. Simmons advanced to a bed on which a fragile-looking, pallid woman was lying, apparently asleep. Very beautiful, notwithstanding her wanness and want of colour; yet with something of the awfulness of a corpse, as she lay there so white and motionless. But she lived. You could see the drapery of the bed gently stir; you could watch the trembling and swaying about of a soft lock of hair that had fallen about her face, as her breath rose and fell in heavy and protracted sighs. Very beautiful! Her long fair hair —of the hue the ancients would have called "honey-coloured" and the old Italian masters have loved with true and intense art-love—floating from her face in undulating lines, encircling her head like the golden nimbus of a saint. How abundant those tresses, how graceful, how admirable, with a ripple on them as of a sea smiling and sparkling in the amber of sunrise!

For some moments Mrs. Simmons stood contemplating the sleeper, almost as though retained by a kind of fascination. Then moved by a sudden thought, she knelt down to look at the woman's left hand—very small, and soft, and of a charming form, resting outside the coverlet. She ventured even to touch the hand, turning it gently so that she might the better examine it. Still the woman slept on.

"No," Mrs. Simmons said to herself, and she was examining, it would seem, more particularly the third finger of the hand. "No, there is no ring."

Then she took up a handkerchief of cambric edged with lace.

"A very pretty handkerchief."

She turned to each corner separately, in search of the name or initials of the owner. In one corner she noticed a small hole cut or torn, it was not quite clear which.

"The name has been cut out. Why, I wonder? Who is she? Why has she come here? What does it all mean? Surely under all the circumstances, there can be no harm in searching her pockets?"

Perhaps, before she had time to answer her own question, Mrs. Simmons was busy with the dress of the sleeper, and had turned over many small articles found in the pocket.

"She's well dressed; quietly, but very nicely; a gold watch and chain, brooch and small earrings, two keys, a port-monnaie, with some gold in it, and some silver coins: what are they? French, I should think; and these? Why, surely these must be Indian; and what's this? A scrap of paper with an address on it, half rubbed out. I can't read the first word. Something House, Kew, it looks like. Why, surely——"

She paused, passing her hand across her forehead, with rather a theatrical manner. Unconsciously, perhaps, she had raised the tone of her voice; perhaps the habits of her life rendered it unavoidable that she should favour loudness of speech and decided gesticulation.

"Surely, she cannot have escaped from an asylum?"

She stood still, glancing upwards in a manner she had found attractive at the Paroquet, as though she had particularly addressed herself to the occupants of the seats in the front row of the gallery.

"No! she is not mad, my life upon it, Soft! She wakes!"

At the Paroquet this would of course have been the cue for the band to have played slow and mysterious music, with muted violins. Mrs. Simmons, with theatrical stealthiness, and as though keeping time to imaginary chords, moved towards the bed.

The woman opened her eyes like dead violets, they were

so beautiful in colour, and yet for the moment light and life were so entirely absent from them.

"Where am I?" she asked, softly, raising her hands languidly to her head. There was a look of trouble, bewilderment, alarm, upon her face.

"Don't be frightened," said Mrs. Simmons; "you are quite safe now."

"Where am I?" she repeated.

"You are quite safe; you are among friends."

"Friends? Have I any friends?" She appeared to be trying to recollect: she shuddered.

"Surely you have friends," said the actress, drawing the bed-clothes round the invalid. Then in answer to her glance of inquiry, she continued, "Am I not your friend?"

"You will help me?"

"To be sure I will," Mrs. Simmons exclaimed, stoutly.

A footstep was heard outside the door.

"Too much talking, I think," said Dr. Hawkshaw, entering.

A thin, gaunt, hard-looking man, with wiry, iron-gray, short-cut hair: with high cheek-bones, and little scraps of whiskers sprouting on their summits. Untidily dressed: a crumpled white cravat twisted round his neck; long cuffs to his coat; when he turned these back, a severe "operation" sort of look was given to his long, sallow, nervous hands—a heavy watch-chain swinging from his fob. His dress was not planned to be professional. When, years back, he had commenced practice, he had assumed the style of attire customary among gentlemen of the middle class: and he had been too busy ever since to study the varyings of fashion, or to make any change in the cut or colour of his clothes. His patients were a little afraid of him at first, for his manner was not immediately conciliating; he was severe in tone and abrupt in action; but they relied upon him the more in the end. There was such an air of strength and soundness about him; and certainly in those small, mobile gray eyes of his, when you had got to know him thoroughly, you could read much kindliness and real tenderness of heart. Above all, you should have heard how the students of St. Lazarus's spoke of him, and how they relished his sturdy, sagacious, eminently practical lectures.

"You're better," he said to his patient. "You've slept pretty well. Still you're giddy, and sickly, and weak, and you haven't a ha'porth of appetite, I should think. However, we'll soon put all that right. How old are you?"

"Eighteen."

"What's your name?"

"Janet," she murmured after a pause.

"Janet what?" he asked sternly, but not rudely. "That's only half a name."

She looked troubled, and turned away her eyes from her questioner: a faint blush dawned on her pale face. Something she said at last, but in a very low voice. The doctor bent down the better to hear.

"Janet Milne?" he inquired, as though doubtful whether he had heard aright.

She bowed her head.

"Well, Miss Janet Milne——" he continued; then he paused as though waiting for correction, looking at her curiously, but she did not speak. "You must be careful how you over-fatigue and frighten yourself again, or the consequences may be even more serious. But we'll take care of you this time, and soon make you well. Mrs. Simmons is an excellent nurse. Keep yourself as quiet as you can. Do you wish to send to any friends or relations to let them know where you are, or tell them how you are going on?"

"No," she answered eagerly.

"You have friends, relations?"

"None."

"Where do you live? where is your home?"

"I have no home."

"Hum!" The doctor withdrew. Out of the room, he spoke to Mrs. Simmons.

"She's telling stories," he said. "Never mind; don't worry her with questions just at present; she's still in a highly nervous state. What has she done? where does she come from? She's young, pretty, isn't she? at least I should say passable. I don't consider myself a judge of such matters. What can have happened to her?"

"I think it must be somehow connected with a love affair," Mrs. Simmons suggested. Her theatrical experiences had taught her that love occasioned many complications—at any rate on the stage.

"Perhaps so. I've heard that love is a dangerous disease ; but I'm not sure of it's diagnosis. It's not in the medical books, and they don't bring the love-sick to the hospital, thank Heaven !" The doctor seemed to be only half in jest.

"People in love, or who fancy themselves in love, do very extraordinary things," Mrs. Simmons observed.

It is possible that her thoughts were recurring to certain remarkable events in her own life.

"So I've heard," the doctor said drily ; "but as far as I can make out, love proceeds in most cases from the stomach, and those suffer the most from it who have weak chests and bad digestions, and don't take sufficient exercise. I *have* heard it attributed to the heart ! but that I don't believe. It cannot be the same thing as fatty degeneration, though it may look like it. Good-bye. By-the-way, if you see Mr. Gossett tell him I'm sorry he wasn't at lecture this morning. That's his voice, I'm sure. Singing he calls that ? Does he, indeed ? Dear me ! I wonder what sort of noise he would make, now, to represent howling or roaring. Good-bye. Take care of Miss Milne. I'll look round to-morrow."

"The shop empty !—where's Simmons ? Oh, if he's gone again to that *Spotted Dog!* What do you want, my little man ? " (This to a customer.) "I'm sure I don't know where to find No. 150 of the *Revelations of a Lady's-maid,* and what *has* become of my part in the *Lone Hut on the Moor, or the Murderer and the Marquis!* I put it down somewhere for half a minute, and now I can't think where I did put it. I hope the children haven't got hold of it—or the cat. Ever so many lengths, and not a line do I know of it yet : and have I—gracious Heaven !—I do believe I have *not* got a clean white muslin frock for the last act. I will *not* go down on my knees on that filthy stage in my new blue silk. I will *not*, I say ; and Nancy, *do* hold the baby's back straight, and mind its precious head ; and have you cleaned the front attic's boots ? And Mr. Gossett ringing for coals and a pint of half-and-half. Oh, dear, dear me ; who would be me, I should like to know, if they could be anybody else ? "

6

Poor Mrs. Simmons, *neé* Arabella Montresor; or, to be very particular, Eliza Perkins!

Some days later Robin Hooper and Mr. Lackington were conversing.

"Now, tell me, Rob," said Mr. Lackington, "is there any more news about the fairy of the fog? You knight-errant, have you been rescuing any more maidens in distress? Have you discovered anything more about her?"

"I have not discovered more about her, for one reason, perhaps, that I have not tried to do so. What right have I, or has anyone, to pry into her history? Was it not enough to know that she was poor and suffering and needing assistance?"

"I'm half afraid of you, Rob, when you put on your chivalric air; I feel like a modern snob running up against a gentleman of the chain-mail period. I confess I'm caitiff enough—isn't 'caitiff' the right word, Rob, under all the circumstances of the case?—to be curious in the matter Gossett tells me she's beautiful."

"She is very beautiful."

"With golden hair, eh? I should like to see her. I should like to make a sketch of her. I've a notion of painting a woman with golden hair dressed in sea-green satin sitting in a punt gathering water-lilies; a fierce red sunset gleaming upon her through very tall rushes. Wouldn't it look well, Rob? I don't know what it would mean in the least; but I think the meaning of a picture should always be left to the spectator, don't you?"

"I don't see why painters should trouble themselves or the spectators with painting conundrums."

"You know you always leave the moral of a fable to be guessed. But about this fairy of the fog. Who is she? How is she? What's she going to do? Do you think she would sit to me for the lady in the punt?"

"Her name is Janet Milne; she has reasons I believe for making no further revelation regarding herself; she is much better; she is still with Mrs. Simmons; she will endeavour to obtain pupils and so earn a subsistence, for she is poor—she has avowed that much; I do not think she would care to sit to you. Now you know as much as I do concerning her. I seek to know no more than she chooses to make known. It seems to me that we are bound to respect her desires in this respect, and if we can aid her in any other way, that we are also bound to do so. I know that *I* will, to the utmost of my power."

"You've the heart of a Bayard, Rob."

"In a very weak and crippled and broken-down body, Jack."

"Has Arnold seen her, this mysterious lady?"

"No. I have told him about her, and he has promised to render his assistance in any plan for her benefit."

"Should I see her if I were to call at Mrs. Simmons's?"

"Probably not."

"Ah! Rob, you are locking up your treasure very securely! Are you afraid lest she should fall in love with any-one else; with me for instance? It sounds very monstrously, of course; but I *have* been loved; women are so weak and illogical; or with Arnold, say? Of course, Mr. Robin Bayard, by all the laws of three volume novels, she *ought* to be in love with you; but if she shouldn't be?"

"For shame, Jack," cried Rob, fervently. "How can you speak in this way of her, of me? Do you respect nothing —no one?"

"I beg your pardon."

"How can you speak of Arnold so?"

"Oh, by-the-way, yes. I forgot about Arnold. He's out of the question, of course; that is, I should think he was. He's received his sentence, poor fellow. We may speak of him as a 'lifer,' I suppose. Have you seen the lady, Rob?"

"Yes; my father's farm is on Mr. Carr's estate. I have often seen her down in Woodlandshire."

"Arnold showed me her picture. He'd painted it himself. Deuced well, too, I can tell you. Arnold would succeed in the fine arts if he had but application. That's the great thing, Rob. It struck me that she was a very nice-looking girl, with superb brown eyes: but she's little, I believe; a sort of chimney-ornament Cleopatra, isn't she, Rob?"

"I don't like the definition; Cleopatra I never admired. Her fierceness, coarseness, muscularity, it seems to me, nearly extinguish her fascination. There is nothing of these

6—2

about Leonora Carr. She is proud-spirited; an only child, an heiress, and has been in some danger of being spoiled. But she is very charming—a sort of Titania from a brunette point of view; very delicate and sprightly, tender and winning. I marvel no more that Arnold should love her, than that she should love Arnold. I think there is every promise of happiness in their union."

" Yes, for them; but for us ? "

Robin looked as though he did not understand.

" There seems to me something selfish about matrimony which people haven't properly taken into account. It's like two people in a large party separating from the rest, sitting down, and getting absorbed in a game of chess, instead of contributing to the general amusement of the company."

" What do you mean ? What would you do? Abolish marriage? I believe, Jack, you are no better than a Mormon," said Robin, laughing.

" Don't you see that Arnold's marriage will abolish *us ?* We may be *his* friends; do you think we shall be Mrs. P.'s? I fancy that when the wife informs the husband that she'd rather not receive his friend Mr. So-and-so, somehow the husband in time leaves off bringing that gentleman home to dinner. Arnold will drop us, Rob, in plain words."

" Arnold will be good and true, as he has ever been," said Robin, hotly.

" Well, well, we shall see. Any news of Hugh Wood?"

' He's gone into the country, to stop at the rectory. I don't think he's very comfortable there. He's not very good friends with his father, I'm afraid. They never get on well together somehow."

" I've a notion about Hugh Wood, which I'll tell you some day. Halloo, do you hear that noise? It sounds like an earthquake; it's only Phil Gossett singing. He's discovered another low note in his voice, an awful depth, it seems to come out of the heels of his boots. How are you, Phil, old man? Now, you fellows, strike up duets while I smoke. I don't know which aids the art-mind the most, music or tobacco; we'll decide to-night. Perhaps one of you has got silver enough to pay for some beer. Thank you, Rob."

CHAPTER VII.

A SCHOOL FRIEND.

"I THINK, Miss Bigg," said Leonora to the school-mistress, "that you do not sufficiently consider the change that has taken place in our relative positions. I am no longer your pupil. I claim to have some influence here. I am about to be connected, by marriage" (she blushed a little, lowering her eyes here), "with the young ladies who have just quitted the room. I shall probably have some voice then in their education. I am also acquainted, intimately in some cases, with the families of others among your pupils. I think, upon consideration, you will decide that it is not advisable to compel me to return to town without seeing little Barbara Gill."

Leo spoke very calmly, without raising her voice, without movement or action. Her tones were very silvery, yet they were firm, decided. Altogether, there was a determined air about the little lady. It was evident that she did not intend to be trifled with or denied. The schoolmistress quailed before her.

"Miss Gill is not well," she said at last, feebly.

"I am aware of that fact. It is an additional reason for my desiring to see her."

Miss Bigg looked uncomfortable. She drew the folds of her shawl nervously together. She complained, in a mutter, that it was "chilly," though her face shone and the stiff curls of her front grew quite dank with heat. She fidgeted with the poet Bigg's sublime work on the table, and nearly pulled the streamers off the bookmarker inscribed "Read, mark, digest." Her head swayed to and fro with a sort of palsied action.

"It is not usual," she began at last, "for any but the relatives of the young ladies under my charge——"

"Pardon me, Miss Bigg, that is not the question. Will you be good enough to inform me whether I am or not to be allowed to see Miss Gill?"

The schoolmistress rolled her handkerchief into a hard tight ball, and with it pressed her eyes by turns severely. There were no tears rendering this proceeding necessary; but it is probably one of the rules of grief that the fewer tears you can produce the more you are bound to apply your handkerchief. For wet mourning cambric is of course desirable—but for dry it is indispensable.

"Leonora! how *can* you?" Miss Bigg sobbed, shaking the words out of herself with an effort, as she rocked to and fro upon her chair. "To think that I should be thus spoken to by a former esteemed pupil! What would my late sister Adelaide have said? What would have been the feelings of my late father, the poet Bigg, upon such an occasion? To think that anybody who had received the blessings of education at Chapone House, Kew Green, should be able afterwards to address me in such a way. How shocking! How awful, I may say! And you, Leonora! above all others! upon whom I have lavished a maternal affection, an unceasing solicitude, beyond anything mentioned in the prospectus or to be expected at an establishment of this nature."

"Miss Bigg," Leo said, quite calmly, "I really think you had better give me an answer. Mamma is waiting in the carriage, and will be anxious to return to town."

"Miss Gill is very ill. There," Dorothea answered pettishly.

"You have had medical advice, of course? What doctor is in attendance upon the poor child?"

"Who do you suppose was to pay the doctor's bill?"

"You have had no doctor? Oh, Miss Bigg, how shameful!" said little Leo, looking very moved and angry.

Dorothea's head shook, like the head of a practicable Chinese figure roughly handled.

"It's very easy to talk about doctors," she jerked out; "to hear *some* people talk one would think that doctors cost nothing. But then *some* people will send for the doctor when their little finger aches. I don't. I never have, and I never will. Let *other* people say or do or think what they may."

Miss Dorothea followed a habit I notice to be favoured by her sex, of resorting to innuendo in her angriest moments.

As certain marksmen hit one mark by aiming at another, so Miss Bigg sought to wound Leo, not so much by a direct and individual attack, as by a general onslaught upon a host of "other people." It is just as well to fire into a covey as to wait and single out a particular bird.

"You tell me, Miss Bigg," said Leo, quite calmly, her voice and manner in charming contrast with the school-mistress's snappishness and loss of temper—"You tell me that little Barbara is seriously ill—so ill that I may not see her—so ill that, as I understand it, you have thought it advisable to separate her entirely from the other young ladies, your pupils : and yet you have not called in medical aid ! Is there not something very strange about this, Miss Bigg ? Does it not strike you that when Mrs. Lomax comes to be informed that a pupil at Chapone House has been treated in this extraordinary way, her confidence in the mistress of the school will be very much shaken, and that she will be prompted at once to remove her children from your care ? "

There was evident indecision in Miss Bigg's proceedings. She wavered between submission and resistance. She was now weak and suppositiously tearful. Anon she was spasmodically strong and angry. Again she brought her tennis-ball of a handkerchief to bear upon her eyes, pressing them painfully.

"I never would have believed, Leonora, that *you* would have turned against me like this—that *you* would have tried to injure me. Your old mistress, who did all she could for your happiness here ; who favoured you beyond any of the other young ladies, till they grew quite jealous on the subject—quite. Were you not allowed to write home oftener? to have more pocket-money? to have more sugar in your tea? Was I ever so strict with you as with everybody else? Didn't I give you when you left, with my own hands, a copy of my late father's sublime work, bound in whole calf? Didn't I inform your dear mamma that you were the best conducted pupil who had ever entered the seminary ? And after all the pains I have taken with your religious and moral culture, to think I should be treated like this ! Threatened even ! and by my most favoured pupil. But I was too partial. I spoiled you. I am rightly punished ;

as we sow so we must reap. I receive the reward of my
weakness, my folly, my injustice. Yet who would have
believed in conduct so unchc-ristian-like emanating from a
pupil of Chapone House ? "

In the extremity of her indignation Miss Bigg put this
question, r.ot to Leonora, but over her head, to where the picture of the poet cooling his bottle-nose over the marble mantelpiece, to where the fancy sketch of the late Adelaide in a
turban, in the character of St. Cecilia, before the patent
mangle and gas pipes, adorned the walls. The appeal was
so emphatic and vehement it was almost a marvel that the
painted semblances of Miss Bigg's departed relatives made
no reply. It is but justice to say, however, that Leonora
was but slightly stirred by it. She rose from her chair.

" I am to understand, then, Miss Bigg, that you refuse my
request ? "

" Don't, my dear child, don't talk to me like that. What
can little Miss Gill be to you ? "

" She is very much to me," said Leonora ; "and I must
see her."

" But if her illness should be something dangerous —
something infectious ? "

" Can it be so, Miss Bigg ? Can there even be a chance
of this, and you have not called in medical assistance ? "

" Ah, Leonora, you little understand how often a person
in my position is made the victim of cruel injustice. I seldom speak upon these subjects. I try to make no difference between my pupils ; if I made a difference in your
case, Leonora, it was not without an effort to the contrary,
and, as I have said, I am punished. I do all I can to avoid
distinctions, even in carving or distributing the gravy at
dinner, or the daily punishments, or the prizes at the close
of the half year. I try to forget that while for one child I
am paid punctually, as sure as the Bank of England, for another I have to make application after application, half-year
after half-year, and still I fail to obtain payment. The
money that has been lost to the school in this way ! and
sometimes the more distinguished the family of the pupil,
the more intimate its connexions with the aristocratic families
of the country, as detailed in that book on the table—*The
Peerage and Baronetage of the United Kingdom* —the more

difficulty, my dear, has arisen in my receiving payment of my accounts."

"I regret to hear all this, of course, Miss Bigg," said Leonora, with a glance of surprise; "but I don't really see what it has to do with the question whether I am or not to see poor Miss Gill."

"Don't, my dear, don't," cried Dorothea. "I'm coming to that. How I contrive to keep my head above water and the seminary open is more, I'm sure, than I can explain. And the young people consigned to me from the colonies— admirably recommended, most unquestionable references— young people handed over to my entire and absolute charge, to board, and clothe, and educate; to maintain even during the holidays; to have every extra; to learn every-thing mentioned in the prospectus; their bringing up to be of the most choice, and elaborate, and expensive character; and yet even for these, would you believe it, the money is often not forthcoming! My dear, it's ruin, positive ruin; a few more consignments of this sort and I shall be actually deprived of house and home. And how can one obtain payment? And what can one do with the children? One must keep them; one can't turn them out of the place; and yet who is to find means for their support?"

"Well, Miss Bigg——"

"Be patient, my dear. Take the case of this child Gill. For four years has she been an inmate of this institution. Her father an officer in India. Most highly recommended to me. The child consigned to me. What could I do but receive it? Could I foresee what would happen? Could I imagine that not one shilling should I receive for the main-tenance and education of that child? I have written letter after letter; each mail carries out a fresh application for the discharge of my account, or at least a portion of it. I receive no reply — not the slightest notice is given to my letters—not a halfpenny of payment made to me. What can I do? Can flesh and blood bear this sort of thing? And yet what redress have I? What am I to do with the child? I must go on keeping her until I hear from India, or until doomsday, I suppose."

"I had no idea of this, Miss Bigg."

"No. I have made a point of concealing these things

from my pupils and from their friends and relatives. It would do no good to the school if these circumstances were made known and talked about. And now, to crown the matter, the child's ill—perhaps has even brought infection into the school. Suppose it's scarlet fever, and every girl catches it, and the school is broken up: what's to become of me then, I should like to know?"

"Why should you think the child's illness infectious? You say you have called in no doctor."

"I can't afford it; that's the simple answer and explanation. There is quite enough money owing to me on Miss Gill's account without a long doctor's bill being added to it. I have done what I can for her; and I've kept her separate from the other pupils. I'm bound to consider them; and for the future——"

"For the future," Leonora interrupted, "*I* will see that you are paid all charges in regard to Miss Gill; and I will see that the best medical advice is obtained for her. And now, if you please, you will show me to Miss Gill's room."

"You persist in seeing her?"

"I have said I will not leave the house until I have done so."

"Booth shall take you to her room," said Dorothea, subdued, as she rang the bell. "I have made the best arrangements for her that were possible under the circumstances. They are not, however, quite so comfortable as I could wish."

Booth entered the room: a middle-aged woman, in a rusty cinnamon-coloured silk dress, a plain frowning woman, who had been many years attached to the establishment, in the character of superior servant or housekeeper, and had in some way, either by persistence in paying her mistress the compliment of imitation, or from the resemblance, said to be produced by constant association, grown to look like a sort of duplicate or cheap edition of Miss Bigg. She had the same hard screwed-up ringlets in petrified coils upon her forehead; the same grim smile—being not so much a smile, indeed, as a cheerless exhibition of teeth and gums; the same forbidding brow and dull black eyes—like unpolished ebony —but she was not nearly so tall as Miss Dorothea, while

she was much stouter in figure. She had endeavoured
to struggle with her contour and suppress her roundness
by means of increased tightness of dress; this imparted
a stuffed, pincushion look to her shoulders and their
vicinity, the notion of that semblance being enhanced
by the fact that pin-heads were to be traced projecting
from various portions of her figure. Upon provocation
she had even been known to produce a dozen or so
from her mouth quite unexpectedly, like a conjuror. She
had been a great favourite of the late Miss Adelaide
Bigg, who had, upon one occasion, spoken of her as "that
inestimable woman, Booth." It had become the fashion
after this to recognise her at every opportunity as an
"inestimable woman;" though this was not the opinion of
the pupils. When the honourable, witty, and pretty Miss
Pincott was a pupil at Chapone House (she was afterwards
the third wife of John Logwood, the second Baron Lambeth,
and distinguished for her zealous patronage of religious
potichomanie, stained-glass windows, poetic literature and
Puseyism), she used to call Booth "Sarnem," and Miss
Adelaide Bigg, who was then living, "Gesler," the young
lady assigning to herself the *rôle* of William Tell, and
heading a mutiny of the other young ladies against the constituted authorities, which resulted ultimately in her removal
from the seminary. These nicknames, however, still lingered
among the school traditions, as, indeed, did the story of
pretty Miss Pincott's revolt. Insubordinate pupils were
often known to speak of Booth as "Sarnem" still; but of
course her fidelity to the heads of the establishment was a
sufficient cause for her being held in severe reprobation by
the young ladies. She was not a very pleasant person—
Booth—from any other than Miss Bigg's point of view.
Her religious opinions, it may be stated, were of a particularly depressing nature. Notwithstanding, she seemed
quite to rejoice in their gloom, much as lovers enjoy dusk.
She described Miss Dorothea as a "gospel-woman," whatever that might be. She called going to church "sitting
under a minister," and indulged occasionally in other phrases
of like mystery. She considered herself and Miss Bigg as
"of the elect," holding probably that they had by an
admirable foresight secured reserved seats in a state of future

bliss, whereas other people must go in with the crush, or take themselves elsewhere. Her sentiments, indeed, in that respect might be described as possessing a decidedly sulphuric flavour.

"Will you please to step this way, Miss Carr?" said Booth : and she conducted Leo from the gaunt drawing-room. They passed up the wide handsome staircase of Chapone House. The upper flights of stairs were shabby-looking, tortuous, ill-lighted, narrow. There was no gay ribbon of many-coloured carpet down the centre, no dapper margin of pure white—mere tawny deal, unpainted, creaking, with unsteady balusters. They were shut from the view of the superior parts of the house by a door kept constantly closed.

Up these dark steps, her silken skirts rustling and whistling angrily against the sides of the limited, ill-lighted path, Leo passed, convoyed by Booth. They stopped at a door, and entered together a small low-roofed attic. The room was clean, but comfortless-looking ; the slanting walls made very acute angles of the side of the chamber, lighted by a small window cut in the ceiling as it seemed ; but, indeed, it was hard to say where the ceiling ended and the walls commenced. It was some few minutes before Leo's eyes became sufficiently accustomed to the light of the room to distinguish that on a small bed in a corner, the only canopy a slope in the whitewashed roof, the figure of a little girl, apparently asleep, lay curled up, a crumpled stream of light flaxen hair upon the pillow, and her thin arms stretched forth, the hands with the palms upwards, and the fingers flaccidly curled.

"Is she asleep?" Leo inquired in a whisper, turning to Booth.

"She's fond of shamming, I think, Miss Carr," Booth answered harshly. "She's often drowsy, though, of late. Come ; wake up, Miss ; you're wanted," she called, in a grating voice, to the child.

"Hush ! don't speak to her like that," Leo interrupted somewhat angrily. She approached the bed and stooped down the better to examine the face of the child—very wan and sharp-featured and pale, save where a blotch of scarlet glowed unnaturally upon her cheek bones.

"Oh, my poor Baby, how you are changed!" Leo cried in a moved voice, the tears leaping to her eyes and her heart in a tremble. "What a little thin hand! Oh, and how it burns! My poor, poor Baby!"

"Yes, she's very feverish. But I think she's getting better. I give her nothing but gruel; she's very weak, or she pretends to be. I think she shams a good deal, to try and get off learning her hymns. But I'm as sharp as she is, that's one comfort."

"Baby, dear," said Leo, softly calling her, and pressing tenderly the wasted burning little hand.

"Come, look sharp," cried Booth.

"You needn't trouble yourself any further, Booth, thank you," said Leo; and there was something in the tone of her voice that made the superior servant draw back.

Slowly the child opened her large blue eyes, fixing them upon Leo, but in a scared, doubting way at first; then, as if shrinking from the conviction they forced upon her.

"Leo?" she murmured at last in a tone of inquiry.

"Yes, Baby, it's Leo come to see you."

"Dear Leo," said the child, and she held out her arms, trying to circle Leo's neck, while her eyes gleamed with a hectic lustre, and she raised her head pouting her parched lips. How well Leo knew the action, and she kissed again and again her little school-friend, hugging her frail form close to her heart.

"Oh, Leo, I thought you would never come. I thought you had forgotten me quite. I thought I should die and never see you again."

"Forgive me, Baby, I've been very wrong to stay so long away from you; but indeed I did not know that you were ill—indeed, I had not really forgotten you—only for the moment, Baby, dear."

"I have so longed to see you: I have so often thought of you. I would have written to you if I could—if Miss Bigg would have let me, and if my hand hadn't shaken so. There's no one now to be so kind to me as you always were, Leo, dear. There's no one now to help me with my geography and my French exercise, as you used to; no one cares for me now, and I've been so sad, and so friendless, and so ill; but I feel better now that I have seen you again,

Leo. You won't forget me again, Leo, will you? Promise me you never will."

"Indeed, Baby, I never will."

And again the thin arms were woven round her neck, and the fevered lips pressed to hers. And after this it seemed how great a pleasure to the poor sick child to interweave her tiny burning fingers tightly with her visitor's, while a smile lit up her wanned features, with yet a wet line of tears upon her sunken cheeks!

"How long have you been ill, my poor Baby?"

"For two weeks I think, dear. I know I have been up here two Sundays, for I heard the bells ringing and the girls getting ready for church. But oh, the time has seemed so long, Leo, so dreadfully long, and I have felt so sick and lonely! I tried hard not to cry, because I knew it was wrong of me, and babyish, and that I am growing a great girl now—and that you wouldn't like me to be crying for so little, would you, Leo? But the tears would come, and even now I can't help crying, though I don't know why quite—for I'm very glad to see you again, Leo. But oh, it was dreadful before you came!"

"I'm sure, Miss Gill, there's been no cause for your crying. Haven't you had a nice room all to yourself?—why, if you'd been a parlour-boarder you couldn't have had more. Here you've been, surrounded with every comfort, and haven't I been for ever and ever coming up to see you, and bringing you your salts, and your gruel, and what-not, all regular and comfortable, and sitting with you asking you your catechism, or hearing you your hymns—for nobody's ever too ill to attend to their religious dooties, you know—nobody; I'm sure its very—very wrong and wicked and ungrateful of you, to be making complaints like this against those as have been wearing themselves out with benefiting you. How can you, Miss?"

So Booth interrupted—the child sinking back with a shudder at the sound of her harsh, coarse voice.

"That will do, Booth," said Leonora, calmly turning to her. "There is no occasion for your remaining here longer. You will leave the room, if you please. I know the way down."

Booth looked very much as though she meditated resist-

ance. Her fierce brows came down lowering over her dull
black eyes, and her head rocked much after Miss Dorothea's
manner. The superior servant paused for a moment as
though searching for a weak place in the enemy's lines.
Certainly she found none. She wheeled round and rigidly
left the room.

"One thing," she said outside, "standing here, I can
make out all they say; if that little slut says more than she
ought, why, I'll let her know, that's all."

"Oh, Leo, how brave you are, to talk to her like that;
aint you afraid of her? She frightens me so, and she is so
cruel and cross; and she says such dreadful things to me
sometimes. Tell me, Leo, do you think I shall die?"

"What, *you*, Baby, so young? What can put such
fancies into your head? No, dear, you'll soon be well and
strong and yourself again. Why shouldn't you?"

"I don't know, but *she* says that very likely I shall die—
that years ago a pupil died here, in this very room, Leo, and
she was younger than I am, and had hair just of my colour,
and she says that most likely I shall go too, just as the
other young lady did."

"It's very wrong and wicked of her, Baby, and you
mustn't believe a word of what she says, and she's a cruel,
bad woman to speak to you of such things."

(Outside the door a superior servant's arm was moving
menacingly.)

"And tell me, Leo, if I die, do you think it's true as she
says, that evil spirits will torture me for ever and ever?
Tell me, Leo; only—only don't say it's true."

And the childish eyes, wide open, gazed piteously,
appealingly, into her friend's face, and Leo felt herself
locked ever so tightly in the wasted arms.

"No, no, my darling Baby," cried Leo, fervidly. "It's
not true, it's not true. Don't think of such things, Baby;"
and then she murmured,—"Oh, how shameful!"

"The hussy! the heathen!" groaned Booth without.

"Oh, Leo, it makes me so glad to hear you say so. I'm
sure that what you say is right, and true. I can believe
every word that you say, Leo. I'll try not to be frightened
any more. I'll try to forget what *she* said. I'm sure what
you say is right."

She looked quite happy in her new faith, putting her whole heart in her belief, as children will do. Who does not envy them the power of doing so?

"It's like what Jenny used to tell me, long—long—oh, ever so long ago."

"Who's Jenny, dear?"

"Jenny was my sister, long ago, in India, when I was quite a little thing, before I came to England—before they sent me here to learn my lessons—but I can remember it quite well. Jenny always told me that when we died we should be more happy than we had ever been; and we should go to join mamma, who died when I was a baby, and who is an angel now in heaven; and she'd be so glad to see us; and we should all be so happy together. Won't that be so, Leo?"

"Yes, Baby, you'll go to join mamma, but not yet. You'll grow to be a woman, yet, as tall as I am—taller, perhaps" (and a smile flitted along the curves of her lips). "But where is Jenny, now?"

"I don't know," said the child, with a sad, bewildered look. "Perhaps Jenny's gone to mamma, without waiting for me. Yet Jenny was very fond of me, and used to nurse me, and kiss me, and romp with me, always. Yes—Jenny and papa; but that's so long ago, now—oh, so long ago. Perhaps they've forgotten all about me now. Yet I don't think Jenny would do that," the child added, meditatively.

"And have you no other friends, Baby, that you can remember?"

"No. I don't think I can remember any more."

"No friends in England? Did no one ever come to see you here?"

"No. Oh, yes—once. The captain of the ship who brought me over. He came once. I used to call him 'uncle,' and he used to make me laugh so; but he never came again."

Some further talk did Leo have with her little friend. Then—

"And now, Baby, I'm afraid I must leave you."

"Must you, Leo! Oh, don't go yet. Five minutes more, Leo. Please, only five minutes. And you'll come again, won't you, Leo?"

" Yes. I'll come again. I'll be sure to — very, very
soon."

"You won't forget, Leo ! Oh, don't forget. I shall be
so, so sad if you forget."

Leo answered with a kiss.

" And you'll be a good, brave girl, and you won't get
frightened again, whatever they may say or do. And then,
if I can—and I think I can—I'll come very soon, and take
you with me. You'll be glad to come with me, won't you,
Baby? And we will be so happy together, and we'll go
down in the country, and make you quite well again ; and
we'll have such fun ; and you shall ride on my white pony,
think of that ! and try and be brave, and get well as soon as
ever you can. Good-bye, dearest !"

"Good-bye, Leo. Kiss me once more. Be sure you don't
forget me. Once more. Good-bye."

" Your ma, Miss," said Booth, outside, " has sent in to
say she's tired of waiting, and hopes you'll be ready to return
to town."

"You must take great care of little Miss Gill, Booth,"
Leo said, in her sweetest accents, not heeding the message,
malignantly delivered—" great care if only for my sake."

There was a sound as of a chinking of money.

"What's money !" Booth was muttering, as she followed
Leo's silken skirts down the staircase. " What's money, I
should like to know, but dross, and filth, and rubbish ? "

It was noticeable, however, that she was found shortly
afterwards putting away carefully certain coins in a green
purse as long as a stocking, decked with sharp steel rings
and tassels.

"I have seen Miss Gill," Leo remarked to Miss Bigg,
nervously grating her mittens together at the foot of the
stairs. " I am distressed at her state. I remember what I
said concerning her. Do you remember it, too. I shall
send down the best medical assistance that can be procured
in London. Meanwhile, you will write to me, if you please,
daily, how she is going on. You will send me, also, a note
of what is due to you on her account, and I will be careful
to speak to papa upon the subject. Pray don't let me have
cause to complain of any negligence as to these matters.
Good-morning, Miss Bigg."

7

The little lady graciously entrusted for a moment two of her fingers to be scratched by Miss Bigg's mittens, and then rustled into the barouche at the door of Chapone House.

"Drive quickly, Andrews. Home, of course," said Mrs. Carr. "Dear me, Leonora, what a long time you have been; you've made me quite tired, and sleepy, and cramped, sitting here by myself. I am afraid we shall be late for dinner, and you know your father hates unpunctuality, especially at dinner. Men are all alike in that respect. Jordan was very angry when he was kept waiting for his meals. I remember on one occasion he left the house because the dinner was rather behind-hand, and declared he would dine off cold meat at a tavern, sooner than wait any longer. I was very much annoyed at the time, I remember. What, that little Miss Gill unwell, is she? I'm sure I'm very sorry—why do you call her Baby? Why, she must be nine or ten years old, I should think. Oh, because her name's Barbara; a foolish name, I think. Yes, I remember her very well. You brought her down to Croxall one Christmas—or was it Midsummer—oh, both was it? A pretty little thing, well mannered, but timid, with red hair, hadn't she—oh, flaxen, was it? Jordan's hair was a bright auburn—a beautiful colour. He was not like you, Nora—not much—just a little about the mouth perhaps, and he had the same way that you have of putting up your chin sometimes. He was a good deal like Arnold in features, only not quite so tall, not with his boots off. *Of course*, the child must have medical advice, the very best, certainly. Very ill, is she? Dear me; poor little thing—poor little soul! Why, my dear, you have got tears in your eyes—don't cry about it, she'll get well again; of course she will. The illnesses I nursed you through when you were a child! But you were always very good when you were ill—very quiet and patient. Jordan was not; he was cross and obstinate, and wouldn't keep in bed, or take his physic. But then he had such a high spirit, and men are always impatient, and lose their temper when they're ill; they can't help it. I always thought that Miss Bigg was very mean. I said she was a screw the first time I ever saw her. I was always afraid that she wouldn't give you enough to eat. It's very wicked not to give children enough to eat. I never liked the woman from the first, although she was

very highly recommended to me. Indeed, I was opposed
to your going to her school, only your father insisted; he
laid so much stress upon the importance of your associating
with young people of your own age, lest you should grow
up odd and old-fashioned, and conceited and spoiled. I
wanted him to educate both you and Jordan at home,
but he wouldn't. He was very firm about it—almost angry
at last, so I gave way. I never opposed his wishes beyond
a certain point; it was not often that he was so obstinate.
So Jordan went to Eton, and you to Miss Bigg. The elder
sister was living then; she was a superior woman to this
one in every respect; she had a better manner, and was
really clever, I believe. No, the poor child mustn't be
left in that way; of course, it's hard upon Miss Bigg, but she
ought to do her duty for all that. She'll be paid in time, I
suppose, unless the child's relations are all dead. Whole
families die oft very suddenly sometimes. I read in the paper
the other day of twelve people being poisoned by eating
horseradish. I never touch it myself on that account, and,
besides, I don't like it. Yes, my dear, I'll make a point of
speaking to your father about it this very evening, after he's
had his nap; he's generally in the mood to listen and do
what I ask him then. And I'll send round to Sir Cupper
Leech the first thing in the morning, to beg that he will go
at once down to Kew, and look at the poor child, and
prescribe for her, and we'll take her away from Miss Bigg at
the very earliest opportunity. Dear me, what a bad habit
Andrews has of pulling up suddenly; he always startles me,
and I'm sure he'll take the wheel off against the lamp-post
some day. I must speak to your father about it. Only five
minutes, my dear, to dress for dinner; don't be longer. I'm
sure that silk will do very well. Your father's fond of that
dress, it's one of the best that Miss Bradshaw ever made for
you," &c. &c.

It is not to be supposed that good old Mrs. Carr delivered
the above sentences in the form of a continuous and set
speech. Her remarks were made from time to time during
the drive from Kew Green back to Westbourne Terrace,
and were interspersed with other observations, not of sufficient importance to be preserved, with interruptions from
Miss Leonora Carr, in the shape of comments and questions,

and, above all, the recital of the illness and sad state of Baby Gill. For convenience' sake only have we welded into one paragraph the gist of the conversation in the barouche, omitting the share of the younger lady.

But Sir Cupper Leech had left London. He was enjoying a physician's holiday. He had stopped at Mayence on a Rhine trip, to test thoroughly the effects of his favourite Steinwein on the Britannic constitution. He was personally occupied in experiments upon this subject. He had some notion of recommending the wine (in pints at luncheon) as an admirable "dirigent, and corrigent, and tonic:" it seemed to him likely to become a fashionable medicine with his aristocratic patients.

Sir Cupper Leech would not return for three weeks or a month. So said his servant (in a handsome livery, a senna-coloured coat, with Turkey rhubarb plushes). But a physician round the corner in Mount Street was attending to Sir Cupper's practice for him.

This proved to be Doctor Hawkshaw, senior physician of St. Lazarus's Hospital, Regius Professor of Phlebotomy and Materia Medica, and author of the celebrated works on "Insanity and Brain Cells," "The Physiology of Fatty Degeneration," "The Pathology of the Stomach," the editor of the new issue of "Pepper on the Kidneys," and other important medical authorities.

Dr. Hawkshaw was very indefatigable. In addition to his own large practice, to his hospital duties, to his medico-literary labours, he seemed always able to do more; to attend to the patients, or deliver the lectures, or visit the hospitals of his colleagues. He never left town; he knew nothing of Steinwein. He was devoted to his profession—his life might be described as one long prescription.

He had been attending a young lady in Coppice Row, on his way to St. Lazarus's Hospital; but he now said that he should call no more, as she was in a fair way of recovery. He opened Mrs. Carr's note addressed to Sir Cupper, and straightway turned his horses' heads towards Kew.

CHAPTER VIII.

MR. LOMAX OF THE WAFER STAMP OFFICE.

THE Honourable Dudley Chalker was in the Highlands. In the north he was the same Dudley Chalker he had been in the south; not different on the elastic heather to that he had been in his spring-seated stall at the opera. Certainly, he was not more conversational: acquired no new power of language. He ejaculated "Aw!" when the Mountain Dew stung his throat and brought the tears from his weak eyes to trickle on to his long moustache, thatching his upper lip so thickly with far projecting eaves, like the roof of a *châlet*. And he murmured "Baw!" when the penetrating mist soaked through his clothes and struck cold upon his cuticle. A few weeks and he was to bend his steps to what it had pleased Lord Dolly to designate "the family dungeon in Wales;" in other words, to Granite Castle, the seat in that principality of the Honourable Dudley's father, Hugh, ninth Baron Sandstone.

Arnold Page had encountered little Lord Dolly at the Junior Adonis Club, Pall Mall, of which institution both were members.

"We've got old Flukey out," quoth his lordship; "had the doose of a job though. The old boy got quite to like his quarters in that lock-up. Said, 'By Jove!' (you know his way), 'he never was so comfortable in his life before; had the best of everything, none of his duns knew where to find him, while the society was first-rate.' Barney Levy didn't behave so very badly in the matter. We all did it between us somehow. Doosid lucky we didn't delay it. There was a whole host of detainers came down an hour after we'd done the trick. Close shave, wasn't it? All Flukey's fault. He wanted such a lot of persuading to come out. You see, when he *does* take an idea into his head—he don't often, I admit—it's no end of trouble to get it out again. He sticks to it, Sir, like glue. Obstinate old

beggar! However, it's all right now. The yachting affair's
coming off. Ever seen his yacht? Pretty little thing, the
Pewit. I call her the *Mudlark.* Flukey don't like it much;
but he *will* hug the shore and run her aground so awfully.
We're off to-morrow; don't know where to. Clipston's
going. Storkford *was*, but he's been missing these three
days, and we don't know where to look for him. If he
don't turn up to-night we shall go without him. I think he's
hiding to avoid us; he does get so dreadfully ill on these
yachting trips. So we all do, for that matter. You're better
engaged, I suppose? Lucky dog, with that pretty Miss Carr,
eh? By George! who wouldn't stand in your boots if they'd
only got a chance? Well, good-bye, old man; wish you
joy. Oh, it won't be immediately. Good-bye. I shall look
you up directly I come back."

And Cupid put to sea in the *Pewit*, under the command
of his friend, Lord Flukemore. A most perilous voyage,
considering that the seamanship of that nobleman was not
of first-rate quality, and that he was as likely as not to steer
his comrades to the bottom. But Englishmen love risky
pleasures: they cannot be always having war and its forlorn
hopes; for one reason, the expense is so enormous; still they
manage to pursue peril by way of pastime, inventing
dangerous *délassements*, less costly, perhaps, but almost
as certain to provide similar chances of a serious issue.

The marble halls and gilded saloons of the Junior Adonis
were deserted. The smoking room had been seized upon
by the whitewashers, and was crowded with scaffolding
poles, by order of the committee, all out of town. There
was hardly anyone to read the newspapers save the waiters.
The magazines were uncut. The porter of prodigious girth
slept throughout the day undisturbed. Buttons kept up a
course of healthy exercise, and wore the nap from certain
portions of his uniform by perpetual sliding down the
banisters. The chief cook was enjoying his vacation at
Hombourg. He wore there a frogged frock-coat, and was
taken for a foreign nobleman *incog.* by more than one travelling Stock-exchange Englishman. The charwoman sat alone
in the scullery, telling her own fortune; it had not been a
very bright one hitherto, for fifty years—but there was to be
a change now; she was to marry well, a rich fair gentleman,

ride in a coach and six, and have eleven children. So said the dirty cards she always carried in her pocket.

London was very empty. The Government of the country was being carried on by one Minister, in whom nobody placed particular confidence. But somehow he seemed to be quite equal to the occasion; at any rate, there was no one in town to question his competency; perhaps it's easy to govern the country in the autumn. The justice of the nation was being distributed by one judge—a puisne, of course, who sat at chambers for half an hour once a week; it was quite enough. There was very little litigation going on, for one reason, I suppose, because the lawyers were all away enjoying themselves—perhaps, as a consequence, the clients were doing the same.

"Are you going down to Oakmere?" asked Robin Hooper of the gentleman residing with him in Sun-dial Buildings, Temple.

"Yes, Rob, I'm going. I put it off from day to day," answered Mr. Arnold Page. "I suppose, because there's something of a duty attached to the thing. They rather bore me at Oakmere in fact; but of course I must go. It's only fit that I should show myself to the tenants, and that sort of thing. I shall go very soon now. Indeed I've just got a letter from my brother-in-law, Lomax, *àpropos* of my going. I don't get on very well with Lomax; but I believe he's a very good fellow, really, and has my interest warmly at heart."

The letter referred to ran thus :—

"*Wafer Stamp Office, Whitehall.*

"My dear Arnold,—I want very much to see you. I was in hopes you would have been down at Oakmere before this. Georgina has had your room ready for the last three weeks. In any case, can you call upon me *here* to-day or to-morrow in the afternoon, before three? I generally leave town for Oakmere by the 3.45 express; but I want to have a little conversation with you upon a matter of business. I'll be sure not to bore you more than I can possibly avoid.

"Your affectionate brother,

"Francis L. Chalker Lomax.

"A. Page, Esq., Sun-dial Buildings."

"Of course I must go and see what he wants," said Arnold, rather moodily. And he went.

There are no distinctions of dress by which we are enabled to detect on the instant the particular grade of a gentleman serving the nation in a Government office. At the bar we have merely to feel the stuff of the advocate's robe to determine whether he be a leader or a junior, or to look for an apparently sore place on his wig, hidden by a circle of court-plaster, to decide if he be or not a serjeant-at-law. In the army or navy we may ascertain rank by counting buttons, or weighing bullion tags, or measuring scraps of lace, or examining if the shoulders be adorned with epaulettes—gold *swabs*, I think the hero (A. B. Seaman) terms them in nautical melodramas. The field-marshal is known more by his white satin ribbons even than his baton. The rear-admiral must announce his position by bearing his flag at the mizen-top-gallant-masthead, while the vice bears his at the fore-top-gallant, and the full-blown admiral his at the main-top-gallant. The coronets of the nobility proclaim their respective titles. We know that the baron may circle his head with six golden balls or pearls, and no more, while the viscount is limited only in this respect by the circumference of his cranium; that the earl may raise the pearls on eight pyramidal points, with a dainty alternation of strawberry leaves, while in the number of these leaves is the superiority of the duke over the marquis asserted. But in the Government office who is to decide which is the underling and which is the official of supreme consequence? There is nothing in the external presentment of the men to aid our selection. The very smartest man I ever knew in my life without exception was Jack Green, of the F. O. The exquisite taste of that man in dress was something marvellous. It would have done honour to a prince of the blood. He was in the choicest society, and he seemed to cast a lustre about any *salon*. He was, of course, conceived to hold an appointment under Government of an extraordinary value and importance. It was in some circles even a moot-point whether he would or not be compelled to go out with the Ministers. I was never surprised at this high appraisement of my friend; he deserved his social successes, all of them, including even the rich wife he ultimately secured. His manners were so distinguished, his cool impudence was so unparalleled, his whiskers were so marvellous, his costume so faultless, while his powers of small talk were quite those of a Cabinet Minister. But all this while—the salary of Jack Green at the F O. was but one hundred and twenty pounds per annum, and not a farthing more. How he contrived to do all he did upon that not large income—and I have good reason for believing that he possessed no further property of any kind whatever—is one of those inscrutable mysteries into which men dare not inquire. Though he looked like a Secretary of State, or at least a head of a department, he was in reality quite a junior clerk. Yet, see to what a pinnacle society raised him, owing to its ignorance of official matters, to the lack of distinctive uniforms in the Civil Service, and to Jack Green's own adroitness, and good broadcloth, and fine whiskers, and conversational powers !

It is not, then, evidently to the men themselves that we must look for outward signs determining their official position. We must cast about for other tests, and eventually perhaps we shall decide that the question revolves itself into one of carpets. For so far as I can make out, the height of official ambition is to sit in a room furnished with a Turkey carpet—after that there seems only the Premiership, or perhaps an archbishopric, worthy of aspiration. The Turkey carpet is the symbol of undoubted superiority and chieftainship in the Civil Service. There may be minor distinctions touching deal desks and Spanish mahogany furniture ; but on the floor the whole business rests. You enter the office at the age of sixteen, say, at a salary of eighty pounds, subject to certain deductions to provide for your eventual superannuation, and your possible widow, and you copy letters from ten till four in a room, the boards of which are bare, several other young gentlemen of your own standing occupying with you the apartment. You advance in age, your salary increases, you progress through cocoa-nut matting, kamptulicon, and Kidderminster, with pauses more or less prolonged at each of these stages, with fewer and fewer comrades sharing your room as you advance, until at last you reach that great official goal—a separate room, with a Turkey carpet. Beyond this pitch of luxury it does not seem possible to ascend—even in the wildest dreams of the most imaginative of our civil servants; and some of them, I assure you, are gentlemen of extreme gifts in this respect.

Mr. Lomax, of the Wafer Stamp Office, was a Turkey carpet man. In age he was about forty, he might even have been a little more, for he was a carefully dressing man, and carefully dressing men, I find, are always rather older than they seem. A handsome man, with a sharp, thin, aquiline nose, large, light blue eyes, the pupil a mere speck that never dilated or lent new light or colour to the rather stony-looking irides, and beautifully arched eyebrows—(he had a habit of smoothing these out with his little finger perhaps to show his superb diamond ring)—it was these, possibly, aided by his small lipless pinched mouth, that gave to his face a certain supercilious expression, which many of his friends accounted very aristocratic. He was tall, slight, stooped a little as he walked, from constant bending over his desk, as he explained. He wore habitually a superfine blue frock-coat with much velvet about the collar; a cravat of a lighter blue, beautifully white linen, his starched wristbands carefully drawn down to his knuckles, his hat glossy as new satin, and his boots brilliantly polished. Winter or summer, he wore light-coloured gloves and carried a neat slim green silk umbrella. He was carefully shaven; only a slight fragment of whisker, the shape of a pine on an Indian shawl, was left on his cheeks: his well-formed chin was decorated with a dimple, and his hair, thinning very much over his white forehead, was yet adroitly arranged, the oiled locks remaining being ingeniously interwoven so as to conceal as much as possible this little deficiency. He had a certain stiffness about the neck; he never turned his head without turning also his whole body; this perhaps interfered with the abstract grace of his movements, but still it imparted a degree of dignity and importance to his manner. A double eye-glass, gold-rimmed, swung from his neck on a broad ribbon; he had a long sight, which rendered it necessary for him to magnify near objects; he always arranged these glasses, securing them by their spring on the curve of his nose, which possessed what engineers call a heavy gradient, before he commenced to read or write; and the action, simple in itself, yet seemed to invest these ordinary occupations with a ceremonious and impressive character. He was a man who, it was evident, had set a high value upon himself, and somehow it happened in most cases that he succeeded in bringing round to an almost identical opinion everybody with whom he came in contact.

The Wafer Stamp Office was proud of its chief—for he was the head of that important branch of the Inland Revenue. And it must not be imagined that it was an easy thing to gain the good opinion of the Wafer Stamp Office considered collectively, or that its applause was given upon insufficient grounds. With the exception, perhaps, of the F. O. (in which of course my friend Jack Green, to whom reference has already been made, is included), the Wafer Stamp is probably the best dressed Government office in London. There was an attempt at one time to set the Admiralty, I believe, above it in point of whiskers, but the ill-advised effort was happily not persisted in. Certainly the manners and habits of the Wafer Stamp officers are of the most distinguished character. Nearly every man of them at some time or·other in his life has waltzed with a lady of title. They never smoke short pipes even in the seclusion of their own apartments. They never carry halfpence or wear cleaned gloves. Even quite the junior clerks come to the office in Hansom cabs, and appear, after four o'clock, in the Row, calmly and securely seated on the most homicidal-looking horses money can hire. These things may not represent quite the exquisite pitch to which matters are carried at the F. O., but it must be conceded that they approach near it.

It was part of Mr. Lomax's duty to despatch to expostulating members of the community long letters on foolscap, setting forth quite a whirl of titles of Acts of Parliament, and an array of. elaborate and argumentative sentences, to convince the objectors how completely and certainly they were liable to be assessed for Wafer Stamp Duty. He had interviews with the public, or such of them as were persistent in the idea of their non-liability, in his snug Turkey carpeted room at Whitehall. He had two manners, two distinct manners, on the occasions of these interviews. He had his grand, solemn, impressive manner, which was very effective indeed, and almost convincing. He waved his paper-cutter like the leader of a slow movement in a symphony as he sat stiffly on his padded Spanish mahogany writing chair. "I assure you," he would say in solemn accents, "the Commissioners have no desire to put a strained interpretation upon the Act under which they derive their powers. I must really ask you to be cautious how you venture to bring, or even to hint, such a charge against the Commissioners. I really cannot consent to sit in this room and hear you so express yourself. I must counsel you at once to pay the amount levied upon you to your district collector without the delay of another hour, or we shall be compelled, however reluctantly, to instruct the Government solicitor to take proceedings. I should warn you also that, under clause 360 of the Act of last session, the Commissioners have power to inflict a fine of treble duty upon the discovery of any attempt at evasion." With a severe glance at his visitor he would ring his handbell with a rigid forefinger. "Good-morning. Door, Pawson" (to the porter), "door; show this gentleman out." And he had his affable, almost jocose, manner. He would stand in front of his fire, with a straddling action of his legs, kicking out his feet now and then from sheer animal spirits and playfulness (like a young horse turned into a meadow), or as though inflicting punishment upon an imaginary foe. "Not liable, my dear Sir, not liable! ha, ha! a good joke: of course you're liable. We're all liable. I'm liable. I'd get off it if I could, but I can't. Pay it, my dear Sir; pay it at once, without further to-do, you'll find it the cheapest in the end. We're terrible fellows here, I can tell you; if we once make an assessment we stick to you—never lose sight of you; and, if you give us any trouble, by George, Sir, we let the Attorney-General and the Lord Chancellor, and all the law officers of the Crown, loose upon you like a pack of hounds. You'll give in *then*. Ha! ha! Take my advice. Give in *now*. Pay it, pay it." And somehow the tax generally was paid. It was hard to say which of Lomax's manners was the most successful.

Certainly it was difficult to resist the charm of his plausibility, of his readiness, of his calm concise way of putting things. His voice firm, yet musical; his articulation very distinct; his smile winning, showing just a flash now and then of his small white teeth; and then the convincing action of his delicate hands waving from his faultless wristbands, the diamond glittering as they sawed the air. He was handsome, aristocratic, clever, and standing on his official Turkey carpet, he had greatly the advantage of his opponent. He had been the younger son of a family, well connected, but not rich. His mother was a Chalker. He had married well; Arnold's sister Georgina, the only daughter of the late General Page, of Oakmere Court, Woodlandshire: not quite so well, perhaps, as he had expected, for the bulk of the general's property, including the land, had gone to his son. But still this was all a long time ago now; the sister was some years older than the brother; children had blessed the marriage; his wife was a clever and accomplished, and had been a very beautiful, woman. The husband had little reason to complain; and he had reached the Turkey carpet stage of official prosperity.

Arnold was ushered by Pawson into the Turkey carpeted room.

"Ah, my dear Arnold, how are you? Glad to see you, my dear boy," cried Mr. Lomax, cheerily (he adopted his jocose manner generally with his brother-in-law, treating him rather paternally and patronisingly, viewing him as a young and inexperienced, and not very gifted, stripling). "How goes on the Temple and our law studies? You're not too assiduous, I'm afraid. Ha! ha! Well, well, we mustn't be too severe upon the young. Perhaps, at your age, I was fonder of play than of work. It's different now —perhaps I can't help myself. Sit down. Pawson, place a chair. Put Mr. Page's hat on the side-table. I'll ring when I want you. Excuse me, while I sign these few letters. There's *The Times* close to you." (Reads) "'Sir, —I have the honour to inform you that the Commissioners ——' Dear, dear! Commissioners with one *s* again. How very careless these young fellows are. Hum—hum—hum. Well, I suppose that will do. You see, Arnold, people *will* object to pay their taxes. Very foolish, isn't it? Yes; of course it is; because they have to pay in the end. Ha! ha! Treble duty, sometimes, for trying to evade.

Hope you don't intend to make any default. I shall show you no mercy, I assure you. I shall send a broker into the Temple, and seize upon all those pretty pictures you have got there. Ha! ha! Here, Pawson, I've signed these letters. Ask Mr. Fitz-Elliott if there's anything more he wants of me? No! Very well, then. Now, Arnold, we've got half an hour to ourselves. I go by the 3.45. Very convenient the Waterloo Station, isn't it?"

"Have you anything particular to tell me?" asked Arnold.

"One or two things; not *very* particular, my dear boy, but I wanted to hear your opinion. By-the-way, Georgina's very angry that you haven't been down to see her for so long a time. You'll have enough to do to make your peace with her when you *do* go, I can promise you. But, as I tell her, the town offers so many attractions to a young man, and it *is* dull at Oakmere—really dull; and then I know the thought of business to be done there has kept you away, I know it as well as possible. You've been frightening yourself with the notion of accounts to be examined, and lists looked into, and new leases to be signed, and interviews with the tenants, and all that sort of thing. Ha! ha! I've done what I could to spare you that. Altogether I don't wonder that you hesitate to quit that snug place of yours in the Temple, where you have every comfort round you, and all your friends and associates at hand, for of course at your time of life it's with the men of your own standing that you want to associate, not with families and fogies—like me, for instance. Yes; for I'm growing a fogy, Arnold—ah! ah! positively a fogy. Well, well, but you must come soon, if it's only to see the great improvements I've been making about the house and grounds. I've thrown out a conservatory in front of the drawing-room window. Georgina keeps her plants there, and her birds, with a fountain in the middle. You can't conceive how very pretty in effect this is. Then I've made a new terrace walk on the left side of the Italian garden. I've rebuilt the pinery, and now I'm throwing out a new wing on the west side of the house. It will be very comfortable in winter; capital parlour and billiard-room, with a charming boudoir above for Georgina; the one on the other side was so terribly cold, and so confined. I'm quite sure," added Mr. Lomax, perhaps in answer to a peculiar expression in the face of his brother-in-law, "I'm quite sure I shall have your hearty approval of all I've done. Of course, these alterations have cost money—that I needn't say; but still I'm sure you'll like them."

"I hope so," said Arnold, rather seriously, "but I have an objection to the old place being pulled about. It always seemed to me to be very complete and comfortable, either for winter or summer; however, perhaps it is my own fault for not being down there oftener than I have been. I had no idea when you spoke of making a few changes, that you had such extensive plans in contemplation."

"My dear fellow, you'll be delighted with them, take my word for it. Georgina has supervised the whole business. She has exerted herself to quite a surprising extent, and you know what exquisite taste she has in things of this kind— really exquisite."

Arnold did not look so satisfied on this head as the husband of the lady. (But then we know how brothers underrate their sisters.)

"Was it to tell me this you wanted to see me?" asked Arnold.

"No, my dear boy, only in part. You've really great natural talent for business, Arnold, if you would only do yourself justice; that remark shows it—that desire to go at once straight to the gist of a matter. Quite right and proper; I applaud you for it. I really do. It's an age of periphrasis, beating about the bush—circumlocution, as people say, laughing at our office manners, and it's very true—very true, indeed. No; what I wanted to say to you was this : I'll put the matter into as few words as possible, for I know *you* don't want to be detained any longer than can be avoided, and I know that *I* want to catch the 3.45 to Oakmere. Ha! ha! well then, look here. The Oakmere property was yours, under your father's will—subject to an annual charge of no great amount in favour of your sister, Georgina, for her life. Now has it ever struck you that the property has been greatly over-valued? No, I dare say not. But I've been looking into the matter. Your father always regarded it as representing a certain income of so much, and he lived up to that amount. You have followed in his footsteps. I can't blame you for so doing. Your expenses have been less than his, still they have been heavy, and the plain fact of the matter is, that you have both been living at a rate in excess of the income arising from the property."

"Is this so?" inquired Arnold, with an air of surprise.

"It is indeed. I have been at some pains to go into the matter. Now, as you must be aware, this state of things cannot go on for long without your feeling the shoe pinch you."

"I had no conception of this."

"Nor had I. Still there is no cause of alarm. The fact is—the plain fact is, that the property has been badly handled—very badly handled; there has been great neglect; there has been a want of supervision. The tenants have had too much their own way, and the estate has deteriorated dreadfully, I must say, since it came into your father's hands, and entirely owing to a bad system of management. No doubt, too, your father was imposed upon by the people about him. He was a man perhaps rather likely to be imposed upon. He was so frank and true and generous himself, that he was very slow to believe ill of anyone. In many points, Arnold, you resemble him remarkably."

"But the remedy?"

"Well, is simple enough—a different system, some retrenchment, a less draught upon the income of the estate, and, what is very important, a liberal expenditure upon the property in the way of improvements. We've fallen behind the age, in fact. We have to deal with land now, as with everything else, upon a very different system to that formerly prevailing. The thing is very clear, only people were some time before they found it out. Improve your property, and you improve your rental. The more money you spend upon your land, the more money over and over again your land will return to you."

Arnold rose and walked about the room rather disturbed in manner.

"I am afraid," he said, "I have to reproach myself with much neglect. I ought to have seen to all this before; it ought not to have been left to you to make these discoveries; but somehow I've fallen into a habit of taking things too much for granted."

"Come, come—you mustn't take a too serious view of the thing; there's nothing to be alarmed about, or to grieve over. It was only likely, that when with my steady business notions—ha! ha! you must give some credit to official habits, Arnold—that when I came to look into the matter I should lay my hand upon one or two little defects and shortcomings like this."

" But what would you have me do now, Lomax ? "

" I'll tell you, very briefly, for the time's running on" (he glanced at his handsome gold watch). "I'll tell you how to improve your property, and without present loss of income, for no man likes retrenchment; I know that very well. We talk of it as an easy thing, but it's really doosid difficult. I ought to know; I've tried it often enough. Ha! ha! Well, look here : in the first place, we must raise money upon mortgage of the Oakmere property."

" Mortgage ! Do you remember how my father used to speak of mortgages ? "

"Yes, yes, my dear boy, I remember; he had old-fashioned ideas upon the subject, and circumstances are really so different to what they used to be. And you will not really be borrowing money, you will be investing it. Now, look here. Say we borrow a sum of fifty thousand upon the estate—at five per cent. We might even get it at four and a half; there are always people who will only lend money upon land—timid investors, say, or trustees who are bound to invest their trust funds upon real government securities. You can always borrow upon land in that way, and at a comparatively low rate of interest. Well, say we raise fifty thousand upon mortgage of the estate ? "

" But wouldn't it do as well," Arnold interrupted, "to borrow of my banker, upon a deposit of the title deeds ? "

Mr. Lomax looked curiously at his brother-in-law for a moment.

"Yes," he said, after a pause, "certainly, that course is open to you. It is quite a matter of opinion. I see myself many objections to borrowing money of a banker in that way. You let him too much into the secrets of the

8

prison-house. One doesn't want one's banker to know everything. And it's a mortgage after all; if *that's* what you're fighting against, it's an equitable mortgage, as you very well know. Besides, suppose he calls in his money, you must go elsewhere for a loan then, and there's—at least I think so — a sense of obligation about borrowing of one's banker—to any important amount. I should say at once go to a third party for the money; an insurance office, or public company with money to lend, for instance. There's the Ostrich, now. I happen to know that the Ostrich would be glad to lend a large sum in this way."

"Well, pardon my interruption; continue, please."

"Well, we raise this money—never mind how at present, we raise it—fifty thousand, say."

"Isn't that a very large sum—more than is necessary?"

"You see the expense is much the same; the examination into title and preparation of deeds much the same, whether you raise five thousand or fifty. But I will show you why I name a large sum. You sink half, say, in the improvement of your property—of course you cannot look for immediate return from *that;* the rest you invest. How? In a way which will bring you sufficient to keep down the interest of the mortgage, and yet leave you a balance of income even above that you are at present enjoying. Invest in railway, mining, insurance companies; I can put you in the way of securing most admirable investments in things of that kind."

"But won't that be speculating?"

"My dear Arnold! You don't call buying Bank stock speculating, do you—because its price varies with the condition of the market? Well, these things I have mentioned are just as safe as Bank stock, though of course they are liable in the same way to fluctuation in value. Now, from peculiar circumstances, I happen to know of some very admirable investments—investments beyond the reach of the general public; for of course there's always a public greedy enough and grasping enough after such things. But, in fact, these investments don't come into the market; they are kept well out of the market by persons well informed in the matter, who know the reason why, and all about it." (He unlocked a drawer in his desk, and took out

a bundle of papers, which he turned over as he spoke).
"Here are some shares now to be had in the Ostrich
Insurance Company — a really splendid thing — safe to
pay twelve per cent., and indeed I see no reason why it
shouldn't pay twenty, or even five and twenty. Then there's
this new Mining Company,—the Dom Ferdinando El Rey
Silver Mining Company, at Tezcotzinco, a most superb
thing. It's close to the Dom Bobadillo, which has paid its
shareholders very nearly ninety per cent.; the income accruing upon its shares, ten pounds paid up only, is something enormous. Then there's the Cape Comorin, Hyder-
abad and Delhi direct Railway, with an imperial guarantee
of six per cent., and the positive certainty of a return of
fifteen per cent. from passenger traffic alone in the course
of a very short time. You know, these things—it's all very
well to talk about speculation—but these things are as good
as gold, as safe as the Bank of England."

"But do I understand you to say that I can obtain
shares in these undertakings without having to pay enormous
premiums?"

"You can have them almost at par—almost at par—
owing—owing to a remarkable train of circumstances—a
recurrence of which is hardly possible."

Arnold, wondering, looked at his brother-in-law. Mr.
Lomax seemed a little nervous and fidgety as his white
hands collected the papers and thrust them into the drawer
again, turning the key upon them. He walked to the
window. Some men, if they have an important communication to make, like always to have their backs to the
light, their faces in shadow. Perhaps Mr. Lomax was of
this way of thinking.

"I may say at once plainly and openly—I really don't
see why one shouldn't be perfectly frank about what—after
all, is simply a matter of business—I may say at once then,
that I can procure you shares in these remarkable investments, the profits accruing from which I consider to be
absolutely certain. In fact, the shares which I propose
should be transferred to your name, stand at present in
mine. And in this way. You may remember, that I was
left guardian of my poor brother George's children. George
had married well, you know—a daughter of Strongbow, the

8—2

great boiler-maker—so under his will I found myself trustee, for the benefit of my nieces, of a very considerable amount of funded property. The land went to his eldest son. Well, I considered myself bound to do the best I could for the benefit of the orphans. I was the surviving trustee, the money stood in my name. I thought they ought to get a better return than the Bank would give them; I sold out; I re-invested the money in these securities, and others of a similar kind. Well, the eldest girl is, as you know, grown up now. She is engaged to be married to young Lord Mardale. Her share of the money left by her father will have to be transferred into the names of the trustees of her marriage settlement. Well, it seems that, strictly speaking, I had no right, in spite of the evident advantages of the change—and the great increase of income to be derived from it—I had no right to invest the money in other than government or real securities—and I am bound therefore to reinstate the sum of money, precisely as it stood originally invested; and you will perceive that I am in fact upon the horns of a dilemma, when I inform you that I am under a pledge —a distinct pledge unfortunately—I cannot think now how I could have been so foolish as to have tied my hands in such a way –a pledge not to bring these securities into the market, because a forced sale, in this way, might give rise to alarming reports, and produce, indeed, disastrous consequences."

"Notwithstanding the eligibility of the undertaking?"

"Notwithstanding even that. You will see, then, that I occupy a situation of some little difficulty. On the one hand, I am bound to buy into the Funds; on the other, I am forbidden to sell out my railway and other securities. I must own that I have laid myself open to a charge of indiscretion."

"What's called a breach of trust, in fact."

"Well, yes; something of that kind; though you will understand that I have been acting—if a little irregularly—still purely with a view to the benefit of my wards. You will see, too, that quite apart even from your own interests—for I desire to put the thing fairly before you—it is a matter of convenience to me to find a private purchaser of these shares."

" Couldn't you take them yourself ? "

" No ; all my available funds are tied up in a way that I dare not disturb."

Arnold hesitated.

" Let me see. Your eldest niece—why, that must be Caroline—wasn't that the girl you proposed to me that I should marry ? "

" Well ; yes. I think I did say something about it once. She's a very charming girl, and very accomplished. I'm sure a very desirable woman for any man to marry."

" And I suppose if I had married her, the question about the change of investments wouldn't have arisen."

Mr. Lomax looked suspiciously out of his light blue eyes. Had he admitted too much ? He quite blushed ; and his white hands shook. He made a dash at his jocose manner, and gained it—very nearly.

" Ha ! ha ! " he laughed with some effort. " Well ; if my brother-in-law had married my niece, you see that in the complication of relationship that would have arisen, perhaps we should have forgotten these little *nuances* of strict right and wrong in the matter of trusteeship. However, that's all over. You're to marry our friend Carr's daughter. Caroline must console herself as well as she can, ha ! ha ! with Lord Mardale, and the money will be reinstated—invested in the name of their trustees in the Funds, or in what securities they please. I shall have washed my hands of it—and these shares, most desirable things, I must say—I only wish I could afford to keep them myself—will stand in future in the name of Arnold Page, Esq., of the Temple, London, and Oakmere Court, Woodlandshire, eh ? "

" Well," said Arnold, slowly, " you see it's a question one can't decide upon on the instant."

" Very true ; at the same time you must remember on the other hand, that the matter cannot be left open very long. You must turn it over in your mind. I should be sorry to influence you either one way or the other—of course, if you don't take the shares some one else will ; at the same time I do think it would be a pity, a great pity, if you were to miss so excellent an opportunity of retrieving your position, and at the same time of improving your estate."

" But there will be calls upon these shares, I suppose ? "

" Well, yes. No doubt, as time goes on, there will be calls on the shares. What then? You'll be able to mee them. They'll give full notice, and you'll be always able to provide the money. Besides, upon your marriage with Miss Carr, there can be no doubt that our friend and neighbour will put you in possession of a very handsome amount, in ready money, paid down on the nail, as people say."

" Do you think he would like his daughter's money to be applied in such a way? "

" How could he object? How could he prevent it? I mean that he could have no possible objection. The advantages of these investments must be patent to everyone. Besides, there's another view I should like you to take of this matter. What do you propose to do with yourself in the future? What career do you think of adopting? You have many elegant and delightful pursuits at present ; literature, music, the fine arts, and so on. Very charming, indeed. But these are simply pastimes, after all ; you must aspire to something beyond these. Of course, you've a very good chance of sitting for Woodlandshire some day. Why not try to qualify yourself for a public and parliamentary life? Say, you take these shares ; you acquire an interest in business undertakings of very considerable importance. What is there to hinder you with your influence and position from stepping into the direction, having a voice in the management of these concerns? I should really like to see you with a little more ambition, Arnold. You don't do yourself justice ; you don't, indeed. You have remarkable intelligence, great natural talent ; you might really distinguish yourself in the conduct of affairs of this kind. I have not the least doubt the Ostrich would be glad to have you on its Board. I am quite sure that the directors of the Dom Ferdinando would see you among them with a great deal of pleasure. Of course my position here as a servant of the Government forbids my dreaming of anything of this kind. But there is nothing to prevent *you*. You would find a directorship after all would take up little enough of your time, while it would be, in a way, educating you for a future share in the carrying on of public affairs. Believe me, you should think twice before you fling away an opportunity of this really valuable kind. Seriously, I must say that your present system of life—so far, of course, as I am able to judge—seems to me of a sadly and dangerously lotos-eating character. You will fall into lethargic habits of mind, from which you will find it very difficult to rouse yourself."

"There's truth in what you say," said Arnold musingly.

"Of course there is, my dear boy; indolence grows on men terribly. Go on like this, and you'll be a fat man before you are five-and-thirty! Ha! ha! one thing, hard work preserves one's figure. Ha! ha! by George "—the watch again)—"I've missed the train! what *will* Georgina say! Well, well, it can't be helped! I must dine in town, that's all, and you must dine with me, Arnold, you must indeed. We've got a new cook at the Mausoleum. Frangipani his name is. Let me see, you belong to the Junior Adonis—Ah! that's a little too fast for me; I find the Mausoleum very quiet and comfortable. We'll take a turn in the park first, though I suppose there's hardly a soul left there now. Pawson, I'm going."

They dined at the Mausoleum accordingly—the Burgundy was excellent.

"What would old Mr. Carr say to my becoming a director of a public company, I wonder!" Arnold asked himself, as he returned to the Temple.

"If he knew that the title deeds were already pledged!" muttered Mr. Lomax, as he took his seat in a late train to Oakmere.

He was well known on the line; the railway servants saluted him with effusion.

CHAPTER IX.

MRS. SIMMONS'S LODGER.

HE notification to the effect that apartments were to be let furnished, and that inquiry concerning them was to be made within, which, as we have shown, had whilom been wafered to the window of a newsvender's shop in Coppice Row, Clerkenwell, was now withdrawn. Mrs. Simmons had secured her full complement of lodgers. The young lady who had been for a few days a patient in the hands of Dr. Hawkshaw, of St. Lazarus Hospital, and a cause of much anxiety to Mr. Robin Hooper and (but in a less degree, by reason of the distractions of his medical and musical studies) to his friend, Mr. Philip Gossett, had become tenant of the vacant rooms, and there was a disposition to agree upon the whole that she was what was called "a desirable lodger." The peculiar circumstances, however, attending her first introduction to the house, though remembered less vividly, were by no means forgotten. Certain mysteries still obscured the motives of much of her conduct, and, of course, there were not wanting in Coppice Row and its vicinage commentators upon these. Coppice Row had never been disinclined to discuss the doings of its friends and acquaintances. The guests, residents for the most part in Clerkenwell, who assembled nightly in the parlour of the "Spotted Dog," and had constituted themselves into a sort of Amateur Committee of Public Safety, keeping a strict and jealous eye upon both the interests of Europe and the privileges of their own immediate parish, and for whose watchfulness no occurrence at home or abroad was either too magnific or too minute ; the conclave at the "Spotted Dog" had had in due course this subject before them for consideration. "Brother" Simmons —for the members of the assembly bestowed upon each other that prefix, probably from some confused association of their proceedings with the formulæ of courts of law and

Masonic lodges (otherwise, they were fond of maintaining a parliamentary tone, though in *that* was traceable at times a decided and undisguisable tap-room fervour) — Brother Simmons had been invited to inform his colleagues fully upon the topic before them. In the peculiar phraseology of the assembly in such cases, he was desired "to contribute to the harmony of the evening," by stating all he knew relative to his wife's lodger. This "harmony of the evening," indeed, seemed to be quite the motto and watchword of the meeting — stress was constantly laid upon it as upon a most precious palladium—just as the words "trial by jury," say, or "civil and religious liberty," are recognised among more important communities as representing institutions pregnant with value. Brother Simmons had responded to that toast (for so, curiously enough, he proceeded to describe the invitation), in an address of considerable length and inconsiderable intelligence. But, in plain truth, Brother Simmons could not give information to the meeting, for the simple reason that he had no information to give. He knew nothing whatever concerning his wife's lodger. The matter was out of his department. And he was the less likely to obtain knowledge on the subject, from the fact that his attendance at the "Spotted Dog" meeting was in direct opposition to the injunctions of his wife. A severe reprimand awaited the return of the newsvender and ex-harlequin to his own fireside. Mrs. Simmons seldom spared her husband. She had found by experience that a merciful or sentimental policy in regard to him was an error that recoiled seriously upon herself. And, after all, there was little enough to be told even by Mrs. Simmons as to the lodger. Dr. Hawkshaw had drawn from her the confession that her name was Milne—Janet Milne. "She's a lady, *that* I know," said Mrs. Simmons, "and the baby's as good as gold in her arms. And the way she takes it from that girl Nancy is quite a picture. A lady every inch of her." Mrs. Simmons was satisfied, then, to ask few questions concerning the new comer. Perhaps her professional duties had begotten in her a certain respect and liking for a mystery. How many melodramas at the Paroquet had hinged upon an awful secret? She looked forward very likely to revelation at the proper time, when the band would have its cue for the appropriate music and the green curtain would loosen in the flies ready to descend and close the drama. She could wait till then.

Miss Milne had entered upon the occupation of the vacant rooms. Her stock of money was slender, as Mrs. Simmons had ascertained when she examined the contents of her lodger's pocket. But the charges in the Coppice Row establishment were not high, and Mrs. Simmons had every confidence, as she stated, in the integrity of the new comer. True : she had no luggage, and expenditure had been inevitable to procure certain wardrobe necessaries. But even then a balance had been left. The purchases had been of the most moderate kind. And the way in which she took the baby from Nancy! with such a delightful regard for the safety of its back ! After that there was no fear that Mrs. Simmons should press harshly for the settlement of her little account for board and lodging.

"A perfect lady," quoth the actress. " I'm sure it's quite a treat to talk with her, after the people one does meet, and the things one has to put up with, and Simmons conducting himself like the monster he is. It's a comfort to have her in the house. And the baby—bless it !—taking to her ever so kindly. I can leave the house with twice the confidence now, without fidgeting myself, as over and over again I have done, with the notion that Nancy has let it fall and bruised its precious head ; or that Amelia's been drinking out of the boiling kettle, or set fire to herself; or that little Jemmy's been breaking every window in the place, or put his sister's eyes out with his peg-top. And to think of her helping me to turn my old green silk, ironing it out with her own white hands, and making it up again for me. Why, it looks for all the world as good as new ; and I'm sure it never fitted me half so well before as it does now. And all done so nicely and simply, without any fuss or bother, or making me feel that she was conferring an obligation, or a favour, or anything of that sort. Poor thing ! so young and so pretty, with such gentle ways about her, and such a sweet soft voice. Yet she must have seen some trouble too, or she'd never look so sad ; and she's very delicate—one can see that at once : so pale, and slight, and starting at every noise, even when the door opens suddenly—as timid as a hare. Wants to be a governess, she says, though she has never given lessons before. Well, I'm sure she'd be a treasure to any family—the best in the land. And such a nice way as she's got with children, managing them so nicely, without any noise, and the poor things getting so fond of her too. Why, there's little Jemmy, who can't bear his lessons as a rule, and runs from his spelling-book like a mad dog from water—why, the child will stand by her side all the morning while she teaches him the French for this, that, and the other; opens his eyes as wide as may be, and gets it all off by heart quite wonderfully. It's the way she has of teaching—that's what it is; and I'm sure it's a first-rate thing for little Jemmy. I know I wish I knew French. Many's the pound a person may make by their knowledge of it. Why, there's young Mobbs, the prompter's son, a mere boy though he *is* married, and his wife, a sweet-tempered young thing, engaged in the ladies' dressing-room at the theatre, and put to bed with twins only last Midsummer,—poor lamb! she never had any talent for the stage, for she's a bad stammer, and her figure's not good, and you must have *that* to succeed at the theatre,—well, young Mobbs is a very clever Frenchman, I'm told; and has constant employment to translate for the theatre. He's as good as a regular engagement to translate from the French; sends in an act a week, and draws his thirty shillings from the treasury for it every Saturday night, regular as clock-work; and he says it only takes him a few hours' work. That's brag, very likely, for young Mobbs *is* conceited. But still, what a splendid thing it would be for little Jemmy, if he should ever be able to do anything as good as that—thirty shillings a week for knowing French! I'm sure you'll be a good boy and stick to your book, and learn as fast as you can, and do all that kind Miss Milne tells you. Won't you, Jemmy? There's a dear child. Kiss his mother, then, precious. And what a sweet singer she is, Mr. Gossett. Ah! you're a judge. I'm sure I never heard such singing. Pure as a bell her voice is. I'm not a musician myself, and I haven't much ear. I never could sing myself, not to speak of. Even in my young days when down at Bath, I always disliked the part of Ophelia on that account. I felt that I wasn't the thing in it. But I know good singing when I hear it as well as anybody; and I'm sure Miss Milne's voice sounds to me the perfection of music. There; I don't care who says it doesn't."

"She's got a very jolly soprano," says Mr. Gossett, thus appealed to. He was sitting in his shirt-sleeves before his piccolo piano. He had been thundering Rossini's *Pro Peccatis*, with superb volume of voice, dwelling on the sonorous bass notes of the music with an intense enjoyment — perhaps dragging the time a little here and there, to exhibit fully the glorious character of his *portamento*. "A very jolly soprano. I heard her give out a little roulade the other day as she came down stairs, accompanying something I was playing on the piano. By George it was beautiful. Perfectly in tune, and exquisitely sweet in quality. Produced, too, without the slightest effort and with no nonsense at all about it; because she could not have known that I could hear her."

"Oh, she's above all that," said Mrs. Simmons, decisively.

"I should like to hear her sing the 'Quand je quitatis,' from *Robert*. Wouldn't it be fine? Or the final trio—with Rob in the tenor part—to my Bertram—how glorious!" And Mr. Gossett twirled up his moustache, thrust his hair behind his ears, rolled his eyes—assumed, in short, his most demoniac expression, and began singing furiously—

> "'Oh tourment! Oh supplice!
> Mon fils, mon seul bonheur,
> A mes vœux sois propice,
> J'en appelle à ton cœur.'

I rather think that would bring the house down — even a frigid London opera audience; don't you think so, Mrs. S. ?"

"How pretty she'd look in the peasant girl's dress," said Mrs. Simmons. "I wear a dress very like that in *The Murder of the Red Barn*, and it's very becoming. I always get two rounds of applause directly I come on in it. Was that the baby crying?"

"And shouldn't I look fine as Bertram—all black velvet and flame coloured lining, and a big cloak to stretch out like bat's wings? By George! I think as soon as I can get any money I'll have the dress made; one can't tell how soon it may come in useful. What o'clock is it? I must be off to lecture. Where did I put that book I was reading— *Madden on Monomania?* Oh, here it is. By-the-way, Mrs. Simmons, if Miss Milne would like to practise on my piano when I am away, it's quite at her service; I dare say she would, particularly if she's as fond of music as I am. I ought to have thought of it before. I shall be home to tea, I dare say, at the usual time. Tell Rob, if he should happen to call when I'm out." And Mr. Gossett hurried away to his medical duties.

" If I dared I'd ask her to give Amelia a musical lesson," said Mrs. Simmons. " People may make money any day by knowing music. There's a brother-in-law of one of the young ladies at the theatre makes an excellent thing of it, accompanying songs at a music hall. I've never heard him, but they tell me he plays beautifully. Yes; I dare say Miss Milne would like to practise now and then on Gossett's piano. I'll tell her of it at once. It would be a first-rate thing for Amelia if she knew music."

Miss Milne availed herself of Mr. Gossett's good nature. She would often play on the piccolo; sometimes she would sing, accompanying herself—growing quite abstracted and forgetful as the music drew her from herself and the present into a marvellous world of its own. The melody over—the charm broken—there were tears in her glowing eyes, and her heart was throbbing almost painfully.

" How exquisite ! " said a voice close to her, on one of these occasions. She sprang away trembling, amazed, frightened. But she smiled soon at her own alarm. Robin Hooper stood at her side.

" Do you like it?" she asked; "it is a simple air by Palestrina, a little old-fashioned, perhaps, but it always seems to me to be full of beauty and tenderness; and it moves me quite absurdly—it makes me forget everything. I must really give over singing it."

" Oh, no," said Robin; " pray, don't do that."

" I am strangely nervous and timid now," she said. " I don't know what's come to me. I used to think I was quite brave at one time, but now "—and she hesitated.

" You've been ill, you know," Robin urged, soothingly ; " you've only just recovered ; you mustn't expect too much all at once."

"But I am well now—well enough to leave here; and I must leave, too, very soon."

"When will you go?" he asked, with some anxiety.

She paused for a few moments, as though struggling with herself.

"You have been very kind to me, Mr. Hooper," she said at length, in a low, hurried tone. "Believe me, I shall never forget your kindness, even if I were to go from here now and never see you again."

He was about to interrupt, but a slight movement of her hand stayed him.

"I have met with great kindness here—not from you only —more than I had any right to expect—more than I can ever hope to repay—great goodness—great forbearance. But there are·many reasons why I should now leave this place and my friends here—for they have been true friends. Perhaps one reason is sufficient. What avails to disguise the fact?—I am poor—I have my bread to earn."

Again he was about to speak—to offer her pecuniary aid, perhaps. She thought so evidently, for the blood crimsoned her cheeks and neck, and she lowered her eyes. Robin felt hot, and trembling, and wretched, seeing this. How he had pained her! Would she ever pardon the gross good nature which was thinking of offering her money? How thankful he was that he had not put his thoughts into words. Forgiveness then had been impossible—quite. But she seemed to be annoyed at her own confusion; perhaps ashamed of the pride from which it sprung.

"I have a deep sense of your kindness," she went on— she had noticed his embarrassment, understood it, and hurried, even at some self-sacrifice, to relieve it—"and I have a deep faith in your willingness to assist me in any way. I shall not forget that the first kind words I heard in this great city came from your lips; and, indeed I should not scruple to beg your aid again, in any shape, should I need it. I am sure I should not have to ask in vain."

"How noble!—how generous!—how good she is!" murmured Robin; "and how she reads my heart! My life is at her service — she may be sure of it — now — at any time."

"It has been unavoidable," she continued, "that some

mystery has surrounded my coming here. I would have had it otherwise, if I could. But at present, this must be so —less for my sake, perhaps, than for others. Some day, perhaps, I may be able to disclose everything; it is due to you who have been so kind to me—to all my good friends here, that I should do so. Suffice it that I am poor and friendless. If I have relations in London," she said, with much agitation, "believe that strong reasons exist for my not applying to them for assistance—for my not making myself and my situation here known to them. Call me still Miss —Milne—Janet Milne—a governess—or one trying so to earn a living."

"You have given lessons before?" Robin asked, timidly.

"No," she answered; "but I must do so now. I can teach music, French, singing. I have lived much abroad. Give me your aid to obtain employment in teaching these things."

"Be sure that I will," cried Robin, fervently, "to the utmost of my power. I will solicit, too, all my friends to assist you. I will ask Arnold Page, he is well connected; and through his sister, Mrs. Lomax, there can be no doubt that we shall be able to find something that may suit you. But do not overtax your strength. Are you sure you are well enough to leave this place yet? Are you sure you can undertake the fatigue of such duties? And pray don't be anxious; you are safe now, and you have friends who will never cease to labour for your welfare."

Earnestly Robin encouraged and soothed her. There was something very winning about the enthusiastic way in which he entered into her plans. Janet's eyes brightened; a smile gleamed upon her lips. A sense of relief and hope came over her, and her usual rather sad, suffering look faded away for the time.

"You are sure to get what you want; I haven't a doubt of it," said Rob. "People will be very glad of such an opportunity; and I know, Miss Milne, that the children that have you for their preceptress will be very lucky children indeed. And when you've gone away from here, you won't quite forget us all—say that you won't. This queer house and all its funny ways—for they are funny, are they not? Mrs. Simmons and the children, and Phil Gossett and his

great bass voice, and—and me. I wish you'd seen Arnold.
He's such a splendid fellow is Arnold. It always does one
good to see him. There! I'm glad to see you smiling at all
the nonsense I talk! And would you have the great kindness to sing that song again, which I interrupted when I
came in, and half spoiled? Thank you. I'm so fond of
music. You see" (a glance at the poor curved foot) "I've
been an invalid myself, and music has been so great a consolation to me. But I'm better now—quite strong and well.
And we'll look in the newspapers every day. You see, it
will be very convenient: we can get them down stairs the
first thing in the morning, and search the advertisements
for something to suit you. There are often advertisements
for governesses who have acquired French abroad. You
must keep up a good heart, Miss Milne; there's not a doubt
that we shall find something to suit you."

Some such conversation had passed between Robin
Hooper and Janet; and we may be sure that he was as
good as his word, and read the advertisement columns of
The Times with an attention he devoted to no other portions
of that wonderful paper, and pestered his friends with
recommendations of Miss Milne as a young lady most competent to give instructions in music, French, singing, and the
ordinary branches of an English education; and desired that
they would be so good as to pester all their friends in the
same way, and especially married ladies and the mothers of
families. Indeed, Robin's interest in Miss Milne was of so
pronounced a character, that it was hardly surprising that his
friends should make it the subject of some comment.

"I think Mr. Hooper comes here oftener than he used,"
Mrs. Simmons remarked, significantly. "It may be because
so many of his friends are gone out of town. Still, I don't
believe that *I'm* the attraction;" and here the good lady
looked very roguish indeed. "Nor you either, Mr. Gossett
—no; nor you, my precious Baby darling. Oh" (with a
change of voice), "no! Baby mustn't tear up my part, or
what will they sat at the theatre!"

"Ah, Rob!" quoth Mr. Gossett, "what it is to be susceptible! You're twisting certain golden tresses round your
heart, and you'll be surprised some day to find you can't
undo the tangle. You'll burn your wings, my little moth, if

you will go so near the candle. You've decided feverish symptoms—quick pulse, eyes over bright, excitable manner. We shall have to make you up a bed in St. Lazarus Hospital. We'll try and do without the knife if we can. As for the lady——"

" I don't like such jests," said Rob, hotly. " There are some things that should be spoken of lightly. Please don't mention *her* again like that. Of me you may say what you will ; only you know, there are chances against my loving or being loved. I'm but a poor sickly cripple. Remember that when you jest : it will give a pleasant sting to what you say."

" My dear Rob, you're really angry ! You know I wouldn't say a word to grieve you for the world."

" Forgive me, Phil ; I lose my temper sometimes, without a cause : I don't know why. Don't say another word about it."

" That's right, old boy ! And now let's have some music. What shall it be—our crack duet from *Robert*, or would you sooner have the one from *Moïse*, your pet ? "

" Wait a few minutes, Phil. I don't think I can sing just yet. My breath's a little short."

But it was true none the less that Mr. Robin Hooper found his way from the Temple to Coppice Row more frequently than formerly.

" Mr. Hooper," said Miss Milne, one day, with a slightly troubled look, her violet eyes turned from him—" Mr. Hooper, can you tell me if it is far from here to this address ? " She handed to him a scrap of paper.

" Kew Green," he read. There was something written above it which he could not quite decipher. " Oh, no ; it is not very far. You can get an omnibus from Piccadilly, or from the Strand. The Brentford omnibus will take you to the foot of the bridge ; or the Richmond will take you over the bridge, across the Green itself."

" I must go there," she said ; " I have wanted to go before. If "——and she stopped.

" Would it not be better that some one should accompany you ? " he began, and then he blushed. " Will she think I am urged by curiosity ? " he asked himself. " Will she think that I want to force my company upon her ? " And

9

he grew quite wretched. "How she will despise me!"
Then he added aloud, "I mean that I think—I have no
doubt—that Mrs. Simmons would be happy to go with you.
Would it not be better so? It will be a protection to you.
You are not very strong yet. You are not used to walking by yourself, perhaps. The crowds in the streets may
alarm you; they are rather alarming at first."

"I came here alone," she said. "You had forgotten
that. No; I will go alone. It is not a very terrible journey," and she smiled. "It was not *that* I wished to say.
But, if anything should happen—if I should not return——"

"Not return!" cried Robin, aghast. "You will not leave
us so suddenly, without saying good-bye even!"

"I think it not likely. I think it most unlikely. Pray
be calm. But," she went on hurriedly, "under a certain train
of circumstances which I must not, which I cannot now
explain, my return might be prevented" (the thought seemed
to make her tremble), "or great difficulties might be placed
in the way of it. Should this be so—pray don't let my
words disturb you so much—I do not apprehend there will
be any cause for this precaution; but, should anything
happen to prevent my return here, you will let me write to
you; and, should I be placed in a situation of difficulty, you
will give me such aid as you can when I shall ask it?"

"Indeed—indeed I will."

"Thank you. Enough! Do not doubt that you will see
me in a few hours; but remember this conversation, should
I not reappear before dark. But not a word of it to Mrs.
Simmons until you hear from me. Good-bye." She put out
her hand: he pressed it reverently.

"What does this mean?" Robin asked himself, when he
was alone again. "Is she in any real danger? Shall I
follow her? Shall I try to pierce this cloud of mystery?
No: she would never forgive me. Yet if harm should
happen to her——," and he paced the room in great anxiety
and trouble, dragging his lame foot after him. "Can *she*
have enemies? Is it commonly possible? Oh, I wish I
had them here, that's all!" And he added after a pause,
"And I wish I was as strong as Phil Gossett." He felt
the muscle of his arm curiously, contemplatively.

Janet stood in the awful presence of Miss Bigg.

That lady was discovered, as usual, in her gaunt drawing-room, studying the calf-bound edition of her parent's sublime work. She marked the place at which her reading had been disturbed, after her accustomed manner, with the embroidered card—"Read, mark, digest," and the green streamers. As usual she exhibited her teeth, under the delusion that she was smiling cordially upon her visitor. But her manner became a little less winning as she began to appreciate the diffident, frightened manner of Janet.

" You desire to see one of the pupils of this establishment ? " she asked, with grim courtesy.

" Yes," was the answer, in a soft, trembling voice. " Miss Gill—a pupil here. Is she well? Tell me that she is well ! "

The schoolmistress started, but recovered herself. Her lips closed. Her efforts at cordiality were checked in mid career. She stiffened herself—a process of congelation came over her—her back seemed to be especially frozen—very hard indeed.

" Why do you wish to see the child Gill ? " she inquired, in her coldest tones ; yet with something of amazement, if not alarm, in her dull black eyes, like burnt-out coals.

" Let me see her," said the visitor, appealingly ; " I am the only friend she has in the world."

" You are not aware, perhaps, that it is one of the rules of this seminary that the pupils shall be visited only by their relations."

" I am her relation——"

" Indeed ! " and Miss Bigg gazed into the trembling eyes of the other with a cruel incredulity and suspicion. " A relation ? "

" Yes, indeed I am—her sister—her only sister."

" Oh ! " Miss Bigg jerked out—apparently not crediting the statement, resolved not to discuss the matter further, but rather to avail herself, as best she might, of the admission of relationship—true or false. " Pray, are you aware that there is a large sum—a very large sum—due to me on account of Miss Gill's education and board in this seminary ? "

" I feared that such might be the case."

9— 2

"Are you prepared to pay the money due?" and Miss Bigg pretended to believe that her visitor was about to settle the account then and there, and took out the keys of her desk, and seized a pen, as though at once to fill up and sign a receipt in full.

"No," answered Janet, "I cannot do this. I have not this money. Indeed I have not. Still, let me see her; pray let me see her!"

And the tears clustered on her eyelashes, like diamond fruit on silken branches.

Miss Bigg was not easily moved. She was revolving in her own mind the consequences, so far as she was concerned, of an interview between the pupil and her sister.

"Stop a minute," she said : "there's no hurry, it seems to me. I have a question or two to put. Where's your father? Where's the father of Miss Barbara Gill, who consigned her to my care a long time back, who was in India then? Where is he now?"

"He is in England now," said Janet, with lowered eyes: "at least I think so."

"You think so. Don't you know? Where do you live?"

"I—I may not tell you."

"Not tell. Oh! ho! this is very pretty. How am I to believe your story? Not tell where you live! Perhaps you call that respectable. Well; opinions differ. I don't, so I tell you—there."

And Miss Bigg forgot her dignity entirely, she was so carried away by her wrath. She grew quite red in the face; her head was shaken violently, as though she were in an express train at its topmost speed ; her figure rocked to and fro, like a ship in a storm, with an appropriate accompaniment of creaking, as of timbers—arising, perhaps, from the tension of the laces and the convulsion of the buckram of that article of attire which generally points out the waist in female figures—and she snapped her grisly fingers in the face of Miss Janet.

"And who's to pay me? Tell me that!" she went on. "Who's to pay for the board and education of this child? Do you suppose that I'm made of gold, that I should find money for such a purpose—and for all these years? It's shameful, it is,—shameful. A wicked, cruel robbery that's what it is. And now you come here—as bold as brass—as cool as ——" (I'm afraid she was so far forgetting herself and her position as to be very nearly saying—"as a cucumber" —an obviously-vulgar simile ; but she stopped herself just in time, fortunately) "as cool as—as anything. You're her sister, are you ? You can't tell where you live, or where your father lives—or won't tell ; isn't that it rather ? Your father a captain ? I don't believe he's any more a captain than I am ; a bankrupt scoundrel and thief, that's what I call him. Why doesn't he pay the money he owes me ? tell me that ; the impostor, the cheat, the swindler ! ——"

And for some time, very angry indeed, Miss Bigg poured forth a well-sustained fire of vituperation into her cowed and trembling opponent. (You see, like love, anger is a great leveller.)

"Let me see her !" appealed Janet.

"And not only must I find money for her education and board, but I must be put to all sorts of trouble besides. I must have all sorts of people coming here at all times of the day—first one then the other—and my servants kept running up and down stairs for this child ; and never to get a halfpenny for her; it's too bad, it is—a great deal too bad ! "

And Miss Bigg brought her clenched hand down heavily upon the sublime work upon the table, regardless of the very expensive binding and of all reverence for her father the poet, in her desire to give due emphasis and force to her words.

"Now it's *you* coming here ! now it's Miss Carr—a conceited hussy, I should like to whip her well. Now it's a doctor from London, coming down express in his own carriage, as if the apothecary from Brentford wasn't good enough. Now it's a Frenchman——"

"A Frenchman !" interrupted the visitor, white with terror, trembling all over.

"Yes, a Frenchman," reiterated Miss Bigg, "bowing, and sniggering, and shrugging his shoulders, and talking his horrid gibberish." (In her anger, Miss Bigg did not perceive how this remark confirmed a current rumour as to her defective acquaintance with the French language.)

"Heaven !" gasped Janet, "has *he* been here, then ? "

"But Miss Mullins made short work of him and his broken English. She could give him as good French as he brought ; and she ought to, considering the salary I pay her. Nothing but carriages coming in at the gates, and knock, knock at the doors, and everybody worried out of their lives with fright ; and all for this   puny, sick child."

" Is she ill ? " interrupted Janet, starting up. " Let me see her ! Don't send me away !—don't, don't, for Heaven's sake ! Indeed, indeed it's not my fault that you have been wronged, as you say ! Indeed, if I had the money, I would pay you ten times over, if need were, only—only let me see my poor little sister ! "

"*If*, indeed ! No ; you've found your way here, and you may find your way back, for all the good you've done. I've had quite enough of your sister ; I don't want you ; and if I had your bankrupt father here—well ! I'd give him a piece of my mind, that's all. There ; it's no use your talking."

" Oh, don't turn from me ! " cried Janet, piteously. " Let me see her, I beg of you—on my knees——"

" Hush get up ; there's someone at the door ; don't be foolish."

Meanwhile, a tall, thin, carelessly-dressed man had entered a room on the upper floor.

"What's the matter ? " he asked sternly.   " Why do you keep that poor child mewed up in this low-roofed place ? "

" She's a bit poorly," answered an ill-favoured woman, carelessly. It was Booth, and she was regarding the patient —poor Baby Gill—not too affectionately. Perhaps the inquiries concerning the child had given trouble to the household at Miss Bigg's seminary. But she aint so bad as she makes out, it's my belief: there's a good bit of shamming about her illness—there always is about most children. She'd try to make you think that she's ever so weakly, just to shirk her hymns and religious dooties."

" Don't be a fool," said the doctor calmly ; " and open that window and let some fresh air in. One can hardly breathe in this place. What is it, my dear?" he went on, turning to the invalid kindly and taking her thin, worn hands into his—large, muscular. "Don't tremble, my dear —don't be frightened. There's no one going to hurt you. It's only the doctor come to take care of you, and make you well again." And he smoothed her silky yellow hair from her burning forehead, and then paused suddenly, looking into her large, feverishly-bright eyes. "Surely I've seen this face before, or one strangely like it. It must be so. But where? In one of the wards of St. Lazarus? I can't think. Bah! what does it matter? Out of the hundred faces I see every day is it wonderful there should be two alike?"

He talked to the child kindly, soothingly.

"There's no shamming here," he went on, with his fingers on her wrist. "Very weak, very feverish. We must put some fat upon these poor cheeks, little one, I think." And he stroked gently her burning face. "You've no appetite, have you, my dear? but you're thirsty. Yes, very thirsty. Don't cry, my dear. We'll soon make you well, if I have to take you away with me in my pocket. That's right—that's a little like a smile, I think." He laid his hand upon her forehead. "We must have no learning hymns or anything of that sort. Here, you woman, I'm speaking to you—no worrying the child about her duty and her collect, or non-sense—do you hear?"

("Awful language!" muttered Booth, to whom these words were addressed. "I wonder a thunderbolt don't fall on him. But these doctors are all alike. They'll suffer for it by-and-by—that's one comfort; and a joyful thought for the elect it is, too.")

He had placed his stethoscope—it was always ready in his hat, he never went anywhere without it—upon the chest of the child. He put his ear to the end of the tube, listening attentively. His was not a face that betrayed much of what was passing in his mind. He had schooled his muscles to maintain a rigidity of expression—a calm, a repose, that nothing could disturb. Only a very close observer could have noted some change in the glance of his bright, kindly, grey eyes. There was a look of sadness, of tender-ness, not traceable in them before. His examination con-cluded, there seemed to be a new gentleness in the way he once more smoothed the soft hair of his little patient, and drew the clothes of the bed comfortably round her.

"You must take care and not catch cold, my dear. What's your name? Barbara Gill, isn't it? Yes. Well, my little Miss Gill, we must do all we can for you, and try and make you well : and you'll be a good little girl, won't you? and do all that I tell you? And we must get some medicine made up for you ; and *you*" (he added, to Booth, in a stern whisper)—"you'd better take care and do all that I tell you, or it will be the worse for you. I'll speak to the schoolmistress down stairs. You need not come down. I know my way, and I'll write a prescription in the drawing-room. You be sure and have it made up at once."

"Bad symptoms," he said to himself, as he passed rapidly down the stairs.

He arrived at the drawing-room just in time to hear a voice cry in piteous tones, "Pray, let me see my sister."

He entered as Janet rose from her knees. He advanced to her kindly—"You here, my dear Miss "——he stopped, a probing gaze fixed upon her. She started back, confused.

"Dr. Hawkshaw !" she gasped, the colour rushing into her face.

"The sister of the pupil up stairs," Miss Bigg said, savagely waving her hand—that awkward gesture implying introduction.

"I have the pleasure of knowing Miss—*Gill*," he said, giving the name after a pause, and dwelling upon it significantly. He stretched out his hand and shook hers warmly. "Miss Gill has been a patient of mine. There is a strong likeness between the sisters."

Frightened at first, Janet now drew some courage from the doctor's friendly manner.

"How did he come to know her, I wonder !" muttered Miss Bigg.

"You wish to see your sister? I have just left her. Come up stairs—this way. I need not trouble you, Miss Bigg—I can show the young lady the way."

Outside the drawing-room door, Janet was about to speak —to express her thanks—her gratitude—to say, indeed, she hardly knew what.

"Never mind, Miss—*Gill*," he said, smiling. "I think

I can keep a secret as well as anyone. Doctors don't tell tales. There is no need of any explanation. Perhaps I know all about it, as it is : and if I don't, perhaps it doesn't very much matter. Be sure I will forget—when I leave here —that my late patient in Coppice Row and the young lady I meet here visiting her sick sister are one and the same person, though their names are different. Not a word, my dear. When you have need of a friend, why you know my address." (He pressed her hand.) "Go in at that door, my dear. Never mind the rude old woman you'll meet there. You'll have the help of another pretty little lady, and I'm sure, together, you'll be more than a match for her."

Janet, engrossed by the object of her mission, had observed neither the handsome barouche, nor the compact brougham—technically termed a pill-box, I believe—standing at the entrance of Chapone House, and evidencing visitors.

She entered the room on the upper floor. A young lady, who had retreated during the attendance of the doctor at the bedside of the patient, had resumed her position there. Janet, pale and nervous, approached the bed.

"Oh, Heaven ! How she is changed !" she said at last, in a choking voice. The tears dimmed her sight. She brushed them away. It seemed to be only with an effort she could recognise the lineaments of her sister in the thin face of the sufferer before her.

"Baby, dearest !" she cried, in a tone of anguish, and she sunk upon her knees at the side of the bed.

"Who is it? Leo, dear, tell me," said the child, with wide open eyes, twining her arms round her friend, and something scared at the agitation of the new comer.

"Don't you know me, Baby? I'm your sister—Jenny— surely you remember Jenny !"

"Jenny !" repeated the child, staring half vacantly.

"Yes; your sister Jenny ! A long while ago—you remember me now? I see you do." Some gleam of recognition shone in the child's large, wondering eyes.

"Kiss me, Jenny," she said, after a few moments. "Yes, I remember you ; that is, I think I do. But you're so big to what my Jenny used to be. Still, you're like her—yes— Jenny had eyes like that. But you're crying. Jenny never

cried—only once—that was when mamma went away to be
an angel. Don't cry—and you'll be kind to me, won't you ?
—as the Jenny of a long time ago used to be—as Leo has
been always. Yet, no; you can never be so good and kind
to me as Leo has been. Dear Leo," and the wasted arms
clung yet more closely to Leo. Janet turned to her with
streaming eyes, her golden hair crumpled, her cheeks tear-
stained.

"You have been kind to my poor little sister. God bless
you for it. And He will—be sure He will. And, indeed,
she has had need of friends. Oh my poor, poor Baby, that
I should see you thus !"

"Could I help being kind to her?" said Leo's soft voice ;
"and it is wrong to praise me so, for I have much to reproach myself with. I have neglected her sadly until now.
I am very glad to see you," she went on, simply, pressing
Janet's hand. "Baby has always been my friend, and you
will be my friend too."

"God bless you !" said Janet, greatly moved. "I owe
you already more than I can ever hope to repay." And she
surrendered herself to a passionate burst of weeping. The
tears clustered in Leo's eyes : for emotion is very infectious.
She rose to withdraw.

"Don't go yet, Leo !" cried the child; "don't leave me
yet. I can't bear to be alone, not even with her—with
Jenny. Don't cry, Jenny ; I am beginning to love you
again—I am indeed—and—and I think I shall be well again
—indeed I do, now that you are both so kind to me."

"My poor, poor sister !"

"Please tell me, Doctor Hawkshaw," quoth Miss Carr,
"is there any danger? When may we move her?"

"There are bad symptoms, my dear young lady,"
answered the doctor. "I can say little more at present ;
and I think you musn't stay too long in the sick room, there
may be risk for you. As to removal—it would be the best
thing to be done, for she is not well attended to here ; but
we must leave it for a day or two. I will come down to-
morrow, if possible. I have left a prescription, with full
instructions. Give my best compliments to your mamma.
And *you* are going to take Miss Gill back to town ? Well,

well; perhaps that will be better. I was waiting to see if I could be useful in that way. We will do all we can for our little patient, be sure of it."

"Get home as quick as you can, John," said the doctor, as he stepped into his carriage. "Poor child! Organic disease, I'm afraid; but it's as well to get her away from that infernal old woman and her hymn-book."

And the doctor, who was never idle, took up a book he had with him in the carriage, and began making, with his gold pencil-case, marginal observations and corrections. They would be useful when a new edition was called for of his valuable work on the Physiology of the Stomach.

There was some excitement in Coppice Row when it was known that Mrs. Simmons's lodger had returned in a superb barouche, and that the charmingly-dressed young lady in it (her bonnet made an immense sensation in the neighbourhood) took a most affectionate farewell of her—even to kissing her—with the words, "I shall see you again very soon. Good-bye, dear."

"You don't know what a relief it is to me to see you back again quite safe and sound," cried Robin to Janet, as she re-entered. "Do you know how I've been amusing myself? I've been reading all the advertisements in *The Times*—not merely those which state that a governess is wanted, but all the others as well. It's interesting; but I did it to kill time until you came back. Look here now, this is a curious advertisement—in the second column;" and he read aloud—"'To JANET.—CHER ANGE, RETURN THEN. WHY WILL YOU NOT? WOULD YOU KILL YOUR INCONSOLABLE ANATOLE?' Hullo! Good Heaven! Why, what's the matter? Hi! Quick! Mrs. Simmons! Some water. Could it refer to her? She's fainted dead away!"

CHAPTER X.

AU CAFE.

HERE are English *quartiers* in Paris, as we all know. For that matter, throughout France, especially along its coasts—it being simply in the nature of things that the Briton should feel at home in the presence of the waves—are there numberless, little, true-blue, stanch, Anglican settlements planted here and there—exotics that have taken firm root in a new soil, without the sacrifice in the remotest degree of the characteristics of their derivation—nay, rather as a matter of principle, clinging the more to national predjudices and opinions, and maintaining national habits and customs, from the fact that they are in a foreign and unsympathising presence, and that it is indispensable, therefore, to demonstrate utterly that Englishmen *will* be Englishmen all the world over under any condition of circumstances. Formally, perhaps, we have surrendered Calais; but we hold the more Boulogne, and many another French seaport, while in the capital we possess, of course, among other properties, the superb quadrilateral stronghold, known as the Hôtel Meurice. And there are French colonies in England, confined, for the most part, to the chief city, however; for the Gallic proclivities are not nautical nor provincial, still less pastoral. It is in London then we must look chiefly for the French *quartier;* and we shall find also German settlements, where a large consumption of sour krout occurs, and of beer, and great smoking, and mystic conversation— philosophical, but foggy; and where the melodies of fatherland, part sung, waken the echoes of the walls; and much simple kindliness and good will, with some proneness to the muddle-headed, prevail. And there are Italian settlements, especially thriving during operatic and southern revolutionary periods; and Greek colonies, addicted to pastry and card-playing, the games being of a kind unknown to northern regions. (It is said that playing with each other, the Greeks play quite fairly. Perhaps when Greeks meet Greeks there are reasons why a different line of conduct is not possible.) It is not only the Jews, therefore, who wander, carrying their country with them and the predilections of their people—their undying love for fried fish, the passover cake, the olive, the old clothes, and the best side of a bargain. Methinks other nations do likewise. The Englishman greets a compatriot in a distant clime—greets him cordially—without prejudice, it is possible, to his privilege of cutting him when they encounter subsequently at home in Pall Mall —and for a season they are friends; and they will rally round them other Englishmen, and they will cherish the customs of their country: forming, indeed, the nucleus of a colony. And so with the aliens sojourning here; so we have Leicester Square; and so we have the *café* in the neighbourhood of that square, to which the reader is now to be introduced.—This way, if you please: the *Café de l'Univers*.

The name was inscribed on the door, over the door, upon the door-posts, the gas lamp, and in gilded letters upon the window panes. The *café* was evidently proud of its name, and thrust it before the spectators at every possible opportunity. An alderman, recently knighted, could not have derived more enjoyment from his title. It was not a large establishment; it might even not unfairly be called a small one. The *Café de l'Univers*, with a little squeezing, might perhaps have accommodated about a score of guests. Plaits of dingy-figured muslin screened the window and the door-admitting light, yet excluding the public gaze. The *café* was eminently French in character. It had not suffered by its change of venue in this respect. It was French from the flower on the ceiling to the pumps of the *garçon*. It might almost have been transplanted direct from Paris. Indeed, there was much of the precarious nature and delicate health of the transplant about it. It was as an *emigré* bereft of his possessions, and considerably pinched by bad fortune, and a comfortless climate. Its state was a little sickly at present —faded, degenerate. What might have looked like splendour in an original state had a certain cheap and tawdry appearance under the change of air and situation. Certainly

the decorations were grand—pretentious; but they were
cheap. You could note the fact in the thin cotton-velvet,
straw-stuffed cushions; in the glaring but inexpensive paper
on the wall; in the gorgeous but green-hued looking-glasses,
and their thinly-gilt, fly-speckled frames; the chipped
crockery; and the marble tables, coffee-stained, and pencilled
with the calculations of the domino-players. But perhaps
noting these things, we are inquiring too curiously. What
did it matter that the prosperity of the *Café de l'Univers*
was not too well assured? Think of the comfort the place
was to the French colony in the neighbourhood. Half-
closing his eyes, or glancing through glasses rose-tinted by
memory and imagination, the exile might here dream that
he was back again in his own beautiful country—might be
led to forget for a time the brumal horrors of this land of
his refuge; his ears were refreshed with the accents of his
own language, uttered by his own countrymen, the rattle of
the dominoes, the clatter of spoons, the tinkling of glasses,
the clash of crockery, and now and then the click of the
ivory balls in collision on the French billiard-board in the
room adjoining. While, for the regalement of his nose, was
there not ever the pungent odour of French cooking
redolent throughout the establishment?

There was a *dame de comptoir*, in black silk, amply
flounced; a lace head-dress, about the size of a pen-wiper,
trimmed with cherry-coloured ribbons; with glossy blue-
black hair, tight to her head; and large, hard, bright eyes.
She wore massive earrings, a coral necklace, a substantial
brooch, bracelets—flexible serpents, with green enamel
heads, and brilliant sham rubies for eyes—and paste rings
upon her large fingers, rather less white than her worked
cuffs, probably from having been washed less carefully. Her
features were large; but she was handsome. It was even
said that there had been no less than three duels among
visitors at the *café* on her account. She was so greatly admired—so loved even—though she steadily refrained from
exhibiting any preference for one of her idolators over the
others. Her age was doubtful. She spoke of her *jeunesse*
in melancholy tones, as of a thing of the past; but it was
by no means certain that she would permit anyone else to
adopt like language. She had experienced sorrows, she

admitted, dabbing tearless eyes with her handkerchief; but, then, most Frenchwomen, according to their own showing, have suffered similarly, without being apparently much the worse ; and one is inclined, in such cases, to pay respect to an established form rather than to expend sympathy upon an individual grief which may be purely suppositious. Her complexion was a mystery : Nature had been greatly assisted —indeed, as has often happened, had called in so powerful an ally as to be overcome, instead of aided. The native hue of the *dame de comptoir* was very nearly lost under the warm coating derived from the rouge-pot, under the plentiful use of the powder-puff; while yet evidences remained prompting unfavourable ideas ; here and there, under the white dust, certain unpleasing rednesses were traceable, just as you may discern the stars for all the white scud veiling them. Still—and, notwithstanding, too, her strong, square animal jaw, gross mouth, and double chin—the lady was an object of great admiration at the *Café de l'Univers.* Was she married or single ? No one knew, though some had theories of their own on the subject. But the question is more English than French : and we have said that the *café* was eminently French. She was called Madame always : Madame Desprès. The *habitués* of the café did not trouble themselves with inquiries touching any Monsieur of that name.

Madame sat at her counter, doing nothing industriously, save when an account was to be received or an order given. A glass-case before her contained brandied cherries ; behind her, ranged upon a shelf, were various liqueur bottles ; at her side, a collection of cigars. She had a grand, calm manner, full of self-possession, and what may be called a laborious smile, too studied to be cordial, and maintaining its set creases upon her fleshy face long after the cause producing it had ceased. She bowed her head to her friends entering or departing, and to the frequenters of the café, with a courtesy which had yet something in it of condescension.

The frequenters of the *Café de l'Univers* were, for the most part, Frenchmen. And the little Gallic colony thrived on cheap, but comfortable terms, for it was one of the advantages of the place, that you really couldn't spend much money in it, however profusely you might be inclined. Yet there were a few English visitors now and then—we shall refer to them more particularly by-and-by—just as there might be in a French settlement of greater extent, in any part of the globe.

The *café* is busy this evening. Louis, the waiter—the *garçon*, of course, I should say—with the close-shaven blue chin and cheeks, and the white apron—has enough to do. Louis, the waiter, who, being a Swiss, seems on that account to cultivate the outward seeming of a mulatto ; who talks fluently any language under the sun, just as the conjuror's bottle is able, on the shortest notice, to produce any liquor you please to call for,—I feel that Louis would be quite equal to replying to me in Chinese, if I could manage to address to him a query in that language ; but there, you see, is my difficulty,—I have really forgotten all my Chinese— (I believe that is the correct mode of confessing ignorance nowadays),—Louis, the waiter, flits from table to table, with his colossal pots of hot coffee (with chicory) and hot milk, and is very busy indeed. There is the clatter of spoons, the rattle of dominoes, the clash of crockery, and the click of the billiard-balls in constant cannonading in the next room. The *Café de l'Univers* is in full swing this evening—is, indeed, quite noisy, while ever and anon a musical clock strikes up a merry waltz tune, not because the hour or the half-hour has come round, but for independent reasons, and at uncertain periods, the music well executed, with an allowance for an occasional wheeziness and uncertainty, as a shirking of particular notes, as in the case of a veteran performer. The little marble tables are nearly all surrounded with guests.

The doors open and close noisily after their manner. Another visitor has entered ; you might know the fact from the gust of fresh air that has rushed into the apartment, rather to the improvement of the general atmosphere of the place. The new comer is an *habitué*. He has removed his hat in compliment to Madame Desprès. She has smiled upon him more radiantly than upon anyone else—so a savage-looking man in a velvet cap has whispered to his neighbour, bald, with a superb beard ; at least, *we* may note that the smile has brought deeper creases into her face. The new comer has even interchanged words with her, has gone so far as to kiss his hand to her. Madame's deprecating gesture seemed to be not so much intended to stay him as to invite him to proceed, and her smile has become even more forcible. She has placed her ringed—not white—hand before her face, not touching it, for fear of disturbance to its surface, and she has ejaculated, " *Fi donc !*" A little further interchange of pleasantries, and the new comer quits the counter, to saunter down the room in quest of a seat. We may note his appearance as he passes.

A very little, very wizened, very old man—yes, old in spite of the profuse clusters of curls which give an unnatural size to his head and fall over his high velvet collar, and hide his ears, and decorate his temples ; a head of hair that is indeed a good deal more than natural—opaque, lustreless, coarse black, like the mane of a horse, without a hint of parting anywhere—without a trace of epidermis ; and (you can see now that he has removed his small grease-polished French hat, so curiously curved as to its rims) towering above his forehead in a dense and lofty toupet. What a strange face !—a tanned yellow in hue, full of deep hollows, covered with a network of wrinkles—a criss-cross of ruts rather, they are so indented, as with a broad-graver, quite an arabesque of age. There is something skull-like about the face, with its large, protruding forehead, its boneless, gristly-fragment-like nose, and the grinning teeth—very uneven these, many missing as in a regiment coming from under fire— the row machicolated, like the battlements of a fortress ; and the eyes, small black specks on a blood-shot ground, restless ever, glittering in their hollows like snakes in caverns. There is something terrible-looking about this *habitué* of the *Café de l'Univers*—this vivified mummy, with his skeleton's head crowned by his exuberant wig, with his manners of gallantry, his young man airs, with his leer and his smile—he has been known to press his trembling claw hand upon his left breast and vow adoration for Madame Desprès. It is reputed that he is constantly producing love verses in French and English. There is a doubt whether he was or not one of the gentlemen who "went out" because of Madame. Be sure he has given his " proofs," that he is prepared to go on the ground again with anyone at any time. Why, there was a tremendous scene at the *café* one evening : ask any of the *habitués*, and you will obtain a recital—but in a low voice, for fear the new comer should overhear. A young man—Auguste —merry, frank, light-hearted, a clockmaker, it was thought, a frequenter of the *café*, had amused himself with ridiculing the old gentleman—*Le Marquis* he was called there amongst themselves : it was a *plaisanterie*, that was all—he was not a marquis. Auguste had puffed in his face tobacco-smoke ; had retained from him his favourite journal ; had trod upon his foot—not accidentally ; had laughed in his face when requested to apologise ; had called him *vieux papa !*—you see ? terms of abuse—*pauvre nigaud, imbécile*, &c. Oh ! the rage of the marquis ! He had spat on the floor, ground his teeth, smashed his wine-glass, trembled with passion, and then he had lanced himself at the throat of the poor Auguste. They were separated, but with difficulty. Madame herself had interfered : she had forbidden Auguste to return. More ; it was very extraordinary ; it was believed that they had met ; and Auguste had not since been seen by his friends. It was not known what had become of him. Truly it was marvellous. Did Monsieur desire to see the *Debats ?*

Yet he did not give promise of being a very formidable antagonist, this little old gentleman. He tottered as he walked ; his back was bowed ; his knees were bent ; he was scrupulously polite ; he removed his hat in recognition of his acquaintances as he passed down the room—for his more intimate associates he had airy gestures and wavings of his hands. He had a favourite seat towards the end of the room, near the stove, and for this he generally made. Since the Auguste episode few were inclined to dispute with him the possession of this seat ; indeed, he was regarded as a privileged guest, although his connection with the *café* had not been of very long standing, or had at least been intermittent. Louis, the *garçon*, seemed to reserve special newspapers for his perusal. Louis was acquainted with the requirements of the visitors ; he brought, without instruction, the daily dose of absinthe or vermouth. Reading his paper, the visitor regaled himself with those peculiar refreshments, taking snuff now and then from a grand enamel and silver-gilt box with a painted porcelain design on the lid, rather more artistic perhaps, than decorous, and stroking a thin tuft he had produced on his sharp chin—a dyed tuft, you could see that; the hairs were quite white at their starting points, though blue-black farther on; running his dusky fingers through his jet locks in the most natural way in the world. He read through tortoiseshell-rimmed glasses—it was wonderful how they could retain their perch upon his shrivelled nose. He enjoyed intensely the caricatures, rather free in character, in a Parisian humorous broad-sheet fastened on to a staff as though it were a flag. He shook with laughter at some of the jokes not too obvious to English intelligence; you could see his head swaying about in his high black satin stock. In the cold weather he wore a cloak of blue cloth, lined with red camlet, gathered closely round the neck, so that it gave rather a hunchback appearance to the wearer, and culminating in a collar of ragged rabbit fur. Beneath this a bottle-green dress-coat of an old fashion, high at the back, short in the waist, with puckers on the shoulders, and long sleeves, the cuffs covering his knuckles; it was plentifully speckled with bright buttons, and was probably quite the mode about the period of peace of Amiens. His close-fitting black trousers were tightly strapped under his highly-polished boots. He was proud of his feet; in leisure moments he might often be seen engaged in contemplating them. Certainly they were neat-looking and well-shaped; albeit there was a suspicion that his boots pinched him. It was thought that his rage against Auguste arose in a great measure from the insult offered to his feet.

There were, as we have said, Englishmen visiting the *Café de l'Univers;* amongst others we may name that promising artist Tom Norris, pupil of the great French artist St. Roche, who had acquired, during a two years' residence in the French capital, and much lounging in the atelier of that eminent painter, a decided French aspect and accent, a contempt for British art—something to the indignation of Mr. Robin Hooper, who knew the gentleman, and had respect for native talent—a taste for Bohemian life from a French point of view—not the most desirable—and little else. Tom Norris, returning to his native England with denationalised opinions and predilections, to his intense joy, discovered the tiny French settlement at the *Café de l'Univers.* He was speedily enrolled as an *habitué.* He

10—2

beat up his friends and acquaintances of the days prior to his labours in the atelier of St. Roche. Artists are the most gregarious of people. Wherever you meet one, you may be sure that there are others not far off—just as lighting upon a grain or two of gold or silver betokens that a mine of the precious metal must be in the neighbourhood. Of course Tom Norris soon carried off his old comrade Timson—a student of the Academy, who received the gold medal for the best drawing from the life, and never since did much else. He came to the surface like a fish for that fly, and then went down again into the depths. Timson—the most good-natured, simple, and amiable of men, who would go anywhere or do anything for anybody ; who had no thought of to-day, not to mention to-morrow, content to live in the past with his medal and best drawing from the life, Timson—who came to the *Café de l'Univers*, and sat down and made himself at home in it, quite as a matter of course, and as though he so achieved the sole mission of his life. And Timson inducted a certain artist-friend, initiating him in the pleasures of Tom Norris's *café*—a certain Mr. Lackington—who somehow brought occasionally in his train a student of medicine and music, by name Mr. Philip Gossett, and now and then, but less frequently, a poor crippled fellow, whom no one could help liking, called Robin Hooper. Even the handsome presence of Arnold Page had sometimes adorned the place.

It was not often that the whole of this party was gathered round one of the little marble tables of the *Café de l'Univers;* but occasionally such an event happened, when there was the noise of very pleasant Britannic conversation wakening the echoes of the place — rousing, but not offending the refugees—giving work to the *dame de comptoir*—and employing, but not in the least destroying the equanimity of Louis, the *garçon*. Nothing, I think, ever would have disturbed the equanimity of Louis, the *garçon*. Waiters are generally tranquil and self-possessed, or they would be probably unfitted for their profession. But the calmness of Louis approached the sublime. He had been engaged at Vienna during the '48 business. But not even a revolution could dethrone Louis from his serenity. He was employed at a *café*, of course. He was communicative on the subject

sometimes, when business was a little dull. The cannonading made a great noise, certainly, Monsieur. On one
occasion a ball entered the *café* and struck a *demi-tasse*
from his hand. He was bearing it to *un Anglais*—a gentleman prisoned in the town by the events of the day. What
did you do, Louis, when the *demi-tasse* was knocked from
your hands? "M'sieu!" says Louis, surprised (but with
calmness) that such a question should be asked, "I brought
another to the *Anglais!*"

Pleasant those talks round the marble table, with the
cigarettes, the coffee, the chocolate, the incidental *petit verre*,
and other cheap delights. The talk of young men, effort-
less, gay, careless, hopeful, light-hearted—it seems to me is
the very best of conversation. The communion of the sages
may be more redolent of wisdom ; but the soundness of age
even cannot compensate for the gossamer grace of youth.
There is *heart* in the talk of young men. Listen to the
fogies in the club smoking-room—can you catch even an
echo of *that!*

"There are comforts about this place," says Robin
Hooper, "and yet there are some things I don't like in it.
That woman at the door, for instance."

"You don't admire her?" cries Tom Norris. "*Mon ami!*
What injustice ! She is superb ! Regard, then, her bust :
it is like the antique." (Having lived two years abroad,
he spoke his native tongue with some difficulty and foreign
accent, and idiomatically. He was rallied about this manner of his a good deal. But that did not affect him much :
he was rather dull at a joke. Jests fall harmless on a
man armed with dulness, as cannon balls from the sides of
an iron-clad ship.) "St. Roche painted a figure like to her.
It represented Revolution—or was it the genius of Liberté ?
I forget. It is no matter. A grand figure, half-nude,
leaning upon a guillotine : in one hand a flaming torch,
in the other a blood-stained—what you call it?—a chopper ?
no ; it is not that—axe—*merci!* Her foot upon a crown ;
upon her head a Phrygian cap. It was *magnifique* truly,
and it was as Madame Després. Therefore, I adore her.
Do you see ? "

"She is like a tigress, I think," continues Robin, "with
her broad jaw, her strong mouth, her glittering eyes.

And there is something stealthy and cat-like about her action. When she smiles, I feel my heart turn quite cold."

"She is grand," says the pupil of St. Roche. "I should like to paint her life-size." (He pronounced the words—of course, because he could not help it—*loife-soize.*) "But in this dog of a country—pardon me, my friend; it is not to abuse your land—which, alas! is also mine—but to express what I think—in this dog of a country, what avails to paint life-size? Bah! it's useless."

"And then," and Robin glances round the room, "all these strange-looking men quarrelling, as it seems, over dominoes and such trifles. How fierce they look! What angry moustachios! What yellow complexions!"

"Well, there *is* a good deal of bile about, I'm thinking," remarks Mr. Gossett. "The foreigner always strikes me as a fine subject for blue-pill. What's that tune the clock has struck up, Rob? La! la! la!—la! la! la! Isn't it an early waltz of Strauss's? I think it is. That fellow playing at billiards in the back room seems to have a decent tenor voice. He began humming just now that beautiful air from *Guido e Ginevra.* It would suit you, Rob; it's a little high, but you could manage it with practice."

"I've been trying all day to make out what my income is derived from my profession," says Timson, meditatively. "The fact is, I've had a paper served upon me by the tax-gatherer."

"What a burning shame!" they all agree.

"Well, you know, I think it *is* hard upon a fellow," Timson goes on. "He never did it before. Why should he begin now?"

"Come to Paris, Timson. There's no income-tax there. France is the real land of freedom!"

"Don't interrupt him, Norris; he's telling a story."

"I dare say you're right, Tom; and most likely I'll go there. I was only about to say, that on looking through my accounts, the conclusion I arrived at was that my profession was a yearly loss to me. I sell nothing, and I have to buy heaps of canvases and paints, brushes and things. I don't know how I do it, I'm sure; because, you know, I've no other money. It's quite a mystery to me how I get on

—how I manage to live at all. Here, Louis, another cup of coffee and a cigar."

" Return, then, with me to Paris. They have love there —in that city, for arts—for artists. You will prosper there, my Timson," says Norris.

Mr. Gossett breaks in suddenly—

" I've discovered such an excellent plan of study. I'm getting up my medical learning at a tremendous pace. It's on a sort of *memoria technica* principle. You can't remember one thing separately, but you remember it in conjunction with something else. Well, I study music and medicine together, just as at school we used to learn Greek through Latin. For instance, there are twelve ribs—an octave and a half; five false ribs—answering to the lines in music; twenty-four vertebræ—or three octaves; four bones in the metacarpus—like the spaces in music; and so on through the whole business. The skeleton's nothing more than an upright grand piano, and I can play what tunes I like upon him. Isn't it a superb idea? I look at his ribs, and I see the whole scale marked out—whole operas composed. I've written out the full description, and I sing it to a Gregorian chant. It's very impressive ; something like this" (sings in a deep bass voice) :—"' The *Tarsus* is composed of seven large bones : a firm and elastic arch—for supporting the body,' and so on. Splendid, isn't it? I shall get on capitally like that. And then, you know, there's descriptive music. Fancy the Pericarditis Polka, with exact imitations of the pulsation of the heart under various forms of disease. The Kidney Quadrilles ; The Varicose Valse ; or—what a sublime opportunity for a composer !—The Stomach Symphony. I defy anybody not to learn upon such a superior system. I shall get through the college as easily as a circus clown through a paper balloon. It's a new discovery. I've a great mind to patent it. My fortune's made. A medical man must succeed who can soothe his patients with song while he cures them with medicine. Many a sick man would jump up and begin to dance if he found me at his bedside singing the drinking-song out of *Der Freischütz.*"

These remarks, noisily delivered — Mr. Gossett was not fond of *sotto voce* singing or speaking — roused many of the exiles, who glanced curiously at the gathering of men round the little marble table, and were confirmed in the notion they had for some time entertained, to the effect that the English were a droll people.

"Who's this coming in?"

"Why, it's Jack Lackington! How are you, Jack?"

"I've had such a dance after you, Rob. I called in the Temple, but I found the oak sported; then I went on to Gossett's, but I missed you again. I thought it just possible you might be here, and I knew I should find somebody I know. How are you, Norris? How's French art getting on? By George! look at that Frenchman over there, how the light falls on his bald head and the rough rim of his beard. I'll make a little study of him, if I can;" and he drew a sketch-book from his pocket. "I might paint him as St. Jerome."

"Yes; and Madame Desprès as the angel," added Norris.

It was noteworthy that while Mr. Lackington was accustomed to idle a good deal in his studio, he was sometimes, out of it, moved by extraordinary inclinations to be industrious, and to be seen busily engaged in most inconvenient places—in crowds, at the theatre, in the streets, at dining-rooms, and, as in the present instance, at the *café*—filling his sketch-books. But perhaps, after all, desultory employment like that is hardly to be regarded as serious work—it is only a preparation for it—not nearer the real thing than mending a pen is to writing. His sketches of this kind were as numerous as they were clever; his finished works were very much more rare. There was about the man some inability to concentrate himself, or he was without any real sense of the value of completion.

"There's that old French poodle here again," he said, looking at the elderly gentleman whose appearance we have described; "he must be an awful age, that old man. If he doesn't take care, I'll make another sketch of him. Timson, I never see you at work of this kind. If you don't stick to your profession, and carry it always about with you, as I do, you'll never get on. There's nothing like application. Do you think, Norris, that fellow's at all likely to be the Wan-

dering Jew ? or, what do *you* say, Rob—Tithonus, perhaps ?
But, Lord, it must be a long time since Aurora cared much
about him. She's quite got over her little weakness by
this time, I should think."

The object of these remarks sipped his absinthe,
apparently quite unconscious that attention had been drawn
to him. The sketch of the bald foreigner had been stopped.
The model had felt a draught and put on his hat—a rusty,
slouched felt hat. Mr. Lackington's plan was interfered
with.

"By-the-way, Rob," he said, turning over the leaves of
the book, "I've stolen a march upon you. I went up into
Gossett's room ; I looked through the crack of the door.
What do you think I saw ?—what do you think I heard ?
Ha ! ha ! Fair Rosamond is discovered. I made this sketch.
I could only get a profile view of her. Do you think it
like ? "

Robin took the book eagerly. Phil Gossett looked over
his shoulder.

"JANET !" he cried, lustily; "and, by Jove ! a capital
likeness ! "

Tithonus threw down his newspaper, surely with needless
impetuosity. He nearly pushed his absinthe off the table.
He rose : there was a strange look in his eyes—a combination of cunning and excitement. He moved towards the
table at which the friends were seated.

"Pardon me, Messieurs," he said, with almost exaggerated politeness, bowing low, pressing his claw hands upon
his breast; "the *Charivari*, is it on your table ? No ; it is
my mistake ; it is the *Moniteur* of last week." He stood
just behind Mr. Gossett as he spoke; he could not
help seeing, between the heads of that gentleman and
Robin Hooper, the sketch they were intent on. "Ah !"
in a voice of rapture, "what a charming head ! it is
superb — angelic. Monsieur is an artist, then ! Ah !
it is exquisite. I am no artist, but I can appreciate.
Pardon me my rudeness, but I could not help seeing.
I adore art. I could not restrain the expression of my admiration."

He spoke fluently in English, though with a foreign
accent. Robin closed the book, with angry abruptness.

His eye met the Frenchman's, and a feeling of alarm, he knew not why, came over him. The Frenchman, smiling and bowing redundantly, returned to his seat. He had seen the sketch. He sat now with his back to the group, absorbed, as it seemed, in the *Charivari*, with which Louis the imperturbable had furnished him. Perhaps the friends were not aware that in this way he could watch very closely their reflections in a green-hued glass opposite. By-and-by, however, he turned round again; he put down his paper; he rubbed his eyes, as though fatigued with reading; he leant upon his elbows, covering his face with his hands. Only by very close observation of him could you discover that he was still watching his neighbours stealthily through his fingers.

Robin shivered. He seemed to have conceived an indescribable, unreasoning repugnance to the man.

"Did you notice him, how he glared at the sketch?" he whispered to Phil. "Why was it produced here? It was shameful—it was cruel! Lackington should be more prudent, more careful. What has she done that her name should be made a by-word in such a place as this? I hate that man!"

"Tithonus?"

"He has got eyes like a reptile. Did you notice them?"

"'Eye of newt and toe of frog,'" muttered Phil Gossett, and he began to hum some of Locke's *Macbeth* music; and then added, "No, by-the-way; his feet are very neat."

"It seems to me that he is capable of anything, that man. There is something absolutely diabolical about his expression."

"Do you think so?" Mr. Gossett asked, his calmness in strong contrast with his friend's excitement. "No. He does not come up to my notion of the diabolical. In the first place he has not got a bass voice, nor a moustache;" and he proceeded to draw a fancy portrait of the Prince of Darkness, for which he might himself have been the sitter.

Lackington's sketch was not again referred to. If Tithonus was listening to hear more of that subject, he must have been disappointed. The conversation had taken a new turn. Tom Norris was relating a wonderful story, which had recently been startling Parisian ateliers; a young artist, a Belgian, a pupil of St. Roche, had been murdered by a Quadroon girl, a *modèle*, in a fit of jealousy it was supposed. She had sharpened a palette-knife, and stabbed him in the back, as, after posing her, he had turned away to his easel. He had fallen dead at once. (Mr. Gossett suggested that the vertebræ had been severed.) He was a young man of much promise, and greatly regretted. The murderess, it was supposed, had escaped in a suit of his clothes, and had reached Algiers; but still there were hopes that she would be captured. It was a wonderful story, full of interesting detail; and Tom Norris was loud in praise of the Parisian police, rather at the expense of the London constabulary, and in favour of the French administration of justice as compared with the English. Indeed, he preferred everything French —even to the accent in speaking English, as we have shown. Is there not, nowadays, rather a denationalising tendency prevalent? Of old, the travelling Briton returned to his native shores, denouncing in round terms, as abominations and absurdities, the manners and customs of foreign nations. But to-day it is rather the fashion for a man to learn so much abroad that he comes back with no inconsiderable contempt for the usages of his friends at home. Perhaps this is because a different class is travelling now. Both modes of conduct may be open to objection; but of the two I think I prefer the first: there's a sturdy, stanch, thorough-going flavour about it. I always feel inclined to shake hands with an Englishman who, having seen some others, pronounces solemnly his opinion that his own is the greatest and most glorious country in the world; and I have besides what amounts almost to a passion for roast beef.

It grew late. The friends broke up their conclave and departed.

The old Frenchman coughed, three times, a peculiar, artificial cough. A man came out of the billiard-room; it was the man Lackington had begun to sketch, with a bald head and ragged beard. He wore a greasy velveteen coat; his clothes altogether were worn and rusty; he had a dirty red scarf twisted round his throat, with no trace of shirt or shirt collar to be seen. He was very thin, with sunken cheeks and prominent, starting-out eyes. He had a half-fed look. He was always in a perspiration, and polishing his head with a torn handkerchief. He approached Tithonus; he stooped down. Tithonus whispered into his ear.

"*Le boiteux ?*" he asked. Tithonus nodded.

"*Le petit diable boiteux !*" he said, with a smile. It was not an attractive smile. The man put on his hat and sauntered out. Certain of our friends were leave-taking outside. Probably their homes were in different directions. The man looked up at the sky as though anxious about the weather. He held out his hand to feel if it were raining. He busied himself with the manufacture of a cigarette. Presently the group broke up. He followed slowly a detachment of it.

"It was she," mumbled Tithonus; and he took from his pocket a ragged book, and made a note in it with a blunt pencil, which he moistened with his tongue to make it mark the more freely. He then leant back in his chair, lost in contemplation. For a long time he remained so without change of position. Then he smiled strangely, and took from his silver-gilt box a copious pinch of snuff.

The hours went by. All the other guests had departed The gas in the billiard-room was turned off. The lights in the outer room had been lowered. Still, Tithonus stirred not.

There seemed to be no desire to hurry him. Louis took no notice of him. He was busy piling up the chairs upon the table, preparatory to the room being swept in the morning. Madame Després had quitted her raised seat; had made for herself a rich cup of chocolate; had enjoyed two small glasses of *parfait amour*. She was now engaged with the pictures of the *Charivari*, the meaning of which it did not appear that she comprehended clearly. Tithonus, motionless, silent, retained his seat. He was evidently a favoured guest. If he had chosen to remain all night, it was probable that he might have had his way. The shutters were up, the outer door of the *café* was closed : Louis had now even removed his apron. He was reading French, English, and German newspapers indifferently.

There was a tap upon the shutters. It was twice repeated. Tithonus rose and moved to the door. Passing Madame, he bowed, removing his hat ; then paused to mumble certain words of compliment. Madame smiled radiantly. He jested. She patted him gaily on the shoulder. He took her large hand, caressed it between his two shrivelled claws, then pressed it reverently to his lips, and so went out. Louis murmured and shrugged his shoulders. Madame sailed towards him.

"*Enfant,*" she said, "you forget : Monsieur Anatole is rich ; Monsieur Anatole is *millionnaire.*"

M. Anatole stood under a lamp-post. The man with the bald head handed him a scrap of paper. M. Anatole read in a low voice :—" 'Mr. R. Hooper, Mr. A. Page (probably the former), Sun-dial Buildings, Temple.' Hem ! There is a mistake, I think," he said. "But we must see. We must not lose the scent now." Again he whispered in the ear of his companion. The man nodded. Soon after they parted.

M. Anatole paused to take a pinch of snuff.

"Never mind," he mumbled. "I shall find her. I put out my hand—so." He extended his arm. "I draw it in —so, and in my clutch—*la chère petite !* Never fear. Who will prevent me ? "

And he walked on leisurely.

CHAPTER XI.

MONSIEUR ANATOLE.

HE Surrey side of the River Thames : beneath the shadow of a celebrated and magnificent hospital for the insane. "A densely-populated district." A narrow, dirty street, ill-built, ill-paved, ill-lighted, in perpetual disagreement with sewerage commissioners and waterwork companies. Children swarming in the gutter, extremely dirty, yet sublimely happy after their manner; pigeons on the roofs, poultry in the front areas, skylarks in the kitchens, rabbits in the back-yards, cats and dogs everywhere.

Fairly in this street, if you made inquiry (as for the purposes of this narrative it is desirable that you should make inquiry) for the house of one Mrs. Birks, you would be bidden to pass along the right-hand side of the roadway until you came to a door with a brass plate upon it—"name of Jugwell,"—and you would be informed that *that* was Mrs. Birks'. The houses, of course, were numbered according to modern practice. But the neighbourhood unconsciously reverted to a former condition of things, and denoted the houses by especial characteristics. In preference to pointing out a particular edifice as No. 10, say, or No. 11, they elected to define it as "the house where Mrs. Jones's mangle were," or "the house with the blackbird in the front airy," or "next door but two to the coal-shed," or "directly oppo*site* to Smith's, the gold-beater's." Mrs. Birks let lodgings. She was a widow : she had been twice married. Her first husband's name had been Jugwell; hence the name on the door-plate.

On the first floor of Mrs. Birks' house, in the front room —small, with a dingy neatness about its fittings, with crumpled chintz curtains, and ragged-seated cane chairs— were two of Mrs. Birks' lodgers. There was a soiled cloth on the table; in the middle a black teapot, with a chipped spout and broken handle. Bread and butter, some withered watercresses, a pewter pot containing beer, a litter of knives, forks, spoons, and crockery completed the furnishing of the table. There was a closeness about the room ; entering it, you felt a strong desire to throw open the windows; the odour of stale tobacco-smoke was strong ; a dull fire burned in the grate; a tall, untidy man in a dull red flannel shirt was on his knees before it, toasting a red herring—a tall, swarthy, muscular man, with a full jaw, rolling black eyes, and a scowling forehead. He rose from before the fire and dashed the fish on the table angrily—noisily.

"There !" he cried, with an oath, "my patience is gone. What a time it takes to cook a herring. Well "—(a shout and an imprecation)—"you have been dipping into this beer at a pretty rate !"

He turned to his companion stretched on the hard horse-hair sofa. He was reading a torn fragment of newspaper ; —it had contained the herring. A fat, blonde man, with a fawn-coloured moustache, and a vacuous expression. He gave a coarse, loose laugh.

"I had the chance, doctor," he said; "I couldn't help availing myself of it."

He spoke thickly, as though his tongue were too large for his mouth—as though the gear and tackle of his voice were not well under control. He laughed again when he had finished.

The man addressed as "doctor" growled threateningly ; then set to work at his breakfast, tearing his food with his hands—devouring ravenously, in rather a wild-beast fashion. Having finished the beer, he refreshed himself with a milder drink contained in the teapot. The man on the sofa con-templating him with a sort of mindless enjoyment of his proceedings.

A third man entered the room.

"*Bong joor, Mounseer !*" said the man on the sofa, with exaggerated mispronunciation.

"Good-morning, my captain," said the new-comer, bowing politely, and pressing a withered, skeleton-like hand upon his breast. It was the small Frenchman of the *Café de l'Univers*—Tithonus—M. Anatole. He wore an old-fashioned blue brocaded dressing-gown, much puffed on the top of the sleeves, high in the collar, with two small buttons close together high up between his shoulders ; on his head, above the profuse black hair, a soiled velvet smoking-cap, plentifully overlaid with tarnished silver cord, and stuck on jauntily at the side. His black specks of eyes turned from the one to the other of the two men. "You are merry this morning, my captain," he said. He moved to the fireplace. Soon he was busy beating up some chocolate (taken from one of the large, side, flap-covered pockets in his dressing-gown) in a little black saucepan, boiling it with milk over the fireplace. Passing the man addressed as the doctor, he stooped down to whisper something in his ear.

"How could I help it, I should like to know?" the doctor cried in reply, savagely, as he thrust a bunch of the withered watercresses into his mouth, having first plunged them into the salt-cellar. I do all I can. I watch him like a dog. But he *will* do it. He was drunk last night. He's half-drunk now. Can I stop him? Can I——" He was going on loudly, in his fierce, boisterous way, when the Frenchman touched him lightly on the arm.

"Hush! Don't talk like that. Be prudént. *That* above all things," he said, and continued his preparations for breakfast. He crumbled his bread, rubbing it between his palms—making a slab sort of soup of his chocolate.

"You two beggars are always plotting together, I think," cries the captain, watching them with his dull, washed-out blue eyes ; "but I don't see that much comes of it all. Make haste and finish that mess, Mounseer, and come and have a game of cards."

And the explosion of foolish, fatuous laughter was repeated.

"In good time, my captain, in good time. You rise early, my captain ; it is an admirable habit; I wish I could do it."

"I learnt it in India ; I can't get rid of it now."

"There are other things you learnt in India," growls the doctor, "and can't get rid of either."

"What do you mean by that?" and the captain rises angrily with a red face, and advances, swaying to and fro. "Look here—I'll have no chaff. I won't stand it. No not from anyone. Don't think I'm afraid of you; and say that again, and, by George! I'll——"

"Sit down, you fool, do!" The doctor stretches out a huge, muscular arm, and the captain finds himself thrust back again on to his sofa.

"Hush! No quarrelling!" cries the Frenchman, calmly, sipping his chocolate. It is strange how the little withered old man seems to awe and command his two burly associates. He eyes them—scrutinisingly, curiously—as the keeper of a menagerie might eye the wild beasts under his control.

"I have news for you, my captain," he said at length, grinning. "I have been to Kew."

"To Kew? Why to Kew?"

"You don't recollect? Is not that a little strange? I have been to Kew to make inquiries. I discovered a young ladies' school there. It is kept by one Miss Bigg; the house is called Chapone House—a droll name."

"Oh, ah! yes—I remember now. Well?"

"Where," the Frenchman continued, "some years ago now, I believe, the daughter of a gentleman in the Indian army—Captain Gill I think the name was—where the daughter of Captain Gill was left as a pupil."

The captain laughed. "Well?" he said.

"The name of the little lady was Barbara—Barbara Gill."

"Is she alive?" The captain lighted a long cheroot with elaborate carefulness.

"Fond parent!" groaned the Frenchman, turning his specks of eyes to the ceiling with mock astonishment. "Yes; she is alive. The account for her education and board at Chapone House is still running. Have no fear on that subject."

"Did you see her?" The captain emitted three puffs of smoke, and watched the blue wreaths float twistingly upwards.

"I did not. She is ill—very ill."

The captain spat on the carpet, then composed himself again comfortably on the sofa.

"Fond parent!" the Frenchman repeated. "Yet stoical—stoical as a philosopher of old Athens; or should I not rather say of Modern Britain? It affords a stronger comparison."

"Shut up," quoth the captain, "or talk what people can understand. You heard of—the other?"

"I did not. So far as I could ascertain, she had not been there. It was contrary to my anticipations, I have no objection to confess."

"By George!" cried the captain, "it's the neatest thing I've known for a very long time! The way that girl has given us the slip—gone from under our very hands—a twist —a double—and the thing done. Doosid neat. I'd back her against any woman in the world for cunning—ay, and pluck, too, for all she looks so timid. Gone—without a clue. Beaten you clean, Mounseer! Gone, without a clue!"

"For that matter, I have a clue."

"An answer to your advertisement, perhaps." (The captain laughed very heartily.) "What fellows you Frenchmen are! Fancy expecting an answer to such an advertisement as that! What nonsense it was—'CHER ANGE! RETURN, THEN. WHY WILL YOU NOT?' Ha! ha! what stuff, isn't it, doctor?"

The doctor grimly smiled; not displeased, perhaps, that the laugh should be against Monsieur Anatole.

"As if she'd care for such a thing as that! As if that would make her stir from her hiding-place. You Frenchmen never will understand Englishwomen."

Monsieur Anatole sighed—a sigh of pity rather than regret—that he should be subjected to such misapprehension, such unappreciation, such obtuse comments.

"Laugh, if you please," he said, "I cannot. It may be that the advertisement was too sentimental. I admit that sentiment is my weak point. Still, I believe in it, and in its effect upon women. If the advertisement was faulty on the ground of its sentiment, it was nevertheless a good fault. And in any case it does not greatly matter. I have a clue —I have two clues."

"You are like the police," the doctor remarked; "they have always a clue—especially when they are losing their prey. The two expressions seem to mean the same thing. And two clues: does that mean that the prey is doubly lost?"

"The police succeed sometimes, though."

There must have been some especial significance in the remark. The doctor scowled fiercely, and his dark swarthy face paled visibly; yet he said nothing. He placed his clenched fists before him on the table, and glanced angrily at the Frenchman.

Monsieur Anatole went on as though he had not fully perceived the effect of his observation. He drew out his large greasy pocket-book. He read from a memorandum—

"'Coppice Row, Clerkenwell.' Do you know that address?"

"I do. What then?"

"It is near the—what do you call it? House of Correction—is it not?"

"Suppose it is; what then?" cried the doctor savagely, rising, and thumping upon the table. "What do you mean by this? Do you want to insult me? By Heaven, if I thought so, I'd—I won't have it. I tell you, I won't have it. I'm not a man to stand any of your infernal nonsense." (The language used on the occasion was a great deal stronger than I dare to set down). "What do you mean by it? How dare you speak to me like this? Have you been setting that idiot Gaspard upon my track? Let me catch him, that's all!"

"Hush! what a noise!" Monsieur Anatole said in a soft voice. "Why this violence? What mistake are you making? I have reason to believe that the person I am in quest of will be found in Coppice Row, Clerkenwell, near the House of Correction. What need is there for you to be roaring out in this way? Who wants to go upon your track, do you think? Do you think Gaspard has nothing better to do? What good would it do anyone to know all about you—where you have been, what you have done—?"

"That'll do; hold hard," cried the other, sullenly; "there's no more to be said about it; only I'm not a man to stand humbug from anyone. Perhaps, it will be as well to bear that in mind."

"You are irritable, *Monsieur le Docteur*," said the Frenchman, shrugging his shoulders till the puffed sleeves of his dressing-gown quite rumpled his black curls.

"Let me alone, that's all—you'd better."

"I was in hopes you two beggars were going to fight. It seems you aint—rather a disappointment to the fancy. I think I'd have backed the doctor for choice. If you're both still game, you can deposit the money with me. I'll see fair."

The captain crowed mirthfully. Monsieur Anatole searched through his pocket-book.

"'Sun-dial Buildings, Temple?' No; I don't think that clue is worth much. Mr. R. Hooper—I think the name is —was traced from there to Clerkenwell. So far so good. I think we are on the scent."

"You make such a fuss about it, that I begin to doubt it," growled the doctor.

"As you please," said M. Anatole.

"And suppose you're right; what then? Say you get her back; what good will it do—to us—to anybody?"

"She'll be off again in double-quick time," laughed the captain.

"It is my affair," Monsieur Anatole answered, solemnly turning to the doctor. "You have no right to inquire into it. I have said that I would find her. I am not often deceived. I shall not be so this time. I shall find her. Trust me; she will not escape."

"And then?"

"Then," and the Frenchman drew himself up, "that is my affair. Don't try to interfere in it. I advise you as a friend."

"You threaten me?"

"No; there is no threatening amongst friends: only kindly warning and good counsel."

"You're so precious fond of your infernal mysteries. However, what do I care? What is it to me? Give us a cheroot, captain?"

"Now, Mounseer, how about that game of cards? Come on."

"One moment, my friend. There is no hurry. Your hand is shaking a little too much at present. By-and-by."

He bent over the doctor again.

"From the 'Ostrich?'" he whispered. "Is there any news? Do they want anything? Hush! Speak softly."

The doctor searched in his pockets. He produced a card. There were some names written in pencil on the back of it.

"Anything about these?" he said. "They'll pay."

Monsieur Anatole read them over slowly in a low voice. "THE REV. PURTON WOOD." He shook his head. "HUGH WOOD—HIS SON." Again he shook his head. "I know nothing of these," he whispered. "Nothing. What is the third name? 'ARNOLD PAGE.' No; nothing. Yet stay. Surely I am not mistaken." He referred to his greasy pocket-book. "Where is Gaspard's memorandum? How curiously facts arrange themselves, and dovetail with each other. Yes; '*Mr. A. Page, Sun-dial Buildings, Temple.*' It is the same, no doubt. Well, well; we will look further into this."

"Come, Mounseer, the cards, the cards!" cried the captain.

"Directly, *mon ami.* Let me finish dressing. It grows late. I will be with you in a moment." And Monsieur Anatole quitted the room. The doctor strode after him, and stopped him on the landing outside the door.

If he had not already received the designation of "the doctor," and you had been in the habit of meeting the man often, and consequently also in the habit—inevitable when one does meet people often, without further acquaintance than that expressed by the phrase "Knowing by sight,"— the habit, I say, of particularising him mentally by some distinct appellation or nickname—I think you would have called him "the shabby man." The title would not have been complimentary perhaps, but it would have been eminently appropriate; for he was a very shabby-looking man—a man who never could have looked anything but shabby. And there are men of this kind who, after even very recent washing—even with yellow soap and a rough towel — still look dirty; upon whose hair the brush and comb seem to be wholly without effect; upon whom a new coat looks rusty and threadbare a moment after it is donned, and clean linen loses on the instant its virginal character, and becomes at once crumpled, and soiled, and dingy. Something of this may be attributable to complexion, or to what a painter (Mr. Lackington?) would, perhaps, term the *texture* of the man; but more to an ineradicable natural untidiness of look and demeanour — to some constitutional inability to give the least attention to the disposal of dress—from some hopeless clumsiness of hand, or distortion of vision, or numbness of feeling, that prevents the detection of inaccuracy in apparel and in the method of its assumption. Hence the number we see about in the world of twisted, wrinkled, creased garments, coats wrongly buttoned, neckerchiefs tortured into ropes or hay-bands, and the front bow wandering away under the right ear, or travelling to vague positions in the neighbourhood of the nape of the neck. There are some men who, if you promoted them from fustian, or even rags, to brocade and velvet, would yet look at home—a native grace and dignity asserting its power, even in that unaccustomed splendour. While others, in tatters or in coronation robes, on a door-step or a throne, look alike dishevelled, and shabby, and ill at ease, and repulsive to the eye. The doctor was of this sort. With coarse, but not ill-shaped features, and plain rather from unpleasantness of expression than defect of form, with a grand figure, although a little high and round-shouldered perhaps, thrust into ill-shaped clothes fitting awry—dragged, torn on, the cuffs turned away from his brawny, nervous hands, his cravat a creased wisp round his great bull throat, his waistcoat unbuttoned, and his flannel shirt bulging forth in front,—I think you would have chosen (under the circumstances I have imagined above) to designate him "the shabby man," if you had not, in-deed, preferred the even more decisive and appropriate title of "the ugly customer." But, as we have seen, Monsieur Anatole and the captain, for reasons best known to them-selves, called him "the doctor;" and to that name he answered.

He placed a strong hand upon the skinny shoulder of Monsieur Anatole.

"Come," he said, sternly; "you know we can't go on like this. The money—when are we to get it?"

"Have patience," the Frenchman answered quietly, as he bent down, seeking to release his shoulder. But the doctor's hand was too heavily, too firmly upon him.

"I *have* had patience. You promised that we should be —be rich."

"We *shall* be rich."

"But *when?* How long are we to wait? I want the money now, at once. I'm sick of waiting."

"Do you suppose that *I* do not want the money now, at once? Do you think that *I* am not sick of waiting? Undeceive yourself."

"Still, you don't answer me. You are all plot and mystery; but what comes of it all? Answer me. How long are we to wait? Name a time. Tell me when this is to end. I'm sick of being chained to that man, watching him like a dog. It's a dog's life. I've had enough of it."

"Bah!" Monsieur Anatole exclaimed. "That a dog's life! A dog may lead a worse life than that; or a man either, for that matter. You'll find it out some day. And you don't fulfil your trust. I have warned you of that before. You let the fool do too much as he likes."

It was evident by their gestures, if not by their words, that they were referring to the captain in the next room.

"I do all I can," the doctor said, gloomily, and with a certain humility about his gloom — a confession of inferiority. "You are always for waiting. You are too careful, it seems to me. They are not very particular at the 'Ostrich.' They are easily satisfied. They don't ask many questions."

"You think he would pass muster? You know he would not. It is not only the 'Ostrich' we have to satisfy. We might manage that. But a respectable medical practitioner? How much depends upon that! Can you find one to sign his papers? Take him as he is now. Why, a finger on his pulse would ruin the whole plan. You know that very well. Look at the questions in the list — *Is he temperate? Is there anything in his health or habits tending to shorten life?* Can you get those questions answered so as to prevent dispute by-and-by—answered by a respectable, trustworthy medical practitioner? You know you cannot at present. We must wait: and he must be watched. A little care and he will recover; a dose of spirits of lavender to steady his nerves: he can face the doctor, and the thing will be done. Then," and Monsieur Anatole treated himself to a hideous grin, "I don't say that you need watch longer."

"This is putting the money off for a long time."

"Bah! is not the game worth the candle? Is it only the 'Ostrich' we want. Why not the money of a dozen other offices? Is not the prize worth running for? You are a child in these things, I tell you; and you cry for money! You would sell for a *sou* down a thousand pounds a week hence! What folly! Well, you shall have money now. I have other schemes in hand. You shall have what you want—now; and by-and-by we shall be rich—enormously rich!—only wait a little, and watch; it is indispensable."

"I tell you I am sick of watching. I have had enough of it: the part doesn't suit me. If he will drink, can I help it, can I stop him? Perhaps I'm too fond of the sport myself. For the doctor's certificate" — he dragged the Frenchman still more closely, and whispered in his ear a brief communication; yet an important one evidently, if only by the expression of Monsieur Anatole's face. There was a curious look in his specks of eyes, as he glanced up at the doctor with the words—

"You know what that would be?"

"One may as well be hung for a sheep as a lamb," said the doctor, with a sullen laugh.

"Hum! It is a good name — Dr. Hawkshaw, of St. Lazarus. It ought to go without question. But the handwriting?"

"I know all about that—I ought to."

"Well, we will see. It is not a bad idea. I will give so much credit; the plan is yours."

"But you'll be in it, remember. Take care of that. There'll be no getting away and leaving me in a hole. By George! if I thought that, I'd——"

"Pooh! You are like a child! What are you talking about? We shall be equal, of course."

The room-door opened.

"What's all this mumbling about? Come, I say, are you going to play cards, or not?" So the captain questioned Monsieur Anatole, noisily.

"Certainly, if you will have it so. I will postpone the completion of my toilette." And he whispered the doctor— "You want money? You shall have some. He has a little left—a little, not much. You understand?"

And Monsieur Anatole sat down to play *ecarté* with the captain; the doctor taking a slovenly sort of interest in the game, lounging behind the captain's chair, smoking a cheroot, and spitting freely about the room.

CHAPTER XII.

ON THE SCENT.

THE hostel of the "Spotted Dog" has already obtained the honour of mention in this chronicle. The reader will recollect that it faced a certain newsvender's shop in Coppice Row, Clerkenwell, and was oftentimes patronised (notwithstanding his wife's adjurations to the contrary) by the proprietor of that shop.

It was a day or two after the events and the conversations we have narrated above.

In the neighbourhood of the "Spotted Dog," Monsieur Anatole stood on the kerbstone, leaning against a lamp-post, and apparently occupied by profound meditations. His one hand clutched his enamel and silver-gilt Louis Quatorze snuff-box; equidistant between the box and his nose; his other hand held suspended a pinch of snuff. Thought had, as it were, paralysed the muscles of his arm, and stopped midway his contemplated nasal refection. Then the thought, escaping into words, gradually relaxed its hold, and removed the injunction from the pinch of snuff.

"It is as Gaspard said," he muttered, sniffing heartily; particular that no grain should escape him; sniffing—the pinch having vanished—from each finger, separately and severally — as animals, their meal disposed of, lick their paws to possess themselves of every lingering trace of their joy. "Gaspard is a fool, but he is honest."

And through wrinkled, semi-closed lids the Frenchman surveyed the shop with the name of "Simmons" inscribed above its entrance, with the fluttering newspapers at its door-posts.

"To think that *mon ange* should have taken refuge there!" he said. "It is strange, yet Gaspard is positive. He is a fool, but he is honest," he repeated. "Was that some one at the window? No; it could not have been. The reflection upon the panes. The windows are not very clean. It is not a very nice place for *la petite*. My sight is not so good as it was. Certainly I could almost have sworn then that some one had appeared at the window. It is possible that my imagination deludes me. Alas! I am the victim always of imagination, of sentiment, of passion."

Yet Monsieur Anatole had not been deceived. Some one had appeared at the window—to retreat from it suddenly, with a start and a scream.

"What's the matter, my dear?" asked Mrs. Simmons, exuberantly, after her manner. "Anything wrong with the baby? Or has a string of Mr. Gossett's piano broke? Why, how pale you've turned!"

"That man!" cried Janet, with a nervous gesture. "Save me from him! Save me! He must not know that I am here!"

"He shall not! Don't be frightened, my dear: there's no cause for alarm. He shall step over my corse ere he shall reach you!"

The language was a little extravagant, perhaps, and the action accompanying it rather violent, and suggestive perhaps of the attitudes to be found in post-Raphaelite epic pictures. But Mrs. Simmons was a woman who meant what she said, even when she spoke most theatrically. Her *pose* had won many a round of applause at the Royal Paroquet Theatre, Hoxton, and on many provincial boards, especially in what Mr. Skelt was wont to call "her favourite character" of Helen MacGregor; engravings of Mrs. Montresor in which assumption being at one time obtainable at the moderate tariff of one penny plain, and twopence coloured.

A tall, bony man, aquiline as to his nose, buttoned up in a tight surtout, meanwhile passed the lamp-post against which Monsieur Anatole was leaning. A gleam of recognition danced furtively in the black specks of eyes.

"Colonel Barker," he muttered, "governor of the House of Correction. There is authority and government in his very nose. The English functionary has always a nose of that pattern. Is it therefore the judicial power is termed always the 'beak?' Ah! my friend, the doctor! One word to the colonel-governor, and should I not obtain the particulars of a beautiful episode in your past? Bah! the fools men are! 'Doctor,' indeed! Imbecile! Pratt —

Monkton—Luce—call yourself what you will, I know you;
I have your history *here*." (He touched his breast—perhaps he referred to the greasy pocket-book lodged in its
neighbourhood.) "You are no match for Anatole. I hold
up my finger so, when I please, and you will go down before it. The fools men are!"

He raised a knotted, thin finger, with a peculiar air of
menace as he spoke; then a strange smile, very forbidding
in character, distorted the numberless hard lines and
wrinkles about the lower half of his face.

"And now," he said, "to see about *la chère petite.*"

He crossed over and entered the "Spotted Dog." It was
as though he were throwing out skirmishers to feel for an
enemy in ambuscade. He did not advance directly to the
assault of the newsvender's. He opened his first parallel,
as it were, in the direction of the "Spotted Dog." Perhaps, he felt that that establishment represented really the
key of the position—the Hougoumont of his Waterloo—
the Malakoff of his Sevastopol; and, securing the "Spotted
Dog," the newsvender's must of necessity fall into his hands,
with all its treasures (including Mr. Gossett's piccolo), and
prisoners male and female (including Mrs. Simmons and the
baby, and, of course, Janet Gill).

A barman, with a tendency to redundant flesh, in a blue
velvet waistcoat, his full face well embossed by a variegated
pattern of pimples, supplied the Frenchman, upon the
bidding of the landlady, with the refreshment he had de·
manded. "Haff-haff," he of course termed, after the
manner of his countrymen, the liquor placed before him.
He took it sipwise, and tried hard not to make faces as he
did so, and to make himself believe that he liked it—that
his long acquaintance with England had really at last grafted
upon him insular tastes. The effort, however praiseworthy,
was only partially successful.

The landlady—the outlines of whose form were something blurred and swollen, like those of a figure drawn on
blotting-paper—age and prosperity and the smell of malt
decoctions having combined to fatten her—acknowledged
by a grand smile—·it took up some room upon her face, but
that was equal to the demand made upon it—the polite bow
of Monsieur Anatole.

"Haffable old gent," she murmured, as she put a brilliant polish on a rummer, and then held it up to the light, closing one eye, as though to concentrate her gaze through it, and test to the uttermost its lustre and cleanness.

"I'm sure I beg your parding."

The Frenchman with another lifting of his hat, had addressed to her an inquiry.

"Name of Simmons?" answered the landlady. "Oh, certainly, I know it. Few better. But which Simmons do you want? Because there's two about here. Is it Simmons the butterman?— which his name is Frank, and his shop jist on your right 'and as you go round the corner ; or is it Simmons the newsman, as lives immediate oppo*site*, and which we calls him 'Arlekin Simmons, for to distinguish him from Frank, and not as any offence is meant, but becos he was once a dancer, and played 'arlekin at the theayter, that's all."

"'Arlequin Simmons," the Frenchman repeated. "Ah ! yes ; that was probably the Simmons he referred to. The newsman over the way. Ah ! yes ; no doubt that was so. Exactly opposite, precisely. Many thanks."

"Not as I iver see him dance myself," the landlady said, "which I don't say as I iver have, becos it's a long time ago since he done it ; but I've seen those as has seen him ; which it's quite as like as not as Mr. Simmons will be here hisself any minit, for his morning pint, which he comes for pretty rigler altogether—leastwise, his three ha'porth and a little cold water at noon, which he takes for his ashmer. Well, I niver ! Talk of the what's-'is-name, and he's afore you. Why, if there aint Mr. Simmons his very self coming in at the door at this self-same moment. How curious things do 'appen !"

A man in a Scoth bonnet entered, fat, wheezy, unhealthy-looking, as a lady's spaniel.

"Morning, Mr. Simmons. Why, if there aint a gent here jist asking after you."

Monsieur Anatole made one of his best bows to the ex-harlequin.

"I had a 'stranger' in my tea at brekfuss !" exclaimed Mr. Simmons. "I knew I should be meeting some un afore night as I didn't know of. Yes, my pint, please 'm, with a dash of hold hale it 't. Your servant, Sir. Pleased to see you. Might you be wanting to see me? Much obliged, I'm sure; but if it's perfessional, why, you see, I've retired for some time now, on account of my 'elth and my ashmer, and for the missus—she's permanent at the Paroquet, and I never interferes in her engagements. Nor in the lodgings—never. I make it a rule, and I aderes to it."

The Frenchman's small black eyes wandered over the rather obese and unwieldy frame of the newsvender, settling nowhere, but making, as it were, a rapid mental sketch of him—a mental memorandum of him—a *précis*, to be registered and put away in the pigeon-holes of his memory for use upon a subsequent occasion. A smile of satisfaction followed the tour of inspection of his eyes—or less a smile, perhaps, than a crease or rut in the lower part of his face— there was nothing very mirthful or genial about it, though it resulted, probably, from some internal sense of comfort.

"An easy task," he said to himself. "He is husband! English husband! Ah! well. The husband is always fool."

And the crease deepened in his rejoicing at his own Gallic epigrammatic proposition.

"You will take a glass with me?" said Monsieur Anatole. "Pardon me, you will?"

"Well, as yer so pressin', I don't mind if I do; but I really don't think as I've the pleasure——"

"Pardon me again. You are 'Arlequin. Do you think I have forgotten that? Ah! it is the character of true genius ever to ignore its own successes—its own power—to forget all in a sublime modesty!"

"Your 'elth, Sir," said the newsvender, who had not quite followed the complimentary apostrophe of the Frenchman—indeed, it had a little frightened him by its unintelligibility. So far as he was concerned, he was glad to get from it to such *terra firma* as drinking "a 'elth"—a thoroughly practical business, about which there could be no possible misapprehension.

"The name of Simmons is a great one in the annals of pantomime. There was a dancer years ago who created an enormous sensation in Paris. His name was also Simmons. He was very agile; very adroit. It is now long since. It was after the peace. Paris was crowded with your compatriots. He appeared in a grand ballet, *La Chatte Meta-morphosée.*"

"Why, it was Great-uncle Jim. I've heard tell of him, though I never see him—not to remember. He died of drink. He would do it; nothing could stop him. He was the smallest man that ever were. Why, they could very nearly sew him up in a real cat-skin. You knew him?"

The Frenchman bowed low, closing his eyes, as though to impart a proper sentimental tone to the proceeding. He signified respect for the late Mr. Simmons—regret for the existing Mr. Simmons's bereavement.

"And you sell the newspapers now! Ah! And your wife lets lodgings! Ah! you have many lodgers?"

"I never interfere with 'em—never. I leave it entirely to my wife—it's her department."

"You have vacancies?"

"No; I think she's pretty well let now. There's Mr. Gossett—there's Miss Milne——"

"*Milne?*"

"Yes; a young lady—quite a lady—as hasn't been with us long—a governess, or something, I believe; but I never interferes."

There was a sudden click in Monsieur Anatole's throat. It was the only evidence permitted to escape of the internal crow of exultation he was enjoying; one note straying from a peal of internal laughter, finding its way to the outside world with difficulty, half-stifled in its passage.

Monsieur Anatole cared to hear little more. Mr. Simmons was flabbily voluble as usual. He drew from himself long straggling sentences, as a conjuror produces from his mouth endless tapes: he wrapped these round Monsieur Anatole: he swathed him in withes of bald talk. The Frenchman heeded not; he knew that he could burst his bonds at will; he had gained his end; he had tracked his quarry. What mattered the wheezy garrulity of Mr. Simmons, great-nephew of Uncle Jim, of *La Chatte Metamorphosée?* Yet he did not hesitate to fill up the glass of the ex-harlequin. For himself, he could proceed no further with his "haff-haff:" he was too much excited, perhaps — perhaps, he did not like it. He regaled himself with a huge pinch from his Louis Quatorze silver-gilt box.

Soon he was rid of Mr. Simmons.

He left the "Spotted Dog." He made a circuit and advanced upon the newsvender's shop from another direction. He crept up the steps stealthily—he knocked at the door.

It was opened almost immediately.

"Miss Milne?" he said. "I desire to see Miss Milne."

A stout matron form, florid, robust, stood before him.

"Miss Milne?" It was Mrs. Simmons who made this inquiry, repeating his words.

"Yes; Miss Milne." And Monsieur Anatole advanced one foot, and prepared to enter the house.

"Well; what is it? *I am Miss Milne,*" said Mrs. Simmons, with superb effrontery; and her massive figure effectually barricaded the entrance. Monsieur Anatole's jaw dropped, like the jaw of a corpse. He gazed for a moment into the resolute face of the actress. He almost quailed before it. He grew quite confused.

"Pardon me," he mumbled, "there must be some mistake."

He went slowly down the steps, as the door was noisily slammed-to behind him.

"Has the fool Gaspard been deceived, or has he deceived me? Have I been on a fool's errand? Or is she really there, and on her guard?" He asked himself these questions as he passed along—growling—keeping up, too, a steady fire of not nice oaths. Fortunately they were, for the most part, in a foreign language, and their hideously imprecatory character was lost to his neighbours and fellow-passengers.

"I've missed rehearsal, and I shall be fined, of course," exclaimed Mrs. Simmons; "but what do I care if I've been of use, my dear, after all your goodness to baby? I'd do it a hundred times over! There, there, let the colour come back to your cheeks; the danger's past now."

Let us enter again, if you please, the *Café de l'Univers* in the neighbourhood of Leicester Square.

It is a few days after the circumstances above set forth.

We hear the usual clink of dominoes; gathered round the little circular marble tables, we find the usual groups —

foreigners, for the most part, with a few Englishmen, but these generally artists, who are never of any particular nationality—cosmopolitans, for the most part, or denizens of that great Bohemia, the neutral territory, on which all people meet on like conditions, with an equal interest in it, on peculiar terms of relationship and brotherhood.

Mr. Gossett puffs his cigarette and tosses back his black snake locks.

" I have been studying Meyerbeer deeply," he cries out, " and at length I have come to a definite opinion upon his case. You see, his music is a regular amalgam ; you have to subject it to an analysis. I find a distinctly Teutonic diathesis, with Gallic complications, and yet a sort of Italian eruption thrown out thickly in every page of his scores. It requires very careful and very peculiar treatment. I don't know a more interesting composer—considered musically."

" And medically," laughs Robin Hooper.

" It is very *extraordinaire*," remarks Tom Norris.

" Look," says Mr. Lackington ; " Tithonus has grown a hundred years older ; or has the Wandering Jew got an abatement of his sentence ? Or has Cagliostro forgotten to have his elixir of life made up—to be taken when the cough is troublesome—or has he lost the prescription ? Look ; St. Jerome is whispering in his ear ! "

" What do you say, Gaspard ? " asked Monsieur Anatole —apparently part of the whispered communication had escaped him.

Again Gaspard stooped down to whisper.

" Gone ! " cried Monsieur Anatole, hoarsely, angry. " Gone ! You have let her escape ! Gone ! Where ? "

Gaspard, in a scared sort of way, pantomimed regretful ignorance.

" Fool ! Imbecile ! Dog ! Beast ! " And a doubled-up claw was shaken in his face.

" You shall pay for this ! " Gaspard shrunk back, scorched and withered, as it were.

Monsieur Anatole rose. He had almost forgotten to take up his Louis Quatorze snuff-box, but he recovered it with an angry snatch. With tremulous haste he quitted the room. He did not pause to raise his hat at the door, after his wont, or to acknowledge, by any of his customary exuberant grimaces, the presence and the glory of Madame Desprès.

"What, then, has Monsieur Anatole?" Louis the waiter whispered the question, waiting at the counter for a glass of absinthe, to be carried into the billiard-room.

"I know not. Perhaps he is in love," Madame Desprès answered with a grand, placid, artificial smile. How steady her hand was. She did not spill even a drop of the absinthe. But she had had much practice in filling small glasses, and her nerves were as steel.

Louis emitted a guttural sound, with a rolling accompaniment of r's. Unquestionably he was annoyed at something.

"Who'll lend me tenpence, or pay for what I've had here?" asked Mr. Lackington of his friends.

"Come to Paris, Jack," Norris cried out; "there is money to be had there: you will never want in that country, where there is, what you call *beaucoup de*——everything. At present, I have no money myself, or I would help you."

So Mr. Robin Hooper settled his friend's score at the *Café de l' Univers.*

CHAPTER XIII.

A SISTER'S LETTER.

Oakmere, Woodlandshire.
Saturday, December 7th, 185—.

"**M**Y DEAREST ARNOLD,

"I think you owe it to your sister—a sister some years your senior—and whom the loss of a mother at an age when, alas, you could hardly appreciate the extent of the affliction that had fallen upon you, compelled to do all in her power to fill the place of the mother taken away, and with a mother's care watch over your progress from infancy to youth and manhood; I think, let me repeat, that you owe it to your sister to keep her informed of your movements. I *do* beg that you will write to me as often as possible, and *at very least I beg that you will favour me with a reply to my letters.* Try, my dear Arnold, to be unfashionable in this respect. Letter-writing is not really 'a bore.' Our ancestors loved and reverenced correspondence. You know the heaps and heaps of letters from and to grandpapa and great grandpapa that we have here in the library. Imitate their example. Somehow I think that the people of the past loved each other more than the people of the present. Certainly, families were held together by stronger ties. I really believe that the world grows colder and harder every day.

" But a truce to this. You will write to me, Arnold, and especially to inform me that you are coming down to us now very shortly. Christmas will now very soon be here, and you *must* be with us then. Remember, I can hear of no denial. You escaped us last year most shabbily. A bachelor's dinner-party in the Albany, even though given by Lord Dolly Fairfield, who, by-the-way, ought certainly to have been with the Southernwoods—I have reason to know that the Marchioness was quite angry at his staying in town—is not sufficient reason for a gentleman's absenting himself from his family at such a season of the year. I am aware that it is very dull here, the state of my health, and the frequent recurrence of those nervous attacks to which I have been unhappily subject through life, render it impossible for me to see much company—preclude me from cultivating to any great extent even the limited society to be found in this neighbourhood. We shall be little more than a family party—Frank and the children and myself, not very amusing or enlivening, I dare say. Still it will only be proper that you should be here. Situated as you are, you should certainly spend Christmas upon your estates ; already you are but too little known here. Your continued absence will really be a source of grievance to the tenants. There is nothing like the master's eye. However, Frank has done much. Indeed his exertions on your behalf, often, indeed, after a severe day's work at that horrid Whitehall office, have been quite unremitting.

"And this reminds me to tell you that your conduct in regard to Frank on the occasion of your flying visit here, some time since, appeared to me to be most extraordinary and unreasonable. Pray endeavour, in future, to retain a better command over your temper. Fortunately Frank's equanimity is remarkable, and he is willing to make every allowance. Still I *do* hope that you will not permit anything of the kind to recur. You cannot, surely, understand the trouble Frank has been at, and entirely on your account. Of *course*, expenditure has been necessary, even large expenditure. You can have no improvement without it. But the advantage of this will be reaped by-and-by. I have no hesitation in saying that the property was going to rack and ruin, and *would have gone*, but for Frank's foresight and judgment and great labours—and what has been his reward ? I quite blush for you, Arnold. As for the money, it is really not possible to conceive that you cannot lay aside even the greater portion of your income to effect these improvements, and others contemplated. The demands upon you must be very few ; it is quite a mystery to me, indeed, what you do with your money. And if you cannot afford to make a trifling sacrifice *now* for the future benefit of your property, how will you be able to manage it when you have a wife and children, and an expensive establishment to keep up, when you sit for the county and *must* spend money? I confess that upon

12—2

these points I am quite at a loss to understand you, and I
must still presume to be surprised at your setting up your
opinion in downright opposition to Frank's. This does
seem to me unconscionable. But I really fail to understand
the young men of the present day; there would seem to be
no limit to their assumption, and self-confidence, and con-
ceit. Age and experience, and business talents, are completely set at naught and defied by them. However, I
have no wish to dwell longer upon what must always be an
unpleasant subject, and I am happy to say that Frank has
too much good sense and, I may add, too good a heart, to
be disposed to take offence at any hasty observations that
you may make, or to judge you harshly in regard to your
demeanour towards him, however intemperate. The alterations and improvements in the house here were indispensably
necessary. The place was becoming barely habitable.
It is all very well to quote certain old prejudices
of poor dear papa's in opposition to change, but
surely it is rather too much to strain the meaning of these
so as to negative all alteration. I suppose if a pane of glass
had been broken, papa would have had it mended, and
in the same way if a new east wing had been required,
or a new drawing or billiard room, or a nursery for my
poor little chicks, do you think he would have hesitated
as to the building of any or all of these? Of course
not. As to the question of the *taste* of the alterations,
you are really grossly wrong. You may have some judgment with respect to paintings, but upon architectural
matters I must say you betray a most marvellous ignorance; you surely cannot have studied even the first principles
of the science. Of course Frank did not rely upon his
own unaided judgment, though I feel bound to say that
he might have done so fairly, for the extent of his information upon these, and indeed upon all subjects, is
only exceeded by his refined modesty in depreciating the
value of his own opinions. He obtained the best architectural advice, and the new buildings have been greatly
admired, and the Court is becoming quite one of the show
places of Woodlandshire. Perhaps, however, you cannot
be expected to recognise thoroughly the excellence of
Frank's improvements until you take up your residence

altogether at the Court. I hope this may not be very immediately however, for the present state of my health would render a present change extremely inconvenient and alarming to me.

"With regard to the cost of these changes, *I* can certify that there has been no needless expenditure, certainly no waste. I do not pretend to say that the new erections might not have been completed at a less cost, if mere cheapness had been considered, and grace and taste put altogether on one side. But I cannot suppose that you would have desired that such a course should be pursued. I should hope you have too much reverence for poor papa's pride in Oakmere Court to propose that it should be made an eyesore to the whole country side, and that the new wing should be an unsightly brick barn, like a railway station or a manufactory, hopelessly ugly, however useful. I consider that the new buildings have cost wonderfully little, their value and beauty, and their enhancement of the property being taken into the account. While upon this subject I may say that your objections to a mortgage upon the estate really seem to me quite childish. My dear Arnold, of what can you be thinking? Papa's objections to the property being encumbered, of *course* could have no reference to money raised for the improvement of the estate. Where do you get these strangely narrow-minded views from? Sometimes it really seems to me that you have become possessed with quite miserly views in regard to the value of money, or do they arise simply from your inexperience and want of acquaintance with the subject? Pray do show yourself in a more amiable light. Become a little tractable. Permit yourself to be guided by Frank, whose knowledge is so wide, whose sense is so sound, and whose desire to promote your benefit is, I know, so singularly fervent.

"I am glad to learn that you have obtained a seat at the boards of those public companies. Frank, I know, thinks highly of them. I am sure you must have long felt the want of sensible occupation—I mean sensible as distinguished from what I must really call the frivolous pursuits in which you have spent only too much of your time. You will, in this way, be thrown among associates of a more influential and important class than you have hitherto been in the

habit of meeting. This will be a great advantage. I am
well aware that a young bachelor is not expected to be very
nice in the selection of his intimates. Society rightly holds
that marriage always acts as a sifter in these matters, and,
therefore, that interference of any other kind is superfluous.
You may derive amusement at present from mixing with the
inferior classes, by becoming the friend of artists and
students, young men with irregular habits, who lead lives
society could not for one moment countenance ; but pray
do not on any account attempt to introduce any of your
strange companions at Oakmere. I really feel myself at
present quite unequal to dealing with such an emergency.
Already we are brought, thanks to you, into a position of
some difficulty. Pray how do you expect us to deal with
our neighbours here—Farmer Hooper and his wife? They
are most respectable people, of course. I have not a word
to say against them on that score, *but, you know, Arnold, as
well as I do, that old Hooper is not a gentleman.* It is very
true that he may be superior to his position, but, after all,
you know, he is simply a farmer and a tenant of old Mr.
Carr's. Your kindness to the poor cripple, his son, does
credit to your heart, though, in some measure, I must say,
at the expense of your head. One thing is quite certain,
however, *I* will not call upon the Hoopers. *I* will not be
the means of placing them in a cruelly false position. Pray
be careful, my dear Arnold, what you do, and remember
that it is indispensably necessary that all injudicious acquaintances *should be dismissed* when you marry or come home
to Oakmere. Of course, I make an exception in favour of
your friend, Hugh Wood. Not that I like him ; for I really
think him one of the most disagreeable young men I ever
met, he is so grim, and gloomy, and *gauche*. But he is the
son of our excellent rector here, a charming man and an
admirable Christian (I wish you would pay more attention
to his delightful discourses), and of course a clergyman is
always, if only from his office, a gentleman. (I admit that
many have only the official title to the distinction.) So
Hugh Wood's claim through his father, the Rev. Purton
Wood, I am ready to concede, though I repeat I dislike him
particularly. Frank says his political opinions are quite
detestable, and upon other subjects his views are of a most free

and dangerous character. What bad taste this is in a clergyman's son! Has he much business at the bar? I should hardly think he had, if, as I have always understood they did, appearance, and grace, and tact formed indispensable requisites to professional success. The tie that binds you to him is to me utterly incomprehensible. But I suppose men's friendships are, and have been always to women, the most inscrutable of mysteries.

"The Carrs have been for some weeks at Croxall Chase. We have, of course, exchanged frequent visits. They regretted very much that you could not stay longer with them at Scarborough. Mr. Carr tells me he has quite given up all idea of leaving England. He says that at his advanced age foreign travel would be too much for him. They remained at Scarborough but a few days after your departure. The weather turned so cold, and the old lady says now that the place never did agree with her. They were a little curious about your new occupations. Too curious, I thought, and I was careful not to afford very explicit information. They are rather strange people; somehow we don't get on very well with them. The old gentleman's manner to Frank seems to me very cold and distant, and I dislike it particularly. But Frank takes it, as indeed everything else, most good-naturedly. He is, I fancy, if anything, a little too easy and yielding in matters where his own dignity is concerned. He says we must make allowances for the little peculiarities of elderly people like the Carrs. Besides, the Carrs cannot be expected to know much about the usages of good society. Money will do many things, but it will never supply the want of birth. Of course, as I need not tell you, their origin was of a most humble kind. Mr. Carr's father, I am given to understand, was quite a common workman t a forge. Mrs. Carr is certainly not very refined. I often wonder that they should have been able to obtain such a position in society as they seem to have secured. They g , or could go anywhere, and Mr. Carr was offered a title by the last administration; having now no son, he declined. I applaud his moderation. Indeed, titles are now, it seems to me, only too easily procurable. Fancy a blacksmith's son with a title!

"Leo rode over to see us yesterday. She was quite unattended. Was not that rather strange? I am surprised that old Mr. Carr allows her to do such things. Of course the distance is very trifling, but it does not look well for a young lady to be riding about, even in this quiet place, quite by herself. Certainly, she looks very pretty in her riding-habit. I don't wonder that men admire her so much as they do. She is of that sort of *brunette* beauty, that is so particularly attractive in extreme youth. I doubt if she will retain her good looks as she advances in life. Little women, I think, as a rule, are seldom pretty after five-and-twenty.

"But I am not surprised at your admiration. Men have always been easily led captive by a pretty face. It was not, perhaps, to be much wondered at, that your intimacy with Leo when she was quite a child should grow with her growth, and develop into something like a serious attachment when you began to find your old playmate changed into a charming young lady, very pleased to waltz with you, and to be your partner all the evening at balls, &c. And of course there is not a word to be said against the match. In a pecuniary point of view, indeed, it is highly advantageous. The child will inherit the whole of her father's property; and that, we know, must be very considerable. Mr. Carr cannot for many years have lived up to anything like his income; he must have put by large sums yearly; in fact, in many things I think the Carrs are quite penurious. Many of the arrangements at the Chase seem to me (and certainly *I* am not extravagant in my views) to be most niggardly. Yes, your wife will be an heiress—so far you will have to be congratulated. And yet I am by no means sure that Leo is quite the kind of woman I should have selected to be your wife. Perhaps it is in the nature of a sister's partiality to be always a little disappointed at a brother's choice. I contemplate your union, I cannot help confessing, with much uneasiness and anxiety. I own I look in vain in Leo for those sterling qualities of the head and heart which I feel are indispensable to happiness in the married state.

Miss Bigg's seminary at Chapone House, Kew Green, was most highly recommended to me. With perfect confidence, therefore, I entrusted Blanche and Edith to her charge. I am afraid, however, that I have been deceived in regard to Miss Bigg. Certainly there has been misapprehension somewhere. It appears that one of her pupils had been attacked with illness of an alarming character. I regret to say that this was kept from the knowledge of the parents of the children under Miss Bigg's charge. It was by the merest accident that the fact came to my knowledge. But Dr. Hawkshaw, who had been attending Lord Hengist for his gout, it appears, had been also in attendance at Miss Bigg's school. The Honourable Miss Hengist was a pupil of Miss Bigg's. Of course, directly the fact came to my knowledge, I sent for my darling children. Their escape has been most miraculous; my intervention was most opportune. They were happily spared; but, I believe, other of the pupils have been less fortunate. I consider Miss Bigg's concealment and want of candour to be most culpable. It is the first duty of a schoolmistress to inform the parents of her charges immediately upon the appearance of any danger. Fortunately, Blanche and Edith have escaped infection; they are quite well, and very glad, you may be sure, to be home again at Oakmere. I hardly think I can permit their return to Miss Bigg.

"It seems that the young lady who was first attacked with the fever was a Miss Gill, the daughter, I am given to understand, of a Captain Gill, of the Nizam's Irregular Horse, but who had formerly been in the regular service— the 600th Light Dragoons, I believe. Was not that Lord Dolly's regiment? I am ashamed to be ignorant on such a subject. A few years ago, and I was well *up*, as you call it, in the *Army List*, and need not have made such an inquiry. An officer's daughter is generally prepared to stand an examination in 'Hart.' But times are changed. Perhaps now I am more qualified to answer questions concerning the Civil Service, and especially the Wafer Stamp Office, Whitehall!

"It is quite time that Leo should be married, if only that an end may be put to the foolish, rash, inconsiderate things that she is incessantly doing. It is a misfortune to be an only girl, and especially with parents so indiscreetly indulgent as are Mr. and Mrs. Carr. Since the loss of their son, they have done all they could to spoil Leo. Will you believe that, in spite of all that could be said or done by those best qualified to counsel her, she had been actually so headstrong and obstinate as to take away that sick girl from Miss Bigg's school and convey her to Croxall Chase—an act of downright insanity; there is no other word for it. It is a mercy the child did not die on the journey. She was in excellent hands where she was: most carefully tended, I am given to understand, by Miss Bigg, a woman of experience in such matters, though her concealment of the fact of the illness was unpardonable.

"Very little seems to be known about these girls. For I forgot to mention that there are two. An elder sister of the child who is ill is now stopping at the Chase. She is certainly interesting, even lady-like looking. Delicate features, pale, thin, with pretty light hair. She is a little awkward and timid in manner, and not very well dressed. She shrank rather strangely, I thought, from all mention of her father or her family; upon which subject I was of course anxious to elicit information. Certainly they must be poor. I fancy she is here *almost* in the capacity of governess. I know she has been giving Leo lessons in singing. But Leo never could sing in time, and no amount of teaching will ever make her. She treats Miss Gill (Janet I believe her name is) quite as an equal. They appear to be great friends. It may do Leo good to associate with so modest and quiet mannered a girl as Miss Gill, but the idea at her age of her having a *paid* companion is rather monstrous, for I presume they have the decency (with all their nearness) to remunerate Miss Gill for her services. Perhaps you may be able to find some one in town who knows something about Captain Gill, formerly of the 600th Light Dragoons. I really hardly know whether the man is or not now living. I always suspect that there is something wrong when people are inclined to be secretive and mysterious about their fathers and mothers.

"*Monday.*

"I had intended to close my letter here, but I find that I have some really important news to add.

"After morning church yesterday (a delightful discourse from dear Mr. Wood), we received intelligence of a sad affliction that has fallen on the poor Marchioness. I am sure I grieve for her as only a mother can. I know what it would be in the case of one of my own darlings. Poor little Lord Marigold died at Gashleigh Abbey early on Saturday morning, after a very few days' illness. He was a most engaging child of ten, and very promising for his age. He died of diphtheria, caught, it is believed, from one of the servants, who now lies in a very precarious state. The servant is said to have been only recently engaged at Gashleigh; she was formerly in the service of the Carrs; still, I cannot think that there is any connection between the illness of the child Gill at Croxall and the death of his poor little lordship. How sad this is, is it not? How terrible a blow to the parents. How true it is that in the midst of life we are in death!

"He was, as you know, the only child of the Southernwoods. Their grief will be extreme. The Marquis was *so* proud of his son. There is, I should think, very little probability of the Marchioness having more children. In that case you will note that Lord Dolly is the next heir to the title. This event is of very great importance to him. I am pleased to think that you have always been on terms of intimate friendship with him. Of course, upon certain of his proceedings, it is not possible to look approvingly— but these will be forgotten now. He was very young at the time. I always thought that there was something very attractive about Lord Dolly. I wonder he has never married. There is no doubt but he will be a good deal sought after now. I used to think one time that he was rather *épris* with Leo. Did you ever have such a fancy? I am not sure that once the young lady herself was not possessed with a *tendresse* for the little nobleman. Perhaps it was before *you* spoke. Did that ever occur to you? But at that time, the chance of being Marchioness of Southernwood seemed sufficiently remote. Now things are changed. The Marquis's health is by no means good.

"The funeral will take place on Friday.

"We have, of course, sent our cards and inquiries. The Marchioness is now more composed, and has passed a tolerable night. Some uneasiness is expressed by the doctors in attendance, as to the state of the Marquis. I shall write a letter of condolence to the poor Marchioness as soon as I possibly can. At present I really do not feel myself equal to it. The shock to my only too fragile nervous system has been dreadful.

"Have you any certain information concerning the movements of Lord Dolly? It seems that he went on a yachting expedition with that dreadful man, Lord Flukemore. They have telegraphed and written to him at the places at which he was last heard of; but their news of him is not very recent. He was a bad correspondent, like too many of the young men of the present day; and not, I fancy, on the best terms with his brother, though I have reason to know that Lord Southernwood has behaved most kindly and considerately towards him on more than one occasion. I know that the Marquis disapproved very much of Lord Adolphus's intimate connection with Lord Flukemore. All things considered, the Marquis's view of the matter is not to be marvelled at. By-the-way, what is Lord F. to do now? His old constituents would have nothing to say to him, and carried the election of his opponent in the teeth of the Government. I hear that an effort will be made to bring him in for an Irish borough. Upon the whole, the dissolution seems to have been a failure. The gains of the Government are very trifling. The general notion seems to be that they cannot possibly last out a session. Frank is very indignant because of a rumour that great changes in the mode of levying the wafer stamp duties are in contemplation.

"I now close my long letter. Be sure that you write soon.

"All unite in kindest love. God bless you, my dear Arnold. I look forward to our meeting at Christmas.

"Ever your affectionate sister,

"GEORGINA SOPHIA LOMAX.

"P.S.—I shall wear complimentary mourning for Lord Marigold. It will be only a proper mark of respect to such near neighbours as the Southernwoods. I shall make no change in the children's dress, however. *Be sure you put on a hatband.*

"ARNOLD PAGE, Esq."

The death of little Lord Marigold was duly chronicled in the first column of *The Times*, in the list of casualties with which that journal commences its setting forth of the news of the day. "On the 7th instant, at Gashleigh Abbey, aged ten years, of diphtheria," &c. &c.

The small coffin—a very chaste thing the undertaker called it—beautifully ornamented with the Southernwood arms, had hardly been completed, when another announcement appeared in *The Times*, and not merely in the first column. A separate paragraph in the body of the paper was dedicated to the event.

This was the death of the Most Honourable the Marquis of Southernwood, "at Gashleigh Abbey, also of diphtheria." The Marquis had survived his only child but a few days. The Marquis was in the thirty-fifth year of his age only.

His titles were set forth, his orders, the posts he had filled. He had succeeded to the title on the death of his grandfather, the fifth marquis (of whom some particulars were furnished at an earlier stage of this history). He would be succeeded by his brother, the Honourable Adolphus George Ernest Alfred, commonly called Lord Adolphus Fairfield, at present away from England, it was believed in the Mediterranean; but special messengers had been despatched, charged to convey to him the melancholy intelligence.

Great expectations had been formed of the late Marquis, now, alas! how bitterly disappointed. His lordship had been regarded as one of the most promising statesmen of the day in the Upper House. In the event of the return to power of the Earl of Birmingham, not a doubt existed but that it had been the intention of that minister to offer an important post in his cabinet to the late Lord Southernwood. A vacant Garter would certainly have been his. All this was over now. The remains of the distinguished peer were interred at Gashleigh Abbey. Many noble families were plunged into great grief, and wore heavy crape for some months.

A small gentleman in deep, glossy new mourning, drove slowly along Piccadilly in a cabriolet, a very small tiger, also in mourning, swinging behind. There was something solemn about the appearance of the equipage. Even the horse was black, and reined in purposely that his pace should be slow and stately, almost funereal.

It was the present Marquis; very recently known to us as Lord Dolly Fairfield.

He looked pale beneath his grim hatband. Still the old ambrosial air was not wholly gone. He was still Cupid, only Cupid who had been too near the ink or the blacking, or who after his separation from Psyche had put on crape, mourning her as dead to him.

The Marquis encountered a friend, and pulled up his big black horse. With a tiny crash the tiger descended to try once more to reach the horse's head. He did not succeed; but you would not from his impassive appearance have known of his failure.

"How are you, Arnold, old boy?" quoth the Marquis to his friend. "Get in and let me take you along somewhere. I've got such a lot to say, and it's such a comfort to have some one to say it to; and somehow, you know, I always cottoned to you. Awful business all this, you know, isn't it? Shocking. I'm only up in town for a day or two. The poor Marchioness can't bear my going away from her, poor thing; she's in a dreadful way, you know. She was awful fond of Southernwood, awful; but I was obliged to come up on business, I really could not help it. And the Abbey is *so* dull now, enough to kill a fellow. I don't know, you know, how we're to get on without Southernwood; never dreamt of such a thing as this, you know, never did. And the poor little boy too! he was such a little brick, that boy, I was no end fond of him, and had such larks with him—and—and you know, I didn't even see him before he died! Such a pretty seat he had too upon his pony, and a stunner for pluck. I shall never forget his taking the park hurdle once—the cleanest thing you ever saw: nearly frightened his father into fits. He never was much on horseback, Southernwood wasn't. Poor old Southernwood, he behaved deuced well to me altogether. I'm awfully sorry about it; and that poor Marchioness, I don't think, you know, she'll ever get over it. It makes a fellow cry only to look at her; I'm horrid cut up, and that's the fact. You know I aint the sort of fellow to make a Marquis of, to sit in the Upper House, and that, you know. I must turn over a new leaf now, I suppose, and there's such a heap of things to do; and I'd never given a thought, you know, to anything of this kind. I hope the Marchioness will be better now the funeral's over; but I don't know what to say about it. Doctor seems to be very anxious about her. I suppose you'll go down to your place at Christmas. I must come over and have a look at you; it does a fellow good somehow to see you. Here we are at the Albany; come in for a moment, for a glass of sherry, do! I've got a lot more to say to you : come along."

And as he wrung his friend's hand you might have seen that the tears had come into his lordship's eyes at mention of his dead brother and nephew; while a painful expression quivered about his smooth round Cupid face. Altogether, indeed, he looked something like a tinted statue of the charming son of Mercury and Venus, out in April weather.

CHAPTER XIV.

AT CHURCH.

T was very cold at Oakmere, county of Woodland-shire ; less the steady inclemency of settled frost than cold, windy, cloudy rawness of atmosphere ; the country streaked and patched here and there as with thin white paint, where there had been a peppering of snow—not in profuse feathery flakes, but small compressed hard globules, as though it had been raining pills : the days very short, the nights long and dreary ; the hedges bereft of their leaves, black as negroes out of their holiday suits, mistletoe in request, and holly, for decorative purposes ; housewives waking up in nightmare paroxysms about mince-meat, and Mr. Redbreast on the window-sills ravenous for a share of the bread and butter of his old friends the young children.

Oakmere Rectory, however, was a warm house. It was not a handsome one. More of a cottage perhaps : its ceilings very low, its rooms very small; but its walls were of considerable width, its thatch roof was thick; and the

Reverend Purton Wood, Rector of Oakmere, fully appreciated the comforts to be derived on winter nights from roaring fires, soft close rugs and carpets, padded couches and chairs, and dense curtains before the windows. In these respects the rectory was even luxuriously furnished and fitted.

The rector had been many years a widower. A portrait of the late Mrs. Wood hung in the drawing-room of the rectory—a rather gaudily painted work, representing a small-featured brunette with a high tortoiseshell comb and a short waist, gloves as long as stockings crumpled upon her round arms, a fan about the size of a three-cornered tart in one hand, and a bunch of jessamine in the other. She had pretty round brown eyes, and shiny red lips. The painting was after the manner of Lawrence. The execution would formerly have been pronounced dashing and artistic. Modern art-critics would probably denounce it as slovenly and sloppy.

Ordinarily a green curtain screened the picture. His wife gone from him, the rector had found that the contemplation of her portrait affected him too painfully; and it did not appear that he had ever recovered himself sufficiently to bear the sight of the picture for any long period. He was now and then to be found gazing at it in rather a studied attitude, his head well tilted back, and one hand thrust into his waistcoat. Perhaps he expected to be found so employed, and preferred therefore to look as impressive as was possible under the circumstances. Some (but these were of his most enthusiastic admirers) had even been heard to assert that there were tears to be seen in his eyes on these occasions. " My poor wife ! " he would say, by way of apology for his weakness, and in explanation of it. " My poor dear Emma ! " And with a trembling white hand,—he would draw the curtain again over the portrait, and with a distressing sigh bring himself back again to consciousness of the world around him, and to resignation under his state of affliction. He had been careful to cherish every relic of his wife. " Everything connected in the remotest degree with my poor Emma is sacred in my eyes," he would murmur, in tones choked by grief: so her work-table still stood in the room ; her piano, an old-fashioned " cottage " inlaid with brass, by Tomkinson ; her harp carefully shrouded—a mis-

shapen ghost—in the corner; the Canterbury loaded with
her music; the faded group of flowers feebly painted by her
when she was quite a girl at a boarding-school, and so on.
And he had embalmed her memory in song; he was at one
time perpetually employed upon monodies to his deceased
partner. (As a young man at Oxford he had been distinguished for his English verse : his fellow students, while
they found endless fault with his Latin hexameters, readily
admitted that he was quite a poet in his native tongue.)
His "Lines to Emma" were quite numberless. Some of
them are to be found engraved on her neat tomb in Oakmere
Church, and are greatly admired in the neighbourhood.
Flowers grow over her grave. The rector tended them for
some time with his own hands. But he found it more convenient afterwards to pay a man to perform this duty for
him. And of late, owing to accidental causes probably,
the grave plants have hardly been so carefully looked after
as of old. His friends assert of him that he has never been
the same man since the death of his wife ; that he has never
lifted up his head, never been seen to smile since the occurrence of that lamentable event. In fact, all those well-
known observations in constant use relative to inconsolable
widowers had been applied at various times by various
people to the Reverend Purton Wood. And yet there were
stories among the very old inhabitants of Oakmere unfavourable to the domestic happiness of the rectory. Poor dear
Emma in her lifetime, it was hinted, in short, had been
rather bullied than not by her husband ; it had been her
turn to weep then. There had been much disappointment
it was said touching the insolvency of her father, which had
interfered with the payment of her marriage portion ; or
there had been some similar cause for the dissatisfaction of
Purton Wood. It is hardly worth while to inquire further
into the matter, which long precedes the date of our narrative, and has little connection with it.

There had been but one child of the marriage—Hugh
Wood—a barrister in the Temple. The reader saw him for
a few moments only in an early chapter when he called at
Mr. Arnold Page's chambers. At present he is at Oakmere,
to spend Christmas with his father at the rectory.

The Reverend Purton Wood was a tall thin man with

pale gray eyes, heavy red eyelids and short sandy hair, interspersed with tufts of white. He stooped as he walked, and his stork-like legs bent at the knees; he was narrow-chested, and his voice was of a treble, almost a falsetto, quality, and produced with some effort: he seemed to jerk out his words by a swaying-about action that set his whole body in motion—a manner noticeable in weak-chested men compelled to exert their voices. In age he was apparently between fifty and sixty. His features were small and delicate, his complexion a freckled pink. He was proud of his teeth, which were white and regular, as he was fond of showing; but a smile with such an object is never very attractive. His long neck was carefully wrapped up in a very wide, very stiff, white cravat, after a comfortless fashion of the past, tied in a very dexterous bow in front. In his Oxford days, Mr. Wood had been quite famous among a certain rather dandified set of scholars and gentlemen as "a man who could tie a cloth." He was particular as to the whiteness of his linen, scrupulous as to the purity and the set of the long wristbands he had a habit of continually drawing towards his knuckles. He had not abandoned one tittle of his starch, of his careful dressing, of his neatness of appearance, during his many years' ministration at Oakmere. The tips of his black cloth boots—his dressing-room was quite a museum of boots—were still splendidly varnished after a receipt presented to him by one of the leaders of fashion in his youthful days; the scent of Windsor soap always lingered about his thin white hands, and when he flourished his delicate cambric handkerchief the room was perfumed with bergamot. But this handkerchief was simply for show and sermons: he carried another for use—a faded yellow bandanna, for he was a snuff-taker, carrying a handsome gold box, the gift of a noble pupil, with whom, after the peace of Amiens, he had accomplished the grand tour.

Sunday morning. Opposite his father at the well-furnished breakfast-table sits Hugh Wood, tall and gaunt, moodily-looking, with rough hair and ragged black whiskers, carelessly dressed in rusty clothes as usual. The rector, his neck very stiff, thanks to his clean cravat, sips his coffee—he always takes coffee at breakfast on Sundays under the notion that it improves and strengthens his voice—holding up the saucer heedfully, lest any soiling drops should fall. Hugh, glowering over a large cup of tea, stirs his spoon round and round in gloomy abstraction. The rector has glanced once or twice in the direction of this proceeding disapprovingly, wincingly.

"Don't, my dear Hugh, don't," says Mr. Wood at last, in rather peevish tones. "You can't think how the grating of that spoon jars upon my nerves and annoys me. Of course you do these things thoughtlessly: but really the neglect of such little *convenances* adds immeasurably to the tedium and worry of life. I'm sure that in my time young men were more careful; it is from attention to small matters that society derives its peculiar charm and polish. Now a great neglect of finish prevails, it seems. What is the consequence? Why, the world becomes more and more steeped in vulgarity every day."

Hugh said nothing, but he put down the spoon. Next he emptied his large tea-cup at a draught—perhaps it *was* rather a large draught. The rector drew in his breath with a hissing sound, as though in pain. He raised his hand as though about to resume the thread of his previous remarks, but he deferred his observations, for he could not but perceive that his son's heavy forehead wore something of a scowl as he pushed back his chair, rose from the breakfast-table, and walked to the window.

The Reverend Purton Wood adjusted his wristbands and toyed with the mourning-ring on his little finger. For some minutes neither spoke.

"By-the-way," said the rector at last, with an affected carelessness, but with a slight addition of colour to his face; "by-the-way, Hugh, perhaps you are not aware that I make it a rule never to send for the letter-bag on Sundays. You see in the country one has to consider example very much. But, of course, there is no reason why you should not quietly walk over to the post-office before service and obtain your letters; especially as it is likely enough a matter of some importance to you not to miss the post."

"Thank you; but I don't know of anything very urgent likely to come for me," Hugh answered, without turning round.

"Still, Hugh, something of importance *may* come. We

13—2

may attend to matters of necessity even on the Sunday. We have authority for that. I really think you had better call, quietly, before service. There will be plenty of time."

Hugh made no reply. His father looked annoyed.

"In fact," he said, with some hesitation, "to tell you the truth, I should really feel obliged if you could make it convenient to call at the post-office, and inquiring for your own letters, ascertain if there are any for me—indeed if you would bring them away with you. I have a particular reason to-day for being anxious about my letters—about one especial letter from London—about Moss's bill," he added, in a low tone, and with a suspicious glance over his shoulder towards the door.

"I thought all that matter had been settled long ago," said Hugh Wood, turning round sharply.

"Hush! No, my dear boy. Not settled. Not altogether settled."

"Then that advance of the Ostrich Insurance Company?"

"Hush! not so loud. My dear boy, I couldn't do everything with that advance. It was not of large amount; there were many pressing claims upon me. I did what I could—I paid off, I compromised some, I pacified others with an instalment. I paid Moss all arrears of interest: but the principal——"

"Are we never to hear the end of Moss and his shameful claim?" Hugh asked, with some violence.

"Don't be intemperate, Hugh—and—and don't address me in that tone." The rector's face reddened. "I'm sure I do all I can. I get no rest for thinking of these things. At this very moment I'm trying my utmost to raise the funds. The Ostrich has another application of mine before it now. I'm expecting daily to have the papers from the office for signature. You will join me in a bond—we insure our lives and assign the policies—and charge your life interest under your uncle's will."

"This is ruin, father."

"Don't say that, Hugh. Haven't I enough to bear? Don't taunt me, Sir: and pray keep your temper."

"But the money I remitted the other day?"

"Hush! There were some things I couldn't postpone. I owed money in the village. People were beginning to talk: I was really obliged to pay. I made sure of hearing from the Ostrich before this, and settling with Moss, and having some money in hand to go on with."

"But how is all this to end? How are we to keep down the interest of these loans, to pay the premiums on these insurances?"

"Now pray be calm, Hugh, and don't irritate me. What is the use of these regrets and reproaches? We shall get on somehow; at least we shall have peace and quiet for a little while; that will be something; and then matters won't go on like this—can't go on like this. The bishop *must* do something for me. I stand very well with him now, though I fear I've lost all chance from the Southernwoods. But the Marchioness is such a Puseyite: and the bishop is so evangelical. But something must turn up. Some one will make me a present, or leave me a legacy. If we can only tide over this dreadful business with Moss all will be well. I'm sure of it. I never was so pestered and worried for money in all my life."

Hugh said nothing, but sat down gloomily and drummed upon the table.

"There, there, Hugh," said his father, with some temper, "pray don't go on like that! You know how it annoys me; and I must say I think you are strangely apathetic about this business. But what do you care? Safe and snug in your chambers in London, what does it matter to you even if an execution is put into my house—if the few poor things I possess are rudely torn from me by bailiffs—if I become the talk and scandal of the whole country side? I suppose you will smoke your pipe, none the less happily, for all that your poor mother's relics even are dragged hence, brutally, by the myrmidons of the law!"

"Don't talk in that way, father," Hugh said, sternly.

"What will you care? You won t lend a hand to help me. You won't try to earn a penny the more."

"I earn all I can. I send you every halfpenny I can manage to scrape up. What good does it do?"

"I'm sure I'm not extravagant, if you mean that," said his father, querulously; "it's not only out of *my* debts that this trouble arises. Think of the expenses entailed upon me by your life at the university."

"I never ought to have gone there—never would have, if I had known the truth."

"Yes. You would take a pleasure in degrading your name; in being apprenticed to a trade: in standing behind a counter. I try to make a gentleman of you. This is the return I get. You won't help me, whatever my need. You know that you could have borrowed this money twice over, if you had chosen. You had but to ask young Page, to have it."

"I couldn't borrow, because I couldn't repay. Least of all of Arnold Page."

"You've some foolish romantic scruple. Page has more money than•he knows what to do with: and if *you* won't ask him, I don't see what there is to prevent *my* doing so."

"I must beg, father, that you will do nothing of the kind."

"You thwart me in every way. I urge you to make some effort to secure an advantageous marriage, but you don't appear to hear me. You can't win a woman by keeping away from her timidly, listlessly. There was more pluck about the young men of my time. The excellent matches some of those fellows made! But *you!* There are not many good things of the kind in the county, but there are some. There was that niece of Lomax's whom you let slip through your fingers—Caroline Lomax, who is to marry Lord Mardale—she was a good match if not a great one. I gave you every sort of opportunity. I paid great court to Mrs. Lomax, a woman who is particularly disagreeable to me, solely on your account, that you might stand well with the family. I furnished you with all sorts of introductions. The Comptons were prepared to make a great deal of you in London—but you never went near them but once. You stood a very good chance at the Carrs'—that little Carr will be worth an enormous sum on the death of her father—she's young, pretty——"

"Pray say no more of this," Hugh interrupted warmly. "You know that Miss Carr will marry Arnold Page—has been some months engaged to him."

"I know that she's not yet married. That's all the young

men of my time ever thought it worth while to inquire about. At one time I did think you cared a little for her."

" Pray don't speak of her, least of all in this way." Hugh's face was crimson, and his voice trembled. " I never had a chance of her love. I—I was never worthy of it—never shall be."

"You must think more of yourself, Hugh, or you will never prosper. You must take more care of yourself, dress better, cultivate acquaintance with eligible people, go more into society—try to make some figure there."

"Are these things to be done for nothing, do you think? Can I do this, and still work hard at my profession—toil to earn money to send home here to meet Moss's claims and keep down the interest on the loans? But don't let us talk further upon this subject; it is waste of time, nothing better."

"That's the bell commenced, isn't it? I must make haste."

So the conversation dropped.

There was nothing very remarkable about Oakmere Church : a simple edifice of early English architecture, with a large chancel in which the square pews of the gentry of the neighbourhood were situate. It was picturesque in summer, with its background of elms : Oakmere park, smooth and green, stretching away to the left, and the dense old yew-tree like a black cloud brooding over the graves, and just permitting, between the opaque streaks of its boughs, a glimpse of the rectory on the right. It was cool and pleasant in summer coming in from the sunny churchyard, when the open doors allowed a draught through the church, and a glimpse of green fields for the reflection of wearied worshippers—perhaps unconsciously finding more religion in the earth and sky without, than in the eloquent discourses of the Reverend Purton Wood within. The sun shone through the painted window over the little loft in which the asthmatic hand organ wheezed out its sacred strains, and the rays, dyed divers hues by the process of fil-tration through the coloured glass, fell at last upon the old clerk at his desk, steeping him, as it were, in a rainbow, and making quite a painter's palette of his bald head. There were interruptions during the summer services. The blackbird's saucy secular music sadly interfered with the reading of the lessons, and the doves in the belfry above cooed intermittent responses all through the litany. The poplars waved their tall slim bodies to and fro before the windows, and the yew boughs pushed against the panes as though they were trying to prise the casement, and obtain an entrance by force. It was a pleasant enough country church in the sunny summer time.

But certainly it was less agreeable in winter. It was bitterly cold then. A roaring fire was kept up in the stove in the centre of the aisle—it nearly roasted the clerk, but it warned no one else. There was, too, a well sustained file-firing of coughs and sneezes all through the service, with now and then a resonant smack breaking in upon the other sounds, when the schoolmaster had found it necessary to administer sudden punishment to a refractory pupil. And the church was very draughty; perhaps it was on this account that the congregation were prone at certain periods of the service to disappear, lurking at the bottom of their high walled pews, and only coming to the surface again in reluctant compliance with rubrical demands.

Those church divisions which agitate and irritate cities are little known and less understood in the country. Few of the congregation of Oakmere Church troubled themselves to inquire to what clerical party their rector was inclined to attach himself. Was he high? or low? or broad? No one knew—I may almost say that no one cared. There was little in his manner of conducting the service to betray party leanings any way. He was certainly pompous, but as much so probably on his own account as on that of his office. He did not place flowers on the altar, but he stuck a good many into his sermons ; he did not wear an embroidered robe, and chasuble, but he was prone to very highly ornamented paragraphs. Some of the ladies of his flock, his most treasured lambs, were continually going about loud in praise of Mr. Wood's charming discourses. "What an eloquent sermon our dear rector gave us—*so* poetical." Mrs. Lomax was of this number. But a good many people before these have fallen into the error of accepting bombast for enthusiasm, and fine words for poetry. And it is curious sometimes to remark that for the very same heads that women are busy preparing crowns of bay-leaves, men are often hard at work constructing the very biggest of foolscaps.

The church is well attended this morning of the Sunday before Christmas. In the rectory pew, just severed from the communion rails by the door of the vestry, there is only gloomy, stern-looking, silent Mr. Hugh Wood. He is not very attentive to the service, I fear. He sits or stands with the others of the congregation, but there is no book open before him. His arms are folded across his chest, and he never takes his eyes from the ground. It would seem almost as though there was some object in his doing this. Immediately opposite to him is the pew apportioned to the dwellers at Croxall Chase. It is filled by old Mr. and Mrs. Carr and their daughter Leonora. They have come a distance of two miles to church in the closed carriage. Beyond is the Oakmere Court pew. If you listen you can hear Mr. Lomax, of the Wafer Stamp Office, joining rather noisily in the responses. His tone is not unlike that he employs in his jaunty, affable, official manner we have already noticed. Mrs. Lomax, in handsome velvet and furs, assists the singing with her shrill, not musical voice. She is never very correctly in time ; but harmony in country churches is quite a secondary consideration—the great thing is to be as noisy as you can in your praise and thanksgiving. Edith and Rosy, late of Miss Bigg's school, are also in the pew, looking rather cold and blue and anxious for the termination of the service ; and with them, too, is Mr. Arnold Page, who is paler and thinner than of yore—so the tenant-farmer congregation nearer the door of the church agree among themselves afterwards. Among these you may remark a very hale and hearty gentleman in a red velveteen waistcoat ; a portly, broad-chested man with mottled cheeks, a thick neck and bright healthy eyes. That is Farmer Hooper of Wick Farm, a tenant of Mr. Carr's. He is the father of Robin Hooper. That pretty-looking little old woman in the warm plaid shawl is his mother. And you can see Robin there also at her side. But he is not very tall and the pew is very high. Certainly a very good attendance at Oakmere Church on the morning of Sunday before Christmas. The Reverend Purton Wood dabs his eyes

with his cambric handkerchief — he was very nearly producing the bandanna, for he took a pinch of snuff in the
vestry when he put on his cassock and brushed his hair and
prepared for the sermon—and glances at his lean knuckles
and draws down his wristbands, and clears his throat, and
lays himself out for oratorical effects and triumphs.

He is about to enunciate his text when he finds the heads
of many of his flock turn away from him. There is a slight
noise at the door. Some one has entered the church,—a
stranger.

Very few strangers ever come to Oakmere Church. The
correct course of conduct to be pursued with regard to a
stranger entering the church, is not exactly known, as it
appears. The occurrence is so unusual that no provision
has been made for it. The tenant-farmers simply stare at
the new-comer. The rector pauses. It is impossible for
him to commence with that figure standing there in the
centre of the aisle. Hugh Wood starts as from a reverie to
appreciation of the difficulty. He signals the bald-headed
clerk. That functionary descends from his desk, and probably from some misconception of the intentions of the
rector's son, he takes the stranger in tow, brings him up the
length of the church, and finally deposits him in the rectory
pew. There is the noise of a book falling down in Farmer
Hooper's pew.

But the interruption has been got over. A slight querulousness and annoyance, the results of it, are traceable in the
tones of the rector's voice as he begins his sermon. But the
stranger is now hid in the rectory pew and the congregation
can give undivided attention, and the rector warms to his
work at last. He fixes his rather colourless eyes upon a
stone cherub, part of a monument to one of the worthies of
the county, on the opposite side of the chancel-arch—this is
after his usual manner ; he preaches all his sermons to the
stone cherub—and he reads it a very ornate jobation, jerk-
ing out of himself treble bursts of florid language : very
charming, very eloquent, and *so* touching, *so* calculated to
benefit his parishioners, as Mrs. Lomax remarks, who
always poses herself as a critic on these occasions—treating
the sermons as merely sent to her for review, and especially
designed for the behoof of others of the community. But

there are many people, apparently, who conceive that religion is better adapted for their neighbours than for themselves, just as there are some doctors who prescribe drugs for others they would never dream of putting into their own mouths.

It is not for me to judge the preacher. I will presume that his sermon was quite orthodox : what the church militant would perhaps describe as "regulation." It was divided into heads : he paused now and then to give his hearers an opportunity of concentrating their coughing : there was a glowing peroration. It contained a great number of what his poorer parishioners called "dictionary words !" not that those were objected to—indeed the good folks were rather the more proud of their pastor in proportion as they understood him the less. And at the conclusion he especially blessed his patient friend the stone cherub, raising his white hands with that object, rather histrionically perhaps.

The stranger sat very still in the rectory pew. Occasionally, however, he would raise his head sufficiently to permit two black specks of eyes to peer restlessly about the church. A little old man in a blue cloak with a red lining and a shabby rabbit fur collar,—wearing a profuse black wig, —carrying a greasy black hat with a curved rim.

The organ crows forth a husky hymn, with the usual abruptness and want of feeling in its method of execution characteristic of all hand instruments. The congregation flock out of church : it is too cold for much lingering in the churchyard for conversational purposes.

"What is the name, Sir, if you please, of the gentleman who preached ?"

The old man whispered his inquiry in the ear of his companion in the pew.

"My father, the rector, the Reverend Purton Wood." And Hugh Wood passed out.

"Why, Robin, lad, what's the matter?" asked Farmer Hooper of his son. "What's worrying you ? what's wrong now ? Why, you're white as a sheet, lad ? Look at him Nance." This he addressed to his wife.

"Let him be, let him be," she said; "the lad's well enough — hale and well now, aint you, Robin? Like enough he's pale, and the weather so cold as it is. But he's strong and well now."

"Poor lad, poor lad," muttered the farmer. "But let her think so : she will do it." Then aloud he added,—"Lean on me, Rob ; you'll get on better so, my lad."

"Let him be," the wife said again ; "he can walk bravely and strongly enough now, can't ye, Robin ? "

It was the farmer's habit of mind rather to exaggerate the want of health, and the deformity of his son : perhaps the result of contrast with his own sturdiness ; whereas the wife was always inclined to make light of her son's crippled state, and to give him credit for quite a fanciful amount of health and strength. But the poor woman loved her one deformed child so dearly ; she deemed him quite perfect both in mind and body. She had no eyes, or seemed not to have, to note his crooked limbs, his curved back, his wan face, and she could not bear to think that her husband snould be always dwelling upon these.

"Go on, father," Robin said. "I'll catch you up in a minute. I can go faster than you think. I want to say a word to Hugh Wood and to Arnold."

"It's that book-learning in London that makes him so pale," said Mrs. Hooper, apologetically, to the farmer as they moved on.

"Poor lad, poor lad," the farmer muttered again. "He grows worse, I think, but the old woman won't let me say so."

"What does he do here ? How dare he come here ? " Robin was asking himself. "The old man of the *Café de l'Univers* ? I must speak to Arnold. Fortunately *she* is not at church."

At this moment Miss Carr left her party to come to him. She put out a little gloved hand, and a kind bright smile adorned her lips.

"How do you do, Mr. Hooper ? " she said to him. "I am very glad to see you again."

("She is very beautiful," Robin thought, "and very good too, I am sure ; but it is for Arnold's sake she speaks to me.")

"How is your poor invalid ? " he asked.

"Very ill, I fear, Mr. Hooper. My poor little Bab l But we are going to have advice from London again."

"And Ja—— Miss Gill?"

"Poor thing, she is very distressed on her sister's account. I could not persuade her to come to church and let me sit with poor Bab. Her attention is unremitting; she loves her sister most tenderly."

Mrs. Lomax swept by.

"How *can* you?" she whispered in Leo's ear. She did not approve of any but a very formal notice being taken of Robin Hooper. "Why does Arnold involve us with these awkward acquaintances of his?"

"We can't let you carry off Arnold to-day, Leo," quoth Mr. Lomax, with patronising cheerfulness: "we can't spare him, can we, little ones?"

Edith and Rosy adroitly placed themselves one on each side of their uncle, with the view perhaps of leading him away captive.

"Take care, Rosy. No romping on Sunday," said Mrs. Lomax, sternly.

"You'll come over to-morrow morning, won't you, Arnold?"

"Yes, certainly."

"Come over, by all means, Arnold," Mr. Carr interposed. "I've something to say to you."

("Why does Hugh Wood always hurry past without speaking?" Leo asked herself.)

"Come, Carr, come Leo, don't stand too long in the cold," said Mrs. Carr.

A few words with Robin, and Arnold was carried off by the Lomax party.

"He's a Frenchman, Sir, I hear." So Robin elicited from the blacksmith of Oakmere. "He came down last night. He's put up at the Crown. No one knows anything about him."

The old man of the *Café de l'Univers*, Tithonus, Monsieur Anatole, lingered in the churchyard. He was the last to leave it. He looked very deathly, with his skull face, moving amongst the graves.

"Not here!" he said, moodily. "I thought she would have been at church. She is *dévote*. I cannot have been mistaken. In any case, it is clear I have business in this neighbourhood"—and he read from a scrap of paper:

"'Arnold Page. The Reverend Purton Wood. Hugh Wood.' Yes," he went on, "I think I shall soon know all about these; and about *la chère petite.*"

CHAPTER XV.

OLD MR. CARR.

ROXALL CHASE was on the confines of the parish of Oakmere, and a very noble property. The original mansion, a beautiful quadrangular structure, with gable ends, porch and Elizabethan windows—turn to the engraving of it in that very interesting work, the *History of the County of Woodlandshire*—was totally destroyed by fire late in the last century. It was replaced by the present edifice, in favour of which there is little to be said; a massive block, coated with stucco, spotted with most unpicturesque windows, and crowned in the most obtrusive manner by numberless stacks of chimneys of great variety of form. It is but fair to state, however, that the inside of the house is very commodious, handsome, and well arranged.

Arnold Page had walked over from the Court. His visit was evidently expected: he was met in the hall by Leo, who greeted him affectionately.

"I am not to detain you," she said, "though I have longed to see you so much, and I have a thousand things to say to you. But I promised papa not to keep you from him. It seems he has something to say to you, something important I should think, by his manner. What can it be about, I wonder? but I won't stop you now. He's in the library. But only promise me that you'll come away as soon as you can; I shall be in the small drawing-room. Promise!"

"I promise, dearest," and he entered the library.

A spacious room well furnished with books; maps covering such parts of the walls as the shelves left vacant;

portfolios upon stands ; heavy oak chairs with green leather cushions, and a large carved oak writing-table, at which sat old Mr. Carr. It was the most comfortable room in the house, with the warmest aspect, the most secure from draughts. There was a glowing fire in the grate, and the softest of Turkey carpets upon the floor. The old gentleman's seat was very near the fire. He was accustomed to retire to this room for some hours' seclusion after breakfast, when he read and answered his letters, amused himself with the newspaper, audited his accounts, and had interviews with his steward, bailiffs, agents, and servants.

"How are you, my dear Arnold? I am obliged to you for coming. I don't find that I move about as easily as I used to, or I would have gone over to see you. Draw near to the fire. It's bitterly cold this morning, and—and you're not looking very well—a little pale and worn and anxious, I think."

A close observer might have noted that Mr. Carr was a little more nervous and hurried in his manner of receiving his visitor than was customary with him. His hands shook a little, as he adjusted his tall flaxen wig, and rising from his writing chair, stood in front of the fire. He moved about from one foot to the other during the pause that followed, as though uncertain how to begin what he had pre-arranged to say.

"I wanted a little conversation with you, Arnold," he commenced at length. "But I must first ask you to be patient and forbearing with me if I should say anything that may be in the slightest degree displeasing to you. You may be sure I would not do this for the mere object of paining you—that I am only doing what I believe to be strictly my duty."

"Pray speak with the utmost freedom, Mr. Carr," said Arnold, frankly.

The old man resumed his seat, and folded his hands together before him. He turned his chair from the table towards the fire ; he bent his eyes upon the ground.

"Your late father, Arnold, was a very dear old friend of mine. We were neighbours and we grew to be friends— fast friends. He was a true gentleman, Arnold. He knew as well as I did that I was not really his equal, that I never could be so; that in birth, in education, in all that gives a man social position—and be sure I am not speaking now of wealth—I was very far beneath him. But he never let me see this; others have, with not half his claims to look down upon me: but he—never. And he gave me his friendship. I think he found me honest and true, as I know I have sought through my life to be; I think, if I may so say, that he prized me for those qualities. He gave me his friendship years and years ago, and he never regretted it. Perhaps you have forgotten that he died with his hand in mine. I have never suffered so much as I suffered then, save when death took from me—but that was long before—took from me—my father—and—once again—when I lost my poor boy, Jordan, my only son, Arnold."

Mr. Carr stopped, for his voice sank and trembled too much for him to be able to continue. Arnold's face wore rather a puzzled look.

"It had been your father's wish," the old man resumed at length, in calmer tones—"it was among the last words I heard fall from his lips—that, at a future time, our two families should be united by marriage. My daughter then was quite an infant, you were a boy growing apace: I could say nothing then. I respected my old friend's project, but I knew that its carrying out did not rest with me; I knew the interference of parents in plans of this kind never has been and never will be of much use. It is not for us to shape just as we please the future of our children. I determined, therefore, that things should simply take their course. It was a great happiness to me to find that without any action on my part events promised to occur precisely as I could wish: in exact accordance with the views of my poor friend. I watched your kindness and your friendship for my little Leo; she was but a child then: I was pleased to think that that kindness, that friendship bade fair to ripen into love. When my consent was asked for your marriage, I gave it freely. I stipulated only that there should be no haste or abruptness. My daughter is yet very young.

"So far all has been well. But now certain circumstances must come under mention. Be patient, Arnold; I will not needlessly wound you. I am greatly anxious for the carrying out of your father's plan; but there is one thing, concerning which I am bound to be still more anxious—that is the happiness of my daughter. I am bound to take every precaution with this object. I am her father, she is my only child now; she is very dear to me, and she is very young.

"I am a quiet man, silent too, apparently abstracted; but I think I notice what goes on around me as well as most people, better perhaps than a good many. And there are some things one cannot help noticing and knowing of, without listening to gossip or tale-bearing, or the ceaseless tattle of the country. Among other things I have not been able to avoid knowing a good deal about what is happening upon a neighbouring property—Oakmere Court."

Arnold reddened, started at the mention of his own estate.

"I fear I have laid myself open to many charges of neglect and mismanagement in regard to Oakmere," he said.

"We cannot expect young men to be perfect landlords all at once: to be immediately awake to the fact that property has its duties and responsibilities as well as its privileges. Your father took pleasure in playing his part as owner of Oakmere. I used to think it a fine sight to see him take the chair at the half-yearly dinner of his tenants. How lustily they cheered him, how fond they were of him, how proud! And they had cause; he was a gallant soldier and a noble gentleman. For his sake they were prepared to render like honours to his son."

"I own my neglect. I ought to have made a point of attending the half-yearly dinners, of making myself better acquainted with my tenants. I am obliged to you for bringing these things to my notice, Mr. Carr. I am sorry you did not do so before."

"I am very unwilling to enter upon these topics. Even now I would sooner look on and say nothing. But I am bound to speak further. You promise yourself to enter upon a new line of conduct. I must warn you to be careful lest King Stork should turn out a worse ruler than King Log. Pardon my bluntness. But is it part of your new

14

plan to dismiss **several old** servants, amongst others the steward who served your late father very faithfully for many years?"

"I know that some changes have been made; I hardly know to what extent. Mr. Lomax has been acting upon my behalf. I am bound to say, that he has rather exceeded his authority; though it is only right that the blame of his so doing should fall upon me."

"Mr. Lomax——" the old gentleman began in rather louder tones than he had yet employed. But he checked himself. "I am an old man of business," he said, calmly, "and I claim to have some experience in business matters. I have many friends in the City and elsewhere, and I hear a good many things—some of them rather curious. It's a good plan in business to watch carefully the faces of the men you are dealing with. You've walked through a forest in this country many times, I dare say, and seen a blaze of white paint upon the trees destined to destruction. Well, in the same way I've gone upon 'Change, and I've noticed the men with a particular look in their faces, in regard to whom I have never been deceived. They were the men who were *going*. Bankruptcy and ruin hung over them. Do you know, Arnold, that I couldn't help keeping my eyes upon you yesterday in church? I ought to have been otherwise occupied, but I couldn't help it, for it seemed to me that your face wore just the look of which I have been speaking."

Arnold quitted his seat. He was about to exclaim something rather loudly, but the old man stopped him by a deprecatory gesture.

"Hush!" he said, "my dear boy, sit down again. Don't be angry with me; don't be in a hurry to quarrel with me. I am not speaking at random—you know that I am not. But indeed I am bound to use plain words. And now ask yourself these plain questions: Is it honest in a man to look forward to marriage as a means of paying his debts with his wife's money? And next, ought I to give my consent to the union of my daughter with such a man?"

There was silence for some minutes, Arnold breathing very heavily, controlling himself with much effort.

" This is very harsh language, Mr. Carr," he said at length, in tones as temperate as he could command.

" Believe me, Arnold, I should be sorry to say more than the occasion fully justified. Let us look a little closer into the matter. I say nothing more about neglect and mismanagement. I will not dwell, though I could, upon the pain it gives me to see your father's good old house dismantled, half pulled down, to be tortured and twisted with improvements, and alterations, and new-fangled additions. This is extravagant, distasteful to me; but it is nothing more. I know little, I ask less, as to your manner and habits of life when you are away from here. I know that it is almost expected of young men of birth, of fortune, of position, that they should lead expensive lives, perhaps viciously expensive lives ; I don't care to look too curiously into such a question. But certainly there should be limits. The Oakmere property has not been yours very many years. It is rather early to be depositing your title-deeds as security for a considerable loan from your bankers ; to be charging your property heavily to secure a large advance from the Ostrich Insurance Company. You wonder that I know this ? My dear boy, it is very hard to keep some secrets. If a man is borrowing money, the fact is known to many more than those he borrows of. There were some very noisy people stopping at the Crown Inn a week or so ago. They made little secret of their mission here. They described themselves as agents on behalf of the Ostrich Insurance Company. They were here, it seems, to survey the estate of Mr. Arnold Page, preparatory to a mortgage. It was nice news for all the village gossips to be discussing. And there are certain other things I should mention. There is no harm in an idle gentleman ; his wealth and position, perhaps, entitle him to idleness, while they prevent any ill consequences coming of it; but an idle gentleman who makes believe to work is likely to do a good deal of mischief to himself amongst others. It was not for you, Arnold, it was not for your father's son, to connect yourself with public companies of an origin and an object, curious, to say the least of them. It was not for you to take your seat at a board of directors, half dupes and half adventurers, if not swindlers. Why should you join the ranks of mere

14—2

'guinea-pig' directors? Why should you back up with
your name and credit a slippery speculation? Yes, I have
a prospectus here—a Silver Mining Company, which is to
pay an enormous dividend, of course. You have some
strange names amongst your colleagues of the direction.
I'm an old City man, Arnold, and I can tell these things,
almost as you can meat, by the smell, whether they are
worth anything or not. It's a bubble company : it mayn't
collapse, like other bubbles ; it may even live and thrive,
just as many a thing begun in a joke ends by being in
earnest. And this is not the only affair of the kind that you
have connected yourself with ! Why should you soil your
clean fingers with this Stock Exchange mire ? The Ostrich
Insurance Company is not a very *nice* company. It is very
fond of risks. There are strange stories as to its dealings
with many young men, the heirs to great properties. It
trades rather disreputably in usury under the respectable
colours of life insurance."

The old man had assumed a tone of irony that was
unusual with him. But it was with an altered voice that he
said,

"It is little pleasure to me to be saying these things.
But you will know whether they are or not justified by
facts."

"I have thought it right to connect myself with certain schemes of, I believe, great public utility. I think,
Mr. Carr, that you have been in some way strangely mis-
informed as to their character." Arnold spoke with some
warmth.

"You tested their worth before joining them?"

"All proper inquiries were made."

"By yourself, or by someone else acting for you?"

"By Mr. Lomax," Arnold said, hesitatingly.

"And you have acted altogether on his report—on his
advice?"

"I have in a great measure."

"I heard so."

Mr. Carr drew back his chair. He checked himself as
he was about to speak, and waited for a few moments.

"Mr. Lomax," he said quietly, "is by far too much
interested in the case to be capable of giving good advice

concerning it. Indeed, under any circumstances, I should take leave to doubt his competency to advise. You know what happens when the blind lead the blind. Why should I hesitate to speak freely? Why should I close my mouth in regard to this man? Arnold, your friend and counsellor, your brother-in-law Mr. Francis Lomax, is a ruined man. He is sinking, catching at straws, anything, to save himself, as sinking men will do. You are the straw—too valuable a straw to be drawn in and sunk by such a man. You must let him go, Arnold! not sink with him."

"This cannot be," Arnold began; "you must be wrong, Mr. Carr. I am quite sure that Lomax——"

"No, you are not sure, Arnold; you know that you are not. It is right to defend your sister's husband, but it is right also to speak the truth. Ask your own heart concerning this Mr. Lomax; at the bottom of all your regard and respect and friendship for him, isn't there distrust? You suspect him while you shut your eyes and surrender yourself to him."

Arnold was silent. He bit his lips while he gazed gloomily at the fire.

"Well? You suspect, let us say. I do more. I *know*. I am less likely to be deceived. He has not married into my family. I can study him from a little distance; out of the spell of his handsome person, his plausible talk, his graceful manner. And as I have said, I am an old man of business, and I know a little of what goes on. I know what all sorts of people are doing. I know all about this gentlemanly, prosperous-looking, successful-seeming Government official. Plainly, he is a ruined man. I *know* that. I *think* he is something worse; but I decline to speak positively. He *may* retrieve himself from a very dangerous position. He *may* replace in time money not his own, of which he has possessed himself in, let us say, an irregular way—money he has speculated with, and which, as a result, is now represented by a bundle of waste paper—shares in public companies, the veriest of bubble companies. He *may* do this if he can persuade you to mortgage your land and hand him the proceeds in exchange for his waste paper shares. He may then continue to look like an honest man in the eyes of the world—not unless."

Arnold sat silent--motionless. The old man watched him carefully, expecting him to speak.

"Well, well," he muttered, "there is no need to hurry him. I have given him something to think about."

And to pass the time, he took up a magazine that was on the desk before him, and began to cut the leaves with a paper-knife.

Arnold was pressing his hands tightly together until his nails quite wounded his palms.

"And—and—Leo?" he said at length, in a low inquiring tone, without lifting his eyes from the fire.

The old man rose and placed his hand gently, kindly upon Arnold's shoulder.

"Don't think harshly of me. It was a great pleasure to me," he said, "to give my consent to the marriage of my daughter with my old friend's son. It will be a great pain to me if anything has occurred, if anything should occur to prevent that marriage. But——"

"But what?" Arnold asked, anxiously, as the old man paused.

"But, as I have said, I have a duty to perform. My friend's son, when I gave that consent, was the master of Oakmere Court, a rich man."

"I have never been, I never shall be, Leo's equal in point of wealth," Arnold interrupted. "I know that I am unworthy of her in that and a thousand other ways."

"Hush, my dear boy, don't mistake me. It's not a question of money," Mr. Carr said rather proudly. "My child's happiness is not a mere matter of bank-notes. I would offer no obstacle to her marriage with a gentleman, however poor, a gentleman who had no regrets to look back upon; who had not muddled away a fine property: who did not bring with him a load of incumbrances. It is not a question of money, it is a question of honesty!"

"Mr. Carr, you insult me!"

"No, Arnold. But you have touched pitch. You mustn't wonder that your hands are defiled."

"You wish to break off my engagement with Leo?"

"I wish for nothing of the kind."

"What then?"

"Pray be calm. I wish this engagement to continue.

But that cannot be if your present line of conduct is to be still pursued."

"What would you have me do?"

"I will tell you. You will take the management of your estate entirely out of Mr. Lomax's hands. You will reinstate the old faithful servants—friends, I might say—of your father's whom this man has dismissed. You will return to the family solicitors in lieu of trusting your affairs to the sharp gentlemen whom, in consideration of the money he owes them, Mr. Lomax has selected for you. You will stop this mortgage with the Ostrich. With a little retrenchment, and the good management resulting from your personal superintendence and residence upon the estate, you will soon find yourself in a position to repay your bankers the advances they have made; a little nursing, and the property will recover of itself. You won't again sign any number of papers Mr. Lomax may shuffle up before you. In fine, ere it becomes too late, you will break with him. You will demand from him strict accounts, and especially in regard to the money obtained on loan from the bankers. And you will withdraw yourself absolutely from these undertakings of great public utility, as you deem them—fraudulent bubbles, as I say."

Arnold walked up and down the room in a state of considerable agitation.

"But if I cannot do this," he exclaimed, "if it is now too late, if it is impossible——"

"It is not impossible, it is not too late," said Mr. Carr, firmly; "but if you refuse to act as I would have you——" and he paused. "No, Arnold," he continued, "I don't forget that I am speaking to the son of an old friend, to a gentleman, although he has been duped into a cruelly false position. How I wish now that I had interfered some time ago to caution you, and said then much of what I have said to-day! But you will not try to force upon me the *rôle* of the harsh parent of the plays; you will not try to make me the antagonist of my child; you will not sow dissension between us. My poor little Leo! You can't think what a joy and a treasure she is to me, Arnold. I know that she has given you her heart, and, perhaps, might be led, if you insisted, to act in opposition to my will, to deem

me her enemy : the thought of such a thing is very grievous
to me. You will not do this ; I will leave the question to
your own honour, Arnold. It is not for me to step in and
say that the engagement should not be carried out. But if
events should occur as I have hinted, why, then, a ruined
man, you will know that you are no fit husband for my
daughter—you will shrink from asking her to share a ruin
your own folly and improvidence have in great part brought
upon you."

" Does she know anything of what you have said to me ?"
Arnold asked, in a low voice.

" Not one word of it."

" Have you thought of what would be the effect upon
her, if this engagement were brought to an end ?"

" I have thought of that, and I know that it would be
great suffering to her ; she is tenderly attached to you ;
it would wound her terribly. But she is very young,
Arnold ; she would recover. The youthful heart can bear
a great deal. How many happy women now have been
miserable enough in the past about their first loves—
the disappointments of their girlhood ? Yet these have
gone and left no trace. And she may have mistaken her
own feelings in regard to you. But I will not urge that
argument."

" No one can desire her happiness more than I do," said
Arnold. " Pray believe in the truth of my love for her."

" I have never doubted it, Arnold."

" I trust I may be able to show you that you have been
deceived in regard to me and my position ; until then,
I will try to be guided by your wishes in regard to Leo.
Only, only," he said, in a hoarse voice, " don't ask me to
resign all hope of her."

The old man pressed his hand.

" No, no," he said ; " don't think so badly of me as that.
But I have a right, I think I have, to impose conditions :
let things go on as they are ; but the marriage must not be
for some time yet, and I must trust to you to put no unfair
pressure upon Leo. If her inclination in regard to you
should undergo a change ; if she should seek to escape from
this engagement ; if she should grow ever so little weary of
it, you must not try to bind her to her promise ; you must

not taunt her with her caprice. It is the privilege of youth to be inconsistent—fickle even. Let her be free. Don't remind her of her word plighted to you. Time works his way in spite of us all. This engagement may die out, quite naturally, of a sort of inanition—no one any the worse for it. Let things take their natural course. But there, I need say no more. In whom should I have confidence if I have none in you,—my old friend's son? And perhaps —perhaps you may retrieve yourself. There—there, keep a good heart, and don't think the worse of me because I have spoken plainly. It's as well that some in the world should speak plainly; and the subject is an important one—it demands out-speaking. Don't think I am cruel, or harsh, or heartless; only I love my Leo, and I am bound to see that her happiness is not imperilled by anyone or anything."

And, the conference ended, Arnold quitted the library.

The old man took up his magazine and resumed his occupation of cutting the leaves. But he stopped after a few minutes in a state of abstraction.

"Poor boy," he muttered, "poor boy—for he is but a boy after all. It has been a sharp lesson for him, but it will do him good. It's as well that he should see all that has happened in a proper light before it is too late. As for that scoundrel Lomax," he rose and poked the fire vigorously: the action seemed to relieve him of the necessity of continuing his remarks. But he couldn't go on with his magazine.

"Poor children," he said after awhile, "they love each other. It would be a thousand pities if anything should interfere to prevent their coming together. A very pretty couple. But," and his voice grew quite stern and harsh as he spoke, "I won't have my father's money and my money going to patch up the shaky reputation of that Whitehall Government office scamp! No, no. Anything but that."

Arnold paused on the mat outside the library, uncertain what to do. He looked pale, very sad and depressed.

"In the small drawing-room, she said; but it were better, perhaps, not to see her. I don't think I could even bear to see her after—after what has happened, after what I have heard. Perhaps I have no right to see her."

Yet he stood hesitating, loath to go, with regretful eyes fixed on the drawing-room door. Then, as though moved by a sudden resolution, he strode rapidly across the hall, opened a glass door and passed out. The air struck very cold after Mr. Carr's snug library. He walked briskly at first, but his steps slackened shortly. He had quitted the drive in front of the house. He was pacing slowly in the flower-garden. Each additional foot of the way separating him from Leo seemed to be as a new difficulty to be surmounted, a new argument against proceeding. He felt greatly inclined to return to the house, to say but two words to her, to see her but for a minute—only to see her— only for a minute. All at once it seemed to him that there was some one on before him in the gravelled path into which he had passed. He caught the glimpse of a woman's skirt turning a corner. It was a cold day for anyone to be walking in the garden. Could it be Leo? It was not unlike one of her heedless proceedings. She was prone to be out of doors at all times, at all seasons, notwithstanding all Mrs. Carr's entreaties to the contrary, and her warnings as to the colds likely to be caught by such means, backed by quotations of precedents furnished by the career of her son, Jordan Carr. Then Arnold remembered that the path he was in led to what was known as the sycamore walk—an avenue of trees sheltered from the cold winds, and a favourite portion of the garden with the inmates of Croxall Chase. Certainly it might be Leo. He hurried on.

As he turned to enter the avenue he was startled by a slight scream, and a cry of surprise, if not alarm. He found himself within a few yards of two persons.

One, a woman, not Leo, but a stranger; pale, fragile-looking, with rippling golden hair, a scared look upon her face, her eyes dilated, her almost colourless lips parted. At a glance he was able to note these facts. She stood in a shrinking attitude, with a trembling, outstretched arm, as though to ward off a terrible danger.

A man had disturbed her in her walk. He had gained the avenue apparently through a breach in the leafless hedge dividing the garden from the meadow land beyond. Arnold re-

cognised him at once. It was the man who had entered
Oakmere Church at the commencement of the Reverend
Purton Wood's discourse; the man who had sat in the
rector's pew on Sunday; and a vague remembrance seemed
to haunt Arnold that somewhere else he had met the man
before.

"*Chère ange!*" said Monsieur Anatole to Janet Gill. He
removed his greasy hat to make an obsequious bow. A
grin curdled over his yellow, wrinkled, wizen face.

"You here!" Janet gasped, shivering; and she went
on in a faint voice, "What is it you want?"

"Pardon me that I have startled you!" he said. "In
my joy at seeing you, I could not resist declaring myself at
once." He stopped for a moment, to grin again, it seemed.
"At length, I find you, then! You have given me some
trouble!"

He advanced to take her hand. She shrank from him
with an expression of extreme repugnance. Turning, she
saw Arnold, and almost unconsciously she moved towards
him. There seemed in the action a mute appeal for
assistance and protection immediately perceptible to
Arnold. He was at her side in an instant.

"Can I be of any service to you?"

She drew courage from his presence.

"Go," she said to the Frenchman in firmer tones.

"Can you ask it, so soon—when we have met but
this moment after a separation so long? You are cruel,
my Janet; you are frightfully cruel."

She trembled. Arnold read the terror in her ghost-pale
face. He frowned, and took a step towards the Frenchman.

"I go," said Monsieur Anatole, hurriedly. "I regret to
have occasioned alarm. I am not unknown to Mademoiselle;
she will vouch for me. Pardon me if I have trespassed on
these lands. I am not of this country, and not *au fait*
at its laws of property. Adieu. You will not take my
hand, Janet? Ah, you are cold to an old friend! But
you will change. You are a little frightened now. You are
pale and sick-looking, my child. We must not expect then
too much from you; but we shall meet again, be sure of it.
Au revoir then. *Monsieur*" (this to Arnold in a tone of

ceremony), "I have the honour to wish you a good-morning."

He removed his hat again, pressing it upon his chest, while he bent himself into a right angle. He looked from one to the other with a strange leering smile upon his shrivelled lips. Then he gathered round him the folds of his blue cloak, stopped to kiss his skeleton hand and nod many times to Janet, broke through the hedge again and disappeared.

"Surely," thought Arnold, "I have seen that man before: but where?"

Janet stood trembling, gazing after Monsieur Anatole. Spell-bound, fascinated as a bird by a serpent; pressing her hands upon her heart. For a moment Arnold thought she was about to fall, and put forth his hand to save her.

"He has frightened you. Suddenness is sometimes very alarming, Miss Gill, is it not? I have heard of you from my friend Robin Hooper, from my sister, Mrs. Lomax. I am known to the Carrs, my name is Page—Arnold Page. I reside near here, at the Court."

She gave him her hand.

"Forgive me for having troubled you. I am not very well this morning, a little over-wearied and unnerved with nursing my sister who is very ill. That man came before me so unexpectedly, when I was abstracted by other thoughts, and——"

"It was shameful of him. He is a stranger here. Do you know him?"

"No—yes, a little only. He has no right to intrude upon me here. I grow faint again. I will return to the house. I thought a turn in the garden would do me good, but I am weaker than I thought."

So they turned in the direction of the house.

"She is very beautiful," Arnold muttered, as he glanced at his companion. "Very beautiful, in spite of her pale-ness. I don't wonder at poor old Rob's enthusiasm. She is not well enough to be left: I must go back with her to the house, even—even if I should see Leo."

But he was not sorry to be able thus to excuse to himself his return.

As they approached the house, the door opened, and Leo came out to meet them; a recollection of his recent conversation with old Mr. Carr came upon Arnold with a painful vividness. For the first time he felt confused and troubled in her presence.

"I could see you from an upper window," said the little lady. "But it is too cold for you, Janet; you must toast yourself over the fire, you look quite perished. Why were you going away, Arnold, without seeing me? What a long time papa kept you talking in the library; I'd half a mind to break in upon you. What could you have to say to each other all that time? and then to go away, although you promised to come to me in the little drawing-room! For shame, Sir! I've a great mind to be very angry with you! Why do you treat me like this? what have I done to deserve it?"

The dash of petulance in her manner seemed to be only half assumed.

"Forgive me, Leo," said Arnold, with some hesitation in his manner. "It was growing late. We found we had so much to say in the library: business talk—mere business talk—it wouldn't interest you. And I promised Edith and Rosy I'd get back early. They wanted me to take them a drive, or go with them for a ride, or something or other, I hardly know what."

"I shall be very angry with Rosy and Edith, very jealous of them. You can tell them so, if they attempt to take you away from me. But come in now. It's so warm and snug in the little drawing-room."

"No, Leo. I think——"

"Oh! Arnold, for shame. *Do* come, if for five minutes only."

"Well, then, for five minutes. No longer, Leo." And they re-entered the house. It had never seemed to Arnold harder to part from her. The charm of her manner, her artlessness, her kindliness, her beauty, had never possessed and swayed him more absolutely than now, when their engagement seemed to be in danger. There was something very entrancing in that infantine grace and gleefulness, that blithesome alacrity with which she drew two chairs close to the fireplace and forced Arnold to sit down at her side, while she stole her soft little hand into his, and nestled her head upon his shoulder, the tender brown eyes glancing up now and then into his face.

"My dear old Ar!" she said. A look of pain quivered for a moment in his face as he thought how dear she was to him : dearer now than he had ever known. How terrible it would be to him to lose her!

The door of the room opened, a head was projected into the room, and a voice said "Oh! I didn't know—" but the voice did not complete the sentence, the head was rapidly withdrawn, and the door was closed again.

"I wouldn't have gone in if I'd thought *they* were there," said old Mrs. Carr outside the room. "People in their case don't like to be disturbed. I know Jordan was dreadfully angry one day because I would go into the room where he was sitting with Annie Courtney. He was engaged to her ; but I never liked her. I always said she was a conceited minx : and she never would have made him a good wife. And she eloped at last with that worthless Captain Rackstraw."

"What are you thinking about, Ar?" asked Leo.

He started from his reverie. He turned to her with a kind smile.

"About you, Leo," he said. But she shook her head.

"A story, Sir. You know it is. You are very pale and sad-looking to-day, Ar. Are you well? Have you been reading too much, keeping bad hours in London? You ought to have come down and led a steady life at Oakmere. Why, you're not going already, I'm sure. You have only sat here for two minutes yet."

"Yes, dearest, I must go now, indeed I must."

"Don't look so sad, or you'll make me sad too. You *must* go? Well, good-bye. But you'll come soon again? Very soon?"

"Very soon. Good-bye."

"And I shall ride over to see Mrs. Lomax, and Edie and Rosy, in a day or two."

He went out, walking rapidly. He pressed his hat upon his brows rather angrily. How desolate the country looked! what a dull road it was back to Oakmere Court, how cold and raw, and wretched the weather! His old, gay, glad, bright manner had quite gone from him to-day. He was certainly, as Leo had remarked, pale and sad-looking, and he bit his lips and frowned almost savagely as he breasted the cold gusts sweeping along the Oakmere road. He was so occupied with his thoughts, that he did not perceive that there was some one approaching him rapidly.

"Hullo, Arnold!" Arnold looked up and found Hugh Wood close to him.

"How are you, Hugh, old man?" he said, with something of a return to his old cheerfulness. "Why, I haven't seen you for this ever so long."

"No. I was in town at the commencement of term; but you were away, I suppose, for I didn't see anything of you. Bad weather, isn't it? But I can't stop indoors. I've been having a chat with Robin, and now I'm out for a constitutional before dinner. You've been up to the Chase, I suppose?" He looked down and began drawing on the ground with his foot, as he said, "By-the-bye, I have to congratulate you, I believe. I ought to have done it before I suppose. But I'm remiss, I know, about these sort of things. I hear that you are going to be married—at least so everyone says about these parts—to Miss Carr."

Arnold winced a little.

"Thank you," he said. "Well, yes. However, it won't be at present, at all events. And perhaps it's rather premature to be talking about it; only they will do that in the country. And you know the proverb, 'There's many a slip——'"

"I thought it was all settled," and Hugh looked at his friend rather curiously.

"Well, it is, in a sort of way; but many things may happen to prevent it. One can't be sure of anything. The lady may change her mind or——" but he stopped. It was hard to talk lightly of such a thing.

"Or you may change yours, I suppose you mean," thought Hugh Wood; but he did not say so.

"Well, I mustn't keep you in the cold. Good-bye, Arnold. Come up and see me at the rectory. The Lomaxes terrify me, or I would call at the Court. Good-bye. A merry Christmas to you. That's the right thing to say, I suppose."

And they parted.

"It's hard to help hating a very prosperous man," said Hugh Wood to himself as he strode on his way; "one feels injured and jarred, and shaken by contrast with him. And yet Arnold's a good fellow too. But he's a spoilt child of fortune, with more money than he knows what to do with: and now with more love, it seems! He can afford to treat her love as a trifle, possession of her as a chance thing or accident that does not much matter either way! Or does he suspect me, and talk like that to trick me? But no, he's above that. I ought to hate him if he should win her, not prizing her love, not giving his own wholly in return! No, that can't be. He *must* love her: and he's a friend, an old college chum, and he's honest, and good, and true, I'm sure. And he'd lend me any sum I needed twice over, if I only chose to ask him. But I couldn't do that; I couldn't to save my life."

Leo had grown thoughtful after Arnold had left her.

"There's something wrong with Arnold," she said, "I'm sure of it. I never saw him so before. He looks oppressed, dejected. What can papa have been saying to him? Has he been scolding him? But why? Why should he? I am the only person entitled to scold Arnold!" And a sunny smile gleamed over her face, to be followed by a look of extreme sadness. "Oh! if he should be tired of loving me!"

She turned quite pale at the thought. "No, no. I mustn't think that. I won't. I've no right to think that. Dear Arnold!"

But somehow the thought would return again and again to vex her.

"I won't tease myself thus. Let me do something to be quit of these fancies. Let me go to my poor little Baby Gill!"

CHAPTER XVI.

OAKMERE COURT.

T the date of her marriage to Francis Lomax of the Wafer Stamp Office, Georgina Page, only daughter of General Page, of Oakmere Court, Woodlandshire, was in full enjoyment of the reputation of being a beauty: she was quite the toast of the county. Lomax, in securing her as his wife, was regarded as a fortunate man, and received the congratulations accordingly of his relatives, the Chalkers. Some expectations, formed perhaps too hastily, had been disappointed. The bulk of the general's property had gone to his son, at the date of the wedding an Eton boy, home for the vacation, permitted to attend the ceremony in an "unattached" character, rejoicing in a round jacket, the whitest of trousers, and the gaudiest of cravats, and the stiffest of shirt-collars, his neck being garnished on that occasion with what used to be known as "stick-ups" for the first time in his life. People talked of Lomax as a good "manager," however. He was said to be always busy "looking after" the affairs of his brother-in-law: and it did not occur to anybody that he neglected to care for his own interests meanwhile. Georgina was likely to have some power over a brother so many years her junior, and though this was liable to decrease as he advanced in life, it was sufficient in the first instance to strengthen her husband's position considerably. Thus, for some years Mr. Lomax had found himself nominally yearly tenant of Oakmere Court, the property of his brother-in-law, in reality fixed there with tolerable security and in possession of considerable power, either by direct usurpation or unavoidably from the absence, indifference, and confidence in him, of his brother-in-law. It was a whispered complaint throughout the neighbourhood that Mr. and Mrs. Lomax gave themselves all the airs of the absolute proprietors of the estate.

The claims of Mrs. Lomax to be ranked as a beauty perhaps could be no longer fairly substantiated. Her features

15

were not less perfectly proportioned and regular, but an un
pleasant rigidity had seized upon them ; her once delicate
and transparent complexion had faded now into a uniform
dull waxen tint ; and the rich flaxen tresses had thinned,
receding from her forehead, always inclined to be over
prominent, and under conditions of greater exposure looking
disagreeably hard and bony, with a tendency to shine as
though it had been glazed.   People talked of her more as a
"charming woman" and less as a beauty.   For she was
decidedly clever, adroit in manner, with that social requisite
(the comfort of which has been a little overrated)—a flow of
conversation.   She was certainly accomplished, understood
dress thoroughly, and before her marriage could play Thal-
berg's fantasias upon the pianoforte, and produce really
creditable imitations of Prout in water-colours.   She had
written stanzas to her sleeping children, and a poem, only a
very limited number of copies printed, strictly for private cir-
culation, and called "Como Revisited."   By-and-by as she
left her youth still further behind her, and her artificial
manner of thought, speech and action, grew upon her, she
became more and more self-possessed and self-venerative, with
an inclination to languor of spirits and an indolent, almost
insolent, disdain of effort or of interest on behalf of anything.
Society now began to speak of her as "an elegant woman."
Her light blue eyes were very glassy now — never knew
dilation, never gained colour or sparkle from exhilaration,
the specks of pupils remained ever the merest specks.   She
complained of her nerves, was fond of the sofa in her
boudoir, and of "putting her feet up," and shrank at the
slightest noise.   In fact she was a good deal like many
other "elegant women," who as a rule I find are generally
nearing middle-age, and not over-pleased with the fact, rejoicing in weak nerves and very delicate health, inclined to
be, to use a harsh word, "scraggy," and leading their hand-
maidens very desperate lives indeed.

Mrs. Lomax was suffering from what she called, as though
she were the original inventor and vested with patent rights
in regard to it, and what was consequently known throughout the household as, "one of her headaches."   She looked
especially old and cross and plain on days when she was
thus afflicted ; people had to be especially careful in their

manner towards her and in their conversation, and to be particular as to the noiselessness of their footfalls; the existence of her maid became more than ever a burden to her, and the children were heedful to put as much space as possible between themselves and their parent. She reclined upon the luxurious sofa in her boudoir, a very handsome room, one of the additions made to the Court under the auspices of her husband. She was shrouded in shawls: she was trying to read, she said, one of a large parcel of books just received from a London circulating library: but she was often obliged to close her eyes and to pat her forehead with a handkerchief well steeped in Eau-de-Cologne. Probably there was nothing very serious the matter with Mrs. Lomax. Dr. Hawkshaw was not her medical attendant. She had seen him once or twice; but she conceived him to be so extremely unrefined, so very wanting in manner, that she really could not, she *could not*, whatever might be the consequences, consult him upon her state of health. Otherwise it is probable that the doctor would have outspoken his opinion pretty sturdily, and prescribed a strong pill which would have put to flight the headache in a very brief time. But there was something "elegant" about her invalid condition, which perhaps made Mrs. Lomax rather nurse her headaches, treasuring them as evidences of birth, and breeding, and culture, as other people cherish pedigrees, diplomas, and examiners' certificates.

"How are you now, Georgy dear," asked Mr. Lomax in a soft voice, touching gently one of her thin, veiny, sallow, white hands.

"A little better, I think, Frank, dearest," she answered with a wan smile, "but I'm but a poor creature, a very poor creature."

The manner of the husband and wife towards each other was a little remarkable. It did not seem to result so much from affection as from a thorough understanding between them. It was scrupulously, studiously polite, with indeed all the outward seeming of tenderness; certain people had at one time even manifested an inclination to set up Mr. and Mrs. Lomax as quite pattern husband and wife. Indeed, they had probably never known what it was to suffer from those differences of opinion commonly known as "tiffs"

15—2

which (I am given to understand) are not unusual in the married state; they had probably never used a harsh word, nor so much as a severe tone, in addressing each other, and yet I fancy this did not arise from the intensity of their mutual regard, but from an extreme and ingrained reverence for the regulations of society : their manner in seclusion was precisely the same as in public, but more from their devotion to the opinion of the world than from any extraordinary cordiality existing between them.   They would as soon have thought of rudeness in private as of bickering in public, or as of eating peas with aid from their knives, or of being helped twice to soup.   It is possible that they were too much oc-cupied with their social duties to have any room or time for the cultivation of more domestic cares and regards.   As it was, their bearing was irreproachable : only it had all the rigid regularity of machine lace, which for all the perfectness of its fashioning is, as we all know, so much less esteemed than the hand-made article : only that a little homeliness, even roughness now and then, would have made it seem so much more natural and so much more valuable accord-ingly.   How estimable in the eyes of Leontes was the statue of Hermione ! but when he took it by the hand, found it was not stone he touched, but true flesh and blood —a woman—and crying, "Oh, she's warm !" strained her to his heart, don't you think he was possessed of some-thing more precious than a whole glyptotheca crammed with art treasures? Well, there was a certain suspicion of stoniness, for all its perfectness, about the regard of Mr. and Mrs. Lomax for each other, which one never could get alto-gether quit of : it never seemed, somehow, able to become flesh and blood, to rise above a particularly low temperature. Yet for all I have said it certainly does seem hard to find fault with people for not quarrelling, and I beg therefore that no-body will run away with the notion that I appraise a hus-band's affection for his wife in proportion to the number of times that he knocks her down.

"What is that noise I hear? has anyone called?   I hear the sound of talking."   And Mrs. Lomax closed her eyes with a wearied look, as though the noise, slight and distant, as of conversation some rooms off, were quite too much for her.

"Yes," Mr. Lomax answered, " the children are a little

noisy, and I can't very well stop them. Leo is here : she came over from the Chase on horseback. I told her I was afraid you would hardly be able to see her."

" Really, I fear I am scarcely equal to it."

" No, dearest, it were better not. I must forbid any needless exertion. It is of no great moment ; she is very happy in the drawing-room, talking to the children. Unfortunately, Arnold has but this moment gone out, to call at the Hoopers'."

" Dear, dear, why will he mix himself up with those people ? What a dreadful thing is a love of low society ! And I very much fear that it grows upon him. I must really make an effort. Mrs. Carr has already some cause of complaint against me, I believe ; I have been out on two occasions when she called. If I deny myself now, they might make a distinct grievance out of the matter, and I should be extremely sorry if any coolness between the families were to arise on my account, though I am sure I take no pleasure in the society of that spoiled child, Leonora."

" If you really feel equal to it, perhaps on Arnold's account——"

" For that matter I never have had, and I never will have anything to do with the engagement."

" It's an advantageous one for Arnold," Mr. Lomax suggested.

" Arnold might have done better, I think. Of course the origin of these Carrs won't bear even thinking about."

" Well, it's a little too late to consider that now, dearest. I'll tell her that you'll see her ; she can come in here. Be sure you don't over-exert yourself, Georgy, and don't unwrap or you may take cold."

And he left the room to return presently with Leo Carr. This duty executed, Mr. Lomax withdrew to the library ; he remembered that he had not quite finished *The Times.* The Whitehall offices were closed for the Christmas holidays ; on such occasions Mr. Lomax, perhaps in common with other Government officials similarly situated, had rather a difficulty in knowing what to do with himself, and in getting through the day.

" I'm sorry to hear you're so poorly this morning, Mrs.

Lomax," said Leo, entering; "but there's no harm, I suppose,
for all that, in wishing you a merry Christmas."

"Thank you, dear, the compliments of the season, of
course," Mrs. Lomax murmured, half closing her eyes, and
the two ladies kissed in rather a cool and ceremonial
manner.

They didn't like each other, it may be stated; but then
under such a circumstance kissing is considered more than
ever indispensable. They did not like each other. Leo
had tried hard to attach herself to Mrs. Lomax, was careful
always to speak of her as "dear Mrs. Lomax," and to think
kindly and fondly of her, for was she not *his* sister? (For
loving *one*, we are anxious to cover the whole family of that
one with our affection, stretching it out like a sheet of india-
rubber, and wrapping them all well round in it. Of course
the collapse comes, and the love shrinks and dwindles into
being hardly enough for the original *one*. Do you remember
how friendly you were with *her* brother; how you tried to
like him, and not to think and know him to be the out-
rageous snob he really was? Well, well, that's all over now.)
But even Leo with her full large heart found the task
difficult; the more love she poured on that cold, hard,
polished surface, the less of it seemed to adhere, the more
it all came slipping off again. And Mrs. Lomax's sentiments
in regard to her brother's betrothed, were not very kindly;
if for no other reason, perhaps because she was jealous of
her. Next to the Marchioness of Southernwood, who, however, was some miles distant, Mrs. Lomax had been inclined
to rate herself as the most influential lady in that division
of the county. But Leo with her wealth and beauty was
gaining unconsciously upon her. If the fact was apparent
to no one else, it was apparent to Mrs. Lomax. Her
importance was dwindling before Leo, like a lump of ice in
presence of the sun.

Leo looked very pretty. With a flush of health upon her
round soft brunette cheeks. Her eyes very brightly gleaming under her dainty, jaunty little hat and curled feather.
A trim collar turned over her crimson neck-ribbon, and a
handsome riding-habit fitting perfectly the charming outline
of her lissom graceful figure. She looked smaller than ever,
perhaps; as it generally happens to small people in riding-

habits to look, but strangely bewitching — though Mrs.
Lomax did not feel the force of the spell, or love the little
lady any the better for her beauty.

"I am very sorry Arnold should have gone out," said
Mrs. Lomax, telling a story very probably. "He should
have known that you were likely to call."

"Yes, it's a great pity, but it's my fault," said Leo,
simply; "I ought to have told him I thought of calling to-
day. Even now he may come in, in time to ride back with
me."

"He's very thoughtless. I'm sure I do all I can to make
him attend more to the *convenances* of the engagement he
has entered into. But it is of little use, I fear; I don't
know what's come to Arnold lately. Haven't you
noticed, Leo, that of late he has looked pale and thin—
anxious ?"

"Yes. He is not looking well. There is certainly a
change in him of late. But I have forborne speaking to
him on the subject. It may be some trifling annoyance after
all. Perhaps I have no right to enquire into it."

"Ah !" and Mrs. Lomax sighed heavily, " years ago what
a good frank open-hearted boy he was. He had few con-
cealments from me then. I used to think he had a great
affection for me—great reliance upon me—great confidence
in me then. I know he was coming to me for ever for
advice under some trifling difficulty, or for assistance, or
for comfort under some petty vexation that yet seemed
very hard to bear. But men are always disappointing the
expectations of those who knew them as children. I do
trust that such may not be the case with my own darlings.
Now all is changed. I see little of Arnold. We have
none of the long cosy confidential chats we used to have
together as brother and sister, now, how long ago ! We
are estranged in some way. How or why I am totally
at a loss to conceive. But the knowledge that such is
the fact is very sad—very painful to me."

It is questionable whether Mrs. Lomax was not inclined
to exaggerate the terms of intimacy and unreserve formerly
subsisting between herself and her brother. At the conclusion of her remarks she raised her handkerchief to her
eyes ; not that there were any tears requiring removal, but

that the action under the circumstances of the case seemed
to be a fitting one, and suggestive of pathos, and moved
feelings in an agreeable way.   Leo said nothing; she looked
serious, and gazed upon the carpet, following with her riding
whip the lines of its arabesque pattern.

"I thought once, Leo, that you would have supplied my
place ; and I confess the thought was a source of comfort to
me—more, of pleasure.   I hoped that you would have
secured the confidence denied to me.   How important it is
that men should have some one to confide in—some one to
whom they can certainly look for sympathy and support.
How great an aid to them !   What an advantage to them,
that haven of refuge and safety—a loving heart !   How
valuable the knowledge that whatever the world may say or
do, whatever may happen, *there* they can ever repose, sure of
sympathy, and tenderness, and affection !"

Mrs. Lomax again removed imaginary tears.   Leo glanced
at her for a moment, something suspiciously perhaps.   Indeed there was a want of honest ring about the tones of her
voice; there was something that suggested affectation and
overcharge; it was hard to question the counterfeit; while
yet it was equally difficult to accept it as genuine.   Leo
remained silent.   Perhaps not knowing exactly what it was
expected of her to say; perhaps unwilling to break the
thread of Arnold's sister's monologue.

" I thought—I hoped, that you would have been all this
to Arnold," Mrs. Lomax resumed, and then paused, evidently
looking for some remark from her visitor.

"And why should I not be all this ?" Leo asked, rather
drily.   Mrs. Lomax shook her head.

"I don't question your desire to serve Arnold, dear,"
Mrs. Lomax said in her sweetest tones ; very busy the while,
as it seemed, searching for the mark in the corner of her
handkerchief; "I don't question your desire to serve him to
the utmost of your power.   I don't dispute the truth of your
love for him——"

" There is no need to do that, I think," Leo interrupted,
quietly, but her lips drew closely together and her eyebrows
approached her eyes.   Mrs. Lomax glanced apprehensively,
but she was reassured by the apparent calmness of her companion, and proceeded.

"Good wishes and true love will go a great way," she said, "but——"

"You mean that I am otherwise incompetent?" For Mrs. Lomax began to pick her way through her words rather particularly.

"Oh! no, dear. I assure you not at all. But perhaps it does not rest so much with the woman in these cases, as with the man; it depends less upon her faith and trust in him than his in her, and——"

"Do you mean that Arnold does not love me?" Leo asked. There was no sign of agitation in her voice, the question was very quietly put. But she turned her brilliant eyes full upon the face of Mrs. Lomax. She left off toying with her whip, and her small hands clenched; and while she waited for an answer to her inquiry, the riding-habit in the neighbourhood of her bosom was somewhat stirred as though her breathing were short.

"No, dear, I should be very sorry to say that, very sorry," Mrs. Lomax answered, languidly, after a moment. "Arnold has known you quite from a child, and always had an extreme regard for you—a great admiration for you, as indeed he could hardly help having." She had while speaking kept her eyes averted from Leo. She looked to see if any favourable effect had followed this compliment; but Leo's face remained unmoved. "I couldn't say that Arnold does not love you. But—" and she hesitated, perhaps not seeing what was to follow her sentence, even if she could perceive the end of it, or rather anxious that Leo might create a diversion by interrupting. But the young lady remained very quiet and silent.

"You see, Leo," she began again, "in our world—perhaps it is a subject for regret, but with that we have nothing to do just now; it's past our altering—in our world there is something more to be considered in marriage than mere love. The position of the parties for instance. When we first became aware of the nature of the engagement subsisting between Arnold and yourself we all hastened, I'm sure, to give it every possible sanction and encouragement; it was a great source of congratulation to us all. There was nothing to be said against it. The children of neighbours and friends, loving and marrying was really charming and delightful and all that, under the circumstances of the case, could possibly be desired. You were both rich. Arnold was without ambition—seemed to have no particular views in life—there appeared to be no possible reason why you should not marry and settle down in this quiet country place, and live upon your estates, very happy, indeed, ever after— quite like people in a fairy tale, quite."

She seemed pleased with her illustration, and lingered over it as though it left a pleasant flavour in her mouth. Then she sat up on the sofa, unsettling some of her shawls, and with her glassy eyes intent upon the polished steel bars of the grate, she continued—

"But if the circumstances of the case have undergone a change: if Arnold has shown an inclination to emerge from obscurity—to quit the seclusion and retirement in which he has hitherto lived, and enter upon a public career; if, as I think, he has now determined to come before the world and devote to purposes of general utility the great talents he possesses; I confess, then, I should come to the conclusion that this marriage was not altogether propitious. I should be disposed to look unfavourably upon the chances of happiness resulting from it. I should begin to regret—and I say it I'm sure with extreme reluctance, even pain—but I should regret that he had not in fact looked for a wife in other quarters."

"You think he will have married beneath him?" said Leo.

"I should be sorry to use such an unfortunate selection of words; which, indeed, ill represent my meaning. But there are other inequalities than those of wealth and position; those of mind for instance. For of course, socially considered, you are on a par. That Arnold should come of an old county family is not a fact, I am sorry to say, that the world is disposed to lay much stress upon nowadays."

"But are not women generally the mental inferiors of their husbands?"

"It often happens so, dear, and perhaps it is as well that that should be the case. Still——"

"Still you think that I should be in his way, that I should interfere with his plans, hinder his advancement, perhaps?"

" I confess that I think you would not enhance his position. Mr. Carr has not cared to cultivate his interest with the county, although he has certainly a large stake in it. He has shrunk from all participation in political conflicts ; in short, my dear Leo, while I think you would be the admirable wife of a simple country gentleman, I fear you are hardly suited to be the partner of a statesman, and that I believe to be Arnold's true *métier*—such the part he aspires to play."

" You are, perhaps, right," Leo said, simply.

" I have offended you ? hurt you ? Pray forgive me if I have been too candid. I should be so sorry if——"

" Indeed not. I am obliged to you for speaking so openly, for explaining to me your views upon the matter."

" Yes, precisely, for after all they are only my views upon the matter. It is possible that they are not shared by Arnold."

" Certainly, that is possible."

" In matters of this kind it is often those who are the most interested who are the last to arrive at the real truth."

" But you think he *will* arrive at it—the truth as it appears to you ? Yes, and more : this depression he is labouring under, you think it results unconsciously to himself from his progress towards the truth, towards the discovery that he has entered into an unfortunate engagement ? "

" I think,—yes. I think very likely that may be as you say," and Mrs. Lomax hesitated, for there was something about the tone of Leo's voice that she did not quite understand.

" Thank you. Dear me, how long I have been here : papa will think me lost. Good-bye."

" Good-bye, my dearest Leo. Don't think too seriously of what I have been saying." Mrs. Lomax rose from the sofa to kiss her young friend with most effusive affection.

" I hope your headache will soon be better."

" Thank you, dearest, I'm sure you're very kind. Good-bye."

A few moments and there was heard the crunching patter of Leo's pony upon the gravel of the carriage drive. She pressed her hat tight upon her forehead, and plied her whip ever so little. The pony bounded off in a gallop along the road to Croxall Chase.

"She hates me, that woman," Leo said, through compressed lips. "Well, I'm afraid I don't love her very much. I'm glad I did not say all I thought of saying to her. I had to keep on muttering over and over, 'She's Arnold's sister, she's Arnold's sister,' or I don't know where I should have been. And she can doubt her brother!"

She sped along the road, a bright light in her eyes, a glorious colour in her cheeks, a stray tress of hair streaming out at the back of her head, and a very brave smile trembling along the lines of her red lips as she said,

"No; if all the world told me he was false, I'd believe him true. My dear old Ar!"

Almost involuntarily, by way of giving emphasis to her words, she plied the whip with unusual vigour, and the pony feeling he might have all his way, so as he did but go fast enough, went on with a rush.

"He loves me! he loves me!" she cried, exhilarated by the pace and the thought; "he has told me so a hundred times, and he can't lie, I know he can't. *He* lie! to *me!* It's not possible!"

She was quiet and calm again as the pony landed her at her father's gate.

"Certainly, though," she said to herself, "he is very sad and oppressed of late. I wonder why?"

Mrs. Lomax had forgotten her headache. For a long time a rather malign smile remained upon her face after Leo's departure; she seemed to be lost in a maze of pleasant thoughts, though still ostensibly engaged examining the mark of her name in a corner of her handkerchief.

Mr. Lomax emerged from the library. He held the newspaper in his hand, and looked a little red about the eyes, as though he had been asleep over it.

"How are you now, Georgy, dear? The poor head better? Has Leo gone?"

"Yes, dearest, she has gone. She bored me rather. And she's not nearly so nice-looking as she used to be."

Mr. Lomax sat down and stirred the fire with an air of

serious interest, as though stirring the fire were one of the events in a man's lifetime.

"By-the-bye, Frank, did it not at one time cross your mind that Carry Lomax, your niece, would have been a desirable match for Arnold?"

"I thought so once. Indeed I hinted as much to Arnold; but he didn't seem to admire her. It doesn't matter now much; she's engaged to Lord Mardale. I suppose the thing will come off early in the season."

"She's a clever girl, and I think she was inclined to like Arnold."

"I think she's quite clever enough to have got over by this time any foolish fancy of that sort."

"Do you know, Frank, I've been thinking about this engagement with Leo."

"Well, what about it?"

"Thinking that perhaps after all it may never come to anything. Nothing would surprise me less than to wake some morning and find the affair broken off."

"Why? Do you judge from something that Leo has said? Is there anyone else in the way, affecting either party?"

"Perhaps it is only my fancy, but it occurs to me that both are a little weary of the business, or, at least, Arnold is. You know he must have gone out this morning on purpose to avoid her."

"Do you think so? Surely that can hardly be the case. I'm sure Arnold would be very foolish if he suffered anything to put an end to the engagement. It's really a good match."

"Oh. I think if Arnold could be brought to appreciate his own advantages, he might look far higher for a wife."

"He could hardly get more money," said Mr. Lomax.

"He might secure a better position by far if he was to connect himself with a family of distinction."

"Yes, but for all that I happen to know that old Carr's money would be useful to him; particularly useful." And Mr. Lomax walked to the window. His wife followed him with her eyes. But the subject was allowed to drop.

CHAPTER XVII.

CHRISTMAS.

N town, over the regulation roast turkey and plum pudding and the prevailing melancholy of the Christmas dinner, it is the fashion to fancy that the country is the place in which the festive season should especially be passed; that the metropolitan dulness is there counterbalanced by a quite astounding cheerfulness. In the country, terribly oppressed by care, and with the additional discomfort of intenser cold, trying to consume a facsimile meal, a counterpart delusion prevails that town is particularly gay and brilliant and happy. Both are right so far as their own gloom is concerned.

Certainly Christmas at Oakmere Court was dull and tiresome enough. I have Arnold Page's warrant for so asserting. There was "no one but ourselves," as Mrs. Lomax expressed it. She would have preferred (at least she said so) to have invited many of their relations and friends from London, and have filled the old house with company. She always especially pitied, she said, the many young men of their acquaintance, who for various reasons would find themselves away from their families on Christmas Day. (I am not sure that these stray gentlemen are the ·most to be pitied of all people on that day. I have a notion that somehow they manage to enjoy themselves upon the whole pretty well, considering.) Mrs. Lomax would have liked to have celebrated Christmas in a thoroughly good and old-fashioned way. Lomax said nothing: probably he saw that there was no occasion to disturb himself; he was well acquainted with the established Government office plan of letting things take their course. Mrs. Lomax soon discovered that she was not equal to such an undertaking, and pleaded the state of her health. Certainly the state of her health was rather convenient to her than otherwise. It invariably prevented her going anywhere or doing anything she did not like. Especially it spared her the expense and trouble of receiving friends at home. I think there must be a good many ladies whose health is equally and conveniently delicate. They avail themselves of the hospitality of their friends, though quite unable "to receive" at home. They are "equal" to any number of balls and parties and dinners, provided always that none of these are required to be cele-brated within their own walls.

Mrs. Lomax was languid and weak during Christmas Day. She enjoyed immensely, however, the delightful discourse of the Rev. Purton Wood. "So appropriate, so nice and fitting," as she declared, "and full of poetry, especially to be appreciated by mothers;" and at intervals during the day she felt called upon, as it seemed, to be spasmodically festive, putting on spurts of cheerfulness, if we may describe her conduct in sporting phraseology. Lomax was bland and smiling and affable, chafing his white hands, and stirring the fires with the care of a surgeon at an operation. Perhaps the day was the most enjoyed by the young ladies home from Miss Bigg's seminary,—Edith and Rosy, who tried hard to persuade Uncle Arnold to romp with them, and to make more of the season, and to be a little more merry, and more like the Arnold Page he had been during former Christmas holidays. He had spoken to Leo for a few moments only as they came out of church.

Mr. Lomax carved the turkey to perfection, raising his white hands high over the bird.

Mr. Lomax was not usually liable to much exhilaration. He prided himself rather upon the evenness of his temper and spirits; but he was not indisposed to recognise the season as a fitting occasion for the relaxation of any extreme opinions upon the subject of becoming demeanour; to regard the holidays given to the functionaries of the Wafer Stamp Office as intended in some sort as an outlet for pent-up exuberance and suppressed emotion. He was particularly cheerful on Christmas morning: something more than blandly affectionate to his wife and children. "Aint master haffable, just," was the exclamation in the still-room and kitchen at Oakmere. He was chatty, even garrulous, as Arnold thought, who, voting him rather a bore, had escaped from the house after church to wander about the park until dinner-time. Mr. Lomax was certainly very talkative, and with something of the nervous restlessness of a man who keeps on talking to you, flying incessantly from topic to topic, to avoid possibly your suggesting some less agreeable subject. You know how the man converses who owes you money of which he is in momentary dread lest you should demand the repayment? Well, Mr. Lomax's manner of talking to Arnold was very like the manner of such a man.

When Mrs. Lomax and the children had withdrawn from the dining-room, he was less than ever likely to escape from the current of talk upon which he had permitted himself to be borne along. Arnold was inclined to be silent—moody even; it was not probable if left to himself, that he would have suggested any subject of conversation, agreeable or otherwise; but Mr. Lomax could not see that. So he was more than ever cheerful, quite enthusiastically so, bade Arnold draw his chair round to the fire, patted him on the shoulder, drank his health, blessed him, in an off-hand man-of-the-world sort of way, which was yet meant to be impressive; talked of his late father the general, with much nodding and shaking of the head to signify emotion, then jerked off to praising the wine, viewing it held up to the light of the roaring fire, smacking his lips. Everything that was possible having been said on that subject, he darted to another. He *would* talk; now it was of himself, and his position in the Wafer Stamp Office, and his chances of advancement. But he confessed to content: he had an excellent appointment, what more could he look for? True, he might aspire to the Cabinet, but was it worth his while? Yes: put it simply in that way, please, was it worth his while to surrender his present advantages for such a prospect? Not at present, at any rate. By-and-by he might think differently, especially with his daughters grown up and married, well married, and so his position strengthened. And then he proceeded to talk politics, and Arnold gaped (behind his hand) until the tears quite filled his eyes.

But, in fact, Mr. Lomax was rather fond of talking politics. He was famed for little addresses on the subject of his opinions, delivered blandly with cool cheerfulness after dinner. He entertained what may be called Government-office political opinions. He always gave vent to these as from an abstract point of view, levelling them at other people, as though, in fact, they concerned himself but in a very slight measure. "Yes," he would say, sharing in the after-dinner men's talk, helping himself to claret (he preferred it to port), "yes, but you must take care what you do; you must regard the tendencies of the age; and undoubtedly it is as you say, very justly, and I don't deny it, among the tendencies of the age, to introduce electoral reform, to extend your franchise. Well, then, I say extend your franchise if you will, only have a proper basis for your franchise; and how can you have that without a thorough re-adjustment of your taxation? Settle your fiscal reform, and then go to your electoral. And here again you must consider the tendencies of the age—undoubtedly these are in favour, I admit it, of direct taxation. When you tax, then, ought you not to enfranchise? Of course, my dear Sir, I'm quite aware that you are opening up a very grave, a very wide question. Very true: how can you finally adjust your taxation? how can you answer for those coming after you? That's very well put: but still it seems to me that you might do it by a reconsideration of your wafer stamp duty, a department of taxation with which, as you know, I am myself immediately connected. Now it does seem to me that in an extension of this tax, you might have found a very admirable economy of taxation. It is not equitably levelled at present, I admit; there are many inequalities, many evasions; still it is a tax that might be made to yield an enormous revenue. Everybody must use wafer stamps, they can't help it, my dear Sir. Try that claret," and so on.

He said little more than this ever in regard to his political convictions; but he elaborated and embroidered his original theme like a pianist playing a fantasia. Considered as political convictions, it will be noted that they might be adapted to the use of either side of the House. If there was a difference at all, I should say that it was in favour of the ministerialist.

Perhaps it was not to be greatly wondered at that Arnold Page wearied at last of this man's plausible, fluent, affable talk : became irritated, as a man might be by a tune, however pretty, played incessantly ; was prompted at last to do

16

anything to interrupt his brother-in-law. Starting as it were from a reverie, he said, abruptly—

"I did not intend to mention the subject to-day; but I don't know that there is any reason why the thing should be postponed : perhaps all that I have to say may as well be said now as at any other time."

"What is it, Arnold?" Mr. Lomax asked, rather anxiously.

"I wanted to speak to you about this projected mortgage with the Ostrich Insurance Company."

"Isn't it rather late to enter upon the subject? I say nothing about its being Christmas Day; of course I am always at your service. But, my dear Arnold, I *did* look forward to a little peace and quiet these holidays ; a little abstinence from business. I've been sticking to it pretty closely at Whitehall lately, I can tell you. But of course if this is something particular you wish to tell me, though I fancy Georgina will be expecting us in the drawing-room directly——"

"What I have to say will not take two minutes. It is simply this — the mortgage with the Ostrich must not proceed."

"Not proceed?" and Mr. Lomax raised his eyebrows to the highest point possible to them. "My dear Arnold, what are you saying ; not proceed ?"

"Not proceed," Arnold repeated, rather sternly.

"But, really, you quite surprise me. This is the most extraordinary thing I ever heard of ; *the* most extraordinary. I never in the whole course of my life met with so remarkable a change of opinion ; though surely, Arnold, it amounts to infirmity of purpose : absolutely surprising, quite sur—prising."

And Mr. Lomax stood up with his back to the fire and began to straddle and prance and plunge about after his good-tempered, jocose manner, so often practised on the official hearthrug at Whitehall.

"It may be as you say. But I have quite made up my mind now. The mortgage shall not go on. I shall get rid as quickly as I can of the mining, railway, and other shares I hold. I have seen reason to change my opinion. I do not scruple to confess as much. I shall resign my seat at the boards of the Dom Ferdinando and other companies. I find myself in difficulties. I must retrench. Economy and good management it seems to me will do great things; and this Oakmere property will surely right itself in a very short time."

The colour faded somewhat from the cheeks of Mr. Lomax. He resumed his seat: he turned his eyes away from Arnold as he said in rather a strained voice, his fingers fidgeting and weaving themselves together,

"I should say that thirty years ago old Mr. Carr was an excellent man of business. I dare say there was hardly to be found in the whole City of London or out of it, a more competent man. But time works great changes. The world has rolled on and left good old Mr. Carr a long way behind, clinging to opinions and prejudices, and mistaken notions of the past. I don't wonder, my dear Arnold, that his views upon questions of business do not happen to be precisely *ours*. I see to whom you have been talking."

And Mr. Lomax ended with rather a triumphant smile, and he nodded many times to the grate, as though he were on very friendly terms with it indeed.

"I did not wish to introduce his name into the discussion," Arnold said, resolutely; "and I should not have done so. However, I am not ashamed to say that I owe it to Mr. Carr that I have taken up with different opinions upon these matters. I have, as you say, been talking with him—my father's good old friend, whose only wish has been to do me a service and a kindness. His notions may be old-fashioned—gone by—out of date. But I share them. He can have no possible interest to serve——"

"My dear Arnold," Mr. Lomax interrupted, rather warmly, "I hope you don't mean to assert—to insinuate for one moment that I have had any object to serve in giving you the advice I have given? And, after all, you are not a child, and you must know that you have acted entirely upon your own judgment. I have certainly furnished explanations, and have been at some pains to make clear to you the existing state of things, and have not hesitated to point out the course I should myself have pursued had I been in your situation. But beyond this I have done little or nothing ; pray be careful to recollect as much. I hope, therefore, you don't plan to bring any charge against *me*, even if matters should not turn out quite equal to my, I may say *our* anticipations."

"There is no need to enter upon that subject," Arnold said, calmly. "I think it is sufficient for the present to state that I desire to make certain changes ; to stay all further proceedings in reference to this mortgage ; to stop all the building projects, which, it seems to me, are seriously damaging this house and grounds—to reinstate those of my father's old servants who have been, I think, somewhat too hastily dismissed. I shall again place myself in the hands of the family solicitors. I shall reside here a great deal more than I have hitherto done ; and I think you must at once make up your mind to terminate your residence here, and prepare to re-occupy your house in town."

There was silence for some moments. Mr. Lomax could not conceal an air of mortification and anger. He bit his lips and began drawing on the carpet with the toe of his boot.

"These are indeed changes, Arnold," he said at length in a low voice. "I hope you may find that you are not adopting them too hastily. I hope you may not have cause to regret them."

He stopped, perhaps expecting Arnold to say something of a more hopeful character. But Arnold did not speak. Mr. Lomax gradually felt his old confidence and ease of manner returning. But his hand shook a little as he helped himself to claret : and he said,

"However, we must talk more upon this subject at another time. It embraces too many considerations, it is altogether too vast to be disposed of at a moment's notice. I'll make a point of going all through it again with you very carefully. Now suppose we go and see what Georgy and the children are doing in the drawing-room."

"One thing more I should mention. The shares I hold ; some of them purchased of you—I presume these can now be taken into the market and sold ?"

Mr. Lomax was silent for some moments and looked rather grave as he said,

"Well, there was an understanding that nothing of that

kind should be done for some time ; a sort of pledge was given that those things should not be brought into the market. I'm afraid the present will be found a very bad time for selling. A sale now to any extent would seriously damage the prospects of these undertakings."

" I would sooner incur a sacrifice than hold these shares any longer."

" Of course," said Mr. Lomax, rather insolently, " if you *will* take up with Quixotic notions—run away with absurd and romantic sort of opinions, you must be prepared to submit to sacrifices—even large sacrifices in maintaining them. That is only to be expected. If you part with these shares you will of course do so just now at a very considerable loss. Some of them I see are quoted at quite nominal prices. I should seriously advise your contriving to hold them, for the present at any rate. That will not be agreeable to you ? Well, but it is only fair I should submit to you whether there is not something due to your colleagues in these undertakings — your fellow shareholders. Are you entitled to depreciate *their* property—to endanger the success of their scheme, by what I must really call a very capricious line of conduct—to play fast and loose with enterprises of really very grave importance? I think there should be some chivalry, and generosity, and honour, even in what appear to be simply matters of business."

" I will consider the objections you urge against my dealing with the shares of which I have unfortunately become the proprietor. At present, I admit, I don't entirely appreciate their force. It seems to me that my co-proprietors would not hesitate to sell, if it seemed good to them. It doesn't occur to me that shareholders are often disposed to consider each other in such matters. I thought that the City rule always was to sell at the highest price and buy at the lowest ; and regard little else besides ? "

" I admit," said Mr. Lomax, with something of a blush, ' that such has been the ordinary way of dealing with matters of this kind. But one doesn't expect gentlemen of property and position to be eager to avail themselves of such practices. I confess I see a certain amount of unfairness in abandoning your partners, for such these people are, strictly speaking, at the present moment. It is very well for rats to leave, as we are informed they do, ships that are sinking——"

"Do you mean that these undertakings are failing?"

"The present time, as I have said, is not very favourable for speculations of this kind."

"Speculations?" Arnold repeated, gloomily.

But Mr. Lomax continued as though he had not heard him.

"Things are flat in the City; decidedly flat. There are even the first drops as of a coming storm—what is known in commercial circles as a panic," and Mr. Lomax shivered in spite of himself. "I hope and I believe that it will pass over, that all will yet be well. If you are determined to get out of these things at all risks, why so it must be. You must be prepared, however, to pay for your sudden change of opinion; we will go further into the details some other time. Now for coffee."

"Stay; this mortgage with the Ostrich——"

"Well, it is a little too late in the day to take exception to that," Mr. Lomax said, with some hesitation.

"You mean that it must go on?"

"I mean that it is already completed."

"Completed?"

"Yes; don't you remember signing the deeds the other day?" Mr. Lomax put the question to the grate in rather a hoarse voice.

"I remember nothing of the kind. Stay; those parchments I signed," and Arnold placed himself in front of the fire to intercept the looks of his brother-in-law—"you said that they were the new leases, at increased rentals, of the Manor and Moor Farms—that the old leases fell in this quarter-day; surely you said so?"

"You must have fancied that I said so. I mentioned, I remember, the circumstance of those leases falling in, but not in reference to the deeds you signed—hardly on the same day, if I recollect rightly: and my memory is very good: a servant of the Government, a man holding the appointments I do, is, indeed, obliged to have a good memory."

"And those deeds?"

"One of them was a mortgage of Oakmere." Mr.

Lomax's voice trembled, nearly failed him : he was barely audible.

"And the title deeds of the estate ? "

" You signed an order to the bankers to deliver the title deeds into the hands of the trustees of the insurance company, after the repayment to the bankers of a small advance made by them some time ago now, upon the security of the title deeds; you may remember I mentioned the subject to you. The Ostrich now hold the only mortgage upon the property."

Mr. Lomax jerked out his explanation, such as it was, hurriedly, nervously, with considerable effort; less, as it seemed, in reply to Arnold's questions than to his stern face and angry glances.

" You have tricked me," Arnold said, calmly, after a pause.

" My dear Arnold ! " Mr. Lomax jumped up, holding out his white hands in a deprecatory manner.

" You have tricked me—cruelly, shamefully."

" Don't insult me, don't talk to me like that. I won't have it." He assumed a blustering, fierce tone, but he trembled visibly.

" Sit down."

" I won't have it—not from you—not from any man. How dare you, Sir——"

" Sit down."

In spite of himself, almost, Mr. Lomax found himself obeying his brother-in-law : he resumed his seat, with restless frightened eyes, with shaking hands. There was silence for some moments, during which he tried to pour himself out a glass of wine, but he spilt half of it, leaving a great red puddle on the white table-cloth, and he stained his white shirt front in lifting the half-filled glass to his lips.

" Why do you speak to me like this ? " this time in more of a whining tone. He grew more and more restless and uneasy under the long silence that was prevailing. But his courage had left him, with his old jaunty manner. " Why do you address such words to me ? "

" You have tricked me. More : you have robbed me." Arnold's hands were tightly clenched, his lips compressed, his brows knit, his whole expression grim and threatening. "You have robbed me."

"Robbed! Don't say that," Mr. Lomax whined.

"What has become of the money received from the Ostrich Insurance Company?"

Mr. Lomax hesitated.

"It was paid in to your account at the banker's," he said, slowly.

Arnold started up. He took a letter from his pocket.

"Explain this then—a letter received this morning from the bank requesting my attention to the fact that my account has been now some time largely overdrawn. Why is this?"

Mr. Lomax drooped. His hair fell—he roused himself with an effort.

"Some mistake, I think," he muttered.

There was a strange smile of contempt upon Arnold's face.

"I bank at the same house," Mr. Lomax went on, in a low voice; "it's possible, just possible, that our moneys have somehow got entangled. I'll look to it the first thing in the morning; indeed I will. Some mistake, of course: the money must have been paid in to my account. The first thing in the morning I'll go to them."

"And I, to consult a solicitor," said Arnold.

"My dear Arnold." Mr. Lomax clasped his hands with a look of agony.

"You've robbed me."

"Don't, don't. For God's sake, don't expose me, don't expose me;" he sunk upon his knees, his white moist face shining in the firelight, his hair quite damp from fear. "I'll do all I can, indeed I will. Give me time, only give me time, and don't, don't expose me." The head of the Wafer Stamp Office presented rather a lamentable spectacle just at that moment, trembling, livid, on his knees before his brother-in-law.

"Tell me," said Arnold, sternly, "does Georgina know of this? Speak the truth."

"No, no, indeed not, not a word of it. She does not even suspect. Don't be harsh with me, Arnold; for Georgina's sake, for the children's, don't expose me. I'll do all I can.

It's not, perhaps, so bad as you think. Part of the money was owing to me, indeed it was, for the shares, you remember. It's not so bad as you think."

" It's worse than you dream of," Arnold muttered.

" For God's sake, don't be harsh with me."

" Get up ; don't kneel to me." He turned away as Mr. Lomax arose, steadying himself by the chair, the mantel-piece. " Ruin, ruin, absolute ruin !" Arnold said, with a groan.

There was a knock at the door, and little Rosy burst into the room, crying aloud in her pretty shrill child's tones,

" Why, papa, why, Uncle Ar, why, what a long time you've been. We've been waiting for you to come in to coffee for ever so long. And, Uncle Ar, you promised to do some drawings for me after dinner. What a shame of you not to come sooner !"

" We're coming now, Rosy," said Arnold kindly, and he lifted the little girl up and kissed her.

" How strong you are," Rosy cries out; " aint I very heavy ?"

" Run and tell mamma we shall be in the drawing-room directly," says Mr. Lomax, and Rosy runs off.

" You'll not tell Georgina ?" and Mr. Lomax turns im-ploringly to Arnold.

" No, perhaps not," and Arnold follows Rosy.

" Have some pity ; don't expose me. I'll do all I can ; indeed, indeed, I will ; Mr. Lomax keeps hoarsely whisper-ing long after Arnold has passed out of hearing.

Mrs. Lomax utters languid expostulations at their delay in coming to the drawing-room. Mr. Lomax has been some minutes after Arnold, who fancies he detects a slight odour of brandy hanging about the Government official as he passes him to stir the fire laboriously after his manner.

" How cold it is changing the room," he says, rubbing his hands, and stooping down over the grate. In the red glow thrown upon his face by the fire, his extreme paleness is not visible. Gradually he recovers himself; his jauntiness is a little spasmodic; there is hardly the customary self-possession about his cheerfulness, but he is tolerably calm now ; his hands tremble less, he is studiously polite to his wife ; even more than usually playful with his children. He looks through a book of comic illustrations with Edith, and adds to her amusement by the exceeding drollery of his remarks. Mrs. Lomax reads her novel by fitful snatches, stopping now and then to talk lazily, to reproach her daughters for their too great noise, especially to remonstrate with Rosy loudly crowing at the very funny drawings that Arnold is executing for her in pen and ink, or to yawn terribly, pressing her thin fingers upon her high bony forehead, and complaining of her poor head.

The children withdraw for the night, Arnold quits the room. He will go and smoke a cigar somewhere, he says, before he turns in.

"Good-night, dearest brother," says Mrs. Lomax affectionately, and she kisses him; "be sure you don't take cold."

The kisses of brothers and sisters are notoriously lukewarm at best. In the present instance no exception presented itself to that general rule. And yet Mrs. Lomax felt her hand pressed kindly by her brother, with, as it seemed, more than usual kindness and intention.

"Dear Arnold," she says, perhaps in more genuine tones than she has employed for some time. Recollection may have taken her back to a past when unalloyed love for a child brother was very warm and tender and glowing in her breast, long before any notion about her being a beauty, or a charming or an elegant woman, any ambition for the applause of the world, or desire to take high rank in society, had disturbed her head or hardened her heart.

"Arnold is not well," she said to her lord afterwards in the seclusion of their chamber; "I never saw him looking so worn and thin. I wonder what can be the matter with him. I think there must be something on his mind. Have you any idea, Frank, what it can be?"

"No, Georgina," Mr. Lomax answered: "I haven't indeed, unless it's the cold: the winter does not agree at all with some people."

"I don't see what he can have to worry him," the lady continued, "unless he has begun to tire a little of his engagement with little Leo Carr. I should not be very much surprised—nor very sorry either. Do you think, Frank, he can have seen anybody in town that he likes better than Leo? do you fancy there can be anything wrong with the engagement on that account? Do you think *that* can be the cause of his looking so poorly?"

"No, my love. I hardly think that can be so;" and the subject was not pursued further.

"I've weathered a good many storms; I think I shall weather this," Mr. Lomax murmured to himself as he drew the bedclothes well round him and calmly drifted to sleep.

Arnold had returned to the dining-room. He unfastened the shutters, threw open one of the windows, and stepped into the garden.

"I can't breathe in the house," he said; and soon the red star formed by the lighted end of his cigar was to be seen passing many many times up and down the garden paths. It was bitterly cold, but he did not seem to heed it. Possibly he was kept warm by his anger, his indignation, and his passionate regrets.

"Certainly Georgina must be considered," he said, repeating the phrase over and over again. "Yes, I am bound to consider her, and her poor children. It is not right that the punishment should fall upon them. The fool I have been! Why did I ever listen to this man? I might have known at once, I did know, that he was false—a hypocrite, a plausible scoundrel. But it's little good calling names now; there is other work to be done." He strode up and down the walk. There was not a sound to be heard but the crunching of his own footsteps upon the gravel. It was a bitter cold night, without wind; the leafless boughs of the trees barely stirred.

"Ruin, absolute ruin! He does not know the cruel wrong he has done me. It is not for money alone, though that is bad enough, but to be tricked like this, and *to lose her!* It is clear to me now. Mr. Carr must have known more even than he told. I must lose her. I am not worthy of her, I must lose her. Heaven! is it to be borne? Dear Leo! I have never felt till now how deeply I love you, how dear you are to me! It will break my heart to give you up. But—but it must be so. I cannot hold you to the engagement. I have no right to ask you to share the fortune of a ruined man, a spendthrift—so I shall seem to the world. No, I am bound in honour not to do this. To be accused of marrying for money! of paying my debts with my wife's portion. I little knew how near old Carr was to the truth when he used these words. How I have fooled away my good fortune. I have only myself to blame. What a trifler I must seem to all, even in my love. Leo will never know how fondly I have loved her. I have so shrunk from expression of my feelings, so toyed with my passion, as though there could lurk something ridiculous about a great, true, honest love, as indeed mine is for Leo. I know it now. The dear little bird, she has stolen into my heart, nestling there, until she has made it hers for ever; and now to lose her through my own cursed folly and indolence, and taking things for granted, and hatred of trouble and exertion of any kind. The money might go and welcome, so far as I care, but that its loss renders me unfit to claim Leo's hand. I am to do nothing; matters are to rest as they are. I am not to remind her of her plighted word. In other words, I am to let her love for me gradually fade and die out. I am to do nothing to keep it alive. While a dozen other suitors are at her feet, bewildering her with their vows and protestations, and turning away her heart from me! I am bound in honour to submit to this, to sit still and see her gradually ebb from me. To do nothing, while, as Phil Gossett would say, my engagement sloughs away."

He smiled very sadly as he spoke.

He re-entered the house.

So passed Christmas Day at Oakmere Court.

CHAPTER XVIII.

ARNOLD'S RIDE.

RNOLD obtained but snatches of fitful, feverish rest. He was haunted by terrible dreams; he awoke in paroxysms of alarm, to lie a long time awake, revolving all the painful thoughts of the previous day. At last it became evident to him that he was now awake, beyond all possibility of going to sleep again for many hours. He tossed about on the bed, rolled his head from side to side in search of a cool place on the pillow : at last he could bear it no longer. It was quite dark, a cold winter's morning : but his head was burning hot. He was seized with a longing to be out of doors again. He got up and dressed, passed quietly down stairs, through the back part of the house into the stables.

He soon found old Williams, his father's groom. Williams seemed to require less rest than any others of the household; he was the last to retire at night; he was the first to appear in the morning. He was going his round as he called it, smoking his first pipe. He was too thoroughly English a servant to manifest any surprise at seeing his young master even at so early an hour. He pulled his scanty forelock of hair, passing his hand over his furrowed forehead; his small sharp eyes sparkled with pleasure.

" It does one good to see you about the stables again, Sir," he said, taking his pipe from his mouth.

Arnold nodded to him kindly.

" How's the asthma, William ? " Arnold asked.

" Well, Sir, I expect it's as well as it ever will be, thank you, Sir."

" Give me a light, Williams."

The old man was eager to comply, flattered by the request. He shielded the bowl of his pipe with his brown horny hands, and drew at his pipe until the tobacco was all a-glow, crimsoning his palms, and patching his face with light. It was quite a little illumination in the dark dense winter morning. Arnold lighted his cigar.

"I'm going out; I'll ride the roan mare, I think."

"Take the black, Sir, he's in prime fettle. Mr. Lomax has been riding the roan, but he don't give the mare a chance, and he don't work her half enough; in fact, the stables is going to rack and ruin for want of work. Mrs. Lomax has a'most given up riding, I think; you'll like the black, Sir, I warrant you will."

"Very well, Williams, as you please."

And Williams disappeared to shout, "Here, you Joe," to some assistant slumbering in one of the lofts. There was soon to be seen the wan light of a lantern glimmering about the stables, and casting ghostly rays of light on the walls of the yard; then the clattering of wooden-soled boots, and presently the ring of iron-shod hoofs, as a beautiful black hunter was brought out.

"Wo ho, old Beaufort!" said Williams, patting the silk-coated flanks with admiring affection. "He don't want the whip much, Sir, when he's warm to his work."

In the frosty air the breath of the men and the horse surrounded the group as with a cloud of steam.

Arnold was off at a hand gallop through the park, out into the high road.

"A pretty seat," said old Williams to himself, gazing after the horseman, though it was only for a few moments he could trace him through the darkness: "he always had a very pretty seat, just for all the world as the old gentleman had before him. So had Miss Georgina, as fine a girl as you ever set eyes on she was then, with cheeks as red as an apple. But that's all over now. That was before she got married and had the megrims. As for this Lomax—well, well, it don't become me to be talking over my betters, and letting 'em down. He rides well, d—n him, I will say that for him, when he likes, though he hasn't given the roan a chance. Ah, it's different to what it used to be in the old gentleman's time. We spent something like a Christmas then: there was an interest took in the stables *then.* The house full of company, and yet a mount for everyone of them. Why don't Mr. Arnold come and see us oftener, and put things square like? Why does he always keep away up in town? The old man never found it dull down here, I'm thinking; but young gen'lemen will be young gen'lemen, I suppose. Please God it will all come right again presently, when he marries. And she's a pretty creature, that Miss Carr, and sits her pony like a little queen, she does. I warrant she'll see that justice is done to the stables; and then this Lomax will clear out—giving himself airs for all the world as though the place belonged to him. I hate to see him astride my horses; he's too sugary and civil by half. Here, you Joe!"

And the old man, wheezing asthmatically, re-entered the stables.

The daylight found Arnold mounted on the black hunter, rattling along the smooth, hard high-roads of Woodlandshire. He could not fail to gather exhilaration from the pace at which he had been proceeding. He had never been possessed by any tendency to gloom or despondency. It was natural to him to contemplate everything from its pleasantest point of view. As he became more and more familiar with the facts of his brother-in-law's dishonesty, so in proportion his alarms and foreboding lost their intensity. He began to think that on the previous night he had been inclined to exaggerate in some degree the extent of his misfortunes, to over-estimate the painfulness of his position. As he rode on, story after story occurred to him concerning men whom he had known, who had suffered from the frauds of others, or from their own recklessness, and who had yet recovered themselves; who had run neck and neck races with ruin, and yet had come in winners. It is true he could not at present estimate the extent of his liabilities. How he cursed a thousand times the hour when he had entered the share-market, and exchanged good bank notes for suspicious-looking documents called stock and share certificates! But surely some of these would turn out of real advantage to him. Of course Lomax's conduct had been shameful, abominable, scandalous, but probably there was something to be said for him; he had been the victim of others, it might be, deceived and imposed upon in his turn; and now he would do his best to set matters right again. Surely he would. Arnold had met with such kind treatment from fortune hitherto, that it was difficult for him to believe that she had now turned against him ; and ever kindly dispositioned, lenient, considerate towards his fellows, he could not be readily brought to judge severely, or to condemn in strong terms the derelictions of his brother-in-law, Francis Lomax. It will be seen that daylight and his morning's ride had dispersed much of the gloom which had oppressed his contemplations of the previous night.

In relation to his engagement with Leonora Carr, however, he certainly experienced greater difficulties.

It is not easy for a prosperous man at once to believe very fervidly in misfortune, to convince himself that the pleasant paths of his life's journey have now come to an abrupt termination, and that for the rest of his days he is doomed to travel over a most bleak and desolate moorland. Arnold had been very happy hitherto—his career had been useless, profitless, likely enough ; but it had been eminently pleasant, and even elegant after its manner. He had seemed removed from the common chances of ill-fortune and disappointment. Even in the matter of his love—contradicting all proverbial precedent—his course had run smooth. He had perhaps been slow to appreciate the charms of Leo Carr : just as he had not appraised readily the strength and extent of his own regard and affection for her. But then he had known her many years, as a plaything, a tiny child to be kissed and romped with ; he was likely to be a little confused as to the precise moment when stepping across an important boundary line the girl took rank as a woman ; when it was no longer possible to fondle and pet without bowing down to adore—proffering the love and devotion of a life. If it were permissible to partition his feeling for her into different stages of growth, it might be said that he loved her first because she was a near neighbour, a toy, a child. Next because she was beautiful ; then, because of herself. More and more, he felt himself subdued by the magic of her charm of manner, her graceful waywardness, her warmth of heart, her great kindness and goodness. And it was an instance of the general prosperity of his career, that he had had but to sue for this beautiful creature's love to receive it instantly to the most absolute extent the most exacting of lovers could have imagined. It had never been possible f....

anyone to doubt for a moment the earnestness and truth of Leo's love.

The circumstances that had now arisen, threatening the issue of his suit, were of a most unlooked for kind. They could only be attributed to his own extraordinary negligence as to his property, and the control over it he had permitted Lomax to obtain, added to that gentleman's fradulent deal-ings, and the questionable investments he had induced Arnold to meddle with. It had never been supposed that Arnold's pecuniary position could equal that of the only child of Mr. Carr, the reputed millionnaire. But the families had long been on terms of intimate friendship ; the marriage had been a favourite scheme with the heads of both houses —it seemed a natural result of the proximity of the estates, and the many years' intimacy of the Carrs and the Pages ; it had been accepted quite as a matter of course by the whole country-side. Even now old Mr. Carr had expressly avoided all peremptoriness in discussing the marriage with Arnold. He had been careful so to pose the question, as it were, that the obstacles affecting its settlements seemed to spring from Arnold. It had been put to him as an appeal to his honour, whether in the greatly altered situation in which, thanks to himself and to Mr. Lomax, he would find his pro-perty, it was fair to require that the agreement should be carried out. If he were really embarrassed, as Mr. Carr suggested, was he entitled to involve in his embarrassments his wife, her fortune and family? The answer was left to him ; his future, so to say, was in his own hands. But there could not be a doubt as to the conduct his own sense of self-respect recommended to him. And a feeling of sadness and sorrow grew upon him the more he pondered the subject.

Still it was undeniable that a more cheerful view of the case was open to him. Mr. Carr's opinion might be fairly questioned. And the marriage was made to depend upon his own position ; and this Arnold had already persuaded himself was respectably hopeful. Perhaps the worst that could happen would be a delay in the marriage until he had extricated himself from his difficulties : until the estate had righted itself. The shares could not be all loss. The in-terest on the mortgage could be easily kept down. A few

17

years' economy and retrenchment, and it might be possible
to pay off the mortgage, or at least a large portion of it. He
should be amply punished for his negligence by the post-
ponement of the marriage—by the present loss in money.
He would have done with Lomax for the future; he would
turn over a new leaf—reside on the estate—look after everything himself and so on. But in truth he did not feel altogether at ease, notwithstanding the large amount of flattering
unction he was endeavouring to lay to his soul; his heart
would ache a little notwithstanding the quantity of balm of
hope he did not cease to pour upon it.

He had turned his horse's head towards home again. He
was skirting Croxall Chase on his Road to Oakmere. Suddenly he heard a voice calling after him his own name. He
looked round, and saw Leo on her pony advancing towards
him at full speed. He started: he felt a little anxious to
avoid her at first. Was doubtful how he ought to conduct
himself—what he should say. The next moment he could
hardly regret seeing her; she was so radiant with health and
spirit and beauty. And in the shadow of the rim of her
round hat her eyes gleamed like stars.

"How are you, Ar?" she cried, in her silver-bright
tones, sending strange thrills to his heart, and putting her
little hand into his. "I was afraid you'd be off at a gallop
again before I could reach you—that black horse has such a
superb stride, poor little Jujube wouldn't have stood a
chance. You are out early, Sir. You can't say that you
came over to see me, because you've gone past the gates. I
suppose you couldn't sleep last night, after your Christmas
pudding, was that it, Ar?" she went on saucily. "Don't
look so grave, please. How's Rosy, and Edith, and all of
them? Did you have a pleasant party yesterday? Hum,
you don't look as though it had been particularly exciting.
I wish you'd dined with us. Not but what we were quiet
enough. Poor mamma's bad with the rheumatism again. I
hope Mr. and Mrs. Lomax are quite well. I ought to have
asked after them before. To tell you the truth, we were
very gloomy yesterday. My poor Baby Gill is sinking, I'm
afraid—I grow very anxious about her. We've sent to town
again for Dr. Hawkshaw. You'll come back with me to
breakfast, won't you, Ar? No? Oh! dear, dear, how little

we see of you now. Won't you? *Do* come. Won't even
devilled drumsticks tempt you? Going round to the Wick
Farm, are you? to see Robin Hooper? Are you quite
sure that's true, Sir, or have you only just thought of it?
Oh, Ar, I wish——"

And the little lady stopped rather suddenly, turning down
her eyes, and was very busy patting her pony's neck.

"Wish what, dearest?" Arnold asked, bending over her.

"No. I have no right to say so. You would not like
me to. You would be offended, perhaps."

"With you, Leo? It's not possible," and he pressed her
hand tenderly. "Say on, dearest."

"Well, this only, Arnold—" she spoke seriously now, in
quite a moved voice—"I will only ask you to be sure that
if you are sad I share your sadness. That if anything I can
do will remove the cause of your sorrow, be sure I will do
it : if I but knew what it was to do ! Oh, Ar, it seems to
me there is something changed of late about us—something
keeping you from me—something that pains and saddens
you. Don't be angry with me, dearest. I am saying more
than I ought, perhaps—more than I ever dreamt of saying ;
only tell me that we are the same to each other as we have
ever been."

"Surely so, Leo," he answered. But there was something in the tone of his voice that made her turn her gaze
for a moment inquiringly into his eyes.

"I ought not to ask, I ought not to doubt, Ar, I know ;
and, indeed, I don't doubt. I find something painful even
in charging myself with doubting. And yet I can't help
thinking, Ar, can't help fearing, I don't know what. I feel
afraid sometimes, like a child in a dark room, without knowing why.'

"Dear little Leo !"

"That's almost one of your own good smiles, Ar. Do
you know that they become more and more rare, Ar, every
day?"

"As one grows older one grows more serious : I suppose
that's the reason, Leo."

"I'm not so sure of that. I think we might grow happier
and merrier every day if we only would. If our lives grow
more and more gloomy, surely we have only to thank our-

17—2

selves for it. I am not sad very often, yet I am sometimes : when I tease myself with questions; when I dread lest I have misinterpreted the past; when I look forward to the future with misgivings. And do you know, Ar," she said, with a charming smile, with yet some lingering sadness in it, " do you know, Ar, that all my hopes of happiness seem somehow to centre in, to rest upon, you ? "

He pressed her hand tenderly again. His heart beat turbulently; the blood rushed into his face. A sense of guilt came over him — a sense of unworthiness—and he quailed before the bright brown eyes. Her happiness wholly in his keeping ! Had he been true to his trust? Had he not perilled all by his folly, his indolence, his imprudence? But she did not notice his uneasiness—too much occupied, perhaps, with her own thoughts. In a low, gentle voice, she went on,

" So when I find that we meet less and less often, that your letters become fewer and fewer, yes, and shorter and shorter, I can't help thinking to myself that if—if you did not ——— Yet no, Arnold, it's only been half a thought after all; and I won't, I can't put it into words, and my tongue would refuse to speak them if I did. And I will keep on saying to myself over and over again—as I have done a hundred times—that my Ar is as brave, and frank, and good, and true as a knight of old; ever has been and ever will be so ; and that it is as wicked as it is foolish to hint a doubt in regard to him. There, will that do, Ar ? "

" Thank you, Leo," he said, simply. And quite in a knightly way he raised her hand to his lips. But he said no more. She seemed a little disappointed at this, and a half sigh escaped her.

" It's cruel keeping you here in the cold," she said, " isn't it? And I see that black horse is in a fidget to be off again. And you won't come back with me to breakfast? You really feel bound to go on to the Hoopers'? I shall grow jealous of Robin Hooper : he sees a great deal more of you than I do, not merely in town, but down here also."

" You know, Leo, there are reasons why I should call upon him as often as possible. Poor Rob is very sensitive. I should not like him to feel neglected down here because his father is a farmer, and not on the visiting lists of the gentry about here. He is so good, so clever; above all, so afflicted. He is my friend too. He mustn't think I shrink from owning him down here."

"You are right, Ar, no doubt. Poor Robin Hooper! I am trying hard to like him, and I think I shall succeed. Yes, he is certainly clever. I read those verses of his in the book you gave me, and I think them beautiful."

"May I tell him so? Good-bye, Leo. Love to papa and mamma."

"You'll come soon again, very soon?"

"I'll be sure to."

"Good-bye."

And once more the ring of the hoofs of the black horse resounded along the road to Oakmere. Leo gazed after her lover, proud of his brave handsome figure, and the ease with which he sat the horse; she smiled as she saw him urge old Beaufort to a gallop and then disappear round a turning in the road. Then the smile faded, and a pained look took its place.

"He never once looked round, and—and he did not kiss me!"

And slowly the little lady turned her pony's head, and, entering the gates of Croxall Chase, passed down the stately chestnut avenue towards her father's house.

Midway between Croxall and Oakmere, a cross-road turning to the right leads to Wick Farm—a large plain house, compact, stone-faced, slate-roofed — in which for many years the Hoopers have been farmers, under long leases from the lords of Croxall Chase. The farm is one of the best on the estate; the Hoopers are greatly respected in the neighbourhood. Their one son, Robin, a poor deformed young man, the country people said, had been made quite a friend of by young Mr. Page of Oakmere. They had lived up in town together studying law, and Mr. Page had been very kind to the poor boy; and they had shared the same chambers in London. A very good thing for young Hooper, all agreed, to be so taken up by the gentlefolks : old General Page had begun it, the good, kind old man—not but what the poor deformed fellow was clever enough, and could likely enough earn his own living if his health would only permit. And, perhaps, after all, there would be no need for him to work. Farmer Hooper was reputed a warm man, a saving man, a trifle stingy even, it might be.

Not far from the farm, Arnold met this old Mr. Hooper, seated on a rough Exmoor pony. The farmer's high-gaitered, long, sturdy legs dangled down, nearly reaching the ground. He touched the pony with a switch he carried, and advanced to Arnold at a sharp trot.

" Morning, Sir," he said.

"How are you, Mr. Hooper?" and Arnold shook hands warmly with the farmer.

" It's coldish this morning; but we must expect it at this time of year. You've been a round on the black, I see?"

"Yes; and I thought I'd come this way home, to ask for some breakfast at the farm, and see how Rob's getting on."

" Well, thank'ee kindly, Sir, the poor boy's much the same, no better and not a great deal worse. I fear he's very sickerly still. I think he'd be better out of London—not but what I'm sure we owe you many thanks for all your kindness to him and care of him there. But, perhaps, it pains him to see everyone so strong and hearty-like in the country. Poor lad: in London, you see, pale faces don't so much matter. It's only fair to humour the poor body as much as we can."

"I thought he'd been better and stronger of late," said Arnold.

" Well, Sir, maybe: can't say I see it myself, though. But the missus says so: she *will* think the boy's as strong as a lion: and it's hard to gainsay her. You see, he's her only one, and the poor soul's mortal proud of him. It's the old story, you see, Sir, of the hen with the one chick."

" I shall find him up at the house."

"Surely you will, Sir. And, I'll answer for him, he'll be glad to see you. You'll excuse my turning back? He's fond of talking of you, Sir. He's a good heart, has our Rob, and he couldn't say better of you than we should care to hear. We think with him, Sir, on that subject; and I'm sure the old woman joins your name in her prayers morning and night; I know it, because I've heard her myself many a time. Next to Rob, Sir, I do believe she thinks better of you than of anyone. Good-morning, Sir, you're sure of a good breakfast up at the farm, I'll answer for the old woman."

As Arnold stopped at the white gate of the Wick Farm, Robin Hooper hurried out to meet him.

"Take your hat, my boy, or you'll be catching cold," cried Mrs. Hooper, following her son. "You're hale and hearty enough now, but you might be laying yourself up again."

Robin, limping as usual, was soon by Arnold's side.

"How are you, Rob? I've come to beg for some breakfast."

"Come in, my dear Arnold, I'm so glad to see you. I've been wanting to see you; I was almost thinking of coming over to see you at the Court. Thank you, mother, but I shan't want my hat. We're coming in; Arnold's come to breakfast with us."

Robin's pale-coloured hair was streaming in the wind: his face was lit up with excitement.

They entered the snug, warm, low-ceilinged parlour of the farm-house. Mrs. Hooper busied herself in preparing quite a sumptuous breakfast for her guest. Robin stirred the fire until it roared and crackled; once or twice he gazed into the face of his friend, wistfully, inquiringly. He began to think that there were traces of care, of painful thought, upon Arnold's brow he had never remarked before.

"Certainly," he said to himself, "Arnold has a sad look; I fancied so a day or two ago. I watched his face in church yesterday. There is a clenched look about his face he used not to have. His expression is now inclined to be rigid, and fixed, and heavy; how bright, and gay, and mobile it used to be! What has happened, I wonder?"

"Let me help you to some of this pie, Arnold," he said, aloud. "I hope you had a pleasant day yesterday."

"Pretty well, old boy," Arnold answered with a smile; "somehow those home festivals are never very brilliant affairs, you know."

"And Leonora, Miss Carr,—she is quite well, I hope?"

"Quite, thank you, Rob. I have seen her this morning. She spoke of you; she was admiring one of your poems."

"She's very kind," and Robin's face crimsoned with pleasure.

"I'm sure my boy's poetry is beautiful," said Mrs. Hooper. She had breakfasted some time ago, and was continually going in and out of the room, anticipating the servant's attendance upon Arnold. "Very beautiful; I never read anything like it. That poetry they put in the *Woodlandshire Mercury*, up in the left-hand corner, isn't near equal to it. Some of it quite made me cry the other day, it was so touching. I don't believe finer poetry was ever written," and she left the room again.

"If the public would only think like authors' mothers, where would be criticism, Arnold?" asked Rob, laughing.

"Mrs. Hooper is right," said Arnold, seriously. "You have made a great advance lately. There seems to be so much more real feeling in your verse than formerly. Feeling is added to fancy now. It is as though you had looked into your own heart, Rob, instead of being content with what others have told you of theirs. What is the secret of it?"

"There is no secret," and Robin turned away blushing very much.

"You must collect all your scattered verse some day, Rob, into a book; I'm sure it will prove a very favourite volume with many."

"I confess that I have thought of doing so," said Rob; then after a pause he added, in a low voice, "My life will be no long one; it need not be, for perforce it must be very useless. I can take no part in the world's struggles; I am compelled to be idle when others are busy. I think a book is better than a tombstone, considered as a memorial. I shouldn't like to be wholly forgotten when I am dead—at least, there are some I should wish to remember me; and if a few only will prize my lines, not for their own worth so much as for their author's sake, if only for that, I should like to leave a book behind me. But I am talking very gloomily for Christmas time. If my mother were to hear me!—my mother who *will* think me a giant in stature and strength." He smiled sadly as he added,—"Poor, dear mother, I believe she has persuaded herself of that in order that she may persuade me."

There was a pause for some moments.

"But you wanted to see me about something? what is it, Rob?"

"Yes, it is most important, and I had nearly forgotten it," said Robin, starting up. "You know, I have told you of the young lady, Miss Gill—I thought her name was Milne; there was some mistake about that, it seems—Janet Gill—at present with Miss Carr, at Croxall Chase?"

"More, Rob, I have seen her; she justifies your admiration, though it was not expressed in very mild terms. But you are right, she is very beautiful."

Robin darted a quick, suspicious glance at his friend; then he resumed,—

"There is some mystery about her: but that matters little, I do not seek to pierce that. But there is danger threatening her."

"Danger, Rob? down here?"

"I feel it, I know it. There is a man here, an old man, a Frenchman—a man we used to see at that *café* in town Jack Lackington is so fond of—whom Jack used to call Tithonus, whose presence here I know means injury to Janet."

"You are right, Rob, I have seen the man down here, his face seemed familiar to me, but I could not then recollect where I had seen him. Yes, it was Tithonus of the *Café de l'Univers.* He is down here, I have seen him, with Janet Gill."

"*With her?*" repeated Rob, trembling with excitement. "I dread that man! I hate that man! what does he do here —what does he want with her—did she know him?"

"Yes, but she seemed strangely frightened at seeing him; I never saw anyone so frightened."

"Why did I not go to Croxall Chase to warn her? why did I not write to her? What a pitiful coward and fool I am! where did she see him?"

"It was in the garden at Croxall. He appeared to have suddenly burst upon her presence. She turned quite faint with terror."

"Oh, help her, Arnold! help her!"

"What does it mean, Rob? what is the mystery? Why should this old Frenchman exercise such power over her?"

"I do not know, I do not seek to know; only if she needs help, should we not give it? You will give it, will you not, Arnold? promise me that you will."

"With all my heart, I promise, Rob."

"We must act at once. I will go down to the Crown, I will see about this Frenchman. Will you see Janet Gill at Croxall and proffer your assistance? Something assures me that she will need it."

"Certainly I will, Rob; I will lose no time about it; I will endeavour to see her this morning."

Robin, left alone, limped up and down the room in a state of great perturbation.

"If he should feel the power of Janet's beauty as I do!" he murmured; "indeed, is it not irresistible? And if she——" he did not finish the sentence; he was shivering as with cold.

CHAPTER XIX.

CAPTAIN GILL'S DAUGHTERS.

POOR Baby Gill was reposing in one of the large, curtained, lofty, luxuriant beds at Croxall Chase. The room was spacious, massively and handsomely furnished, on the warmest side of the house, and with the prettiest look-out, for just below was the large flower garden, beautifully kept. Old Mr. Carr took an especial pride in his flowers; his gardener carried off the best prizes at the Woodlandshire Horticultural Show, triumphing even over the gardeners of Gashleigh Abbey. But it was winter now, and the flower-beds were desolate. A glorious fire glowed in the grate, and the windows were wadded to keep the cold out.

There was such a waxen paleness on her face, her breathing was so slight, she lay stretched out so still and motionless, it was as though she were already dead. As Janet bent down to kiss the wasted face of her child-sister, one might have fancied that she did so to test whether the poor soul were yet warm and living. Baby Gill murmured something in her sleep, stirred a little, but she did not wake. Janet rose and turned away : it was to prevent her burning tears falling upon the sleeper.

"My poor, poor Bab," she sobbed, "my own darling sister!" And she sank upon her knees, remaining so for some time, rapt in prayer.

She was pacified then, and she brushed the tears from her eyes, and smoothed her golden hair from her forehead. Then she sought to place the pillows of the bed more comfortably for the invalid, to draw the draperies of the bed well round her, to shield her from all possibility of draught ; and again she paused to bend over and contemplate the thin pale face. How sunken were the cheeks, how hollow the eyes, how prominent seemed all the bones of the face— a beautiful face, though all the exquisite bloom of childhood had gone from it, though it was aged terribly, though the mould of the features was marked and defined as in maturity ; and the long flaxen tresses were cut quite short. Dr. Hawkshaw had insisted that this sacrifice should be made during the height of the fever from which poor Bab had been suffering. Her little hands, once pink and plump and dimpled, were now thin and transparent, lined with blue veins, and white as marble.

"I have only Bab in the world," said Janet, "and if she should be taken from me ! Oh, God, it will be more than I can bear ! My poor sister ! It has been for her I have suffered all I have suffered, and for her I would go through all again. But if I am to lose her? Can it be? can it be? No. Heaven will not permit it ; surely Heaven will not permit it. Oh, if she should be dying !"

It was in vain she endeavoured to shut out the thought : in vain she tried to force herself to hope. One glance at the white face of the sleeper tore away all the fond dreams with which she had sought to muffle her fears, set her heart aching anew, opened to her a long vista of despair and desolation. Yes, Baby Gill was dying. All fever had gone, but her strength had given way in the struggle. She was cool and calm, but all force had left her. Her constitution had yielded. She was dying of the effort to recover. She could hardly raise her hand: her voice was an almost inaudible whisper ; she could not keep awake, she was lying helpless, half dead, lethargic, dreamy, sinking into death as into a sleep more than ordinarily sound.

There was a light tap at the door. Noiselessly Janet went to it : she admitted Leo into the sick-chamber. Leo grasped her hand. The brown eyes gleamed with an anxious inquiry more eloquent than words.

"She is still asleep," said Janet in a low, sad voice, the tears starting to her eyes. "Heaven only knows whether she will ever waken."

Leo drew the poor girl close to her and kissed her affectionately.

"Hope always, Janet," she whispered, "all may yet be well. The issue is in His hands. Don't cry, dearest. You have need of all your courage, Janet. The train must have come in by this time. I have sent a carriage to the station to meet it. We must have Dr. Hawkshaw here very shortly. I know he will not fail us. I wrote to him myself. Keep up a brave heart, Janet. Hope always for the best."

"I have only Bab in the world," Janet repeated in a heart-broken murmur. "If she is taken from me, I have nothing to live for—nothing to love or care for, no one to love or to care for me !"

"Don't say that, Janet ; we are your friends here : we shall never cease to love you. You will never leave us. For my poor Baby's sake, my own dear little school friend ; for your own sake, too, my dearest, bravest Janet. You will remain with us always !"

Janet pressed her friend's hand, but shook her head mournfully.

"But Bab will recover," Leo went on, "I feel sure she will. Dr. Hawkshaw can do wonders ; our poor little Bab will get well again soon, very soon ; and then how happy we shall be again, only think !"

"You are very good to me, Leo," said Janet, smiling through her tears. "I hardly thought there could be so much kindness left in the world. Perhaps I have had but too good reason to doubt the world. But you—you are an angel. The devotion of a life could but repay the debt I owe to you. Oh, if I can ever serve you in my turn !"

"Hush, you must not talk like that; I must not hear you."

There was a slight noise outside the door. Leo opened it as quietly as possible.

" What is it ? "

A servant stood outside. They were informed that there was below some one waiting to see Miss Gill; some one who desired to see her particularly. The visitor had been shown into the small drawing-room.

"Go, Janet," said Leo, " I will watch poor Baby. It may be some one from Dr. Hawkshaw. If he could not come himself he would send some one on whom he could rely. Hope for the best."

Janet glanced at the sick child: she was still asleep. Leo had taken up her station by the bedside. Janet felt that her sister was safe in Leo's charge. She quitted the chamber and passed down the stairs. She paused for a moment to collect herself, as it were, she then turned the door-handle of the small drawing-room and entered. Seeing no one she advanced into the centre of the room. She turned as she heard a sound behind her.

"*Petite ange !*" said a voice. She started, trembled, leant upon a chair to save herself from falling.

Monsieur Anatole was standing with his back to the door, intercepting her return that way, bowing, smiling, redundantly.

" Pardon me," he went on, "pardon me for intruding upon you, for forcing myself upon you, but I had no alternative. I have much to say to you, dear child, much that I *must* say to you. And you must hear me. You shall not say ' Go !' to-day in that tone, usually so sweet, but which at times you can compel to be so severe, so frightfully severe. There will to-day be no *preux chevalier* to interrupt us, rushing foolishly to proffer assistance that is not required. For we are friends, are we not *mon enfant*, old friends ? We have need of a long, long talk together. Don't look towards the bell-rope. Think : let there be no *esclandre*. There are things we know of which perhaps your grand friends here—they are grand, are they not ? yes—and rich —the house is superb,—true it is English taste, which is not a recommendation,—well, which perhaps your friends here had better not know. Family secrets should be kept in the family. Is it not so ? "

" Yes. That is so," she answered, shivering, possibly without knowing much what she was saying.

Monsieur Anatole smiled : he bowed low.

" You will compose yourself," he said ; "there is no hurry, you will take time."

He drew out his silver-gilt box and took a pinch of snuff with great deliberation, still smiling extravagantly, dusting carefully his face and the breast of his coat afterwards with an old silk handkerchief. There was a jaunty youthfulness about his air as he did this, strangely opposed to the extreme age of his looks. He then stood in an artificially graceful attitude—one of his claw-like hands half hid in his waistcoat, the other resting upon his hip ; one of his shrivelled legs straight, the other advanced in a curve. He paused for a few moments, his eyes fixed on his small neat feet, and deriving pleasure from his contemplation of those extremities.

" I will wait your pleasure," he said at length, in a mincing voice ; " only you will understand, dear child, that we must come at last to the object of our meeting."

He turned his reptile eyes upon her. She started back, then with an effort calmed herself—strove with her fears, clasped her hands, and stood before him as erect as she could.

" Go on. Say what you will, and leave me as soon as may be. There is some one here, very ill, at whose bedside I should be even now attending—from whom it is a pain to me to be absent."

She spoke in a low, oppressed tone, but with tolerable firmness.

" I am very sorry. *Pauvre petite.* Is she so ill then ? The little sister ! I share your sorrows, my Janet. Be sure of it, now and always."

" Enough ! " she answered, with an impatient gesture. " For her sake I have borne much. For her sake I am prepared to bear more even. You have found me—what is it you wish ? " There was indignation and disgust in her glance.

" She asks me what I wish ! " Monsieur Anatole apostro-

phised the ceiling. "Can she not guess? Does she not
know that it is once more to tell her of my boundless love
for her—a love which carries me out of myself: a love which
intoxicates, which maddens me—which renders me capable
of anything. You hear me, my Janet?"

"I hear," she answered faintly, shuddering.

"Yes, you hear! you know of my love—my devotion—
my passion, my Janet; and you will be mine? Is it not so,
beautiful child?"

"No no, no; a thousand times no!"

He went on as though he had not heard her.

"My first youth is gone, I know it. It is the deep-seated
love of maturity that I offer you, sweet infant, a love without fickleness—without change. I am no longer of that age
to which love is a trifle, unappreciated, misused—woman a
toy, to be grown tired of, neglected, ill-treated. No, I have
passed through those things there. I have committed follies,
indiscretions, perfidies even: who has not? As a young man,
fêted, caressed, admired, spoiled by success, I have been
thus guilty, I know it: I own it, with shame. But this is
no longer possible to me: all is now changed. It is a
grand love I offer to you, my Janet, whole, honest, superb."

"For Heaven's sake, let me hear no more of this!" she
cried, piteously.

He smiled, bowed, but he resumed,

"In every way my love promises to lead to happiness;
on all sides I find reason to believe that success will attend
our marriage. Ours will not be one of those unfortunate
unions consecrated by the Church, it may be, but which
nevertheless the eyes of parental authority have viewed with
severity—which the parental heart has refused to sanction.
My suit, as you know, dear child, has the cordial approval
of your excellent father—an officer as brave as he is honest,
as handsome as he is brave. You know that I have this
approval?"

"I do know it."

"My own parents, it is my deep regret, no longer live
to bless a union in which they would have taken a holy
pride. Sweet mother, noble father, how you would have ap-
proved my choice! how you would have welcomed to
your pure hearts my Janet, my wife!"

He affected to brush away a tear, though the relatives for whose loss he expressed such poignant lamentations, to judge by his own age, must have been dead many years, probably before Janet had entered the world.

"What then remains?" he asked. "But one word from you, sweet angel—a word you will not, I know, I am sure you will not hesitate to pronounce. Speak, my Janet."

He advanced towards her as he spoke.

"Stand back!" she cried with a scream, raising her hands.

"You are frightened without cause, my little one!" He smiled grimly. "You will be mine?"

"No," she answered firmly; "it is time to end this dreadful mockery. I tell you, no! You have heard my answer; and now leave me. I am not so friendless as you think; do not dare to come here again; do not dare to follow me further. If I touch this bell, I can summon to my aid those who will drive you from the house. Go!"

He sat down deliberately: the chair he selected, an easy reclining chair, being between Janet and the door. He crossed his legs—he began to pat his hands together as though he were occupied with mild aristocratic applause, as in a stall at the opera.

"Brava! brava!" he cried, languidly; "well played, my Janet. You have a great talent I find, quite an unexpected talent for the sentimental high comedy. But ask yourself a question or two, dear infant—consult probability a little. Do you think that it is likely that I should take all this trouble to find you out—and there has been trouble I admit; your escape was well managed; you have kept concealed very well; I wish to do you justice in that respect —but do you think I should take all this trouble, yes, and bear all this expense, and there has been considerable expense,—in tracking you—and all for nothing? to leave you again — to depart when with an action impressive and charming, and a sweetly commanding tone, you bid me go? Do you not see that I am now by this development of a new talent, if by no other tie, bound more than ever to remain—bound never to quit you? No, my Janet, I tell you plainly, I have found you and I shall not go!"

"Have you no pity?"

" Pity ? It is not of pity we are talking, but of love ! "

" I will hear no more, no more ! "

" Pardon me : you will. So excellent a daughter will not, I am sure, act in downright disobedience to the will of her father ! "

" My father ! He is not himself. You know he is not. He has been the victim of a shameful and wicked conspiracy. He has been but an instrument in the hands of others. He no longer knows what he says—what he does. He is your dupe and victim."

" Hard words, my Janet, cruel words indeed, considering of whom they are spoken—to whom they are spoken—an affectionate father ! a devoted lover ! Ah ! beautiful angel, the divine William Shakspeare, your great English poet, was right when he said—I don't remember the passage precisely, but it was about a thankless child and a snake's tooth. Very superb passage ! and it fits the present occasion marvellously. Think again, my Janet. You will not disobey this fond father ? It will be better not, for many reasons."

There was something half bantering, half threatening in the air with which he spoke these words ; there was a subdued malignity in the tone of his voice that appeared to alarm Janet terribly. As though some invisible bonds were tightening round her, she moved about with a writhing, painful action, to free herself and escape. She shrank from the gaze of Monsieur Anatole.

" Yet why should I hesitate ? " she murmured. " Has he played a father's part to me ? What has he done that I should make this frightful sacrifice ? No, no, I cannot." And then in louder tones she added, " No, I will not yield ! Go, Sir, do your worst."

" You will not yield ? I may do my worst ? Poor child ! Do you know what that worst is ? "

He smiled as he thrust his right hand into the tail pocket of his coat and drew out his black, greasy, swollen pocketbook. He held it in front of him while he tapped it playfully with the skeleton fingers of his left hand, as though it were a miniature piano, and he were performing upon it a merry tune.

" I know that you are a villain ! " said Janet, with passion. " I know that you are capable of any enormity : I know that you have made this poor man your dupe, that he is helpless in your hands, ruined by you beyond all hope. Gambler and cheat that you are, I know that I have been as much bought and sold as ever negro slave was bought and sold. My father is not himself, is no longer in his right mind, or this would not have been, could not have been. But enough has been done. I quitted my home—home! what a mockery there is in the word—never to return to it. I deny my father's right to dispose of me. Go, Sir; you have your answer : do your worst ! "

"What a pretty thing it is to see a woman in a passion ! " he observed calmly. He chuckled over this for some time, enjoying the notion amazingly. Then he added, with more harshness than he had yet employed, " But, perhaps, it is time to be serious. You are clever at calling names, my Janet. I am a gambler and a cheat, is it so ? Well, well. What will it please you to call papa ? We will say nothing as to his fondness for this," he imitated the action of drinking, "for, after all, that may be considered merely as an amiable weakness to which many of his compatriots are as prone as he is. But I think we can bring more severe charges against papa. I think I have it in my power ; I think the means are in this pocket-book to bring poor papa to a rather strict account. Eh, my Janet, what do you say ? Poor papa ! Gallant Captain Gill : admirable soldier, brave cavalier, dashing *sabreur* — those are fine titles, are they not? Can you picture to yourself, sweet infant, poor papa stripped of those titles, as a bird is stripped of its pretty plumage in a poulterer's shop ; poor papa standing in the dock—it is so called, I think, — the dock of the prisoners at the Old Bailey, while a venerable judge proclaims to him the sentence of the court ; and, my faith, a terrible sentence ! poor papa, denounced openly, held up to public shame as a thief, a forger, a felon ! Ah, it is terrible, is it not, my poor little child ? "

With a smothered scream, Janet had bowed her head, hiding her face in her hands. Monsieur Anatole smiled triumphantly.

"It is bad, is it not? but not so bad as formerly. Now it is transportation, my Janet, for life ; it may be at the least, my infant, penal servitude for years and years. Poor papa !

I can see him now, with his hair cut so short, my Janet, his brave moustache gone; in a vile prison dress; toiling till he is near to death with fatigue, the poor man; and for associates, ah! *mon Dieu!* what wretches! This is so now, my Janet. Of old—ah! it was frightful. Think, dear angel, the black cap upon the head of the judge — the terrible sentence—the white cap over the face of the prisoner —the barbarous, yelling mob—the rope round his neck— the adroit knot under his ear—a bolt drawn—— Ah! no, no. Poor man, I can tell no more. It is too horrible."

It is not possible to describe the force he gave to this description by means of his gesticulation; how, as he spoke, he seemed to act the whole scene—conjuring up all its terrible details and accessories. Now, by his looks and actions, representing the solemn judge; now the terror-stricken criminal; anon, a mocking demoniac in the imaginary mob, then the executioner going through the motions of tying a rope, of fixing it, and ending with a guttural groan and gasp, and a drooping attitude, that were frightfully real. Janet cowered away from him, sick with terror, speechless, panting for breath.

"Poor papa!" he said, sneeringly, at last, after watching her closely with an air of satisfaction, at the manifest effect of his performance. "You will not permit him to be punished? You will aid me in concealing his little failings and misdoings? You will make it worth my while to be silent, will you not? We will put it in that English business-like way if you prefer it. You will give me your love, will you not? You will, so, bribe me to silence. For can I betray the father of the woman I adore—of my wife! *Grand Dieu!* it would be impossible!"

She remained with her face covered, overcome by her fears or lost in thought.

" And you, dear infant," he continued, bending over her, "you could not bear to be pointed out by the world, to be known to all — yes, even by your dear, good, kind, rich friends here—to be known as the daughter of a forger, a convicted felon! Ah! it would be frightful, would it not, my Janet?"

"If it were only for myself," she murmured, abstractedly, not addressing him, but speaking aloud with apparent un-

18—2

consciousness; "if it were only for myself it would not matter! But for Bab, but for my poor Bab — my poor sister!"

He started with a look of discovery. A new sparkle came into his eyes, a cruel smile wreathed about his lips.

"Ah, yes, for this little sister; this poor suffering little sister; you will have pity for her if not for poor papa, if not for yourself, my Janet. You will not let them speak ill of her, you will not doom her to this disgrace—to be taunted ever, followed by insults—the daughter of a felon! Poor little child! What has she done that she should be so treated? Certainly, I think it would kill her. Poor little suffering sister. You will save her, will you not, my Janet?"   •

"My poor Bab!" she cried, with a voice of agony. "Oh, have mercy! have mercy!" And she flung herself on her knees at his feet. "Have some pity. Oh, for God's sake, have some pity!"

The door opened suddenly, and Leo entered, very pale. She glanced from one to the other.

"Why do you kneel to him, Janet?" she asked. She assisted Janet to rise, and kept hold of her hand. She gazed steadily at the Frenchman. "What does this mean? Why are you here?" But she did not wait for an answer. "Courage, Janet," she said. "Dr. Hawkshaw has come."

"*Oh, la belle brunette!*" muttered Monsieur Anatole. He packed away his pocket-book.

He bowed to Leo, a leer of admiration wrinkling up his face. He moved from the door, as, at a sign from Leo, Janet passed him and went out.

"Be calm, be brave, dear Janet," whispered Leo; "the good doctor is now with our poor Bab. Be sure he will do all that is possible to be done for her, for us."

Leo closed the door; she turned to Monsieur Anatole,—

"What have you said to her?" she asked, sternly. "Why have you frightened her? did you come here to insult her, at such a time as this?"

"Pardon me, my Miss," the Frenchman answered; "you do me wrong, I am the friend, the very dear friend of Miss

Janet who has just left us; there is nothing in the world I would not do to serve her."

"It looked like it just now, when she was kneeling at your feet, trembling all over, pale as a ghost."

"Ah! she misunderstood me, that is all. You see Miss" (he pronounced the word *mees*), "there is a story involved in the matter which it is possible I am not at liberty to relate."

"I do not desire to pry into anybody's secrets; but if I thought you had insulted her, poor child, well, I should like to have you whipped from the place : nothing would please me better, and there are people here who would do it; but no, you are an old man, I see."

"Old?" he repeated, in a tone of injury, of indignant expostulation. "I am called old? ah, I see, in the sense in which you apply the term, it is not objectionable. Yes. I am the old friend of Miss Janet Gill, the old friend of her family; that is so. I am here charged to convey to her the wishes of her family—of her father, the Captain Gill. I can understand that it will be painful for her, for you : it is always painful to part from those we love—doubtless it will be a great grief to you to lose our Janet, but it is unavoidable : I am instructed by her father to make all the arrangements necessary for her departure from here. She will come with me without loss of time ; I may say, at once."

"What! you wish to take her away?"

"You have divined my wishes."

"But it cannot be. She does not wish to go with you—she shall not go."

"I am sure," said Monsieur Anatole, with smiling deliberation, "you are yourself too excellent a daughter to desire that she should act in opposition to her father's will."

"You tell me that it is at his request she is to leave here, with you?" she eyed the Frenchman with a great scorn.

"That is so, I give you my word," he answered, bowing.

"I don't believe it," Leo said, simply.

Monsieur Anatole scowled.

"Her father, the excellent Captain Gill, can be produced if need be. You can learn from him his views in regard to his daughter."

" He is here ? "

" He will be here, should his presence be necessary. A father's feelings must not be trifled with ; he can, if need be, invoke the aid of the law. He will be curious to learn what reason exists for the detention from him of his child, his dear Janet."

A piercing scream rang through the house : a prolonged scream as of acute hysterical agony.

"*There* is a reason," said Leo, pale with excitement. " I fear the worst has happened ! "

She hurried away quickly, mounted the stairs, entered the room on the first floor looking out into the garden, Baby Gill's bed-room.

" Go to her ! " said Dr. Hawkshaw, as Leo entered.

She turned to find that Janet had fallen senseless on the floor ; she sprang to her aid.

The doctor was at the bedside of his patient ; the head of Baby Gill seemed to recline upon his arm, his fingers were upon her wrist. There was a look of deep pity, of extreme tenderness upon his calm, thoughtful face. He withdrew his arm, permitting the child's head to fall slowly back upon the pillow. He smoothed the straying short-cut hair from the forehead, waxen white ; he disposed the slight arms by the side of the wasted still warm body, straightening the tiny, child's fingers. One last look at his poor little patient —motionless, beautiful in spite of the many sad traces of premature decay imprinted upon the young and delicate features—asleep—but asleep and at rest, her troubles and trials over for ever : and gently, slowly, reverently the doctor drew the sheet over the body of dead Baby Gill.

" Yes," he said, in a low, moved voice ; " all is over. I can do nothing here now : the child is dead."

He turned to where Leo was raising the head of Janet, bathing her temples.

" Poor thing," he said, " I was too abrupt in telling her ; but I thought she had been better prepared for this sad issue. I have been expecting it for some time : I knew that the chance of the child's recovery was very, very faint. Let me do that for you, Miss Carr, your hand trembles too much. Don't *you* faint, my dear ; ring for one of the servants ; your mamma, I fear, is not very well able to move.

There, she is getting better; but the room is a trifle too hot, that fire throws out a tremendous heat. See if you can open that window, my dear, if only for a few inches; open it at the top."

Slowly Janet drew breath—sighed; her pallid lips parted.

"Is it true?" she asked, in a tone barely audible. Her eyelids quivered, her eyes half opened.

"It is better to let her know the worst at once," said the doctor. "Yes, my dear Miss Gill," he went on, "it is true. Be comforted; she died without pain. Her earthly troubles are over. God has taken her to himself. The poor child has suffered very much, would only have lived longer to have suffered still more; she is at rest for ever now."

Leo, her eyes full of tears, bent down to kiss the white face of Janet.

"Be comforted, Janet, *my sister*," she whispered in a tone of deep tenderness.

CHAPTER XX.

A FOND FATHER.

ONSIEUR ANATOLE, left alone in the small drawing-room at Croxall Chase, paused for a few moments, busy biting his lips, lost in thought. Presently it seemed as though he had arrived at a determination. He buttoned his coat, moved to the window, opened it and stepped out, not closing the window behind him. His footsteps were inaudible upon the turf as he went round the angle of the house, and stopped when he found himself facing a close group of fir-trees that formed a thick dark green screen concealing a sweep of the carriage drive from the view of anyone at the front windows. He put two of his fingers a long way into his mouth and gave a prolonged shrill whistle, after the manner of boys in the street. The whistle was answered by a shout, and presently there emerged from behind the fir-trees a shabby-looking dog-cart drawn by a powerful iron-grey mare. The driver was tall, muscular, swarthy; by his side sat a stout red-faced man, with bloodshot light eyes, a shaggy yellow moustache, and a vacuous expression. He waved his hands and laughed with noisy jocosity as he perceived Monsieur Anatole.

"Ah, doctor, you are punctual. I thank you!" said the Frenchman to the driver of the cart. "Ah, my dear captain!" and he shook hands with the second man.

"How are you, Mounseer?" laughed the captain. "By George, you'd make a good figure to scare the birds, you would!" He enjoyed his own joke immensely.

"Hush! No noise!"

"You've kept us a devil of a time," said the man addressed as "doctor," "and it's beastly cold."

"I don't know what we should have done without that bottle of brandy I was so prudent as to bring with me." And the captain lifted a large flask to his lips, maintaining it there in a tilted position for some time.

"Hush! get down, take care you don't fall. You can come into the house, there's a good fire in this room."

Monsieur Anatole led the way to the window which he had left open, and conducted the two men into the small drawing-room, closing the window after them.

"I suppose, doctor, the horse will stand quiet?" he inquired.

"Perfectly. Not a doubt of it."

"If not I'll send one of the grooms round." He stirred the fire, throwing on more coal, and stood warming his back. He pointed to two chairs.

"Be seated," he said, with a wave of his hand. The doctor sat down in the chair nearest to him, a very frail, light, *papier-mâché* chair: it looked quite unequal to the weight it supported. The captain chuckled, selected a well-padded couch, and flung himself upon it.

"Listen, Captain Gill," said Monsieur Anatole, pointing a finger at the recumbent officer, and speaking with some severity, "don't forget your mission here. You have come to demand your daughter, Janet Gill, you know, and you don't go away without her. You have brought a carriage for her conveyance from here. Any luggage that she may have can be despatched afterwards to an address that shall be furnished. You will stick to that text. You may add to it; but you must not depart from it in the slightest degree. You don't go away without her, remember that. If any difficulty arises—mind, I apprehend none—but if any should arise, remember that we are here to assist you. Do you understand?"

"All right, Mounseer," answered the captain.

At this moment the door opened and Janet entered.

She was strangely pallid, her features rigid, a wild light in her eyes. She stood in the presence of the three men: her father, Monsieur Anatole, the doctor.

"*Chère ange,*" muttered the Frenchman.

"Well, Janie, my girl," said the captain. And he laughed, got up lazily, and advanced to her roughly, to kiss her as it seemed. But something in her glance awed him, stopped him.

"What do you look at me like that for, my girl?" he asked, irresolutely. "Don't you know me? Can't you see who it is?"

" Do you know what has happened ? " she inquired in her turn, with some solemnity.

"Don't talk like that, don't try to frighten a fellow. Don't puzzle me with riddles," he said, coarsely, "I hate them. Speak out plainly if you've got anything to say, or else shut up altogether, and come along. That's my advice."

She stopped with an air of shrinking from him. Then she took courage again.

" I *will* speak out. Your daughter—my poor, poor sister —Barbara, is no more. She has died within these last few minutes. She now is lying up stairs, still warm, quite dead. Do I speak plainly enough ? "

He drew back, rather cowed, shocked, perhaps, even more by her manner and her looks, than her words.

"Poor little Bab," the captain exclaimed, moving towards the fireplace, in truth to escape the piercing eyes of Janet, fixed upon him with a wild earnestness, a concentrated questioning.

Janet shivered ; she pressed both her hands upon her left side, as though in pain.

"Oh, father," she cried at last, in a tone of appealing tenderness, "have you no feeling ? Have you no heart ? "

He only answered by a foolish stare, hardly comprehending her question, as it seemed, gazing at her with wonder.

" How can you speak like this of your poor, dead child, of my own darling Bab : have you no pity ? Try and be yourself once more ; oh, try and think of the past, of the mother who died bequeathing to their father's care her two poor children, dying happy because she believed that he would do all that man could to fulfil that sacred trust. Try and think of her living—loving you—and you, father, worthy of her love : try and do this, father. Oh God, make him understand me ! "

He seemed dazed, confused ; he was rubbing his forehead with his hand, listening to her, yet failing, as it appeared, to see the application of her words.

" I'm sure, Janie, I'm very sorry," he said at last, "very sorry, for all that's happened ; for you, you know, and the other poor child, Bab. Yes, my girl, and for your poor mother, you know. Don't cry, my girl, because you know crying never did anybody any good—never; crying won't bring back the dead. It can't, you know."

And he began to wipe away some tears that were trickling down his own puffed, red face. His eyes were always very weak and moist; it could hardly be said that his tears were wholly due to his grief.

"Remember what you came here to say, and to do," the Frenchman whispered, stealthily nudging the captain's arm.

"Yes, by George, you're right. I'm glad you reminded me. Well, Janie, you know, it's very sad and melancholy, and a great pity, and all that; but it can't be helped, and all the crying in the world won't bring back Bab, nor your mother either, who's been dead this ever so long; you know that just as well as I do. So now we'll come to business, if you please. It's some time since you gave me the slip. But now we've found you out you must just come back again. You're my daughter, you know, and you've no right to give your old father the go-by—your father who loves you, you know, and that sort of thing. And you can have your luggage sent after you, you know, to an address which shall be furnished. There, I think I've said everything that's necessary; so now, if you please, we'll start."

He paused with some abruptness, and sank back upon the sofa.

Janet did not speak.

"You have heard the remarks of your excellent father, dear Janet?" asked the Frenchman, in a fawning tone.

"I have heard," she answered, scornfully.

"And you will come with us?"

"Can you ask it? Are you so lost to every feeling of humanity? I do not speak to *him* now" (she pointed to her father). "I see that he is in no state to understand this or any other subject. I see that he is but a puppet in your hands—moving as you direct; speaking, parrot-wise, the words you have taught him. I speak to *you*—I will not go from here. I will not be torn from the bedside of the poor dead child up stairs. It shall be my task to pay to her remains the last sad honours, to kiss for the last time her cold lips, to see the dreadful lid close over her dear face for ever; the coffin lowered into the earth; to weep and pray

over my dead darling's grave. I will not go until all this
has been done."

"But *then,* Janet," Monsieur Anatole resumed; "will you
come *then?* The funeral over, will you pledge yourself,
will you give me your word to join your father at the place
he may appoint?"

She waited for a few moments, engaged as it were in a
struggle with herself.

"No!" she answered; "I will not do this; I will not
leave my good, true friends here, to trust myself again in
your hands. You have threatened me—you have threatened
him. Do your worst."

"I *will* do my worst," said Monsieur Anatole, with a
malignant scowl; "if you are quite sure that you have the
courage to bear it. I have hinted to you how the consequences will affect poor papa—may affect yourself. They
made you hesitate a little while since; they are not trifles—
you will hesitate again, I think; they will humble you. Do
you remember? you were on your knees to me a little while
ago."

"It was for *her,*" Janet replied; "for my poor dead
sister, don't think it was for myself."

"And for him?" The Frenchman pointed to the
captain.

"You must do your worst. I would save him if I could;
but not at the price you demand. I cannot do it."

She was very pale as she spoke, panting for breath; her
voice very low-toned, sinking to a whisper.

"We've had enough of this talk, I think," the doctor
growled out. "For one I'm quite tired of it. It's very
well for girls; but it's rather wearisome to men. The trap's
very near—for two pins I'd have my arm round that girl's
waist in one moment, and in another have her out there in
the trap, and off down the road. They'd have to go quick,
those that wanted to catch me. Why don't one of you give
the word for this being done? What do you say, captain?"

"Help!" cried Janet. In a moment, Leo Carr entered
the room. She was accompanied by her father. Leo at
once placed herself by the side of her friend, whispering
words of comfort and encouragement in her ear.

Old Mr. Carr, very calm and composed in his manner—

the slight tremor in his voice when he spoke was habitual with him, probably the result of age,—advanced to the centre of the room. He waited for a few minutes, as though endeavouring to understand the situation of the affairs in which he was called upon to act. He looked from Monsieur Anatole to the captain, from the captain to the doctor.

"To what," he said, quietly but peremptorily, "am I indebted for the honour of your presence here?" There was an uncomfortable silence for a few moments.

"We are the friends," said Monsieur Anatole at last, stepping forward and constituting himself the spokesman of the party, "the friends of the young lady resident with you —Miss Gill—and we called to see her."

"Her friends? and she has to cry for aid, in anticipation of violence offered to her by you."

"It was a misconception, altogether a misconception. She is timid, easily alarmed : she might be sure that she has nothing to dread from us—her father and her friends. It was a mistake on her part."

"And a mistake on yours, I presume, to admit your associates into my house through that window—not the usual means of entrance to a gentleman's house—a house to which you are all entire strangers. You were not unseen. From my chair in the study I could obtain a fair view of your proceedings."

But Monsieur was not easily abashed. He bowed, smiled, pressed his hand upon his heart.

"I am a foreigner, I am not of this country," he said. "I may be forgiven for not being thoroughly acquainted with all the minutiæ of its social etiquettes. I took the shortest road to bring my friend here." He pointed his right forefinger towards the captain, his left forefinger he waved about, indicating the apartment in which they stood. "I trust there may be found in the urgency of the occasion excuse for the possibly unceremonious nature of my conduct. Think, Monsieur—try to picture yourself in the situation of my esteemed friend, Captain Gill : a father eager to see his child—some time separated from her. Should you have been very heedful by which entrance you reached her, so that finally you pressed her to your heart?"

It was a little unfortunate that, by way of comment upon the Frenchman's observations, the captain had fallen back upon the sofa in a stupid sleep. The doctor shook him with an extreme violence.

"What is it?" cried the captain, savage at being disturbed so rudely. "Can't you let a fellow alone?"

"He is overcome," Monsieur Anatole interrupted, "with the fatigues of his journey here, and still more with the sad news of the blow that has fallen upon him. Still we have no claim to trespass further upon your hospitality. With much gratitude for the kindnesses she has received at your hands, Captain Gill will now resume the guardianship of his daughter Janet. She will accompany him to town—a carriage has been brought for her conveyance from here."

"Janet cannot 'quit us in this way, at such a time as the present," Leo whispered to her father.

"Have no fear," he answered, in a low voice. Then aloud to the captain, "It is impossible," he said, "that your daughter can be removed from here with this abruptness—especially after the sad event that has but now occurred. I may say at once that I will not permit it. She is herself far from well—certainly in no fit state to be called upon to undertake the sudden journey you propose."

"I am here to demand my daughter, and I don't go away without her," said the captain, with stupid doggedness, thumping his fist upon the table.

"I will *not* go; do not let them take me away," cried Janet, in a broken voice, to Mr. Carr.

"No, my dear, don't be frightened; they shall not," he said.

"My excellent friend Captain Gill will return to make all arrangements that may be necessary for the interment of the poor little girl who is no more. He conceives that he best consults his surviving daughter's happiness by removing her at once from a scene likely to seriously affect both her mind and body. He is probably the best judge, under the circumstances, of the right course to be taken in regard to his daughter Janet. I presume, Sir, you will offer no obstacle to his plan?" Monsieur Anatole spoke with some insolence.

"Carriage at the door; any luggage can be sent to an address to be afterwards furnished," the captain muttered.

"You will allow Miss Gill to depart with her parent and friends?" the Frenchman asked.

"I shall do nothing of the kind," Mr. Carr said, simply, "and I beg that you will at once quit my house."

"I must caution you," Monsieur Anatole continued, "how you act in disobedience to what I believe to be the law of this country. You are a magistrate; you should be better informed than I am. You will take care how you detain a child from the custody of her lawful guardian—her father."

"I will bear all risk," Mr. Carr replied, with a smile. "Miss Gill chooses to remain, and I doubt the competency of her father to undertake the office of guardianship. You will accept that answer as final, if you please; and you will at once leave this house, where I do not scruple to tell you that you are not welcome; that your presence is an intrusion."

He took Janet's hands into his, pressing them kindly. He was startled to find how cold they were.

Monsieur Anatole crossed the room and stooped down to whisper in the ear of the doctor.

Leo had watched them eagerly. She removed her gaze from them for one moment as she perceived outside the window two figures advancing along the carriage drive in front of the house. She started with pleasure as she recognised them, re-opened the window, and made a signal for them to enter.

Of the two persons who now came upon the scene, the first was Arnold Page, who at once greeted Leo warmly, and took up his station at her side. The other was a gentleman attired in the deepest black, but yet the intense gloom of his mourning did little to diminish the fresh roseate bloom of his complexion, the brightness of his eyes, the trim daintiness of his flaxen curls, in close rings all over his head like gilded chain mail. A very small gentleman, with a lithe, little figure, his tiny hands in the closest fitting of black kid gloves.

It was the Marquis of Southernwood, at one time known to the reader of this history as Lord Dolly Fairfield.

"How d'ye do, Miss Carr—hope you're quite well? long time since I've seen you, isn't it? How d'ye do, Mr. Carr?

hope Mrs. Carr's quite well. Met Arnold, and couldn't
resist, you know, coming in to see how you were, just in a
quiet, friendly sort of way. Dreadfully dull at the Abbey,
quite moped to death there, the poor Marchioness quite
unequal to seeing anyone, and very unwilling that I should,
you know. Who have we here?" he asked in a whisper,
as he surveyed through his eyeglass Monsieur Anatole, the
doctor, and the captain. "By George! here's an odd lot!"
he said to himself; "one would think old Carr had been
arrested, and that these were the bailiffs; but that can hardly
be either. Well, that *is* a queer old Frenchman in the wig.
It's as good as a play to look at him." Then aloud: "I hope,
you know, that I am not in anybody's way here, or anything
of that sort?" .

"No. Please don't go," Leo said to him, in a tone of
urgency that struck upon his ear rather pleasantly.

"I won't on any account," he answered, with some
fervour.

"We are interrupted," Monsieur Anatole recommenced.
"It is unfortunate, but it is indispensable that we should
adhere to the terms of our demand—my excellent friend the
Captain Gill——"

"Captain Gill?" the Marquis repeated, as though asking
himself a question, his eye following the direction of Monsieur Anatole's hand, and resting upon the crimson, vacant,
leering face of the man half dozing on the sofa.

"Captain Gill formally insists upon his daughter being
given up to him," said Monsieur Anatole.

"Yes, enough of shilly-shallying. Give up the gal and
let's get off. I'm sick of sticking here," cried the doctor,
coarsely.

"Give her up, to be sure," the captain hiccupped.
"Come along, Janie, my lamb." At this moment it seemed
that he caught the eye of the little nobleman, who had not
once withdrawn from him an eager gaze of scrutiny, and
curiousness, and interrogation. The captain started, rubbed
his hands over his forehead, his eyes, stared hard, at last
evidently paled and trembled.

"You will quit my house, and at once," said Mr. Carr,
firmly, pointing to the window.

"Little Lord Dolly, by the living jingo!" cried Captain

Gill, and he slowly rose from the sofa and staggered away some feet.

"Yes, Captain Gill, you're quite right," said the Marquis of Southernwood, very quietly, and yet with a certain threatening in his manner. "You know me, and I know you. Take my advice and clear out—you and your precious friends,—clear out before you're kicked out. You've no business in Mr. Carr's house, as you very well know. Go, and don't be in a hurry to come back again."

"You won't blow upon me ? You won't be hard upon a fellow, will you though, Lord Dolly ? Now don't," whined the captain, as he stood at the window, with one foot in the room and the other in the garden.

"Be off, or I don't know what I shall do," remarked his lordship. The captain disappeared with a deprecatory groan.

"You will yet permit me to observe——" Monsieur Anatole recommenced, tapping his snuff-box ; he was ill at ease, though he affected comfort and quietude.

"Don't be a fool, Mounseer," the doctor cried out noisily. "Can't you see the game's up ? Come along." He seized hold of the Frenchman's greasy hat, and thrust it violently upon his head. It was more like bonneting him than anything else ; it crushed the curled wig, and nearly hid his eyes. Then the doctor, in spite of angry remonstrances and cries and sundry struggles, fairly dragged, nearly carried, Monsieur Anatole out of the room.

"Get up," he said, strengthening the direction with an oath, as he pushed the Frenchman up the steps of the dog-cart. "I always thought you'd make a mess of it. You must try some other dodge. All right, captain ? "

"All right !" the captain cried, sulkily. And the dog-cart left Croxall Chase.

"I thought I knew the fellow's face," the little nobleman was saying in the small drawing-room ; "but I couldn't at first recollect where I had seen him. It's some years ago, now. He was our paymaster. I know he tried hard to pigeon me when I was in the Crimea. One of the very worst sort of fellows I ever met with. But that's about the least thing he did. The man's an awful scamp and vagabond. He's broke now ; but I should think he was with-

19

out exception the very biggest blackguard in the whole
service. I beg your pardon, Miss Carr, for using such language, but he was, out and out. Why, that man, when he
was in India——"

"Stop, stop," whispered Leo, "she's his daughter."

But it was too late. A sob, a moan, a stifled scream, and
Janet Gill had swooned away. Arnold was only just in time
to save her from falling with some violence.

"What a stupid sort of fellow I am!" cried his lordship.
"I never thought about that, or I'd have bitten off my
tongue rather than said what I did. Who'd have dreamt of
that thief having such a daughter!"

"Poor Janet!" said Leo, tenderly, "how she must have
suffered. Can you hold her, Ar? Are you sure? Will
you ring the bell, please, Lord Dolly? I beg your pardon."

"Don't mind, Miss Carr," cries the Marquis; "it's a pity
to balk yourself. You'd better say Dolly still, I'm more
used to it, and it's shorter."

"How fortunate it is that Dr. Hawkshaw is still here,"
said old Mr. Carr.

Mrs. Carr was in one of the rooms on the first floor.
She was well wrapped up in shawls, reclining in the easiest
of chairs, commanding the view from the window, and yet
not far removed from the fire. Dr. Hawkshaw was with
her.

"You know, my dear Madam, if you don't do what
you're told, you can't expect to get well," he said, rather
austerely.

"Well, doctor, I'll try; but I hate medicine. I always
did: so did my poor Jordan, I remember. Why, he once
bit a piece out of the wineglass rather than take his senna."
She turned to the window. "Dear me, why, who can those
three men be driving through the park?"

"I don't know, I'm sure," Dr. Hawkshaw answered.
"Yet stay." He rubbed his eyes and looked more carefully.
"Now I come to think of it, surely I do know one of them
—the one who is driving."

But the subject dropped, for Mrs. Carr had sunk back in
a doze.

CHAPTER XXI.

CHEZ MR. LACKINGTON.

MR. LACKINGTON had pitched his art-tent in a suburban district, north-west of London. Perhaps it would be more correct to say that his tent had been there pitched for him by somebody else. In fact, he had been a fellow-student with, and most intimate friend of, that celebrated painter Stippleman —before success, and above all, a rich wife came to Stippleman. She came to him literally, a lady amateur, with a fortune ; her taste in art being præ-Raphaelite—almost, indeed, præ-Cimabuesque—she was so severe, and archaic, and rigid. She fell in love with Stippleman's straight, lean, up-and-down sort of figure — his vacant expression, and gamboge-coloured thirteenth-century beard —as he stood awkwardly painting her portrait; and she took him away from his easel and married him instantly ; and his pictures rose in price and won excellent places afterwards. But before this happened, he had been joint tenant with Lackington of a small, shabby, comfortless studio, in Omega Street, Camden Town. Stippleman had, of course, taken the place ; and moved in at once with his lay figure, his carpet-bag, and his eternal associate Jack Lackington— he could no more leave him behind than his clothes or his palette. They seemed to be linked together as firmly as the Siamese twins—no man would ever have dreamed of sundering them. But the lady amateur made short work of the operation. She haled off Stippleman to a neighbouring Gothic church — fearfully Early-English in architecture — where, with the aid of a mediæval-looking curate, something like an incarnate brass-rubbing, she made the painter her husband. Lackington would, perhaps, have been pained and grieved at this separation if he had been a little less indolent. " Rather shabby of Stip, I think," he complained a few times to two or three intimates. " He might have given a fellow notice : and

19—2

I'd have gone and lived with him in his new crib— a regular swell place he's got now. I don't suppose his wife would have minded; or I'd even have got married myself, if some one would have looked out a wife for me. One thing, he's left me the lay figure, and it's almost as good a companion as Stip, for he wasn't much of a fellow to talk. He was wonderfully clever, though, was Stip, wonderfully clever. Did you ever see that picture of his of a woman with red hair feeding a cockatoo? By Jove, I believe it to be quite without a parallel in art. It's out and out, the most awfully jolly thing *I* ever saw. Oh, no, I'm only a duffer by the side of Stip—he's a genius!"

Mahomet, we are taught, felt himself and his mission to be secure when he had obtained *one* disciple? But is there ever any difficulty about the one disciple? Is there such a thing as a *minority of one?* I fancy there are plenty of seconds in the world—that no man need ever be without backers. Preach what doctrines you like, some one will believe; commit what absurdities, some one will applaud; be as insolvent as you may, some one will accept your bills, some one will discount them; go mad, and there are plenty of medical certificates of your sanity. There is a law of endless division, we are told: Nature descends to infinite smallness, as a great humorist has pointed out to us, citing a bluebottle as his example. Yes; even a bluebottle has parasites, marvelling at the importance and grandeur, and admiring the superb buzz of the big fly. And those parasites, pray haven't *they* parasites? A man need not be a Johnson to have a Boswell. Hasn't some one Boswellised Boswell, and won't Boswell's biographer in time have a biographer? So, while Stippleman was bowing before the head of *his* creed in art, Lackington was adoring Stippleman, lauding his genius, and loudly calling upon the world to appreciate the lustrous beauty of his works, — "Wonderfully clever fellow, Stip," — imitating his method and handling, and following in his footsteps. And while these things were going on, wasn't little Tom Piper—a fledgling in the profession, a probationer at the Academy—wasn't he making Jack Lackington *his* exemplar, crying, "Wonderfully clever fellow, Lackington," pronouncing his art achievements to be "awfully jolly," and "jewels of

colour ;" sitting at his feet—a disciple, a believer ; copy-
ing his manner when he painted, and his indolence when
he didn't; perhaps, even more than his master, prone to idleness, for the imitator is always inclined to over-do (as a
bad portrait-painter exaggerates and magnifies facial peculiarities so that there may be no mistake as to the likeness) ;
smoking more pipes of stronger tobacco, borrowing halfpence when Lackington borrowed silver (perhaps Stippleman had loans of gold, and *his* idol, bank-notes), and
generally cheaper, and shabbier, and more worthless than
his pattern, like a piratical reprint of a book not good in
the beginning. And little parasitical Tom Piper—hadn't
he parasites ?—only I must draw a line somewhere, please.
I cannot take upon myself the responsibility of introducing
some people to the reader—and I don't know that Tom
Piper's admirers would be very eligible acquaintances.
Surely, I am bound not to bring more doubtful company
into this book than I can possibly help bringing.

Omega Street, Camden Town, was situated in what is
generally called an unfinished neighbourhood, which
means, of course, a very uncomfortable place. Incom-
pleteness is never pleasing. Think of the half-shaved
man ; imagine the woman whose unhooked dress yawns
at her back a ghastly gap—these are not creditable objects.
And a street snapped off short, barred by an ugly hoarding,
or blockaded with stacks of bricks, is not an attractive sight
neither. Mounds of earth piled up for unknown purposes,
deep trenches—sad traps and pitfalls to the traveller—
puddles of stagnant water, puddings of mire and mortar
and cement, stumps of houses—records of ambition that
brought brankruptcy and imprisonment to the builder ;
carcass erections, bristling with scaffolding poles like hair
standing on end, the wind whistling through the skeleton
windows and doors, and round the groups of London Arabs
huddling in the cellars, pic-nicing miserably on garbage,
midst fragrant oyster-shells, till the policeman turns on them
a circular glare from his lanthorn, and the light disperses
them as dawn the ghosts ; the heaps of broken tiles and
fractured gallipots, that will collect on these occasions ; and
the enclosures " where rubbish may be shot," which seems
to mean always that dead dogs and cats may congregate

with other nastinesses, and where the old battered hat and the worthless, worn-out one shoe, are ever present. These are some of the items of the prospect obtainable from the "eligible modern residence," in an unfinished neighbourhood. Of course, by-and-by, Time "makes a good job of it," as people say. That is, he generally does so : though I believe there are some "unfinished neighbourhoods" that never will be finished. Certainly there are carcasses I knew quite as a baby, that are carcasses still—and very dirty, and disreputable, and decomposed carcasses, too—at this present time. But, as a rule, we recognise the new suburb in time. A certain period, of course, is suffered to elapse, as with all new states, for the district to assert itself, settle its government, and appoint its beadle ; and then we are willing to concede that it is part of London, and to enter it on the metropolitan map, and in the Post Office Directory, and to establish relations with its vestry ; and this without a thought as to the untidiness that marked the outset of its career.

"I've lived in a good many neighbourhoods, Jack," quoth Mr. Philip Gossett, of St. Lazarus's Hospital, visiting his friend, "but I don't remember ever getting into such a queer place as this. It looks as though it had been dissected, and some of the best limbs carried off."

"Mind that puddle, Phil ; it's rather deep. They drowned a whole family of kittens in it yesterday. I admit it's not a nice place, but then it's cheap," Mr. Lackington answers simply. "You can't have niceness and cheapness too, I believe. You'd be surprised how little I pay."

"Yes, so's your landlord, I should think."

It was said jestingly : but the remark contained, like some other jesting remarks, a large leaven of truth.

The artist generally prides himself upon the picturesque disorder of his studio. Art-critics have often commended "litter" as a valuable pictorial attribute, and indubitably a sort of beauty is attached to the unkempt. But there was little attractiveness about the want of order manifest in Mr. Lackington's painting-room. It was unfurnished, naked-looking, cold, and damp. There was a gaunt rectangular stand of gas-burners supplied by means of a coil of flexible tubing. The apparatus had a painful resemblance to a gibbet, with ropes all complete. Its object was to enable Mr. Lackington to work at night: an advantage of which he seldom availed himself. In fact, as a rule, the man who gets through but little work in the day-time, is not likely to do much at night. There were no decorative fittings, so dear to the artist ordinarily: no bits of armour, carved furniture, fragments of drapery. For plaster casts the painter had a supreme contempt. The walls and ceilings were patterned with damp stains, and upon certain articles in the room, especially upon a stack of old boots and shoes in one corner, there was quite a thick coating of green mould. There were a few millboards and canvases, none of any large size, turned with their faces to the wall, covered with dust, and spoiling gradually from mildew. The mantelpiece was strewn with paints, brushes, bottles, old letters, cigar stumps, pipes, cards, half-pence, bits of string, a dirty shirt-collar, a boot-lace, a penny bottle of ink, tobacco (loose), a quill pen (split up), and a box of matches (upset). In the middle of the room was a ragged square of carpet, and on this an easel very weak in one of its legs, and supporting itself by means of a chair crutchwise. Visitors were often liable to the accident of moving this chair, unconscious of the service it was performing, and so of bringing down the whole machine with a crash. Upon the ledge of the easel there was generally a small canvas, upon which the painter was presumed to be employed. He never produced large works: it has been shown that he was not very industrious. If he ever commenced a picture of importance, he was sure to abandon the scheme before it was half completed; when he would reduce the dimensions of his canvas, and cutting out such portion as he had finished, sell it as a fragment, or a design, or a study, just as it stood. He was by no means without talent. He had been highly estimated for some time as "a man of promise." But then there are so many men of promise; perhaps people misjudge and overvalue *promise;* and those who are praised for their promise are often unambitious—satisfied with even that small measure of success. Jack Lackington, in spite of his promises, had performed very little. " If he would but work ! " exclaimed his friends and admirers ; " if he would but work ! " How often one hears that sort of exclamation ! and always, as it seems, in reference to the men who, somehow, never *will* work.

"Ah, Jack! if you would but work!" good little Robin Hooper would say to the painter, quite earnestly.

"So I will, Rob, old boy, some day, if it's only on your account. I'm glad to see you up here—it cheers a fellow up. If I had half-a-crown, I'd send out for some beer. The slavey has to go about half-a-mile to fetch it; but I dont spare her on that account. She's a tendency to fat. I'm sure exercise must be the best thing for her. There's nothing like exercise for keeping down fat."

"Well, you ought to be fat, if want of exercise would make a man so."

"Ah! Rob, you will be personal. Never mind. You see I exercise my mind; that's how it is. The artist is seldom fat—he thinks too much, and does not thrive enough, until he becomes an Academician, and gets his meals regularly. Corpulence comes with success. It's the penalty men pay for being prosperous. Don't meddle with those canvases, old boy, unless you want to get into a devil of a mess with dust and mould."

"Why don't you finish this, Jack? It's a very charming picture."

"Which have you got hold of?—excuse my rising to see."

"A girl in yellow satin, crying, with a broken tambourine in her hand; a rainbow in the sky, and what looks like a battle going on on the horizon. I don't know what it means."

"I'm sure I don't. I think it's nice, but I could never make up my mind clearly as to what I intended to do with it. Some one told me it was full of 'a precious infinite of symbolism.' I think I was frightened by that remark, and put the thing away in consequence."

"You ought to finish it. Ah! if you would but work, Jack."

"I shall finish it, never fear. The painter must never be hurried. That's one of the most important maxims of the profession. I shall go on with that picture some day—when I'm in the humour. You see, Rob, art-feeling is of necessity mobile; it has'nt the quietude of a fixed star, so much as the restlessness of a comet; it proceeds, however, upon a prescribed orbit. One must, of course, avail oneself of, and look out for, its return; but, meanwhile, what can one do but wait? It would be dreadful to try and work in a wrong frame of mind. What good could one hope to do?"

"There are long intervals between the returns of comets, I think, as between your periods of toil, Jack. I'm afraid you have taken up the theory of Mr. Muddle, the carpenter. 26,672 years ago you were at work upon this picture, and 26,672 years hence you will be at work upon it again; and it won't be any more finished than it is now."

"Thank you, Rob. I love satire. I don't even mind it's being at my own expense. You see it doesn't involve money out of pocket. But the fact is, you don't understand the artist mind—few people do. When it may appear to the ordinary observer to be the most idle, it may be really the most industrious. You mustn't estimate the artist's work by counting his pencil-strokes. It would surprise you, very likely, if you could know how truly busy I sometimes am, when, to all appearances, I am leaning back in this chair, as I am now, indolently smoking a pipe—enjoying myself: that's my body, but my mind is working within, Sir, like a steam-engine—very like a steam-engine. I'm sure I wonder I've never blown up; many of my imaginings are very combustible."

"Jack, you talk this stuff over and over again, until you half believe it, it seems to me. You must work with the grain, if you can, against it, if you can't; it's only shutting your mouth a little tighter, and working a little harder. People grow gray waiting for the right mood in which to accomplish their great deeds. If the mood won't come to you, you go to it: that's my advice."

"By Jove, Rob, you're quite a moral teacher; and there's a ray of sunlight fallen upon your head and a flush glowing in your cheeks—I'd make a sketch of you if I had not broken my pencil. You see what I get by having a studio with this aspect, instead of the horrid conventional north-east light. I should never have had that gleam lighting up your hair upon the old plan. I like as much sun as I can possibly get. I sometimes sit here and watch him peep in at that window, and then gradually glide round the room and disappear. You can't think how interesting it is—how full of art-value : and really it's a good day's work, say what you will about idleness. But what were we talking about before we got on to this subject ? Oh, moral teaching. Well, that doesn't promise much. Suppose we turn to something else. By-the-way, how's Arnold ? Is he still in town ? "

" Yes. But I see little of him—too little. He is much occupied, I fancy, about some business with his brother in-law."

" Mr. Lomax ? I know him. I've met him at Arnold's once or twice. Can't say I admire him. He's polite, and civil, and aristocratic-looking, of course. He's in some way connected with Lord Sandstone, isn't he ? I believe his mother was·a Chalker. But he seems to think that the whole duty of man consists in being a Government servant, and that the Wafer Stamp Office is the pivot upon which the globe revolves. He considers it quite a freak of nature—an eccentricity trenching upon lunacy— that anybody should elect *not* to devote life to sitting on a Government stool, writing upon Government foolscap, Wafer Stamp Office imbecilities. He looks upon people otherwise occupied as a distinct and inferior race—as Simiadæ, in fact ; but he condescends to be interested in their habits and manners, and asks questions as he would of a keeper at the Zoological, and interjects now and then a ' Dear me !' or, ' How curious !' ' How interesting !' ' Really !' or, ' You surprise me !' He alluded to me once .as an ' artist person,' poor man ! and afterwards was good enough to express a mild regret that he had never learnt drawing. He's a precious creature, is Lomax. Do *you* like him, Rob ? "

" Candidly, I don't," Rob answered, laughing. " But you see one must suffer him for Arnold's sake. It isn't much to do for Arnold, after all, considering all things."

" Arnold is a tremendous swell, Rob, as we very well know. It does me good to contemplate Arnold. I find that doing so braces my artistic faculties. Do you know, Rob, I've discovered that Arnold's nose is a bit of the most perfect drawing that ever was seen. I couldn't make out for a long time what was the charm that made me always

delight in looking at Arnold. Some people kindly thought
to assist me, and suggested that it might lie in his claret
or his cigars, which are good, I allow cheerfully, and the
idea was therefore creditable and reasonable. But no; it
was beyond that, and suddenly the thing came upon me
like a revelation. Arnold's nose is perfection! I don't go
in for Greek art much, as you know, and therefore I am
uttering quite a tame opinion when I declare that, in
point of nose, he beats the Apollo hollow. He's very
handsome, besides; but his nose is a *chef d'œuvre*, quite."

"I don't know whether you're in jest or in earnest,
Jack Lackington," Robin said, reddening; "but this I
know, that Arnold Page is my good true friend, and I
don't like even seeming to laugh at him behind his back."

"My dear Rob! Pray don't come down upon me in
that severe manner. I call upon you to admire Arnold's
nose quite seriously, as a superb achievement on the part
of nature, and you tell me I am laughing behind his back.
What a confusion of ideas, even from a merely anatomical
point of view! Well, well. Will you have a pipe? No.
I forgot, you don't smoke."

It was some months later than any of the events hitherto
chronicled. It was the spring time : other artists had been
toiling greatly for the exhibitions : sitting for many hours
daily crumpled up in unhealthy attitudes before their easels,
or erect, ceaselessly advancing and retreating as though bent
on bayoneting their canvases, accordingly as they affected
microscopic or dashing styles of execution. Mr. Lackington did not permit himself to be much moved by the considerations that so greatly agitated his art-brethren. Early
in the season he had assigned to himself the task of painting
a picture to be exhibited at the Academy. Nearly every
year he entered upon a similar undertaking. As he went
on, however, he discovered that sufficient time would not
remain for him to complete the work he had begun, by the
period prescribed. He had made a like discovery on many
former occasions. He then resigned himself to the condition of things in which he found himself situated. He
"took it easy" as he confessed; his mind was at rest on
the subject—he did not hurry with his work—it may almost
be said that he altogether ceased to work. And the state of

a cessation from toil seemed to be infinitely more agreeable to him than the state of toil. It is true he was not likely to gather laurels from the Academy, but then he despised the Academy. He sent for exhibition some minor production, generally the only completed portion of his abandoned undertakings of the previous season ; in fact, as a rule, the only finished works bearing the name of Lackington, were fragments of other, larger and unfinished, canvases. It was only by the sale of these excerpt pictures and of sketches professedly unfinished, that Mr. Lackington received any of the emoluments of his profession : and his receipts, as the reader has probably concluded, were not large in amount.

Mr. Lackington's proceedings in regard to his painting for the Academy were sufficiently well known among his friends and associates, and the experience of a course of years did not give rise to any lively faith as to the probabilities of a change in the artist's method of life ; yet, owing to a sort of superstition or obstinacy of credulity, or to the force of long habit and custom, there prevailed a practice of visiting Mr. Lackington in his studio a short time before the date of sending in to the Academy works to be exhibited, with the view of inspecting his productions. Perhaps the best excuse for the thing rested in the fact that much pleasure resulted from the meeting in the artist's studio of a number of his intimates—all for the most part mutually intimate. Jack was delighted to see his friends, although the object of their visit had become purely fictitious—farcical even. They came ostensibly to view works of art which did not exist, as they very well knew ; which never would exist, as they might also be well assured. Of art-talk there was enough and to spare : of art-fact there was little or none. And yet there was considerable enjoyment both for the visitors and the visited.

On the particular occasion of which I desire to make mention, there was something more to bring Jack's friends together than the old formal notion as to inspecting his pictures. The company were not brought together simply by the old tacit, spontaneous idea of visiting the painter at that special period of the year—they were assembled by invitation. Jack had announced himself to be in funds. It seemed that a new dealer had appeared in the studio world ;

he had made proposals to Mr. Lackington, and had become the proprietor of a hoard of very unfinished sketches of all sorts of things made at all sorts of times. The amount received by the artist was so unexpected, and appeared to him to be so inexhaustible, that he thought it right to summon his friends to his rooms to assist in its expenditure. They were faithful friends; they did not hesitate to rally round him. All the gas-burners were lighted in the gaunt studio; there was a great array of bottles and tumblers on the table at the side of the room; the atmosphere was heavy with tobacco-smoke; there was much and noisy conversation, with loud bursts of laughter breaking through it now and then. The effect was altogether very genial and pleasant to all concerned—except the other lodgers in the house.

There was great shop talk, of course. It was not of much consequence after all that there were no pictures by Mr. Lackington to be considered: there were plenty more pictures by other painters to be talked about and over. What about the pictures going to the Academy? What had the Bayswater fellows got to send? What had the Langham men been after? How did the Camden Town colony come out? Would it be a decentish sort of exhibition, did fellows think, even with the absence of McChrome, and Dogman, and Nudely, and Verditer, and the other swells who weren't going to send? And how about that picture of Fritter's? And what had Botter got this year? and Hatchman, and Stencil, and Kniggleton, and the rest of them? And what an awfully jolly thing that is of Stippleman's, cry some. Beastly rotten, declare others; for there are many opinions upon art questions, especially in art circles. "Very sweet," "boshy," "charming," "execrable," "full of thought," "utterly inane," "stunning," "idiotic;" these are some of the words employed by the disputants: "wonderful clever fellow, Stip;" "out and out duffer;" and so on. But be sure that Mr. Lackington defends his idol with great zeal and obstinacy—that is, he would have so defended his idol if he had been a little less indolent.

Robin Hooper's pale, delicate-featured face was to be seen in one corner of the room, and now and then his musical, tender-toned voice was to be heard, and generally, it should be stated, in defence of some of the reputations

that were being assailed. Artists profess to deprecate
violent criticism, but to hear them speak of their contemporaries one would think they rather advocated vitriolic abuse
or insane laudation. They never let anyone down easy, as
the phrase is. They always hoist their man up to the
seventh heaven or hurl him down bodily to the lowest
Tartarean depths. Robin ventured now and then mild pro-
tests against these tremendous decisions; but he found that
there was little appeal, that he was not much attended to.
He consoled himself with the reflection that his friends were
possessed of much less blood-thirsty and savage natures
than might at first be imagined : while he could not resist
the enjoyment offered by the genial oddity of the whole
scene. He had, too, a great regard for Jack Lackington,
loved him for his very foibles, and had helped him in
a thousand ways, and would be ready to do so again and
again for ever. And, of course, Tom Norris was there—the
pupil of the great St. Roche—and Tom Norris's faithful
friend and shadow, Timson.

"Yes, Rob, and I expect Phil Gossett, and perhaps
Arnold; he said he'd come if he possibly could, although
he's very busy. Heaven knows what about ! Fancy Arnold
busy ! It's rather a new idea, isn't it ? You know everybody in the room, don't you, Rob ? The little man with
the trim whiskers ? Oh, that's Binns. Yes, his is a new
face. He's a good little sort. He fancies he's strong upon art.
Oh, these little men ! Between you and me, he's rather a
flat : I hope our fellows won't find him out and chaff him.
But he's bought a sketch or two of mine on my own terms ;
says he's fond of artists' society, so I thought it civil to ask
him. I think he's a clerk in an insurance office or something of that sort. Go and talk to him, Rob, only don't
mention pictures, and get away from him when he begins a
story of an adventure of his upon Monte Rosa—he's an
awful bore with that story. There's nothing in it : only the
end of it is always such a long way off. I don't think
Alpine travel can be more tiresome to do than it is to hear
about ; but then I'm an indolent man. I think the true
picturesque is to look up at mountains, not down from them.
What do you say, Rob ? What do you think of mountain
climbing and jumping over *crevasses ?* " (Robin smiled, a

little sadly, perhaps, with a glance at his foot. How apt
men were to forget his deformity! But he said nothing,
and Mr. Lackington continued.) "I'm disposed to think
there should be an Act of Parliament to put down dangerous
entertainments, such as tight-rope dancing, trapeze swinging,
and Alpine travelling. I don't see the fun of a lot of men
all tied together, like the tail of a kite, or a rope of indif-
ferent onions, being dragged up a mountain side, only to
come down again with their intellects well shaken together,
more muddled even than when they went up. Ah, Rob,
it's only emptiness that ascends,—bubbles and balloons, for
instance. Let me lie on my back in a valley! But then,
as I've said, I'm an indolent man; and I don't care about
my muscles getting as hard as nails, I don't see that they'd
be any more useful to me. Talk to Binns, only avoid
Monte Rosa and the fine arts. Hullo, here's Phil! How
are you, old boy? you *are* late!"

"Detained up at Clerkenwell by a P. M.," says Mr.
Gossett, entering.

"What's been the matter? Mix yourself a tumbler of
something."

"My landlord fallen down dead in an apoplectic fit,
that's all. Been busy with the inquest. Where are the
liquors?"

"What, Simmons? Here you are, whisky, gin, brandy."

"Yes, Jemmy Simmons, the harlequin. (Which do you
say is the whisky?) They've made believe to cut him up
in pantomimes often enough. The thing's been done in
earnest at last. (Two lumps of sugar, please.) I felt half
inclined to mince him up into diamonds in the regular comic
scene way."

"Don't be horrid, Phil."

"Shall I sing a *De profundis* for him? My voice is in
first-rate order. Are you sure that water boils? I *have*
seen harlequins made into sausages. I do hope that in this
case——"

"You'd better be quiet; Robin can hear you. But you
students have no bowels. What good actors doctors are!
They always affect to have feelings."

"Poor Jemmy Simmons! It was drink did it. (This is
uncommon good whisky. It's rather strong; but I won't

risk adding more water.) The poor missus is in a dreadful state, quite knocked over. I suppose she was fond of him, though they never seemed to agree—a dreadful scamp, I'm afraid. But he was an interesting case. I never cut up a harlequin before. I think I should like to try a pantaloon next. Why, you've got quite a large party, Jack. Who's this coming up stairs?"

"Why, it's never—yes, it is though—Hugh Wood! Whatever brings him here?" And Mr. Lackington advanced to meet the incoming guest. "How are you, Hugh? I'm sure I'm very glad to see you here. I did not ask you, because I didn't think that you cared about this sort of thing. However, it's all the kinder of you to come unasked. What will you drink?"

"Thank you, Lackington. I owe you many apologies. But—— is Arnold here?" Hugh Wood was very pale; his eyes moved about restlessly; he spoke with a nervous agitation very unusual with him.

"No, he's not here at present; but I expect him."

"I called at his chambers, but I couldn't find him. I heard that he was coming here, so I came on. I want to see him particularly, very particularly." He spoke quite breathlessly, fidgeting with his hands.

"Pray stay," urged Jack Lackington, for Hugh Wood seemed inclined to go at once. "You'll find Robin in the corner. (What a long talk he's been having with Binns. But Rob would manage to get conversation out of a plaster cast.) Pray stay, Hugh, I've not a doubt but that Arnold will drop in presently. It's not very late." And then he asked to himself, "What the deuce can be the matter with Hugh Wood? I never saw him in such a state before. He can't have been drinking. By-the-way, that reminds me. I'll mix myself another tumbler." He had not hitherto been particularly abstemious, and the pleasures of the evening began to tell upon him a little.

Hugh Wood was muttering—

"Yes. I must see Arnold. I must see him, and I must ask him to help me. It goes sadly against the grain; but there is nothing else to be done now. I would do anything to avoid this. He is the last man I ought to apply to; but I can't help it. And Arnold is so good and kind, I'm sure he will do all I ask. It will be a mere nothing to him. Ah! he has come."

Arnold entered the room; there was something like a shout of welcome as he made his appearance, he was so thoroughly a favourite. He was shaking hands heartily with man after man, quite in his old cheery, winning way.

"No. I can't expect to be able to speak to him here. He will never be free. These men will never give me the chance. I will .wait. I must manage to leave when he does, and speak to him on the way home." So Hugh Wood said to himself as he watched the cluster of men surrounding Arnold Page, sunning themselves as it seemed in his glad, handsome, bright presence.

Yet he was hardly the Arnold Page of old. He had grown very thin, his face was worn, and there were decided lines about his mouth and on his forehead; his hair seemed to look scantier, and in certain lights there seemed to be a tinge of gray here and there robbing the brown curls of their lustre.

"How are all you fellows?" he said. "I'm deuced glad to see you again. How are you, Norris? How are you, Timson? Well, Jack, where are these bottles you talk so much about?"

There was something hectic and strange and over excited about his manner, so all agreed afterwards.

"Take care, Arnold," said Rob, at his elbow, "you'll find that brandy tremendously strong."

"Never mind, Rob. What does it matter?" he said. Certainly he'd prepared for himself a very strong mixture. Robin looked at him curiously, with wonder, almost alarm in his eyes.

"Bravo, Arnold! This is something like an evening, isn't it? 'Fill up your cup and fill up your can.'" And Mr. Lackington's manner gave token of a little inebriation. "I suppose you know we can't expect to see you often doing *this* sort of thing. Benedict, the married man, will have to give up his tumbler among other things. By George, what a pity! I feel quite eloquent upon the subject. I should like to make a speech: and I will too. I'll make a speech and propose your health. We'll do it with all the honours,

20

three times three, till we make Camden Town ring with it.
By George, we *will* make a row! Your health, and the
future Mrs. A. P., the prettiest girl in England —
Leonora——"

"Stop!" cried Arnold, angrily. "Don't make an infernal
ass of yourself, Jack Lackington."

"What do you mean? What are you looking like that
for? Why, you're as white as a sheet! Why do you grip
my arm like that? You hurt me!"   •

Certainly there was a strange look upon Arnold's face as
he pulled his friend a little on one side.

"Read that," he said, and he tore from his pocket a
newspaper, crumpled, yet folded so as to give prominence
to a particular paragraph. "Read that, and don't, don't,
for God's sake, speak of my marriage again."

He turned away to see if they had been overheard, or to
hide the expression of cruel anguish that was writhing upon
his face. But it did not appear that they had been noticed.
Binns had got upon his Monte Rosa hobby. Everybody
had been so cautioned against the narrative of his adventure
upon that mountain, that of course everybody was anxious
to hear it.

Amazed, scared, sobered, Jack Lackington looked over
the newspaper. It was a copy recently published of the
*Woodlandshire Mercury, and Stoneshire and North Hillshire
Flying Post.* His eye at once lighted upon these lines :—

"We have the pleasure to inform our readers, that from
private intelligence just received, we are enabled to state
that a marriage is on the *tapis* between the Most Honourable the Marquis of Southernwood and Leonora Agnes, the
lovely and accomplished daughter of John Jordan Carr,
Esq., of Croxall Chase, Woodlandshire, and Westbourne
Terrace, London."

"But is this true, Arnold?" Jack Lackington asked, in a
low, agitated voice.

"Don't ask me. I can't speak of it now. Where's the
brandy?" Jack Lackington wrung his hand, with an
emotion no one would have believed him capable of.

"Where's Arnold?" inquired Hugh Wood. "He's not
gone, surely?"

"Yes, he left two minutes ago."

"I want to see him particularly. I must follow him. Good-night, Lackington."

"You'd better not, Hugh, I think. Arnold is—not very well, he was complaining of his head. Better let him get home quietly."

"But I *must* see him, it's most important." And he hurried away. He came up with Arnold a few yards down the street. He had stopped to light a cigar.

"My dear Arnold," said Hugh Wood, breathlessly. "Pray forgive my following you—pardon my abruptness. But I have something very particular to say to you. I am in great trouble—I have much need of your assistance. You will not refuse me, I am sure, when you know all."

"What is it, Hugh, old boy? I shall be very glad if I can be of any use to you," Arnold said, kindly.

"You are very good to say so—I——" but he stopped.

Two men advanced, shabbily dressed, ill-looking.

"Mr. Page, I'm thinking?" said one, in a tone of inquiry.

"Yes. I am Mr. Page."

"Very sorry, Sir. But we have a dooty to perform. It isn't for much; I dare say you can soon manage to settle it."

A few minutes afterwards Hugh Wood re-entered the painter's room.

"What's the matter, Hugh? Did you overtake Arnold? Have you seen a ghost?"

"I have seen something that has amazed me as much. He told me to tell you. Bade me make no secret of it. I can scarcely believe it even while I speak it, though my own eyes have just had proof of the thing."

"What is it?"

"Arnold Page is arrested!"

"Arrested?"

"Yes. Arrested for debt!" said Hugh Wood; and he added in a lower voice, "And at this time of all others!"

CHAPTER XXII.

DURESS.

"WELL," remarked Mr. Lackington, "I *am* astonished. Arnold arrested! Arnold, of all men! Why, here have I been in debt all my life and no one has ever paid *me* the compliment of arresting me. No creditor in his wildest dreams,— and creditors have very wild dreams—they are generally persons of great imaginative power—no creditor ever once presumed to hope that he could do himself any good by arresting *me*. You see you can't get blood out of a stone. That the fact is so universally acknowledged, is a great comfort for the stone. It saves it no end of inconvenience, and pressure, and squeezing. *I* am left at large—poor, embarrassed, in debt, and yet free—while Arnold, whom I have always looked upon as a millionnaire, a man who might fairly have sat for the portrait of Crœsus—Arnold, whose life seemed to me to be one enormous balance at his bankers'—Arnold is ignominiously arrested and carried to a sponging house! It can't be, Rob; the thing's not commonly possible; there must have been some frightful mistake: or Arnold must have done the thing on purpose, to try a new experience of life, just as kings have before now played at being beggars for an hour or two by way of amusement; or he got arrested as a polite way of avoiding Binns' story about Monte Rosa, which seems to have frightened all the men away. He's such a tremendous gentleman is Arnold, he would rather undergo any amount of personal inconvenience than wound the feelings even of Binns. Don't look so serious, Rob. The thing isn't true. It's only a fairy tale. The genius of the ring has disappeared behind a cloud. Let's clap our hands three times; if you know an incantation say or sing it, and he'll emerge supreme and effulgent as ever. Where are you going, Rob?"

"To Arnold. He mustn't be alone; he mustn't think **that**

we fall away from him now he's in trouble." Robin spoke very seriously.

"Stuff, Rob. Stay where you are. Arnold told Hugh Wood particularly, that no one was to come to him to-night. But to-morrow morning he hoped to see some of us ; and to be out in the course of the day."

"Poor Arnold !" said Robin, tenderly.

"Don't take too gloomy a view of the thing, Robin. It will all come right in the end. Why do you shake your head ?"

"I fear all this is more serious than you have any idea of. Arnold has not been himself of late. I couldn't help seeing that, though I did not like—I felt I had no right, to question him on the subject. There has been something hanging over him, oppressing him terribly. I fear we have only as yet the first drops of the shower—there may be worse to come. It is not merely a question of money, Jack."

"You are right, Rob : I had forgotten." And Mr. Lackington's tone became more subdued. "He has really cause for unhappiness. I did not know it until he spoke of it himself half an hour ago. It is ten times worse than any mere money loss, though I should be the last to speak lightly of considerations of that sort. You knew that the engagement had come to an end ?"

"I feared so. I heard from home lately. There was great talk of it in the country : they were full of it. But they did not know the particulars. Poor Arnold ! How he must suffer under all this. I can't bear to think of it."

"But it will come right. I have faith in Arnold's luck. Dame Fortune has been so kind to him all his life that I'm quite sure she won't have the heart to leave him now." But Robin shook his head.

"If it were only the money !" he said.

"Well, yes. A man can be tolerably happy without money ; instance myself," cried Jack Lackington. "I've none, and I'm not particularly miserable that I know of. Perhaps it's the brandy-and-water keeps me up ; but I even feel particularly jolly at this moment : though, of course, I'm sorry for Arnold."

Rob looked at him rather curiously.

"I am, Rob. Put away that very unusual, sarcastic ex-

pression, please, for a more fitting occasion. Don't accuse
me of holding with some one or other that there is something not altogether disagreeable to us in the misfortunes of
our friends. It isn't that we like their misfortunes: because
we don't; but we like them better, because of their misfortunes. Don't you feel that you care more for Arnold
now than ever you did? Isn't he brought somehow ever so
much nearer to you by reason of his troubles? Before, he
seemed to be mounted upon such a pedestal of good luck
that I couldn't reach up to him, much less shake hands with
him. Now he's down, he seems to me more human, more
mortal, and I can get my arms well round him and hold
him to my heart. Brave old Arnold! Down on his luck;
locked up in Chancery Lane. I feel like a brother to
him!"

"Decidedly it's the brandy-and-water," Robin remarked
quietly.

Meanwhile Arnold resigned himself quietly to a state of
durance in a Cursitor Street sponging-house. He did not
permit himself to be violently dejected at the unpleasantness of his situation. There was much passive courage at
the bottom of his *insouciance;* and perhaps he had been so
long a time suffering under a dread of coming trouble, it
was a positive relief to him to find himself contending at
last with a real and tangible misfortune. About a vague,
shapeless apprehension of evil there is something more
dreadful always than in the evil itself. A great misfortune
had overtaken him at last—there was no mistake about it—
in the shape of a sheriff's officer. He resigned himself to
the care of that functionary; and the key was turned upon
him : the barred windows were in front of him. He felt
something as a recruit feels on the eve of a long-expected
engagement; sick with waiting; pale, not from fear, but
from suspense ; grateful at last to hear the roar of the cannonading commencing, and to know that he was certainly
in for the real thing at last; free to tighten his belt, moisten
his palms the better to grasp his weapons, clench his teeth,
draw a good long breath, settle his bonnet firmly on his
brow, and prepare to meet the enemy.

And this with no experience of misfortune, with no positive knowledge as to the extent of his trouble, with **no**

correct appraisement of his real position; only with a
suspicion, daily taking more and more shape and greater
ugliness, that matters were going very wrong indeed—that
ill-luck had followed upon the heels of ill-luck, and that
there was no help for it now but to stand at bay. He had
been careless, indolent, negligent, apathetic; he was reap-
ing the crop of trouble his own folly had sown. He had
trusted in others, had let things take their chance, and had
been tricked, duped, swindled; half laughing and conscious,
half unsuspectingly trusting—too true and honest himself to
take the trouble to question others—too apathetic and easy-
going and heedless of consequences. Well, he had shut
his eyes to some purpose. He now opened them in a
sheriff's lock-up house. Yet it was of little use now to sit
and cry, wring his hands, and do nothing. There had been
enough of doing nothing as it was.

He was an Englishman; with plenty of pluck and
activity when you could once bring him to believe that
need was for both of these. Prosperity had made him a
little sluggish; even if this were not in some measure innate
and constitutional. He would never get up and hit a man
if he could do it sitting down. In his old days at Oxford,
he had been known as a fellow who played always a waiting game—though that, it might be, was as much owing to
indolence as intention—who never did much until he was
thoroughly warmed to his work. When his colleagues
spoke of his sparring, it was generally to laud the noble
way in which he took his punishment: at first playing a
good deal—too much many thought—with his adversary,
treating the thing too much as a joke, not careful enough
of himself, getting up smiling when he went down, but
always somehow coming out winner in the end; for his left
fairly in play, there was very little standing up against it—
as all confessed—a hard hitter when he chose; only he did
not, the lament ran, choose often enough or early enough
in the game.

He did not yield, then, to his misfortune. His step did not
lose its elasticity, his eye its brightness; the look was still
open, frank, and cheery, though the face was a trifle thinner
and more careworn than of old. When a cloud of anguish
oppressed him, it was not to be attributed to the misfortune

that had made him a prisoner. Robin Hooper's quick perceptions had lighted upon the real cause of trial. "If it were only the money," Arnold groaned now and then, unconsciously repeating Robin's words. "If it were only the money!" And his thoughts travelled to Croxall Chase, and returned much the worse for the journey, loaded with a gloomy picture; his Leo the wife of another! And he could say nothing! do nothing! he had no right to blame anyone but himself. *There* was the real sting of his grief.

It was some comfort even to turn from this sorrow to his money embarrassments; on the plan of counter-irritation, perhaps. He stirred himself. It was late at night, but he wrote letters to be delivered the first thing in the morning —one to his brother-in-law, to be left at the Wafer Stamp Office, Whitehall; the other to his solicitors, who had acted for the family for many years, Messrs. Holroyd and Hopegood, Lincoln's Inn Fields, requesting at once their advice and assistance.

He had heard of sponging-houses often enough—certain of his artist friends had quite famous stories to tell concerning them; and he had read of them in modern novels: never dreaming that he should himself become so intimately acquainted with a place of the kind as to be locked up in one, a guest of the sheriff's officer. He half smiled; the position was so strange, and new, and curious. The place was hardly so prisonlike, so comfortless, as he had imagined it would be. The rooms were certainly small and close, and the numberless bars had rather a monotonous and wearisome effect; while generally there was a want of air and some absence of cleanliness about the house. But the people of the place were very civil—didn't look wonderingly at him, as he had feared they would; forgetting how accustomed they must be to all descriptions of prisoners for debt. They were civil, and respectful, and obliging, perhaps because of that prosperous moneyed look about him, which not even the atmosphere of a lock-up could tarnish, much less deprive him of altogether. He went to bed, lying awake some hours: but ultimately he slept soundly enough. It takes a good deal to deprive a thoroughly healthy man of his sleep, and Arnold had hardly known a day's illness in the whole course of his life.

He was not very early in the morning : he had rather a
habit of rising late. He was offered a private sitting-room,
but he declined it; he thought the public room might
furnish some amusement. He had little secretiveness or
love of concealment; besides, the chance of being recognised by any of the other lodgers seemed to be too remote
to be worth considering. He felt as though he were staying
at an hotel of far too shabby a character for any of his
friends or acquaintances to be tenants of it also.

He entered the coffee-room on the following morning.
He found himself in the presence of a fellow prisoner.
" Business was very slack," the attendant admitted, in a
tone of deep regret, and an accent guttural, nasal, Jewish.
" There aint but vun other gent in the 'ole 'ouse besides
yerself."

The other captive was at breakfast, with his back to the
door. The table-cover was rather creased, spotted, and
stained ; a black coffee-pot was yielding blacker coffee,
strongly chicorised ; there were two dingy-looking eggs in
cracked egg-cups ; and a violent odour of red-herring per-
vaded the room. The man who sat at the table, surrendering himself to the vigorous enjoyment of these dainties, was
very tall, thin, narrow-chested, with tufts of white in his
sandy hair. He was clothed in black, closely buttoned to
the chin, and wore a wide cravat of black silk, apparently
wound many times round his crane neck, and tied in a
minute bow in front. He turned round as Arnold entered
the room, exhibiting a small-featured, freckled, pink face,
with weak eyes and white teeth. He started up in some
confusion, and advanced, holding forth two long, white, wel-
coming hands.

" My dear Mr. Page," he said, in a high falsetto voice,
" now this is really kind of you, truly good ! " And the pink
of his complexion deepened to crimson.

Arnold, with much amazement, recognised the Rector of
Oakmere, the Rev. Purton Wood. He was next conscious
of his hands being vehemently grasped and shaken.

" Real Christian kindness : and the difficulty I had to
persuade Hugh to go to you ! I knew that I was right.
I felt convinced that there would be no hesitation on your
part."

"I fear there has been some mistake," said Arnold, as soon as he had a little recovered from his surprise.

"Yes, my dear Mr. Page, of course there has been a great mistake, a cruel mistake, of which unfortunately I have been the victim. Pray forgive me if I have not hitherto done you justice. I have not made allowances. Those of my cloth are apt to take perhaps too severe views of things. We have been parted a good deal, in spite of our being near neighbours at Oakmere, notwithstanding I am the rector of that place. We shall know each other better in the future. I hope your dear sister is quite well. I hope my excellent friend Lomax is quite well. I have been compelled to be absent of late much more than I could have wished, getting a substitute to do my duty, or simply driving in on the Sunday morning; very unwillingly, I confess, for I have all my life set my face strenuously against Sunday travelling,—opposed it to the utmost of my power,—it can so generally be avoided! But in an unfortunate hour, suffering under a merely momentary pecuniary inconvenience, I was so imprudent—I admit it freely, I avow my fault, no one can condemn my conduct more severely than I do myself—I was so weak and thoughtless as to obtain money upon my note of hand, given to a Jew, one Moss, a bill discounter——"

"Pray, Mr. Wood, do not——"

"My dear friend, I must insist! In justice to myself, it is only right that you should be furnished with the particulars of this unhappy business. I know nothing of business; the many calls upon my time during a long life of earnest toil, though I say it, have been of how different a nature! I am a mere child in affairs of this kind—quite helpless in all matters of a pecuniary kind. I fear I neglected to do what I ought; I permitted time to elapse. It seems I was not ready at some precise moment with a sum of money that was expected of me. I really find a difficulty in explaining, even in myself comprehending, how the thing occurred: and I fear I am using all sorts of untechnical terms. But I found myself sued upon the bill and served with what I think is called a writ. I let things take their course, presuming that at last they would leave me at peace; but this Moss grew very angry, and was unwearying in his

persecution of me. My furniture he could not touch, it was
secured by a bill of sale—I believe that to be the correct
title of the document, the nature of which I am quite at a
loss to understand—a bill of sale given to a third party—"

" Really, Mr. Wood—— "

" One moment longer and I have done. Moss then
sought to arrest me. You know we are on the borders of
Woodlandshire; I was down in another county, coming
over to the service on the Sunday, and returning the same
day. That terrible Moss! He had writs of execution out
against me in three counties—I was taken yesterday afternoon. Pray be warned by my example, my dear young
friend : never put your name to a bill ! However great
your necessity, never do that ! I sent Hugh on to you at
once. He is not all I could wish; it is with deep pain I
have so to speak of my own son, my only son. He is intemperate, headstrong, disinclined to make allowances. I regret
to say that we had a very distressing meeting here yesterday
—a cruel scene. I fear very high words passed between us.
I must avow that I have hardly that absolute command
over my temper I could wish—it is constitutional, I suppose.
I trace the same defect, in a very aggravated form, in my
son ; but I persuaded him at last to seek you out. He
found you at last, of course ; he followed you, I presume,
though it grew too late last night to do any good."

" But, Mr. Wood, I must really——"

" Yes, yes ; quite right, my dear Mr. Page—may I say,
Arnold? Surely yes. I knew your poor father intimately.
I have known you quite from a child. My dear Arnold,
then, you will require security : quite right ; I prefer even
that that should be so. I will join my son Hugh in a bond
to secure to you the repayment of the advance. After all,
the sum is a very small one, a mere bagatelle, though
swollen with interest and law expenses." The Rector of
Oakmere paused at length to take snuff from his handsome
gold box, closing its lid with a sharp click, by way of full
stop to his sentence, flourishing his yellow bandanna, while
his weak grey eyes watched Arnold with a restless eagerness.

" I am sorry you would not permit me to interrupt you
before—that you have not spared me the pain of this confi-

dential communication. I have already stated there is some mistake—some misapprehension."

"You have not seen Hugh?" the rector asked, quite breathlessly.

"I saw him for a few minutes only, last night. But——"

"He said nothing of my cruel position here; he did not solicit your assistance to extricate me?"

"No. He had hardly the opportunity of so doing. We were not alone—and even if he had——"

The rector stamped angrily upon the floor as he turned away from Arnold, and bringing his white fists down with a heavy thump upon the table, he made the fragments of red-herring, the dingy eggs, the battered service, and the black coffee-pot reel and shiver with his violence.

"That's Hugh all over, that's Hugh to the life—selfish, obstinate, pigheaded! He'd see his own father rot in a gaol, before he'd stir his little finger to aid him. What does he care! He was stayed, I suppose, by some infernal non-sense about obligation : or his wretched timidity and shy-ness, or some idiotic scruples of that sort. That's Hugh: meanwhile, I'm to go to the dogs. I'm to be ruined. I'm to die in the gutter. Who will care? I, a clergyman too—a Fellow of my college, before I was fool enough to marry. It serves me right."

"Hush, hush, Mr. Wood. Pray be calm."

"And I'm sure I've not been extravagant." His wrath dwindled into peevish whining here. "I'm sure my own expenses are of the most moderate kind. No man could live more simply. It's seldom that I take more than a pint of wine a day. I have speculated a little now and then, and been unfortunate. But my son's education has ruined me. His college bills, his thoughtless extravagance, his ruinous expenditure!"

"No, no, Mr. Wood," Arnold interrupted, gently, but firmly. "I knew Hugh at Oxford. We were in the same set. No one could have been more moderate, or temperate, or simple in his mode of life than he was : he set us all a good example."

"But you'll help me, Arnold, won't you?" the rector asked, suddenly changing the subject. "I well know you will. Your father's old friend—your neighbour and clergyman, the poor unhappy father of your old college friend, Hugh. You'll help me; a very small advance will help me out of this. And if I can only satisfy Moss, I'm sure I can arrange with the others. I know they will give me time, or perhaps take a composition."

" I'm sorry to tell you, Mr. Wood, that I am more in the situation of one needing assistance than able to give it," Arnold said, gravely.

" What do you mean? Why are you here?"

" Like you, Mr. Wood, I'm arrested for debt."

The rector gave a long, low whistle. It was rather a vulgar method of expressing surprise, but he seemed able to divest himself at a very short notice of the elaborate artificial polish of manner in regard to which he had acquired some fame in certain circles.

" I have heard strange rumours about you down at Oakmere," he said, with some violence of tone; "but I hardly thought they could be true. You're badly hit, then? You've melted down that pretty little property the old general left? or is this only a stroke of ill-luck, which you'll get over? You won't stop here though, I suppose. Surely you can manage better than that?"

Certain it is, that either the consciousness of impecuniosity, or else the fusty atmosphere of a sponging-house, has a soiling effect upon most men. The Rev. Purton Wood spoke now with a jaunty coarseness of look and action, a disregard of social conventions, an abandonment of all respect, both for himself and for others, that seemed to arise from long intimacy with debt and difficulty, and would have sat well on one of the most confirmed and permanent of prisoners in the Old Fleet, or the abolished Bench.

" I have done what I believe to be the best, if not the only thing to be done by a man in my situation," said Arnold, drily. " I have sent for my solicitor."

" But your marriage will pull you, I should think," Mr. Wood continued; "that little Carr will have no end of money. It can't be true, that rumour I heard the other day, that the engagement between you was all off?"

Arnold made no reply. There was little need. Two visitors just then entered the room. One was Hugh Wood. He glanced uneasily from his father to Arnold.

"He knows all now," he muttered. He shook hands with Arnold, and then proceeded to listen to a long petulant address from his father, whispered in a corner of the room. He received a string of reproaches with much patience and forbearance, biting his lips the while, but saying little in reply. He brought *The Times* newspaper for his father, and a packet of letters. The Rector of Oakmere was soon busy tearing open the envelopes, perusing the contents through gold-rimmed glasses.

The other visitor was known to Arnold. He was young Mr. Hopegood, the solicitor, junior partner in the firm of Holroyd and Hopegood, Lincoln's Inn Fields. There was no longer a Mr. Holroyd in the firm; he had been dead some years. Old Mr. Hopegood and his son, young Mr. Hopegood, were the only partners. The latter gentleman was advancing towards middle age. A pleasant-looking, fresh-coloured, well-dressed man, who always wore bright kid gloves and a glossy hat, and took a pleasant view of his profession and of life generally. It always fell to his share of the business to attend clients placed in lugubrious positions, weighed down by Chancery suits, suffering under adverse verdicts, imprisoned for debt. His bright presence illuminated these tenebrious situations, just as a cheerful doctor benefits a depressed patient. His cheery view of his profession and of life stood him in good stead with clients in difficulties. You caught unconsciously something of his hopeful way of looking at things; and began to regard with him the Lord Chancellor as rather a good joke than not; the Court of Bankruptcy as very like a picnic party, or private theatricals; and being locked in prison merely a form of change of air, and going out of town. He was a first-rate lawyer to consult in a sponging-house. The grimy coffee-room grew quite a gaily furnished apartment,—it might have looked on to a flower-garden instead of a narrow whitewashed bar-roofed yard—under young Mr. Hopegood's auspices. For the other branches of the profession, where dignity, solemnity, almost severity, were required—these invariably received the attention of Mr. Hopegood, senior, whose grave manner and silvered head had an imposing and quite pictorial effect at will-makings, the signing and sealing of heavy mortgages, and at weddings.

It was quite as good as having a bishop at the altar, the
securing Mr. Hopegood, senior, for the ceremonious scene
of completing the settlements.

"How do you do, Mr. Page?" said Mr. Hopegood,
junior, with easy grace. "I hope I see you quite well? I
got your note but a quarter of an hour ago. You see I
haven't lost any time. It doesn't do, you know, in these
cases. Who'd have thought, you know, of meeting you
here? Well, well; you know stranger things than that have
happened. Queer places these, aint they? Convenient,
though. Like a bad hotel, eh? Dear, and not too comfortable. Yes; the accommodation is not in proportion to
the charges : two guineas a night, say. You never set foot
in one of these places before? No, I dare say not. But
they're dying out. We shall have no more lock-ups soon.
It's quite worth while coming to see what they're like, while
you can, before they're finally abolished. However, a few
hours are quite enough, eh? I should think so. Well,
about this little matter of yours. It's a great pity it should
have happened; because one thing of this kind is generally
sure to bring upon us a host of others ; and then, you know,
we shall be rather in a mess, or something very like it.
Fortunately, this is but a small amount. And I'll see about
it, and do my best, and you need be under no apprehension
as to the result. I am glad you sent to us at once; because,
in these cases, loss of time is loss of everything. To tell
you the truth, I had rather an inkling of what was going on,
and I was prepared for it. No, no ; you mustn't put questions to lawyers ; and you mustn't ask me what I'm going
to do now. You must be content with the door being
opened, and your walking out a free man. Now, will you
excuse me for half an hour? Will you try and amuse yourself for that time in this queer old place? That's right.
I'll not be more than half an hour—perhaps not so much ;
and then you can say good-bye to Mr. Solomon. Only" (he
sunk his voice to a whisper here), "take care where you
go! Be prudent for a short time. I dare say the storm will
blow over; storms often do. I wouldn't go much to Sun-
dial Buildings just now, if I were you, nor down to Oakmere. I'm not sure that I would not try the sea-breezes
across the Channel. Hush! Good-bye!"

Mr. Hopegood, junior, waved his brightly gloved hand and was gone. The Rev. Purton Wood and his son were engaged in another part of the room. It seemed that the father had paused in the perusal of his letters to have a low-voiced explanation with Hugh relative to Arnold. Apparently Mr. Wood was satisfied that no blame could rest with his son. Indeed, Arnold's presence as a prisoner was a sufficient reason for no application for pecuniary aid having been made to him. The rector was more calm, less peevish, as he resumed his examination of his correspondence.

"This is from the bishop's secretary. I fancy I know the handwriting;" and Hugh pushed an unopened letter across the table to his father. "Yes; and surely that's the bishop's seal. The letter has been forwarded from Oakmere on to my chambers. It's marked *immediate*."

The rector snatched up the letter, inspected the seal through his glasses, then broke it hurriedly. He glanced over the writing.

"The archdeaconry of Binchester!" he cried, angrily. "What's the good of that to me? I won't take it! After waiting all these years, to be offered the archdeaconry of Binchester! The bishop ought to be ashamed of himself. I won't have it! Nothing shall induce me!"

"It's better than Oakmere, isn't it?" Hugh asked.

"Don't be a fool, Hugh!" his father said warmly. "How can you ask such stupid questions? Yes, of course it's better than Oakmere. Nothing could be much worse than that. But it's not what the bishop ought to have done for me. It's most ungrateful of him—most disgraceful, after the years and years I've waited; and the man who was my junior at Oxford; was my fag at Harrow. And he presumes to offer me the deanship of Binchester! And he knows my situation—he must know it: how I've been pinched for money; cramped in every way for years. It's most insulting! Why, the Southernwoods would have done more for me, if I had only cultivated my acquaintance with them a little more. Why, Hugh, you used to know that little Lord Dolly. You must have met him often enough. You must know him quite well enough to ask him to give me something. There are some very good things—really good things in the gift of the family. Now he's the Marquis, he might be got to do me a good turn."

But the rector could detect little encouragement of this proposition in the face of his son. He turned again to the study of the bishop's letter.

"Not his own writing even," he muttered, gloomily. "Oh! the insolence of office! Employing his secretary to write to his old college friend! Well; I'd better accept it, I suppose. I believe it's worth a good deal; and, perhaps, if Moss were to see this he'd let me out. I'd give a new bill to include the judgment he's got on the last, and to have a small advance to go on with. There are some things I must pay before leaving Oakmere."

He mused over this for some time, abstractedly folding up the letter, weighing it in his hand, then tapping with a corner of it on the table. An idea seemed to occur to him. He looked up.

"By-the-bye, Hugh—" he said—"stoop—lower. I don't want *them* to hear. There's another chance for you now—a good one. Do you know that Page's engagement with that little Carr is broken off?"

"Is this so?" asked Hugh, his breath very short, his face pale, his eyes wide open.

"Yes; Arnold almost said as much. And I heard it spoken of last Sunday at Oakmere. The girl's free. There's nothing to prevent you now going in and winning; only you mustn't lose time. There'll be plenty more after her. Indeed they say already that Lord Dolly's up at the castle sufficiently often. Of course the Carrs will try to hook the Marquis: but that doesn't signify. I'm sure a fine, tall, well-built young fellow, going in for the thing in style, would be safe to cut out that little whipper-snapper."

"It can't be true!" said Hugh, in an agitated voice, after a pause. "She loves Arnold: I'm sure of it. In any case, I haven't a chance, nor the ghost of one. It's folly to think of such a thing."

"You're an ass, and a coward, Hugh," his father said, passionately. "You expect everything to be done for you, and do nothing yourself. I'm sure I've toiled hard enough for you. I'm sick of it. What do you hope to get by hanging back like a cur? Do you think a pretty girl like that, with a load of money, will come and fall at your knees, and beg you to marry her? I'm ashamed of you!"

Hugh made no reply, though his lips trembled a little. A few minutes later his father said, in a more subdued tone,—

"Well, you'd better go on to Moss; tell him what's happened. And make the best arrangement you can with him."

As his son quitted him, the rector unfolded *The Times,* and was soon fully occupied with the news of the day. Arnold walked up and down the room, humming a tune or chatting with Mr. Solomon (or his assistant, who always answered to that name : there was some mystery about the real Solomon, it was supposed; no one could indeed be quite sure that he had ever seen him, though many had heard of him). Arnold was deriving considerable amusement from the information concerning men and things, afforded him by his Jewish janitor. There was novelty, if not absolute freshness, in views of life from a sheriff's officer's stand-point.

Mr. Hopegood, junior, returned within the time he had named. He was more cheerful than ever. He announced to Arnold that he was free.

"Only pray be careful," he said, pressing his gloved hand gently upon Arnold's arm, and with a subtle expression of face. "Pray be careful. Don't show too much. This is a trifle, and it's settled. By-and-by we may have to deal with more difficult matters. Take my advice, and keep quiet, out of the way. Go up that back street into Holborn, and take a cab. Good-bye."

Arnold took leave of the Rector of Oakmere; but he was so absorbed in his newspaper, that he hardly looked up.

"Good-bye," he said, almost abstractedly. "I shall be out myself in half an hour, at the most. Hugh's now settling with Moss."

It was rather pleasant, Arnold thought, even after so very brief a term of captivity, to hear the iron-clamped door of the lock-up close noisily, and to know that he was on the free side of it. He drew a long breath; there seemed to be more air in Cursitor Street that morning, he fancied, than usual—air of a quite pure, bracing, health-

ful character. Perhaps it was by contrast with the atmosphere of Mr. Solomon's house, which was certainly rather
loaded and thick.

"Arnold," cried some one behind him, as he turned out
of Cursitor Street. He looked round with a start. In
another moment he was shaking hands heartily with Robin
Hooper, who had limped hurriedly up to him.

"My dear Arnold," cried his friend fervidly, "how glad
I am to see you! I have hardly slept a wink for thinking
of you. I've been planning all sorts of ways of helping
you. But you're free, Arnold? You're sure you are?"

"It looks like it, Rob, doesn't it?" Arnold said with
a smile. "My manacles have been struck off. Would
you like to see the terrible marks they've left on my
wrists?"

They crossed Holborn, turning down Gray's Inn gateway,
to avoid the noise, for they could scarcely hear themselves
speak. They were soon walking up and down the large,
quiet, barrack-yard-looking square of Gray's Inn.

"I was going, Arnold, if you'd have let me, and indeed
you must have,—I was going to write down to the old dad
at home, Arnold. He's plenty of money, though he doesn't
much care to part with it. But he would in such a case as
this; I'll answer for him. He'd have been glad to help
you."

"You're very kind, Rob; but Hopegood has managed it.
I hardly know how. It was a small affair, but," he added,
wearily, "I fear it's the beginning of greater mischief. I
wish I could see to the end of it all; but I can't."

"What do you mean, Arnold?" asked Robin, looking up
appealingly into his face.

"I mean ruin, Rob," he said, simply, very sadly. He
felt Robin's hold upon his arm tighten : then that a tremble
ran through the poor cripple's frame as he said, in a moved
voice,

"Not ruin, Arnold; don't say that. I know that there
has been of late much to make you unhappy. I have
watched your face sometimes when you have forgotten
my presence. I could see that there has been something
distressing you terribly. You have smiled with an effort,
and there has been not quite a true ring about your gaiety.

21—2

I have asked no questions. It was not for me to add to your pain by pressing upon your wounds. You have been cruelly used, tricked, cheated of your happiness. I did not think that she would stoop to such conduct. But——"

"Not a word against her," Arnold interrupted with some warmth. "The engagement is at an end by my doing, not hers. I released her from her promise because, as an honest man, I could not ask for its fulfilment. She is free, free to give herself to whom she will. God grant that she may be happy in her choice; she can be nothing more to me : we are parted for ever."

"And you love her still? Yes, I see you do; and the engagement is over, with no chance of its renewal?"

"With no hope whatever. Don't ask me more, Rob. I have told you all I can. It is my own doing. I have been foolish, weak, mad—yet try to think as well of me as you can. I may not tell you more. There is a secret, but it is not wholly mine. Pity her, poor child ! pity us both. But think of our love as over for ever." And Arnold turned away his head.

"Yes," said Robin, pensively, "this is ruin indeed."

"Don't let us speak of this subject again, Rob. Accept it as settled. I hardly intended to have said so much. But it is right you should know that she is blameless. Don't let anyone accuse her, Rob. They may say what they will of me, they are welcome to, and indeed I deserve all that can be said. But not one word against my poor Leo ! I may have seemed to you cold about my love—to have trifled with it. But indeed I loved her, Rob. Perhaps I did not know how fervently until now. We won't speak of this again. Fortunately I have many things now to occupy me. I am deeply involved, Rob, I fear. Heaven knows whether I shall save anything out of the wreck of my fortune."

"But you have friends, Arnold, who will do all in their power to assist you."

"I mustn't make bad worse, Rob. I must not pull down those who hold out helping hands to me. I must bear my troubles as I can. Give up everything and start afresh in the world, as hundreds of men have done before me. That reminds me. Where are we going—what am I to do? I am told not to go near the Temple, nor down to Oakmere, for fear of arrest. I must take lodgings somewhere; or I must ask some friend to give me house-room for a few days."

"Let me see," says Rob meditatively; "there's Lackington, at Camden Town." Then he remembered that Lackington's opinions, expressed on the previous night, might not sound very pleasantly in Arnold's ears; and he doubted the painter's discretion in the matter of out speaking. "Yes, it would be the very thing," he cried out suddenly, "if you wouldn't mind."

"Mind what, Rob?"

"Why, they're rather shabby, and humble, and the neighbourhood's not a very nice one. But I think you'd be comfortable, and you'd have Phil Gossett for company; and no one can help liking Phil, though, perhaps, his piccolo is rather a nuisance to an unmusical man. I mean Mrs. Simmons's lodgings in Coppice Row."

Arnold thought the proposition an admirable one.

"It is so important that he shouldn't be left alone," Robin said to himself, "and I can trust Phil; and no one will dream of looking for Page of Oakmere in Coppice Row."

They found Mrs. Simmons in deep crape, her face less rubicund than ever, notwithstanding the contrast afforded by her large new widow's cap with its long floating lappets in front.

"You're very kind to think of me, Mr. Hooper, in my trouble. It's like you. I'm sure I'll do all I can to make Mr. Page comfortable. Oh, yes, I've plenty of room in the house. Lodgers are fond of clearing out the minute a death happens in a place. And I've been so ill myself that I could barely stand or speak. My poor Jemmy's death was so shocking sudden. But we shall get on better now the inquest is over; they buried him this morning, a simple funeral, but crowds of the profession followed. People have been very kind to me. Nothing can equal Mr. Gossett's goodness; nothing. Never so much as laid a finger on his piano the whole week. And the sweet letter I had from that dear Miss Gill; it would do your heart good to read it. I suppose she saw the paragraph in the paper. A very nice paragraph it was. Certainly, poor Jemmy was a beautiful dancer as a young man. I never saw his equal. He was not a good husband; and it was the drink that carried him off at last. I used to talk to him pretty sharply when he was here. I can't help feeling sorry for it now, though I know he deserved every word of it and more; he didn't use me well, but I've been so miserable since he's gone that I've hardly known what to do. Yes, I'm in hopes we shall get on pretty well. The children are wonderfully clever with the newspapers and publications. I think we shall be able to manage, though we shall miss him terribly at first. Poor Jemmy! It quite brings the tears into my eyes only to mention his name. To think that there's his Scotch bonnet hanging up, and he'll never again be able to put his head in it! I'm not in the bill of the Paroquet until the day after to-morrow; they've been very considerate. It will be hard at first taking off my crape and going into colours. I'm to play in the *Maid of the Wreck*. I quite dread it. I wouldn't mind so much if it was a laughing part: but it's a piece with a strong crying interest, and the audience will expect to have their feelings worked upon tremendously, and if I once begin crying I know I shall think of my poor Jemmy, and my nerves will give way, and I shan't be able to recover myself. One thing, there's enough to occupy one with all these children's mouths to feed, and the lodgers to attend to, and my parts to learn, and the job to make both ends meet. No, Sir, Mr. Gossett's not in at present. I expect him in the afternoon."

So Mr. Arnold Page, of Oakmere Court, became a lodger in the house of Mrs. Simmons, of Coppice Row.

CHAPTER XXIII.

TEARS.

THE Lomax household seems to have been going on much in its usual way. The customary eight o'clock breakfast; the departure of Mr. Lomax to his Whitehall office by the express train; the children's dinner at one o'clock, when Mrs. Lomax takes her luncheon—generally a substantial one; the return of Mr. Lomax from the performance of his official duties; a stroll about the gardens and grounds; the late dinner at seven, coffee at nine, and then to bed. A change on Sundays. The dinner-hour earlier; and attendance at the two services at Oakmere Church; otherwise, the daily programme of the family, as above set forth, was strictly adhered to week after week throughout the year. There might be slight incidental interruptions of this simple line of conduct; but even these were barely of sufficient importance to distinguish one day from another. There were walks, and rides, and drives, and the interchange of ceremonious visits with the families of the gentry in the neighbourhood. Now and then there were visitors staying in the house, but seldom more than one or two at the same time, though the old house could almost have lodged a garrison. Arnold would come down from town for a few days now and then; but he always seemed glad to hurry back again, and was, indeed, while at Oakmere, incessantly occupied, sitting up late at night over his papers and writings, and very anxious about his letters when the letter-bag came in from the post-office. "Mr. Harnold don't get on well with Lomax, and no wonder either," the footmen agreed amongst themselves. Mrs. Lomax's headaches had been more and more frequent, increasing so much of late that her maid had given warning. Mr. Lomax was less agreeable than of old: he had grown nervous, and fidgety, and petulant. The spring of his affable, jocose manner seemed to have broken; or there was a screw loose somewhere in its machinery; anyhow, it did not work nearly so well; it was nothing like so comfortably under control as it used to be. The butler remarked, too, that he had taken to drinking a great deal more wine after dinner than had been usual with him, and he seemed to suffer from an extraordinary antipathy to strangers. The appearance of some unknown person advancing along the carriage drive set him trembling dreadfully, and swearing and screaming to his servants that he was not at home to anyone, and that he was not to be interrupted on any account whatever.

Perhaps the most unchanged inmates of the house were little Edith and Rosy, late pupils of Miss Bigg, who were enjoying the incoming spring exceedingly.

Outside the Court house there were but few events of interest to be registered. There had been some marvelling throughout the parish at the repeated absences of the Rev. Purton Wood, and a whisper was floating about to the effect that his son had been "going on" rather in London, giving the excellent rector a great deal of trouble. A picturesque addition to Oakmere churchyard had excited much admiration. Miss Carr had erected a white marble cross to the memory of the late Barbara Gill. There had been objections taken at first by some of the most severely critical of the villagers, to the effect that the memorial was "papish." But it was agreed, at length, that, under all the circumstances of the case, the objection should not be persisted in. A simple inscription set forth the name and the dates of the birth and death of Captain Gill's daughter and Barbara.

And there had been another change. Miss Gill had quitted Croxall Chase, in spite of the earnest entreaties of the Carrs. She had undertaken the duties of governess in the family of Mr. Lomax. Her rate of remuneration was moderate, extremely moderate; Mrs. Lomax herself admitted as much. But then, as she urged, it was the first situation that Miss Gill had undertaken. She brought no character of any kind with her to Oakmere. Her presence at Croxall was only attributable to what Mrs. Lomax must really call a piece of Quixotism on the part of Leonora Carr, who seemed to take quite a pleasure in doing odd and eccentric things. Some of them very questionable in point of taste (but, then, how she had been brought up ; her own way in everything !) Miss Gill was probably competent; but Mrs. Lomax had no guarantee or assurance to that effect. None knew really anything about her, and it was feared that some of her relations were quite disreputable people. But after the disgraceful manner in which Miss Bigg had behaved, it was clearly impossible that the children could be again trusted to her care : and there was a sort of charity in employing Miss Gill ; though her position at the Court could, of course, only be regarded as experimental— and so on. Mrs. Lomax had a good deal to say upon the subject. Perhaps one chief reason of the engagement was comprised in the fact that Miss Carr was strongly opposed to Janet going to Oakmere Court.

"What does that little Leo mean by interfering in matters in which she can have no possible concern?" Mrs. Lomax demanded. And instantly she acquiesced in proposals which had originated with Janet. Mrs. Lomax was in great doubt at first as to the light in which she should regard her new governess. She was inclined to dislike her, from the fact of her long sojourn at the Chase under the protection of the Carrs. "But she seems a modest, gentle girl ; pale, nice-looking ; a very creditable governess in appearance, ladylike and retiring ; and she manages the children well, and they certainly seem to like her." So, upon the whole, Mrs. Lomax decided that her governess was a treasure ; and having made up her mind on the subject she retired to her boudoir, to lie down, and nurse and make much of one of her own patent and peculiar headaches.

Leo had strongly combated Janet's notion of becoming a governess, and especially in the household of the Lomaxes. "She won't appreciate you, Janet. She can't," Leo declared, in reference to Mrs. Lomax. "I don't like her, although she *is* Arnold's sister. I have tried to, very hard indeed, but I can't manage it ; and I don't think that you'll be able to either, my Janet. But mind, you must promise me that if you are not happy there, or if she ever says a word to you that she ought not to say, you will come back here again, mind that. This is your home, Janet, never forget that ; and I'm your sister, dear, now ;" and she drew Janet towards her and nestled her head upon Janet's shoulder—there was a wonderful intermingling of golden and rich brown tresses—and kissed Janet's pale cheeks so heartily that there rose through there surface quite a flush of warm colour. "But indeed," she went on, "I don't see why you need quit us at all, why you can't stop with us always—when we've all grown to be so fond of you, Janet. I never saw mamma take such a fancy to anyone as she has taken to you. I won't say anything about myself, because, you know, I'm no one. Only I shall miss you dreadfully if you go, you naughty, beautiful, cruel, darling Janet."

"I must go, Leo," Janet said simply, with a tremor in her soft voice. "For many reasons it is not right that I should remain here idle. I must do my duty. It is only fitting that, placed as I am, I should seek to earn my own living. Don't. think me ungrateful, Leo; I shall never forget your kindness to me ; and, above all, to her who has been taken from us. I shall never cease to thank you for that. I shall always owe you a great debt of gratitude. For Mrs. Lomax, I have every cause to be thankful that she has engaged me at all. I was fortunate to learn that she contemplated engaging a governess for her children. I will endeavour to do my duty. They seem nice, clever children. I don't think I shall have any difficulty in regard to them."

"If Edith and Rosy don't treat you well, Janet, tell me, and I'll see to them. I think I could make those girls afraid of me if I chose," said Leo, with a severe air; and then she kissed her friend, and tied round her neck a small gold cross—gold and turquoise—which Janet was bidden ever to keep for Leo's sake.

Finally Janet quitted Croxall Chase and took up her residence at Oakmere Court.

The dog-cart started from the Court regularly in the afternoon to meet Mr. Lomax at the railway station. One day, however, Mr. Lomax did not arrive by the train he ordinarily came down by. The servant who had brought over the dog-cart was a little at a loss to know what to do ; whether to drive back to the Court or to wait at the station the arrival of the next train.

"If I stop here,' he argued, "I may be wanted up at the

house, and get a wigging for loitering ; and if I go off I
may miss master, and if he has to walk over, or to hire a
trap, there'll be the deuce and all to pay."

Influenced, perhaps, by the popular delusion to the effect
that beer quickens the intelligence, or moved by the maxim
which instructs men in doubt to have a drink, he sauntered
over to the Railway Hotel—a small, terribly new-looking,
white-brown brick-built public-house — to refresh himself
with a glass of Woodlandshire ale.

Just then he heard his name loudly vociferated by one of
the porters attached to the station.   He turned ; a letter
was handed to him.   It had been brought down by the
guard of the London train : he had received it from one of
the messengers of the Wafer Stamp Office.   The letter was
marked upon the outside, " To be delivered immediately."
It was in Mr. Lomax's handwriting, addressed to his wife.
The servant rode rapidly back to the Court with the letter.
It was brought to Mrs. Lomax, nursing her headache in her
boudoir.   We will take the liberty of looking over her
shoulder as she reads.   A few lines only, hurriedly written,
hurriedly blotted,—

" MY DEAREST GEORGINA,—

      " Circumstances have occurred which will detain
me in London this evening.   Don't be under any alarm.
Business matters which I cannot leave.   I shall dine at the
club, and get a bed most likely at Long's.   Treat the thing
as a matter of course.   Don't let the servants or the neighbours see you uneasy.   If by any chance Arnold should be
with you tell him *on no account to go near* the Temple.   I will
write again if I should be unable to see you to-morrow.
Kiss the children for me.

      " Ever, my dearest Georgina,
        " Your affectionate husband,
           " FRANCES L. CHALKER LOMAX.'
" *Wafer Stamp Office, Whitehall,*
   " *4 o'clock, Friday.'*

Mrs. Lomax, when there was no one looking at her, was
not very readily alarmed.   She read her husband's letter
through twice, without much emotion—without turning a

hair, to use a sporting phrase. She did not even alter her reclining attitude upon the sofa as she read. Certainly she did not start to her feet after the manner of impressionable people receiving a communication of more or less importance.

"Office business, I suppose," she said at last. "What else can it be? I suppose it's more pressing than usual, or Frank would not have written in this tone." And she rang the bell: her maid entered from the adjoining dressing-room.

"Pull up that blind, Morris. I don't think the sun comes in now. My head is a little better. Put the eau-de-Cologne nearer. I will have a cup of tea when the children have theirs. Be kind enough to tell Miss Gill so, and the dinner need not be served to-day. I don't feel equal to it, and Mr. Lomax is detained in town on business. He will not be able to come down to-night. That will do, Morris."

"Frank is really too conscientious. He is quite a martyr to his office," Mrs. Lomax said to herself. "I am sure I don't know why he should wear himself out in this way. Government won't thank him one bit the more. Government won't do anything the more for him. But really he seems to have quite a passion for work. He will make himself seriously ill if he goes on like this. He is really too conscientious."

She had so frequently made use of this set form of speech that it seemed at last as though she seriously believed in its truth. She had found it effective to rustle about in society representing her husband as the victim of official toil. People were permitted to imagine that the Government of the country was in a great measure carried on by Mr. Lomax, and that he was in some way, no one clearly understood how, a member of the Cabinet, though his name did not appear publicly in the official lists. But Mrs. Lomax was *au fait* at certain of the secrets of social success: she knew that if you assumed a high tone, and were sufficiently vague in your statements, the people around, decidedly impressed, would draw upon their fancy a good deal concerning you, crediting you with a vast amount of importance: for a good many are reverent in such matters precisely in proportion as they are ignorant.

Mrs. Lomax took a cup of tea in the school-room with the governess and the children. It enabled her to study Miss Gill a little more for one thing. But she said little ; languidly rebuking Rosy once or twice for clattering with her teaspoon. The repast concluded, Mrs. Lomax retired again to her boudoir, and listlessly examined the last packet of books from the library.

" Yes, Miss Gill is decidedly pretty. Beautiful, Arnold says, but that's absurd ; men who set up for possessing taste are for ever committing themselves to such extravagant opinions. With more colour and style she would certainly be very prepossessing. She seems unconscious of her good looks ; one sometimes finds that in persons of her class : they are unaware of how much mischief they might do to man, as they say horses are. I think her system of education is good. She saves me a great deal of trouble, and she never answers me ; and how important that is in one's dependants and inferiors."

At her usual hour Mrs. Lomax retired to rest. She was not haunted by any unpleasant dreams ; she was not hindered from sleep by any terrible fancies affecting her husband ; she passed a very comfortable night. Probably she was satisfied that Frank was able to take care of himself. Certainly, however, she was unaware that a strange rumour was going round the village ; something to the effect that two strange men were stopping at the Crown Inn, armed with instructions from the sheriff of Woodlandshire, touching the arrest of Mr. Lomax. The rumour might or might not be true ; the Crown Inn was much disapproved of among the gentry of the neighbourhood ; the landlord was discountenanced : he was branded as "ill-conditioned," and his house denounced as the eyesore of the village. The Crown had been a reputable house once, but it had been demoralised by the workpeople when the railway skirted Oakmere, and had never been reputable since ; had been the scene of Saturday-night revels ; many "navvy" dances, fights, and frolics, that had shocked the propriety of the parish ; and it was said that the landlord (J. Skittler) had left off attending church and devoted himself to betting on horse-racing, cardplaying, and other low pursuits.

It was soon after breakfast on the following morning that

Leo's pony was to be seen cantering along the avenue leading to the Court. Rosy Lomax escaped from her French
irregular verbs to hurry to the entrance and greet Leo warmly
after her manner.

"How are you, Rosy?" Leo said, as she descended—then
to the groom, "Walk him about, George, please, he's very
warm." She entered the house. "It's mamma I want to
see, Rosy. I want to see her at once : I shall find her up
stairs, I suppose? Don't you come. I know you're playing
truant from Miss Gill. I know the way."

She gathered the long skirts of her habit skilfully together,
and hurried up stairs. She was encountered by Morris, who
was compelled—the young lady would take no denial—to
lead her at once to Mrs. Lomax's boudoir. Morris had
faintly suggested Miss Carr's waiting in the drawing-room
until Mrs. Lomax could see her. But Miss Carr had thrust
this proposition abruptly on one side.

Indeed, there was something peremptory about Miss
Carr's manner this morning. Her brows were clouded, her
eyes were bright, her lips were compressed closely, and the
colour of her cheeks had gathered into two angry patches ;
she was otherwise very pale. She hurried into the boudoir.

"Excuse my disturbing you so early," she said at once
to Mrs. Lomax, without further greeting, laying—flinging
rather—her riding whip on the table and tearing off her
fawn-coloured gauntlets ; "but I was anxious to see you as
soon as possible."

"Not quite so loud, Leo, please," cried Mrs. Lomax,
with an affected air of drowsy entreaty ; "think of my poor
head—and I have had a very disturbed night. You can go,
Morris ;" and then she asked herself, "What can the child
possibly want? How rude she is ! What does she mean
by disturbing me in this way?"

"Where is Arnold?" Leo asked, with some suddenness,
and without much heed to Mrs. Lomax's appeal.

"I don't know, indeed," Mrs. Lomax answered. "Who
should know, if you do not? I seldom see him—seldom
hear from him. He seems to have quite forgotten that he
has a sister, ever anxious about him. But why do you ask,
Leo? What is the matter? Why do you look at me so
strangely?"

"There is some mystery about Arnold. What is it?"

"My dear child, you are applying to the very worst person in the world for information on such a subject. I am sorry to say that I know very little indeed of Arnold's movements. Do not *you* hear from him? Has he not written to *you* even?"

"Yes," said Leo, and her lips trembled as she spoke. "He has written to me at last. I heard from him this morning." She undid some of the hooks of her riding-habit, and took a letter from her bosom. "The post brought me *this*," she went on. "It is in reference to it that I have come on here at once—as quickly as I could. Plainly, I don't understand the letter." She laid it before her on the table.

Mrs. Lomax peered at her visitor through her half-closed eyelids. She noted—not without an ill-repressed smile of satisfaction, it must be admitted—that there was a strange tremor in her voice ; that the sparkle in her eyes might arise from tears—it was not easy to be certain on the subject, because the flap of her hat threw the upper part of her face into shadow—that her bosom was heaving quickly, angrily. It did not seem as though the aperture left where the hooks of the riding-habit had been unfastened could be closed again very readily, there was such a raging storm within.

"I shall be happy if I can assist you in any way," Mrs. Lomax said, drawlingly. "I can generally read Arnold's writing pretty well. His meaning is generally clear enough. May I look at the letter?" And she put forth her hand to take it.

A look of pain crossed Leo's face : a look of anger : then, with a nervous, jealous eagerness, she seized the letter again, and thrust it back into her bosom, and held her hand over it as though to protect and keep it there.

"No," she said, with something of a childlike simplicity in her tone ; very soft now, though, full of deep, suppressed feeling. "No : I couldn't bear anyone to read it but myself. It's all mine. I couldn't let you see it. Perhaps Arnold wouldn't like it." She was obliged to raise her hand to her face now ; the tears had overflowed her eyes, clustered on her long close silky lashes, swung there for a moment, then fell, making a course for themselves down her cheeks, dripping finally on to the bosom of her riding-habit, just over the place where the letter was hid—the letter that had caused her grief. "It's a cruel letter," Leo said, "a cruel letter."

"I'm sure Arnold would write nothing improper," Mrs. Lomax observed stiffly, as she watched, not sympathetically, the tears drop down, one by one.

Leo checked herself, clenching her hands as though to struggle sturdily with her weakness.

"Arnold would do nothing that is unworthy, I know that," she said, firmly; "no one better. I can't show you this letter, Mrs. Lomax. But I will tell you plainly, shortly, what it is about. Plainly, then, it puts an end to my engagement with Arnold. All is to be *broken off* between us. I believe that is the correct term to employ. This is not much to you, Mrs. Lomax; but it is a great deal to me. I remember you one day confessed to me that it would not be greatly disagreeable to you if the engagement were so to end: that you were inclined to think that Arnold might have made a better choice; to fancy that he had been mistaken in the state of his feelings to me. Is it not natural for me now to inquire as to the share you may have had in bringing about a result you were candid enough to own you desired?"

"Indeed, Leo——"

"Have you influenced Arnold in any way? Answer me simply, please."

"I have not," said Mrs. Lomax, cowed a little by the stern tone of her visitor, by her almost imperious manner.

"You greatly overrate any influence that I may have over my brother," Mrs. Lomax continued. "How could I induce him to take such a step? By what possible means? Such a thing could not be."

"You are right. It could not be," Leo said, musingly.

"I am surprised at the news you bring, as I am shocked, pained. However much I may have regretted the step Arnold took in entering upon this unhappy engagement, I was prepared to wait and to accept its issue cheerfully when the proper time arrived. Certainly I would not have interfered, upon any consideration, to disturb an arrangement deliberately come to, and on which your happiness so greatly depended. I may have spoken to you with more candour than was judicious; but pray acquit me of resorting to any underhand measures to attain an end I desired, I admit, but I certainly did not expect."

Leo bowed her head. Amidst Mrs. Lomax's regrets and protestations, there was an undertone of triumph that was very hard to listen to patiently, while yet there was little in her remarks to which exceptions could fairly be taken.

"Forgive me, Mrs. Lomax, if I have spoken too hastily. It is only natural that I should endeavour to discover why Arnold desires to end our engagement."

"Does the letter assign no reason?"

"It speaks of an inevitable necessity, of unforeseen difficulties, to which he is compelled to yield."

"I hope that this may be so."

"You doubt it then?" Leo asked, quickly.

"No. Only it is strange, I think, that we should neither of us have heard anything of these unforeseen difficulties, this inevitable necessity. What can he mean?"

Leo's breath was very short. Her heart beat so loudly, she pressed her hand upon her side as though to still it.

"Arnold would not lie!" she said, with clenched teeth.

Mrs. Lomax was silent.

"Arnold would not lie!" Leo repeated. "Something serious has happened, or he would not write thus to me. I have never doubted his truth. I do not doubt it now. If our engagement is to end, I believe it will pain him almost as much as it will pain me. But why should it end? What can interfere to prevent it? And yet the terms of the letter are clear enough. Too, too clear! He speaks of parting from me for ever, says we can never more be to each other as we have been. Tells me I am free, and trusts that I may be happy. Happy! and never to see him more! What have I done that he should write like this to me?"

"I am very sorry for you, Leo," said Mrs. Lomax; and she was so far wrought upon by the poor girl's passion as to rise, take from the mantelpiece a *flacon* of eau-de-Cologne, and push it towards her.

Faint sympathy is as damning as faint praise. For Leo's heartache, Mrs. Lomax proffered the consolation of—scent on her pocket-handkerchief! But the poor girl only drew

22

fresh courage from the covert insolence of this attempt at condolence, as brave hearts always grow braver in the hour of trial.

"I do wrong to give way like this," she said, recovering command over herself. "I am forgetting where I am, to whom I am speaking. And you can tell me nothing, then? You know nothing of these difficulties to which your brother alludes?"

"Nothing, Leo; unless——"

"Unless what?"

"You will pardon me, Leo, for a suggestion that may seem little flattering to yourself. But you know why most matches are broken off? Because, as time goes on, the parties concerned discover that they have overvalued their regard for each other; or rather, that they have mistaken what was simply regard, for love. Unfortunately, too, men are very fickle—they outgrow their emotions very rapidly; indeed, they are too apt to transfer their attachments. They bow low before one altar to-day: before another to-morrow."

"You would have me infer——"

"I am merely—in the bewilderment of this affair—suggesting a solution; doubtless far-fetched and improbable. But Arnold *may* love another."

Leo winced, as though from a lash.

"It is not possible," she said, in a choked voice.

"Pardon me," Mrs. Lomax continued. "You mean not *probable*—it is quite possible that Arnold may have formed another attachment. How little we really know of the conduct, resorts, modes of life, of our brothers and sons living away from us! Who can tell into what indiscretions Arnold's life alone in London may have betrayed him! He is certainly of a susceptible nature, keenly alive to the perilous fascinations of beauty. Young, handsome, rich, a favourite in society, courted on all sides, might he not fall an easy prey to the arts and manœuvres of some designing woman? Upon what paltry inducements have men been known to make sacrifice of their every hope of happiness!"

"This is not true of Arnold," said Leo.

"I wish I could share your confidence, my dear Leo. I fear, in these matters, Arnold is inclined to be weak. He has something of an artistic—a poetic temperament, a sense of the beautiful, only too readily appealed to, too easily led captive. It was only the other day I heard him—but, perhaps, it is mischievous to repeat what, after all, can only be a trifling matter, an affair without serious meaning, though really, in his situation, he should have been more discreet."

" What do you mean, Mrs. Lomax ? "

" As I have been so unfortunate as to commence I suppose I must conclude ; but it may be nothing, after all. Pray don't let it distress you, Leo. I heard him speak, the other day, of the beauty of the governess of my children— of Miss Gill—in terms of the most extravagant eulogy ; employing quite a lover's words, with quite a lover's manner——"

Mrs. Lomax stopped with a startled look. They both turned, attracted by a slight noise at the door. Their gaze fell upon the figure of Janet Gill standing in the doorway. Her face was scarlet : it was evident that she had unintentionally overheard Mrs. Lomax's speech, had become aware of the story of Arnold's admiration.

She had approached the boudoir of Mrs. Lomax upon some mission connected with her charge of Edith and Rosy. " Would it disturb Mrs. Lomax if they were now to commence their practising, or should they first take their morning walk, or should Miss Edith now have her singing lesson ? " Mrs. Lomax and Leo had been so engaged in their conversation that they had not been conscious for some moments of the presence of Janet. Her cheek was still flushed, her whole frame trembling, when, having received an answer to her inquiry, she regained the school-room.

" Mamma's been scolding her," Rosy whispered to her sister. " I knew she was cross ; I could see she was when I went in to say good-morning."

" It was unfortunate that she should be so near when I had occasion to mention her name," Mrs. Lomax recommenced, when Janet had withdrawn. " I don't think, though, that she could have heard me ; I was speaking very low."

Perhaps Leo had her own opinions upon the subject : she said nothing. The interruption had the effect of terminat-

22—2

ing an interview, which Leo now regretted she had ever
sought ; but she had yielded to her first impulse to seek to
gain news of Arnold from his sister. She now perceived
that no good could be gained by prolonging the conversation.
Mrs. Lomax administered further doses of that sort of consolation which rather irritates than soothes suffering ; she
expressed abundant hopes that all might yet be well, for
Leo's sake and for Arnold's, while her looks and manner
were in flat contradiction of her speech. Finally, they
parted, with that icy cordiality prevalent in cases where
people are on very intimate terms while they dislike each
other particularly, notwithstanding.

The pony had it all his own way on the road back to the
Chase. He walked on leisurely, permitting himself even to
stumble, now and then, in a slovenly, sluggish way, without
receiving the punishment of the whip Leo usually awarded
on such occasions, and which the pony was something
astonished at not receiving. But she was lost in
thought.

"Yes ; she is very beautiful. If he should have
ceased to love me—if he should love Janet ! " And she
shivered.

She reached home, and saw the pony led away to the
stable ; still she did not enter the house. She remained for
some time leaning against the pillars of the entrance, her
eyes fixed upon the horizon, but without speculation in
them ; they were possessed by her cares, they were dimmed
with tears. Over all one thought was ruling her absolutely,
coming to her in different shapes and ways, presenting itself
in new aspects, under all sorts of disguises ; then, in a
moment, baring itself again, falling upon her with its terrible
force—each blow striking her in the same one vulnerable
place, with still the same agonising dread.

"If he should not love me ; if he should love Janet ! "

There was a sort of clockwork regularity in the way this
thought came to her, was dismissed, returned again, again
and again. It pained her terribly ; she quite writhed under
it. She who had known so little sorrow : to whom grief was
as appalling as it was new. And this thought that would
not quit her, that seemed to rob her of all hope of happiness, that wounded her self-esteem so mercilessly, that

deprived her of her trust in Arnold, in his truth and honour, in his love ! That gone, it seemed to her that she should lose with it all sense of right, all faith in justice, all belief in good. If for one moment she was able to clutch firmly at the hope—"He is true, he never could deceive me !" somehow she let it go again, directly afterwards, with a moan—"If he should not love me, if he should love Janet !"

It was so inexplicable that he should abandon her with this cruel abruptness ; that "unforeseen difficulties" should arise. What difficulties? If he loved her still there could be no difficulties interfering to prevent her happiness. "But if he did not love her"—indeed it seemed the only reasonable explanation of his letter; but how agonising the thought was !

Still in her riding-habit, she left the entrance and strolled into the flower-garden, now standing still as a stone for some minutes, now walking hurriedly, lashing the flowers with her whip, pale and angry, or tearing her gloves into strips. Then she entered the house to change her dress, pausing first to read once more that strange, dreadful letter. It grew quite crumpled and worn, that letter—it had been folded and unfolded, read and re-read, so often. She read it again, crying over it passionately. She had dismissed her maid and locked her door, purposely to surrender herself to her sorrow. Then she smoothed her hair, and washed from her face the traces of her tears, peering into her mirror to ascertain whether her eyelids were so swollen and red as to betray her. Then she read the letter, and cried again.

"How cruel he is !" she moaned piteously, with a child's simplicity. "If he knew how it pains me, this horrid letter, he would never have written it. He never could."

Then she so longed to tell some one of it. She could not bear to keep this secret horror locked in her own poor heart ; it seemed to be burning its way out, gnawing its bonds as it were, and struggling to be free. How precious, too, would sympathy be to her—real sympathy, the sympathy of some one who loved her, who would lighten her grief by sharing it, who would pour oil into her wounds, whisper hope in her ears, and so lull her to peace and rest again ! And who could do this, if her mother could not?

She entered the room usually occupied by Mrs. Carr—a handsomely furnished room, from which Mrs. Carr now seldom stirred, for she had aged very much of late, was crippled by rheumatism, was drowsy and listless. She occupied a large cushioned chair, placed midway between the window, when the sun was shining into the room, and the fireplace, and deriving warmth from both. For she was constantly complaining of cold now; and, indeed, had grown rather querulous and peevish altogether.

Leo kissed her mother affectionately, and was then made to draw a chair nearer and listen to a long story about the old lady's ailments, intermingled with a lamentation concerning the advantage taken of these by the household, to neglect their duties. Mrs. Carr took her daughter's little hands, and caressed them as she spoke, and then wandered into reminiscences of her dead son, and forebodings that she should never live to see her daughter married to Arnold. "Why did Arnold stay so long away? Why did he never come to see them now?" And Leo found she could not speak to her mother on the subject. She could not be sure of her attention, still less of her sympathy, for Mrs. Carr controlled and concentrated her ideas now with difficulty. "She will not understand me. Poor mamma!" and she kissed and quitted her.

"I don't know what's come to Leo," the old lady said to herself; "the child's very different of late. I suppose she feels moped down here. There are no companions of her own age now that nice good girl, Miss Gill, has left us. I think she was foolish to go to Mrs. Lomax, who won't use her well. But, poor thing, I dare say she felt a want of occupation after the death of her sister. She had just the coloured hair that Jordan was so fond of. If Leo falls ill I must send at once for Dr. Hawkshaw. I'm sure he's done me more good than anyone. But I'm a poor, ailing old woman now. I'm not long for this world I fear. Perhaps this place doesn't agree with me. I always told Carr it was damp. But he will have it that it's so beautifully drained. Men are so obstinate." She rang the bell. "I'll have my arrowroot now," she said to the servant, "with just a teaspoonful of brandy—and—put coals on. Why don't you look to the fire when you come into the room."

Leo wandered through the large house, in a mournful, objectless way, pausing here to open her work-box, there to take down a book from a shelf; now to scribble with a pencil in her drawing-book; now to strike a few chords or play a fragment of a tune on the piano. At last she entered the library. Her father was bending over the newspaper, reading sedulously through his double glasses, after his wont. He looked up, and nodded to her kindly as she approached.

"Well, my little Leo, and what can I do for you?" he asked, and he circled her with his arm, and drew her towards him. "Have you come to cheer up poor old papa in his study? Give me a kiss, my darling."

"Oh, papa, I'm very, very sad," she said, and her eyes filled again with tears.

"Why, what a sigh. Sad? What, you, my Leo? No, it isn't possible. What's the matter? Is the pony gone lame?"

"About Arnold, papa," and she nestled close to him, and laid her head on his shoulder, while she took his hand and pressed it to her lips.

"What about Arnold, dearest?" he asked, in a more serious tone.

"He has written to me—read;" and she drew the letter again from her bosom. Mr. Carr resumed his glasses. She shifted her position a little, so that she might the better watch his face as he read.

Mr. Carr slowly perused the letter, dwelling, as it seemed, upon some of the words in it: then laid it on the desk before him.

"Well, papa?" she cried, gazing into his face with a piteous look of inquiry.

"You are right, dearest," he said, slowly but tenderly; "it is very sad. Poor Arnold: I expected no less from him."

"You expected this letter, papa? You knew that he would write it?"

"No, Leo; not that. But I knew that the difficulties to which Arnold alludes might arise. It seems that they have arisen."

" But what are these difficulties, papa ? "

" My dear, Arnold does not detail them. It is not fitting, therefore, that I should do so even if I could—and I may say at once that I cannot. I have only a general acquaintance with the subject to which he refers."

" And you think that it must be as he says, that our engagement must end ? "

" I fear it must be as he says."

" Oh, I could never bear it ! " she cried, in a voice of anguish. Her father winced and his hands shook.

" Dearest," he said, " we have all troubles to bear, and we must bear them without repining. Strength will be given to you to endure, my Leo, it may be, even a more severe trouble than this. Don't cry, my darling." She could not speak for some moments for her sobs.

" But to lose Arnold like this !—for I know not what reason ! And to think that he may love another ! Does he break our engagement because he loves another ? Tell me—only—only don't say that you think he loves another."

He smiled as he smoothed her soft hair from her forehead and kissed it.

" No, Leo ; I don't think that Arnold has written this letter because he loves another. I think that is hardly possible. Ask yourself the question, dearest, when you look in the glass," he whispered, " and you may satisfy yourself on that subject. Besides, Arnold is a true and worthy gentleman. Surely you haven't forgotten that. He is not capable of a meanness, of a cowardice."

" Oh, thank you, papa."

" Whatever happens, dearest, think of him as an honourable gentleman. He may be suffering now as much as you are. Perhaps in releasing you from this engagement he was thinking less of himself than of you. It may be for your sake, Leo, for your surer happiness."

" But I don't want to be happy without Arnold. I don't want to be released from my engagement," she said softly to him.

" We must let Arnold do his duty, Leo, and we must do ours ; even though it should be the parting from Arnold for ever. Yes, Leo, for ever ! It seems very terrible, poor child; but you would be brave when the time came, and bear it bravely? Wouldn't you, my little Leo?"

She waited, lost in painful thought, weaving her fingers together round her father's hand.

"I think—" she said at last, in a subdued tone. "Yes," she went on. "Do you know, papa, I think I could bear a great deal if, if I was quite sure that Arnold really loved me!"

"My poor Leo!" said the old man tenderly; and he pressed her to his heart.

Just then a servant knocked at the study door. He came to announce that a visitor had called at Croxall Chase— "The Marquis of Southernwood."

CHAPTER XXIV.

THE RETREAT FROM OAKMERE.

"HOW d'ye do, Mr. Carr?"

"I am very pleased indeed to see your lordship," said the old gentleman cordially, yet with something of an old-fashioned formality in his welcome. "Mrs. Carr is still too unwell to see visitors. You will excuse her absence."

"I'm sure I'm very sorry."

"Poor thing, she is quite a martyr to rheumatism. My daughter will be here directly."

"I shall be delighted to see Miss Carr. Cold spring, isn't it? Thank you, Lady Southernwood is tolerably well; her health was never very good. I'm in hopes, as the warm weather comes on, we may be able to move her abroad. Poor Southernwood's death was a dreadful shock to her, and coming so close upon the loss of the little boy; and the weather is so much against invalids."

The conversation went on in thorough English fashion for some minutes. The weather subject discussed and exhausted, they proceeded to the contents of *The Times* newspaper.

"Yes," said the Marquis of Southernwood, "I was up in town for a few days. I only got back to the Abbey last night. Fellows were talking about it a good deal at the clubs. Quite a panic, they say, in the City. Some of the men deuced hard hit by the smash-up of that Silver Mining Company. I heard that Arnold Page was in it; a heavy sufferer, some fellows said. I hope it mayn't be true. Such a good sort of a fellow as Arnold is; but they were telling all sorts of stories about him. How d'ye do, Miss Carr?"

Leo had entered while he was speaking. She looked pale, but composed, her eyes very bright. She must have heard some part of the little nobleman's observations, his praise of Arnold probably. It earned for him a charming smile and a gentle pressure of the hand.

"She's awfully pretty, that girl," he said to himself. Perhaps his admiration was in some measure to be read in his glance. Leo blushed a little as her eyes met his. His thoughts flew off from her to Arnold again. It was by a natural process he turned from Leo to the man she was engaged to marry."

"I am sorry we don't see more of Arnold down here in Woodlandshire. Oakmere isn't at all a bad sort of place, nicely situated, very pretty country. A man might be very jolly there; especially such a jolly sort of fellow as Arnold."

It was apparent to his lordship immediately afterwards, by something he read in the faces of Mr. Carr and Leo, that his remarks were in some way unfortunate, or that their subject was ill-chosen. But he was at a loss to discover exactly what awkwardness disfigured his speech.

"I've been going, somehow, too fast, I suppose; I must stop my horse : riding too close upon the hounds," he muttered. "I shall drive them to mischief if I don't take care." He wandered from the hunting to a racing metaphor. "Is Arnold scratched then for the great stakes? Can it possibly be that the favourite has bolted? And was that woman up at the Court, with all her rigmarole talk, really trying to give me the tip in a quiet sort of way? Certainly I was blazing dull about taking her meaning."

It was evident that Mr. Carr and his daughter had become

embarrassed by the allusions to Arnold: his lordship couldn't fail to appreciate the fact. When conversation is thus run into a knot, the way is not to stop to untie it, but to start fresh with another line. Just as in arranging one's cravat, if the bow can't be managed at once, it little avails to struggle with the mischance: one must take up a new piece of muslin. The Marquis was not easily disconcerted: he was not shy, and he possessed considerable volubility; a man with such advantage is not soon placed *hors de combat* in conversation. He soon changed the topic.

"I did not come out this morning intending to pay visits. It was quite a chance my calling. I'm very fortunate to find you at home. I came out to try a horse of Chalker's. Did you notice him, Miss Carr? I should like you to see him; Chalker wants me to buy him. You know Chalker? I think he's Lomax's second cousin, or something of that sort. Chalker rides heavy, you know, and says the horse isn't near up to his weight. He's very showy to look at, but I don't think he's good for much more than a park hack. I doubt his hunting very much. I wouldn't trust him over timber; and I don't like his hind-leg action. One thing, this isn't much of a hunting county; at any rate, not in this division. Poor Southernwood, you see, didn't care about it, and didn't encourage it much. Perhaps we may be able to manage a reform one of these days. But if the thing once goes down it's rather difficult to get it up again. Chalker isn't a bad sort of fellow; but he's rather a flat at a horse. Not that his pace is bad if you can get him to keep it up. He's a chestnut. I called at Oakmere and saw Mrs. Lomax. Not very well, she said. Lomax was away on business of some kind. She hadn't seen anything of Arnold lately."

It was unfortunate that his lordship should have taken the conversation as it were a canter in a circus, stopping again very much where he had started, on the subject of Arnold; and now the confusion of Leo had much increased, for she was asking herself the question, whether by any possibility Mrs. Lomax could have spoken to the Marquis on the subject of Arnold's letter—could have revealed the fact that the engagement was broken off. Her cheeks crimsoned at the thought. Mr. Carr adjusted the apex of

his wig, and walked to the window to look at the chestnut,
the property of the Honourable Dudley Chalker. A groom
stood at the head of a tall, rather leggy, horse, champing
its bit proudly and leisurely, waiting for its rider outside
the porch.

"I'm sorry you're so far off the Abbey," his lordship
resumed, with a puzzled glance at Leo's blushes; "it's a
good long ride over here. Lady Southernwood isn't able to
see anyone yet. I hope she may soon. It's very dull at
the Abbey; but she likes me to be there. I run up to town
for a day or two now and then, but I never stay long. Will
you give my kind regards to Mrs. Carr? I hope she'll soon
be better. Good-bye. Just you look at the chestnut for a
moment, Miss Carr. I shall ride over again soon, to see
how Mrs. Carr is."

He took Mr. Chalker's steed a turn before the windows,
caracoling a little to exhibit the chestnut's advantages, perhaps to display his own admirable horsemanship, though he
looked very small mounted so high, waved his little closely
gloved hand, removed his glossy hat from his sunny curls,
and disappeared behind the clump of firs on the margin of
the carriage drive, at a brisk trot.

"Yes," he said to himself, "there can be no doubt about
it. That woman, Mrs. Lomax,—by George, what a jaw she
has!—meant to put me up to a wrinkle. The engagement
must be off! Arnold must be out of the running! But
why, I wonder? How's it come about? It can't be *his*
fault? How can *he* have come to grief? He's never been
extravagant; he's kept steadily out of a bad set of men; he
never betted, or very seldom; because he never cared much
about it: more for fun than anything else; he never played.
I can't make it out. Oakmere was always said to be no end
of a good property; that is, of course, in a moderate sort
of way; and quite unencumbered when it came to him.
What mess can he have got into? Women always liked
him, they could hardly help it: but he wasn't much of a
flirt, only in a joking way. He always held his own: knew
what he was about. It can't be his doing. The little girl's
an out-and-out good match for any man. He can hardly
be such a fool as to have thrown her over! Has the old
governor put a stopper on it? But I don't see the pull of

his doing that. Old Page, I believe, was a great friend of his. It bothers me completely, I own. Would they let him go simply because he's dropped money in that Silver Mining Company? I must get at the truth of the matter. If need be, I'll see Arnold. There's no girl I like better than that little Carr. Lady Southernwood's always at me to marry now I've come into the title. I wouldn't spoil old Arnold's game for the world; but if it's quite clear that he's out of the betting, I don't see why I shouldn't fairly go in and win. She's a dear little girl, and I can't help thinking sometimes that she rather likes me. Of course there'll be no end of chaff about the notion of my getting married. Even Chalker, who aint very witty and that, he'd have something to say. But, lor', all that don't matter much when a fellow once makes up his mind. And I am pretty well used to chaff, I am; they're always at me, because I'm a little un, and good-natured, I suppose; and, after all, one has to come to marriage at some time or other."

So Lord Southernwood cogitated as he rode back the chestnut from Croxall Chase to Gashleigh Abbey. Apparently he had some considerable difficulty in deciding upon the merits of Chalker's horse. "It's clear he aint a bad roadster," he was always saying; and yet he was constantly taking out the horse for renewed trials of his qualities in this respect, invariably selecting as the scenes of these judicial investigations the cross-country roads between the Abbey and the Chase. He was taken, besides, with an extraordinary interest in the state of health of old Mrs. Carr. He seemed never satisfied that he received due information concerning her. Three times a week he would call at the Chase to prosecute his inquiries, and to express his sympathy for the old lady. On each occasion he would return more and more impressed with the conviction that Mr. Carr was an extremely pleasant, intelligent, kindly old gentleman, and that there was something wonderfully charming in the limpid brown eyes of Miss Carr. He had never seen in his life such stunning—such beautiful eyes, he meant to say. And what a soft little hand she had, and what a lovely red mouth —and wasn't her figure perfect, and her foot—and how well she put on her things—and what a jolly seat she had on that little white pony! And it was remarked at the Abbey that his lordship's appetite wasn't anything like what it had been. A clipper—no end of a clipper—if I could only be sure that Arnold was really out of it, and that I could honestly go in on my own hook! I never loved any woman as I love her. By George! there's nothing I wouldn't do if she asked me. I thought I'd been hit befoie once or twice, but, lor', it was nothing to this. I'm in for it seriously this time—no mistake at all about it. By George! it's time I found out about Arnold, though. I shouldn't like to do any thing shabby—I never have yet, that I know of— only why isn't the old boy down here to look after himself, and hold his own? Certainly, I'll go up to town, and make sure, to-morrow, or the next day, or, at any rate, on Monday."

Meanwhile, the chestnut was galloped again to Croxall, and further kind inquiries made respecting Mrs. Carr's rheumatism. Even the old lady, recumbent amongst her cushions, found some amusement in these repeated visits. "Bless the little man," she said; "he's very good to give himself so much trouble. One would think he was an apothecary, he comes so often." And she rang the bell. "I think I'll have an egg now beat up in a glass of sherry."

It is not to be supposed that the neighbourhood failed to notice Lord Southernwood's proceedings. As the chief magnate of the county it was natural that he should be the object of considerable attention. The intimacy with the Carr family was much canvassed and remarked upon. The visits of a marriageable bachelor at a house in which one of the tenants is a marriageable spinster involve one inevitable conclusion. People who are not clever at putting two and two together can generally manage to put one and one together, as it were, and to conclude that matrimony must necessarily represent the sum of the transaction. The gossips of the place stated at once that Mr. Carr's daughter would be the future Marchioness of Southernwood. If there had existed any other plan for the disposal of the lady's hand, such was now entirely at an end. Gossips have always short and convenient memories, and rumour is not particular as to the exact dovetailing of details. The *Woodlandshire Mercury and Stonyshire and North Wiltshire*

Flying Post—a most admirable and largely circulated agricultural newspaper—had some months since informed its readers of an approaching marriage between Arnold Page, Esq., of Oakmere Court, Oakmere, son of the late General Page, C.B., &c., and the only daughter of J. J. Carr, Esq., of Croxall. Without contradicting or further referring to this statement, the editor now connected the lady's name with that of the Marquis of Southernwood. It would be difficult to say how this report crept into the printer's office and was put into type. The statement was certainly premature. At the time of its appearance in the columns of the *Mercury* there was little other foundation for it than the frequent visits of Lord Southernwood at the Chase, his trials of the chestnut, his inquiries as to Mrs. Carr's health, and the country gossip these facts had originated. But there are some editors so anxious to put their readers in possession of early information that they will boldly guess at truth, and risk the course of events affirming or negativing their courage and cleverness. Just as there are some liars who set up for being truth-tellers, or even soothsayers, because the facts of to-day have not absolutely contradicted their fictions of yesterday.

Mrs. Lomax had received further intelligence concerning her absent lord—a few lines to say that he was still detained in town by his official duties. The Chancellor of the Exchequer, he said, had complied with a motion in the House for some important returns in connection with the Wafer Stamp Office, and the whole department were employed upon them day and night. He hoped shortly to return to Oakmere ; in any case he would write a long letter in a day or two.

" Poor Frank ! how he slaves for that horrid office !" Mrs. Lomax went about the house exclaiming. " He is sure to be seriously ill after all this—a reaction *must* come. No man can stand such constant wear and tear. I am sure he is growing quite old and thin-looking of late, owing to his ceaseless exertions for the Government. They really ought to do something for him ; or else I am sure I should advise his at once retiring from the service. He is not suited to an office of that kind. He is too anxious—too assiduous— too conscientious !"

Meanwhile, it was strange, certainly, that in reply to many inquiries made day after day at the Wafer Stamp Office, Whitehall, the only information to be obtained was to the effect that Mr. Lomax was in the country—absent from business—by reason of ill-health.

Some days later, the post brought Mrs. Lomax a letter. It was on foreign paper; it bore the post-mark of Paris; there was a flattered profile of Napoleon the Third upon the postage-stamp. The letter was from Mr. Lomax, dated from an hotel in the Rue de Richelieu.

"DEAREST GEORGINA,—*Burn this when you have read it*, but don't be alarmed. I have been compelled to come over here owing to many pressing claims that have recently come upon me. A most unfortunate combination of circumstances has placed me in a very painful position, out of which I don't see immediately the means of extricating myself. In the first place, however, it was important to gain time. This could only be by my absenting myself from England. Things have happened very cross indeed; and a panic has almost hopelessly depressed the share market at the very moment when I was looking for a rise in prices to recover myself. *I fear Arnold will be a great loser.* I hope he will manage to avoid arrest. I endeavoured to give him warning; but I had enough to do to effect my own escape.

"Pray, dearest Georgina, do not let this distress you too much. Hope for the best. You must summon all your courage to meet this most unfortunate state of things. I cannot yet give you any information as to how long I shall remain here. But I will write again very shortly. And now as to the best course for you to take under the circumstances. It will be necessary for you to quit Oakmere at once. Without a doubt the furniture will be seized in the course of a day or two; indeed, I very much fear that Arnold's creditors will bring the whole place to the hammer. It will be a thousand pities that the Court should go out of the family. But what is to be done? There is such a terrible scramble always in cases of this kind; and creditors are always so cruelly rapacious. It is heavily mortgaged, and if there is a forced sale I fear there will be a very poor margin after settling the claims of the mortgagees. One thing there is no fear about : the annuity payable to you, and charged upon the estate. It is most unlucky that Arnold should somehow have selected this precise moment for quarrelling with the Carrs. I have heard, too, that upon some squeamish pretext, he has been so weak as to release Leo from her engagement. How monstrous a piece of folly this seems to me, I need not inform you. Of course old Carr will do all he can now to widen the breach—if not to break off the marriage altogether. If Arnold had but secured Leo's fortune, he still might defy the storm. But bad luck always seems to set in for such a long run. As I have said, Arnold will be a heavy loser ; but I think he may manage yet to keep out of the Bankruptcy Court, especially if he has taken my warning, and absented himself in time. Creditors are much more inclined to compromise when their debtor keeps them at arm's length. If he once lets them close in upon him, it's all up with him. Pray keep up your spirits, Georgy dearest, and for all our sakes try to put as good a face upon this matter as you can. Leave Oakmere as quietly as possible. I parted with the house and furniture in Great Upper Eaton Place some time since, at a time when I was much pinched for money, though I think I have not mentioned the circumstance before. I should recommend, therefore, your looking for a nice furnished house somewhere in the neighbourhood of Regent's Park. You need not stint yourself in regard to rent. Suspicion—which it is our interest to allay as much as possible—might be aroused by your taking too small or too cheap a house. There will be no rent to be paid for some months ; it will be quite time enough to trouble ourselves as to the amount due when the time for payment arrives. Give out that Oakmere does not agree with you, or that you desire to be nearer London in order to obtain masters for the children. Of course take Miss Gill to town with you, and don't dismiss the servants at the Court : they are Arnold's servants, not ours, remember. In fact, do all you can to cover our retreat. Should you find yourself pushed for means, I fear I must ask you to convert your jewels into money ; but do this as quietly as you can. I would send you a cheque, but that I drew out

23

the balance of my account, overdrawing, in fact, as much
as I dared, to supply myself here ; but you will find some
loose gold, I think, in the drawer of the escritoire in my
study.   Break it open, if you can't find the key.   You
will remove all portable valuables from the Court—
especially the plate; it will be judicious to retain possession
of these as long as possible, and they may be overlooked
by the creditors.   It will be as well to settle any small
bills that may be due from us in the village ; it will not cost
much, and it will have a good effect.   You might almost
ride up to town ; by which means you will secure carriage
and horses for London ; they can be sold at any time
if found troublesome ; and the luggage could follow you by
train.

"Remember! *Everything left in the Court will be utterly
lost to us*—because I make no doubt that the creditors
will seize everything in a very short time; but there
is no organisation amongst them, and a great deal may be
done if one has the start of them in matters of this kind.
Write to me what you propose doing.   You had better for
the present address all letters to the post-office here.   Excuse
the haste and, I fear, incoherence, of this letter.   I am
writing as fast as I can to save the post: and I jot down
remarks and suggestions, without much order, just as they
come into my head.   You will bear in mind that the odium
of the seizure and sale of Oakmere must fall on Arnold ;
by no possibility can we avert this.   A little more or less of
scandal carried to his account cannot much signify, therefore.
There will be no harm, consequently, in permitting people
to think that though *we* are to some extent sufferers, *the ruin*
is Arnold's—that we quit Oakmere because of his misfortunes.   You can even speak of his unhappy speculations
having been made in direct opposition to my counsel—to
his neglect of the advice of those so much more likely to
be informed on a subject of so vital an importance, and so
on.   If this sort of notion but be spread about—which will
really hurt Arnold in no way—it will materially strengthen
our position.   I will write again very shortly.   I am
quite confident that you will do everything for the best.   I
trust your head has not been troubling you.   Make a
few visits in the neighbourhood before quitting the

Court, and explain your departure in the way you think most desirable. And with love and kisses to the children,

"Believe me, dearest Georgina,
"Ever your affectionate husband,
"FRANCIS L. CHALKER LOMAX."
" P.S.—*Be very careful to destroy this letter.*"

Mrs. Lomax had some right to be startled by this strange and unexpected communication. If she commenced her perusal reclining on the sofa, she concluded the letter in a much more energetic position. She had started to her feet. She was clutching the mantelpiece: the paper fell on the ground, as she raised her hand to press her forehead, throbbing now with something beyond accustomed aches. Next she read through the letter again : her intelligence seemed at first paralysed by her surprise, and she seemed unable to grasp at the meaning of her husband's words. What did she know of, how could she be expected to understand, pecuniary embarrassment—she who, as General Page's daughter, Arnold's sister, Francis Lomax's wife, had never had a wish ungratified, if money was in any way depended upon in the matter? Her husband fled to avoid his creditors, Arnold irretrievably ruined, Oakmere Court to be abandoned—sold to the highest bidder—perforce, the old house and estate gone from the family for ever ! It was was hardly credible. And the frightful suddenness of all this. She might well be shocked.

She had not possessed the slightest conception or suspicion of the mischief that had been impending ; and this notwithstanding the very cordial understanding and confidence that had appeared to exist between her husband and herself. She knew that he was a proprietor of shares in various undertakings—speculated, indeed—without having any very clear notion that speculation implied almost equal probabilities as to loss and gain. Life had always, to her mind, represented affluence—a well furnished table, good society, horses and carriages, a perpetual balance at the bankers'. She could not understand a sudden taking away of all these things any more than the abrupt lopping off of her limbs. She had, of course, heard and read often enough of loss,

23—2

and bankruptcy, misfortune, creditors, ruin — but without once dreaming that such influences could ever draw near to her detriment, could ever affect her in any way. She deemed them as visitations which might afflict other people; but she thought herself in some way secured and fortified against any such ill chance. She had brought herself, by some process of thought, to an active belief that she had been, as it were, vaccinated by fate, and rendered proof aginst the attacks of misfortune, as she had been, when a child, secured against the evils of small-pox.

Arnold ruined! The thought could not but be very painful to her. She had a considerable affection for her brother, though she had been a good deal in the habit of plastering over her feelings with sham sentiment, very dangerous to their vitality; just as other ladies are prone to spoil the beauty of their complexions by injurious coatings of rouge and pearl-powder. But, in truth, after all her frothy talk and artificial decorations of the subject had been cleared away, there certainly remained a genuine foundation of regard for Arnold. It was very sad. Ruined! and, in some way, she knew not how precisely, ruined by her husband. She could not but see *that*, though Mr. Lomax had forborne to make any clear confession on the subject; and had she done nothing to further the completion of the catastrophe? The marriage which — her husband admitted as much — might have saved Arnold, had she not done all in her power to postpone and prevent? Had she not sought to mine Leo's love for and confidence in Arnold? Had she not endeavoured to effect a breach in their engagement, and to widen the division between them by every artifice her ingenuity could suggest, even to the calling in the aid of Leo's jealousy, to ensure the success of the scheme? Had she not hastened to inform little Lord Southernwood—not directly, but at least by suggestions—that the engagement was at an end? only that his lordship had seemed obtuse on the subject, influenced perhaps by his own attachment to Leo, his regard for his friend Arnold, or his want of confidence in himself and his own merits. Yes, unwittingly perhaps, but no less certainly, she had hurried Arnold's downfall.

As to her husband's position, there seemed to be less

precise information. But it was clear, according to his own statement, that he had left the country to avoid arrest, and it was not possible to say how long his expatriation might endure. However, there was work to be done, and she must nerve herself to do it.

Beneath Mrs. Lomax's affectation of languor and ill-health there was much greater strength of character, much more cleverness than, perhaps, many people would have been disposed to admit. Perhaps she was in something of the same case as the old Roman conspirator, who came on the stage in his nightcap, and said, " I'm not sick, if there's anything going on worth being well for." Perhaps she drew strength from the occasion : clearly it was no time for one of her headaches now. She bathed her temples, dined with Miss Gill and the children, the while calm, placid, cheerful, but with dignity ; ordered the barouche, fortified herself with one or two extra glasses of sherry, and went forth to pay a round of visits.

The courage which women so constantly exhibit in periods of peril, even in cases where men are sometimes terribly cowed and cast down, presents a circumstance worthy of more consideration and comment than I can here afford to give to it. Is it that, possessing less imagination than man, as well as less reason and foresight (I am not flattering the sex now, am I?), they are the less likely to magnify their danger, less likely to appraise it with any exactness ; or are they moved by a greater faith, amounting to a strange sort of confidence that what they desire will somehow be brought to pass? But I must leave the reader to ponder this little matter at his leisure.

More or less conscious of the disasters that had fallen upon her family, Mrs. Lomax paid visits to her friends in the neighbourhood, including Mr. and Miss Carr, Mrs. Carr being still unable to receive visitors.

Mrs. Lomax took occasion to mention, in the course of her conversation, that she was about to quit Oakmere Court ; for one reason, that her brother had views in regard to it which, while she regretted, she was powerless to avert. She fancied that he might even part with possession of the property altogether. But she was without certain information on the subject. Such a proceeding would be, of course, opposed to the wishes of Mr. Lomax and herself. But, indeed, she was not sorry, for many reasons, to quit the country for a time. She rather looked forward to a season in London. They thought of taking a furnished house in town for some months : their own house, in Eaton Place, was unfortunately let : they couldn't very well turn out an excellent tenant, or make him suffer for their change of plan. No ; she should not see much of the gay world. She was not particular as to the situation of the house, so that there was plenty of room in it—with children plenty of room was so desirable. She was the more anxious to be in town, because she couldn't bear to be alone in the country, and Mr. Lomax would be absent from her for some little time, she feared. He had been very busy of late, terribly over-worked, he really was too conscientious—tried to do too much. But the financial department of the Government had been very much occupied of late. She believed some important changes were in contemplation, but she really did not understand the matter much, though Mr. Lomax had kindly tried to explain the matter to her. She had always been but a poor creature at figures. Mr. Lomax was at present abroad. It was in connection with his official duties —he was entrusted, she believed, with the settlement of some kind of Continental commercial treaty, but she knew nothing of the particulars ; it was a position of great res-ponsibility ; the time he would be absent was very uncertain, it depended upon so many things. In London she should be so much nearer to her own doctor ; it would be so great a comfort to her, for her health had been anything but good of late, her headaches were dreadfully frequent in their re-currence, and had of late increased in violence. There were drawbacks, too, as to the education of children in the country. Miss Gill was giving her every satisfaction ; her attention was unremitting ; she was really quite a treasure ; but Edith and Rosa were of an age now when the assistance of masters was imperatively required, and Oakmere was so inconveniently situated for anything of that kind—and so on. She entertained her acquaintances with a very plausible narrative, and everybody appeared to be perfectly convinced that under the circumstances the departure of the Lomaxes from Oakmere was, although much to be lamented, still un avoidable. Even old Mr. Carr seemed to be quite satisfied on this head; at least no one noticed that there was a certain strangeness in the smile he wore as he listened to Mrs. Lomax, bowing his head, shaking hands with her, and afterwards conducting her to her carriage with so much old fashioned courtesy. Leo had kept watchful eyes on the visitor, but had taken but little part in the conversation; but she greeted very warmly, kissing them profusely, Edith and Rosy, who had seats in the barouche, and had learned with great glee that they were very soon to quit Oakmere for London. "And we shall go shopping, and have new dresses," said Edith. "Yes," cried Rosy, "and see 'Punch and Judy' in the street, and go to the Z'logical Gardens; and, perhaps, papa or Uncle Ar will take us to the play. Won't it be fun?"

Certainly Mrs. Lomax showed herself equal to the occasion. She managed the retreat from Oakmere very cleverly, exhibiting very adroit generalship; carrying off her baggage and munitions of war so completely, that not so much as a silver spoon fell into the hands of the enemy. And there seemed to be no suspicion touching the motive of her flight. If Mr. Carr was better informed on the subject than other people, he held his peace (the old gentleman had almost a genius for reticence and reserve), and the family credit was not impeachable in the neighbourhood. The petty claims in the village were duly satisfied; there could be no further trouble on their account. Mr. Lomax was not without the wisdom of this world. He knew that the small creditors are always the more troublesome; that people are given to put down their sovereigns carelessly, while they struggle with earnest effort for the possession of halfpence; that it is difficult to believe in great losses, but everyone is anxious to guard against little misfortunes; and that when to a man with large debts and little money, occurs the question, "Whom to pay?" unless he is inclined to defy society altogether by crying, "No one!"—he will answer wisely, "I will pay those small near creditors, in contact with me, invested, therefore, with greater powers of annoyance—those of my own household, my servants, tradespeople, the water-rates—it's dreadful to have no water in the cistern! I will provide for the fleabites, which are immediate, inevitable.

I will run the risk of being devoured alive, which is remote, and perhaps, after all, problematical."

Notwithstanding, therefore, the suddenness of their movements, the Lomax family quitted Oakmere, as it were, under a triumphal arch, with *éclat*, without suspicion; and the shutters were closed in many of the windows of the house, which put on, as though in mourning for the departed, a desolate, forlorn, uninhabited look.

" Can anyone be dead, I wonder ? "

The gentleman who muttered this inquiry had come down from London by the train. He contemplated the altered aspect of the house with some apprehension.

" If she should have escaped me again ! " It was Monsieur Anatole who spoke.

He rang a bell at a side door of the house; some time elapsed before his summons received any attention.

" The family have left for town." Such was the information he finally obtained.

Monsieur Anatole was evidently enraged; he trembled as though palsied; he swore many oaths in a foreign tone, and shook a sallow knuckly fist menacingly in the air. Finally, he ground his heel into the gravel-walk before the house, and, turning his back upon Oakmere, resumed the road back to the nearest railway station.

"*O petite !*" he mumbled angrily, "if my love goes to turn to hate ! "

Lord Southernwood made very praiseworthy efforts to learn something of Arnold Page and his movements, even at last to going up to town to prosecute inquiries concerning him. But " fellows at the club " would give no information. Page hadn't "turned up at the Junior Adonis for ever so long." There was an idea prevalent that he had left England, "doosid hard hit and that," by the smash up of the Dom Ferdinando El Rey Silver Mining Company; but it was thought that he would show up again in time, when the thing had blown over a bit. And "fellows at the club" asked Lord Southernwood, in his turn—" Was it true that Arnold's affair with that little Carr was all off? And, supposing that to be the case, what an awful sell it was of

Arnold, wasn't it though? And what a pity he hadn't married her at the end of last season; he might have made it
all right with her money. And what a nice little girl she
was—fellows all liked her; little, you know, but no end of
pretty." Lord Southernwood could arrive at no positive
information concerning his friend.

He even ventured into the Temple, and found his way to
Sun-dial Buildings, after some little difficulty and considerable discussion with a beadle in an orange cape, and a knot
of porters in very short aprons, and with pewter badges
almost as big as cheese plates in front of them. (Why do
Inns of Court porters always wear short aprons and pewter
badges?) He had visited Arnold once or twice in the
Temple in the old prosperous days, but the organ of locality
was not highly developed in his lordship's phrenological
economy, and he had always had great difficulty in discover-
ing Sun-dial Buildings. Perhaps the Temple is rather
intricate and bewildering to strangers.

But Arnold's chambers reached, there was little gained.
The black outer door was closed. He had the pleasure of
reading his friend's name in white paint outside, and of
slipping his card through the letter-slip, hearing the feeble
sound of its fall into the letter-box within, and that was all.
The gentleman was away, the porters thought—had not
been seen in the Temple for some days past. Mr. Hooper,
the gentleman as lived with him, it was surmised, was often
at the chambers, though probably not there at present.
Lord Southernwood returned to the West End, rather dis-
consolate. He took council with some of "the fellows at
the club." It was suggested that Arnold might be keeping
out of the way for reasons which all appreciated: "But,
you know, they can't take a fellow on Sunday, can they?"
said some one. "Write and ask him to dine with you on
Sunday."

Lord Southernwood was grateful for the suggestion. He
wrote a line to the Temple, begging Arnold to dine with
him in the Albany on the following Sunday—for one reason,
that he had something particular to say to him.

"If he's in town," said his lordship, "no doubt Hooper's
in the secret, and takes care of his letters. I remember
Hooper, now I come to think of it. Good-natured little

hump-backed man : never could make out why Arnold cared about him. I'll send the letter to the Temple."

In the course of a few posts Lord Southernwood received a reply from Arnold, rather abruptly worded, as he thought. His invitation was declined, without any assigned reason : but if his lordship particularly desired to see Arnold Page, he was requested to call on a specified evening, at a given address in Coppice Row.

"He seems rather savage, poor old boy," remarked Lord Southernwood; "down on his luck, I suppose. Well, a man does get a little put out when he is up a tree. I know what it is myself. I must try and cheer him up. But where the doose is Coppice Row? Never heard of such a place ; give you my honour—never. But suppose a hansom will be able to find it. • Does any fellow know where Coppice Row is ? "

And there were various guesses :—Bloomsbury, Paddington, Bermondsey, Peckham, &c. Some "fellows," indeed, were quite anxious to back their opinions heavily.

Mr. Robin Hooper still resided at the chambers in Sun-dial Buildings, and took care of Arnold's letters, conveying them to him stealthily. But Mr. Hooper was a good deal absent during the day. He could settle to nothing, as he said — could not read, could not write — for thinking of Arnold. He was paler, more delicate-looking than ever. He was constantly at Mrs. Simmons's house, or visiting Jack Lackington's studio, or at the Café de l'Univers, marvelling at Tithonus, still an *habitué* of the place. At night he sat alone in the rooms in Sun-dial Buildings : amidst all the luxurious comfort of their fitting up they seemed, in Arnold's absence, very cheerless and wretched.

"I shall be almost glad to leave them now," he said ; "though I have been very happy here, too. But Arnold says he must give them up; that he can never afford to keep them after what's happened. Poor Arnold! it sounds very strange, his talking in that way. I grow very nervous about him. I almost wish that he were safe out of England. I feel sure that they are trying to arrest him. It's a bad, dreadful business ; it's killing him. I never saw a man so changed. Certainly it is hard for him to bear—to lose his fortune, and to lose *her.* Yes, and he loves her very dearly; more than I ever thought he could love. I haven't done him justice in that respect; but he didn't do himself justice, either. He was so fond of looking at everything from such a gay, pleasant, lighthearted point of view, one got to think him incapable of deeper feelings. He seemed to think that everything in life was but a jest. I know now he thought very differently all the while; but it's a sort of fashion for men to affect not to be in earnest. Poor Arnold! And how can she bear to give him up at a word, in a moment? But do people ever love as they are loved?"

Slowly he unlocked a drawer, taking from it a carefully folded sheet of paper. He opened it: it contained a slight pencil sketch—he must have begged or borrowed, perhaps stolen it from Jack Lackington—certainly it had been cut out of his sketch-book. It was the drawing of Janet Gill he had exhibited one night at the Café de l'Univers.

"Yes," said Robin Hooper, contemplating the drawing very sadly, "it is very hard to love without hope."

CHAPTER XXV

THE MARQUIS OF SOUTHERNWOOD.

MR. PHIL GOSSETT remained faithful to Mrs. Simmons in her affliction. He still lodged on the first floor of her house in Coppice Row.

"I can do just what I like, that's the great advantage of it," as he would often confess. "It's not a quiet house, and the situation can't be called first-rate. But then I like noise too much myself to complain of it in others; and I haven't far to go to St. Lazarus's; and that's a great comfort, when you come to think of early lectures in the winter. And I can study all night, if I think proper—I don't often go out—or smoke all night, or play the piano all night. There's nobody to find fault; nobody who can't sleep through it. Isn't that jolly to think of? And the children cry and laugh, and the widow rehearses melodrama in the back parlour, and I play up here my loudest on the piccolo, or practise my deepest and severest bass songs— you can't think how stunning it is altogether. It will be a great treat to you, Arnold."

Arnold smiled. Mr. Gossett's good-humour was irresistible: and it was hard to say that he did not believe every word of his praises of the Coppice Row establishment, in which he pursued his studies of music from choice, and medicine from necessity.

"I've got several songs you haven't heard," he continued. "But you won't be charged anything extra on that account. Hullo! here's your visitor. Now don't hurry the *tempo!* Your pulse, I see, is moving from *allegro* to *allegretto.* No slurring of the difficult passages. And if in the middle of the discussion you feel inclined for a song—music, you know, hath charms, &c.—shout out for me, and I'll come in and sing the 'Piff-paff,' or something equally soft and soothing. I'll just fill my pipe before I go."

Mr. Gossett was speaking very much at random concerning the visit Arnold was about to receive. He was unacquainted with the exact relation in which Arnold stood to the Marquis of Southernwood, but he could perceive that his friend was under some excitement in expectation of the interview.

Lord Southernwood, in the charge of a hansom cabman, had been conveyed to Coppice Row. He surveyed, through his eye-glass, a neighbourhood entirely new to him. Occasionally he lost that command he was accustomed to maintain over his astonishment, and was unable to resist the utterance of an explosive " By Jove ! "

He leaped lightly from his cab at the private door of the widow Simmons's house, and considerably over-paid the cabman, under the impression, probably, that he must have come a long journey of many miles from the West End of London.

·"First floor, if you please, Sir," said Mrs. Simmons, in reply to his inquiry for Arnold Page, and after a scrutinising glance at the visitor.

She was quite aware that her lodger did not desire to be " at home " to everyone; not at all astonished at his wishes in that respect. Perhaps former lodgers had entertained similar views as to the importance of retirement from the world.

"What a dear little man ! " she exclaimed, as his lordship ascended the dark, tortuous stairs ; " fresh as a daisy, and light as a feather. And what a little foot; I don't believe I could get into his boots. Why, he don't look a bit bigger than that little Miss Bilberry at Bristol, when she played Captain Charlotte on her benefit. What a mite she was ! Though, certainly, she'd a very neat leg. One thing, I've been so accustomed to see such tall men. Ah ! my poor Jemmy ! He *was* a fine man once ! and a love of a figure, too ! A sweet harlequin, though he wasn't a good husband ; and took too much, I must say, though he's the father of my children. But I shall never look upon his like again— never ! Nancy, you good-for-nothing girl ! what do you put the kettle on for, without any water in it ? Do you want to burn the bottom out ? " &c.

If Arnold had been disposed to any severity of feeling in regard to his old and intimate friend, Lord Dolly, he would certainly have found it difficult to restrict himself to such a

state of mind in the presence of his lordship. The frank
cordiality, the warmth of attachment, the cheery good-nature,
manifest in his visitor's looks and manner, would have been
sufficient to disarm a man far more inclined to acrimony and
rigour of judgment than was Arnold Page. Certainly it is
difficult to think unkindly of a friend in his presence; and
there are so many men whose charms of manner prevail
against all considerations of more important gracelessness.
Contemplating little Lord Southernwood, with his "Cupid"
airs, his hearty laugh, his silky curls, his pink and white
complexion, his eye-glass, his unconsciously frank and open
method of speech; his utter unreserve upon all and every
topic; it was as hard to condemn him upon any question,
as it would be to treat harshly a child, or a schoolboy, or a
pretty woman. •

"How are you, Arnold, old boy? Deuced glad to see
you. Awful time since we've met. Hardly expected to
find you in this odd corner. You've not a very brilliant
look out: though it might be worse, mightn't it? The
prison's gloomy—House of Correction, is it? But then that
public over there looks no end of cheerful. One would
think they sold gas, they put such a lot in the window.
Well, and how have you been getting on? And what have
you been doing with yourself? You don't look particularly
well; pale and thin, I think. However, that don't matter
much, does it? Part of a fellow's training. I'm sure I'm
very glad to see you."

"Your lordship's very kind to say so," Arnold began, in
rather dry tones.

But how could he talk sternly to the little man who was
shaking him by the hand with such unaffected fervour.

"You must keep your pecker up, you know, Arnold.
You've been unlucky, haven't you? At least, I hear fellows
saying so. Some infernal public company; always the way,
somehow. When they get a gentleman in the City, they
generally manage to fleece him. But, you know, things
never turn out so bad as they look. You'll pull through;
fellows always do pull through. I've known so many cases
of this kind. You're quite right to keep quiet, though. Go
abroad; the thing will blow over—things always do blow
over, somehow."

"Yes; I'm thinking of going abroad almost immediately, but——"

"I'd stick to Paris, I think. I wouldn't try Hombourg, or any of those places. They're too tempting, too risky; and the run of luck is evidently against you just now. Keep in Paris. You'll find the society very pleasant; mixed, but amusing. Keep there till things can be got square over here."

"If they succeed in making me bankrupt—I learn that that is contemplated—I must, of course, surrender. In any case, I give up everything—everything! It's as well to speak quite plainly on the subject. It's as well that there should be no misunderstanding. My lord, our positions are greatly changed since we first met, some years ago now. Henceforth we are little likely to be thrown together; but you may know at once that I am ruined—completely ruined."

"Oh, no; not so bad as that comes to, old fellow. Something must be done for you. Keep abroad. We can at least attach you to an embassy somewhere, or something of that sort. Fellows live very comfortably at the embassy. Or why not a consulship? That kind of thing somewhere —just for a time: till things are put right here—which, of course, they will be, only we must give them time. By George! I'll force the Government to give you something. They're in a doose of a hurry for my vote; but I'd go into Opposition if they won't do anything for such an old friend as you are, Arnold."

"Your lordship is very kind; but I could not, for many reasons, accept such a thing—least of all could I permit your intervention on my behalf in such a matter."

"How do you mean, old fellow, I don't quite see?"

"I don't wish to say anything wanting in courtesy or in temper; we've been on such good terms in the past, that it's not worth while that—indeed there is no reason why— we should quarrel now."

"Quarrel, old man? Oh, dear, no, of course not," said his lordship—a little confused, it may be, and troubled with some forebodings that their conversation promised to contain certain elements of danger.

"But I think I am right in saying that your visit here— made at your own desire, not mine—was for some other

object than to tender your services to me; though, indeed,
I should wish you to understand that I am anything but
ungrateful for these."

Lord Southernwood coloured a little, and looked on the
ground.

"You see, Arnold," he said, hesitatingly, and then
stopped, hardly knowing how to proceed, or what he had
purposed to say.

"You come here, not to pry into my hiding-place, to look
with your own eyes upon my fallen state, to satisfy yourself
as to my poverty and disgrace—not to do these, I know.
I neither wish to be insulting nor unjust; nor was it simply
to proffer me aid that you came here. Pray let us go at
once to a subject we must arrive at sooner or later. I have
seen *this*."   •

He produced and presented to the Marquis the copy of
the *Woodlandshire Mercury*, which contained the paragraph
before referred to, setting out that a certain marriage was
on the *tapis*, &c.

"I didn't know of this. I give you my honour I didn't
know of this," cried Lord Southernwood, considerably
excited. "I never saw this before. It wasn't in *The Times*
—it wasn't in *Bell's Life*—and—and I never see any of the
other papers."

"But is it true?" Arnold asked sternly.

"No, it's not true; they ought not to put such things in
the paper. By George, it ought not to be allowed. How
do they get hold of such things? who the deuce writes
them? It's too bad. 'Pon my soul, it's too bad. I give
you my honour I didn't know that such a thing had appeared in print."

"But is there no ground for this statement?" His lordship paused for a little, in evident embarrassment; his glass
fell from his eye.

"Look here, Arnold, old man. Don't be too hard upon
a fellow: don't be in too great a hurry to think badly of me.
You've, perhaps, a right to turn round a little upon fellows
just now; but don't try to get me in a corner. I'm not a
cur; I never did anything yet very shabby to anybody, not
that I know of, and I aint going to begin now. I'm quite
willing to speak out plain and that, if you'll only let me and

listen to me. I've admired *her* all along—I have, upon my honour: but I never dreamt of more than that, till the story went about that you were out of the thing, altogether out of it, don't you know?"

"Well, my lord?"

"Give me time, old man; and if you'd call me Dolly once more, it would really be rather a treat and a comfort, and that sort of thing. Well, since I've heard that story, I own things have seemed rather different, and I've been down in the neighbourhood, don't you know? and I've seen more and more of her; and I couldn't help it, but I got to think more and more of her every day, and perhaps overdid it and went over there too often. But I was out trying a horse of Chalker's, and somehow the brute would always gallop that way, and it was awful dull at the Abbey; and, perhaps, I called there more than I ought, and I'm sure I'm very sorry if I've done wrong." He waited a moment, perhaps to see if Arnold would speak, but he remained silent, biting his lips, his eyes bent on the carpet. His lordship contemplated his companion through his eyeglass, which he had resumed, as he continued—

"And now, Arnold, if you'll only tell me that that story is all wrong, that the engagement is not at an end, though it may be standing over for a time; if you'll only tell me this, I'm sure I'll do all I can to make amends; I'll never go near the place again, never speak of her, try not to think of her. I'll go out of the country if you like, to Italy, or anywhere — it don't matter to me, you know; or I'll go down and punch that editor's head; I'll do anything you like to mention to put things square again. Duelling and that's rather out of fashion, you know, or if it had been any comfort to you to have had a shot at me, I'm sure I should have been very happy to have stood up to you. A fellow ought to do all he can to make amends for a shabby thing; only for what that newswaper fellow writes, why it is not true—there hasn't been a word said of anything of the kind."

"And she encouraged your visits?" Arnold asked, gloomily. It was curious how they both avoided all mention of the name of the person in reference to whom the discussion arose.

24

"She is the same as ever," Lord Southernwood said, with some enthusiasm in his manner; "only, perhaps, a little quieter and sadder in her ways. We were always friendly and that, and I could always find something to say to her, when I wouldn't open my mouth before some other women. She was always kind and jolly, you know, and laughed when a fellow tried to say anything amusing, and helped him out when he got into a hole in his conversation. I think she liked me a little always, and things are pretty much about the same as ever they were—only—only I think I care more for her than I ever used to, more than I ever cared for any woman in the world."

Arnold raised his eyes for a moment to regard his friend, then lowered them, as he said, in a low voice—

"My engagement is at an end—for ever. We are not likely to meet any more; we can never be anything more to each other. In the future it can matter little to me whom she loves, whom she marries."

There was silence for some minutes. Lord Dolly was the first to speak.

"I suppose, though, old fellow," he said slowly, "you'd find it doosid hard not to hate the man who becomes her husband."

Arnold frowned; but presently a cloud seemed to clear from his face.

"I love her, though—though I may never look upon her face again,"—his voice trembled very much as he spoke— "I hope she may be happy, very happy, in her future husband; and no, I will not hate him, not if he wins her love, not if he loves her—a true loyal gentleman who will prize, at its proper value, the treasure trusted to his keeping; who will devote to her his life; who will be good and generous, and loving and tender to her always, whatever happens. No! I couldn't hate such a man."

Lord Southernwood looked at his friend very disconsolately.

"He can't mean me," he said to himself; "Arnold always was rather beyond me." And he leant his head upon his hands, resting his arms upon his knees, a picture of gloom, dejection, intense melancholy. Arnold moved towards him.

"Give me your hand, Dolly," he said, in a kindly, though rather tremulous voice; "it was of you I was thinking. Win her love if you can. I think I could trust her happiness to your keeping."

"By George!" cried his lordship, much moved, "do you really think so, Arnold?"

"You love her, Dolly?"

"I do, upon my soul; and I'll try and deserve her, and be worthy of her, and all that. I'm a better sort of fellow of late, you know, than I used to be. All strictly proper since I got the peerage; the Upper House, you know; that sort of thing. I've been very steady of late, living at the Abbey with the Marchioness, who's been urging me to marry, and who'll be delighted to hear of this, who's a very good, kind woman, though melancholy—but that's only to be expected—and very religious and that, and who'd be very glad to see her at the Abbey, and who'd be sure to make much of her and love her no end, as indeed who could help doing? And, indeed, I'll do all that man can do to make her happy. I will indeed. I know I don't deserve such good fortune; but I've reformed. I'm better behaved, ever so, than I used to be. And that case at Brompton—you know what I mean—has been given up now, quite; for good and all. I did the right thing, and got out of it, and I'm deuced glad. And I'll go on straight and proper now; you see if I don't. What a trump you are, Arnold! You know I've been deuced miserable about this. I was so afraid that you'd cut up rough; and it did so look as though I'd been playing a shabby trick, hitting a man when he was down, you know. But you'll promise me you'll think as kindly of me as you can? Will you, now? and there can be no reason why we shouldn't be friends still, as we have been all through."

Arnold shook his head gloomily.

"Ah, but by-and-by," his lordship continued, "you'll think better of things; and you'll find that you'll pull through your difficulties; and we shall see you prosperous and happy yet."

"No," said Arnold, with some bitterness; perhaps the very manifest happiness of his visitor jarred upon him and wounded him; don't trouble yourself to dream such dreams

24—2

concerning me and my future. I'm utterly ruined and broken down, beyond all getting up again. Indeed, I don't know what will become of me. What is a man of my age to do when ruin like this comes upon him? I'm too old even to enlist," and he smiled with a strange sadness.

"Poor old boy!" murmured his lordship, and he began to appreciate the fact that his presence, under existing circumstances, was perhaps likely to be a source of some pain to his friend. "He's sadly down upon his luck just now. I can do him no good. I'd better go. And then he added aloud, "You'll let me see you again before you quit England, Arnold? please do."

"Why not?—if you wish it. Though what good can come of our meeting? But my stay is very uncertain. I may start immediately, or I may be prevented leaving at all for a very long time. It matters very little either way."

"But we don't part in anger?" his lordship asked, appealingly.

"Certainly not, Dolly. Good-bye."

"And—may I tell her that I have seen you? May I repeat what you have said on *that* subject?"

"Anything you will, Dolly."

Lord Southernwood breathed freely.

"You're a great trump, Arnold. Good-bye. God bless you, old fellow. I hope things will soon come square again. I'm sure they will." And he hurried out to look for a cab, to be carried back again to the West End of London.

"Something must be done for Arnold," he kept on saying to himself; "of course something must be done. The Government must be bullied, if need be. I'll play up all sorts of games in the House if something isn't done. I'll astonish the weak nerves of the peers. I'm quite capable o doing it."

He lit a cigar. Under the soothing influence of his smoke his thoughts drifted away from Arnold and his misfortunes to more pleasant topics.

"That darling little child! that sweet little Leo!" he said to himself. "How I do love her! How happy I shall be if I can ever call her mine! And there ought to be no doubt about it now. I ought to be the favourite now at long odds. With Arnold scratched, I ought to win in a canter. If I can only persuade her to love me ever so little ; and she *does* like me. Only there seems a long step from laughing with a fellow, and chaffing and gossiping, and that, to downright loving him—decidedly a long step."

"What does it matter now?" Arnold asked himself very sadly. And he sank into a chair, leaning forward, staring at the carpet, biting his lips, his nails. Then he hid his face in his trembling hands, rocking himself to and fro in great grief. For some time he was left alone, a prey to bitter reflections.

"May I come in?" asked some one at the door, who entered as he put the question. It was Phil Gossett.

"Has the visitor gone? I just wanted to fill my pipe again ; and I think I left my tobacco-pouch on the mantel-shelf. I've been nursing the baby in the parlour behind the shop, and telling the children stories till I've drained my memory and my imagination quite dry. Holloa! Arnold, don't look so sad, or you'll make me miserable too. Here, let me play you something on the piccolo to cheer you up. What shall it be ; 'Ruddier than the Cherry?' or would you like something dismal, 'The Wanderer,' say ; or the 'Maniac,' with prodigious theatrical effects."

"Thank you, Phil," said Arnold, grimly. "Something gay and light-hearted, to suit the occasion. Play 'The Wedding March ;' and sing anything you like—'Three Jolly Postboys,' or, 'He's a Jolly Good Fellow ;' anything with mirth and jollity about it."

Mr. Gossett looked at his friend with rather a puzzled air.

"Don't play anything of the sort, Phil," said a third person. Robin Hooper entered the room. "Arnold doesn't mean it, I know, by the sound of his voice."

And he went and took Arnold's hand, pressing it kindly. He gazed in his face ; he read its worn, suffering look, so strengthened and intensified during the last half-hour.

"Dear Arnold," he began. Then it occurred to him that, perhaps, silence was better suited to the case than spoken sympathy.

"Poor old Rob," Arnold said in a moved voice, returning the pressure of his hand. Then, after a pause, he went on, hoarsely, "I must end this, Rob. I must get away from here as soon as may be, or I shall go mad. Let me go at once !"

"Well, perhaps it will be better so," Rob whispered, slowly and thoughtfully ; " there are men constantly watching the Temple. I am afraid of being followed. I think it may be as well to make a move."

A plan was soon agreed upon.

Some few hours later Robin took an affectionate leave of Arnold at St. Katherine's wharf, on board the *Baron Osy* steamer, bound for Brussels. It was Sunday morning as Arnold steamed down the Thames, away from his creditors.

Old Mr. Carr had come up to town for a few days. He had interviews with Sir Cupper Leech and Dr. Hawkshaw touching the state of health of Mrs. Carr. And he went into the City. He was one of those old gentlemen who are never comfortable unless they can go now and then into the City. Why they go, what they do when there, I have never been able to understand. Perhaps a committee of bankers and brokers picked from Birchin Lane and Throgmorton Street might be able to afford information on the subject.

" Lincoln's Inn Fields," said old Mr. Carr, as the footman assisted him to mount into the carriage again ; " the offices of Messrs. Holroyd and Hopegood. Andrews knows on which side of the square to find them."

Soon the carriage stopped again. The footman was sent into the offices to make inquiries. He returned immediately with information.

" Mr. Hopegood was out—Mr. Hopegood, junior, was in —would be disengaged in two minutes."

" It's the young man I want to see," said Mr. Carr quietly, as he got out of the carriage. Mr. Hopegood, junior, was soon at liberty.

" How do you do, Mr. Carr ? " he asked, smiling, rubbing his hands, leading the way to his quiet snug room, about which there was a lingering odour as of sherry. (The wine was hidden in the bookcase, behind Barnwell and Alderson's Reports, on the second shelf. The lawyer professed to keep the wine for the refreshment of very depressed clients, but it did not appear that he refrained from referring to it now and then himself, quite as often, I should say, as to the volumes of Reports screening it; and certainly he was never depressed himself.)

"Pray be seated, Mr. Carr. Unseasonable weather, is it not?" and then he asked himself, "What does the old fellow want, I wonder? He's a good client—though he doesn't give us all his business. Deuced shrewd old dog!" then aloud, "I'm sorry my father is out, Mr. Carr; but he's just gone round to the Rolls for a few minutes."

"I am glad to see you, Mr. Hopegood," said the old gentleman; "I hope your father is well. You can do perfectly well all that I want. Better than your father, indeed. I want but to put a few questions, to obtain a little legal assistance. We can manage this, I fancy, without our being under the necessity of mentioning names at all."

"Certainly, Mr. Carr."

"There is always an awkwardness about mentioning names. Let me put my case then in this way. A.'s estate is mortgaged—heavily mortgaged to B. A. is seriously indebted to C., D. and E. I don't want to introduce more technicalities than I can avoid. Upon the petition of C., D. and E., A. is made bankrupt. You follow me?"

"Exactly."

"Now, will the fact of the bankruptcy necessitate the sale of the mortgaged estate, upon the chance, that, if sold, it may produce enough to pay off B., and leave a balance for distribution among the other creditors?"

"No. The assignees of the bankrupt may not deem such a course advisable. There may be many reasons against it. For instance, B., the mortgagee, might refuse concurrence in the sale."

"In this case we may take it that B., the mortgagee, *would* refuse concurrence."

"You see if B. throws difficulties in the way, possessing, as he probably does, the sole means of verifying the title, and refusing to produce these, or to satisfy any intending purchaser in regard to the title, what are we to do? The assignees of A. have no more power in the matter than A. would have if not bankrupt. He might file a bill to redeem, compelling B. to take his money back and re-convey, and then the estate might be sold. But I fancy the assignees would rather shrink from going to the Court of Chancery;

Leo.

they would weigh the certainty of the expense against the chance of profits arising from the sale when it took place—and, indeed, they could not go to the court without the consent of all the creditors, or a majority of them after a meeting held, or with the express sanction of the Commissioner. You see that the probable result would be that the estate would not be sold."

"I see; provided B. would not assist."

"Exactly."

"I am obliged to you, Mr. Hopegood. I think I understand the matter very clearly, thanks to your assistance. I think, too, that we need be under no immediate apprehension in regard to A.'s estate." He rose to go: he shook hands with Mr. Hopegood, junior, but as he moved towards the door, he turnéd and said,—

"But one thing more. Suppose the case to stand as I have put it, with this addition, that B. becomes bankrupt as well as A. What then becomes of the estate?"

"Ah! then, my dear Sir, the estate is in serious peril. B.'s assignees will collect all his assets—will realise his securities—they would call in this money—foreclose the mortgage—sell the estate."

"And all this would be done rapidly?"

"Very rapidly. Legal wheels have been well greased by reform. We can proceed at a great pace now."

"Thank you. I understand perfectly. When B. is bankrupt, we must look out a-head. Good-morning." And he took his departure.

"Home," he said to the footman, who imparted the information to the coachman, and the carriage rolled away from Lincoln's Inn Fields.

"A clever old file that," said Mr. Hopegood, winding red tape round his fingers mechanically, as he pondered over his conversation with old Mr. Carr; "he'd have succeeded as a lawyer. I wonder now what his little game is?"

He took out the sherry from behind Barnwell and Alderson to warm and quicken, perhaps, his imaginative faculties, and he passed a silk handkerchief over the bumps of casuality on his forehead, as though to polish them up for the occasion.

" To secure Oakmere Court, and annex it to Croxall? I shouldn't be surprised. I always did think that country neighbours preyed upon each other, like big fish upon little ones. It's astonishing how the love of land grows upon a man, particularly his native land. Certainly there is nothing like freehold property. It's such a comfort being away to look at it, and sit down on it, and walk on it, up and down, and over it. Compare it to investing in railways ! To have nothing but a few beggarly scraps of paper in a tin box, and to call *them* money and capital. Bah! give me land, with a long deed of conveyance and a fat abstract of title— that's business, that is, and pleasure too."

It may be as well to say here, that thanks to creditors C., D. and E., Mr. Arnold Page was made bankrupt ; all proper formalities being regarded—a docket being struck, a petition to the Chancellor on the part of the creditors being presented, and a fiat being opened. (I cannot attempt to explain to the reader the meaning of all this legal slang. I must ask him to take for granted that it is correct.) Arnold Page's name appeared in the list of bankrupts in the *London Gazette*, and a day was appointed at which he was required to surrender himself, and submit to be examined, and otherwise comply with the requirements of the bankrupt laws.

CHAPTER XXVI.

TWO OF A TRADE.

IN the shabby lodging over the water—the reader has already contemplated the slovenly, slatternly, disreputable "interior"— two men sat, leaning over a small Pembroke-table, on which were strewn various written and printed documents. One man— he has been known to us rather by the sobriquet of the "doctor" than by any other title—had taken off his coat, probably for great coolness, or that it impeded the free movement of the muscles of his arms : there are some men never happy when completely attired, who cannot even eat their dinners without removal of upper garments and generally much unbuttonment. He sat in his shirt-sleeves —they did not obtrude evidence of recent washing—unfastened at the wrist, and exposing his brawny, hairy, sinewy arms and hands, terminating in blunted, bitten, horny, not clean finger-ends. He wiped every now and then his red, blotched, dank forehead with a crumpled, ragged, dull coloured cotton handkerchief. He was smoking the stump of a clay-pipe, black from use and dirt; the tobacco of a most unfragrant strength. He puffed great clouds intentionally, as it seemed, in the face of the companion opposite to him at the table—laughing coarsely and brutally when the smoke made the other man cough, or the accumulating density of it caused him to rise from his seat and beat about with his thin grisly hands to disperse the vapour. The other man was Monsieur Anatole. His greasy pocket-book was in front of him. He occasionally took a pinch of snuff from his silver-gilt box, with the free painting on its lid.

"It is a pity," said the Frenchman in reply apparently to some observation made by his companion ; "you are a man of great ability, but of little ambitions. You take a small shopkeeper's view of transactions. You do not appreciate what I may call the political economy of investment and speculation. You lay too much stress upon the system of small profits and quick returns. It seems to be simple and wise—it is really foolish and rash. What avails it always to be at work drawing in your net? you will catch more fish by waiting. One good haul is better than ten bad ones; and you will have toiled very much less. Be sure I am giving you the best advice for you and for myself."

And Monsieur smiled—his old smile, full of a strange mocking meaning—sinister, menacing.

"You give me plenty of jaw—I know that Mounseer. Plenty of words, deuced little else," the other man answered rudely. "You're for ever telling me to wait and wait; we're to grow rich by-and-by. Meanwhile I starve. I'm sick of waiting, I tell you. I want money and I'll have it."

"Bah! it is folly to gather an unripe harvest!"

"But we shall wait and lose all. Wind up now, I say. We shan't get all we expected. But we shall make a good haul. We shall make sure of the money from the Ostrich, at any rate."

"It will be very rash; suspicion will certainly be excited; attention will be drawn to us. No; we must wait. I tell you we *must*."

"But there will be money wanted; there will be premiums to be paid."

"Well, they shall be paid if need be. What is your English proverb which bids you not to lose your ship for a hap'orth of tar?"

"You have money, then?" cried the doctor, starting up angrily.

"No," the Frenchman answered, with some uneasiness. "I have already told you I have none. But I will endeavour to procure some. I will borrow, I will obtain money for the premiums by some means."

"It seems to me you're trying to cheat me. Look out, if that's the case. It's my belief you are making a purse for yourself out of the partnership funds. By Heaven! if I thought that"—and the doctor brought a clenched black fist heavily down upon the table.

"Don't be foolish. It will benefit you very little to quarrel with me. Do you want to dissolve partnership? Take care; this policy is in my name, it stands as assigned to me in the books of the company." He pointed to a large folded document before him. "You will be entitled to one half—when the life of the assured drops—and the policy becomes payable. But it will rest very much with me as to the proportion you will receive."

"If I thought you meant to cheat me!" growled the doctor.

"Be assured, my friend, I mean nothing of the kind. But our plans are not yet complete. There are the other policies to be obtained."

"Yes; but I fear "—the doctor spoke hesitatingly—" fear there will be some hitch about the other policies."

"Ah! how so?"

"Mind, I have been fulfilling my part of the arrangement. I was to do all I could to effect insurance upon *his* life." (He jerked his thumb over his shoulder, as though to indicate some one in an adjoining room.) "You were to take what steps might be necessary to make the amounts insured become payable; you know what I mean," he added, in answer as it seemed to another of Monsieur Anatole's smiles. "I couldn't do that, I own myself. I'm no coward, but I couldn't do that. A man who's chummed with me a long time now; whom I've eaten and drank with, the last especially; whom I like rather than not. I couldn't——"

"Hush!" Monsieur Anatole interrupted softly. "Why speak of such things?"

"Well, I've done my part, as far as I could. Some of the policies have been obtained. I've taken care of him, patched him up, got him through the examination. But of late he has not been well enough to pass."

"Because you have neglected your trust. Because you have not watched him. You have not taken proper care."

"I have done all I could, and I tried a bold stroke yesterday. I went in his stead to an office of repute. It is better not to mention names. I underwent examination for him! I borrowed his name for an hour or two. I cleaned myself, dressed myself respectably, and marched before a board of directors; was examined by a medical officer, who seemed satisfied with the captain's health, though he thought there might be an additional premium to pay, perhaps, on account of long residence in India."

"It was very bold," the Frenchman remarked, thoughtfully; "it was too bold!"

"It may be so; because I can't go on with it; because I can't go to that office again; because in coming away from it, I met some one who, I have since ascertained, is connected with it; who may have recognised me; made inquiries; given warning."

"Ah!" cried the Frenchman, drawing in his breath as though in pain, "if that should be so?"

"It will be better, as I have said, to make sure at once if we can; the time has come for you to fulfil your part of the engagement."

"No; if suspicion has been excited it will be more than ever necessary that we should wait until it is allayed. We must do nothing; we must keep very quiet; we must pay the premiums that are falling due. It would be very clumsy work to bring on a crisis at such a moment. To draw all eyes upon us. Bah! it would be madness!"

"You find excuses for waiting in everything, it seems to me," the doctor growled, sulkily. "Suppose I refuse to wait?"

"Why trouble me with so unlikely a supposition? I think, my friend, that you have lost your wits since your meeting with Dr. Hawkshaw? Is not that the name of the gentleman you encountered on the steps of the insurance office?"

"What do you mean by that?" cried the doctor with an oath.

"Bah! you know what I mean!"

"Have you set spies upon me? Have you had me followed?"

"Sit down. Don't enrage yourself needlessly."

"Take care," cried the doctor. "I'll have no nonsense; I'll stand none of your infernal humbug, Mounseer. I know you. I know all about you."

"Sit down," Monsieur Anatole repeated, and this time with an air of command that influenced even his turbulent companion, who shrunk back involuntarily into his chair. "Sit down. Don't talk like an imbecile. You don't know

me ; or if you do, you know nothing by which I can be
affected. No ! I have lived some years." He chuckled
grimly. "I have followed pretty well my own devices, and
yet I defy the world to bring to my charge anything of
which the law can lay hold. And I have lived under very
particular governments ; and I have lived to see and take
part in many strange events. For you, my friend, I think
you have been less fortunate."

"I don't understand you," muttered the other, moodily,
gnawing his fingers.

"Pardon me. But you do. You may search through the
archives of the police for my name in vain ; that is," he
added, as though correcting himself, "in connection with a
conviction. I have wandered in many lands. A speculator, an
entrepreneur, a gambler even. I will not gainsay you. I have
lent money ; I have borrowed money : I have discounted
the bills of others ; I have had my own bills discounted ; I
am a traveller. It was in India I made the acquaintance
of our admirable friend in the next room. I had money
transactions with him. He became a client of mine ;
introduced me to his daughter, the amiable Janet, for
whom I conceived a regard tender as it was supreme.
Let that pass. What more do you know of me, my friend ?
Nothing. It is folly for you to pretend it. But for
you——"

"Shut up, can't you ?" growled the other, between his
teeth.

"But for you," Monsieur Anatole continued, without regard to the interruption, taking snuff with calm pertinacity ;
"but for you—it is altogether different. As I have said,
you possess an extraordinary ability ; but you have never
known how to apply it. Will it please you to be called by
your real name, Pratt, or your assumed name Monkton, or
Luce ? I believe there are some others, but it is needless
to remind you of them. And it is immaterial, so far as we
are now concerned. Your first error — at least the first
which brought your name on the books of the police—was
a curious one. It arose from your great talents, from your
extreme want of caution ; and the stake was a very small
one, a poor fifty pounds ; and detection so imminent ! You
passed an examination before the College of Surgeons, in

the name of another, for whom you endeavoured illegally and mischievously—because an incompetent surgeon can do so much harm to his fellow-creatures—most mischievously, to obtain a diploma. It seems you are clever at passing examinations for. others. But you were detected at the last moment. Was not Dr. Hawkshaw one of the examiners? It would be curious, if it should be reserved for him to discover you now as a counterfeit Captain Gill. Let us hope that he did not do so, did not remember you. Years have passed, and you have much changed. Years passed by you—how? In prison, I think. I have the particulars in my pocket-book. Certainly, part of the time in the House of Correction, Cold Bath Fields—eighteen months, if I remember rightly. Next you were in trouble about an assault—a rather murderous assault; then I think you were lodging in Horsemonger Lane Gaol (what a frightful name that is!), convicted upon a charge of embezzlement; afterwards you were sentenced to transportation, for an offence which the English law calls arson, committed with the view of defrauding a fire insurance company. Well, it now seems that you are turning your attention to fraud in connection with life insurance. You are a just man. You like to rob all alike: it is only fair. I have but to add one circumstance, then I will stop. I am sorry to have bored you, as you English say—but it occurs to me, doctor, otherwise Samuel Pratt, born of respectable parents at Homerton, aged forty-three, that you have returned from transportation in a manner unexpected by the police, unlawfully, without a ticket-of-leave. Is that so?"

"It's a lie!"

"No, it is not. I only asked you out of politeness, not because I didn't know. But you are right to deny it; denial is always, or nearly always, the safest plan in any case."

The doctor—Samuel Pratt, as his real name appeared to be—had paled very much during the Frenchman's narrative; his sinewy grimy hands trembled, though he clasped them together as though to restrain himself and obtain command by an effort over his nerves. His eyes rolled, taking stealthy glances only at the Frenchman, unable to meet boldly his fixed reptile gaze.

"Why, why do you tell me all this?" he asked at length,

querulously, rather than with his usual courageous rudeness.

"My friend, it has seemed to me necessary that we should
thoroughly understand each other," said Monsieur Anatole;
"and you have been inclined to force this line of conduct
upon me. I have suffered very much. I have overlooked
very much. I am not a complaining man; it is very disagreeable to me to be finding fault. I have been willing to
make allowances for the manner of your nation, always
coarse, gross, defiant — what you call bullying. You
threaten me; I smile. You insult me; I laugh: but you
attempt to upset my plans; I rise, then, and I upset you—
figuratively, of course, I mean. I have endavoured to avoid
this, but it is no longer possible for me to do so. So, then,
at last, I speak out. I warn you. I let you know. I tell
you plainly that I am the master, and that I will be obeyed.
Do you hear me, my friend?"

"I hear you, curse you!"

"Ah, you are rude; it is your insular manners; you have
to be pitied more than blamed. No matter. For the future
you will not dictate to me. You will obey me in everything.
If I say 'Wait,' you will wait without a murmur. Have no
fear; you shall have your full share of the profits of our
partnership. But you will learn this fact: you will repeat
it over and over again to yourself until you remember it,
until it is graven very deep in your memory; it is this "—
he stooped to whisper in Pratt's ear:—"*I* am the master,
and I will be obeyed, or——"

"Or what?" asked Pratt, with a shudder he could not
control.

"Oh! you wish for the alternative? You are curious, my
friend. Well—or I will go to that window. I will fling it
up. I will beckon to that man below; the man in the
shiny hat, the shiny cape: he is busy just now with the
servant washing the doorstep over the way; but he will
hear me if I call; he will do his duty if I say to him,
pointing to you: 'Policeman, that man is Samuel Pratt,
escaped convict: you will arrest him. You will take him
to the nearest station-house. You will lock him up very
tight, till he is again brought up, again sentenced;' but not
again to escape, they will take good care of that."

"You forget I could split upon you; blow all your schemes to the air," said Pratt.

"Pardon me, my friend. I do not forget. I know that you might talk. I know that you might say many things; but I know also that you would not be believed. I know that your accusation against a citizen of France, as I am, in intimate connection with the Government of this country, as I am—I know that your talk would be disregarded, laughed at. Have *I* to fear a charge brought against me by a convicted felon, an escaped transport? It is folly! I fear you not. No, Samuel Pratt, you have great abilities. I admit it; but you cannot cope with me. What could you say, after all? That insurances have been effected upon the life of our excellent friend with sinister motives. Bah! prove your words. True, I have effected insurances: or policies in his name have been assigned to me. What then? I am a creditor of this worthy gentleman's. I have naturally an interest in his life, or, which you will, I am about to become his son-in-law. I am affianced to his daughter Janet. Again, I am permitted to have an interest in his life. For his state of health, what does that matter? What do I know? I am not medical, and I have not appeared in the matter. He has been examined by the officers of the company. It is nothing to me. What do creditors ever know of the state of health of their debtors? What do the habits of fathers-in-law signify to sons-in-law? Tell me, my friend? Point out to me, if you can, a flaw in my conduct upon which the police can put a finger. Bah! I defy you."

Mr. Pratt seemed to be silenced, if not convinced. He drummed upon the table.

"There's one thing you forget," he said, at last, fiercely. "Open that window to shout to the bobby, and I fling you out neck and crop: or I get my hands round your throat, not to let go in a hurry!"

Monsieur evidently winced at this speech. Perhaps he was not physically brave, or he had underrated the ferocity of which his comrade was capable. He recovered himself, however, as he said jauntily, with a laugh—

"For shame! you don't do yourself justice—not common justice; and a gentleman who has had the advantage of a medical education! Fie! It would be all very well for a labourer on a railway, a mere navvy, poor creature—he knows no better; but for you, who have passed an examination at the College of Surgeons, I did not believe you capable of such folly. I thought you, a man of your ability, quite above tying a rope so tightly round your own neck. You would stoop, then, for the sake of a petty vengeance, to a murder of the stupidest, the commonest, the grossest kind! I had a higher opinion of you?"

The jeering audacity of these remarks rather cowed the other man; he began to feel himself unequal to, outbid by, the Frenchman.

"Stow it, Mounseer, do—it makes a fellow's flesh creep to hear you talk; while to hear you laugh goes through one like a knife." ·

"The knife again! Truly, my friend, you have coarse ideas and associations," laughed Monsieur Anatole again.

"But we will 'stow it,' then, as you say. Only you will remember, for the future, *you* will obey; *I* am the master!"

"All right!" growled Pratt. They shook hands upon it; the small skinny claw of the Frenchman seemed quite lost in the great black fist of the doctor.

"We shall get on better for this," said Monsieur Anatole, cheerfully; "we have cleared the air; we can breathe now more freely." And he gathered together the papers on the table, including the policy of insurance, and thrust them into his capacious pocket-book.

"Only don't try to sell me," said Pratt, with a resumption of some of his old insolence.

"Only· be obedient——" and the Frenchman pointed meaningly to the window as the doctor raised his black hands with a clutching action.

The door opened, a third man entered the room.

"Well, and how does our excellent friend, Captain Gill?" inquired Monsieur Anatole, with a leer.

Captain Gill looked like a man but recently out of bed. He was only half-dressed; his hair straggling over his puffed face; ordinarily red and bloated, now pale, almost livid. His eyes were bloodshot, staring; his expression vacant and wild.

"I say, you know," he began, "a fellow can't stop here.

We must get out of these lodgings at once. Why, they've got snakes in the house ; snakes and crocodiles, and all sorts of creeping things, and they've got into the bed-room ; they have, 'pon my soul. Crawling about the bed-clothes, under the bed, you know. It's horrid. A fellow can't stand it, you know. I daren't go into the room again. I wouldn't go there for any money."

He glared about him. His eyes settled at last upon a black bottle on the mantelshelf. He made a staggering dash at it, secured it, and held it to his lips.

" Take it from him," said Monsieur Anatole, in a low voice of command.

" Gently, old boy, that'll do !" and the doctor wrenched the bottle from the captain's hands. Monsieur Anatole smiled, as he said to himself—

" He's getting very ripe for an accidental death ! What do I say ? Lock him for an hour in a room with a bottle of cognac, and he would make a neat suicide of it; but not suicide as it would be understood by an insurance company. And there would be no one to blame, no one. Keep an eye on him," he said aloud. And he took his hat and went out whistling.

" If I thought that he meant to sell me ? " Mr. Pratt sat brooding over this idea, every now and then clenching his black fist to shake them threateningly at vacancy.

The Dom Ferdinando El Rey Silver Mining Company at Tezcotzinco had given promise of being a very prosperous undertaking. Its capital was to be 500,000*l.*, in 50,000 shares of 10*l.* each ; an amount of ten shillings per share to be paid on the application for allotment, twenty shillings per share on the allotment, and a call of 5*l.* per share six months afterwards. The scheme was very favourably received by a speculative public. Some three-fourths of the shares had been applied for almost before the prospectus had been fairly issued. The object of the company was to work the celebrated mines at Tezcotzinco, long known as among the richest in the world, and closely adjoining the Dom Boba-dillo mines, which had returned such enormous profits to the proprietors. The working of the mines would be extremely simple, neither pumping nor lifting being required.

Evidence in possession of the Board of Directors exhibited a money value of discovered ore equal to several millions sterling. The vein, or lode, extended across an entire mountain ridge; was of the enormous thickness of from eighteen to twenty feet, and, in some places, was of still larger dimensions. The company proposed to itself other sources of revenue. It would open up immense tracts of luxuriant land for cultivation; it would construct a railway from the mines to the nearest navigable river, and widen and improve the seaport, which it was proposed to purchase absolutely. The soil was of an amazing fertility; the climate pure and salubrious; the mountain-sides were clothed with primeval forests, abounding in timber adapted for all building, naval, and cabinet-making purposes; the whole region was enriched with all the treasures of the tropics. It was computed that by their trade in cochineal, dyewood, fruits, and lignum-vitæ, the proprietors would realise an enormous profit upon their outlay. A lease of the Tezcotzinco mines for a term of 999 years, with full right to work all the mines already discovered, or thereafter to be discovered by the company, of gold, silver, copper, lead, and other ores, extending over an area of seventy square miles, had been purchased for an amount to be paid partly in cash and partly in shares of the company. The promoters of the undertaking were to be remunerated largely out of the first moneys that should come to the hands of the company (which was completely registered), and applications for shares were to be made by a given date, upon an accompanying form. An Irish nobleman had been secured for chairman, and there was an imposing array of directors, bankers, brokers, solicitors, agents, managers, &c.

Such is an abridgment of the original prospectus of the Dom Ferdinando Mining Company. The name of Arnold Page, Esq., of Oakmere Court, Oakmere, Woodlandshire, and of the Temple, London, did not appear in the first list of directors. He was added to the Board, under the power which had been reserved from the first of increasing the number of the directors. The influence of his brother-in-law, Mr. Lomax, a large proprietor in the undertaking, seemed to be sufficient to effect this little arrangement, and

Arnold Page sat weekly at a large baize-covered table in a dim house in a murky street in the City, and tried to persuade himself that he was becoming useful in his generation, and that he understood the affairs of the Dom Ferdinando. He sat before a sheet of blotting-paper with a pen in his hand, anxious, it seemed, by way of doing something, probably, to add his signature to anything that came in his way; it was occupation; it saved him from going to sleep; it very nearly prevented him from yawning. He was a regular attendant at the meetings of the Board, moved by his new-born desire to be of service, to be industrious, to abandon the pleasant grace of his old lotus-eating life, and to give a helping hand to the progress of the world. And he really had faith in the worthiness of the company; believed the glowing reports of the agents and correspondents at Tezcotzinco: examined the long lines upon lines of figures that jostled each other in the computations and calculations of the managers, and put implicit trust in the promise that the results would realise to the full the sanguine expectations of the promoters. Many weary hours he devoted to the business of the company. He was quite "a mod-el derack-terr," as the secretary (a Scotchman) more than once informed him, with a grin, intended for cheerfulness, but really ghastly in its effect. Very likely, thus employed, Arnold had often thought longingly of his now less frequent pleasant gossips with Lord Dolly at the Junior Adonis, or the old chats upon art with Jack Lackington, or of listening to the charming tenor of Rob blended with the bass of Mr. Gossett in an operatic duet; more often still of the delicious meetings with Leo, now growing fewer and fewer, all by reason of his unremitting attention to his official duties. It was but sorry consolation, after all, for missing these things, to reflect that he was, in his brother-in-law's words, "qualifying himself for parliamentary life," "acquiring an interest in business undertakings of considerable importance," "educating himself for a future share in the carrying on of public affairs." A director of the Dom Ferdinando Silver Mining Company, —indeed, he was—thanks to Mr. Lomax's introduction—a member of the boards of other companies. It is not necessary to go into detail concerning these, or to cumber

these pages with useless repetitive narratives touching what
may be called Arnold's City career. The Dom Ferdinando
may be taken as a fair sample of the schemes with which it
was his evil fortune to be connected.

It is not to be supposed, however, that *he* only, as an
individual, fell among thieves ; that he was the only honest
man at a table of rogues. There were other gentlemen
reputable as himself who had permitted their names to
ornament the prospectus of the Company, influenced very
much by motives similar to his own ; a want of occupation,
a desire to be useful ; though, perhaps, far more than he
did, they cared for the remuneration attached to the post
of director. A Board seems to be always composed of
King Logs and King Storks, the Storks being in a minority,
and yet managing somehow to rule, and finally to devour
their associates. One thing, the chairman couldn't lose
much. It has been said that he was an Irish peer : and,
moreover, he never attended the meetings of the Board.
The Storks were glib, shrewd, mysterious men, intimately
acquainted with the management of public companies, who
seemed to qualify for their seats at the Board by allotting
themselves shares and owing the company the amount due
in respect of the allotment ; who quite overawed the Logs
by their superior information upon business topics, and bewildered them by the use of a language—it might be called
Stock-Exchangese — which no efforts of the Logs could
render into intelligible English. The Logs were, for the
most part, retired military men, troubled with the notion
peculiar to retired military men : that they are intimately
acquainted with business affairs, and valuable members of a
commercial community. With what bewildered, dazed,
fuddled looks they watched the proceedings before them !
Brave old gentlemen ! yours is a humiliating position ; and
very dear at the price, though bought at two guineas an
attendance, and an excellent lunch, served by the company's
porter. Certainly it is a sad spectacle ; and yet a laughable
practical joke, to see two Indian colonels inspecting the
books and auditing the accounts of a mining company.
" This is the ledger, is it ? Ah ! And this the cash-book ?
Dear me ! Beautifully written. This the day-book — the
journal—the bill-book. Ah ! I see. Yes. You copy from

one into the other. *Post*, you call it? Exactly. Very nice, indeed. I suppose they add up all right?" And they retire to the Occidental Club, agreeing over their mulligatawney, that the Dom Ferdinando is a wonderful company—wonderful, by Jove! That accounts are extraordinary things—quite extraordinary, by gad! And they sign a balance-sheet ("Dam rum-looking thing," they mutter), and report to the proprietors that they have examined the books and accounts of the company, and find everything to be in a highly satisfactory and flourishing condition.

It has been stated that the undertaking had been well received by the public; but an arrangement of that sort is simple and easy enough. The promoters of a company take steps to ensure its triumphant reception, just as a manager buys bouquets to hurl to his new prima donna, or hires claqueurs to applaud in the pit, pre-determining a tremendous success. By-and-by, of course, comes the reaction —a drop in the receipts, a vacuum in the treasury, empty benches. That can't be helped: bring out your next novelty, and dismiss your prima donna; get out of the company; get up another; bolt with your profits—with anything else you can lay your hands upon, if need is. The market had been skilfully manipulated; the prospectus made its appearance at a period when, according to the City intelligence of the newspapers, money was particularly easy. The shares were at one time quoted at a high premium, the result, it was generally believed, of some very adroit bulling manœuvres conducted by a secret committee of the Storks of the Board. But there had been something hectic about the business. The shares seemed liable to great fluctuations in price; the quotations were as unsteady as the pulse of an unhealthy man. The weekly share-list showed extraordinary variations in value; the shares going up and down as suddenly and uncertainly as the barometer in squally weather. The pilots, who had weathered Capel Court storms, began to shake their heads as they considered the Dom Ferdinando; they began to think the ship wasn't altogether sea-worthy, and to look to escape by means of the boats, selling out at once, and securing such small premiums as could then be obtained. It was, perhaps, about this time that Mr. Lomax

began to feel uncomfortable qualms: he had sadly over-
bought; in the event of a sudden rush over the side of the
ship becoming necessary, he had certainly cumbered himself more than sufficiently to sink him. He transferred a
large share of his risk to his brother-in-law. There was a
lull, a partial recovery: perhaps there was relenting on the
part of the " bears; " or they had made enough for a time,
satisfying their expectations, or not caring to kill the golden
goose outright. The ship rode on tolerably well; nobody
particularly caring to ascertain exactly how much the leak
was gaining on the pumps. A few months and there was a
great cry, a strange bubbling sound; money was very tight,
it seemed, and the ship was settling down bodily.

I am anxious not to weary the ready with the minutiæ of
the misfortunes of this dreadful Dom Ferdinando company.
Information touching the collapse of bubble companies is
to be gathered from many and convenient sources. In the
columns of the newspaper are to be found revelations identical with the story of this shameful undertaking. I refer
the reader to these. The case was a very glaring one. It
seemed to be streaked in all directions with fraud, as a
human body with veins. It was so leavened with
chicanery, that the whole affair bore the aspect of a
gigantic swindle. It was very hard for innocent men to
disentangle their innocence from the débris of dishonesty. It was harder still to answer the question ceaselessly screamed out by an infuriated body of swindled
proprietors—What has become of our money? No one
seemed to know; only that there was nothing left. Not a
halfpenny in specie, and a terrible list of liabilities. The
large sums received from the shareholders had ebbed away
through the fingers of the directors, and sunk, as it were,
through some great hole in the floor beneath the board-room
table. There was endless confusion. The books of the
company were handed over to professional accountants; but
there was no one who could give any explanation. The
Storks, to a man, had disappeared; for the most part, in
some mysterious way, enormously enriched by the whole
business. Whether the company thrived or failed, sunk or
swam, in its poor days as in its palmy, these clever gentlemen managed somehow to derive benefit from the under-

taking, and then at critical moments contrived to elude pursuit and to suddenly disappear, pretty much as ingenious evil spirits down trap-doors in pantomimes. *Sauve qui peut* had been the cry as on the occasion of other crises, and many had made good their escape. The agent at the mouth of the mine; the manager and director in London; the Scotch secretary; every underling who, by any means, could thrust his finger into the pie, upon the chance of a sovereign sticking to it as he withdrew it, these had clean gone, past all finding out. There remained—upon whom to wreak the wrath of the proprietors—the wretched Indian colonels, and the other King Logs of the Board of Directors; including, of course, Mr. Arnold Page, of Oakmere Court. And as a tribe of Choctaws, infuriated at the escape of certain of their victims, determine that the remainder shall be put to worse and worse torture, to more and more horrible punishment, so the shareholders cried out for condign vengeance to be visited on the heads of the poor Log directors. They were made bankrupts, to a man. Every farthing they possessed was seized upon, and they stood awaiting the terrible examination before the Commissioners; the brow-beating of a host of opponents; the butts of the newspapers, serious and comic; to be questioned upon all sorts of things; betrayed into contradictions; teased with inquiries concerning matters of which they knew nothing, when they should have known so much; bewildered with the books and papers shown to them, certified by them, signed by them, innocently, ignorantly, of course, yet guiltily and fradulently, as their opponents persisted; worried pitilessly, like noble quarry at the mercy of curs. Poor souls! They were paying a heavy price for the two guinea attendances and the excellent luncheons. And our Arnold was of these; utterly ruined, surrendering everything, asking only to be set free to starve!

Monsieur Anatole was sitting in the *Café de l'Univers.* He waited until the other guests had departed. He then approached the *dame de comptoir.* Madame Després received him with a superb smile. They proceeded, as it seemed, to serious converse. Monsieur Anatole drew from his pocket-book a ragged bundle of papers; Madame

Després handed him in.exchange a dirty canvas bag probably containing money; finally Monsieur Anatole took his departure.

He did not know that a man had watched him through the plaits of the muslin veiling the glass door. The man was Pratt. He escaped just in time to avoid encountering the Frenchman.

"At least I know one place where to find him," growled Pratt, as he retreated. "But how does he get money from that woman?"

Louis, the waiter, sat scowling at a marble table, reading, or affecting to read a coffee-stained *Indépendance Belge*. Madame took his hand: he snatched it from her.

"He is a millionnaire," she said, with an air of apology. "He is a supreme speculator. He has undertaken to negotiate for me an investment, which will repay to me a profit enormous—superb! We shall be rich, Louis. We shall be *rentiers*. I hold ten shares in the company of the silver mine of Dom Ferdinando. It is an enterprise sublime—glorious! Ah! how I long for that old black pocket-book of Monsieur Anatole!"

CHAPTER XXVII.

PUNISHMENT.

P and down, up and down the sycamore avenue in the garden at Croxall Chase paced Leonora Carr.

Of late a change had come over her looks. An expression of suffering, of sorrow, was now upon her face. She was very pale. The small delicate features seemed smaller, more delicate than ever; yet the brown limpid eyes were surely larger, with such an earnest appealing piteousness in their gaze : though prone now to fill with tears upon very slight provocation—a chance word, a sad thought, a mournful memory. The rich brown hair looked more than ever luxuriant and profuse, perhaps because it was less heedfully tended — thrust back negligently from her forehead, and suffered to fall in thick twisted loops about her neck, and even on her shoulders. How slight now, yet how charmingly lithe her beautifully proportioned figure : to which thinness could never give angularity ; there was such softness in its outline, such a tender grace in its every movement. She seemed to have grown taller, perhaps from a certain calm stateliness that had recently come to her, replacing that girlish mobility of expression, that vivid fervour of manner for which she had been at one time remarkable.

She was not alone. A visitor had called at the Chase— Lord Southernwood. He had ridden over from the family seat of the Southernwoods at Gashleigh. The London season had commenced ; but the Carrs had not left Croxall, the state of health of Mrs. Carr not permitting of her removal ; and Lord Southernwood was at no loss to account for his still lingering in the country ; for instance, the wishes of his sister-in-law, the bereaved Marchioness ; the recent demise of his brother—surely these were sufficient reasons for his absence from the gaiety of town ? though it is possible they might not altogether explain his visits at Croxall Chase, which had become of late more and more frequent.

Leo and his lordship had been for some time in the garden, occupied evidently with a conversation of much interest.

"And those were the very words he used?" she asked, in a choked voice, as Lord Southernwood finished speaking.

"Yes, indeed, Miss Carr, as near as I can recollect them."

"Poor Arnold," she said, and the tears rushed into her eyes; "and yet," she added half aloud, "could he have ever given me up like this if he had loved as I have?"

"I'm very sorry, very sorry indeed, if I have said anything to pain you. I am, upon my soul, Miss Carr," urged his lordship, piteously.

"No, no; it is only right that I should be told, that I should know all. You must not wonder that it has made me sad, very sad; for I have loved Arnold so dearly! Could I help it? I may speak of it to you, who are his friend—yes," she went on in her simple, touching tones, "and my friend, too, are you not? I have known him so long now, so very long, ever since I was quite a child. I remember his father also. Good old General Page! such a noble-looking old man, with quite white hair, a great friend of papa's, who never came over to see us but he remembered to bring toys or sugar-plums for me; and he would make me hunt in his coat-tail pockets for them, and pat my head and smooth my hair—so good, and tender, and loving to me always. And Arnold was so like him; and he'd come to romp with me, and was never tired of doing all he could to please me—was never rude or rough with me as some boys are when they play with children. Do you think I can ever forget these things? I have been used to be petted and made much of, spoiled perhaps; but I can never forget those who were so kind to me; and was it wonderful that I should grow up to love him? Is it strange that I should now be terribly pained when he is sad and in trouble? And when he told me of his love, and asked me for mine, he knew it was his before he asked for it, and it seemed only natural and of course, that I, who had loved him all my

life, should be his wife at last. And this is to end now, and
we are to be nothing more to each other, and we are never
to meet again, never!"

She stopped, overcome by her emotions. Lord Southernwood could do nothing but watch her tenderly, with a
reflection of her suffering upon his face. He did not dare
to say more; indeed, he was accusing himself of brutality
for having said as much as he had, bringing those tears in
the eyes of the woman he loved. He looked very wretched,
and what chance was there, he asked himself, of a successful
issue to his suit? How could he hope for the love of this
poor sufferer, whose love had already been given so wholly
to another—to Arnold, and was his still? How could it be
otherwise?

"I do wrong to give way like this," Leo said, quickening
her steps as she brushed away the tears from her eyes. "I
do but pain you, and I do no good to myself, or indeed to
anyone. Pray forgive me. I shall grow stronger soon. I
shall learn to forget, perhaps."

"I'm sure if I could do anything, Miss Carr, I would,"
said his lordship, in sad accents. "If I could serve Arnold
in any way, if he would only let me, Heaven knows I'd
do it."

"I know you would," she exclaimed, and almost involuntarily she gave him her hand. He received it blush-
ingly, holding it with a timid reverence.

"Such a good, true fellow as Arnold has always been.
All the fellows liked him; so cheerful, and jolly, and that,"
his lordship stammered.

"Thank you," she said, with kindly eyes, "for speaking
so of him. I like to hear you praise him. I could always
listen to praise of him. There, I'm better now. I think
I'll go in now. They'll wonder in the house what has
become of me."

She turned to leave him.

"And—and you'll think over what I've been saying,
please, Miss Carr," he urged, with a rueful, imploring air.
"You won't forget. You'll try to think as well as you can
of me, please. I'm not like Arnold, I know; I'm miles off
him; but I love you, indeed I do. I never loved anyone
as I love you. I'll do all I can to make you happy. I——"

"Hush!" she said, half closing her eyes, like one in acute pain; "no more now, please; no more now."

"But I may hope, ever so little? please tell me that. Don't drive me mad; let me hope that some day, a long time hence——"

"Oh, hush!" she repeated; "not another word of this now; not for a long, long time. I'll try, indeed I will. You've always been so kind to me. I'm sure you will be so still. You've been his friend and mine, Lord Dolly, dear Lord Dolly; and I have always liked you, and I'll try—only let me go, please let me go now, and don't speak of this;—not for a very long time."

She broke away as he took one of her hands and pressed it to his lips. Another moment and she had left him to enter the house, and remove as best she could all traces of her recent emotion from her face.

Lord Southernwood took out his handkerchief and wiped his forehead.

"What a darling she is! how I love her! By Jove, I would do anything she told me. Perhaps it *is* rather hard to be able to win smiles from her only when I praise *him*. But isn't it natural? He is a good fellow, and I couldn't say a word against him, not if I tried ever so. It is natural that she should love him; but I think she will love me too —a little, in the end. I'm sure she will! How I love her! I'd jump over the moon if she asked me to; at least, I'd try to do it. There's no folly or insanity I would not do, if she bade me, to see a smile upon her dear little lips, to catch a bright glance from those jolly eyes—how they run through and through a fellow! I'm going mad I think—mad with love, I think; and I'm trembling all over, like a jelly. I never felt anything like it before."

Some months have elapsed.

It is necessary that we should register certain changes that have meanwhile taken place in the situation of divers of our friends.

The chambers in Sun-dial Buildings have been given up; the fittings and furniture have been sold for the benefit of the estate of Arnold Page, a bankrupt. The premises bear a wholly different aspect now, tenanted by that rising advocate, Bellows, Q.C., of the Northern Circuit, member for the borough of New Gateford, who will probably be offered the Solicitor-Generalship on the break-up of the present administration, and the formation of a new ministry. All comforts and luxuries have been rigidly abolished, and the rooms are gradually resuming the appearance they boasted prior to their occupation by Arnold, and in the life-time of old Mr. Tangleton, the special pleader. It may be stated that the many pictures which had ornamented the walls did not fetch very high prices when brought to the hammer; the works of art executed by Mr. Lackington realising such insignificant sums as seriously to discompose that artist, affording him an excuse for abstinence from labour during many days.

Arnold had returned from the continent in due course, and surrendered, in compliance with the requirements of the bankruptcy laws. Of course he was no longer subjected to personal restraint or molestation. But he had to attend a long series of wearisome examinations before the Com missioner. He was greatly occupied with the preparation of his schedule, in endeavouring to aid his legal advisers, Messrs. Holroyd and Hopegood, in the arrangement of his accounts. It was a tedious business; partly owing to the inextricable confusion in which he had permitted his affairs to fall, partly in his own inability to understand his own position, or to render any explanation upon various heads, or to recollect a thousand things which of course he ought to have recollected particularly. There were adjournments, and adjournments, and adjournments, until the readers of the newspapers began to cry aloud at last, asking each other how much longer they were to be bored with these repeated reports concerning the proceedings of the Bankruptcy Court, "IN RE PAGE." It was a time of terrible trial, of humiliation, of suffering, for Arnold. He bore it with great patience, with as much composure as he could possibly command; evincing an earnest desire to render all the assistance in his power to his numberless creditors, surrendering every half-penny he possessed, doing all that was possible for him to do in atonement for his sins of omission and commission, of neglect and folly. The extent of his liabilities seemed to him to be enormous—was entirely beyond his comprehension. He failed to grasp the facts of the entanglement in which he found himself struggling; he stood amazed at the long lists of debts—debts of which he had not the remotest conception. The Commissioner's mode of dealing with him was not unkind. He even took upon himself to compliment the bankrupt upon the frankness of his confession, and his apparent desire to afford aid to his assignees; while he yet lifted up his hands at the profligate rate of the expenditure, and animadverted upon the manner of life of young men of the present day in strong terms, accurately reported in the newspapers of the next morning, though the applause which followed the observations in court was of course immediately suppressed. (Why applause is to be disallowed when speeches are permitted which manifestly bid, and bid high, for applause, is of course one of those mysteries a non-legal public can never hope to penetrate.) "The bankrupt, a young man of intelligence, of education, who had mixed with the world, who was presumed to have some acquaintance with business habits—who, at any rate, had ventured to thrust himself into a position of serious importance and grave responsibility—had yet been guilty, according to his own account, of the childish imprudence of attaching his signature to documents, of whose contents he knew nothing—absolutely nothing; he had not even read them over, barely looked at them. It seemed almost hopeless, under these circumstances, to arrive at a proper understanding of the bankrupt's case. In reference to this Silver Mining Company, of which so much had been heard in the course of these proceedings—he (the learned Commissioner) made bold to say that a grosser case of positive fraud and villany (applause, aggravated rather than put down by the greater noise of the ushers)—he would repeat, of positive fraud and villany, than was represented by this Silver Mining Company, he had never met with in the whole course of his professional existence, which was not of yesterday, as everybody in that court was well aware. Though he did not desire to add to the pain which the bankrupt must necessarily feel in the unfortunate position he then occupied, by attributing to him a guilty participation in the most iniquitous transactions of that company: indeed, it was evident that he was a serious loser rather than a gainer by his connection with it : still, in reference to his conduct as a member of the direction of the company, he was bound to say that the bankrupt had laid himself open to censure of the gravest kind. He (the Commissioner) would say nothing—though there was plenty to be said—on the subject of the bankrupt's betrayal, by his negligence and inefficiency, of the trust reposed in him by his co-proprietors. He had been assiduous in his attendance at the meetings of the Board, but for any good he had done by such means he might as well have been a thousand miles away. The man who was unable to protect his own interests was powerless to watch over the concerns of others. Why, it actually appeared by the statements that had been made in that court—and he confessed, in spite of the extraordinary nature of the evidence, that he could not resist putting implicit faith in it—it positively appeared that the bankrupt, in compliance with a resolution passed by the Board, of which he was a member, to the effect that the directors should issue promissory notes or bills of exchange on behalf of the company, the bankrupt, he repeated—and, it was alleged, other directors, not now before the court,—had been so imprudent and' ill-advised as to be led to affix his name to a number of such bills without remarking that there was no mention of the bills being given on behalf of the company, thus actually pledging his individual personal credit to bolster up the decaying reputation of this nefarious undertaking. So scandalous a case of unreasonable imprudence, to say the least of it, had never come before him (the Commissioner). The liability thus incurred by the bankrupt was of an amount that was absolutely frightful ; and it was to be relieved of such and other liabilities,· that the bankrupt now came to that court. The case must stand adjourned. There must be a production of further accounts. Protection to the bankrupt would, of course, be continued. But in the present state of this case it was not possible for the court to adjudicate."

Mortified, heart-sick, terribly oppressed, Arnold left the court to take counsel with his solicitor. It needed all Mr. Hopegood junior's good-humour to cheer his client in the slightest degree.

"We must do the best we can. We'll show fight yet.

26

We'll have another round with the Commissioner. He's giving way, I can see that. He wants to settle the case, only there's been such a confounded opposition, he's obliged to take time. But he's with us—I can see that. That speech to-day showed it. Very satisfactory I call it. He's always rather partial than not to the bankrupt who gives him an opportunity of making speeches. Suppose we have a glass of sherry? How oppressively hot the court was, and how full! They never will ventilate law-courts enough. Somehow there seems always an objection to letting too much light and air in upon law matters. Ha! ha! Don't fear, Mr. Page. We shall be all right. Another glass! Do!"

During the progress of adjudication upon his disastrous affairs, Arnold, at the request of his sister, had taken up his residence in the house she had secured in town after her masterly evacuation of Oakmere. Mrs. Simmons learnt with regret that her lodger was not likely again to occupy her apartments in Coppice Row. Mr. Gossett greatly missed his companion, the kindly critic and the patient auditor of his vocal efforts. Mr. Lomax was still absent from England. It was now boldly stated that his connection with the Wafer Stamp Office had altogether ceased, although it was not clear as to whether he had or not been dismissed the service; the more general impression being to the effect that he had been permitted to retire upon a superannuation allowance. Mrs. Lomax averred that her husband's health was no longer equal to the severe requirements of his official career, and that, acting upon the advice of his medical attendant, and in compliance with her earnest solicitation, he was at present restrained to a milder climate in the south of Europe, awaiting the restoration of his energies, recruiting his faculties, enfeebled by overwork and excess of devotion to the Government. The gentlemen who had been his colleagues at Whitehall, whether occupants of rooms in which cocoa-nut matting, or kamptulicon, or Kidderminster, or Turkey carpets decked the floors, agreed amongst themselves that, "Somehow Lomax had gone a-mucker;" a statement which, possibly for its vagueness and incomprehensibility, considered publicly, was satisfactory and congenial to their official minds. It was tolerably notorious, however, that Mr. Lomax was not likely for some con-

siderable time to come to appear again upon the scenes he
had been accustomed to adorn ; and all sorts of motives
were assigned in explanation to this absence, more or less
flattering in their nature according as they proceeded from
friends or enemies, from apologists or censors.

Mrs. Lomax, comfortably settled in a small but genteel furnished house on the outskirts of the Regent's Park, no longer
deemed it necessary to maintain the rigid regard for appearances she had manifested prior to her departure from Oakmere. She availed herself of the independence, the reticence,
the isolation, so easy of attainment when you are one of a
million in town, so difficult when you are one of a dozen in
the country. She made but few of her London friends
aware of her arrival. She entered at once upon a less
expensive mode of life. She did not go into society ; she
entertained no company. She gave up her carriages and
horses, dismissed all unnecessary servants. To the limited
circle to whom any explanation was due or desirable, she
gave out that she was regulating her life in accordance with
what she considered correct under the circumstances of her
husband's absence from the country ; the growing up of her
children, now, as she said, of an age when the unremitting
attention and devotion of a mother was more than ever
desirable ; and the unfortunate position in which her brother
had found himself placed. She affirmed, that these things
considered, a state of seclusion and retirement was in the
best taste. There was no escape from the publicity of
Arnold's difficulties ; it did not avail, therefore, to deny
these in any way. But she made out the best case she
could, hinting to the most curious of her intimates, that her
own resources were crippled by the sacrifices she had made
to avert the disasters which had come upon her brother ;
while she yet looked forward to a resumption at no
distant date of the position she had surrendered, expressing
herself most contented with, and resigned to, her present
retired manner of existence. She spoke often now of her
duty—she was fond of remarking that the mother of a
family *must* make sacrifices. And she wore cleaned gloves
for the first time in her life, and had several of her silk
dresses *turned.*

It is not to be questioned, that in the bosom of Mrs.

26—2

Lomax there existed for her brother as warm an affection as she was probably capable of, though beneath the weight of the sham sentiment and artificialness which had become part of her nature, it breathed with difficulty, was semi-petrified, endured long cataleptic suspensions of vitality. She sympathised with his sufferings under his reverse of fortune, and this quite apart from the fact that inconveniences were entailed upon herself by his embarrassments. She was earnest in her entreaties that he would take shelter in her newly-acquired house. Of course, Arnold, dear, so long as I have a home, you will have one too ; whatever he has done, it is not for a sister to desert her brother ; if I were reduced to my last crust, be sure that half, if not the whole of it, would be yours, my poor Arnold." There was, nevertheless, something irritating in the patronising generosity of her manner. She either chose to ignore, or was really unaware of the fact, that her husband had largely contributed to her brother's ruin ; and occasionally in her expressions of affection and outbursts of sentiment, mingled certain peevish regrets and complaints that were very galling to Arnold. " I make no reproaches," she would say ; " I make no reproaches. It is not for a sister to sit in judgment upon her brother ; and, of course, it is not to be expected that I should understand all the intricacies of this dreadful business. I confess it is to me an impenetrable mystery, how all this money could have slipped through your fingers ! I am afraid you have been dreadfully extravagant, Arnold. I am afraid you have neglected Frank's good offices ; so competent as he has always been to advise upon business topics. And now you are dependent upon me, and the poor annuity charged upon the estate and payable under my settlement ! Of course, I am only too happy to be able to assist you, even though the fortunes of my own poor dear children may be crippled to furnish you with means. I know what duty a sister owes to her brother ; " and so on. Of course this was hard to bear ;— not the less so from the consideration that Arnold had been doing all in his power to screen Lomax. It had been unavoidable that his name should be mentioned in the course of the bankruptcy proceedings ; it was not to be concealed that large sums of money had passed from the

bankrupt's possession into the hands of his brother-in-law.
"It is a pity that we haven't this Mr. Lomax here," the
Commissioner had observed upon more than one occasion.
"I should like to have put a few questions to him. There
has been either collusion or robbery, I won't say which."
But Arnold shrank from exculpating himself at the expense
of his sister's husband. "For her sake, for the children's,
let me say as little as I can about him." And a long
penitential letter which Lomax had addressed to him, imploring not to be betrayed, beseeching his pity and forbearance, a letter which contained a full confession of a long
list of rogueries of which Arnold had been the victim, he
had committed to the flames ; for he found the temptation
growing upon him, when Mrs. Lomax became too querulously
kind and charitable in her dealings with him, to silence her
by producing her husband's letter. "No," he said, as he
watched the confession turn to tinder in the grate; "for
her own sake, for the children's, she shall not know from
me that her husband is a scoundrel." So he endured on,
without a word, taking his punishment, severe though it
was, very manfully.

But upon one subject Mrs. Lomax said nothing : the
engagement with Leo which she had done so much to
terminate. She was fully conscious of the mischievousness
of her conduct, though she considered it now, perhaps, past
all reparation. She never opened her lips upon the matter.
The Carrs were still in the country. She had not seen Leo
since the departure from Oakmere. Secretly, she could
not but reproach herself for breaking off a match, which, she
was disposed to think, but for her interference, would have
taken place, and in effect have wholly retrieved Arnold's
fortune. She was unaware, perhaps, how far he had of himself retreated from a position he believed he could not
hold with honour. But certainly, she had done all she
could to sap Leo's faith in him, to encourage the pretensions
of a dangerous rival, the Marquis of Southernwood.

So Arnold was an inmate of the Regent's Park house.
Had Mrs. Lomax forgotten that he was thus brought into a
position of some danger? She had herself at one time
found it convenient, for purposes of her own, to charge him
with undue admiration of her governess, Miss Janet Gill.

He was now under the same roof with that young lady; constantly, it could not be helped, subjected to the perils of her society; and he was in a condition of mind which aggravated the risks he was running. He had suffered very much; he had been terribly wounded in the encounter from which he had just emerged. It is always those barely convalescent from one disorder who are so liable to fall a prey to another. And it was certain that he admired Janet Gill very much. Had Mrs. Lomax forgotten these things?

In the midst of his troubles he had received a letter from Leo. It was kindly if somewhat timidly worded, containing no reference to the engagement, treating that apparently as at an end, and yet, as it were, seeking to build a friendship out of the salvage of a destroyed love, as one might erect a cottage in the country with the stones of a dilapidated palace. It expressed sincere sympathy for him, in terms so simple and earnest, that he had perhaps been more touched by them had they come to him at some other time. But while under the fire of his examination in the Bankruptcy Court, he seemed to have no time to attach true value to her attempts at comfort. Perhaps, too, situated as he was, he found it necessary to gain strength to endure, by hardening his heart as much as possible. He sometimes tried to beat out all tenderness from his heart, as a man will stamp out fire—heedless what harm his foot may do, so long as he can extinguish the flame. He sought to forget: as though the first part of a life history could be as easily put away from one as the early pages of a book can be torn out and destroyed. He continued a long struggle with memory, in which he often came worst off. If he ever triumphed it was only for a time. There came a terrible eaction. "The past is past," he would sometimes say. 'Soon I shall be able to look back half wondering, half doubting, was I ever rich? did I ever love? I shall see *her* Marchioness of Southernwood, in the crimson velvet robes of her order—with a cape furred with miniver pure, three rows and a half of ermine, and a train a yard and three-quarters on the ground. She will roll down St. James's Street in the lumbering Southernwood family chariot on the way to the drawing-room of her sovereign—while I stand among the mob on the kerbstone splashed by her wheels, as

I ask myself, looking across the chasm that divides us, Can it be, that I ever thought I possessed her love—ever strained her to my heart—ever thought to call her wife?—What an idiotic dream all this will then seem! And yet I did love her; and I believed that she loved me. Let me not blame her: what has happened is of my doing, not hers. She has duties to perform—duties to her social station, to her wealth, to her beauty. Her position in society is the more precious to her because it has been honestly fought for and won by her father and grandfather. How can I expect that she should step down to lift up the bankrupt and beggar in the kennel, who has come to grief, thanks to his own folly? No, I held my happiness in my hand, but not tightly enough—my fingers relaxed one by one, and it escaped from me like a butterfly. I have been like a gambler, who begins with a great run of luck, and staggers from the table at last, ruined and disgraced. I have lost fortune, love, and honour too, perhaps, in the world's eyes. I know that I am suspected of fraud, yet God knows I have made all the atonement possible. I have given up everything, and by-and-by the struggle will be for a bare living!" Certainly he was going through a stern ordeal. Men have suffered as much often enough. There has never been lack of suffering in the world, the while there has been plenty of happiness and courage, and goodness too, and strength to bear. But there is great danger of emerging from such trouble either utterly cowed and spirit-broken, cast down past all lifting up again, without self-respect, bereft of the dignity of misfortune, or else cold, cynical, grim, morose, selfish. The alternative is not pleasant, and Arnold Page, graduating in the school of adversity, was in some peril of taking up poor Timon's cry, "I am misanthropos, and hate mankind!"

He sent no reply to Leo's letter, crumpling it in his hand. "Let it end," he said. Perhaps he expected to hear something from her father; but nothing came; and poor Leo waiting heart-sick for a letter, crushing her face against her pillows, wetting them with her tears, was suffering cruelly.

"No letter from him. Another day has gone, and no letter! Does he not know that at a word from him I would fly to him, I would cling close to his heart, and never—never leave him?" And the next day she would be summoned to the drawing-room, to receive that constant visitor at Croxall Chase, the most honourable the Marquis of Southernwood. And she seemed to read in her father's eyes, though he never opened his lips upon the subject, a desire that the pretensions of the visitor should not be discouraged.

On the break-up of the establishment in Sun-dial Buildings, what had become of our friend Robin Hooper? Well, he had secured a temporary residence in a house in Omega Street, Camden Town, inhabited, as to its first-floor, by that distinguished artist, Mr. Lackington.

"To think that those gems of art which Arnold bought of me should go for a mere nothing," sighed the painter, as he sat smoking before a blank canvas, or watching the sunlight glide round his room and fade away. "And Arnold paid very respectable prices for them, I remember."

"It was a mere accident, Jack," urged Robin; "you mustn't let it interfere with your work."

"But, my dear fellow, if the public has quite made up its mind to undervalue one's work, what is the good of working? Besides, the look of the thing : one would think I had overcharged Arnold."

"Arnold never thought so. Never will think so. He valued the pictures highly, though, poor fellow, he was obliged to let them go with the rest. And, after all, he has too many other things on his mind to be occupied with this subject, poor fellow."

"I remember Hugh Wood talking to me about it. He's a hard man, is Hugh Wood. He told me I was very selfish one day; it was in reference to those very pictures, and Arnold's patronage of my easel. By-the-way, it reminds me, Arnold's match with Miss Carr is quite off, I suppose?"

"Entirely, as I understand," said Robin; "it seems strange that money should make any difference. I thought at one time that love strengthened more, that people were brought closer together, in misfortune; but it seems not so, at least not in the fashionable world."

" That's the nearest approach to a sneer I ever found you guilty of, Rob; one would think you were a contributor to a newspaper : accusing the upper classes of want of feeling ! Why, you'll speak disrespectfully of bishops next."

"I was wrong," said Robin; "I had no right to say that. At least, I know that Arnold wouldn't have suffered me. I suppose, therefore, that it is quite right, and in the nature of things, that his troubles should separate him from the woman he loves."

" But will it better Hugh Wood's chance ? "

" What do you mean ? "

" I mean that Hugh Wood is in love with Leonora Carr."

" Do you really think so ? " and Robin mused upon the subject. "Perhaps it may be so. The fact would explain much of Hugh's apparent hardness and severity. I remember to have heard a rumour to the effect once in the country; but it was traced to his father, the new Archdeacon of Binchester. He was rather given to romancing, and sentiment, and fine talk. His taste in that way broke out now and then in his pulpit. Poor Hugh ! How much disappointed love there seems to be in the world." Robin sighed.

" You think he has no chance ? "

" None whatever. Hugh is poor. His father's perferment won't help him. I should suppose the young lady has never given him a thought. Besides, there can be no doubt that she will marry Lord Southernwood. Arnold has said as much himself."

" Poor old Arnold. I tell you what I'll do, Rob, I'll set to work——"

" I'm very glad to hear you say so."

" Hear me out. I'll paint those pictures over again, and make a present of them to Arnold. I think it will please him."

" I'm sure it will, Jack. You've a great deal of good in you, Jack, if you would only let it come out."

Perhaps it would have been difficult to abstain from applauding the painter,—to have pondered at that moment whether justice had not a lien upon his labours that should have interfered with their devotion to purposes of generosity.

Was there any reason other than his friendship for the painter that could have brought Robin Hooper to reside in Omega Street, Camden Town? Could he have given a thought to the circumstance that the studio was at no great distance from the Regent's Park, while the park was very near to Mrs. Lomax's new house? Could he have counted upon the probability that the children of Mrs. Lomax would often, under the charge of their governess, Miss Gill, promenade in the pleasant enclosures adjoining the gardens of the Zoological Society? Certainly he made early discovery of the fact of these promenades, availing himself thereof, and renewing his acquaintance with Janet. She received him with the gentle kindness of her ordinary manner, enhanced by a lively gratitude, a keen memory for his services in the past. He found himself upon the footing of an old friend. The children recognised him as an Oak-mere neighbour, and soon prattled to him freely enough, or listened while Robin, limping as he walked between them, drew upon his imagination, and invented wonderful fairy stories for their amusement. And was there no incentive to his efforts in the fact that Janet was listening too? It was very dangerous work, Mr. Robin, so far as your own peace of mind was concerned. You were taking pains to sow, the while you knew you could but reap for all your pains a harvest the richer in affliction. Over and over again he had avowed his consciousness, that to *him*, crippled and de-formed, love was, must be, hopeless, futile, impossible. And yet was he not exposing himself more and more to danger; was he not baring his heart to the blow? He knew, very soon, that he loved Janet; was convinced as soon of the folly of his love; and yet did not fly, yet lingered near her, her presence but giving fresh vitality to his passion. He was acting as those foolish invalids who foster a passing malady until it becomes a confirmed organic disease. He knew that he loved; knew, too, with the jealous quickness, the avid perception of a lover, that the woman he loved, loved another; and yet he loitered near her, aggravating his suffering, intensifying his passion.

" She loves him," he said to himself, " she loves him ; or

why did her face flush, her eyes kindle, when I but chanced to mention his name? Well," he went on sadly; "it is only natural, I suppose. A woman's love is drawn towards Arnold, it seems to me, almost in spite of herself. And she must see so much of him now,—now that she is beneath the same roof. I ought to have known this, to have been more prepared for this; and yet, surely, there is something cruel about it—something very hard to bear. If she but knew how much I loved her! But that's madness!"

And there were others who had discovered that the Regent's Park had become a resort of Miss Janet Gill's.

"Gaspard was right. She is to be found here nearly every day, as it seems. He is a faithful creature, is Gaspard. I must do something for him; I must speak highly of the poor fellow in certain quarters. He deserves encouragement, promotion. Ah, behold her! It is as I expected, she is here to-day."

Monsieur Anatole was the speaker. He was standing in a secluded part of the park, but in such a position that he could command a view of the gate at which Janet and her pupils were accustomed to enter.

He had made certain changes in his dress. A deep crape band encircled his curved greasy hat; he wore a black coat; and round his neck a high, creased white cravat. He was, in fact, attired in mourning. Could it be that, to counteract the paleness of his face, consequent upon contrast with the deep gloom of his dress, he had slightly tinged the summit of his cheek bones with some artificial bloom? Those thin carmine clouds surely had in them something more than natural, and they were inconsistent with the prevailing sallowness of the other parts of his face; their youthful glory was so flatly contradicted by the labyrinth of crow's feet and entanglement of wrinkles in their immediate neighbourhood. The dense, luxuriant black wig had been, it seemed, freshly anointed; the curls were more than ever clotted together, matted and interwoven beneath the surface, glossy as a newly lacquered boot. Monsieur Anatole never looked so young—or so old.

The pupils were a little in advance. They did not note the approach of the Frenchman. He removed his hat ceremoniously. Janet started as she recognised him—but more from surprise than fear. She did not now betray the alarm, the extreme trepidation she had manifested on former occasions.

"Dear Janet," he said, bowing low, "you will pardon my thus intruding myself upon your notice, interrupting your contemplations."

She made no answer, watching him with a grave, offended air.

"But I have sought you with an important object."

"Not to renew a matter at an end for ever. Not to weary me again with a suit to which you have received a final answer?"

"Alas! I comprehend to what you refer. No, my Janet: I will, since you desire it, refrain from touching upon that subject. I will leave it to some happier occasion. You are hard with me, cruel; still I do not despair. To true love there is no such word. I come to speak to you of your father, the excellent Captain Gill."

"Say what you have to say, and leave me."

"Ah, my Janet, prepare yourself for a severe trial. Life is uncertain : life is full of troubles. Be assured, beautiful angel, of my sympathy, my devotion. But you cannot doubt of these. The orphan should find in every man a father, a friend, a lover. I will be all to you now, my Janet, do not fear."

"What does this mean?"

"The brave soldier will never draw sword again. The dashing *sabreur* is no more!"

"My father is dead?" She turned very pale. Her breath was very short, as she asked the question.

"Alas! yes, my Janet; the Captain Gill is dead." He waited for a few minutes, peering at her through his fingers. He had taken his hat off as he announced his news, and assumed a theatrical attitude expressive of grief, his eyes covered by his hand. Janet did not speak.

"I am aware," said Monsieur Anatole, "that between you and your admirable parent there had been of late differences of opinion. Some discontinuance, it may be, of the affections which should ever unite a father and a child. Alas, that there should ever be these family divisions; and yet they would seem to be inevitable! But these will now be forgotten."

There was something so false and mocking in the tone and manner of this man, that natural sorrow could not show itself in his presence. Tears seemed stanched by his influence : as bleeding is stayed by caustic.

"When did he die? and where?" Janet asked, nervously.

"In prison ; three days since. Poor man, his free, gallant, noble spirit confined within the walls of a debtors' gaol—it was terrible! He was very poor ; there are many expenses to be borne, in order that due respect may be paid to his remains. I would cheerfully find money for these if—if, indeed, I were able. But, alas ! I have made large payments lately. I have incurred serious losses ; and it might not be agreeable to you that I should take upon myself this expenditure."

"This is all the money I have in the world," she said. She took out her portemonnaie, and, opening it, shook the contents into his claw-like hand, held out before her, compressed into the form of a cup.

"This is but little, my Janet." He eyed it mockingly. She shuddered.

"What more can I do?" she asked, in a tone of despair.

"Ah ! the pretty ornament on your neck—the cross, gold and turquoise—you will add that. I will convert it into money."

It was the cross Leo had given her. Slowly and sadly she took it from her neck and handed it to Monsieur Anatole.

"Take it," she said. "You will let me know when the funeral has taken place. Then, you will never see me again."

And she left him.

"Edith," said Rosy to her sister, "did you see Miss Gill give a lot of money to a beggar? How good she is."

"He wasn't a beggar."

"He was; one of those beggars who try to look like clergymen, and sell sealing-wax. I've often seen them in the streets."

If Monsieur Anatole had known that his careful toilet would thus be spoken of by so juvenile a critic !

CHAPTER XXVIII.

HE house occupied by Mrs. Lomax was situate in a road divided from the park by a winding canal, crossed here and there by small light suspension bridges : a semi-detached house, of modern structure, and of cheap Italian architecture.

Soon after her return with her pupils from their morning promenade, Janet was informed that Mrs. Lomax desired to see her for a few minutes in the back drawing-room. This apartment had been devoted to much the same purposes as the boudoir at Oakmere. It was regarded as sacred to Mrs. Lomax's repose, and to the nursing of her headaches. Many of the decorative articles of furniture had indeed been brought from the original boudoir, especially the china and glass ornaments ; so that, with the blinds down, and the mistress of the place in her accustomed attitude of languor, the back drawing-room near the Regent's Park bore a considerable resemblance to the lady's sanctum at Oakmere Court.

Mrs. Lomax acknowledged, by a slight movement of her head, the entrance of Janet.

" I am sorry to seem to be finding fault in what I am about to remark, Miss Gill. I shall be even more sorry if I occasion you pain by the course I propose to myself to follow. Still, plain speaking is very desirable at all times, and indispensably necessary on very many occasions."

Mrs. Lomax paused for a moment, as though waiting for an acknowledgment of the truth of her proposition. Janet bowed slightly.

" I must admit that I shall lose your assistance in the education of my children with considerable regret. Still I am compelled to inform you that the time has come for our separation. I must beg you, therefore, to look elsewhere for an engagement as governess."

Janet received this announcement with some surprise.

"May I ask the reason for your taking this step, Mrs. Lomax?"

"Under the circumstances, I have no objection to your inquiry; at the same time, I guard myself—you will so understand me, if you please, Miss Gill—from any admission of a right on your part to question me. You have acted with much imprudence, Miss Gill. I don't desire to use words needlessly harsh or displeasing to you. I lay nothing further to your charge, therefore, than extreme thoughtlessness. But you have so far forgotten what is due to me and to my children as to allow some one to accompany you during your walks in the park. This person, a young man named Hooper, is the son of a farmer near Oakmere. It is not for me to pronounce upon his conduct. He has received much kindness—foolish kindness, I may say—from my brother; who even permitted him to reside in his chambers in London. My brother Arnold is not very discreet, and certainly in this case, his pity for the young man's affliction— he is, as you know, sadly crippled and deformed—got the better of his judgment. This young Hooper's station in life should have prevented my brother from admitting him to terms of intimacy and friendship. Kindness to our inferiors and to the unfortunate is, of course, desirable, commendable; but there must be limits. The young man has presumed to become the companion of yourself and my children; he has permitted himself to address them upon terms of equality. I believe he has even called them by their Christian names. I am at a loss to understand how you could have suffered such things to go on. Your conduct has been seriously reprehensible."

"I regret that you should think so," Janet said, calmly. "I received great kindness from Mr. Hooper some time ago now: kindness I can never forget."

"That may be, Miss Gill," Mrs. Lomax admitted, with a severe air. "It is a matter upon which I must decline to enter. I cannot allow my children to associate with this young man. I must recommend you to take warning from this affair in any future engagement you may hold."

Janet bowed; lowering her head, perhaps to conceal the curl of her lip, the flush upon her cheeks.

"And it is on this account you desire me to go?" she asked.

Mrs. Lomax hesitated a little.

"Yes," she said, at last; "on this account. But I deem it my duty to address you also on another subject; and I don't wish to conceal from you that it affords an additional motive for my bringing our agreement to an end."

She paused to refresh herself with her scent-bottle. Invigorated, but still languid, and with half-closed eyes, she resumed—

"I refer to the presence of my brother in the house."

Janet started at this unlooked-for beginning.

"As I have said, my brother, Arnold, is not very discreet. Perhaps he has not yet arrived at a period of life when one is entitled to look for much discretion. I don't wish to attribute blame to you, Miss Gill. I am aware that a governess is often placed in a position of some embarrassment from the attentions of visitors and others not sufficiently mindful of her real station in the household. My brother's conduct in this respect has not escaped my observations. He has certainly sought your society far more than there was any occasion for. Of course it is not possible to prevent communication between two persons resident beneath the same roof. But considering his position and your own, I fear you have rather encouraged——"

"Pardon me, Mrs. Lomax——" Janet began, a little warmly.

But Mrs. Lomax was not to be interrupted.

"One moment, Miss Gill, if you please. I do not wish to pain you in any way. I am quite aware that your experience as a governess is very limited. It is very excusable if, placed in a position of some difficulty, owing to the thoughtlessness of others, you have been at a loss how to act. The attentions paid to you by my brother Arnold were, no doubt, as agreeable as they were flattering. But it seems to me it would have been more prudent in you to have at once prevented any repetition of them. I am sure your own good sense would have pointed out to you a plan of accomplishing this, which would have been without offence on the one hand, while it would have been effectual on the other. Young men are very careless how their conduct may be understood or misunderstood; how attentions that really mean nothing may be accepted as meaning a great deal. Of course, in your position, a young woman is entitled to do the best she can for herself; it is only natural that she should be ambitious. Governesses have frequently made very advantageous marriages. But I have my duty to perform. I have to caution you as to your future conduct. I must ask you to relinquish any hopes you may have entertained with regard to my brother. I shall now be happy to hear anything you may desire to say on this unpleasant subject before we dismiss it finally."

Janet's face was crimson, and her voice trembled as, with evident effort, she said—

"I will say but this, Mrs. Lomax: that you have misunderstood me, that you have not done me justice. Let all be as you wish."

"Thank you. We will regard the matter as settled, if you please. I am far from wishing to inconvenience you. You will let me know as soon as you have heard of anything likely to suit you. I shall be happy to report favourably of your ability to impart instruction."

Janet quitted the room. She hurried to her small bedroom at the top of the house. There, alone and secure, she surrendered herself to a passionate burst of tears.

"How cruel she is!" she exclaimed. "Yet surely *he* does not know of this. No, no! I wrong him by the thought. He is too good and generous. I must go—I must never see him more! Would I had never seen him. Have I, then, no friend in the world?"

She thought of Leo, and put her hand to her neck to feel for her cross. Missing it, the memory came to her of how she had disposed of it, and why. And she wept afresh.

"I am alone, then, in the world—quite alone! My poor father dead!" She shuddered. "But he never loved me! —he never could have loved me!"

Her long rich golden hair had come streaming down at the side of her face. She moved to the small glass near the window to rearrange the stray tresses. It was impossible for her to avoid seeing that she was beautiful.

"How pale I am! how sad I look!" she said; and then

27

in a low suppressed tone, " Oh, if *he*—if Arnold would love me a little ! "

It was the morning after the interview between Mrs. Lomax and her governess.

Again Janet had set forth for a walk with the children in the Regent's Park. They had passed over the suspension-bridge, but had not yet crossed the carriage drive and entered the enclosed part of the park. A quick footstep behind them caused Rosy to look round abruptly.

" Why, here's Uncle Ar come to walk with us," she cried, clapping her hands.

" You be quiet, Rosy, and walk on with Edith. I've something to say to Miss Gill. I'm going to ask her if you've been good lately, and if she can let you off your French exercise this afternoon."

" Oh, thank you ! How nice ! " And she put up her face to be kissed previously to marching on with Edith, in advance, as it were, of the main body of the party.

" Forgive me, Miss Gill," said Arnold, turning to Janet, " for intruding upon you here. And indeed I fear I have to ask your forgiveness in other respects. I was yesterday, by a mere accident, in the front drawing-room, and could not help overhearing a great deal of a conversation between yourself and my sister which was carried on in the back room. I will not tell you how grieved I was to hear what I did hear."

Janet trembled, and her face flushed. She did not trust herself to speak.

" I am sure we shall all feel your loss very much. To me it will be more especially painful, because, as it seems, your leaving us is attributed to what my sister is pleased to term indiscretion on my part. I will not stop to ask whether this may have been so or not. I know it would avail little for me to attempt to correct the opinions Mrs. Lomax has adopted upon this subject—even if you could be prevailed upon after what has happened to stay with us; and I think I know enough of you to say that that is not likely. But at least you will pardon me my share, whatever it may have been, in your dismissal, cruel and foolish as I must ever think it."

He spoke in a low tone, with some embarrassment, for

the subject involved considerations of a delicate nature. But in his manner there was a kindness that approached to tenderness. Janet's heart throbbed unsteadily.

"Indeed," she said, as calmly as she could, "I have nothing to forgive." She put out her hand as she spoke; the gesture was half mechanical. Her face crimsoned as she was made aware of what she had done, by finding her hand enfolded in Arnold's.

"You are generous—kind to say so." He held the hand longer than there was any real occasion for, or he would never have become conscious that it was trembling a good deal, sending, as it seemed, strange thrills through his frame. At particular moments, in certain conditions of the heart, there is something very electrical about the unexpected encounter of hands—something very perilous to future peace of mind. He released his fluttering prisoner at last, unconditionally; it is always a difficult matter to know what to do with prisoners. Janet's hand fell down to her side; one moment, and she was in an agony at its captivity; now there was positive pain about its freedom. She did not know what to do with it. She was in the plight of those nations which, we are told, are unfitted for liberty, and rejoice in despotism.

"I fear," said Arnold, "I am now without such little power as I ever possessed to be of use to you. But I trust you will not quit my sister's house until you are sure as to the safety of your next step. I will engage—at least I can control Mrs. Lomax so far—that your residence with us, while it lasts, shall be made as agreeable to you as possible. But I trust that you have other friends who can be far more useful to you."

She shook her head sadly.

"I am alone in the world. I had but one living relative —my father—and—and he could not have helped me. Now he is taken from me."

"Captain Gill is dead?"

"Yes. I learnt of it only yesterday. I cannot pretend to regret it as a child should regret a parent's loss; for my father had not been himself for some time. He was very ill in India. He became the victim of very strange associates. I think his mind became affected—seemed to lose all interest in, all regard for, his children. He tried to force upon me a marriage—but I will not speak of these things. They are over now for ever. All his errors are atoned for now. I will try always to think of him as I remember him years ago—not—not as he was of late!" And she shuddered.

She had been speaking hurriedly, as though glad to enter upon any topic that promised avoidance of the danger that lurked about such proceedings as the joining of hands or the meeting of glances accidentally laden with tenderness.

"And have you no one to whom you can now apply for advice and assistance?"

"Yes; I have one friend who I know will assist me. Leo—Miss Carr."

Arnold started.

"You are, right," he said, in a strained voice. "Leo will do all she can for you. She will be always good, and kind, and true. Let her know how you are situated. I am sure you will not have to ask in vain for her aid."

Janet raised her eyes to look into his face. Much of the story of his engagement was of course known to her; and perhaps there was something more than the feminine curiosity natural under the circumstances, which prompted her, as she watched him, to ask herself the question—"Does he love her still?"

There was certainly a little awkwardness in being caught with that expression of anxious inquiry upon her face.

"Well, Uncle Ar," said Rosy, returning, "are we to be let off our exercises? Are we to have a half-holiday this afternoon?"

Janet replied to the question. Histrionic talent seems to come quite naturally to women.

"Yes;" said Janet, smiling. "Mr. Page has interceded for you. You are forgiven your lessons, but only for this afternoon. You must work very hard to-morrow to make up for lost time to-day."

Rosy hurried off to convey the pleasant intelligence to Edith.

"Pray, count me also your friend," said Arnold, availing himself of the opportunity eagerly, with some abruptness. "Pray believe me sincerely interested in your welfare, and that I will do all in my power to secure it. Pray believe this. I am your friend, always your friend, Janet—Miss Gill, I mean."

He quitted her, crossing the road, and entering the enclosure.

"She is very beautiful," he said to himself. "There is something very winning about that gentle voice, that graceful repose of manner, those deep, melting blue eyes. How happy the man will be who gains her love. What happiness to come weary, and wounded, and deeply troubled, to rest upon that true, tender, loving breast. Poor Janet! She has seen great sorrow; and is yet patient, and enduring, and calm. I'm sure I trust she may be happy. What does Georgina mean by treating her so cruelly? Well, all I can do to help her, Heaven knows I will do!"

He was so occupied with these thoughts that he failed to perceive that there was someone walking at his side and endeavouring to arrest his attention. He turned, however, when he felt a light touch on his arm, and found Robin Hooper limping along close to him.

"Ah! Robin, old fellow, how are you?" he cried; "what do you do here? Have you come into the park to meditate upon future poems? Are these lime-tree avenues genial to the muse? How does Camden Town suit you? and how is Jack Lackington? and what is he doing now? You see I have a thousand questions to put to you."

He did not appear to notice—but then he was, perhaps, talking a little at random, absorbed by other considerations, wrought upon and elated by rather intoxicating considerations—he did not notice that Robin bore upon his face traces of excitement, and moved along with greater difficulty, seemed more lame and crippled, than ever.

"You have just left Miss Gill—Janet Gill?"

"Yes; that's so, Rob."

"I saw you. I have been watching you for some minutes."

Arnold gazed at him rather suspiciously — curiously. There was an acrid tone in Robin's voice, a querulousness about his manner.

"What's the matter, Rob?" he asked. Robin breathed hard, waited for a few moments; he hardly seemed able to speak.

" Take care what you do, Arnold," he said at length.

" Why, what do you mean, old boy ? What's gone wrong ? What's the matter ? "

" Don't be cruel, Arnold. Don't trifle with her. I know that men think lightly of these things, make sport of them, seem to think there is a pleasure in playing upon a woman's feelings ; touching upon certain notes, and then listening coldly and critically to the effect produced ; employing words, and phrases, and tones, that really mean nothing, and yet which seem to mean so much ; giving a strange language to a sensitive woman to construe, as it were, and laughing at the mistakes she is led into by her ignorance, her weakness, her trustfulness."

" What *is* this all about ? What are you driving at, my dear Rob ? " '

" I have noticed this before to-day, often. The net seems very negligently spread, but the birds are secured by it not the less certainly. I don't accuse you, Arnold. But *her* happiness is at stake, however much you may trifle with the game. It may be pleasant to you—to me, I own, it seems very hateful—to tender trash to a woman and watch while the poor soul takes it unsuspectingly and treasures it in her heart as something beyond all price."

" Will you be a little more explicit, Rob ? " Arnold asked.

" It is difficult to speak more plainly on the subject, painful to allude to it at all ; and I know that so much rests with your nature, Arnold, and you are hardly to be held accountable for it. You are always, unwittingly, it may be, so picturesque in the presence of women, so attractive, so winning, because you are so subdued, deferential unto tenderness. You are misleading, while you are not dreaming of anything of the kind. Your voice softens, your tone becomes so sympathetic, you seem to concentrate your interest ; what woman can help exaggerating her ideas of your regard for her, giving significance to commonplaces, attaching importance to trifles ? "

" This might be flattery, Rob, if you were less serious, less angry."

" Bah ! Don't speak like that, Arnold. I will be plain with you since you wish it. You are trifling with the feelings of Janet Gill ! "

" Robin ! " cried Arnold, with a start.

" I have tried not to think so. Heaven knows I would rather not think so. But I cannot altogether close my eyes. I have watched you. Yes, and I have watched her, when she has least suspected me. I have tested her ; I am not deceived. I would not speak like this, if I were not sure. She is hardly herself aware of it, I think."

" What do you mean ? " Arnold asked again, rather because Robin had paused and it seemed necessary to say something, than because he was wholly conscious of what he was saying.

" Do you require to be told ? " said Robin, in a pained voice. " Be it so, then. She loves you ! "

Arnold was silent. He bent his eyes upon the ground, he pressed his hand upon his heart.

" No," he whispered hoarsely, at length. " You are wrong, Rob ; you must be wrong, I think. It cannot be."

And yet, could he help drawing some comfort from Robin's statement ? To be loved, loved by Janet ! What a pleasant haven of rest seemed open to him in the fact of her love. How doubly precious, after the disappointments he had endured, after his sufferings, the harassing trials of his misfortunes. He was greatly in the mood—as most hapless lovers are, fresh from a recent trouble—greatly in the mood to be won by this unexpected love dawning suddenly upon him.

" She loves you ; she loves you ! " Robin seemed to find a morbid pleasure in the pain the confession caused him. " You are my friend, over all. I have never forgotten it—I can never forget it—only, don't trifle with her. Be kind to her, for her own sake, for yours, for mine. Don't let her give you her heart, to take it back again, broken, crushed. I can say no more. Be true, be generous, if only because she loves you, as I know, I am sure she does. Good-bye, I can say no more now."

And painfully excited, Robin moved away, and had soon disappeared from the park.

" Can this be ? " Arnold asked himself, and he flung himself into a seat.

He remained for many hours in the park. Again and again he went over the circumstances of his acquaintance with Janet, to see if any ground for Robin's charge could be discovered. "Have I misled her in any way?" he asked himself. "Have I even by accident induced her to believe that I love her? Poor child! If this be so, I must make all the reparation possible. And if she loves me——" but for some time he did not even mentally complete this sentence. But he brooded over the fragment.

"Do I love her?" he asked himself, seeking to probe his own feelings on the subject. "No," he answered, with some hesitation. "Not—not as I loved, as I love Leo. But do I love her sufficiently? Do I love her enough to justify my encouragement of her affection? Enough"—he went on after a pause—"enough to marry her? Why may I not make her mine, for ever, and be happy with her, as I should be; who can doubt it? She is as poor as I am: at least the question of money can never come between us to part us. Our positions are equal so far; if, indeed, a governess is not rather degraded by marriage with a bankrupt. To quit England for ever: thousands of miles away, where men will know nothing about me—will care nothing —there to work for my living, and for Janet, to toil and to die. To go away never to return, with Janet as my wife, earning her love honestly, loving her in my turn—humble, hardworking, contented, happy. Would not this be the best? Indeed, I think it would."

So for a long, long time he discussed the question with himself. Now convinced, dismissing the subject as settled; now doubting, beginning anew, going over all his arguments again and again; wearying himself terribly, and leaving off at last perhaps not much nearer adjustment than when he commenced. He rose and quitted the park depressed in spirit, with an aching head, a heavily laden heart.

It was not only Robin Hooper who had witnessed the interview between Arnold Page and Janet, had noted, among other circumstances attending it, his pressure of her hand, his reluctant relinquishment of it. A handsome barouche had been rolling along the road at the precise moment of that meeting of hands. The carriage contained one person; a lady, leaning back, richly dressed, but pale and delicate-looking, with an air of languor and dejection about her. It was Leo.

She started as she recognised Arnold and Janet, turned paler than before, frowned, bit her lips, shivered, and then had passed on. The footman looking back by chance a moment afterwards, fancied his young mistress must have some painful fragments of dust in one of her eyes—certainly she was holding her handkerchief to her face.

The Carrs had come up to town; were again in Westbourne Terrace. It was found desirable that Mrs. Carr should be within immediate reach of the best medical advice. Her state of health was precarious; but she had borne the journey to London tolerably, and it was thought that she was improving. Sir Cupper Leech, Dr. Hawkshaw, and other physicians had met in consultation concerning her. They were of opinion that their patient would yet do well, if only her strength could be kept up.

The Marquis of Southernwood was also in London; but was not seen much in public. He had only shown himself once or twice at the Junior Adonis; but it was rumoured that he was a frequent visitor in Westbourne Terrace; constant in his inquiries as to the health of Mrs. Carr.

He had not, however, ventured to renew his suit to Leo. He noticed with pain that the young lady looked pale, and worn, and sad; that her old glad bright manner was exchanged now for a calmness that was almost apathetic; a quietude that seemed to arise from extreme listlessness and weariness. People said that she was worn out with attendance upon her mother, a great invalid. The Carrs had been out very little during the season, on the same account, it was alleged.

It was not, then, in the character of an affianced lover that Lord Southernwood came so constantly to Westbourne Terrace; he stood in the position of a trusted and intimate friend. There was something touching, as Leo could not but often acknowledge to herself, about the kindness of his forbearance. He attempted to constrain her in no way; he never even hinted at his suit; suppressed all mention of his love. Yet there was a lover's homage in his manner, an infinite respect, a hushed tenderness, that must have appealed to the heart of any woman. And there was necessarily growing, day by day, in Leo's mind, a stronger and stronger conviction that she was parted from Arnold for ever—that the engagement was ended, past all revival or renewal.

Lord Southernwood found her one day in the drawing-room, returned from a drive in one of the parks.

She was trembling nervously, oppressed, terribly cast down. He had never seen her so before. His simple words of kindness and sympathy, so hearty, so truthful, touched her deeply, and, in a moment, the tears were dimming her soft limpid eyes. Something he read in her glance which sent the blood rushing to his heart tumultuously; and he ventured to allude to a subject which it had been agreed between them was not to be again mentioned.

"I am so sad," she murmured faintly; "I am utterly wretched. Be very kind to me; promise me you will."

He drew her towards him. How radiantly happy he looked! he pressed her to his heart; and for a moment his lips touched hers.

Then he was furiously ringing the bell calling for assistance. Leo had swooned in his arms.

Janet had continued her walk within the park with her pupils. Returning home she remembered that she had been entrusted by Mrs. Lomax with some trifling commissions, for the execution of which it was necessary for her to quit the park to enter a street of shops in the neighbourhood. On her way she had to pass a large corner public-house, much frequented as a resting and refreshment place for omnibuses and cabs. She noticed that a small crowd was then collected, and, to avoid being hustled and inconvenienced, she was about to leave the pavement for the road. Just then, there was a sudden surging in the group and an opening, through which she was enabled to perceive the cause of the excitement. It was not a very unusual object in a London street. A man was clinging to a lamp-post, shouting, singing, screaming, stamping with tipsy vehemence. His clothes were torn, stained with mud; his hat was in the gutter, a shapeless mass. He was a puffed-looking stout man, with a red face, straggling light hair upon his forehead, and a shaggy yellow moustache. She recognised him in a moment, hardly able to suppress a cry of terror. It was Captain Gill! It was her father.

A shabby, tall, burly man came stumbling down the steps of the public-house, seized the captain by the collar of his coat, and was soon struggling to thrust him into a cab ; the captain resisting with a drunken obstinacy. The tall man was of course Pratt " the doctor." Ultimately he succeeded in his endeavours, and the cab drove off with its unsavoury occupants amidst the jeers and laughter of the crowd.

Janet proceeded on her way.

" I have been tricked. I have been robbed ! " she said. " My father lives still, then. Heaven forgive me, but it is almost in my heart to wish that he were dead ! "

And some time afterwards she went on,—

" If Arnold knew. If he had seen the sight I saw to-day. What would he think ? How could he love me ? No—it would be impossible. He would shun me ; he would hate me. Yes ; I must leave this place—must leave Arnold as soon as possible."

She hid her face in her hands.

CHAPTER XXIX.

HE Venerable Archdeacon of Binchester wrote sometimes to his son, Hugh Wood, barrister-at-law, occupying very dingy apartments up three pair of stairs, in a close old court in the Temple. The longest and most important portions of these letters were generally to be found in the postcript. I am enabled to furnish an extract from the correspondence of the archdeacon. The following lines, at the period of their receipt by Hugh Wood, occasioned him considerable embarrassment :—

"I am happy to say that I am settling down here very comfortably. The people in the neighbourhood seem to be very fairly impressed with the respect due to a dignitary of the Church. Still, strange as it may seem to you, my dear boy, I find myself at the present moment considerably pressed for money. I would very much rather avoid, if possible, any further dealings with Moss. I have too unpleasant recollections in connection with the last affair. Can you assist me? Even twenty or thirty pounds would do. . Shall you be surprised to hear that I have been seriously contemplating a change in my condition? But, indeed, I weary of my life of solitude. I long for a partner in my declining years. Why should this not be so? The engagement between young Page (who seems to be absolutely ruined—I suspected what was coming when I last saw the misguided young man in town,) and old Carr's daughter, if it ever really existed—and I have always entertained doubts on that subject—seems to be now wholly at an end. As *you* are so disinclined to move in the matter, what is to prevent *me?* There is a trifling disparity as to age, but I don't attach any importance to that; it is, indeed, as nothing, weighed against the importance the lady would gain, the high position she would secure as the wife of an archdeacon. In this country a woman's heart turns naturally to the clergy. I confess I see no reason why the affair should not be brought about. However, I cannot just now quit this place. My arrival is too recent. I have made a very favourable impression, and I must not risk losing it. The Carrs, I find, are now in town. Will you take an opportunity of sounding the young lady, as delicately as may be, upon the subject?"

Speedily, however, Hugh was able to convince the archdeacon that his plan could not possibly be carried out. He forwarded to Binchester a copy of the *Morning Post*, in an important column of which journal was to be found an official announcement of the approaching marriage between the most honourable the Marquis of Southernwood and the daughter of Mr. Carr, of Croxall. Of course the editor of the *Woodlandshire Mercury* had something to say upon the subject. "Did we not some time ago put our readers in possession of this important information?" And he was enabled to conclude his paragraph with a glowing eulogium of the superior intelligence of the provincial as compared with the metropolitan press.

Yes, it was now true beyond all question. Leo was engaged to be married to Lord Southernwood.

"God grant you may be happy in your choice, my little Leo," said old Mr. Carr, as he kissed her, nestling tearfully in his arms.

For the present Mrs. Carr was not informed of what had happened. She was so weakly that it was feared serious consequences might attend the communication to her of any news of importance. This, at least, was Dr. Hawkshaw's opinion.

Hardly a day passed now but Lord Southernwood was in Westbourne Terrace. He was in splendid spirits; how he laughed and prattled! how proud he was of his affianced wife! how he studied to please her, to anticipate her lightest thoughts and wishes! how he loaded her with presents! how he astonished Chalker by his vivacity, his volubility, his restlessness! And the fellows at the Junior Adonis learnt of it now, and discussed it freely after their manner, agreeing finally to give their approval, and to vote that Cupid had got into a good thing, and was doosid lucky and that, in having secured that doosid pretty little Miss Carr, whom they all to a man admired. What presents he brought to please her ! It seemed as though he was for ever fitting superb necklaces round that soft throat. (What a time he was fastening the clasp ! but then it's a really difficult thing to arrange a necklace upon a warm human neck, when love and admiration are distracting one's attention, and interfering with the business.) And now he was pressing, sliding the very prettiest of rings upon the tiny fingers ; now circling the delicate wrists with bracelets, and rewarding himself with kisses ; or in watching his own image in miniature mirrored in her eyes ;—a very dainty amusement. He was supremely happy.

And Leo ? She was very busy. Was there not the wedding *trousseau* to prepare and supervise ? Was it possible for her not to take an interest in the vital questions arising at every turn in connection with clothes and millinery ? Was it possible for her, a woman—and a pretty woman, too—to rest unmoved while her marriage finery was strewing the house ; in the presence of those enormous parcels from the mercers', from the mantua-makers ; while her path was crowded with lace of all kinds, in all sorts of arrangements, with silks, velvets, satins, flowers, feathers ; and all conditions of trades, and workpeople pausing for her instructions, imploring to be noticed and commanded ? Could she avoid being affected in some measure by a light-heartedness so contagious as Lord Dolly's, so persevering, so ceaseless ? Could she, notwithstanding all that had passed, remain wholly calm and apathetic in the presence of a love so whole, so unremittingly fervent ? No. There were times when her gaiety rivalled even his ; when she met him with the gleefulness of a madcap school-girl ; when her silvery laugh added music to his mirth ; when she persuaded herself—wondering a little the while, it may be—that she could pay him back wholly and honestly love for love ; and her interest in her bonnets, in her gloves, her thoughtful researches into quite the inner mysteries of the toilet and the wardrobe, satisfied even the most sanguine and jealous expectations of her lady's-maid : and when she would take a pride—a natural woman's pride—in dressing her best ; in looking her best ; in wearing her choicest smiles ; decking herself with her brightest glances ; and all to please him—

for his sake. Yet there were times, too, when these things were not possible to her—when she would sit speechless midst her finery; cold at heart, with shattered nerves, shuddering, sick with dread, and hopelessness and sorrow; breaking into wild sobs and passionate tears, and not daring to ask herself the reason of these; praying for the end; longing for the marriage-day to come and go, that such a wrench might be given to the method of her life that change or looking back would be then futile, impossible, and her fate would be accomplished for good or evil, beyond all remedy.

Something like this had been her mood the day when she felt herself touched upon the shoulder, and a gentle voice said—

" Leo ! "

She looked up. Janet Gill stood before her.

To welcome the visitor most cordially, to receive calmly, smilingly, her congratulations on the approaching marriage, to draw her attention to certain of the dresses, and the decorations that were to grace the occasion, were but natural duties to perform immediately at the outset of Janet's visit, to the hindrance of any other thoughts arising in Leo's breast, in reference to the interview she had witnessed in the park between Janet and Arnold, and any suspicions and jealousies thereby occasioned. Leo's affection for Janet was great ; they had been closely united in the love they had both felt so strongly for poor little Baby Gill, lying dead in Oakmere churchyard. To listen with interest to Janet's story of her dismissal by Mrs. Lomax was a task readily executed, without preoccupation or *arrière pensée.* None the less was she prepared to enter into her friend's future arrangements, or to proffer all the assistance that could be rendered.

" I never liked Mrs. Lomax. Of course you must not remain there a day longer than can be avoided, Janet. O course something that will suit you a great deal better must be immediately obtained for you. I will speak to Lady Lambeth on the subject. I know she will interest herself about it at once. She is helping me with my *trousseau.* She was a pupil of Miss Bigg's. I know her intimately. She was then the Hon. Miss Pincott. She is Lord Lambeth's third wife. Her own children, perhaps, are too young yet to need a governess, but she is sure to know of some family wanting one. I am really glad that you are leaving that dreadful Mrs. Lomax. I am sure you have not been happy there ; but how came she so foolish as to lose you ? "

Janet explained Mrs. Lomax's charge concerning Robin Hooper, but she suppressed all mention of another subject upon which Mrs. Lomax had founded a complaint. Was Leo stirred by an intuition? The blood rushed to her face, as, fixing her eyes upon her friend, she said in a low voice,

" And Arnold ? " For a moment Janet was confused— could make no reply.

" He is well ? Tell me, Janet."

" Yes, he is well ; but he has suffered very much."

" Poor Arnold ! " Leo said softly, with a sigh. Then, presently, " What is he going to do ? "

" He talks, so I have heard, of quitting England never to return."

" Never ! " and Leo started, and a look of suffering crossed her face. It was Janet's turn now to contemplate her. Involuntarily, perhaps, her eyes turned from Leo and rested upon some of the marriage finery which strewed the room. Perhaps Leo noticed this.

" Don't despise me, Janet," she said, in a voice that sounded so full of suffering that Janet sprang to her side at once.

" What do you mean, Leo ? " she asked ; and then to herself she added, " It is, then, as I expected ; she loves him still ! If there were no other reason, would not this be enough to keep me apart from him for ever? She who has been so good to me ; who so loved poor Baby—dear Leo ! "

Leo was seized with a sudden trembling. She clutched Janet's arm.

" Tell me," she whispered hoarsely; " you love Arnold." She repeated the question, seeing Janet pause.

" No," said Janet with an effort. " No, indeed not."

" You are sure ? "

" Arnold can never be anything to me—never."

" Never—but if he sought your love ? "

" No, he will not; he must not do so. It cannot be ; my

love can never be his !" Then she murmured beneath her
breath, "God help me : what am I saying ?"

Leo took her friend in her arms and kissed her : then
burst into tears and hid her face upon Janet's shoulder.
"Oh, Janet, pity me ; I am very wretched."

They were disturbed almost immediately, and Leo had to
conceal as best she could all trace of recent emotion.
But it seemed as though she were accustomed to these
sudden calls being made upon her, as she was used to
interruptions—to being incessantly required to attend to *this*
question, to decide upon *that*. The position in which she
was placed brought upon her so many occupations. A
servant announced that there were two ladies waiting to see
her in the drawing-room. Leo repaired thither.

A tall limp woman in crumpled black threw back a rusty
veil, and disclosed to Leo's surprise the not pleasant features
of her whilom preceptress, Miss Dorothea Bigg, of Chapone
House, Kew Green. She was accompanied by that "inestimable woman" Booth (the "Sarnem" of the seminary,
according to the Hon. Miss Pincott), who recognised the
presence of the ex-pupil by a sharp sniff and a grim courtesy,
the defiance of the former, as it were, effectually contradicting any submissiveness that might be attributed to the
latter.

"My dear Leonora," said Miss Bigg, with a renewal of
her old frightful attempts at a smile, and rising from the
comfortable chair she had taken possession of on her entry ;
"how pleased I am to see you ; always delighted to meet
again any of my old pupils, but especially you, dear, such a
favourite as you always were, too. I've come to offer my
'umble congratulations. You remember Booth—your old
friend Booth"—(Booth was here subjected to a convulsive
twitching about the region of her nose—her method perhaps
of negativing such a statement), "Booth couldn't rest until
she too had offered her 'umble congratulations. We read of
it in the papers. So gratified. I'm sure, it must be a great
source of happiness to your dear ma, to your excellent pa.
And so, dear, from being simply Miss Carr you'll become
the Marchioness of Southernwood ! Dear me. What a
change ! And how very nice, and gratifying, and pleasant
to all concerned. He's quite a young man the Marquis, I

28

believe. I should *so* like to see him. I *have* heard that he's been a little wild, the Marquis; but of course that will be all over now. But they *do* say that he was rather dissolute at one time. Young noblemen will be, you know dear, a little wild. I suppose the other affair is quite off—Mr. Page, I think the name of the gentleman was; some relation of the gentleman whose children were at one time under my care, the Miss Lomaxes; and very sweet children they were, I'm sure. I remember you once called with your dear ma and took them a drive to Richmond. Mrs. Lomax was Mr. Page's sister, I believe. But of course it was quite right to put an end to that arrangement. Why, dear me, I saw the gentleman's name appearing quite often in the news-paper. He'd been very unfortunate, I suppose, to say the least of it. . Of course you could have nothing to say to him after that. Why, his name was in the police courts, I think; quite amongst the lowest criminals, wasn't it, Booth?" (Booth vehemently affirmative.) "Why, he was brought up charged with bankruptcy at the Old Bailey, or some such place. Wasn't he, Booth?" (Booth chuckles triumphant in the distinctness of her memory of the case.) "But of course you see nothing of him now. I'm sure I hope I haven't distressed you in any way by mentioning the unhappy affair, dear. But you know how deeply interested I am in anything that concerns the welfare of my pupils. I'm sure if they were my own children, I couldn't feel more for them, and I couldn't rest, dear, until I had called to offer my 'umble congratulations upon your approaching marriage with the Marquis of Southernwood. How pleased my poor sister Adelaide would have been. I don't re-member any pupil of Chapone House making a more dis-tinguished match, although very many of the pupils have been most intimately connected with the aristocracy. My 'umble but sincere congratulations, dear."

"I am much obliged to you, Miss Bigg," said Leo, for-mally.

"And I hope, dear, you will think no more of any little estrangement there may have been between us," said Miss Bigg. "I know that there was a difference of opinion con-cerning one of the inmates of Chapone House. I refer to little Miss Gill. Now, alas! no more. But such is life!"

(Booth grunted acquiescence that such *was* life—raised her rusty kid-gloved hand for a moment to let it fall again upon her knee—an action presumed by many people to express eloquently sympathy, and pity, and emotion generally.) " You will try and forget my share in that melancholy business ? "

" Certainly, Miss Bigg."

The schoolmistress moved about uneasily in her chair. There was in Leo's manner a calmness and a coolness that did not much encourage the visitor to proceed. Booth sniffed significantly, and looked at the ceiling. Miss Bigg fidgeted with her gloves, dabbed her eyes with her cambric handkerchief, in case there should be any tears thereabouts —there were none—and then continued :

" You are not aware, perhaps, how much I have suffered on account of Miss Gill. Her illness did dreadful mischief to the school. There was quite a panic among the parents ; they hurried away their children, most inconsiderately, I must say. I did all I could, but at length I was obliged to give way. Now, I have parted with my interest in Chapone House. The brass plate is off the door. The celebrated seminary for young ladies exists no more. I grieve to say the establishment has been converted into a preparatory school for little boys.

" Indeed." It was certainly provoking that this important news should affect Leo in so small a way.

" And I'm ruined. I hardly know what to do. At one time I thought even of entering the service of a widower as housekeeper. Perhaps, dear, with your numerous ac- quaintance, you may know of some such situation likely to suit me."

" No, Miss Bigg. I do not."

Miss Bigg again dabbed her dry eyes with her hand- kerchief. She then produced from her shawl a square parcel.

" I am endeavouring to raise a small sum by means of the sale of an edition of my late father's sublime work, *The Course of Life*, a soul poem, in twenty cantos. I have here a list of subscribers, containing the names of the most dis- tinguished among the nobility, clergy, and gentry." (She placed before Leo a sheet of foolscap paper closely written

28—2

upon.) "I hope, dear, you will allow me to put your name down as a subscriber for a few copies. Perhaps you could also persuade the Marquis to subscribe. His name would ornament the list, and would be the means of attracting others. The book, I need hardly say, is an invaluable one. It is well know to every pupil at Chapone House. At page 342, you will find some very precious lines addressed to a young woman entering the married state—they are peculiarly apposite, dear, to your present position. Indeed, consolation and advice may be found in my father's poem adapted to almost every station in life."

"It's a Gospel work," said Booth. "No woman should be without it. Many a soul has been saved from perdition by it." And she looked as though she rather grudged Leo the excellent chance that was being offered to her.

"How many copies shall I put down to you, dear?" asked Miss Dorothea, in her most inviting tone.

But here they were interrupted. Two gentlemen briskly entered the room : Lord Southernwood and Dr. Hawkshaw.

"What's all this about?" asked the doctor, looking round.

"Buying books?" said his lordship, cheerfully. "What are they about? Shall I get you a dozen or so of them, Leo? *The Course of Life?* Eh? A soul poem? What's that mean? My eyes! What a lot of it. It don't look very amusing reading."

"At page 400 there's some excellent advice to scoffers," said Booth, bitterly.

"Oh, indeed!" said Lord Southernwood ; and to himself he added, "Severe old bird!"

The doctor had taken up the volume, and also the list of subscribers, in spite of an effort Miss Bigg had made to secure the latter.

"It teems with the most exquisite poetry," said Miss Bigg, chafing her hands, rather with the air of a tradesman recommending his wares.

"It looks as though it did," the doctor remarks, dryly. "But somehow I don't think I care much for poetry. It seems to me that poetry is too often prose with its stomach out of order, and wanting physic very badly indeed."

"It's my late father, the poet Bigg's sublime work—full of

piety, the salvation of many a sinner," Miss Bigg said, indignantly.

Booth added, " And so stirring."

" It may be. But I don't think I'm to be stirred—*by a spoon*," and the doctor smiled grimly. " I hope I'm too solid."

He turned to the list of subscribers, and read from it.

" The Lord Chancellor, 10 copies ; the Archbishop of Mesopotamia, 12 copies ; Lord Bethesda, 20 copies ; the Bishop of Binchester, Lord Lambeth, Dr. Grawler, D.D., the Rev. T. Pott, the Bishop of Otaheite, Mr. Trimmer, M.P. Hulloa ! Dr. Hawkshaw, M.D., 6 copies."

Miss Bigg shrank back as the doctor turned his sharp eyes upon her.

" It's a mistake, I think," she stammered. " Or else, you were put down, in anticipation of your approval."

" Which you'll never get," said the doctor sternly, " I tell you so at once. I know something of the poet Bigg, and I wouldn't have any of his rubbish in my house, not if you paid me for it. It's my impression that he was an immense humbug ! "

" Oh, why don't the ground open and swaller him up ? " groaned Booth.

" Take my advice. Don't go on with this sort of thing. There's a class of people well known to the police, and recognisable by others, under the title of begging-letter impostors. Try not to be mixed up with them : though many of your proceedings bear a strange resemblance to theirs. For this list, I believe it contains very many mistakes similar to the one you have made in connection with my name. So we'll dispose of it at once." (He tore it up.) " And now, I think there's no one here who wants a copy of this precious book, and therefore you'd better go."

Booth uttered an explosive " Oh, indeed ! "

Miss Dorothea Bigg glanced round her, but she saw that her chance of obtaining subscribers to the sublime work was not just then very promising. Leo had withdrawn with his lordship to a window, where they appeared to be holding quite a confidential discussion. The schoolmistress gathered up her books, and with a severe courtesy quitted the room.

Dr. Hawkshaw was summoned up stairs to attend his patient, Mrs. Carr. She had been dozing a little; and there had been some doubt at first about disturbing her. She was so reduced in strength that rest was very valuable to her. The physicians had agreed that if she were asleep when they paid their visit they would return to see her at a later period of the day. Dr. Hawkshaw found Sir Cupper Leech engaged in serious conversation with old Mr. Carr. They were leaning against the mantelpiece in the small dressing-room adjoining the chamber occupied by the invalid.

Presently the nurse who had been attending in the sick-room was despatched to inform Leo that Dr. Hawkshaw desired to speak to her. She quitted Lord Southernwood hurriedly, and found the doctor waiting for her on the landing of the staircase. She was in some alarm, seeing him look very grave and pale.

"Don't be frightened, my dear," he said, kindly and gently, "but your father desired me to speak to you. He is rather unnerved this morning; he did not feel equal to it himself. It is no longer to be disguised that our poor patient is in great danger. Pray be calm, my dear—be brave. It will afflict papa so terribly if you give way. Take courage. Yes, my dear, I fear the worst. She has awoke in a state of extreme exhaustion, and we have agreed that unless a very extraordinary change takes place there is no hope of her rallying. Don't cry, my dear. Be as brave as you can, for her sake, and for poor papa's, upon whom the blow will fall very, very heavily. When you have a little recovered yourself we will go into the bed-room. She is quite herself now—quite calm and sensible; though, poor soul, so exhausted, that she can hardly speak. I have been expecting this, though it has come upon us much more suddenly and rapidly than I had looked for. She is sinking fast. I fear in a few hours all will be over. There, there's a brave girl. Dry your eyes; and now we'll go into the bed-room.

Leo suffered herself to be led into the bed-room. She had but a dreamy consciousness of what she saw there, her sight was so dimmed, her brain seemed so bewildered. She had afterwards a vague memory of the stately florid figure of Sir Cupper Leech at the side of the bed ; close to him her father, pale, shaking, leaning upon the bed for support ; and the face of the invalid, wasted, waxen-looking, death-stricken. She stooped down to kiss the faded lips, the sunken cheeks, the shadowy hands stretched out helplessly on the counterpane. She had never once dreamt of her mother's illness terminating fatally ; yet now the conviction came to her that day by day the evidence, as it were, had been accumulating, and the proven fact was before her : she stood in the solemn presence of Death ! The awful change was going on under her eyes, and the good, kindly, loving lady was to be taken from her for ever. She could not speak ; her tongue seemed paralysed, petrified ; the tears gathered in her eyes, till the whole scene seemed to swim before her ; she could only bend lower to press again and again soft kisses upon her mother's face.

Dr. Hawkshaw kept his hand upon the dying woman's wrist. Every now and then the physicians exchanged sadly significant glances.

" She is trying to say something," said Dr. Hawkshaw. " Listen, my dear, stoop down."

" God bless you, Leo, dear. God give you happiness, my darling. Always love your husband—love Arnold. Be a good wife to him. I've always loved Arnold ; he always reminded me so of my poor Jordan. Don't cry, my dear. You'll take care of our little Leo, Carr ! God bless you, dear. You've been a good husband to me."

More she said, or tried to say ; but nothing further was audible or intelligible. Only a moan now and then announced that the sufferer still lived.

Soon Doctor Hawkshaw was to be seen stepping into his brougham, rather worn and depressed, looking as befitted a man who had been fighting with death, and been worsted in the conflict. In the absence of any order being given, the coachman always understood that he was to drive home to the doctor's residence in Mount Street. For some minutes the doctor was so preoccupied that he failed to notice which way he was being taken.

" Poor woman ! The end came sooner than was expected. But when a constitution once gives way, at her time of life —well—well—it's all over now. Everything possible was

done for her. There's more in Sir Cupper than I was at
one time inclined to think. Let me see. Where do I call
now?" (He consulted a note-book.) "Ah! yes; I can
take it on my road to St. Lazarus. Hobson!" to the coachman) "Bow Street—the police-office. It's time I said something to my friends there about this man Pratt. He's no
business to be at large, and he can be up to no good. In
fact, I happen to know that he's up to a great deal of
harm."

The death of Mrs. Carr was duly chronicled in the first
column of *The Times.*

The marriage of Lord Southernwood and Miss Carr was,
of course, postponed for many months. Mr. Carr and his
daughter, after the funeral, left town again, and lived in
strict retirement at Croxall Chase.

"Awful sell for Cupid, the affair being put off," the fellows
at the Junior Adonis agreed.

It was dull enough now in the neighbourhood of Oakmere; the hand of affliction pressing heavily upon the
inmates of Croxall; the Court shut up, with rather a doubt
prevailing as to whom it belonged. The fine old house—
square, with two wings projecting beyond the centre, red
brick, with stone coignes and window-cases, and a sculptured
open parapet, concealing the roof, from which rise the
octagon columnal chimneys—the old house had been
stripped of its furniture. There was a drift of leaves disfiguring the roads and paths; the lawns were neglected;
moss and weeds spotted and blotched the gravel walks.
There were no lights in the windows now; the shutters
were closed. Some of the panes of glass had been
broken—but who was to pay for mending them? The
pleasant clatter of horses' hoofs was no longer to be heard
in the stable-yard, round the paving-stones of which rank
fringes of grass were growing. No sound of human voice,
no, nor bark of dog, greeted the ear now; all was deserted,
dreary, wretched. In a short time the neighbourhood would
be giving the place the credit of being haunted—of being
possessed by ghostly visitants from another world. It was
already said to be in Chancery : which was a step in the
supernatural direction. Young Mr. Page, it was freely,

though sorrowfully, stated, was a ruined man. And the Lomaxes had given the place up; but then nobody regretted that fact much.

A very worthy gentleman had succeeded the Rev. Purton Wood. That was the only grain of comfort to be discovered around the general dismalness of the state of things in Oakmere.

And Arnold, where was he?

He had obtained his certificate from the Commissioner in Bankruptcy. He had determined to quit England for ever, and had written a letter to Janet Gill, asking her to go with him as his wife.

CHAPTER XXX.

A CATASTROPHE.

MONSIEUR ANATOLE, with a stealthy glance over his shoulder—it had become, with him, an habitual action to look round him suspiciously, as though he expected to find himself watched or followed—and as noiselessly as he could—there was always a cat-like quiet about his movements—inserted a shiny latch-key in the door of the house over the water, admitted himself, and passed up stairs to the front room of the first floor.

A half scream of surprise greeted him, a noisy start, a volley of oaths.

"How you frighten a fellow," cried Captain Gill, angrily; "creeping in like a ghost or a thief. I wish you wouldn't, Mounseer. You don't know how it knocks me over. Sets my heart beating, quick and noisy, like an undertaker's hammer!"

"Indeed! like an undertaker's hammer?" repeated Monsieur Anatole, as with a leering grin he surveyed his friend.

The captain was wiping his forehead with a ragged silk

handkerchief, his hands trembling violently; his eyes glistening, bloodshot, and strangely restless. He was only half dressed; had a beard three or four days old on his chin; his collar and shirtbuttons were unfastened, and his thick bull-neck and huge chest were bare and exposed. Perhaps he had torn them open to breathe the better; he was panting noisily, like an asthmatic person. Presently he began shivering; rubbing his hands together, but with a fidgety, uncertain motion, as though his muscular action was not thoroughly under control, gazing round him as though with an inane terror of something or somebody.

"I wish to Heaven you'd take me out of this place," he said at last, in a feeble, scared tone of voice; "you don't know how it gives me the horrors. It oughtn't to be allowed. Millions of creeping things, all about, on the floors, on the walls. Yes "—he looked up and shuddered—" and on the ceiling too. By George, they come dropping down on a fellow like rain." He got up and changed his seat. " Insects are bad enough; but when you come to reptiles, when you get on at last to devils, who can stand it? How they writhe, and wriggle, and glide, and slide about. Whichever way you turn you find one of them, and so d—d near to you." He started up with a wild scream.

" By George! I wouldn't sit where you are sitting, not for any money. You've got into the very worst place in the room. They're so thick on that sofa, you couldn't put a pin down without sticking it into one of them. How they twist about, and wink, and grin, showing their infernal sharp teeth and forked tongues."

"Nonsense! nonsense!" said Monsieur Anatole, taking a pinch of snuff.

"Why don't you take me somewhere else? I can't stand it; I can't, indeed. This isn't a fit lodging for an officer and a gentleman. Where's the doctor? He promised me I shouldn't stay here. Where is he?"

" I don't think we shall be troubled much more with the doctor." And Monsieur Anatole smiled significantly.

" By-the-way,—what was it?" And the captain rubbed his head, and seemed trying to recollect. " I had something to tell you about the doctor; though I can't think what it was. Dear me! what was the doctor's name? I never

could quite make out. He was always rather shy about
his name. Luce, wasn't it? Though sometimes it seemed
to be something else. I met him first of all at a dram-shop
—though I forget where—at some sea-port place, soon after
I came back from India through the continent with Janet.
Ah! I wonder what's become of Janet. You were to have
married her : but the thing never came off, somehow; and
then she bolted. Perhaps she's dead. Who knows? But
the doctor; what was it about the doctor? I played cards
with him, I know, and I lost. I was always so doosid
unlucky at cards, as you well know,—at least, you ought to.
You've had a good lot of my money altogether; all of it, I
might say. Let me see. Ah! I remember. You keep out
of the way of the doctor : that was what I wanted to tell
you. By George! he is in a way about you—quite raving.
I couldn't help laughing. He said he'd wring your ugly old
French head off. That was like him, wasn't it? And I
think he'd do it, too! He's a desperate sort of chap, is the
doctor. He said you'd robbed him, tricked him, blown
upon him; that was what he said."

"He's an imbecile!"

But Monsieur Anatole seemed a little moved by what he
had heard. Perhaps he was of those natures which are
morally courageous and physically timid. Anyhow, it was
not pleasant to learn that the doctor meditated violence ;
especially as it was tolerably well known that, if possible,
he was a man who would, in such a case, act up to his
word.

"I'd advise you to keep out of his way. I think a blow
from that fellow's great fist would pretty well kill a man.
Have you cheated him? There was always something up
between you two fellows. I never could make it out. Some
dodge for raising the wind somehow; by insurance on my
life. I know it was precious little I ever got by it; though
you gave me a good deal of trouble, and cut me off my
grog, and patched me up to go before the doctors.

He laughed noisily.

"You're better," said Monsieur Anatole.

"No, I'm horrid bad; especially at night. I can't sleep
a wink. Who could, I should like to know, with all those
infernal snakes and things crawling about a fellow? I should

like a screw-up of something, but there isn't a drop in the
house ; and I've no money to send out for anything ; and
they've stopped my tick at all the publics about here."

" Try that," and Monsieur Anatole produced a full-sized
black bottle from the tail pocket of his old-fashioned dress-
coat.

The captain snatched at the bottle, uncorked it, and
drank from it, though there were glasses upon the mantelpiece within reach of his arm.

"And strong, too, by George ! "

He was seized with a fit of coughing.

" Yes, it's strong," Monsieur Anatole remarked, and he
walked to the window. He stood there for some time, apparently lost in thought, contemplating abstractedly the passing
incidents in the street. Then he turned for a moment, and
his eyes were fixed on the bottle, wandering afterwards to
the captain, and then from him back again to the bottle.
Presently he turned his back again upon his friend, and he
took a pinch of snuff as he again looked from the window.
A group of children, rather ragged, and not very clean, pale
and thin, yet not unhealthy-looking, with gleaming round
eyes and profuse hair—the peculiar properties of street
infancy—were surrounding a large, battered, headless,
wooden toy-horse, upon which,—amidst much noise and
laughter, and wrangling, and crying, and merriment, with
occasional accidents, bruised foreheads and grazed legs, and
the variety of emotions usual under such circumstances,—
they were alternately enjoying rides. For a little while the
Frenchman watched the game, unable to restrain his interest or his amusement at certain of the serio-comic
features of the proceeding. Then he broke off into a low
muttering.

" It's a smaller stake than I had thought to play for.
But the game grows a little dangerous. Perhaps it would
be as well to rise from the table while I can rise a winner.
I had hoped to make a far grander *coup*—to have come off
with a fortune, and retired from business for ever ; affluent,
happy, with *la chère petite* as my wife. It was a folly taking
that man Pratt into the affair. A good cat's-paw ; but I
trusted him, I yielded to him too much : it is owing to him
that these other companies have refused the insurance ; it

is due to his mismanagement that suspicion has been roused; and—and I have found it necessary to take steps for his removal,"—he smiled grimly — "to give his old friends of the police information concerning him; he will trouble me no more." He consulted his watch. " By this time I think I must be secured. Well! shall I rise from table? Are not the chances a little against me if I remain?" He contemplated his friend for a moment. "No, I can do nothing further with him : it is too late. No office would look at him now—not even the most greedy for business, the most anxious to swell the number of their policies. There is only the Ostrich Insurance then. But the amount will be wholly mine; there is no longer the imbecile Pratt to cry for a division with me. I can prove, if need be, an interest in the life of the deceased. He is my debtor; I possess overdue bills of his. All is *en règle*. The premiums just due, have been paid, thanks to Madame Desprès and to *la chère petite*. It was a trick, but it was necessary to obtain money from her. And it is, after all, but antedating the departure of her excellent father, the brave captain, by a very little. The question remains : Shall I take this money now, or shall I wait? No, I will not wait. The man Pratt may talk, may try to do me a mischief; it is probable—it is even natural."

He turned round to glance once more at the captain, who had remained speechless at the table. Then he resumed his hat and slowly went out.

" Decidedly, I will let things take their course."

The captain watched the departure of Monsieur Anatole with a strange expression of cunning and interest, listening to his footsteps as he passed down stairs, to the noise of the street-door closing, hastening to the window to make sure that he was really walking down the street. Then the captain burst into a shriek of wild laughter, peal after peal, noisy, shrill, insane.

" Mounseer has forgotten the brandy !" he said. And he raised the bottle to his lips.

There was quite a gay smile upon the Frenchman's puckered old face, a jaunty strut in his walk, as, with an approving glance at his small neat feet, and a heedfulness that no speck of mud should mar the lustre of his boots, he left the Lambeth side of the river, crossed one of the bridges, and soon found himself in the Strand.

"It's a lovely afternoon," he said. "I will promenade myself into the park, or I will sit in the sun and watch the sky, and the water, and the birds, and the little English children with their nursemaids."

Further for his amusement, and in case the other resources should fail him, he purchased a cheap evening newspaper, which he folded into a small compass and thrust into his pocket.

It was pleasant and sunny, as the Frenchman slowly sauntered along the brink of the ornamental water in St. James's Park. He was in no hurry, was not pressed for time : he seemed a thorough idler, with very little on his mind. Small matters arrested, even absorbed, his attention. He slowly took out his tortoiseshell-rimmed eye-glasses, polishing them with his handkerchief, and read with deliberation the notice at the park entrance as to the hours of opening and closing the gates ; the enjoinment upon visitors to protect the water-fowl, and the list of persons who had recently been found guilty of sleeping in the park, cutting the seats, injuring the shrubs, and other misdemeanours, with the dates of their convictions and the punishments awarded them by the magistrates. He noted a slight difference in time between the clocks of the Horse Guards and of the tower of the Houses of Parliament ; he studied with manifest admiration the twin towers of the Abbey, their beautiful gothic tracery, now lit up by the flush of the sunset ; he was particular in his selection of a seat ; he was attracted by the extreme tameness of a cluster of particoloured ducks, and watched them feeding from the hands of a family of children in short-flounced full-skirted dresses ; he felt in his pockets, and discovered some crumbs, with which, in his turn, he began to feed the birds, and amuse himself. It was thus he was reminded of his newspaper, which he had almost forgotten. He took it out, resumed his seat, and commenced very leisurely to unfold it and scan its contents.

Certainly he was in no hurry ; although it was now an hour and more since he had quitted his lodgings and his friend, the captain. He was not greatly interested in his newspaper, neither : he often looked up from it as some one passed in front of the seat on which he was sitting, as a boat glided away upon the water, as the water-fowl's unmusical clamours struck upon his ear. He turned lazily from column to column, from page to page : decidedly a very desultory reader.

At length something caught his eye as he was turning over the paper ; something important, as it seemed. He quite started : he uttered a cry of surprise ; he snatched at the paper, tearing it in his eagerness to get at a particular part of it, midway in one of the columns. He had missed it in glancing down that column before. A very short paragraph, headed with the words " This Day ; " and underneath, in capital letters, " The Ostrich Insurance Company."

He turned pale as he read ; he trembled ; he gasped for breath ; his eyes grew dim ; the letters danced before him ; he was obliged to wait for a few moments to try and regain his composure, to obtain command over his shaking hands. No wonder he could not read, with the paper jogging up and down in front of him like that. He removed his hat to wipe his wet forehead, disturbing his wig recklessly in the process. Again he took up the paper, struggling to master its few brief sentences on the subject of the Ostrich Insurance Company.

The paragraph set forth that for the past day or two, although, for obvious reasons, there had been forbearance in giving them publicity, there had been sinister rumours in the City seriously affecting the insurance company, and the character and proceedings of its officials ; that now the worst suspicions had been confirmed. The offices of the company were closed, though they had been surrounded all the morning by an angry crowd of claimants, creditors, and insurers. That the greatest excitement prevailed ; that the company was said to be hopelessly insolvent, while it was believed that an investigation into affairs would disclose a series of the most nefarious and disgraceful proceedings on the part of the directors. It was feared (the newspaper went on to state) that another instance would be disclosed of gross imposture and fraud on the part of a public company. When would the public be warned ? &c. &c. Here was another case, &c. &c. It was but the other day, &c. &c., ending with a neat reference to a certain celebrated Silver Mining Company. The managing director and the secretary were alleged to have absconded, taking with them the books of the company, and all the available assets. Of course, steps would be immediately taken to ensure their pursuit and arrest. Meanwhile, as was to be seen by reference to another column of the paper, a petition had been presented to the Court of Bankruptcy, for the immediate winding-up of the concern. It was believed that the policies of the company were not worth the paper upon which they were written; and that the more the affair was examined, the more it would be found disastrous to the creditors, and shameful to all concerned. The office had been conducted on what was known as the mutual system; so that the insurers were, in fact, partners in the undertaking.

Monsieur Anatole was at length able to master and to understand the news contained in the paper he had purchased. He glanced round him wildly; he crushed the paper into a large creased ball, and crammed it in his pocket; he rose, and set off, walking as rapidly as he could.

"If it should be too late?" He kept on repeating this sentence over and over again. "If it should be too late? If it should be too late?"

He went on mechanically, choosing the shortest way, returning to his lodgings. Now walking quickly, now half running. It did not seem to occur to him—he was too much occupied to think of it—that he might have proceeded much more quickly by taking a cab. "If it should be too late?"

He was panting, trembling with nervous excitement, perhaps, too, from fatigue; as he again produced his latchkey his hand shook so that he made several ineffectual attempts to fit the key in the keyhole. Every minute seemed to him then of an enormous value, and yet there was always something occurring to hinder his progress. He had thought so all the way of his return—troublesome obstacles at every turn. Now he had been unable to cross, owing to a cluster and confusion of vehicles. Now he had been impeded and hustled by an unexpected throng of passengers in the street. Now he had nearly slipped on some orange-peel. Now he was stumbling over the projecting foot of a sleeping beggar. What new agonies he derived at each of these occurrences! he grew angry, feverish, half mad under them; and over and over again he repeated, and when he was silent some one else took up the cry and dinned it in his ear, in both ears, while the echo of it seemed reverberating all round him : "If it should be too late !"

He mounted the stairs with a strange, undefined sense of alarm; he opened the door of the room on the first-floor. He was too frightened at first to enter. All was silent. He took courage, though even yet he was afraid to look round him; he entered the room with some dim consciousness that in another moment his wandering eyes would alight on some frightful object, something terrible. Was he alone in the room ?

No; in another moment he heard a rustling behind him, a frantic cry, a peal of horrid laughter; then a hand upon his shoulder, a grip upon his neck, and he was struggling for his life with a half naked madman—his friend Captain Gill.

He would have been flung down at once, by the force and impetus of the attack, but for the table. It saved him from falling, though its sharp edge came with painful violence against the small of his back, and his head, thrust suddenly down, struck smartly upon the hard, polished surface. Then a jerk, an effort; he raised himself for a moment; the table, pushed by this action, rode away upon its castors, and the two men, rolling down together, fell with a heavy thump. Each had as close a grasp of the other as he could secure, but the Frenchman was underneath; he had been taken at a disadvantage, in point of strength he was terribly overmatched, and for the first moment or two he was nearly paralysed by the paroxysm of alarm under which he was labouring. He began to perceive, however, that he was engaged in a deadly wrestle with a man who was deaf to all cries for mercy, who was mad, whom it was necessary to oppose with all the force he could summon. He gave one scream for help, it was echoed by a mocking yell from the madman, and then with something of the courage and strength of despair he nerved himself for the

29

encounter. So they rolled, and tossed, and struggled upon the floor,—panting, growling, tearing, snarling, struggling: it was more like a fight between two wild animals than between human beings. Monsieur Anatole felt that he was mastered by his terrible foe, yet still he struggled on in hopes that assistance might arrive and the tide of battle be turned in his favour. But his strength was leaving him: he grew more and more faint. If he had ever felt any doubts about his age they must have been effectually cleared away at that moment. He was a poor infirm old man. Another cry for help died away in his parched throat. The madman's hand was twisted in his cravat, draggling it painfully tight; he could feel the sharp knuckles driving into his neck; already his mouth opened, his face was distorted, his eyes were starting from his head in the agonies of strangulation. He felt his head raised repeatedly by the madman's hold upon his neckerchief and then struck violently upon the floor. The pain was acute, he felt half stunned, the room seemed to swim round, and fiery stars to dance before his eyes. He roused himself for a final effort. He had fixed both his hands in his foe's thick crumpled matted hair; his fingers were tightly wreathed in it. He tore at it violently, and then released one hand to dash it with all his force in the captain's face. Pained, blinded, he loosened his grasp of the Frenchman's neck: Monsieur Anatole moved, endeavouring to rise; he felt the hot, noisome breath of the madman beating upon his face. Another moment and he was free; his foe was shaking upon the floor, shrieking with hysterical laughter, holding in his hand the dense, black, curl-clustered wig of the Frenchman.

He was off instantly, staggering to the door, passing a shivering huddle of people on the landing who had been afraid to enter the room, although roused by the noise of the struggle,—half flinging himself down the stairs, hurrying out into the street. Pale, livid, trembling, panting for breath, his clothes torn and twisted, and his head bare, how old he looked now! how more than ever skull-like his face! There was not a hair to be seen upon that yellow, shining crown, terribly red and bruised and battered in places where it had come in contact with the floor and the table. A very old, half-crazed, terror-stricken man, running down the street as fast as he possibly could, with a tail of amazed children crying, screaming, jeering after him. How weak he was! He fell down more than once, to stagger up again more stunned and shaken, and hurry on. At last, feeling his limbs give way under him, he staggered into a cab, but he could not speak. In vain the driver sought to question him as to the direction in which he would be driven; he could give no answer; could only wave one hand in a scared, half-mad way, which seemed to urge nothing so much as immediate movement. The cabman drove off at length, at a rapid pace, in the direction of the Middlesex side of the river.

Monsieur Anatole needed not to have been in such a hurry, in such dire apprehension. In the street he had quitted a crowd now stood round an object in the gutter; a half-naked creature, bleeding, shattered, muddy, lifeless. With a madman's sagacity and cleverness, the captain had discovered the quickest way of reaching his runaway foe. He had heard the Frenchman's footsteps in the street, and had hurled himself against the window, cutting himself frightfully with the broken glass, and falling, with awful force, upon the pavement below.

It was some hours later in the evening. Many guests circled the little marble tables of the *Café de l'Univers.* Madame Desprès was still the gorgeous ornament of the *comptoir.* Louis was occupied as ever with his colossal coffee and milk pots. There were many *habitués* there, and a sprinkling of strangers. The musical clock interrupted now and then the buzz of conversation, accentuated, as it were, by the occasional click of the billiard balls, or the rattle of dominoes. Mr. Lackington made furtive sketches of picturesque *emigrés.* Tom Norris was loud as usual in his advocacy of French art. Timson was still unable to demonstrate that his profession was in the slightest degree remunerative. Phil Gossett still meditated dosing the foreigner freely with blue-pill; and Binns, who had joined the assemblies at the *café,* introduced by Jack Lackington, had made two or three attempts to relate yet once again the story of his adventures on Monte Rosa.

"How often, Lackington, are you going to sketch that

29—2

Frenchman with the bald head and the ragged beard?" asked Tom Norris.

"Hush!" cried Binns. "Here's another bald head!" They looked up.

"Tithonus!" they whispered to each other, in a puzzled sort of way.

A cab had stopped at the door of the *café*. Monsieur Anatole had been driving about a considerable time, as it seemed. At last he had collected his scattered senses, and given a coherent order to the cabman. He poured an uncounted heap of silver into the man's hand, and tottered from the cab into the coffee-room. There was a general movement of amazement at the strange sight he presented. Madame rose from her seat. Louis put down his pots and rushed forward, as though to render assistance.

Certainly there was something strange, weird, alarming about this little old man, with his corpse-like face, his bald bare head, his fixed glazed eyes, his parted lips, his dazed, frightened, insane expression. He shuffled as he walked, dragging his limbs painfully after him, making but slow progress. Louis, serene again in a moment, turned to polish the guest's accustomed table, to dust his usual chair.

Suddenly a man rose from a seat at the side of the room and confronted Monsieur Anatole. The Frenchman stopped; had some difficulty in recognising the person who hindered his advance. A heavy hand was laid upon his shoulder: the coarse, black, nervous hand of a tall, shabby-looking, burly, swarthy man—Pratt, "the doctor."

Monsieur Anatole shivered, ejaculated a strange guttural sound, more like the croak of a reptile, or the hoarse cry of a bird of prey, than a human utterance, staggered, threw up his arms, and fell back heavily. There was an immediate rush towards him.

"Give way," cried the rich deep voice of Mr. Gossett. "I'm a medical man. Stand back, open the door. Give us all the air you can."

He ripped up the buttons of the Frenchman's coat, tore away the ligatures from his neck. There was a froth upon his lips, and a stain of black blood. The medical student felt his pulse, listened at his heart, prepared to open a vein in his arm; sprinkled water in the livid, twisted, wrinkled face. Madame Desprès was on her knees (in a calm, graceful attitude—Tom Norris found time to note and admire it, even at such a moment—but he was always an artist !) rendering all the assistance in her power. Louis had brought cushions, water, cognac ; kept back the crowd ; was ceaseless in his attentions.

"It's no use," said Mr. Gossett, as he wiped his lancet ; " it's all over."

There was a slight struggle in the crowd, the noise of a scuffle, then a peculiar clicking sound. Some persons from the street had joined the group in the *café* round the body of Monsieur Anatole.

"You're our prisoner, Mr. Pratt ; no mistake about it. It's too late to resist." The doctor had been skilfully handcuffed almost before he was aware of it. His attention had been absorbed by the spectacle before him. He was in the custody of three police officers. He permitted himself to be taken from the *café*, and sitting in a cab—it was Monsieur Anatole's cab—he was at once removed to the police station.

"We've been after you some days. Returning home without a ticket : and there are other charges. You've managed well to keep out of our way so long."

"I reserve my defence," he said, with an oath and a coarse laugh. "There would, perhaps, have been a worse charge against me if that Frenchman had lived five minutes longer. The coward ! Why he was killed by the very look of me."

"And you call this a land of liberty ! " cried Tom Norris with an air of contempt. "A man arrested in a public coffee-room ; never saw such a thing in Paris."

"By-the-bye," said Binns, "I think I know that man they took away."

"Tell us about him. Who was he ? "

"Stop," interrupted Jack Lackington. "You didn't meet him on Monte Rosa ? "

"No ; in the City."

"All right. Go on."

"I haven't much to say. It's only this. He was pointed out to me the other day as connected with that Insurance

Company that's just smashed up—the Ostrich. He 'made inquiries' for them, as it's called; a sort of secret agent. If anyone applied to insure or to borrow, that man was set to work to find out what he could concerning the applicant. It's done by many offices."

"He was a kind of private spy—that was his profession?"

Binns admitted that such was his belief.

"And there are spies, then, in this land of liberty?" cried Tom Norris. "What an infamy! There are no spies in Paris."

The Frenchman with the bald head, Mr. Lackington's model, was bending over the body of Monsieur Anatole. The Frenchman was Gaspard.

"Yes; he is quite dead," he said, contemplating the corpse. "Perhaps it is as well; perhaps it has saved trouble to us others. He has permitted too much his private pursuits to interfere with his public duties. He has been warned more than once on that subject, and I had received some instructions concerning him. He commenced to weary the authorities."

"What authorities, Monsieur?" inquired Jack Lackington.

Gaspard contemplated his questioner for a moment, and then, in a theatrical attitude, with a sham devotional air, he pointed upwards.

"He'd paint very well in that *pose*," muttered Mr. Lackington. "I wish he'd give me a sitting."

"Ah!" cried Gaspard, after a moment's pause, feeling in the pockets of the deceased; "where, then, is his snuff-box? his pocket-book?"

The body had been removed, to await an inquest. The last guest had departed. The *Café de l'Univers* was closed for the evening.

Louis approached the *dame du comptoir*. He was very angry; his sharp white teeth could be seen grinding together, his eyes rolled beneath his scowling, depressed, black brows.

"You are an imbecile, Hortense," he said, savagely. "You have permitted yourself to be tricked—fooled." He held up before her Monsieur Anatole's pocket-book.

"Pardon me, my friend," she whined humbly; "I did it always for the best. What is it, then? Was he not then rich, this Anatole? was he not a successful enterpriser—a great financier—rich—a millionnaire? Why do you frown upon me, my Louis, my friend?"

"He was a cheat, a chevalier of industry, a thief, a coward, a beast! I have gathered all from Monsieur Gaspard. He was a *mouchard*, a robber, a brigand; and he was poor, truly a beggar! He was without a *sou*. He has given you worthless papers in exchange for your good gold! For his pocket-book! It is full of trash—of rubbish. Thus I finish it."

And he thrust it into the stove used for heating the coffee.

"Have pity, have mercy, *my husband!*" cried Madame Desprès, in a voice of agony.

"Bah!" And he thrust her from him with brutal violence. She sobbed noisily. But his anger was not mollified by her tears.

"And for all we have lost, for all we have surrendered, we have but this to show! How cruel! It is pretty, but it is not gold!" and Louis took snuff from Monsieur Anatole's silver-gilt box.

CHAPTER XXXI.

THE "KANGAROO," A I,—FOR PORT PHILIP.

OME months have passed. The weather is beginning to grow cold, autumn is gradually yielding to winter. The summer decorations of cut paper, artificial flowers, and willow shavings, are being removed from the grates, and people are coming round again to the opinion that, after all, the best "ornament for your fire-stoves" is comprehended in a heap of blazing coals. Certainly, a very ruddy fire lights up the rather gloomy, shabby old room occupied by Mr. Hugh Wood in the Temple. I think bachelors are generally the first to begin fires; they are very cheap comforts, and they are so conveniently and pleasantly associated with hot tumblers and boiling kettles, warm, cosy conversations, feet on hob or fender, pipe in mouth, celibate joys, which, of course, Benedict abandons when matrimony condemns him to a bright poker and a footman to smother the fire with a downpour of fuel.

And in the glow of the fire you forget the gloom of the place. Otherwise Mr. Wood's chambers are not particularly cheerful or comfortable — a rambling, ramshackled, low-ceilinged set, with many odd-shaped rooms, and great black cupboards, and uneven floors and creaking boards; much dust, very little clean paint or whitewash, and abundant cobwebs; situate in a grimy court, ill paved and ill lighted. But Mr. Wood was not a Temple dandy—(there are such things). The chambers were cheap; in fact, he had for his money even more room than he wanted. It was for that reason, perhaps, he sub-let part of his premises. When Mrs. Lomax gave up her town residence, and proceeded to join her husband on the continent, her brother, Mr. Arnold Page, was very glad to become the tenant of his friend, Hugh Wood. The rooms were now occupied by these gentlemen jointly, and their names are duly inscribed over the door.

The reader will remember that Arnold Page had been called to the bar prior to the date of his first appearance in this chronicle. He had been endeavouring to avail himself of such of his professional emoluments as were to be obtained ; he always spoke in grateful terms of the kindness and assistance he received at this period of his career at the hands of Hugh Wood. But it is necessary to state that his success had not been very considerable.

Clearly the man who has attained maturity without ever having earned a guinea has no light task before him when necessity compels him to begin to toil for his bread. Perhaps Arnold had very much more than average ability ; but he had never had occasion to employ it for his own advantage. Speed and mettle are of no great avail to a horse that is never to run a race ; never to be taken from grazing on pleasant pastures for nobler work. He had talent, undoubtedly ; he had the capacity for success as a toiler— but he had never toiled ; he was born to good luck, as everyone had at one time declared—born with a silver spoon in his mouth. Page, of Oakmere, with an income of some thousands, of a county family, the son of General Page of Waterloo fame—this was all over now. And he had to follow a profession he had taken up in the first instance without seriousness, quite capriciously. At all times there seems to be a wide chasm between the cleverness of the amateur and the skilled labour of the regular workman ; perhaps because the latter has been investing his life in the business, while the former has been merely risking his leisure. It is very difficult to raise money on dillettanteism : and the rate of discount is alarming. Commerce will have its bond, insists on full legal measure. Drawing-room triumphs pale and dwindle exposed to the more searching criticism of a wider and colder arena. Arnold had great taste, and judgment, and accomplishments, considered as one who comes into the market as a buyer ; but when he sought to set up his stall as a seller, the case seemed different, somehow. He could draw and paint ; his ability for art was even remarkable ; but he had never served the necessary apprenticeship, he had not undergone that novitiate of study and toil which alone could give real worth to his productions, and these were with all their cleverness incomplete ; promising in one who had the power to advance beyond the point where promise ceases and actual performance begins : but this he had not. He was skilled in music ; he had written pleasant trifles in prose and verse ; he had even been printed, and for a few things paid. But to live by such means ! to gain bread by all this unfocussed ability. It was a very hard task.

He had secured a stray brief or two ; his old solicitors had kindly put some not important draughting business in his way ; he had earned money by noting cases in court for certain law reports. Hugh Wood had been of use to him by obtaining introductions of this kind, and had procured the insertion of various papers of Arnold's in a magazine upon which Mr. Wood was himself employed. It is not to be supposed that these evidenced any startling ability. They were, perhaps, simply average articles. Almost every well-educated gentleman with good sense and good taste can, if need be, produce a certain sort of literary work of respectable worth. But Hugh Wood was loud and hearty in his praise and encouragement.

"You'll succeed, old fellow ! make no doubt of it. Of course the fight at first is rather hard. I know what that is. I speak from experience. I've had struggle enough for money in my time : no man has been more pinched, I should think."

"I never heard of your difficulties before, Hugh," Arnold said.

"College debts, you know. That sort of thing."

"Nonsense ! You were not in an extravagant set."

"Well, anyhow," Hugh continued, evasively, "the difficulties existed ; but I've got over them now—that is, nearly," he added in a low voice.

He had received that morning a rather urgent letter from the Venerable Archdeacon : but it had come after a considerable interval of silence.

Arnold was hardly convinced. His progress was necessarily slow ; he began to think that his antecedents interfered with his prospects ; he reverted often to his old plan of quitting England. At last, rather suddenly, he announced that he had taken a passage in a ship bound for Port Philip, and the day for weighing anchor was now very near at hand.

An advertisement in *The Times* announced that the ship would very shortly depart. " For Port Philip direct, the magnificent, new, river-built, clipper-ship *Kangaroo*, 1,000 tons, A 1 at Lloyd's, loading in the East India Docks, J. Stunsell, commander. This splendid vessel is fitted with all the latest improvements, and presents the best opportunity for the shipment of fine and season goods ; will receive goods until the 25th, unless previously filled. Has a spacious and elegant saloon ; her cabins are lofty and airy, and she will carry an experienced surgeon. For terms of freight and passage, apply to Messrs. Black, Ball and Co., Billiter Square, E.C."

Mr. Page had secured a cabin in the *Kangaroo*, and had made many visits to Blackwall concerning it, and had been very busy with his outfit, and made great purchases of literature to be read on the voyage, and was altogether much occupied with his plans. He was subject to great bursts of elation, and high spirits, and hopefulness, concerning his future career, with occasional relapses into deep dejection and fits of regret at quitting England and the friends remaining to him out of the wreck of his property.

Hugh Wood's chambers were filled with half-packed boxes, bags, clothes, all the paraphernalia of a long voyage, and the luggage a man takes with him when he purposes to quit his native land, never to return.

" A few more hours," said Arnold, " and then good-bye to England ! " He had been assuming of late the regular emigrant tone, charging his country with the misfortunes· which were with more reason attributable to himself, born of his own conduct.

" Have you heard anything of *them ?* " Hugh asked. There had been, it seemed, a sort of tacit agreement between them that the Carrs should be always referred to as *them*.

" No."

" Do they know of your departure ? "

" They may, but not from me. Does it matter now ? I wrote to *her* upon the death of the old lady—I had no right to, perhaps—a few lines, merely expressive of sympathy and condolence, poor child."

" You received no answer ? "

"Yes; she thanked me simply, kindly. And so that was over."

And he resumed his occupation. He was turning over the contents of a large mahogany desk, committing various letters and papers to the flames; odd and useless documents, bills, and notes relating to long past small events (smaller than ever they seemed to him in his present mood), preserved at the first rather by accident than design. Hugh was sitting at the same table, in front of the fire, smoking, turning over the leaves of a book, now and then glancing at the proceedings of his companion.

By-and-by Arnold came to a letter. He paused as in doubt whether to burn or to keep it. He read it through.

"She was right," he muttered; "she knew my heart better than I did. And yet I thought I loved her wholly, truly. I was not worthy of her. She deserved something better than the poor after-crop of love I proffered her. I don't think happiness could have come of our union. She plainly charges me with misconstruing my own feelings. She was right; and yet I thought she loved me, too. Was it therefore she discovered the false ring about my offer? detected the unsoundness of my heart? God grant that she may be happy. She is a prize well worthy of any man's efforts. Poor Janet! God bless her!" And after a few moments' further musing, he thrust the letter into the fire and watched it consume. Hugh looked from his book and watched it also.

A further tossing of worthless papers into the fire, and then he paused again in his labours. He had arrived at a carefully folded-up packet of letters. He poised them in his hand, but he hesitated; he could not bring himself to destroy them.

"Dear little letters! No, I can't burn these. Why should I? Why should I not keep them for ever? the sole relics of a love that is lost. Besides " (and he smiled sadly), "they'll take up very little room in my luggage: although they take up so much room in my heart." He contemplated them with a sorrowful fondness, then pressed them to his lips.

The letters were—need it be said?—from Leo. Simple productions enough, very likely; girlish, childish even, certainly not very brilliant or intellectual, but frank and

natural, because they were written by one who really loved
—who was not pretending, or studiously posing herself as a
loving woman, as women will do who don't love, but who
wrote trustingly, as she spoke ; her words commonplace
enough, yet precious, they came so warm and fresh from her
heart. If ever a sentence halted, be sure it was because it
was laden heavily with tenderness and affection : and each
line was of value, ordinary as it seemed, for she had strung
upon it such jewels of love : converting, as it were, mere
twine into a glorious necklace of pearls.

He could not burn them. He shrank from the very idea
of such a thing now; and for greater security he pressed the
letters to his heart. And by-and-by he was brushing his
eyes with the back of his hand, as though his vision was
somehow obscured by tears ; and presently he leant over
his desk, hiding his face in his hands.

"He loves her still," muttered Hugh Wood, gazing
through the smoke of his pipe at his friend, and putting
down his book, of which he had not read a line. "He
loves her still ; and he has been mortifying himself like
a martyr of old, as if that ever did anybody any good."
He arose. "Don't disturb yourself," he said. "I'm going
out for half an hour. It is not late ; and I promised to call
upon a man in Pump Court." Arnold hardly looked up,
and Hugh Wood hurried away.

He did not go to Pump Court, however. He went in
a totally opposite direction, quitting the Temple, and turning into the Strand, where he hailed a cab, and drove off.

It was early on the following morning. Hugh Wood
had left the chambers immediately after breakfast. Arnold
was still busy with preparations for his departure.

"A very few more hours, now," he said ; and he began
to meditate how his numerous packages were to be conveyed down to the *Kangaroo* at Blackwall.

There was a little clattering tap of the miniature brass
knocker on the door of the chambers. He opened it.

"Leo !" he cried, with a start.

She was veiled, was in deep mourning. She did not
speak. She put out a small gloved hand ; he could feel,
as he grasped it, that she was trembling violently. Hardly

knowing what he was doing, he closed the door, and led her into the sitting-room. Her eyes rested for a moment on the half-packed trunks, on the untidy helter-skelter of things about the floor, on the table, on the chairs.

"Oh! Arnold!" she said, in a moved, strained voice; "and you were really going without a word—without one good-bye. How could you?" He saw that her eyes had filled with tears; the sight set his heart beating terribly; for some moments he could not speak.

"Forgive me, Leo," he said at length. She gave him her hand again, then sank into a chair.

"And you are going immediately?"

"Yes, almost immediately."

And then there was silence for some time. She lifted her veil, and sat watching the fire, trying, as it seemed, to take off her glove, but she did not give attention enough to the proceedings, or, as it seemed, strength for so small an effort even had left her.

"Going away, and for ever," she said, mournfully, more as though she were speaking to herself than addressing him.

"Yes, Leo, for ever."

"My poor Arnold." And she fairly burst into tears. He advanced towards her, then stopped, and leant against the mantelpiece. She recovered herself after a few moments and she dried her eyes. Then she stole a glance at Arnold's white sad face, noting with pain the lines of care upon his forehead; how his cheeks were sunken; how hollow his eyes were; how thin he looked; how much he had aged and wanned altogether; he seemed intent upon the ragged rug, upon which he was standing speechless, motionless, before her.

"I have not done wrong, surely I have not done wrong in coming here?" she said suddenly, with a start, her face crimsoning. "You are not sorry to see me, Arnold?"

"No, Leo; how could you think so?"

And then a half smile gleamed across her face, and she remembered that she had been frightening herself all the way down to the Temple with the dread lest Arnold should address her as "Miss Carr." She had forgotten this when she met him in the doorway; and now the thought returned only to demonstrate to her how foolish, how groundless, had been her alarms. He called her " Leo," simply, as he had done ever since she could remember.

" Sit down, Arnold, let us talk over this matter quietly, let us draw to the fire ; a fire begins to get very comfortable this cheerless weather, does it not ? sit down by me." And she put her hand into his ; there was no glove upon it now, it was warm, and soft, and trembling within his like a little bird ; disturbing him greatly. And he began to ponder as to when he had last held that little hand in his. What a long, long time ago it seemed !

" And so you are going to emigrate, to settle in Australia ? " she said in calmer tones than she had yet been able to command. " I only heard of it last night."

" Only last night ? "

" Late last night. Hugh Wood came on purpose to tell me. I shall always like him for that."

" Ah ! I remember now ; I know now why he went out. But he did right."

" You are glad now to see me before you go ? " she asked, half-doubtful still.

" Yes, indeed, Leo. I think it very, very kind of you. I shall never forget it."

" And yet you would have gone away without seeing me."

" I was wrong, Leo. But I did it for the best. I thought," he went on in a low voice, " I thought the sight of you, the parting with you, would be too painful to bear." She shivered.

" And you think you will get on well in Australia ? " she asked, after a short pause.

" I hope so, Leo. I will try with all my might. I shall work very hard to make a name for myself in the new world."

" But you won't forget your friends here at home, Arnold ? "

" Have I any ? " he asked, with some bitterness. But he repented his question when he perceived how cruelly he had pained her.

" Pardon me, Leo ; I may think of you as my friend, may I not ? "

"Always, Arnold. Be sure of it. We have been friends for so long, fast friends; we must not stop now, when we are parting, when you are going away for ever as you say. Don't try to forget me; promise me you won't, and think of me kindly, Arnold, as one who—who was a good, true friend always. Promise me this."

"I could not forget you, Leo, if I would; and I would not, Leo, believe me. I was wrong to think of going without seeing you, without a parting word. But it was not that I wished to forget you."

"You are not angry with me, not really angry? You have not been?"

"No, indeed not."

"Oh, Arnold, we have been very wrong to let so cruel a division grow up between us. Nothing ought ever to have endangered our—our friendship; misfortune ought not for one moment to have severed us, but only have drawn us the closer together. Who would have believed in the old, old time, that months and months would pass without our meeting; that you were suffering, and I was not by to give you such comfort as in my poor childish way I could; that you were to be quitting England and I to know nothing of it all; that but for a mere accident, I may say, you would have gone away for ever without seeing me, without my telling you once, assuring you, that I could never forget you; that you would always, always be very, very dear to me, not less in the present and the future than in the past."

He raised her hand tenderly and pressed it very softly against his lips. They were sitting over the fire, gazing into the embers, their chairs very near together.

"Must you go, Arnold?" she asked, in a soft plaintive voice.

"Yes, Leo, I must indeed."

"But you will come back?" He shook his head.

"You will write to me—sometimes—often—to tell me how you prosper?" He hesitated.

"Will it be wise to do so, Leo?" he asked gravely.

"I could not bear to think, Arnold, that you had forgotten me," she said, with a tremulous voice.

"Do not fear, Leo. Besides, these will bear me company; these will constantly remind me of you." He took from his breast the packet of letters. "Though—though, perhaps," he added ruefully, "I ought not to keep them now. I ought to give them back to you." She started as she recognised scraps of her own writing appearing here and there amongst the folds of the letters, then she smiled kindly and her eyes gleamed as she pressed them back gently upon him.

"Keep them," she said, simply. "I, too, have a packet something like that, which I shall keep for ever."

Arnold breathed quickly. He did not trust himself to speak, or to look at her. He felt the blood mounting to his head, and his sight grew dim. For some time neither spoke, as they sat together over the fire in Hugh Wood's chambers. One of her hands still rested in his. Then he felt the other upon his arm; presently it stole to his shoulder, as she bent her head down and murmured, very tenderly,

"No, Arnold, you must not go; I cannot bear it; it will kill me." He sighed, trembling.

"You must not go—for my sake." He strove to speak, he released her hand.

"Arnold!" she cried, in passionate, swooning tones, "you will not go—promise me you will not go—for I love you. Oh, Arnold, you cannot doubt it."

"Leo," he began hoarsely, pressing his hands upon his forehead; but he felt the room swimming round him—he rose, leaning upon the table for support; he could not continue.

"You love me?" she said with painful agitation; "tell me you love me, Arnold?"

"I have loved you, I shall love you always, Leo; but what does it avail? Oh! Leo, it is cruel to try me like this. You know," he cried, hoarsely, "that you are lost to me for ever. That to bid me hope now is only to drive me to a greater despair in the future. If there were nothing else to part us—you are not free—you are to be the wife of Lord Southernwood."

"No, Arnold, it is over; I am free—have pity, Arnold, for I love you so much—forgive me—love me——"

And then she was woven round by Arnold's arms, her tears were dried upon his breast—she was strained against

30

his fiercely beating heart, and he was kissing fondly her forehead, her eyes, her lips.

"Dearest Arnold."

"My own darling little Leo!"

After a little while they grew more composed—more reasonable; though still his arm was round her, still she had very
tight hold of his hand.

"But what will be said of me—what will be thought?"
Arnold asked.

"Does it matter very much, Arnold, what is said, what is
thought? People can only say, dear, that we loved each
other very much—a great deal too much for either of us to
think of quitting the other. After that,—I don't think we
will care much what they add, after that."

"But I am so poor, so very poor, Leo, and you——"

"You are so proud, you mean, Sir," with a mock air of
scolding him. "If you are happy, what does it matter how
you are made happy? You are not ashamed to owe your
happiness to one who loves you as I do? For money, what
is that to us—how can it affect our love? If I were poor,
should you be changed towards me? if I had been in need,
should I not have come to you for aid sooner than anyone?
Such a thought ought never to have parted us,—and it never
shall again."

"You are very generous, darling; you are nobler, kinder,
better in every way than I am. You are a little angel, Leo,"
and here they kissed again. In fact, their observations were
quite punctuated with kisses and caresses just at this period.
"But you have not told me. Lord Dolly——"

"I behaved shamefully, cruelly; but what could I do? it
was soon after poor mamma's death : some months ago now
—she mentioned you quite at the last. That made me very
sad and thoughtful,—she was so fond of you, Arnold,—and I
felt more and more each day that the marriage must not,
could not, take place. And at last,—it was painful to me,
because I could see how terribly he suffered—I told him
that I could never be his wife——"

"And he?"

"He was very brave—very good, and generous, and noble,
as he has always been. He was deeply hurt, but he forgave
me, he released me—besought me to do as I thought best;

said he valued my happiness far above his own, and many kind unselfish things. I felt that I loved him more at that moment than I had done at any former period of the engagement. But oh, Arnold, the sense of relief I felt afterwards when I knew that I was not to be his wife—that I was free ! I was half mad with joy. It was cruel of me, because poor Lord Dolly was suffering sadly. I shall never forget how sad, crushed, he looked, how utterly despairing, as he kissed my hand for the last time—said good-bye, hoped I should always be happy, and then hurried from me; I could hear him sobbing as he went away."

"Poor Lord Dolly !"

"I loved you very much or I could never have been so cruel, Arnold. Still I did not know what to do. I did not dare to write to you; I hardly know why now, but I was afraid; I thought perhaps you had ceased to care for me— to think of me !"

"Leo !"

"And I could learn so little of you, until last night, and then I determined to come here; and when I found that you had kept my poor little letters—that you loved me still a little——"

The sentence was interrupted; she was pressed so closely against his heart that further speech was hardly possible.

"And you didn't love Janet Gill, then? only a very little ?" she whispered with saucy slyness.

Arnold's cheeks flushed as he replied,—

"Not more than you loved Lord Dolly! And—pity me ! I knew not what I did. I thought you were lost to me." Then again,—

"Dear Arnold !"

"Darling little Leo !"

"And papa ?" he asked, presently.

"He's waiting for me now. He came down here with me; but he said he thought the stairs would be rather too much for him, and that I'd better go alone—what an old darling he is !—so he's in the carriage, in Temple Lane, isn't it called? I'm afraid," she added, with a charming blush, "he'll think I've kept him waiting a very long time; perhaps we had better go to him at once."

Old Mr. Carr looked from one to the other of them,

30—2

with sly kindly glances. He shook hands warmly with Arnold.

"You've been a long time, Leo, persuading Arnold to come down and see me. I suppose you have been studying law in the barrister's chambers: the Marriage Act, perhaps: I thought you were never coming, and I've been wanting my lunch terribly. Jump in and lunch with us, Arnold, and dine too. I don't suppose Leo will let you go in a hurry again. There has been no peace in the house of late, entirely on your account, I can tell you. Home, Andrews."

It was after dinner, when they were over their wine, that the old gentleman said to Arnold,—

"So you *would* do all you could to shield that Whitehall scamp!"

"He was my sister's husband," said Arnold. "For her sake, for the children's——"

"You were obstinate: you paid a heavy price. Well, well, you take after your father. The general was obstinate; he knew how to stand to his guns, as the foe found at Waterloo. However, things have turned out better than might have been expected. You will not lose Oakmere."

"It is already lost," said Arnold, with a sigh.

"Not quite. I stand in the shoes—so far only as Oakmere is concerned, thank Heaven!—of the Ostrich Insurance Company. When you come to look at the terms of Leo's marriage settlement, you will find that in marrying that young lady you will reinstate yourself pretty much in your old position, as the proprietor of Oakmere, in right of your wife."

"Oh, Mr. Carr! this is too generous."

"Stop. There are certain conditions to precede that arrangement. I think I must follow Laban's example, and ask Jacob to serve for Rachel. We've had enough of playing with business: but you can begin to work really, if you will. I've still an interest in the iron foundry—a partner's share. We can make room for you, I think, in the counting house, and, perhaps, by-and-by, we can slip you into the firm—there's nothing but a clear head wanted. The business has produced nothing but honest men, hitherto; though I say it. There will be no reason why it should do anything else while you are in it. The partners grow old. There will be plenty to do ; but you'll soon find yourself at home with the work. It's better than being a director of a sham company. But we won't say anything more about that—that's all past ; you've been in the fire and you come out tempered, not destroyed. Your father wasn't ashamed of having an iron-founder for his friend ; you won't be ashamed of being one yourself, or of marrying the daughter of one, especially when she restores you such a property as Oakmere, and adds to it such another as Croxall. No more business to-night : not a word. Pass the claret. We'll drink her health. I can tell you that our friends, Holroyd and Hopegood, will have great pleasure in preparing the settlements on the marriage of Mr. and Mrs. Arnold Page. The names will look well in gold letters on a tin box in their office. And now we'll go into the drawing-room, and ask Leo to play us a tune ; she'll be very angry with me for keeping you from her all this time. One more glass ; you're a little pale and shaky still ; but I think you're going on very well now."

Certainly he was a lucky dog ! Clearly he must have been born with a silver spoon in his mouth !

Hugh Wood returned to the chambers in the Temple.

"Gone ! And left no trace ? Yes ; this," and he took up a lady's kid glove, and contemplated it curiously, as though he took much interest in the manner of stitching used in the manufacture of gloves. " I think I have lost a tenant," he said after some time; " and I think the *Kangaroo,* A 1, for Port Philip, has lost a passenger. It's my doing," he sighed heavily. " I little thought at one time that I should contribute so much to the union of Arnold Page and Leonora Carr. However, if I have made two persons very happy indeed, it will be a rather pleasant reflection for some time to come. And I think Arnold deserved to be happy ; he's a good fellow, let who will speak against him. He has taken fortune's buffets and rewards with equal thanks—or very nearly so. For her—— no ; I won't trust myself on that subject, except to say, God bless her ! may she be happy." And he lighted his pipe. " I have done enough work for to-day ; and I've something to think about."

The *Kangaroo,* A 1, for Port Philip, in due course weighed anchor ; but Mr. Arnold Page had forfeited his passage.

POSTSCRIPT.

WHEN the green baize curtain has descended on the closing scene of the Christmas piece, and the *dramatis personæ*,
illumined by red fire, have been all safely landed in the
Bower of Golden Artichokes, amid the Fairy Realms of Perpetual Whirligigs ; after there has wholly vanished from the
keen vision of the pit that admirable, final group, properly
pyramidic in composition, and presumed to represent the
domestic comfort and normal manner of life of the pantomime family on the cessation of their theatrical toils ;
when the columbine mounts on the shoulders of her spangled
lover, who, with widely extended legs, finds precarious footing on the respective hips of the clown and pantaloon, themselves fixed in attitudes of no inconsiderable violence ; the
while the leanest of sprites literally makes no bones about
twisting himself into any pose conceivable by the most
fanciful artist in human arabesque, and performs in the fore-
ground the gyrations of an incarnate Catharine-wheel—after
all this, there is yet one more drop added to the brimmed-
up cup of pleasure presented to the lips of the holiday folks ;
they are yet called upon to recognise with mirthful applause
one little supplemental proceeding on the part of a chief
performer. The clown protrudes his comic face between
the curtain and the proscenium, with a cry of "Good-night !
Come again to-morrow !" He succeeds in blowing up the
expiring flame of laughter into one final flicker. Bless the
honest smooth-faced schoolboys, who echo aloud the jester's
parting good wishes ; who have yet left in their aching,
rotund bodies a genuine crow of sturdy mirth, and who give
it freely, heartily. But then the clown is always thoroughly
en rapport with the schoolboy.

Very much after the manner of the Jack Pudding of the
pantomime, the novelist, it would seem, is prescriptively
expected to reappear after the drop has fallen upon his
concluding *tableau*, to utter yet more last words ; to afford

further information touching his characters; their fates and
futures: to bid his readers, one and all, "good-night"—
albeit, the prime events being ascertained and settled, and
the heroine comfortably deposited at last in the arms of the
hero, he can hope to kindle but slight interest by any
addenda he may choose to tack on to his chronicle. But
in this we perceive one of the conditions distinguishing
narrative fiction from the methods of the high walks of the
drama. Who presumes to express interest in the background figures of the tragedy? Who would dare to summon
the author of *Hamlet* to give us detailed histories of his
minor personages? "Take up the bodies," says Fortinbras.
"Go, bid the soldiers shoot!   And so, a dead march; a
bearing off of the corpses; a peal of ordnance shot off—and
an end.   We may know no more.   What became of
Horatio?   Did he marry the player-lady, who had increased
in stature by the altitude of a chopine?   In what manner
did Osric conduct himself in his after life?   Were his last
days anything like Brummell's?   Did those twin snobs
Rosencrantz and Guildenstern fall out prior to their
execution, or manifest any change in that surprising
unanimity which distinguished them during the play?   Did
the actors recover from the disastrous failure of their performance at Elsinore?   Did the second clown improve at
all in the guessing of riddles?   These things, had the poet
been a novelist, he would have been bound to inform us.
As it is, we are compelled to go without the information.
Certain ladies and gentlemen, I hear, have held spirit-
rapping conversations with the immortal bard, and received
important communications from him; but I never could
find out that these had reference to any of the important
subjects I have suggested.   I only know that my very dear
William has never manifested himself at my dining-table
(though there has always been a knife and fork laid for
him), and in regard to any curiosity I may have entertained
on the above and kindred topics arising out of his works—
his opinion as to his commentators, for instance—it seems
to me that he has cared—well—not a rap!
  These preparatory observations being submitted to the
calm consideration of the reader, I proceed to register a few
notes concerning certain of the persons and incidents in

this book. It cannot be, however, that I should definitely close the history of each of my characters seriatim. The events narrated have happened in our own day; no very long time back. Nearly all of our friends are still living; and while there is life, there is likely to be vicissitude. I have not the means to provide fortunes for them all, or to remove them beyond the possibility of future attacks of adversity. The wolf may be driven from the door, and driven a great distance off, but it is hard to say, for all that, that he will never, by any chance, find his way back again.

The *Café de l'Univers* has closed its doors, and Madame Desprès and her husband Louis the waiter, have disappeared. It is not known whether the motives of their departure arose from pecuniary or political difficulties. At one time I know it was certainly the fashion to regard the *café* as a hot-bed of disaffection. The English *habitués* were prone to the opinion that every foreign gentleman in the place was strenuously opposed to existing institutions, cherished revolutionary ideas of a most sanguinary character, and was an exile from his native land solely by reason of the want of harmony between his own views and those of his government. But this could not always have been the case, as we all know. Men are fugitives from the country of their nativity for other than political reasons: or why are there so many English at Boulogne? I remember that I was myself much deceived in this way in regard to a frequenter of the *café*, a small olive-coloured man with the largest moustache I ever saw—it was really a phenomenal moustache—and was quite as much entitled to a newspaper paragraph registering its proportions as any colossal gooseberry that ever was seen or even heard of; he rolled his fierce black eyes unceasingly, and in a manner terrible to behold; he smoked cigarettes for ever, to the great danger of his moustache, removing the paper tubes from his mouth now and then the more conveniently to grind his teeth or to spit upon the floor with the greater virulence, the while he amused himself with one of the simple pastimes dear to his nation and in vogue at the *café*. I remember that I attributed to this man ideas of a most objectionable character. It seemed to me that nothing could be more agreeable to him than a merciless *battue* of crowned heads, or to plant a ribbon-decked tree of

liberty, watering it with aristocratic gore, the while was con-
structed a fraternal, revolutionary, terrorist government,
each member of which (*sans culottes* of course) was bound
to wear a blood-red bonnet of liberty and a tricoloured sash.
I was deceived. For all the atrocity of his appearance, and
the fury of his manners, the man was simply a respectable
shopkeeper in an adjoining street, and one of the most
bland and obliging of bootmakers—wearing spectacles even
in his shop and oftentimes nursing a baby!—I ever encountered. It is possible, therefore, that many other guests
of the *café*, credited with revolutionary mania by casual
English visitors, were, after all, not more harmful; for it
seems to me the aspect of foreigners is often tried by a false
test, and an erroneous judgment is so attained. A Briton
with the appearance of my friend the bootmaker would
have been without doubt a highly alarming personage; but
the fact of the bootmaker being a Frenchman completely
alters the case. Ferocity of aspect is a continental
humour; and is yet perfectly innocuous. It doesn't really
mean anything like what it looks to mean: quite as much
as it is republican and revolutionary, it is indeed imperial.
And we have all known for some time that the Empire is—
Peace.

Of our friends who were accustomed to assemble round
the little marble tables of the *café* we have a few items of
news to chronicle. Tom Norris has returned to his land
of adoption—France—taking with him his old comrade
Timson. They occasionally send over for exhibition in
London important works, very much after the manner of
the late eminent French artist, St. Roche, the preceptor
and idol of Mr. Norris. I regret that I am unable to
record that these productions have met with very ready
appreciation in this country—I mean, of course, appreciation
in ready money—though they have been greatly admired by
certain art-critics. Binns, the clerk in the Insurance Office,
has married and taken up his residence at Islington. From
the front windows of his house he commands views of the
canal and the New River, and he is within easy hail of
Sadler's Wells Theatre. It is whispered that his wife was
the only person who could be found to hear to the end the
story of his important adventure on Monte Rosa, and, as a

consequence, she got her reward—in marriage. However, she has probably forbidden any repetition of the story now, for Binns has of late studiously avoided all reference to it. Mr. Gossett has passed all his examinations, and now appears before the world as a full-blown medical practitioner. He has lately undertaken the post of surgeon on board an emigrant ship bound for Vancouver's Island. It is possible that he may be afterwards spoken of in terms something similar to those contained in the evidence of the witness in *Black-eyed Susan*, called to inform the court concerning the moral character of the prisoner, poor William : " Why, as to his medical qualifications, Sir, as to his medical qualifications, why, he played the pianoforte like an angel ! " But, for all that, I know that if circumstances ever call me to Vancouver's Island—and I fervently trust they never may— I should endeavour to secure a passage by the ship which carries Mr. Gossett as its surgeon. For I think an overdose of music would be preferable to one of medicine : while I should fancy that one of Mr. Gossett's incantation songs would be as efficacious as anything in driving away sea-sickness.

Mr. Lackington has quitted Omega Terrace, Camden Town, and secured Mr. Gossett's apartments in Coppice Row. I cannot say that he is much more industrious than of old, but as he is quite as happy, perhaps, it doesn't much matter. And hopes are entertained that he may ultimately catch from her example something of the perseverance and assiduity of widowed Mrs. Simmons, his landlady. She takes great interest in Jack, as the friend of her old and valued lodgers, Arnold Page and Phil Gossett ; and it is possible that she may in time induce him to work a little more regularly ; indeed, it will now be really his own fault if he doesn't prosper, for people are beginning to inquire for his pictures, and he can sell much faster than he can produce. " Don't talk about not being in the mood, or waiting for inspiration," says Mrs. Simmons to her lodger ; " set to and work, and it will come all right, mood and inspiration and all. Nicely I should be *goosed* if I were to wait at the wing of the Paroquet, and not go on till I felt inspired ! And what would become then, do you think, of my poor dear Jemmy's blessed children ? I go on, anyhow, and I soon warm with my part, and do all I know to bring down the applause, and I generally get it; I always do my best. and work hard, and the public know it, and like me for it. And I've had my salary raised of late, for they wanted to buy me off to the opposition theatre, the Vulture in Shoreditch, but I wouldn't go. I shall stick to the Paroquet as long as I can." (And indeed the actress is to be seen nightly on the boards of that establishment working very hard indeed.) "What would you like for dinner, Mr. Lackington, and do you want any of the children to sit to you?" The only change to be noted in the Coppice Row arrangements consists in the relinquishment of the tobacco and snuff business. "I can't attend to that, Sir; I haven't the heart now my poor Jemmy's gone; and it would be such a dreadful thing to have the children going sneezing all about the place, or learning to smoke, or falling into any of the bad habits or goings on of their poor father. No, please Goodness, we won't have that. The man that smokes, drinks—I never knew the rule to fail; and to think of that precious infant there, that sits smiling at me, and sucking his thumbs like a little king, as though he knew all I was talking about, bless him! to think of *his* ever taking to going over the way to that horrid Spotted Dog, as my poor Jemmy used to, and coming home in that dreadful state, and smelling that strong of spirits, that it filled the whole house; no, bless him, he'll never do it; he'll never break his poor mother's heart, will he? a darling. He's got quite his father's eyes: not what they were of late; but when he was steady at Bath, long ago now, the prettiest harlequin that ever was seen on a stage to my thinking, let who will say he wasn't!" Poor Mrs. Simmons!

Janet Gill's services, upon the urgent recommendation of Leo Carr, were secured by Lady Lambeth. She was engaged to aid her ladyship in the bringing up and education of her young family, and entered at once upon the discharge of her duties. But she found that she was more particularly required to act as companion to her ladyship. Her position in the Lambeth household was a perfectly comfortable one, and the air of suffering which had at first distinguished her, gradually yielded to the kindly and sympathetic treatment she received. Her unremitting attention to the children during a period of sickness greatly endeared her to Lady Lambeth, who was profuse in acknowledging the merits of her friend. Upon the decease of Lord Lambeth, which happened recently, Janet withdrew with the young widow and her children to the family seat in the country. There are two subjects upon which Janet never speaks : one is in connection with the history of her father, and the other regards a certain letter she received from Arnold Page, and the reply she sent to it. As to this last, she has never ceased to congratulate herself, albeit it was not without deep pain she brought herself to reject the suit of a man, whom, she admitted to herself, she really loved.

Robin Hooper lives now almost altogether in the country, the solace of the declining years of his father and mother. He has seen, Janet but seldom ; perhaps assured of the utter hopelessness of his passion, he showed the wisest courage in avoiding its object as much as possible. But there have been compensating circumstances attending his suffering ; not merely in the fact that his presence at the Wick Farm gives real pleasure to his parents, though the farmer still persists in considering his state as utterly hopeless, just as the farmer's wife continues to over-estimate his strength and sturdiness, and to disregard his deformity. It must be remembered that Robin is a poet, and a published collection of his songs has achieved for him no mean fame ; the merits of his muse have received recognition from a large public. May not much of his success be attributed to the real feeling imported into his verses? Would there have been as much feeling if his love had triumphed in a commonplace sort of way? Is it not almost desirable that poets should not be too happy, in order that they may learn in suffering what they teach in song? But doubtless time will bring to Robin alleviation of "the pangs of despised love"—the love being, as he knew, without hope from the very first.

It is not possible to disguise the fact that the Marquis of Southernwood experienced a cruel disappointment when he found himself under the necessity of withdrawing his pretensions to the hand of Miss Carr. " It was an awful sell for Cupid," as the fellows of the Junior Adonis agreed in the smoking-room when the matter came before them for discussion; "they never saw any fellow so cut up—never By George! an awful sell!" "Well, it was all that—I don't deny it," his lordship confessed to one or two intimates. He looked very rueful; the colour for once had gone from his cheeks; his eyes had lost a good deal of their wonted sparkle; and his hyacinthine locks were ill-arranged and out of curl. "But what was a fellow to do?" ("Baw!" from the person he addressed.) "You know, Chalker, old boy, you'd have done just the same." ("Aw!" from Chalker.) "The poor dear little thing, you know, I couldn't bear to see her crying, and miserable, and that. I aint at all a fellow of that sort, you know: never could stand a woman crying—it always knocked me over. It wasn't flattering to a fellow's vanity, you know, to be told he wasn't loved, or cared for, or that sort of thing. But, of course, she couldn't help that. I dare say she'd tried all she knew, poor thing, and when she found she couldn't manage it, why, of course, it was only right of her to tell me. And I won't have a word said against her by any man. She's a good, dear little soul—and—and—by George! I'll never love another woman—I never will—and, in fact, I never can, not as I loved her. It was my own fault. I'd no right to cut in. I think I deserve all I got. I knew A. P. was in the case. I knew that she cared for him. I ought to have seen that I'd no chance coming after him. Only I loved that girl! 'pon my soul I did. I don't think I shall ever get over it. I don't think there's such another miserable beggar breathing as I am. Do I look bad, Chalker? But it don't seem to me that I care for anything now, or what I do, or what becomes of me. By Gad, you know a thing of this sort is enough to shut a fellow up for life, 'pon my soul it is! And she did look so devilish pretty when she was crying. I don't think I ever loved her so much as I did then—and the poor little thing wanted to go down on her knees to me; but of course I could not stand that— and then what a relief it was to her when I told her that it was all right—that everything should be as she wished—that the affair should not go on—that sort of thing. I dare say you think me a d——d fool, Chalker, old boy, but I cried liked a child. By Gad! I did. I couldn't help it. Well! what shall we do? Let's talk of something else. Let's do something, or go somewhere. I know I wish I could drive the whole thing out of my head, but I suppose I can't; only I'll never love another woman, I know that—never!"

His lordship retreated to Gashleigh Abbey to receive the condolements of his sister-in-law, the Marchioness, who was inclined to be exceedingly angry with Miss Carr for her cruel conduct. But his lordship would not listen to any charge being brought against Leo, stoutly maintaining that she was thoroughly justified in all she had done, and taking upon his own shoulders all the blame that could arise out of the matter. Indeed he was compelled to inform the Marchioness that he would at once quit the Abbey if another word were spoken to the detriment of Miss Carr; whereupon her ladyship was silent; and I think after a little time secretly applauded the chivalrous behaviour of his little lordship, and more recently forgave Leo for her share in his suffering.

It must be confessed that Lord Southernwood "went a little wild," as people say, about this time. He urged, in explanation, that he really hardly knew what he did. Certainly his proceedings were a little desperate. "I was out of my mind, you know—I do believe I was—just then, or I never should have been such a fool as to back Asparagus for the Cesarewitch; fancy putting an awful pot of money on such a brute as that! Of course I lost it. But I didn't care about that time what money I dropped." It was, perhaps, in compassion for his chapfallen state that a party of his friends projected a continental tour with a view of cheering him up. "It was pretty jolly," as he afterwards explained, "and we got on very well altogether: there was Flukemore, and Clipstone, Storkfort, and Chalker, and we went I don't know where, and saw everything, and managed very well. We told off two fellows to fatigue duty—Flukemore and Chalker: the one had to get up *Murray*, to tell us where we were and what we were looking at; and we put the other on to *Bradshaw*, so that we might be all right as to trains and steamboats, and that. It was a very good plan, and saved us all trouble, and I think I've come back, on the whole, better than I went."

There is one subject upon which, if he would, Lord Southernwood could have given us, no doubt, very important information. I mean in regard to the history of Captain Gill, deceased. But he maintained considerable reserve. He could never be brought to say much more than this : "Well : yes, I knew him ; but, for the sake of his daughter, it's perhaps as well to keep dark about him. He was a bad lot—I'll say that. He was our paymaster, and his accounts got into a frightful muddle ; and some of the fellows suffered severely by him. But we agreed to hush it up. We none of us wanted the thing to get into the papers. There had been great irregularities. There was little doubt but that he'd committed felony, and might have been pulled up for it at any time. He was not a nice man, and he'd got mixed up with a strange set : a French money-lending Jew—something of that sort. And it was said that he suffered from a *coup de soleil.* But my own opinion was that it was all along of brandy ; and he got worse and worse ; and at last he bolted. And it was said that the Frenchman had got an extraordinary influence over him. But I never understood it thoroughly, and perhaps the less that's now said about it, why, the better for all concerned ; it's not a pleasant subject, and it's all done with now. Let's talk of something else."

The Times of no very recent date registered in its first column the demise of the Venerable Archdeacon of Binchester, better known to us as the Rev. Purton Wood, late rector of Oakmere. He was stated to have died "universally regretted." I fear that his estate was found by his administrator, his son, Hugh Wood, to be very considerably involved. But it was remarked that, after the decease of his parent, Mr. Wood seemed to be much less pressed for money than he had hitherto been.

And Mr. Lomax, and his wife ?

Well, the secretary of the Wafer Stamp Office has never returned to England. He has been seen at various continental cities and watering-places ; but I think he has been rather avoided by the English residents and visitors there. He has tried his two manners upon the foreigners with whom he has come in contact; but I don't know positively which he has found the more successful. He appears to have been in possession of ample means, and would probably have taken a respectable position in society, but that every now and then unpleasant rumours concerning him travelled about. He has pretended to represent, in some vague way, the Government of which he was formerly the servant. But it was noticed that the British consulate establishments, at whatever place he appeared, afforded him no sort of countenance. He was joined at last by his wife, who had been advised to travel, as a means of counteracting the headaches to which she had become more than ever subject. The children are now permanently in charge of their relatives, Uncle Arnold and his wife, the present occupants of Oakmere Court. I believe Edith and Rosy are very happy where they are, and becoming rapidly accustomed and resigned to the prolonged absence of their parents. We are not much in the way of hearing particular news of Mr. and Mrs. Lomax; but a short time ago there was current in club smoking-rooms a story to which all friends of the family are requested to give the most positive contradiction. It was something to the effect that an Englishman very like Mr. Lomax in person had been publicly horsewhipped for cheating, or trying to cheat, at cards. In fact, there existed various stories, all having for their chief point a charge against Mr. Lomax, seriously affecting his integrity. Was it in confirmation or in explanation of these sinister reports that a statement followed, to the effect that it had been found necessary to place him under personal restraint, that various recent proceedings of his had been marked by a really alarming eccentricity, and that it was feared that symptoms of a decided softening of the brain had manifested themselves? Certain of the faculty were at no loss to discover an explanation of this disorder, which they unhesitatingly attributed to the frequent railway journeys undertaken by the patient to and from Whitehall at the time when he was resident at Oakmere Court, the house of his brother-in-law. It is added that no hopes are entertained of his recovery, and that the general state of his health does not promise for him a very protracted period of suffering. Whatever his condition, however, Mrs. Lomax continues with her husband.

Oakmere Court has regained its old comfortable aspect under the auspices of its present tenants. Many of our friends assemble there at Christmas time, and on other holiday occasions. Mr. Gossett has sung his best songs in the drawing-room of the Court. Mr. Robin Hooper has recited his verses, while Hugh Wood has applauded : and Mr. Lackington has been seen sketching in the pleasant avenues of the park. The mistress of the Court is pleased to welcome heartily all these to her halls. More pleased still was she when Janet Gill plucked up heart enough to spend her holidays with her old friends. What long conversations the ladies enjoyed together ! especially one day when they drove over to Croxall to visit the room in which had died a poor little school-girl very dear to both of them, and afterwards journeyed to Oakmere churchyard to view once more the grave of poor little Baby Gill.

Concerning Miss Bigg and her companion, Booth, the Gesler and Sarnem of Chapone House, Kew Green, I have nothing further to communicate. It is conjectured that they are still engaged in promoting the sale of the poet Bigg's soul poem, *The Course of Life*, in twenty cantos. Dr. Hawkshaw, indefatigable as ever, states that he has taken effective means to prevent his name being placed in the list of subscribers to the work, while he has a private conviction that the ex-schoolmistress will be found to figure some day in the police reports as a begging-letter impostor, when he hopes the magistrate will not be in a lenient mood.

Old Mr. Carr is hearty and happy, well satisfied with the son-in-law who has toiled so earnestly for the iron-founders as now to take his place in the list of partners ; who has worked hard to deserve all the good things fortune has showered upon him. And especially pleased is the old gentleman with his grandchildren, now very clamorous in the nursery. "If only my poor wife had lived to see our darling's babies ! How happy it would have made her ! Well, well. It little matters how soon I am taken away to join her. My child is very,

31

very happy with her husband and her children. Thank
Heaven ! "

"Amen ! " said some one, reverently, at his side ; and he
found his hand pressed tenderly by his son-in-law.

"What have I ever done to deserve all this happiness ? "
Arnold would sometimes ask himself. It must have been,
as people had said of him from the first, he was a very
lucky dog ! He was born with a silver spoon in his
mouth !

And yet something must be due to the great good there
is in the fellow ! Hear how his father-in-law sings his
praises, and consider how devoted are his friends to him ;
how attached his tenants ; how his children cling to him ;
above all, how his wife loves him. Surely, he could not
win all these and keep them, without some merit of his
own ?

He is not often in London now. His time is divided
between his estate at Oakmere and his business at the iron-
foundry ; and I think I may say for certain now, that he
has abandoned all notion of representing Woodlandshire in
Parliament ; he declares openly his unfitness for public
life, though the chances in favour of his election, if he
would only present himself as a candidate, are now better
than ever. Even more persistent is he in his determination that he will never again, under any circumstances,
accept a seat at the board of direction of any public
company whatever.

And Leo ? Be sure that she is happy if her husband
is ; happy with all that supreme happiness of a woman
who is loved as fondly as she loves.

I close these records with a publication of two rumours
that have just reached me, they refer to two marriages
as likely to be solemnised now very shortly.

I give the reports precisely as I have heard them. I
have no time to enter into any discussion as to their
probable truth.

One is to the effect that the Marquis of Southernwood is about to be united to the widowed Lady Lambeth
(formerly the Honourable Miss Pincott).

The other points to a union between Hugh Wood and
Janet Gill. It is certain that these two were seen to be a

good deal together during their recent visit to Oakmere, when the Christmas holidays were kept in a highly festive way.

I will simply add a hope that both rumours may prove to be true.

THE END.

31—9—68] [PRINTED BY W. H. SMITH AND SON, 186, STRAND, LONDON.